THE SHARING

THE
SHARING
KNIFE

Beguilement
Legacy

Lois McMaster Bujold

FANTASY

THE SHARING KNIFE, VOLUME ONE: BEGUILEMENT
Copyright © 2006 by Lois McMaster Bujold

THE SHARING KNIFE, VOLUME TWO: LEGACY
Copyright © 2007 by Lois McMaster Bujold

Published by arrangement with
Eos Books, an imprint of HarperCollins Publishers
10 East 53rd Street
New York, NY 10022

ISBN: 978-0-7394-8490-6

First SFBC printing: June 2007

Visit the SFBC online at http:/www.sfbc.com

PRINTED IN THE UNITED STATES OF AMERICA

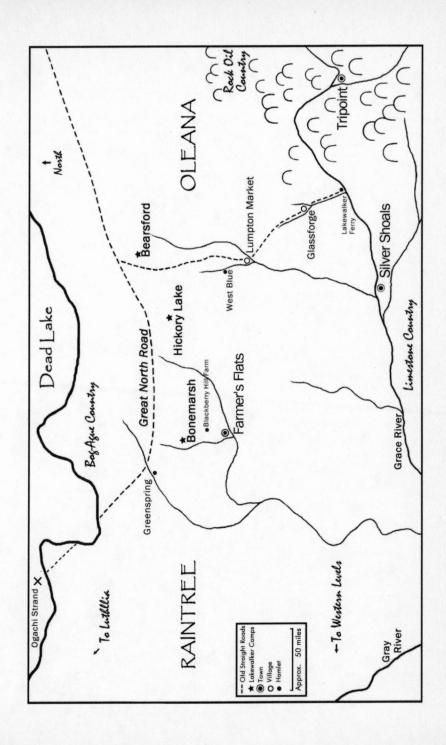

THE SHARING KNIFE

Contents

BEGUILEMENT

1

Fawn came to the well-house a little before noon. More than a farm-stead, less than an inn, it sat close to the straight road she'd been trudging down for two days. The farmyard lay open to travelers, bounded by a semicircle of old log outbuildings, with the promised covered well in the middle. To re-solve all doubt, somebody had nailed a sign picturing the well itself to one of the support posts, and below the painting a long list of goods the farm might sell, with the prices. Each painstakingly printed line had a little picture below it, and colored circles of coins lined up in rows beyond, for those who could not read the words and numbers themselves. Fawn could, and keep accounts as well, skills her mother had taught her along with a hundred other household tasks. She frowned at the unbidden thought: *So if I'm so clever, what am I doing in this fix?*

She set her teeth and felt in her skirt pocket for her coin purse. It was not heavy, but she might certainly buy some bread. Bread would be bland. The dried mutton from her pack that she'd tried to eat this morning had made her sick, again, but she needed something to fight the horrible fatigue that slowed her steps to a plod, or she'd never make it to Glassforge. She glanced around the unpeopled yard and at the iron bell hung from the post with a pull cord dangling invitingly, then lifted her eyes to the rolling fields beyond the build-ings. On a distant sunlit slope, a dozen or so people were haying. Uncertainly, she went around to the farmhouse's kitchen door and knocked.

A striped cat perching on the step eyed her without getting up. The cat's plump calm reassured Fawn, together with the good repair of the house's faded shingles and fieldstone foundation, so that when a comfortably middle-aged farmwife opened the door, Fawn's heart was hardly pounding at all.

"Yes, child?" said the woman.

I'm not a child, I'm just short, Fawn bit back; given the crinkles at the corners of the woman's friendly eyes, maybe Fawn's basket of years would still seem scant to her. "You sell bread?"

The farmwife's glance around took in her aloneness. "Aye; step in."

A broad hearth at one end of the room heated it beyond summer, and was crowded with pots hanging from iron hooks. Delectable smells of ham and beans, corn and bread and cooking fruit mingled in the moist air, noon meal in the making for the gang of hay cutters. The farmwife folded back a cloth from a lumpy row on a side table, fresh loaves from a workday that had doubtless started before dawn. Despite her nausea Fawn's mouth watered, and she picked out a loaf that the woman told her was rolled inside with crystal honey and hickory nuts. Fawn fished out a coin, wrapped the loaf in her kerchief, and took it back outside. The woman walked along with her.

"The water's clean and free, but you have to draw it yourself," the woman told her, as Fawn tore off a corner of the loaf and nibbled. "Ladle's on the hook. Which way were you heading, child?"

"To Glassforge."

"By yourself?" The woman frowned. "Do you have people there?"

"Yes," Fawn lied.

"Shame on them, then. Word is there's a pack of robbers on the road near Glassforge. They shouldn't have sent you out by yourself."

"South or north of town?" asked Fawn in worry.

"A ways south, I heard, but there's no saying they'll stay put."

"I'm only going as far south as Glassforge." Fawn set the bread on the bench beside her pack, freed the latch for the crank, and let the bucket fall till a splash echoed back up the well's cool stone sides, then began turning.

Robbers did not sound good. Still, they were a frank hazard. Any fool would know enough not to go near them. When Fawn had started on this miserable journey six days ago, she had cadged rides from wagons at every chance as soon as she'd walked far enough from home not to risk encountering someone who knew her. Which had been fine until that one fellow who'd said stupid things that made her very uncomfortable and followed up with a grab and a grope. Fawn had managed to break away, and the man had not been willing to abandon his rig and restive team to chase her down, but she might have been less lucky. After that, she'd hidden discreetly in the verge from the occasional passing carts until she was sure there was a woman or a family aboard.

The few bites of bread were helping settle her stomach already. She hoisted the bucket onto the bench and took the wooden dipper the woman handed down to her. The water tasted of iron and old eggs, but was clear and cold. Better. She would rest a while on this bench in the shade, and perhaps this afternoon she would make better time.

From the road to the north, hoofbeats and a jingle of harness sounded. No creak or rattle of wheels, but quite a *lot* of hooves. The farmwife glanced up, her eyes narrowing, and her hand rose to the cord on the bell clapper.

"Child," she said, "see those old apple trees at the side of the yard? Why don't you just go skin up one and stay quiet till we see what this is, eh?"

Fawn thought of several responses, but settled on, "Yes'm." She started across the yard, turned back and grabbed her loaf, then trotted to the small grove. The closest tree had a set of boards nailed to the side like a ladder, and she scrambled up quickly through branches thick with leaves and hard little green apples. Her dress was dyed dull blue, her jacket brown; she would blend with the shadows here as well as she had on the road verge, likely. She braced herself along a branch, tucked in her pale hands and lowered her face, shook her head, and peered out through the cascade of black curls falling over her forehead.

The mob of riders turned into the yard, and the farmwife came off her tense toes, shoulders relaxing. She released the bell cord. There must have been a dozen and a half horses, of many colors, but all rangy and long-legged. The riders wore mostly dark clothing, had saddlebags and bedrolls tied behind their cantles, and—Fawn's breath caught—long knives and swords hanging from their belts. Many also bore bows, unstrung athwart their backs, and quivers full of arrows.

No, not all men. A woman rode out of the pack, slid from her horse, and nodded to the farmwife. She was dressed much as the rest, in riding trousers and boots and a long leather vest, and had iron-gray hair braided and tied in a tight knot at her nape. The men wore their hair long too: some braided back or tied in queues, with decorations of glass beads or bright metal or colored threads twisted in, some knotted tight and plain like the woman's.

Lakewalkers. A whole patrol of them, apparently. Fawn had seen their kind only once before, when she'd come with her parents and brothers to Lumpton Market to buy special seed, glass jars, rock oil and wax, and dyes. Not a patrol, that time, but a clan of traders from the wilderness up around the Dead Lake, who had brought fine furs and leathers and odd woodland produce and clever metalwork and more secret items: medicines, or maybe subtle poisons. The Lakewalkers were rumored to practice black sorcery.

Other, less unlikely rumors abounded. Lakewalker kinfolk did not settle in one place, but moved about from camp to camp depending on the needs of the season. No man among them owned his own land, carefully parceling it out amongst his heirs, but considered the vast wild tracts to be held in common by all his kin. A man owned only the clothes he stood in, his weapons, and the catches of his hunts. When they married, a woman did not become mistress of her husband's house, obliged to the care of his aging parents; instead a man moved into the tents of his bride's mother, and became as a son to her family. There were also whispers of strange bed customs among them which, maddeningly, no one would confide to Fawn.

On one thing, the folks were clear. If you suffered an incursion by a blight bogle, you called in the Lakewalkers. And you did not cheat them of their pay once they had removed the menace.

Fawn was not entirely sure she believed in blight bogles. For all the tall tales, she had never encountered one in her life, no, nor known anyone else who had, either. They seemed like ghost stories, got up to thrill the shrewd listeners and frighten the gullible ones. She had been gulled by her snickering older brothers far too many times to rise readily to the bait anymore.

She froze again when she realized that one of the patrollers was walking toward her tree. He looked different than the others, and it took her a moment to realize that his dark hair was not long and neatly braided, but cut short to an untidy tousle. He was alarmingly tall, though, and very lean. He yawned and stretched, and something glinted on his left hand. At first Fawn thought it was a knife, then realized with a slight chill that the man had no left hand. The glint was from some sort of hook or clamp, but how it was fastened to his wrist beneath his long sleeve she could not see. To her dismay, he ambled into the shade directly below her, there to lower his long body, prop his back comfortably against her tree trunk, and close his eyes.

Fawn jerked and nearly fell out of the tree when the farmwife reached up and rang her bell after all. Two loud clanks and three, repeated: evidently a signal or call, not an alarm, for she was talking all the time in an animated way with the patroller woman. Now that Fawn's eyes had time to sort them out in their strange garb, she could see three or four more women among the men. A couple of men busied themselves at the well, hauling up the bucket to slosh the water into the wooden trough on the side opposite the bench; others led their horses in turn to drink. A boy loped around the outbuildings in answer to the bell, and the farmwife sent him with several more of the patrollers into the barn. Two of the younger women followed the farmwife into her house, and came out in a while with packets wrapped in cloth—more of the good farm food, obviously. The others emerged from the barn lugging sacks of what Fawn supposed must be grain for their horses.

They all met again by the well, where a brief, vigorous conversation ensued between the farmwife and the gray-haired patroller woman. It ended with a counting over of sacks and packets in return for coins and some small items from the patroller saddlebags that Fawn could not make out, to the apparent satisfaction of both sides. The patrol broke up into small groups to seek shade around the yard and share food.

The patrol leader walked over to Fawn's tree and sat down cross-legged beside the tall man. "You have the right idea, Dag."

A grunt. If the man opened his eyes, Fawn could not tell; her leaf-obstructed view was now of two ovals, one smooth and gray, the other ruffled and dark. And a lot of booted leg, stretched out.

"So what did your old friend have to say?" asked the man. His low voice sounded tired, or maybe it was just naturally raspy. "Malice confirmed, or not?"

"Rumors of bandits only, so far, but a lot of disappearances around Glassforge. With no bodies found."

"Mm."

"Here, eat." She handed him something, ham wrapped in bread judging by the enticing aroma that rose to Fawn. The woman lowered her voice. "You feel anything yet?"

"You have better groundsense than I do," he mumbled around a mouthful. "If you don't, I surely won't."

"Experience, Dag. I've been in on maybe nine kills in my life. You've done what—fifteen? Twenty?"

"More, but the rest were just little ones. Lucky finds."

"Lucky ha, and little ones count just the same. They'd have been big ones by the next year." She took a bite of her own food, chewed, and sighed. "The children are excited."

"Noticed. They're going to start setting each other off if they get wound up much tighter."

A snort, presumably of agreement.

The raspy voice grew suddenly urgent. "If we do find the malice's lair, put the youngsters to the back."

"Can't. They need the experience, just as we did."

A mutter: "Some experiences no one needs."

The woman ignored this, and said, "I thought I'd pair Saun with you."

"Spare me. Unless I'm pulling camp guard duty. Again."

"Not this time. The Glassforge folk are offering a passel of men to help."

"Ah, spare us all. Clumsy farmers, worse than the children."

"It's their folk being lost. They've a right."

"Doubt they could even take out real bandits." He added after a moment, "Or they would have by now." And after another, "If they are real bandits."

"Thought I'd stick the Glassforgers with holding the horses, mostly. If it is a malice, and if it's grown as big as Chato fears, we'll need every pair of our hands to the front."

A short silence. "Poor word choice, Mari."

"Bucket's over there. Soak your head, Dag. You know what I meant."

The right hand waved. "Yeah, yeah."

With an *oof,* the woman rose to her feet. "Eat. That's an order, if you like."

"*I'm* not nervy."

"No"—the woman sighed—"no, you are not that." She strode off.

The man settled back again. *Go away, you,* Fawn thought down at him resentfully. *I have to pee.*

But in a few minutes, just before she was driven by her body's needs into entirely unwelcome bravery, the man got up and wandered after the patrol leader. His steps were unhurried but long, and he was across the yard before the leader gave a vague wave of her hand and a side glance. Fawn could not see how it could be an order, yet somehow, everyone in the patrol was suddenly up and in motion, saddlebags repacked, girths tightened. The whole lot of them were mounted and on their way in five minutes.

Fawn slipped down the tree trunk and peered around it. The one-handed man—riding rear guard?—was looking back over his shoulder. She ducked out of sight again till the hoofbeats faded, then unclutched the apple tree and went to seek the farmwife. Her pack, she was relieved to see in passing, lay untouched on the bench.

Dag glanced back, wondering anew about the little farm girl who'd been hiding shyly up the apple tree. There, now—down she slid, but he still gained no clear look at her. Not that a few leaves and branches could hide a life-spark so bright from his groundsense at *that* range.

His mind's eye sketched a picture of her tidy farm raided by a malice's mud-men, all its cheerful routine turned to ash and blood and charnel smoke. Or worse—and not imagination but memory supplied the vision—a ruination like the Western Levels beyond the Gray River, not six hundred miles west of here. Not so far away to him, who had ridden or walked the distance a dozen times, yet altogether beyond these local people's horizons. Endless miles of open flat, so devastated that even rocks could not hold their shape and slumped into gray dust. To cross that vast blight leached the ground from one's body as a desert parched the mouth, and it was just as potentially lethal to linger there. A thousand years of sparse rains had only begun to sculpt the Levels into something resembling a landscape again. To see this farm girl's green rolling lands laid low like that . . .

Not if I can help it, Little Spark.

He doubted they would meet again, or that she would ever know what her—mother's?—strange customers today sought to do on her behalf and their own. Still, he could not begrudge her his weariness in this endless task. The country people who gained even a partial understanding of the methods called it black necromancy and sidled away from patrollers in the street. But they accepted their gift of safety all the same. *So yet again, one more time anew, we will buy the death of this malice with one of our own.*

But not more than one, not if he could make it so.

Dag clapped his heels to his horse's sides and cantered after his patrol.

The farmwife watched thoughtfully as Fawn packed up her bedroll, straightened the straps, and hitched it over her shoulder once more. "It's near a day's ride to Glassforge from here," she remarked. "Longer, walking. You're like to be benighted on the road."

"It's all right," said Fawn. "I've not had trouble finding a place to sleep." Which was true enough. It was easy to find a cranny to curl up in out of sight of the road, and bedtime was a simple routine when all you did was spread a blanket and lie down, unwashed and unbrushed, in your clothes. The only pests that had found her in the dark were the mosquitoes and ticks.

"You could sleep in the barn. Start off early tomorrow." Shading her eyes, the woman stared down the road where the patrollers had vanished a while ago. "I'd not charge you for it, child."

Her honest concern for Fawn's safety stood clear in her face. Fawn was torn between unjust anger and a desire to burst into tears, equally uncomfortable lumps in her stomach and throat. *I'm not twelve, woman.* She thought of saying so, and more. She had to start practicing it sooner or later: *I'm twenty. I'm a widow.* The phrases did not rise readily to her lips as yet.

Still . . . the farmwife's offer beguiled her mind. Stay a day, do a chore or two or six and show how useful she could be, stay another day, and another . . . farms always needed more hands, and Fawn knew how to keep hers busy. Her first planned act when she reached Glassforge was to look for work. Plenty of work right here—familiar tasks, not scary and strange.

But Glassforge had been the goal of her imagination for weeks now. It seemed like quitting to stop short. And wouldn't a town offer better privacy? *Not necessarily,* she realized with a sigh. Wherever she went, folks would get to know her sooner or later. Maybe it was all the same, no new horizons anywhere, really.

She mustered her flagging determination. "Thanks, but I'm expected. Folk'll worry if I'm late."

The woman gave a little headshake, a combination of conceding the argument and farewell. "Take care, then." She turned back to her house and her own onslaught of tasks, duties that probably kept her running from before dawn to after dark.

A life I would have taken up, except for Sunny Sawman, Fawn thought gloomily, climbing back up to the straight road once more. *I'd have taken it up for the sake of Sunny Sawman, and never thought of another.*

Well, I've thought of another now, and I'm not going to go and unthink it. Let's go see Glassforge.

One more time, she called up her wearied fury with Sunny, the low, stupid, nasty . . . stupid fool, and let it stiffen her spine. Nice to know he had a use after all, of a sort. She faced south and began marching.

2

Last year's leaves were damp and black with rot underfoot, and as Dag climbed the steep slope in the dark, his boot slid. Instantly, a strong and anxious hand grasped his right arm.

"Do that again," said Dag in a level whisper, "and I'll beat you senseless. Quit trying to protect me, Saun."

"Sorry," Saun whispered back, releasing the death clutch. After a momentary pause, he added, "Mari says she won't pair you with the girls anymore because *you're* overprotective."

Dag swallowed a curse. "Well, that does not apply to you. Senseless. And bloody."

He could feel Saun's grin flash in the shadows of the woods. They heaved themselves upward a few more yards, finding handgrips among the rocks and roots and saplings.

"Stop," Dag breathed.

A nearly soundless query from his right.

"We'll be up on them over this rise. What you can see, can see you, and if there's anything over there with groundsense, you'll look like a torch in the trees. Stop it down, boy."

A grunt of frustration. "But I can't see Razi and Utau. I can barely see you. You're like an ember under a handful of ash."

"I can track Razi and Utau. Mari holds us all in her head, you don't have to. You only have to track me." He slipped behind the youth and gripped his right shoulder, massaging. He wished he could do both sides together, but this touch seemed to be enough; the flaring tension started to go out of Saun, both body and mind. "Down. Down. That's right. Better." And after a moment, "You're going to do just fine."

Dag had no idea whether Saun was going to do well or disastrously, but

Saun evidently believed him, with appalling earnestness; the bright anxiety decreased still further.

"Besides," Dag added, "it's not raining. Can't have a debacle without rain. It's obligatory, in my experience. So we're good." The humor was weak, but under the circumstances, worked well enough; Saun chuckled.

He released the youth, and they continued their climb.

"Is the malice there?" muttered Saun.

Dag stopped again, bending in the shadows to hook up a plant left-sided. He held it under Saun's nose. "See this?"

Saun's head jerked backward. "It's poison ivy. Get it out of my face."

"If we were this close to a malice's lair, not even the poison ivy would still be alive. Though I admit, it would be among the last to go. This isn't the lair."

"Then why are we here?"

Behind them, Dag could hear the men from Glassforge topping the ridge and starting down into the ravine out of which he and the patrol were climbing. Second wave. Even Saun didn't manage to make that much noise. Mari had better land her punches before their helpers closed the gap, or there would be no surprise left. "Chato thinks this robber troop has been infiltrated, or worse, suborned. Catch us a mud-man, it'll lead us to its maker, quick enough."

"*Do* mud-men have groundsense?"

"Some. Malice ever catches one of us, it takes everything. Groundsense. Methods and weapon skills. Locations of our camps . . . Likely the first human this one caught was a road robber, trying to hide out in the hills, which is why it's doing what it is. None of us have been reported missing, so we still may have the edge. A patroller doesn't let a malice take him alive if he can help it." *Or his partner.* Enough lessons for one night. "Climb."

On the ridgetop, they crouched low.

Smoothly, Saun strung his bow. Less smoothly but just as quickly, Dag unshipped and strung his shorter, adapted one, then swapped out the hook screwed into the wooden cuff strapped to the stump of his left wrist, and swapped in the bow-rest. He seated it good and tight, clamped the lock, and dropped the hook into the pouch on his belt. Undid the guard strap on his sheath and made sure the big knife would draw smoothly. It was all scarcely more awkward than carrying the bow in his hand had once been, and at least he couldn't drop it.

At the bottom of the dell, Dag could see the clearing through the trees: three or four campfires burning low, tents, and an old cabin with half its roof tumbled in. Lumps of sleeping men in bedrolls, like scratchy burrs touching his groundsense. The faint flares of a guard, awake in the woods beyond, and someone stumbling back from the slit trenches. The sleepy smudges of a few horses tethered beyond. Words of the body's senses for something his eyes did not see nor hand touch. Maybe twenty-five men altogether, against the patrol's sixteen and the score or so of volunteers from Glassforge. He began to sort through the life-prickles, looking for things shaped like men that . . . weren't.

The night sounds of the woods carried on: the croak of tree frogs, the chirp of crickets, the sawing of less identifiable insects. An occasional tiny rustle in the weeds. Anything bigger might have been either scared off by the noise of the camp below, or, depending on how the robbers buried their scraps, attracted. Dag felt around with his groundsense beyond the tightening perimeter of the patrol, but found no nervous scavengers.

Then, too soon, a startled yell from his far right, partway around the patroller circle. Grunts, cries, the ring of metal on metal. The camp stirred. *That's it, in we go.*

"Closer," snapped Dag to Saun, and led a slide downslope to shorten their range. By the time he'd closed the distance to a bare twenty paces and found a gap in the trees through which to shoot, the targets were obligingly rising to their feet. From even farther to his right, a flaming arrow arced high and came down on a tent; in a few minutes, he might even be able to see what he was shooting at.

Dag let both fear and hope fade from his mind, together with worries about the inner nature of what they faced. It was just targets. One at a time. That one. And that one. And in that confusion of flickering shadows. . . .

Dag loosed another shaft, and was rewarded by a distant yelp. He had no idea what he'd hit or where, but it would be moving slower now. He paused to observe, and was satisfied when Saun's next shaft also vanished into the black dark beyond the cabin and returned a meaty *thunk* they could hear all the way up here. All around in the woods, the patrol was igniting with excitement; his head would be as full of them as Mari's was in a moment if they didn't all get a grip on themselves.

The advantage of twenty paces was that it was a nice, short, snappy range to shoot from. The disadvantage was how little time it took your targets to run up on your position . . .

Dag cursed as three or four large shapes came crashing through the dark at them. He let his bow arm pivot down and yanked out his knife. Glancing right, he saw Saun pull his long sword, swing, and make the discovery that a blade length that gave great advantage from horseback was awkwardly constrained in a close-grown woods.

"You can't lop heads here!" Dag yelled over his shoulder. "Go to thrusts!" He grunted as he folded in his bow-arm and shoved his left shoulder into the nearest attacker, knocking the man back down the hillside. He caught a blade that came out of seeming-nowhere on the brass of his hilt, and with a shuddering scrape closed in along it for a well-placed knee to a target groin. These men might have fancied themselves bandits, but they still fought like farmers.

Saun raised a leg and booted his blade free of a target; the man's cry choked in his throat, and the withdrawing steel made an ugly sucking noise. Saun followed Dag at a run toward the bandit camp. Razi and Utau, to their right and left, paced them, closing in tight as they all descended, stooping like hawks.

In the clearing, Saun devolved to his favorite powerful swings again. Which worked spectacularly bloodily when they connected, and left him wide open when they didn't. A target succeeded in ducking, then came up swinging a long-handled, iron-headed sledgehammer. The breaking-pumpkin sound when it hit Saun's chest made Dag's stomach heave. Dag leaped inside the target's lethal radius, clutched him tightly around the back with his bow-arm, and brought his knife up hard. Wet horrors spilled over his hand, and he twisted the knife and shoved the target off it. Saun lay on his back, writhing, his face darkening.

"Utau! Cover us!" Dag yelled. Utau, gasping for breath, nodded and took up a protective stance, blade ready. Dag slid down to Saun's side, snapped off his bow lock and dropped it, and raised Saun's head to his lap, letting his right hand slide over the strike zone.

Broken ribs and shattered breathing, heart shocked still. Dag let his groundsense, nearly extinguished so as to block his targets' agony, come up fully, then flow into the boy. The pain was immense. *Heart first.* He concentrated himself there. A dangerous unity, if the yoked organs both chose to stop instead of start. A burning, lumping sensation in his own chest mirrored the boy's. *Come on, Saun, dance with me . . .* A flutter, a stutter, a bruised limping. Stronger. Now the lungs. One breath, two, three, and the chest rose again, then again, and finally steadied in synchrony. Good, yes, heart and lungs would continue on their own.

The stunning reverberation of Saun's targets' ill fates still sloshed through the boy's system, insufficiently blocked. Mari would have some work there, later. *I hate fighting humans.* Regretfully, Dag let the pain flow back to its source. The boy would be walking bent over for a month, but he would live.

The world returned to his senses. Around the clearing, bandits were starting to surrender as the yelling Glassforge men arrived and broke from the woods. Dag grabbed up his bow and rose to his feet, looking around. Beyond the burning tent, he spotted Mari. *Dag!* her mouth moved, but the cry was lost in the noise. She raised two fingers, pointed beyond the clearing on the opposite side, and snapped them down against her armguard. Dag's head swiveled.

Two bandits had dodged through the perimeter and were running away. Dag waved his bow in acknowledgment, and cried to his left linker, "Utau! Take Saun?"

Utau signaled his receipt of Dag's injured partner. Dag turned to give chase, trying to reaffix the bow to its clamp as he ran. By the time he'd succeeded, he was well beyond the light from the fires. Closer . . .

The horse nearly ran him down; he leaped away barely before he could be knocked aside. The fugitives were riding double, a big man in front and a huge one behind.

No. That second one wasn't a man.

Dizzied with excitement, the chase, and the aftershock of Saun's injury, Dag bent a moment, gasping for control of his own breathing. His hand rose to check the twin knife sheath hung under his shirt, a reassuring lump against his chest. Dark, warm, mortal hum. *Mud-man. We have you. You and your maker are ours . . .*

He despised tracking from horseback, but he wasn't going to catch them on foot, not even with that dual burden. He calmed himself again, down, down, *ours!, down* curse it, and summoned his horse. It would take Copperhead several minutes to blunder through the woods from the patrol's hidden assembly point. He knelt and removed his bow again, unstrung and stored it, and fumbled out the most useful of his hand replacements, a simple hook with a flat tongue of springy steel set against its outside curve to act as a sometimes-pincer. Tapping out a resin-soaked stick from the tin case in his vest pocket, he set it in the pinch of the spring and persuaded it to ignite. As the flare burned down to its end, he shuffled back and forth studying the hoofprints. When he was sure he could recognize them again, he pushed to his feet.

His quarry had nearly passed the limit of his groundsense by the time his mount arrived, snorting, and Dag swung aboard. Where one horse went another could follow, right? He kicked Copperhead after them at a speed that would have had Mari swearing at him for risking his fool neck in the dark. *Mine.*

⁂

Fawn plodded.

Now that she was finally coming out of the flats into the southeastern hills, the straight road was not as level as it had run since Lumpton, nor as straight. Its gentle slopes and curves were interspersed with odd climbs up through narrow, choked ravines that slashed through the rock, or down to timber bridges replacing shattered stone spans that lay like old bones between one impossible jumping-off point and another. The track dodged awkwardly around old rockfalls, or wet its feet and hers in fords.

Fawn wondered when she would finally reach Glassforge. It couldn't be too much farther, for all that she had made a slow start this dawn. The last of the good bread had stayed down, at least. The day threatened to grow hot and sticky, later. Here, the road was pleasantly shaded, with woods crowding up to both sides.

So far this morning she had passed a farm cart, a pack train of mules, and a small flock of sheep, all going the other way. She'd encountered nothing else for nearly an hour. Now she raised her head to see a horse coming toward her, down the road a piece. Also going the wrong way, unfortunately. As it neared, she stepped aside. Not only headed north, but also already double-loaded. Bareback. The animal was plodding almost as wearily as Fawn, its unbrushed dun hair smeared with salty crusts of dried sweat, burrs matting its black mane and tail.

The riders seemed as tired and ill kept as the horse. A big fellow looking not much older than her actual age rode in front, all rumpled jacket and stubbled chin. Behind him, his bigger companion clung on. The second man had lumpy features and long untrimmed nails so crusted with dirt as to look black, and a blank expression. His too-small clothes seemed an afterthought: a ragged shirt hanging open with sleeves rolled up, trousers that did not reach his boot tops. His age was hard to guess. Fawn wondered if he was a simpleton. They both looked as though they were making their way home from a night of drinking, or worse. The young man bore a big hunting knife, though the other seemed weaponless. Fawn marched past with the briefest nod, making no greeting to them, though out of the corner of her eye she could see both their heads turn. She walked on, not looking back.

The receding rhythm of hoofbeats stopped. She dared a glance over her shoulder. The two men seemed to be arguing, in voices too hushed and rumbling for her to make out the words, except a reiterated, "Master want!" in rising, urgent tones from the simpleton, and a sharp, aggravated "Why?" from the other. She lowered her face and walked faster. The hoofbeats started again, but instead of fading into the distance, grew louder.

The animal loomed alongside. "Morning," the younger man called down in a would-be cheerful tone. Fawn glanced up. He tugged his dirty blond hair at her politely, but his smile did not reach his eyes. The simpleton just stared tensely at her.

Fawn combined a civil nod with a repelling frown, starting to think, *Please, let there be a cart. Cows. Other riders, anything, I don't care which direction.*

"Going to Glassforge?" he inquired.

"I'm expected," Fawn returned shortly. *Go away. Just turn around and go away.*

"Family there?"

"Yes." She considered inventing some large Glassforge brothers and uncles, or just relocating the real ones. The plague of her life, she almost wished for them now.

The simpleton thumped his friend on the shoulder, scowling. "No talk. Just take." His voice came out smeared, as though his mouth was the wrong shape inside.

A manure wagon would be just lovely. One with a lot of people on board, preferably.

"You do it, then," snapped the young man.

The simpleton shrugged, braced his hands, and slid himself off right over the horse's rump. He landed more neatly than Fawn would have expected. She lengthened her stride; then, as he came around the horse toward her, she broke into a dead run, looking around frantically.

The trees were no help. Anything she could climb, he could too. To get out of sight long enough to hide in the woods, she had to outpace her pursuer by an impossible margin. Might she stay ahead until a miracle occurred, such as someone riding around that long curve up ahead?

He moved faster than she would have guessed for a man that size, too. Before her third breath or step, huge hands clamped around her upper arms and lifted her right off her pumping feet. At this range she could see that their nails were not just dirty but utterly black, like claws. They bit through her jacket as he swung her around.

She yelled as loud as she could, "Let go of me! Let go!" followed up with throat-searing screams. She kicked and struggled with all her strength. It was like fighting an oak tree, for all the result she got.

"Well, now you've got her all riled up," said the young man in disgust. He too slid off the horse, stared a moment, and pulled off the rope holding up his trousers. "We'll have to tie her hands. Unless you want your eyes clawed out."

Good idea. Fawn tried. Useless: the simpleton's hands remained clamped on her wrists, yanked high over her head. She writhed around and bit a bare, hairy arm. The huge man's skin had a most peculiar smell and taste, like cat fur, not as foul as she would have expected. Her satisfaction at drawing blood was short-lived as he spun her around and, still without visible emotion, fetched her an open-handed slap across the face that snapped her head back and dropped her to the road, black-and-purple shadows boiling up in her vision.

Her ears were still ringing when she was jerked upright and tied, then lifted. The simpleton handed her up to the young man, now back aboard his horse. He shoved at her skirts and set her upright in front of him, both hands clamped around her waist. The horse's sweaty barrel was warm under her legs. The simpleton took the reins to lead them and started walking once more, faster.

"There, that's better," said the man who held her, his sour breath wafting past her ear. "Sorry he hit you, but you shouldn't have run from him. Come on along, you'll have more fun with me." One hand wandered up and squeezed her breast. "Huh. Riper than I thought."

Fawn, gasping for air and still shuddering with shock, licked at a wet trickle from her nose. Was it tears, or blood, or both? She pulled surreptitiously at the rope around her wrists uncomfortably binding her hands. The knots seemed very tight. She considered more screaming. No, they might hit her again, or gag her. Better to pretend to be stunned, and then if they passed anyone within shouting distance, she'd still have command of her voice and her legs.

This hopeful plan lasted all of ten minutes, when, before anyone else hove into sight, they turned right off the road onto a hidden path. The young man's clutch had turned into an almost lazy embrace, and his hands wandered up and down her torso. As they started up a slope, he hitched forward as she slid backward, shoved her bedroll out of the way, and held her backside more tightly against his front, letting the horse's movement rub them together.

As much as this flagrant interest frightened her, she wasn't sure but what the simpleton's indifference frightened her more. The young man was being nasty in predictable ways. The other . . . she had no idea what he was thinking, if anything.

Well, if this is going where it looks, at least they can't make me pregnant. Thank you, stupid Sunny Sawman. As bright sides went, that one stank like a cesspit, but she had to allow the point. She hated her body's trembling, signaling her fear to her captor, but she could not stop it. The simpleton led them deeper into the woods.

Dag stood in his stirrups when the distant yelling echoed through the trees from the broad ravine, so high and fierce that he could barely distinguish words: *Let! Go!*

He kicked his horse into a trot, ignoring the branches that swiped and scratched them both. The strange marks he'd read in the road a couple of miles back suddenly grew a lot more worrisome. He'd been trailing his quarry at the outermost edge of his groundsense for hours, now, while the night's exhaustion crept up on his body and wits, hoping that they were leading him to the malice's lair. His suspicion that a new concern had been added to his pack chilled his belly as the outraged cries continued.

He popped over a rise and took a fast shortcut down an erosion gully with his horse nearly sliding on its haunches. His quarry came into sight at last in a small clearing. *What . . . ?* He snapped his jaw shut and cantered forward, heedless of his own noise now. Pulled up at ten paces, flung himself off, let his hand go through the steps of stringing and mounting and locking his bow without conscious thought.

It was abundantly clear that he wasn't interrupting someone's tryst. The kneeling mud-man, blank-faced, was holding down the shoulders of a struggling figure who was obscured by his comrade. The other man was trying, simultaneously, to pull down his trousers and part the legs of the captive, who was kicking valiantly at him. He cursed as a small foot connected.

"*Hold* her!"

"No time to stop," grumbled the mud-man. "Need to go on. No time for this."

"It won't take long if you just . . . hold her . . . still!" He finally managed to shove his hips inside the angle of the kicks.

Absent gods, was that a *child* they were pinning to the dirt? Dag's ground-sense threatened to boil over; distracted or no, the mud-man must notice him soon even if the other had his backside turned. The middle figure surged upward briefly, face flushed and black curls flying, dress pulled half-down as well as shoved half-up. A flash of sweet breasts like apples smote Dag's eyes. *Oh.* That short rounded form was no child after all. But outweighed like one nonetheless.

Dag quelled his fury and drew. Those heaving moon-colored buttocks had to be the most righteous target ever presented to his aim. And for once in his accursed life, it seemed he was *not too late*. He considered this marvel for the whole moment it took to adjust his tension to be sure the arrow would not go through and into the girl. Woman. Whatever she was.

Release.

He was reaching for another shaft before the first found its mark. The perfection of the *thunk,* square in the middle of the left cheek, was even more satisfying than the surprised scream that followed. The bandit bucked and rolled off the girl, howling and trying to reach around himself, twisting from side to side.

Now the danger was not halved, but doubled. The mud-man stood abruptly, seeing Dag at last, and dragged the girl up in front of his torso as a shield. His height and her shortness thwarted his intent; Dag sent his next shaft toward the creature's calf. It was a glancing hit, but stung. The mud-man leaped.

Did this one have enough wits to threaten his prisoner in order to stop Dag? Dag didn't wait to find out. Lips drawn back in a fierce grin, he drew his war knife and pelted forward. Death was in his stride.

The mud-man saw it; fear flashed in that sullen, lumpy face. With a panicked heave, he tossed the crying girl toward Dag, turned, and fled.

Bow still encumbering his left arm, the knife in his right hand, Dag had no way to catch her. The best he could do was fling his arms wide so that she wasn't stabbed or battered. He lost his skidding balance on her impact, and they both went down in a tangle.

For a moment, she was on top of him, her breath knocked out, her body's softness squashed onto his. She inhaled, made a strained squeaking noise, yanked herself up, and began clawing at his face. He tried to get out words to calm her, but she wouldn't let him; finally he was forced to let go of his weapon and just fling her off. With two live enemies still on the ground, he would have to deal with her *next*. He rolled away, snatched up his knife again, and surged to his feet.

The mud-man had scrambled back up on the bandit's horse. He yanked the beast's head around and tried to ride Dag down. Dag dodged, started to flip his knife around for a throw, thought better of it, dropped it again, reached back to his now-twisted-around quiver, and drew one of his few remaining arrows. Nocked, aimed.

No.

Let the creature keep running, back to the lair. Dag could pick up those tracks again if he had to. One wounded prisoner would test the limits of what he could handle right now. A prisoner who was, most definitely, going to be made to talk. The horse vanished up the faint trail leading out of the clearing that paralleled the course of a nearby creek. Dag lowered the bow and looked around.

The human bandit too had disappeared, but for once, tracking was not going to be any trouble. Dag pointed to the girl, now standing up a few yards away and struggling to readjust her torn blue dress. "*Stay* there." He followed the blood trail.

Past a screen of saplings and brush lining the clearing, the splashes grew heavier. By the boulders of the creek a figure lay prone and silent in a red puddle, trousers about his knees, Dag's arrow clutched in his hand.

Too still. Dag set his teeth. The man had evidently tried to drag the maddening shaft out of his flesh by main force, and must have ripped open an artery doing so. *That wasn't a killing shot, blight it!* Wasn't supposed to be. *Good intentions, where have we met before?* Dag balanced himself and shoved the body over with one foot. The pale unshaven face looked terribly young in death, even shadowed as it was by dirt. No answers now to be squeezed from this one; he had reached the last of all betrayals.

"Absent gods. *More* children. Is there no end to them?" Dag muttered.

He looked up to see the woman-child standing a few paces back along the blood trail, staring at them both. Her eyes were huge and brown, like a terrified deer's. At least she wasn't screaming anymore. She frowned down at her late assailant, and an unvoiced *Oh* ghosted from her tender, bitten lips. A livid bruise was starting up one side of her face, scored with four parallel red gouges. "He's dead?"

"Unfortunately. And unnecessarily. If he'd just lain still and waited for help, I'd have taken him prisoner."

She looked him up, and up, and down, fearfully. The top of her dark head, were they standing closer, would come just about to the middle of his chest, Dag judged. Self-consciously, he tucked his bow-hand down by his side, half out of sight around his thigh, and sheathed his knife.

"I know who you are!" she said suddenly. "You're that Lakewalker patroller I saw at the well-house!"

Dag blinked, and blinked again, and let his groundsense, shielded from the shock of this death, come up again. She blazed in his perceptions. "Little Spark! What are you doing so far from your farm?"

3

The tall patroller was staring at Fawn as though he recognized her. She wrinkled her nose in confusion, not following his words. From this angle and distance, she could at last see the color of his eyes, which were an unexpected metallic gold. They seemed very bright in his bony face, against weathered skin tanned to a dark coppery sheen on his face and hand. Several sets of scratches scored his cheeks and forehead and jaw, most just red but some bleeding. *I did that, oh dear.*

Beyond, the body of her would-be ravisher lay on the smoothed stones of the creek bank. Some of his still-wet blood trickled into the creek, to swirl away in the clear water in faint red threads, dissipating to pink and then gone. He had been so hotly, heavily, frighteningly alive just minutes ago, when she had wished him dead. Now she had her wish, she was not so sure.

"I . . . it . . . " she began, waving an uncertain hand at, well, everything, then blurted, "I'm sorry I scratched you up. I didn't understand what was coming at me." Then added, "You scared me." *I think I've lost my wits.*

A hesitant smile turned the patroller's lips, making him look for a moment like someone altogether else. Not so . . . looming. "I was trying to scare the other fellow."

"It worked," she allowed, and the smile firmed briefly before fleeing again.

He felt his face, glanced at the red smears on his fingertips as if surprised, then shrugged and looked back at her. The weight of his attention was startling to her, as though no one in her life had ever looked at her before, really looked; in her present shaky state, it was not a comfortable sensation.

"Are you all right otherwise?" he asked gravely. His right hand made an inquiring jerk. The other he still held down by his side, the short, powerful-looking bow cocked at an angle out of the way by his leg. "Aside from your face."

"My face?" Her quivering fingertips probed where the simpleton had struck her. Still a little numb, but starting to ache. "Does it show?"

He nodded.

"Oh."

"Those gouges don't look so good. I have some things in my saddlebags to clean them up. Come away, here, come sit down, um . . . away."

From that. She eyed the corpse and swallowed. "All right." And added, "I'm all right. I'll stop shaking in a minute, sure. Stupid of me."

With his open hand not coming within three feet of her, he herded her back toward the clearing like someone shooing ducks. He pointed to a big fallen log a way apart from the scuffed spot of her recent struggle and walked to his horse, a rangy chestnut calmly browsing in the weeds trailing its reins. She plunked down heavily and sat bent over, arms wrapped around herself, rocking a little. Her throat was raw, her stomach hurt, and though she wasn't gasping anymore, it still felt as though she couldn't get her breath back or that it had returned badly out of rhythm.

The patroller carefully turned his back to Fawn, did something to dismantle his bow, and rummaged in his saddlebag. More adjustments of some sort. He turned again, shrugging the strap of a water bottle over one shoulder, and with a couple of cloth-wrapped packets tucked under his left arm. Fawn blinked, because he seemed to have suddenly regained a left hand, stiffly curved in a leather glove.

He lowered himself beside her with a tired-sounding grunt, and arranged those legs. At this range he smelled, not altogether unpleasantly, of dried sweat, woodsmoke, horse, and fatigue. He laid out the packets and handed her the bottle. "Drink, first."

She nodded. The water was flat and tepid but seemed clean.

"Eat." He held out a piece of bread fished from the one cloth.

"I couldn't."

"No, really. It'll give your body something to do besides shake. Very distractible that way, bodies. Try it."

Doubtfully, she took it and nibbled. It was very good bread, if a little dry by now, and she thought she recognized its source. She had to take another sip of water to force it down, but her uncontrolled trembling grew less. She peeked at his stiff left hand as he opened the second cloth, and decided it must be carved of wood, for show.

He wetted a bit of cloth with something from a small bottle—Lakewalker medicine?—and raised his right hand to her aching left cheek. She flinched, although the cool liquid did not sting.

"Sorry. Don't want to leave those dirty."

"No. Yes. I mean, right. It's all right. I think the simpleton clawed me when he hit me." Claws. Those had been claws, not nails. What kind of monstrous birth . . . ?

His lips thinned, but his touch remained firm.

"I'm sorry I didn't come up on you sooner, miss. I could see something had happened back on the road, there. I'd been trailing those two all night. My patrol seized their gang's camp a couple of hours after midnight, up in the hills on the other side of Glassforge. I'm afraid I flushed them right into you."

She shook her head, not in denial. "I was walking down the road. They just picked me up like you'd pick up a lost . . . thing, and claim it was yours." Her frown deepened. "No . . . not just. They argued first. Strange. The one who was . . . um . . . the one you shot, he didn't want to take me along, at first. It was the other one who insisted. But he wasn't interested in me at all, later. When—just before you came." And added under her breath, not expecting an answer, "What *was* he?"

"Raccoon, is my best guess," said the patroller. He turned the cloth, hiding browning blood, and wet it again, moving down her cheek to the next gash.

This bizarre answer seemed so entirely unrelated to her question that she decided he must not have heard her aright. "No, I mean the big fellow who hit me. The one who ran away from you. He didn't seem right in the head."

"Truer than you guess, miss. I've been hunting those creatures all my life. You get so you can tell. He was a made thing. Confirms that a malice—your folk would call it a blight bogle—has emerged near here. The malice makes slaves of human shape for itself, to fight, or do its dirty work. Other shapes too, sometimes. Mud-men, we call them. But the malice can't make them up out of nothing. So it catches animals, and reshapes them. Crudely at first, till it grows stronger and smarter. Can't make life at all, really. Only death. Its slaves don't last too long, but it hardly cares."

Was he gulling her, like her brothers? Seeing how much a silly little farm girl could be made to swallow down whole? He seemed perfectly serious, but maybe he was just especially good at tall tales. "Are you saying that blight bogles are *real*?"

It was his turn to look surprised. "Where are you from, miss?" he asked in renewed caution.

She started to name the village nearest her family's farm, but changed it to "Lumpton Market." It was a bigger town, more anonymous. She straightened, trying to marshal the casual phrase *I'm a widow* and push it past her bruised lips.

"What's your name?"

"Fawn. Saw . . . field," she added, and flinched. She'd wanted neither Sunny's name nor her own family's, and now she'd stuck herself with some of both.

"Fawn. Apt," said the patroller, with a sideways tilt of his head. "You must have had those eyes from birth."

It was that uncomfortable weighty attention again. She tried shoving back: "What's yours?" though she thought she already knew.

"I answer to Dag."

She waited a moment. "Isn't there any more?"

He shrugged. "I have a tent name, a camp name, and a hinterland name, but *Dag* is easier to shout." The smile glimmered by again. "Short is better, in the field. *Dag, duck!* See? If it were any longer, it might be too late. Ah, that's better."

She realized she'd smiled back. She didn't know if it was his talk or his bread or just the sitting down quietly, but her stomach had finally stopped shuddering. She was left hot and tired and drained.

He restoppered his bottle.

"Shouldn't you use that too?" she asked.

"Oh. Yeah." Cursorily, he turned the cloth again and swiped it over his face. He missed about half the marks.

"Why did you call me Little Spark?"

"When you were hiding above me in that apple tree yesterday, that's how I thought of you."

"I didn't think you could see me. You never looked up!"

"You didn't act as though to wanted to be seen. It only seemed polite." He added, "I thought that pretty farm was your home."

"It *was* pretty, wasn't it? But I only stopped there for water. I was walking to Glassforge."

"From Lumpton?"

And points north. "Yes."

He, at least, did not say anything about, *It's a long way for such short legs.* He did say, inevitably, "Family there?"

She almost said *yes,* then realized he might possibly intend to take her there, which could prove awkward. "No. I was going there to look for work." She straightened her spine. "I'm a grass widow."

A slow blink; his face went blank for a rather long moment. He finally said, in an oddly cautious tone, "Pardon, missus . . . but do you know what *grass widow* means?"

"A new widow," she replied promptly, then hesitated. "There was a woman came up from Glassforge to our village, once. She took in sewing and made cord and netting. She had the most beautiful little boy. My uncles called her a grass widow." Another too-quiet pause. "That's right, isn't it?"

He scratched his rat's nest of dark hair. "Well . . . yes and no. It's a farmer term for a woman pregnant or with a child in tow with no husband in sight anywhere. It's more polite than, um, less polite terms. But it's not altogether kind."

Fawn flushed.

He said even more apologetically, "I didn't mean to embarrass you. It just seemed I ought to check."

She swallowed. "Thank you." *It seems I told the truth despite myself, then.*

"And your little girl?" he said.

"What?" said Fawn sharply.

He motioned at her. "The one you bear now."

Flat panic stopped her breath. *I don't show! How can he know?* And how could he know, in any case, if the fruit of that really, really ill-considered and now deeply regretted frantic fumble with Sunny Sawman at his sister's spring wedding party was going to be a boy or a girl, anyhow?

He seemed to realize he'd made some mistake, but to be uncertain what it was. His gesture wavered, turning to open-handed earnestness. "It was what attracted the mud-man. Your present state. It was almost certainly why they grabbed you. If the other assault seemed an afterthought, it likely was."

"How can you—what—*why*?"

His lips parted for a moment, then, visibly, he changed whatever he'd been about to say to: "Nothing's going to happen to you now." He packed up his cloths. Anyone else might have tied the corners together, but he whipped a bit of cord around them that he somehow managed to wind into a pull-knot one-handed.

He put his right hand on the log and shoved himself to his feet. "I either need to put that body up a tree or pile some rocks on it, so the scavengers don't get to it before someone can pick it up. He might have people." He looked around vaguely. "Then decide what to do with you."

"Put me back on the road. Or just point me to it. I can find it."

He shook his head. "Those might not be the only fugitives. Not all the bandits might have been in the camp we took, or they might have had more than one hideout. And the malice is still out there, unless my patrol has got ahead of me, which I don't think is possible. My people were combing the hills to the south of Glassforge, and now I think the lair's northeast. This is no good time or place for you, especially, to be wandering about on your own." He bit his lip and went on almost as if talking to himself, "Body can wait. Got to put you somewhere safe. Pick up the track again, find the lair, get back to my patrol quick as I can. Absent gods, I'm tired. Mistake to sit down. Can you ride behind me, do you think?"

She almost missed the question in his mumble. *I'm tired too.* "On your horse? Yes, but—"

"Good."

He went to his mount and caught up the reins, but instead of coming back to her, led it to the creek. She trailed along again, partly curious, partly not wanting to let him out of her sight.

He evidently decided a tree would be faster for stowing his prey. He tossed a rope up over the crotch of a big sycamore that overhung the creek, using his horse to haul the body up it. He climbed up to be sure the corpse was securely wedged and to retrieve his rope. He moved so efficiently, Fawn could scarcely spot the extra motions and accommodations he made for his one-handed state.

Dag pressed his tired horse over the last ridge and was rewarded on the other side by finding a double-rutted track bumping along the creek bottom. "Ah, good," he said aloud. "It's been a while since I patrolled down this way, but I recall a good-sized farm tucked up at the head of this valley."

The girl clinging behind his cantle remained too quiet, the same wary silence she'd maintained since he'd discussed her pregnant state. His ground-sense, extended to utmost sensitivity in search for hidden threats, was battered by her nearby churning emotions; but the thoughts that drove them remained, as ever, opaque. He had maybe been too indiscreet. Farmers who found out much about Lakewalker groundsense tended to call it the evil eye, or black magic, and accuse patrollers of mind reading, cheating in trade, or worse. It was always trouble.

If he found enough people at this farm, he would leave her in their care, with strong warnings about the half-hunt-half-war presently going on in their hills. If there weren't enough, he must try to persuade them to light out for Glassforge or some other spot where they might find safety in numbers till this malice was taught mortality. If he knew farmers, they wouldn't want to go, and he sighed in anticipation of a dreary and thankless argument.

But the mere thought of a pregnant woman of any height or age wandering about in blithe ignorance anywhere near a malice's lair gave him gruesome horrors. No wonder she'd shone so brightly in his groundsense, with so much life happening in her. Although he suspected Fawn would have been scarcely less vivid even before this conception. But she would attract a malice's attention the way a fire drew moths.

By the time they'd straightened out the definition of *grass widow,* he had been fairly sure he had no need to offer her condolences. Farmer bed customs made very little sense, sometimes, unless one believed Mari's theories about their childbearing being all mixed up with their pretense of owning land. She had some very tart remarks on farmer women's lack of control of their own fertility, as well. Generally in conjunction with lectures to young patrollers of both sexes about the need to keep their trousers buttoned while in farmer territory.

Old patrollers, too.

Details of a dead husband had been conspicuously absent in Fawn's speech. Dag could understand grief robbing someone of words, but grief, too, seemed missing in her. Anger, fear, tense determination, yes. Shock from the recent terrifying attack upon her. Loneliness and homesickness. But not the anguish of a soul ripped in half. Strangely lacking, too, was the profound satisfaction such lifegiving usually engendered among Lakewalker women he'd known. Farmers, feh. Dag knew why his own people were all a little crazed, but what excuse did farmers have?

He was roused from his weary brooding as they passed out of the woods and the valley farm came into sight. He was instantly ill at ease. The lack of cows and horses and goats and sheep struck him first, then the broken-down places in the split-rail fence lining the pasture. Then the absence of farm dogs, who should have been barking annoyingly around his horse by now. He stood in his stirrups as they plodded up the lane. House and barn, both built of weathered gray planks, were standing—and standing open—but smoke rose in a thin trickle from the char and ashes of an outbuilding.

"What is it?" asked Fawn, the first words she'd spoken for an hour.

"Trouble, I think." He added after a moment, "Trouble past." Nothing human flared in the range of Dag's perceptions—nor anything nonhuman either. "The place is completely deserted."

He pulled up his horse in front of the house, swung his leg over its neck, and jumped down. "Move up. Take the reins," he told Fawn. "Don't get down yet."

She scrambled forward from her perch on his saddlebags, staring around wide-eyed. "What about you?"

"Going to scout around."

He made a quick pass through the house, a rambling two-story structure with additions built on to additions. The place seemed stripped of small objects of any value. Items too big to carry—beds, clothes chests—were frequently knocked over or split. Every glass window was broken out, senselessly. Dag had an idea how hard those improvements had been to come by, carefully saved for by some hopeful farmwife, packed in straw up from Glassforge over the rutted lanes. The kitchen pantry was stripped of food.

The barn was empty of animals; hay was left, some grain might be gone. Behind the barn on the manure pile, he at last found the bodies of three farm dogs, slashed and hacked about. He eyed the smoldering outbuilding in passing, charred timbers sticking out of the ash like black bones. Someone would need to look through it for other bones, later. He returned to his horse.

Fawn was gazing around warily as she took in the disturbing details. Dag leaned against Copperhead's warm shoulder and swiped his hand through his hair.

"The place was raided by the bandits—or someone—about three days ago, I judge," he told her. "No bodies."

"That's good—yes?" she said, dark eyes growing unsure at whatever expression was leaking onto his features. He couldn't think that it was anything but exhaustion.

"Maybe. But if the people had run away, or been run off, news of this should have reached Glassforge by now. My patrol had no such word as of yesterday evening."

"Where did they all go, then?" she asked.

"Taken, I'm afraid. If this malice is trying to take farmer slaves already, it's growing fast."

"What—slaves for what?"

"Not sure the malice even knows, yet. It's a sort of instinct with malices. It'll figure it out fast enough, though. I'm running out of time." He was growing dizzy with fatigue. Was he also growing stupid with fatigue?

He continued, "I'd give almost anything for two hours of sleep right now, except two hours of light. I need to get back to the trail while I still have daylight to see it. I think . . . " His voice slowed. "I think this place is as safe as any and safer than most. They've hit it once, it's already stripped of everything valuable—they won't be back too soon. I'm thinking maybe I could leave you here anyway. If anyone comes, you can tell them—no. First, if anyone comes, hide, till you are sure they're all-right folks. Then come out and tell them Dag has a message for his patrol, he thinks the malice is holed up northeast of town, not south. If patrollers come, do you think you could show them to where the tracks led off? And that boy's—bandit's—body," he added in afterthought.

She squinted at the wooded hills. "I'm not sure I could find my way back to it, the route you took."

"There's an easier way. This lane"—he waved at the track they'd ridden up—"goes back to the straight road in about four miles. Turn left, and I think the path your mud-man took east from it is about three miles on."

"Oh," she said more eagerly, "I could find that, sure."

"Good, then."

She had no fear, blast and blight it. He could change that . . . So did he want her to be terrified out of her mind, frozen witless? She was already sliding down off the horse, looking pleased to have a task within her capacity.

"What's so dangerous about the mud-men?" she asked, as he gathered his reins and prepared to mount once more.

He hesitated a long moment. "They'll eat you," he said at last. *After everything else is all over, that is.*

"Oh."

Subdued and impressed. And, more important, believing him. Well, it hadn't been a lie. Maybe it would make her just cautious enough. He found his stirrup and pushed up, trying not to dwell on the contrast between this hard saddle and a feather bed. There had been one unslashed feather mattress left inside the farmhouse. He'd noticed it particularly, while shoving aside a little fantasy about falling into it face-first. He swung his horse around.

"Dag . . . ?"

He turned at once to look over his shoulder. Big brown eyes stared up at him from a face like a bruised flower.

"Don't let them eat you, either."

Involuntarily, his lips turned up; she smiled brightly back through her darkening contusions. It gave him an odd feeling in his stomach, which he prudently did not attempt to name. Heartened despite all, he raised his carved hand in salute and cantered back down the lane.

Feeling bereft, Fawn watched the patroller vanish into the tunnel of trees at the edge of the fields. The silence of this homestead, stripped of animals and people, was eerie and oppressive, once she noticed it. She squinted upward. The sun had not even topped the arch of the sky for noon. It seemed years since dawn.

She sighed and ventured into the house. She walked all around it, footsteps echoing, feeling as though she intruded on some stranger's grief. The senseless mess the raiders had left in their wake seemed overwhelming, taken in all at once. She came back to the kitchen and stood there shivering a little. Well, if the house was too much, what about one room? *I could fix one room, yes.*

She braced herself and started by turning back upright anything that would still stand, shelf and table and a couple of chairs. What was broken beyond mending she hauled outside, starting a pile at one end of the porch. Then she swept the floor clear of broken plates and glass and spilled flour and drying food. She swept the porch too, while she was at it.

Beneath a worn old rag rug, ignored by the invaders, she found a trapdoor with a rope handle. She shook the rug over the porch rail, returned, and stared worriedly at the trap. *I don't think Dag saw this.*

She bit her lip, then took a bucket with a broken handle outside and collected a few live coals from the still-smoldering whatever-it-had-been, and started a little fire in the kitchen hearth. From it, she lit a candle stub found in the back of a drawer. She pulled up the trapdoor by its rope, wincing at the groaning of its hinges, swallowed, and stared at the ladder into the dark hole.

Could there be anyone still hiding down there? Big spiders? . . . Bodies? She took a deep breath and descended.

When she turned and held up the candle, her lips parted in astonishment. The cellar was lined with shelves, and on them, untouched, were row upon row of glass jars, many sealed with hot rock wax and covered with cloth bound with twine. Food storage for a farm full of hungry people. A year of labor lined up—Fawn knew exactly how much work, too, as preserving boiled foodstuffs under wax seals had been one of her most satisfying tasks back home. None of the jars were labeled, but her eye had no trouble picking out and identifying the contents. Fruit preserves. Vinegar pickles. Corn relish. Stew meat. A barrel in the corner proved to hold several sacks of flour. Another held last year's apples packed in straw, terribly wrinkly and by now only suitable for cooking, but not rotted. She was stirred to enthusiasm, and action.

Most of the jars were big, meant for a crowd, but she found three smaller ones, of dark purple fruit, corn relish, and what she trusted was stew meat, and hauled them up into the light. A kerchief full of flour, as well. A single iron pan, which she found kicked into a corner under a fallen shelf, was all that was left of the tools of this workplace, but with a little ingenuity she soon had flatbread cooking in it over her fire. The jar of meat proved to be, probably, pork cooked to flinders with onions and herbs, which she heated up after she'd freed the pan of her bread circles.

She caught up on days of scant rations, then, replete, set aside portions made up for Dag when he returned. Clearly, judging from his lady patrol leader and his general build, he was the sort of fellow you had to capture, hog-tie, and make remember to eat. Was he just a goer, or did he live too much inside his own head to notice his body's needs? And what all else was that head furnished with? He seemed driven. Considering the almost casual physical courage he'd displayed so far, it was unsettling to consider what he might fear that pushed him along so unceasingly. *Well, if I were as tall as a tree, maybe I'd be brave too.* A skinny tree. Upon consideration, she wrapped the meat and the preserves in rolls of flatbread so that he might eat while riding, because when he came back, it was likely he'd be in a hurry still.

If he came back. He hadn't actually said. The thought made a disappointed cold spot in her belly. *Now you're being stupid. Stop it.* The cure for bad sad thoughts was busyness, right enough, but she was getting dreadfully tired.

In one of the other rooms she found an abandoned sewing basket, also overlooked by the raiders, probably because the mending that topped it looked like rags. They'd entirely missed the valuable tools inside, sharp scissors and good thimbles and a collection of fine iron needles. Were the blight bogle's—malice's—mud-men all men then? Did it make any mud-women? It seemed not.

She decided she would sew up some of the slashed feather ticks in payment for the food, so it wouldn't feel so stolen. Sewing was not her best skill, but straight seams would be simple enough, and it would put an end to the messy, desolate feather wrack drifting about the place. She hauled the ticks out onto the porch, for the light, and so she could watch down the lane for a tall—for whoever. Needle and thread and fine repetitive work made a soothing rhythm under her hands. In the quiet, her mind circled back to this morning's terror. Dwelling on it started to make her feel sick and shaky again. As an alternative, she wrenched her thoughts to Lakewalkers.

Farmer to a Lakewalker didn't mean someone who grew crops; it meant anyone who wasn't a Lakewalker. Townsmen, rivermen, miners, millers—bandits—evidently they were all farmers in Dag's eyes. She wondered at the implications. She'd heard a story about a girl from over to Coshoton who had been seduced by a passing Lakewalker, a trading man, it was said. She had run away north three times to Lakewalker country after him, and been brought back by his people, then hanged herself in the woods. A cautionary tale, that. Fawn wondered what lesson you were supposed to draw from it. Well, *Girls should stay away from Lakewalkers* was the one obviously intended, but maybe the real one was, *If something doesn't work once, don't just repeat it twice more, try something else,* or *Don't give up so soon.* Or *Stay out of the woods.*

The nameless girl had died for thwarted love, it was whispered, but Fawn wondered if it hadn't been for thwarted rage, instead. She had, she admitted to herself, had some such thoughts after that awful talk with Stupid Sunny, but it wasn't that she'd wanted to *die,* it was that she'd wanted to make him feel as bad as he'd made her feel. And it had been rather flattening to reflect that she'd not be alive to properly enjoy her revenge, and even more flattening to suspect he'd get over any guilt pretty quick. Long before she'd get over being dead, in any case. And she'd done nothing that night after all, and by the next day, she'd had other ideas. So maybe the real lesson was, *Wait till morning, after breakfast.*

She wondered if the hanged girl had been pregnant too. Then she wondered anew how the tall man had *known,* seemingly just by looking at her with those eyes, their shimmering gold by sudden turns cold as metal or warm as summer. *Sorcerers, huh.* Dag didn't look like a sorcerer. (And what did sorcerers look like anyhow?) He looked like a very tired hunter who had been too long away from home. Hunting things that hunted him back.

A girl baby. Maybe he was just guessing. Fifty percent odds weren't half-bad, for appearing right, later. Still, it was an encouraging thought. Girls she knew. A little boy, however innocent, might have reminded her too much of Sunny. She hadn't meant to be a mother so soon in her life at all, but if she was going to be stuck with it, she would very well try to be a good one. She rubbed absently at her belly. *I will not betray you.* A bold promise. How was she to keep a child safe when she couldn't even save herself? *Also, from now on, I will be more careful.* Anyone could make a mistake. The trick was not to make the same one twice.

She eventually ran out of ripped fabric, patience to brood, and the will to stay awake. Her bruised face was throbbing. She hauled the repaired ticks back inside and piled them four deep in a corner of the kitchen, because the next room was still a disheartening mess and she hadn't the energy left to tackle it. She fell gratefully onto the pile. She had barely time to register the musty scent of them, and reflect that they were overdue for an airing anyhow, when her leaden eyes closed.

Fawn woke to the sound of steps on the wooden porch. *Dag back already?* It was still light. How long had she slept? Blearily, she pushed up, eager to show him the overlooked treasures in the cellar and to hear what he'd found. Only then did it register that there were too *many* heavy steps out there.

She should have been overlooked in the cellar—*I could have thrown a couple of those mattresses down there*—She had just time to think *What good is it to not to make the same mistakes twice when your new ones'll kill you all the same?* before the three mud-men burst open the door.

4

When the faint path he was following up into the hills turned into something more resembling a beaten trail, Dag decided it was time to get off it. Groundsense or common sense or sheer nerves, he could not tell, but he dismounted and led his horse aside into the woods to a small glade well out of sight and hearing of the track. He hardly needed to lay on suggestions of not-wandering-away; even Copperhead, with his rawhide endurance and his temper, was so tired as to be stumbling. But then, so was Dag. Feeling guilty, he tied the reins up out of the way of front hooves, but left the saddle on. He hated to leave his mount so ill tended, but if he came back in a tearing hurry, there might be no time to fool with gear. Or to hesitate to ride the beast to death, if needs drove hard enough. *Tomorrow, or the day after, we shall all take a better rest. One way or another.*

He did not return to the trail itself but shadowed the track a dozen paces off in the undergrowth. It was slow work, ghosting like a deer, each footfall carefully laid, constantly alert. Not a mile farther on he was glad of his prudence, freezing in a tangle of deadfall and wild grapevines as two figures came thumping openly along the path.

Mud-men. A fox and a rabbit, at a guess, and he hardly needed his inner senses to tell; they were crude, perhaps early efforts, and marks of their animal origin still showed on their hides, their ears, their misshapen faces and noses. It was highly tempting to try to do something with that combination, awaken them to their true-selves and let nature take its course, but the attempt would cost him his cover, perhaps open him to their master beyond. This was no time for games. Regretfully, he let them pass by, grateful that their clumsy new forms included human limitations on their sense of smell in trade for human advantages of hands and speech.

He first knew he was drawing close to the lair by the absence of birds. *This is a day for absences.* He drew his groundsense in even more tightly as the first yellowing, dying weeds began to rustle underfoot. *I wasn't expecting this till miles farther in.* The lair was much closer to the straight road than he'd thought it could possibly be. It was shockingly clever, in a malice so—supposedly— young, for it to send its first human gulls to take prey so far from its initial bastion. *How did we overlook this?*

He knew how. *We are too few, with too much ground to cover and never time enough.* Widen the teeth of the sweeps, speed the search, and risk clues slipping past unobserved. Go slow and close, and risk not getting to all the critical places in time. *Well, we found this one. This is a success, not a failure.*

Maybe.

By the time he reached a vantage he was crawling like a snail, nearly on his belly, scarcely daring to breathe. Every herb and weed around him was dead and brittle, the soil beneath his knees was achingly sterile, and his tightly furled groundsense shivered in the dry shock of the malice's draining aura. *Indeed, it's here.*

At the bottom of a rocky ravine, a creek wound from his right, ran straight below him, and curled away on his left. Not one living plant graced the cleft for as far as he could see in either direction, although the dead bones of a few trees still stood up like sentinels. A camp, of sorts, lay along the creek side: three or four black campfire pits, currently cold, piles of stolen supplies scattered haphazardly about. On the far side of the creek, a couple of uneasy horses stood tied to dead trees. Real, natural horses, as far as Dag could tell. Ill kept, of course.

The space below might accommodate twenty-five or fifty men, but it was nearly deserted at the moment. Exactly one mud-man was asleep on a pile of rags like a nest. Dag wondered if any of the absent company might be men his patrol had captured last night. Which implied that the patrol might well arrive on its own at any time, pleasant thought. He did not allow himself to dwell on the hope.

Partway up the other side of the ravine a shelf of overhanging rock created a cave, perhaps sixty feet long and shielded in front by a smooth gray outcrop of stone pushing up almost to meet the overhang. No telling from here how far back in it went. Paths ran out either end, down to the creek and up over the rise behind.

The malice was inside, at the moment. So was it mobile yet, or still sessile? And if mobile, had it undergone its first molt? And if it hadn't, how frantic would it be to gather the necessary human materials to achieve that? A malice's initial hatching body was even clumsier and cruder than a mud-man's, which generally seemed to irritate it.

Dag opened his shirt and felt for his sharing knives. He pulled the strap over his head and stared a moment at the twin sheaths. The stitched leather was slick with wear and dark with old sweat. He ran one finger over the thread-wound hilts, one blue, one green, drew and contemplated six inches of polished bone blade. Touched it to his lips. It hummed with old mortality.

Is this the day your death is redeemed, Kauneo my love? I have borne it around my neck for so long. As you willed, so I do. This was a vicious malice, big and getting bigger fast. It would nearly be worthy of her, Dag thought. Nearly.

He drew the second, empty bone blade and laid the two back to back. *They come in pairs, oh yes. One for you and one for me.* He slipped them away again.

Mari too bore sharing knives, and so did Utau and Chato, gifts of mortality from patrollers before them. Mari's current set was a legacy from one of her sons, he knew, and as dear to her as these to Dag. The patrol was well supplied. Who used theirs on a malice was not normally a matter of drawing straws, or heroics, or honor. Whoever first could, did. Any way they could. As efficiently as possible. It wasn't as though there wouldn't be another chance later.

Dag's ground was quivering at the drain from the malice's presence, an effect that would bleed over into his body if he lingered here much longer. Sensitive young patrollers were often so disturbed by their first encounter with a malice's aura, it took them weeks to recover. Dag had been one such. Once.

Now: go. Back to the horse, and gallop like a madman to the rendezvous point.

Yet . . . there were so few creatures in the camp. The opportunity beckoned for a, so to speak, single-handed attempt. Down the ravine side, fly across the creek, up into that cave . . . it could all be over in minutes. In the time it took to bring the patrol up, the malice too might draw in its reinforcements (and where were they now, doing what mischief?), turning the attack into a potentially costly fight just to regain a proximity he had right now. Dag thought of Saun. Had he lived the night?

But with his groundsense thwarted, Dag couldn't see how many men or mud-men might be hidden in the cave with the malice. If he went charging in there only to present his head to the enemy, the difficulties his patrol must then face would grow vastly worse. *Also, I would be dead.* In a way, he was glad that last prospect still had the power to disturb him. At least some.

He lowered his face, fought for control of his hastened breathing, and prepared to withdraw. His lips twisted. *Mari will be so proud of me.*

He started to push back from the edge of the ravine, but then froze again. Down a path on the other side, three mud-men appeared. Was that first one a—where had this malice found a *wolf* in these parts? Dag had thought the farmers had reduced wolf numbers in this region, but then, this range of rugged unplowable hills was a reservoir for all sorts of things. *As we see.* His eyes widened as he recognized the second in line, the escaped raccoon-man from this morning. The third, huger still, must once have been a black bear. A flash of familiar dull blue fabric over the giant bear-man's shoulder stopped his breath.

Little Spark. They found Little Spark. How . . . ?

A more or less straight line over the hills to the valley farm from here was the short leg of a triangle, he realized. He had run two long legs, to get from the farm back to where he'd first lost the raccoon-man's traces, then work his way here.

They found her because they went looking, I bet. It accounted for the rest of this malice's absent company; like the two he'd passed on the trail, they had doubtless all been dispatched to comb the hills for the escaped prize. And the malice and its mud-men already knew about the valley farm if they'd recently raided it. Must have known for a long time; his respect for this one's wits notched up yet again, for it to leave such a nearby tempting target alone, unmolested and unalarmed, for so long. How much strength had it gained, to dare to move openly now? Or had the arrival of Chato's patrol stampeded it?

The blue-clad figure, hanging head down, twitched and struggled. Beat the back of her captor with hard little fists, to no visible effect, except that the bear-man shrugged her hips higher over his shoulder and took a firmer grip on her thighs.

She was alive. Conscious. Undoubtedly terrified.

Not terrified enough. But Dag could make it up for her. His mouth opened, to silence his own speeding breathing, and his heart hammered. Now the malice had just what it needed for its next molt. Dag had only to deliver to it a Lakewalker patroller—and one *so* experienced, too—for its dessert, and its powers would be complete.

He wasn't sure if he was shivering with indecision or just fear. Fear, he decided. Yes, he could run back to the patrol and bring them on in force, by the tested rules, be *sure*. Because the Lakewalkers had to win, every time. But Fawn might be dead by the time they got back.

Or in minutes. The three mud-men vanished behind the occluding rock wall. So, at least three in there. Or there could be ten.

To get in and out of that cave . . . No. He only had to get in.

He didn't know why his brain was still madly trying to calculate risks, because his hand was already moving. Dropping bow and quiver and excess gear. Positioning his sharing-knife sheaths. Swapping out the spring-hook on his wooden wrist cap for the steel knife. Testing the draw of his war knife.

He rose and dropped down over the side of the ravine, sliding from rock to rill as silently as a serpent.

It had all happened so fast . . .

Fawn hung head down, dizzy and nauseated. She wondered if the blow she'd taken on the other side of her face would bruise to match the first. The mud-man's broad shoulder seemed to punch her stomach as it jogged along endlessly, without stopping even when she'd been violently sick down its back. Twice.

When Dag came back to the valley farm—*if* Dag came back to the valley farm—would he be able to read the events from the mess her fight had left in the kitchen? He was a tracker, surely he'd have to notice the footprints in plum jam she had forced her captors to smear across the floor as they'd lunged after her. But it seemed far too much to expect the man to rescue her twice in one day, downright embarrassing, even. Imagining the indignity, she tried one more time to break from the huge mud-man's clutch, beating its back with her fists. She might have been pounding sand for all the difference it made.

She should save her strength for a better chance.

What strength? What chance?

The hot, level sunlight of the summer evening gave way abruptly to gray shadow and the cool smell of dirt and rock. As her captor swung her down and upright, she had a giddy impression of a cave or hollow half-filled with piles of trash. Or war supplies, it was hard to tell. She fought back the black shadows that swarmed over her vision and stood upright, blinking.

Two more of the animal-men rose as if to greet her three escorts. She wondered if they were all about to fall on her and tear her up like a pack of dogs devouring a rabbit. Although she wasn't entirely sure but what that shorter one on the end might have *been* a rabbit, once.

The Voice said, *"Bring her here."*

The words were more clearly spoken than the mud-men's mumblings, but the undertones made her bones feel as though they were melting. She suddenly could not force her trembling face to turn toward the source of that appalling sound. It seemed to flay the wits right out of her mind. *Please let me go please let me go let me go letmego . . .*

The bear-man clutched her shoulders and half dragged, half lifted her to the back of the cave, a long shallow gouge in the hillside. And turned her face-to-face with the source of the Voice.

It might have been a mud-man, if bigger, taller, broader. Its shape was human enough, a head with two eyes, nose, mouth, ears—broad torso, two arms, two legs. But its skin was not even like an animal's, let alone a human's. It made her think of lizards and insects and rock dust plastered together with bird lime. It was hairless. The naked skull was faintly crested. It was quite unclothed, and seemingly unconscious of the fact; the strange lumps at its crotch didn't look like a man's genitals, or a woman's either. It didn't *move* right, as though it were a child's bad clay sculpture given motion and not a breathing creature of bone and sinew and muscle.

The mud-men had animal eyes in human faces, and seemed unspeakably dangerous. This . . . had human eyes in the face of a nightmare. No, no nightmare *she* had ever dreamed or imagined—one of Dag's, maybe. Trapped. Tormented. And yet, for all its pain, as devoid of mercy as a stone. Or a rockslide.

It clutched her shirt, lifted her up to its face, and stared at her for a long, long moment. She was crying now, in fear beyond shame. She would deal with Dag's rescue, yes, or anybody's at all. She would trade back for her bandit-ravisher. She would deal with any god listening, make any promise . . . *letmegoletmego* . . .

With a slow, deliberate motion, the malice lifted her skirt with its other hand, twitched her drawers down to her hips, and drew its claws up her belly.

The pain was so intense, Fawn thought for a moment that she had been gutted. Her knees came up in an involuntary spasm, and she screamed. The sound came so tightly out of her raw throat that it turned into near silence, a rasping hiss. She lowered her face, expecting to see blood spewing, her insides coming out. Only four faint red lines marked the pale unbroken skin of her belly.

"*Drop* her!" a hoarse voice roared from her right.

The malice's face turned, its eyes blinking slowly; Fawn turned too. The sudden release of pressure from her shirt took her utterly by surprise, and she fell to the cave floor, dirt and stones scraping her palms, then scrambled up.

Dag was in the shadows, struggling with three, no, all five of the mud-men. One reeled backward with a slashed throat, and another closed in. Dag nearly disappeared under the grunting pile of creatures. A shuffle, a rip, Dag's yell, and a mess of straps and wood and a flash of metal thudded violently against the cave wall. A mud-man had just torn off his arm contraption. The mud-man twisted the arm around behind Dag's back as though trying to rip it off too.

He met her eyes. Shoved his big steel knife into the nearest mud-man as though wedging it into a tree for safekeeping, and ripped a leather pouch from around his neck, its strap snapping. "Spark! *Watch* this!"

She kept her eyes on it as it sailed toward her and, to her own immense surprise, caught it out of the air. She had never in her life caught—. Another mud-man jumped on Dag.

"Stick it in!" he bellowed, going down again. "Stick it in the malice!"

Knives. The pouch had two knives. She pulled one out. It was made of bone. Magic knives? "Which?" she cried frantically.

"Sharp end first! Anywhere!"

The malice was starting to move toward Dag. Feeling as though her head was floating three feet above her body, Fawn thrust the bone knife deeply into the thing's thigh.

The malice turned back toward her, howling in surprise. The sound split her skull. The malice caught her by the neck, this time, and lifted her up, its hideous face contorting.

"No! No!" screamed Dag. "The *other* one!"

Her one hand still clutched the pouch; the other was free. She had maybe one second before the malice shook her till her neck snapped, like a kitchen boy killing a chicken. She yanked the spare bone blade out of its sheath and jammed it forward. It skittered over something, maybe a rib, then caught and went in, but only a couple of inches. The blade shattered. *Oh no——!*

She was falling, falling as if from a great height. The ground struck her a stunning blow. She shoved herself up once more, everything spinning around her.

Before her eyes, the malice was *slumping*. Bits and pieces sloughed off it like ice blowing from a roof. Its awful, keening voice went up and up and higher still, fading out yet leaving shooting pains in her ears.

And gone. In front of her feet was a pile of sour-smelling yellow dirt. The first knife, the one with the blue haft that hadn't worked, lay before it. In her ears was silence, unless she'd just gone deaf.

No, for a scuffle began again to her right. She whirled, thinking to snatch up the knife and try to help. Its magic might have failed, but it still had an edge and a point. But the three mud-men still on their feet had stopped trying to tear the patroller apart, and instead were scrambling away, yowling. One bowled her over in its frantic flight, apparently without any destructive intent. This time, she stayed on her hands and knees. Gasping. She had thought her body must run out of shakes in sheer exhaustion, but the supply seemed endless. She had to clench her teeth to keep them from chattering, like someone freezing to death. Her belly cramped.

Dag was sitting on the ground ten feet away with a staggered look on his face, legs every which way, mouth open, gasping for air just as hard as she was. His left sleeve was ripped off, and his handless arm was bleeding from long scratches. He must have taken a blow to his face, for one eye was already tearing and swelling.

Fawn scrabbled around till her hand encountered the other knife hilt, the green one that had splintered in the malice. Where was the malice? "I'm sorry. I'm sorry. I broke it." She was sniveling now, tears and snot running down her lip from her nose. "I'm sorry . . ."

"What?" Dag looked up dazedly, and began to crawl toward her one-handed in strange slow hops, his left arm curled up protectively to his chest.

Fawn pointed a trembling finger. "I broke your magic knife."

Dag stared down at the green-wrapped hilt with a disoriented look on his face, as if he was seeing it for the first time. "No . . . it's all right . . . they're supposed to do that. They break like that when they work. When they teach the malice how to die."

"What?"

"Malices are immortal. They cannot die. If you tore that body into a hundred bits, the malice's . . . self, would just flee away to another hole and reassemble itself. Still knowing everything it had learned in this incarnation, and so twice as dangerous. They cannot die on their own, so you have to share a death with them."

"I don't understand."

"I'll explain more," he wheezed, "later . . ." He rolled over on his back, hair sweaty and wild; dilated eyes, the color of sassafras tea in the shadows, looking blankly upwards. "Absent gods. We did it. It's done. *You* did it! What a mess. Mari will kill me. Kiss me first, though, I bet. Kiss us both."

Fawn sat on her knees, bent over her cramps. "Why didn't the first knife work? What was wrong with it?"

"It wasn't primed. I'm sorry, I didn't think. In a hurry. A patroller would have known which was which by touch. Of course you couldn't tell." He rolled over on his left side and reached for the blue-hilted knife. "That one's mine, for me someday."

His hand touched it and jerked back. "*What* the . . . ?" His lips parted, eyes going suddenly intent, and he reached again, gingerly. He drew his hand back more slowly this time, the lunatic exhilaration draining from his face. "That's strange. That's very strange."

"*What?*" snapped Fawn, pain and bewilderment making her sharp. Her body was beaten, her neck felt half-twisted-off, and her belly kept on knotting in aching waves. "You don't tell me anything that makes sense, and then I go and do stupid things, and it's *not my fault.*"

"Oh, I think this one is. That's the rule. Credit goes to the one who does, however scrambled the method. Congratulations, Little Spark. You have just saved the world. My patrol will be so pleased."

She would have thought him ragging her mercilessly, but while his words seemed wild, his level tone was perfectly serious. And his eyes were warm on her, without a hint of . . . malice.

"Maybe you're just crazy," she said gruffly, "and that's why nothing you say makes sense."

"No surprise by now if I am," he said agreeably. With a grunting effort, he rolled over and up onto his knees, hand propping him upright. He opened his jaw as if to stretch his face, as though it had gone numb, and blinked owlishly. "I have to get off this dead dirt. It's fouling up my groundsense something fierce."

"Your what?"

"I'll explain that later" —he sighed—"too. I'll explain anything you want. You're owed, Little Spark. You're owed the world." He added after a reflective moment, "Many people are. Doesn't change the matter."

He started to reach for the unbroken knife again, then paused, his expression growing inward. "Would you do me a favor? Pick that up and carry it along for me. The hilt and the bits of the other, too. It needs proper burying, later on."

Fawn tried not to look at his stump, which was pink and lumpy and appeared sore. "Of course. Of course. Did they break your hand thing?" She spotted the pouch a few feet away and crawled to get it. She wasn't sure she could stand up yet either. She collected the broken bits in his torn-off sleeve and slid the intact knife back into its sheath.

He rubbed his left arm. "Afraid so. It isn't meant to come off that way, by a long shot. Dirla will fix it, she's good with leather. It won't be the first time."

"Is your arm all right?"

He grinned briefly. "It isn't meant to come off that way either, though that bear-fellow sure tried. Nothing's broken. It'll get better with rest."

He shoved to his feet and stood with legs braced apart, swaying, until he seemed sure he wouldn't just fall down again. He limped slowly around the cave collecting first his ruined arm contraption, which he wrapped over his shoulder by its leather straps, then, fallen farther away, his big knife. He swiped it on his filthy shirt and resheathed it. He rolled his shoulders and squinted around for a moment, apparently saw nothing else he wanted, and walked back to Fawn.

Her sharpening cramps almost doubled her over when she tried to rise; he gave her a hand up. She stuffed the pouch and rolled sleeve in her shirt. Leaning on each other, they staggered for the light.

"What about the mud-men? Won't they jump us again?" asked Fawn fearfully as they came out on the path overlooking the dead ravine.

"No. It's all over for them when their malice dies. They go back to their animal minds—trapped in those made-up human bodies. They usually panic and run. They don't do too well, after. We kill them for mercy when we can. Otherwise, they die on their own pretty quick. Horrible, really."

"Oh."

"The men whose minds the malice has seized, its fog lifts from them, too. They revert."

"A malice enslaves men, too?"

"When its powers grow more advanced. I think this one might have, for all it was still in its first molt."

"And they'll . . . be freed? Wherever they may be?"

"Sometimes freed. Sometimes go mad. Depends."

"On what?"

"On what they've been doing betimes. They remember, d'you see."

Fawn wasn't entirely sure she did. Or wished to.

The air was warm, but the sun was setting through bare branches, as though winter had become untimely mixed with summer. "This day has been ten years long," Dag sighed. "*Got* to get me off this bad ground. My horse is too far away to summon. Think we'll take those." He pointed to two horses tied to trees near the creek and led her down the zigzag path toward them. "I don't see any gear. Can you ride bareback?"

"Usually, but right now I feel pretty sick," Fawn admitted. She was still shaking, and she felt cold and clammy. Her breath drew in as another violent cramp passed through her. *That is not good. That is something very wrong.* She had thought herself fresh out of fear, a year's supply used up, but now she was not so sure.

"Huh. Think you'd be all right if I held you in front of me?"

The unpleasant memory of her ride with the bandit this morning—had it only been this morning? Dag was right, this day was a decade—flashed through her mind. *Don't be stupid. Dag is different.* Dag, on the whole, was different from any other person she'd ever met in her life. She gulped. "Yeah. I . . . yeah, probably."

They arrived at the horses, Fawn stumbling a little. Dag ran his hand over them, humming to himself in a tuneless way, and turned one loose after first filching its rope, shooing it off. It trotted away as if glad to be gone. The other was a neat bay mare with black socks and a white star; he fastened the rope to her halter to make reins and led her to a fallen log. He kept trying to use his left limb to assist, wincing, then remembering, which, among all Fawn's other hurts, made her heart ache strangely.

"Can you get yourself up, or do you need a boost?"

Fawn stood whitely. "Dag?" she said in a small, scared voice.

His head snapped around at her tone, and tilted attentively. "What?"

"I'm bleeding."

He walked back to her. "Where? Did they cut you? I didn't see . . ."

Fawn swallowed hard, thinking that her face would be scarlet if only it had not been green. In an even smaller voice, she choked out, "Between . . . between my legs."

The loopy glee that had underlain his expression ever since the killing of the malice was wiped away as if with a rag. "Oh." And he did not seem to require a single further word of explanation, which was a good thing, as well as being amazing in a man, because Fawn was out of everything. Words. Courage. Ideas.

He took a deep breath. "We still have to get off this ground. Deathly place. I have to get you, get you someplace else. Away from here. We'll just go a little faster, is all. You're going to have to help me with this. Help each other."

It took two tries and considerable awkwardness, but they both managed to get aboard the bay mare at last, thankfully a placid beast. Fawn sat not astride but sideways across Dag's lap, legs pressed together, head to his left shoulder, arm around his neck, leaving his right hand free for the reins. He chirped to the horse and started them off at a brisk walk.

"Stay with me, now," he murmured into her hair. "Do not let go, you hear?"

The world was spinning, but under her ear she could hear a steady heartbeat. She nodded dolefully.

5

By the time they arrived at the deserted valley farm, both the back of Fawn's skirt and the front of Dag's trousers were soaked in too-bright blood.

"Oh," said Fawn in a mortified voice, when he'd swung her down from the horse and slid after her. "Oh, I'm sorry."

Dag raised what he hoped was an admirably calm eyebrow. "What? It's just blood, Little Spark. I've dealt with more blood in my time than you have in your whole bitty body." Which was where this red tide should *be*, blast and blight it. *I will not panic.* He wanted to swing her up in his arms and carry her inside, but he did not trust his strength. He had to keep moving, or his own battered body would start to stiffen. He wrapped his right arm around her shoulders instead, and, leaving the horse to fend for itself, aimed her up the porch steps.

"Why is this happening?" she said, so low and breathy and plaintive he wasn't sure if it was to him or herself.

He hesitated. Yes, she was young, but surely—"Don't you know?"

She glanced up at him. The bruise masking the left side of her face was darkening to purple, the gouges scabbing over. "Yes," she whispered. She steadied her voice by sheer force of will, he thought. "But you seem to know so much. I was hoping you might . . . have a different answer. Stupid of me."

"The malice did something to you. Tried to." Courage failing, he looked away from her gaze to say, "It stole your baby's ground. It would have used it in its next molt, but we killed it first." *And I was too late to stop it.* Five blighted minutes, if he had only been five blighted minutes quicker . . . Yes, and if he'd only been five blighted seconds quicker, once, he'd still have a left hand, and he'd been down that road and back up it enough times to be thoroughly tired of the scenery. Peace. If he had arrived at the lair very much sooner, he might have missed her entirely.

But what had happened to his spare sharing knife, in that terrible scramble? It had been empty, but now he would swear it was primed, and that should not have happened. *Take on your disasters one at a time, old patroller, or you'll lose your trail.* The knife could wait. Fawn could not.

"Then . . . then it's too late. To save. Anything."

"It's never too late to save something," he said sternly. "Might not be what you wanted, is all." Which was certainly something he needed to hear, every day, but was not exactly pertinent to her present need, now was it? He tried again, because he did not think his heart or hers could bear confusion on this point. "She's gone. You're not. Your next job is to" *survive this night* "get better. After that, we'll see."

The twilight was failing as they stepped into the gloomy shadows of the farmhouse kitchen, but Dag could see it was a different mess than before.

"This way," Fawn said. "Don't step in the jam."

"Ah, right."

"There's some candle stubs around. Up over the hearth, there's some more. Oh, no, I can't lie there, I'll stain the ticks."

"Looks flat enough to me, Little Spark. I do know you should be lying down. I'm real sure of that." Her breathing was too rapid and shallow, her skin far too clammy, and her ground had a bad gray tinge that went hand in hand with grave damage, in his unpleasant experience.

"Well . . . well, find something, then. For in between."

Now was not, definitely *not,* the time to argue with female irrationality. "Right."

He poked up the faint remains of the fire, fed it with some wood chips, and lit two wax stubs, one of which he left on the hearth for her; the other he took with him for a quick exploration. A couple of those chests and wardrobes upstairs had still had things in them, he dimly recalled. A patroller should be resourceful. What did the girl most need? A miscarriage was a natural enough process, even if this one was most unnaturally triggered; women survived them all the time, he was fairly sure. He just wished they had *discussed* them more, or that he had listened more closely. Lie flat, check, they'd got that far. Make her comfortable? Cruel joke . . . *peace.* He supposed she'd be more comfortable cleaned up than filthy; at any rate, he'd always been grateful for that when recovering from a serious injury. *What, you can't fix the real problem, so you'll fix something else instead? And which of you is this supposed to aid?*

Peace. And a bucket and an unfouled well, with luck.

It took more time than he'd have liked, during which to his swallowed aggravation she insisted on lying on the blighted kitchen *floor,* but he eventually assembled a clean gownlike garment, rather too large for her, some old mended sheets, an assortment of rags for pads, actual soap, and water. In a moment of ruthless inspiration, he broke through her reticence by persuading her to wash his hand first, as though he needed help.

She still had the shakes, which she seemed to take for residual fear but which he recognized as one with the chilled skin and grayness in her ground, and which he treated by piling on whatever blanketlike cloths he could find, and building up the fire. The last time he'd seen a woman coiled around her belly that hard, a blade had penetrated almost to her spine. He heated a stone, wrapped it in cloth, and gave it to Fawn to clutch to herself, which to his relief seemed finally to help; the shakes faded and her ground lightened. Eventually, she was arranged all tidy and sweet and patient-like, her curl around the stone relaxing as she warmed, blinking up at him in the candlelight as he sat cross-legged beside the tick.

"Did you find any clothes you could use?" she asked. "Though I suppose you'd be lucky to find a fit."

"Haven't looked, yet. Got spares in my saddlebags. Which are on my horse. Somewhere. If I'm lucky, my patrol will find him and bring him along sometime. They had better be looking for me by now."

"If you could find something else to wear, I bet I could wash those tomorrow. I'm sorry that—"

"Little Spark," he leaned forward, his ragged voice cracking, *"do not apologize to me for this."*

She recoiled.

He regained control. "Because, don't you see, a crying patroller is a very embarrassing sight. M' face gets all snively and snotty. Combine that with this blue eye I've got starting, and it'd be like to turn your stomach. And then there'd just be another mess to clean up, and we don't want that now, do we." He tweaked her nose, which was on the whole an insane thing to do to a woman who'd just saved the world, but it worked to break her bleak mood; she smiled wanly.

"All right, we're making great progress here, you know. Food, what about food?"

"I don't think I could, yet. You go ahead."

"Drink, then. And no arguments with me about that one, I know you need to drink when you've lost blood." *Are losing blood. Still.* Too much, too fast. How long was it supposed to go on?

Candlelight explorations in the rather astonishing cellar yielded a box of dried sassafras; uncertain of the unknown well water, he boiled some up for tea and dosed them both. He was thirstier than he'd thought, and set Fawn an example, which she followed as docilely as a naive young patroller. *Why, why do they do whatever you tell them like that?* Except when they didn't, of course.

He sat against the wall facing her, legs stretched out, and sipped some more. "There would be more I could do for you on the inside, patroller tricks with my groundsense, if only . . ."

"Groundsense." She uncurled a little more and regarded him gravely. "You said you'd tell me about that."

He blew out his breath, wondering how to explain it to a farmer girl in a way she wouldn't take wrong. "Groundsense. It's a sense of . . . everything around us. What's alive, where it is, how it's doing. And not just what's alive, though that's brightest. No one quite knows if the world makes ground, or ground makes the world, but ground is what a malice sucks out to sustain itself, the loss of which kills everything around its lair. In the middle of a really bad patch of blight, not only is everything once alive now dead, even rocks don't hold their form. Ground's what groundsense senses."

"Magic?" she said doubtfully.

He shook his head. "Not the way farmers use the term. It's not like getting something for nothing. It's just the way the world *is,* deep down." He forged on against her frankly blank look. "We use words from sight and touch and the other senses to describe it, but it isn't like any of those things, really. It's like how you know . . . Close your eyes."

She raised her brows at him in puzzlement, but did so.

"Now. Which way is down? Point."

Her thumb rotated toward the floor, and the big brown eyes opened again, still puzzled.

"So how did you know? You didn't see down."

"I . . . " She hesitated. "I felt it. With my whole body."

"Groundsense is something more like that. So." He sipped more tea; the warm spice soothed his throat. "People are the most complicated, brightest things groundsense sees. We see each other, unless we close it down to block the distraction. Like shutting your eyes, or wrapping a lantern up in a cloak. You can—Lakewalkers can—match our body's ground to someone else's body's ground. If you get the match up really close, almost like slipping inside each other, you can lend strength, rhythm . . . help with wounds, slow bleeding, help with when a hurt body starts to go all wrong down into that cold gray place. Lead the other back to balance. Did something like that for a patroller boy last—ye gods, last night? Saun. I have to stop thinking of him as Saun the Sheep, it's going to slip out my mouth someday, and he'll never forgive me, but anyway. Bandit whaled him in the chest with a sledgehammer during the fight, broke ribs, stunned his heart and lungs. I whacked my ground into a match with his right quick, persuaded his to dance with mine. It was all a bit brutal, but I was in a hurry."

"Would he have *died*? But for you?"

"I . . . maybe. If he thinks so, I'm not going to argue; might finally get him to give up those overblown sword moves of his while he's still impressed with

me." Dag grinned briefly, but the grin faded again. More tea. "Trouble is . . . ''
Blight, out of tea. "You've taken a wound to your womb. I can sense it in you,
like a rip in your ground. But I can't match it to lend you anything helpful
through our grounds because, well, I haven't got one. A womb, that is. Not
part of my body *or* its ground. If Mari or one of the girls were here, they could
maybe help. But I don't want to leave you alone for eight or twelve hours or
however long it would take to find one and bring her back."

"No, don't do that!" Her hand clutched at his leg, then drew back shyly as she
coiled more tightly on her side. How much pain was she in? *Plenty.*

"Right. So, that means we have to ride this thing out the farmer way.
What do farmer women do, do you know?"

"Go to bed. I think."

"Didn't your mother or sisters ever say?"

"Don't have any sisters, and my brothers are all older than me. My mother,
she's taught me a lot, but she doesn't do midwifery. She's always so busy with,
well, everything. Mostly I think the body just cleans itself out like a bad
monthly, though some women seem to get poorly, after. I think it's all right if
you bleed some, but bad if you bleed a lot."

"Well, tell me which you're doing, all right?"

"All right . . . '' she said doubtfully.

Her expression was so very reserved and inward. As though painfully trying to listen to the marred song of her own body with a groundsense blighted
deaf. Or futilely looking for that other light within her, so bright and busy just
this morning, now dark and dead. In all, Dag thought Fawn had been much too
quiet ever since they'd left the lair. It made him feel unsettled and desperate.

He wondered if he ought to invent a few sisters for himself, to bolster his
authority in the matter. "Look, I am a very experienced patroller," he blath-
ered on into that fraught silence. "I delivered a baby single-handedly on the
Great Lake Road, once." Wait, was this a good tale to tell now? Perhaps not,
but it was too late to stop. "Well, not single-handedly, I had two hands then,
but they were both pretty clumsy. Fortunately, it was the woman's fourth, and
she could tell me how to go on. Which she did, pretty tartly. She was not best
pleased to be stuck with me for a midwife. She called me *such* names. I stored
'em up to treasure—they came in right useful later on, when *I* was dealing
with feckless young patrollers. Twenty-two I was, and so proud of myself after,
you'd think I did all the work. Let me tell you, next bandit I faced after that
didn't look *nearly* so scary."

This won a watery chuckle, as he'd hoped. Good, because if he'd gone
with the fictional sisters, she might have asked their names, and he didn't think
his invention would last so far. His eyelids felt as if someone had attached lead
weights to them when he wasn't looking. The room was beginning to waver
unpleasantly.

"She was one straightforward lady. Set me an example I never forgot."

"I can see that," murmured Fawn. And after a quiet moment added, "Thank you."

"Oh, you're an easy patient. I won't have to shave you in the morning, and you won't throw your boots at my head because you're cranky and hurting. Bored cranky patrollers who hurt, world's worst company. Trust me."

"Do they really throw boots?"

"Yes. I did."

A yawn cracked his face. His bruises and strains were reporting for duty, right enough. Reminded of his boots' existence, he slowly drew up his feet and began to undo his laces. He'd had those boots on for two—no, four days, because he'd slept in them night before last.

"Would you feel more comfortable if I went out to sleep on the porch?" he asked.

Fawn eyed him over her sheets, now pulled up nearly to her lips. Pink, those lips, if much paler than he would have liked to see them, but not gray or bluish, good. "No," she said in a curiously distant tone, "I don't think I would."

"Good . . . " Another yawn split the word, and others crowded after: "Because I don't think . . . I could crawl through all that . . . sticky jam right now. Softer here. You can have the inside, I'll take the outside." He flopped forward facedown in the tick. He really should turn his head so he could breathe, he supposed. He turned toward Fawn, that being the better view, and eyed what he could see of her over the hillock of stuffed cloth. Dark curls, skin petal-fair where it was not bruised. Smelling infinitely better than him. A surprised brown eye.

"Mama," he muttered, "the sheep are safe tonight."

"Sheep?" she said after a moment.

"Patroller joke." About farmers, come to think. He wasn't going to tell it to her. Ever. Fortunately, he was growing too bludgeoned by his fatigue to talk. He roused himself just enough to stretch over, pinch out the candle, and flop again.

"I don't get it."

"Good. 'Night." His rueful consciousness of that short curving body separated from his by only a couple of layers of fabric was intense, but very brief.

❧

Fawn woke in the dark of night on her right side, facing the kitchen wall, with a weight across her chest and a long, lumpy bolster seemingly wrapped around her in back. The weight was Dag's left arm, she realized, and he must be dead asleep indeed to have flung it there, because he always seemed to carry it subtly out of the way, out of sight, when he was awake. His chin was scratching the back of her neck, his nose was buried in her hair, and she could feel her curls flutter with his slow breath. He lay very solidly between her and the door.

And whatever might come through the door. Scary things out there. Bandits, mud-men, blight bogles. And yet . . . wasn't the tall patroller the scariest of all? Because, at the end of the day, bandits, mud-men, and bogles all lay strewn in his path, and he was still walking. Limping, anyhow. How could someone scarier than anything make her feel safer? A riddle, that.

If not precisely trapped by his menace, she did find herself pinned by his exhaustion. Her attempt to slip out without waking him failed. There followed disjointed mumbled arguments in the dark about a trudge to the privy versus a chamber pot (he won), the change and care of blood-soaked dressings (he won again), and where he would go to sleep next (hard to tell who won that one, but he did end up on the tick between her and the door as before). Despite a new hot stone, her gnawing cramps ordained that he was asleep again before her. But the unlikely comfort of that bony body, wrapped like a fort wall around her hurting, assured that it wasn't so very much before.

When next she awoke it was broad day outside, and she was alone. Yesterday's agony in her belly was reduced to a knotting ache, but her dressings were soaked again. Before she had time to panic, boot steps sounded on the porch, accompanied by a tuneless chirping whistle. She had never heard Dag whistle, but it could be no one else. He ducked in through the door and smiled at her, gold eyes bright from the light.

He must have been out bathing by the well, for his hair was wet and his damp skin free of blood and grime, leaving all his scratches looking tidier and less alarming. Also, he smelled quite nice, last night's reek—although it had been reassuring to know exactly where he was even from several feet away in the dark—replaced with the clean sharpness of the lost farmwife's homemade soap, rough brown stuff that she had nonetheless scented with lavender and mint.

He was shirtless, wearing a pair of unbloodied gray trousers clearly not his own cinched around his waist with a stray bit of rope. She suspected they came about a foot short lengthwise, but with the ends tucked into his boots, no one could tell. He had an uneven tan, his coppery skin paler where his shirt usually fell, although not nearly as pale as hers. He favored long sleeves even in summer, it seemed. His collection of bruises was almost as impressive as her own. But he was not so bony underneath as she'd feared; his long, strappy muscles moved easily under his skin. "Morning, Spark," he said cheerily.

The first order of business was the repellent medical necessities, which he took on with such straightforward briskness that he left her almost feeling that blood clots were an achievement rather than a horror. "Clots are good. Red, spurting blood is bad. Thought we'd agreed on that one, Spark. Whatever the malice ripped up inside you is starting to mend, that says to me. Good work. Keep lying down."

She lay dozily as he wandered in and out. Things happened. A ragged white shirt appeared on his back, too tight across the shoulders and with the sleeves rolled up. More tea happened, and food: the remains of the pan bread she made yesterday rolled around some meat stew from the cellar. He had to coax her to eat, but miraculously, it stayed down, and she could feel strength starting to return to her body almost immediately because of it. Her hot stones were swapped out regularly. After a second longish expedition outside, he returned with a cloth full of strawberries from the farmwoman's kitchen garden and sat himself down on the floor beside her, sharing them out in mock exactitude.

She woke from a longer doze to see him sitting at the kitchen table, mulling glumly over his hand contraption laid out atop it.

"Can you fix it?" she asked muzzily.

"Afraid not. Not a one-hand job even if I had the tools here. Stitching's all ripped, and the wrist cap is cracked. This is beyond Dirla. When we get to Glassforge, I'll have to find a harnessmaker and maybe a woodturner to put it right again."

Glassforge. Was she still going to Glassforge, when the reason for her flight had been so abruptly removed? Her life had been turned upside down one too many times lately, too fast, for her to be sure of much just now. She turned to the wall and clutched her stone—by the heat, he'd renewed it again while she'd slept—tighter to her aching, emptying womb.

In the past weeks, she had experienced her child as fear, desperation, shame, exhaustion, and vomiting. She had not yet felt the fabled quickening, although she had gone to sleep nightly waiting intently for that sign. It was disquieting to think that this chance-met man, with his strange Lakewalker senses, had gained a more direct perception of the brief life of her child than she had. The thought hurt, but pressing the rag-wrapped stone to her forehead didn't help.

She rolled back over and her eye fell on Dag's knife pouch, set aside last night near the head of her feather mattress. The intact knife with the blue hilt was still in its sheath where she'd shoved it. The other—green hilt and bone fragments—seemed to have been rewrapped in a bit of scavenged cloth, ends tied in one of Dag's clumsy one-handed knots. The fine linen, though wrinkled and ripped and probably from the mending basket, had embroidery on it, once-treasured guest-day work.

She looked up to see him watching her examine them, his face gone expressionless again.

"You said you'd tell me about these, too," she said. "I don't guess it was just any bit of bone that killed an immortal malice."

"No. Indeed. The sharing knives are by far the most complex of our . . . tools. Hard and costly to make."

"I suppose you'll tell me they aren't really magic, again."

He sighed, rose, came over, and sat down cross-legged beside her. He took the pouch thoughtfully in his hand.

"They're human bone, aren't they," she added more quietly, watching him.

"Yes," he said a little distantly. His gaze swung back to her. "Understand, patrollers have had trouble with farmers before over sharing knives. Misunderstandings. We've learned not to discuss them. You have earned . . . there are reasons . . . *you* must be told. I can only ask that you don't talk about it with anyone, after."

"Anyone at all?" she puzzled.

He made a little jerk of his fingers. "Lakewalkers all know. I mean outsiders. Farmers. Although in this case . . . well, we'll get to that."

Roundaboutly, it seemed. She frowned at this uncharacteristic loss of straightforwardness on his part. "All right."

He took a breath, straightening his spine a trifle. "Not just any human bones. Our own, Lakewalker bones. Not farmer bones, and most *especially* not kidnapped farmer children's bones, all right? Adult. Have to be, for the length and strength. You'd think people would—well. Thighbones, usually, and sometimes upper arms. It makes our funeral practices something outsiders are not invited to. Some of the most aggravating rumors have been started around stray glimpses . . . we are *not* cannibals, rest assured!"

"I actually hadn't heard that one."

"You might, if you're around long enough."

She had seen hogs and cows butchered; she could imagine. Her mind leaped ahead to picture Dag's long legs—*no.*

"Some mess is unavoidable, but it's all done respectfully, with ceremony, because we all know it could be our turn later. Not everyone donates their bones; it would be more than needed, and some aren't suitable. Too old or young, too thin or fragile. I mean to give mine, if I die young enough."

The thought made an odd knot in her belly that had nothing to do with her cramping. "Oh."

"But that's just the body of the knife, the first half of the making. The other half, the thing that makes it possible to share death with a malice, is the priming." The quick would-be-reassuring smile with this did not reach his eyes. "We prime it with a death. A donated death, one of our own. In the making, the knife is bonded, matched to the intended primer, so they are very personal, d'you see."

Fawn pushed herself up, increasingly riveted and increasingly disturbed. "Go on."

"When you're a Lakewalker who means to give your death to a knife and you're close to dying—wounded in the field beyond hope of recovery, or dying at home of natural causes, you—or more often your comrade or kin—take the sharing knife and insert it into your heart."

Fawn's lips parted. "But . . ."

"Yes, it kills us. That's the whole point."

"Are you saying people's souls go into those knives?"

"*Not* souls, ah! Knew you'd ask that." He swiped his hand through his hair. "That's another farmer rumor. Makes so much trouble . . . Even our ground-sense doesn't tell us where people's souls go after their deaths, but I promise you it's not into the knives. Just their dying ground. Their mortality." He started to add, "Lakewalker god-stories say the gods have . . . well, never mind that now."

Now, there was a rumor she *had* heard. "People say you don't believe in the gods."

"No, Little Spark. Somewhat the reverse. But that doesn't enter into this. That knife" —he pointed to the blue hilt—"is my own, grounded to me. I had it made special. The bone for it was willed to me by a woman named Kauneo, who was slain in a bad malice war up northwest of the Dead Lake. Twenty years ago. We were way late spotting it, and it had grown very powerful. The malice hadn't found many people to use out in that wilderness, but it had found wolves, and . . . well. The other knife, which you used yesterday, that was her primed knife, grounded to her. Her heart's death was in it. The bone of it was from an uncle of hers—I never met him, but he was a legendary patroller up that way in his day, fellow named Kaunear. You probably didn't have time to notice it, but his name and his curse on malices were burned on the blade."

Fawn shook her head. "Curse?"

"His choice, what to have written on his bone. You can order the makers to put any personal message you want that will fit. Some people write love notes to their knife-heirs. Or really bad jokes, sometimes. Up to them. Two notes, actually. One side for the donor of the bone, the other for the donor of the heart's death, which is put on after the knife is primed. If there's a chance."

Fawn imagined that bone blade she'd held being slowly shoved into a dying patroller woman's heart, maybe someone like Mari, by . . . who had done it? Dag? Twenty years seemed terribly long ago—could he really be as old as, say, forty?

"The deaths we share with the malices," said Dag quietly, "are our own, and no others'."

"Why?" whispered Fawn, shaken.

"Because that's what works. How it works. Because we can, and no one else can. Because it is our legacy. Because if a malice, every malice, is not killed when it emerges, it just keeps growing. And growing. And getting stronger and smarter and harder to get at. And if there is ever one we can't get, it will grow till the whole world is gray dust, and then it, too, will die. When I said you'd saved the world yesterday, Spark, I was not joking. That malice could have been the one."

Fawn lay back, clutching her sheets to her breast, taking this in. It was a lot to take in. If she had not seen the malice up close—the rock-dust scent of its foul breath still seemed to linger in her nostrils—she was not sure she *could* have understood fully. *I still don't understand. But oh, I do believe.*

"We just have to hope," Dag sighed, "that we run out of malices before we run out of Lakewalkers."

He held the sheath-pouch down on his thigh with his stump and pulled out the blue-hilted knife. He cradled it thoughtfully for a moment, then, with a look of concentration, touched it to his lips, closing his eyes. His face set in disturbed lines. He laid the knife down exactly between himself and Fawn, and drew back his hand.

"This brings us to yesterday."

"I jabbed that knife into the malice's thigh," said Fawn, "but nothing happened."

"No. Something happened, because this knife was not primed, and now it is."

Fawn's face screwed up. "Did it suck out the malice's mortality, then? Or immortality? No, that makes no sense."

"No. What I think"—he looked up from under wary brows—"mind you, I'm not sure yet, I need to talk with some folks—but what I think is, the malice had just stolen your baby's ground, and the knife stole it back. Not soul, don't you go imagining trapped souls again—just her mortality." He added under his breath, "A death without a birth, very strange."

Fawn's lips moved, but no sound came out.

"So here we sit," he went on. "The body of this knife belongs to me, because Kauneo willed me her bones. But by our rules, the priming in this knife, its mortality, belongs to you, because you are its next of kin. Because your unborn child, of course, could not will it herself. Here things get really . . . get even more mixed up, because usually no one is allowed to will and give their priming till they are adult enough to have their groundsense come in fully, about fourteen or fifteen, and older is stronger. And anyway, this was a farmer child. Yet no death but mine should have been able to prime this knife. This is a . . . this is a right mess, is what it is, actually."

Though still shaken by her sudden miscarriage, Fawn had thought all decisions about her personal disaster were behind her, and had been wearily grateful that no more were to be faced. It was a kind of relief, curled within the grief. Not so, it seemed. "Could you use it to kill another malice?" Some redemption, in all this chain of sorrows?

"I would want to take it to my camp's best maker, first. See what he has to say. I'm just a patroller. I am out of my experience and reckoning, here. It's a strange knife, could do something unknown. Maybe unwanted. Or not work at all, and as you have seen, to get right up to a malice and then have your tools fail makes a bit of a problem."

"What should we do? What *can* we do?"

He gave a rough nod. "On the one hand, we could destroy it."

"But won't that waste . . . ?"

"Two sacrifices? Yes. It wouldn't be my first pick. But if you speak it, Spark, I will break it now in front of you, and it will be over." He laid his hand over the hilt, his face a mask but his eyes searching hers.

Her breath caught. "No—no, don't do that. Yet, anyhow." *And on the other hand, there is no other hand.* She wondered if his sense of humor was gruesome enough to have had exactly that thought as well. She suspected so.

She gulped and continued, "But your people—will they care what some farmer girl thinks?"

"In this matter, yes." He rolled his shoulders, as though they ached. "If it's all right with you, then, I'll speak of this first with Mari, my patrol leader, see what notions she has. After that, we'll think again."

"Of course," she said faintly. *He means it, that I should have a say in this.*

"I would take it kindly if you would take charge of it till then."

"Of course."

He nodded and handed her the leather pouch, leaving her to resheathe the knife. The linen bag, however, he picked up to put with his arm contraption. His joints crackled and popped as he stood up and stretched, and he winced. Fawn sank back down on the tick and stole a closer look at the bone blade. The faint, flowing lines burned brown into the bone's pale surface read: *Dag. My heart walks with yours. Till the end, Kauneo.*

The Lakewalker woman must have written this directive some time before she died, Fawn realized. Fawn imagined her sitting in a Lakewalker tent, tall and graceful like the other patroller women she'd glimpsed; writing tablet balanced on the very thigh that she must have known would come to bear the words, if things went ill. Had she pictured this knife, made from her marrow? Pictured Dag using it someday to drink his own heart's blood in turn? But she could not ever, Fawn thought, have pictured a feckless young farmer girl fumbling it into this strange confusion, a lifetime—at any rate, Fawn's lifetime— later.

Brow furrowed, Fawn slipped the sharing knife out of sight again in its sheath.

6

To Dag's approval, Fawn dozed off again after lunch. *Good, let her sleep and make up her blood loss.* He'd had enough practice to translate the gore on the dressings to a guess as to the amount. When he mentally doubled the volume to make up for the fact that she was about half the size of most men he'd nursed, he was very thankful that the bleeding had plainly slowed.

He came in from checking on the bay mare, now idling about in the front pasture he'd repaired by pulling rails from the fence opposite, to find Fawn awake and sitting up against the back kitchen wall. Her face was drawn and quiet, and she pulled bored fingers through her curls, which were abundant, if tangled.

She peered up at him. "Do you own a comb?"

He ran his hand through his hair. "Does it look that bad?"

Her smile was too ghostly for his taste, though the quip was worth no more. "Not for you. For me. I usually keep my hair tied up, or it gets in an awful mess. Like now."

"I have one in my saddlebag," he offered wryly. "I think. It sifts to the bottom. Haven't seen it in about a month."

"That, I do believe." Her eyes crinkled just a little, then sobered again. "Why don't you wear your hair fancy like the other patrollers?"

He shrugged. "There are a lot of things I can do one-handed. Braiding hair isn't one of them."

"Couldn't someone do it for you?"

He twitched. "Doesn't work if no one's there. Besides, I need enough other favors."

She looked puzzled. "Is the supply so limited?"

He blinked at the thought. Was it? Shrewd question. He wondered if his passion for proving himself capable and without need of aid, so earnestly undertaken after his maiming, was something a man might outgrow. *Old habits die hard.* "Maybe not. I'll look around upstairs, see what I can find." He added over his shoulder, "Lie flat, you." She slid back down obediently, though she made a face.

He returned with a wooden comb found behind an upended chest. It was gap-toothed as an old man, but it served, he found by experiment. She was sitting up again, the cloth-wrapped hot stone laid aside, another promising sign.

"Here, Spark; catch." He tossed the comb to her, and studied her as she jerked up her hand in surprise and had it bounce off her fingers.

She looked up at him in sudden curiosity. "Why did you call *Watch!* when you threw the knife pouch at me?"

Quick, she is. "Old patroller training trick. For the girls—and some others—who come in claiming they can't catch things. It's usually because they're trying too hard. The hand follows the eye if the mind doesn't trip it. If I yell at them to catch the ball, or whatever, they fumble, because that's the picture they have in their heads. If I yell at them to count the spins, it goes right to their hand while they're not attending. And they think I'm a marvel." He grinned, and she smiled shyly back. "I didn't know if you had played throwing games with those brothers of yours or not, so I took the safe bet. In case it was the only one we got."

Her smile became a grimace. "Just the throwing game where they tossed me into the pond. Which wasn't so funny in winter." She eyed the comb curiously, then started in on the end of one tangle.

Her hair was springy and silky and the color of midnight, and Dag couldn't help thinking how soft it would feel to his touch. Another reason to wish for two hands. The smell of it, so close last night, returned to his memory. And perhaps he had better go check on that horse again.

In the late afternoon, Fawn complained for the first time of being hot, which Dag seemed to take as a good sign. He claimed he was sweltering, set up a padded seat out on the shaded porch floor, and permitted her up just long enough to walk out to it. She settled down with her back against the house wall, staring out into the bright summer light. The green fields, and the darker greens of the woods, seemed deceptively peaceful; the horse grazed at the far end of the pasture. The burned outbuilding had stopped smoldering. Clothing, hers and his from yesterday, lay damply over the fence rail in the sun, and Fawn wondered when Dag had laundered it. Dag lowered himself to her left, stretched out his legs, leaned his head back, and sighed as the faint breeze caressed them.

"I don't know what's keeping my patrol," he remarked after a time, opening his eyes again to stare down the lane. "It's not like Mari to get lost in the woods. If they don't show soon, I'll have to try and bury those poor dogs my-self. They're getting pretty ripe."

"Dogs?"

He made an apologetic gesture. "The farm dogs. Found 'em out behind the barn yesterday. The only animals that weren't carried off, seemingly. I think they died defending their people. Figured they ought to be buried nice, maybe up in the woods where it's shady. Dogs ought to like that."

Fawn bit her lip, wondering why this made her suddenly want to burst into tears when she had not cried for her own child.

He glanced down at her, his expression growing diffident. "Among Lake-walker women, a loss like yours would be a private grief, but she would not be so alone. She'd maybe have her man, closest friends, or kin around her. In-stead, you're stuck with me. If you" —he ducked his head nervously—"need to weep, be sure that I wouldn't mistake it for any lack of strength or courage on your part."

Fawn shook her head, lips tight and miserable. "Should I weep?"

"Don't know. I don't know farmer women."

"It's not about being a farmer." She held out her hand, which clenched. "It's about being *stupid*."

After a moment, he said in a very neutral tone, "You use that word a lot. Makes me wonder who used to whip you with it."

"Lots of people. Because I *was*." She lowered her gaze to her lap, where her hands now twisted the loose fabric of her gown. "It's funny I can tell you this. I suppose it's because I never saw you before, or will again." The man was carrying out her revolting blood clots, after all. Before yesterday, the very thought would have slain her with embarrassment. She remembered the fight in the cave, the bear-man . . . the deathly breath of the malice. What was a mere stupid story, compared to that?

His silence this time took on an easy, listening quality. Unhurried. She felt she might fill it in her own good time. Out in the fields, a few early-summer insects sang in the weeds.

In a lower voice she said, "I didn't mean to have a child. I wanted, wanted, something else. And then I was so scared and mad."

Seeming to feel his way as cautiously as a hunter in the woods, he said, "Farmer customs aren't like ours. We hear pretty lurid songs and tales about them. Your family—did they cast you out?" He scowled; Fawn was not sure why.

She shook her head harder. "No. They'd have taken care of me and the child, if they'd been put to it. I didn't tell them. I ran away."

He glanced at her in surprise. "From a place of safety? I don't under-stand."

"Well, I didn't think the road would be *this* dangerous. That woman from Glassforge made it, after all. It seemed like an even trade, me for her."

He pursed his lips and stared off down the lane to ask, even more quietly, "Were you forced?"

"No!" She blew out her breath. "I can clear Stupid Sunny of that, at least. I wanted—to tell the truth, I asked *him*."

His brows went up a little, although a tension eased out of his shoulders. "Is there a problem with this, among farmers? It seems quite the thing to me. The woman invites the man to her tent. Except I suppose you don't have tents."

"I could have wished for a tent. A bed. Something. It was at his sister's wedding, and we ended up out in the field behind the barn in the dark, hiding in the new wheat, which I thought could have stood to be taller. I hoped it might be romantic and wild. Instead, it was all mosquitoes and hurry and dodging his drunken friends. It hurt, which I expected, but not unbearably. I'd just thought there would be . . . more to it. I got what I asked for but not what I wanted."

He rubbed his lips thoughtfully. "What did you want?"

She took a breath, thinking. As opposed to flailing, which was maybe what she had been doing back home. "I think . . . I wanted to *know*. It—what a man and a woman do—was like some kind of wall between me and being a grown-up woman, even though I was plenty old."

"How old is plenty old?" He cocked his head curiously at her.

"Twenty," she said defiantly.

"Oh," he said, and though he managed to keep the amusement out of his voice, his gold eyes glinted a bit.

She would have been annoyed, but the glint was too pretty to complain about, and then there were the crow's-feet, which framed the glint so perfectly. She waved her hands in defeat and went on, "It was like a big secret everyone knew but me. I was tired of being the youngest, and littlest, and always the child." She sighed. "We were a bit drunk, too."

She added after a morose silence, "He did say a girl couldn't be got with child the first time."

Dag's eyebrows climbed higher. "And you believed this? A country girl?"

"I *said* I was stupid about it. I thought maybe people were different than heifers. I thought maybe Sunny knew more than me. He could hardly know less. It's not as if anyone talked about it. To me, I mean." She added after a moment, "And . . . I'd had such a hard time nerving myself up to it, I didn't want to stop."

He scratched his head. "Well, among my people, we try not to be crude in front of the young ones, but we have to instruct and be instructed. Because of the hazards of tangling our grounds. Which young couples still do. There's nothing so embarrassing as having to be rescued from an unintended ground-lock by your friends, or worse, her kin." At Fawn's baffled look, he added, "It's a bit like a trance. You get wound up in each other and forget to get up, go eat, report for duty . . . after a couple of hours—or days—the body's needs break you out. But that's pretty uncomfortable. Dangerous in an unsafe place to be so unaware of your surroundings for that long, too."

It was her turn to say, "Oh," rather blankly. She glanced up at him. "Did you ever . . . ?"

"Once. When I was very young." His lips twitched. "Around twenty. It's not something most people let happen twice. We look out for each other, try not to let the first learning kill anyone."

A couple of days? I think I had a couple of minutes . . . She shook her head, not sure if she believed this tale. Or understood it, for that matter. "Well, that—what Sunny said then—wasn't what made me so mad. Maybe he didn't know either. Even getting with child didn't make me mad, just scared. So I went to Sunny, because I reckoned he had a right to know. Besides, I thought he liked me, or maybe even loved me."

Dag started to say something, but then at her last statement stopped himself, looking taken aback, and just waved her to continue. "This has to have happened to other farmer women. What do your folk usually do?"

Fawn shrugged. "Usually, people get married. In kind of a hurry. Her folks and his folks get together and put a good face on it, and things just go on. I mean, if no one is married already. If he's already married, or if she is, I guess things get uglier. But I didn't think . . . I mean, I had nerved myself up for the one, I figured I could nerve myself up for the other.

"But when I told Sunny . . . it wasn't what I'd expected. I didn't necessarily think he'd be delighted, but I did expect him to follow through. After all, I had to. But" —she took a deeper breath—"it seems he had other arrangements. His parents had made him a betrothal with the daughter of a man whose land bordered theirs. Did I say Sunny's folks have a big place? And he's the only son, and she was the only child, and it had been understood for years. And I said, why didn't he tell me earlier, and he said, everyone knew and why should he have, if I was giving myself away for free, and I said, that's fine but there's this baby now, and it was all going to have to come out, and both our parents would make us stand up together anyhow, and he said, no, his wouldn't, I was portionless, and he would get three of his friends to say they'd had me that night too, and he'd get out of it." She finished this last in a rush, her face hot. She stole a glance at Dag, who was sitting looking down the lane with a curi-ously blank face but with his teeth pressed into his lower lip. "And at *that* point, I decided I didn't care if I was pregnant with *twins,* I wouldn't have Stupid Sunny for my husband on a *bet.*" She jerked up her chin in defiance.

"Good!" said Dag, startling her. She stared at him.

He added, "I'd been wondering what to make of Stupid Sunny, in all this tale. Now I think maybe a drum skin would be good. I've never tanned a human skin, mind you, but how hard could it be?" He blinked cheerfully at her.

A spontaneous laugh puffed from her lips. "Thank you!"

"Wait, I haven't done it, yet!"

"No, I mean, thank you for saying it." It had been a joke offer. Hadn't it? She remembered the bodies strewn in his wake yesterday and was suddenly less sure. Lakewalkers, after all. "Don't really do it."

"Somebody should." He rubbed his chin, which was stubbled and maybe itchy, and she wondered if shaving was something he didn't do one-handed, either, or if it was just that his razor was in the bottom of his lost saddlebags along with his comb. "It's different for us," he went on. "You can't lie about such things, for one. It shows in your ground. Which is not to say my people don't get tangled up and unhappy in other ways." He hesitated. "I can see why his family might choose to believe his lie, but would yours have? Is that why you ran off?"

She pressed her lips together, but managed a shrug. "Likely not. It wasn't that, exactly. But I'd have been lessened. Forever. I would always be the one who . . . who had been so stupid. And if I got any smaller in their eyes, I was afraid I'd just disappear. I don't suppose this makes any sense to you."

"Well," he said slowly. "No. Or maybe yes, if I broaden the notion from just having babies to living altogether. I am put in mind of a certain not-so-young patroller who once moved the world to get back on patrol, for all that there were plenty of one-handed tasks needing doing back in the camps. His motives weren't too sensible at the time, either."

"Hm." She eyed him sideways. "I figured I could learn to deal with a baby, if I had to. It was dealing with Stupid Sunny and my family that seemed impossible."

In the exact same distant tone that he'd inquired about Sunny and rape, he asked, "Was your family, um . . . cruel to you?"

She stared a moment in some bewilderment, trying to figure out what he was picturing. Beatings with whips? Being locked up on nothing but bread and water? The fancy seemed as slanderous of her poor overworked parents and dear Aunt Nattie as what Sunny had threatened to say of her. She sat up in mortified indignation. "No!" After a reflective moment she revised this to, "Well, my brothers can be a plague. When they notice me at all, that is." Justice served, but it brought her back to the depressing notion that it was all something wrong with her. Well, maybe it was.

"Brothers can be that," he conceded. He added cautiously, "So could you go home now? There no longer being a"—his gesture finished, *baby,* but his mouth managed—"an obstacle."

"I suppose," she said dully.

His brows drew down. "Wait. Did you leave some word, or did you just vanish?"

"Vanished, more or less. I mean, I didn't write anything. But I would think they could see I'd taken some things. If they looked closely."

"Won't your family be frantic? They could think you were hurt. Or dead. Or taken by bandits. Or who knows what—drowned, caught in a snare. Won't Stu—Sunny confess and turn out to help search?"

Fawn's nose wrinkled in doubt. "It's not what I'd pictured." Not of Sunny, anyway. Now relieved of the driving panic of her pregnancy, she thought anew of the baffling scene she'd likely left behind her at West Blue, and gulped guilt.

"They have to be looking for you, Spark. I sure would be, if I were your"— He bit off the last word, whatever it was, abruptly. Chewed and swallowed it, too, as if uncertain of the taste.

She said uneasily, "I don't know. Maybe if I went back now, Stupid Sunny would think *I* had been lying. To trap him. For his stupid farm."

"Do you care what he thinks? Compared to your kin, anyway?"

Her shoulders hunched. "Once, I cared a lot. He seemed . . . he seemed splendid to me. Handsome . . . '' In retrospect, Sunny's face was round and bland, and his eyes far too dull. "Tall . . . '' Actually, short, she decided. He was as tall as her brothers, true. Who would come up maybe to Dag's chin. "He had a good horse." Well, so it had appeared, until she'd seen the long-legged beasts the patrollers all rode. Sunny had shown off his horse, making it sidle and step high, making out that it was a restive handful only an expert might dare bestride. Patrollers rode with such quiet efficiency, you didn't even notice how they were doing it. "You know, it's odd. The farther away I get from him, the more he seems to . . . shrink."

Dag smiled quietly. "He's not shrinking. You're growing, Spark. I've seen such spurts in young patrollers. They grow fast, sometimes, in the crush, when they have to get strong or go under. Takes some adjusting after, be warned— like when you put on eight inches of height in a year and nothing fits any-more."

An example not, she suspected, pulled out of the air. "That was what I wanted. To be grown-up, to be real, to matter."

"Worked," he said reflectively. "Roundaboutly."

"Yes," she whispered. And then, somehow, finally, the dam cracked, and it all came loose. "*Hurts.*"

"Yes," he said simply, and put his arm around her shoulders, and snugged her in tight to him, because she had not cried all that night or day, but she was crying now.

Dag studied the top of Fawn's head, all he could see as she pressed her face into his chest and wept. Even now, she choked her sobs half to silence, shuddering with their suppression. His certainty that she needed to release the strain in her ground was confirmed; if he'd been forced to put it into words for her, he might have said that the fissures running through her seemed to grow less impossibly dark as her sorrow was disgorged, but he wasn't sure if that would make sense to her. Sorrow and rage. There was more erosion of spirit here, going back further, than the malice's destruction of her child.

His instinct was to let her weep the grief out, but after a time his worry roused anew as she clutched her belly once more, a sign of physical pain returning. "Sh," he whispered, hugging her one-armed. "Sh. Don't be making yourself sick, now. Would you like your hot stone again?"

Her clutch transferred to his sleeve and tightened. "No," she muttered. She briefly raised her face, mottled white and flushed where it was not dark with bruises. "'M too hot now."

"All right."

She ducked back down, gaining control of her breathing, but the tight stress in her body didn't ease.

He wondered if her abandonment of her family without a word was as appallingly ruthless as it seemed, or if there was more to the tale. But then, he came from a group that watched out for each other systematically, from partnered pairs through linkers to patrols to companies and right on up in a tested web. *I sure would be looking for you, Spark, if I were your*— and then his tongue had tangled between two choices, each differently disturbing: *father* or *lover. Leave it alone. You are neither, old patroller.* But he was the only thing she had for a partner here. So.

He lowered his lips toward her ear, nestled in the black curls, and murmured, "Think of something beautifully useless."

Her face came up, and she sniffed in confusion. "What?"

"There are a lot of senseless things in the world, but not all of them are sorrows. Sometimes—I find—it helps to remember the other kind. Everybody knows some light, even if they forget when they're down in the dark. Something"—he groped for a term that would work for her—"everyone else thinks is stupid, but you know is wonderful."

She lay still against him for a long time, and he started to muster another explanation, or perhaps abandon the attempt as, well, stupid, but then she said, "Milkweed."

"Mm?" He gave her another encouraging hug, lest she mistake his query for objection.

"Milkweed. It's a just a weed, we have to go around and tear it out of the garden and the crops, but I think the smell of its flowers is prettier than my aunt's climbing roses that she works on and babies all the time. Sweeter than lilacs. Nobody else thinks the flower heads are pretty, but they are, if you look at them closely enough. Pink and complicated. Like wild carrot lace gone plump and shy, like a handful of bitty stars. And the smell, I could breathe it in . . . " She uncurled a little more, unlocking from her pain, pursuing the vision. "In the fall it grows pods, all wrinkled and ugly, but if you tear them open, beautiful silk flies out. The milkweed bugs make houses and pantries of them. Milkweed bugs, now, they aren't pests. They don't bite, they don't eat anything else. Bright burnt-orange wings with black bands, and shiny black legs and feet . . . they just tickle, when they crawl on your hand. I kept some in a box for a while. Gathered them milkweed seeds, and let them drink out of a bit of wet cloth." Her lips, which had softened, tightened again. "Till one of my brothers upset the box, and Mama made me throw them out. It was winter by then."

"Mm." Well, that had worked, till she'd reached the tailpiece. But nonetheless her body was relaxing, the lingering shudders tamping out.

Unexpectedly, she said, "Your turn."

"Uh?"

She poked his chest with a suddenly determined finger. "I told you my useless thing, now you have to tell me one."

"Well, that seems fair," he had to allow. "But I can't think of . . . " And then he did. *Oh*. He was silent for a little. "I haven't thought of this in years. There's a place we went—still go—every summer and fall, a gathering camp, at a place called Hickory Lake, maybe a hundred and fifty miles northwest of here. Hickory nuts, elderberries, and a kind of water lily root, which is a staple of ours—harvesting and planting in one operation. Lakewalkers farm too, in our way, Spark. A lot of wet work, but fun, if you're a child who likes to swim. Maybe I can show . . . anyway. I was, oh, maybe eight or nine, and I'd been sent out in a pole-boat to collect elderberries in the margins, around behind the islands. Forget why I was by myself that day. Hickory Lake sits on clay soil and tends to be muddy and brown most of the time, but in the undisturbed back channels, the water is wonderfully clear.

"I could see right to the bottom, bright as Glassforge crystal. The water weeds wound down and around each other like waving green feathers. And floating on the top were these flat lily pads—not the ones whose roots we eat. Not planted, not useful, they just grew there, probably from before there ever were Lakewalkers. Deep green, with red edges, and thin red lines running down the stems in the water. And their lily flowers had just opened up, floating there like sunbursts, white as . . . as nothing I had ever seen, these translucent petals veined like milky dragonfly wings, glowing in the light reflecting off the water. With luminous, powdery gold centers seeming flowers within flowers, spiraling in forever. I should have been gathering, but I just hung over the edge of the boat staring at them, must have been an hour. Watching the light and the water dance around them in celebration. I could not look away." He gulped a suddenly difficult breath. "Later, in some very dry places, the memory of that hour was enough to go on with."

A hesitant hand reached up and touched his face in something like awe. One warm finger traced a cool smear of wet over his cheekbone. "Why are you crying?"

Responses ran though his mind: *I'm not crying,* or, *I'm just picking up reverberations from your ground,* or, *I must be more tired than I thought.* Two of which were somewhat true. Instead, his tongue found the truth entire. "Because I had forgotten water lilies." He dropped his lips to the top of her head, letting the scent of her fill his nose, his mouth. "And you just made me remember."

"Does it hurt?"

"In a way, Spark. But it's a good way."

She cuddled down thoughtfully, her ear pressed to his chest. "Hm."

The smell of her hair reminded him of mown hay and new bread without being quite either, mingled now with the fragrance of her soft warm body. A faint mist of sweat shimmered on her upper lip in the afternoon's heat. The notion of lapping it off, followed up with a lingering exploration of the taste of her mouth, flashed through his mind. He was suddenly keenly aware of how full his arm was of round young woman. And how the heat of the hour seemed to be collecting in his groin.

If you've a brain left in your head, old patroller, let her go. Now. This was not the time or the place. Or the partner. He had let his groundsense grow far too open to her ground, very dangerous. In fact, to list everything wrong with the impulse he would have to sit here wrapped around her for another hour, which would be a mistake. Grievous, grievous mistake. He took a deep breath and reluctantly unwound his arm from her shoulders. His arm protested its cooling emptiness. She emitted a disappointed mew and sat up, blinking sleepily.

"It's getting hotter," he said. "Best I'd see to those dogs." Her hand trailed over his shirt, falling back as he creaked to his feet. "You'll be all right, resting here a while? No, don't get up . . ."

"Bring me that mending basket, then. And your shirt and sleeve off that fence, if they're dry enough. I'm not used to sitting around doing nothing with my hands."

"It's not your mending."

"It's not my house, food, water, or bedding, either." She raked her curls out of her eyes.

"They owe you for the malice, Spark. This farm and everything in it."

She wriggled her fingers and looked stern at him, and he melted.

"All right. Basket. But no bouncing around while my back is turned, you hear?"

"The bleeding's really slowed," she offered. "Maybe, after that first rush, it'll tail off quick, same way."

"Hope so." He gave her an encouraging nod and went inside to retrieve the basket.

Fawn watched Dag trudge off around the barn, then bent to his ripped-up shirt. After that, she sorted through the mending basket for other simple tasks that she could not spoil. It was hazardous to mess with another woman's system, but the more worn and tattered garments seemed safe to attempt. This stained child's dress, for example. She wondered how many people had lived here and where they had got off to. It was unsettling to think that she might be mending clothes for someone no longer alive.

In about an hour, Dag reappeared. He stopped by the well to strip off his ill-fitting scavenged shirt and wash again with the slice of brown soap, by which she concluded that the burial must have been a hot, ugly, and smelly job. She could not picture how he had managed a shovel one-handed, except slowly, apparently. He was pretty smooth at getting the bucket cranked up from the well and poured out into the trough, though. He ended by sticking his whole head in the bucket, then shaking his hair out like a dog. He had no linens to dry himself with, but likely the wetness beading on his skin felt cooling and welcome. She imagined herself drying his back, fingers tracing down those long muscles. Speaking of keeping one's hands busy. He hadn't seemed to mind her washing his hand last night, but that had been by way of medical preparation. She'd liked the shape of his hand, long-fingered, blunt-nailed, and strong.

He sat on the edge of the porch, accepted his own shirt from her with a smile of thanks, rolled up the sleeves, and pulled it back on once more. The sun was angling toward the treetops, west where the lane vanished into the woods. He stretched. "Hungry, Spark? You should eat."

"A little." She set the mending aside. "So should you." Maybe she could sit at the kitchen table and at least help fix the dinner, this time.

He sat up straight suddenly, staring down the lane. After a minute, the horse at the far end of the pasture raised its head too, ears pricking.

In another minute, a motley parade appeared from the trees. Four men, one riding a plow horse and the others afoot; some cows in a reluctant string; half a dozen bleating sheep held in a bunch by desultory threats from a tall boy with a stick.

"Think someone's made it home," said Dag. His eyes narrowed, but no more figures came out of the woods. "No patrollers, though. Blight it."

Wordlessly, still eyeing the men and animals in the distance, he rolled down his left sleeve and let it hang over his stump. But not the right sleeve, Fawn noticed with a pinch of breath. All the lively amusement faded out of his bony face, leaving it closed and watchful once more.

7

The farm folk spotted the pair on the porch about the time they exited the lane, Fawn guessed by the way they paused and stared, taking stock. The stringy old man on the horse stayed back. Under his eye, the boy made himself busy taking down some rails and urging the sheep and cows into the pasture. Once the first few animals spread out in a lumbering burst of bawled complaint, quickly converted to hungry grazing, the rest followed willingly. The three adult men advanced cautiously toward the house, gripping tools like weapons: a pitchfork, a mattock, a big skinning knife.

"If those fellows are from here, they've just had some very bad days, by all the signs," Dag said, whether in a tone of warning or mere observation Fawn was not certain. "Stay calm and quiet, till they're sure I'm no threat."

"How could they think that?" said Fawn indignantly. She straightened her spine against the house wall, twitching the white folds of her overabundant gown tighter about her, and frowned.

"Well, there's a bit of history, there. Some bandits have claimed to *be* patrollers, in the past. Usually we leave bandits to their farmer-brethren, but those we string up good, if we catch 'em at it. Farmers can't always tell. I expect these'll be all right, once they get over being jumpy."

Dag stayed seated on the porch edge as the men neared, though he too sat up straighter. He raised his right hand to his temple in what might have been a salute of greeting or just scratching his head, but in either case conveyed no threat. "Evenin'," he rasped.

The men sidled forward, looking ready either to pounce or bolt at the slightest provocation. The oldest, a thickset fellow with a bit of gray in his hair and the pitchfork in his grip, stepped in front. His glance at Fawn was bewildered. She smiled back and waved her fingers.

Provisionally polite, the thickset man returned a "How de'." He grounded the butt of his pitchfork and continued more sternly, "And who might you be, and what are you doing here?"

Dag gave a nod. "I'm from Mari Redwing's Lakewalker patrol. We were called down from the north a couple of days ago to help deal with your blight bogle. This here's Miss Sawfield. She was kidnapped off the road yesterday by the bogle I was hunting, and injured. I'd hoped to find folks here to help her, but you were all gone. Not willingly, by the signs."

He'd left out an awful lot of important complications, Fawn thought. Only one was hers alone to speak to: "Bluefield," she corrected. "M' name's Fawn Bluefield."

Dag glanced over his shoulder, eyebrows rising. "Ah, right."

Fawn tried to lighten the frowns of the farmers by saying brightly, "This your place?"

"Ayup," said the man.

"Glad you made it back. Is everyone all right?"

A look of thankfulness in the midst of adversity came over the faces of all the men. "Ayup," the spokesman said again, in a huff of blown-out breath. "Praise be, *we* didn't suffer no one getting killed by those, those . . . things."

"It was a near chance," muttered a brown-haired fellow, who looked to be a brother or cousin of the thickset man.

A younger man with bright chestnut hair and freckles slid around to Dag's left, staring at his empty shirt cuff. Dag feigned not to notice the stare, but Fawn thought she detected a slight stiffening of his shoulders. The man burst out, "Hey—you wouldn't be that fellow Dag all those other patrollers are looking for, would you? They said you couldn't hardly be mistook—tall drink of water with his hair cropped short, bright goldy eyes, and missing his left hand." He nodded in certainty, taking inventory of the man on the porch.

Dag's voice was suddenly unguarded and eager. "You've seen my patrol? Where are they? Are they all right? I'd expected them to find me before now."

The red-haired fellow made a wry face, and said, "Spread out between Glassforge and that big hole back in the hills those crazy fellows were trying to make us dig, I guess. Looking for you. When you hadn't turned up in Glassforge by this morning, that scary old lady carried on like she was afraid you were dead in a ditch somewheres. I had four different patrollers buttonhole me with your particulars before we got out of town."

Dag's lips lifted at that apt description of what Fawn guessed must be his patrol leader, Mari. The boy and the skinny graybeard on the horse, once the fence rails were replaced, drifted up to the edge of the group to watch and listen.

The thickset man gripped his pitchfork haft tighter again, although not in threat. "Them other patrollers all said you must have killed the bogle. They said that had to be what made all them monsters, mud-men they calls 'em, run off like that yesterday night."

"More or less," said Dag. A twitch of his hand dismissed—or concealed—the details. "You're right to travel cautious. There might still be a few bandits abroad—that'll be for the Glassforge folks to deal with. Any mud-men who escaped my patrol or Chato's will be running mindless through the woods for a while, till they die off. I put down two yesterday, but at least four I know of got away into the brush. They won't attack you now, but they're still dangerous to surprise or corner, like any sick wild animal. The malice's—bogle's—lair was up in the hills not eight miles due east of here. You all were lucky to escape its attentions before this."

"You two look like you collected some attentions yourselves," said the thickset man, frowning at their visible bruises and scrapes. He turned to the lanky boy. "Here, Tad—go fetch your mama." The boy nodded eagerly and pelted back down the lane toward the woods.

"What happened here?" Dag asked in turn.

This released a spate of increasingly eager tale-telling, one man interrupting another with corroboration or argument. Some twenty, or possibly thirty, mud-men had erupted out of the surrounding woods four days ago, brutalizing and terrifying the farm folk, then driving them off in a twenty-mile march southeast into the hills. The mud-men had kept the crowd under control by the simple expedient of carrying the three youngest children and threatening to dash out their brains against the nearest tree if anyone resisted, a detail that made Fawn gasp but Dag merely look more expressionless than ever. They had arrived at length at a crude campsite containing a couple dozen other prisoners, mostly victims of road banditry; some had been held for many weeks. There, the mud-men, uneasily supervised by a few human bandits, seemed intent on making their new slaves excavate a mysterious hole in the ground.

"I don't understand that hole," said the thickset man, eldest son of the gray-beard and apparent leader of the farm folk, whose family name was Horseford. The stringy old grandfather seemed querulous and addled—traits that seemed to pre-date the malice attack, Fawn judged from the practiced but not-unkind way everyone fielded his complaints.

"The malice—the blight bogle—was probably starting to try to mine," said Dag thoughtfully. "It was growing fast."

"Yes, but the hole wasn't right for a mine, either," put in the red-haired man, Sassa. He'd turned out to be a brother-in-law of the house, present that day to help with some log-hauling. He seemed less deeply shaken than the rest, possibly because his wife and baby had been safely back in Glassforge and had missed the horrific misadventure altogether. "They didn't have enough tools, for one thing, till those mud-men brought in the ones they stole from here.

They had folks digging with their hands and hauling dirt in bags made out of their clothes. It was an awful mess."

"Would be, at first, till the bogle caught someone with the know-how to do it right," said Dag. "Later, when it's safe again, you folks should get some real miners to come in and explore the site. There must be something of value under there; the malice would not have been mistaken about that. This part of the country, I'd guess an iron or coal seam, maybe with a forge planned to follow, but it might be anything."

"I'd wondered if they were digging up another bogle," said Sassa. "They're supposed to come out of the ground, they say."

Dag's brows twitched up, and he eyed the man with new appraisal. "Interesting idea. When two bogles chance to emerge nearby, which happily doesn't occur too often, they usually attack each other first thing."

"That would save you Lakewalkers some trouble, wouldn't it?"

"No. Unfortunately. Because the winning bogle ends up stronger. Easier to take them down piecemeal."

Fawn tried to imagine something stronger and more frightening than the creature she had faced yesterday. When you were already as terrified as your body could bear, what difference could it make if something was even worse? She wondered if that explained anything about Dag.

Movement at the end of the lane caught her eye. Another plow horse came out of the woods and trotted ponderously up to the farmyard, a middle-aged woman riding with the lanky boy up behind. They paused on the other side of the well, the woman staring down hard at something, then came up to join the others.

The red-haired Sassa, either more garrulous or more observant than his in-laws, was finishing his account of yesterday's inexplicable uproar at the digging camp: the sudden loss of wits and mad flight of their captor mud-men, followed, not half an hour later, by the arrival from the sunset woods of a very off-balance patrol of Lakewalkers. The Lakewalkers had been trailed in turn by a mob of frantic friends and relatives of the captives from in and around Glassforge. Leaving the local people to each other's care, the patrollers had withdrawn to their own Lakewalkerish concerns, which seemed mainly to revolve around slaying all the mud-men they could catch and looking for their mysterious missing man Dag, who they seemed to think somehow responsible for the bizarre turn of events.

Dag rubbed his stubbled chin. "Huh. I suppose Mari or Chato must have thought this mining camp might be the lair. Following up traces from that bandit hideout we raided night before last, I expect. That explains where they were all day yesterday. And well into the night, sounds like."

"Oh, aye," said the thickset man. "Folks was still trailing into Glassforge all night and into this morning, yours and ours."

The farmwife slid down off the horse and stood listening to this, her eyes searching her house, Dag, and especially Fawn. Fawn guessed from the farm men's talk that she must be the woman they'd called Petti. Judging by the faint gray in her hair, she was of an age with her husband, and as lean as he was thick, tough and strappy, if tired-looking. Now she stepped forward. "What blood is all that in the tub out by the well?"

Dag gave her a polite duck of his head. "Miss S—Bluefield's mostly, ma'am. My apologies for filching your linens. I've been throwing another bucket of water on them each time I go by. I'll try to get them cleaned up better before we leave."

We not *I,* some quick part of Fawn's mind noted at once, with a catch of relief.

"Mostly?" The farmwife cocked her head at him, squinting. "How'd she get hurt?"

"That would be her tale to tell, ma'am."

Her face went still for an instant. Her eye flicked up to Fawn and then back, to take in his empty cuff. "You really kill that bogle that did all this?"

He hesitated only briefly before replying, precisely but unexpansively, "We did."

She inhaled and gave a little snort. "Don't you be troubling about my laundry. The idea."

She turned back to, or upon, her menfolk. "Here, what are you all doing standing about gabbing and gawking like a pack of ninnies? There's work to do before dark. Horse, see to milking those poor cows, if they ain't been frightened dry. Sassa, fetch in the firewood, if those thieves left any in the stack, and if they didn't, make some more. Jay, put away and put right what can be, what needs fixin', start on, what needs tomorrow's tools, set aside. Tad, help your grandpa with the horses, and then come and start picking up inside. Hop to it while there's light left!"

They scattered at her bidding.

Fawn said helpfully, pushing up, "The mud-men didn't find your storage cellar—" And then her head seemed to drain, throbbing unpleasantly. The world did not go black, but patterned shadows swarmed around her, and she was only dimly aware of abrupt movement: a strong hand and truncated arm catching her and half-walking, half-carrying her inside. She blinked her eyes clear to find herself on the feather pallet once more, two faces looming over her, the farmwife's concerned and wary, Dag's concerned and . . . tender? The thought jolted her, and she blinked some more, trying to swim back to reason.

"—*flat,* Spark," he was saying. "Flat was working." He brushed a sweat-dampened curl out of her eyes.

"What happened to you, girl?" demanded Petti.

"'M not a girl," Fawn mumbled. "'M twenty . . ."

"The mud-men knocked her around hard yesterday." Dag's intent gaze on her seemed to be asking permission to continue, and she shrugged assent. "She miscarried of a two-months child. Bled pretty fierce, but it seems to have slowed now. Wish one of my patrolwomen were here. You do much midwifery, ma'am?"

"A little. Keeping her lying down is right if she's been bleeding much."

"How do you know if she . . . if a woman is going to be all right, after that?"

"If the bleeding tails off to nothing within five days, it's a pretty sure bet things are coming back around all right inside, if there's no fever. Ten days at the most. A two-months child, well, that's as chance will happen. Much more than three months, now, that gets more dangerous."

"Five days," he repeated, as if memorizing the number. "Right, we're still all right, then. Fever . . . ?" He shook his head and rose to his feet, wincing as he rubbed his left arm, and followed the farmwife's gaze around her kitchen. With an apologetic nod, he removed his arm contraption from her table, bundled it up, and set it down at the end of the tick.

"And what knocked you around?" asked Petti.

"This and that, over the years," he answered vaguely. "If my patrol doesn't find us by tomorrow, I'd like to take Miss Bluefield to Glassforge. I have to report in. Will there be a wagon?"

The farmwife nodded. "Later on. The girls should bring it tomorrow when they come." The other women and children of the Horseford family were staying in town with Sassa's wife, it seemed, sorting out recovered goods and waiting for their men to report the farm safe again.

"Will they be making another trip, after?"

"Might. Depends." She scrubbed the back of her neck, staring around as if a hundred things cried for her attention and she only had room in her head for ten, which, Fawn guessed, was just about the case.

"What can I do for you, ma'am?" Dag inquired.

She stared at him as if taken by surprise by the offer. "Don't know yet. Everything's been knocked all awhirl. Just . . . just wait here."

She marched off to take a look around her smashed-up house.

Fawn whispered to Dag, "She's not going to get settled in her mind till she has her things back in order."

"I sensed that." He bent over and took up the knife pouch, lying by the head of the pallet. Only then did Fawn realize how careful he'd been not to glance at it while the farmwife was present. "Can you put this somewhere out of sight?"

Fawn nodded, and sat up—slowly—to flip open her bedroll, laid at the pallet's foot. Her spare skirt and shirt and underdrawers lay atop the one good dress she'd packed along to go look for work in, that hasty night she'd fled home. She tucked the knife pouch well away and rolled up the blanket once more.

He nodded approval and thanks. "Best not to mention the knife to these folks, I think. Bothersome. That one worse than most." And, under his breath, "Wish Mari would get here."

They could hear the farmwife's quick footsteps on the wooden floors overhead, and occasional wails of dismay, mostly, "My poor *windows!*"

"I noticed you left a lot out of your story," said Fawn.

"Yes. I'd appreciate it if you would, too."

"I promised, didn't I? I sure don't want to talk about that knife to just anyone, either."

"If they ask too many questions, or too close of ones, just ask them about their troubles in turn. It'll usually divert them, when they have so much to tell as now."

"Ah, so that's what you were doing out there!" In retrospect, she could spot how Dag had turned the talk so that they had learned so much of the Horsefords' woes, but the Horsefords had received so little news in return. "Another old patroller trick?"

One corner of his mouth twitched up. "More or less."

The farmwife came back downstairs about the time her son Tad came in from the barn, and after a moment's thought she sent the boy and Dag off together to clean up broken glass and rubble around the house. She surveyed her kitchen and climbed down into her storage cellar, from which she emerged with a few jars for supper, seeming much reassured. After setting the jars in a row on the table—Fawn could almost see her counting stomachs and planning the upcoming meal in her head—she turned back and frowned down at Fawn.

"We'll have to get you into a proper bed. Birdy's room, I think, once Tad gets the glass out. It wasn't too bad, otherwise." And then, after a pause, in a much lower voice, "That patroller fellow tell the straight story on you?"

"Yes, ma'am," said Fawn.

The woman's face pinched in suspicion. "'Cause he didn't get those scratches on his face from no mud-man, I'll warrant."

Fawn looked back blankly, then said, "Oh! *Those* scratches. I mean, yes, that was me, but it was an accident. I mistook him for another bandit, at first. We got that one straightened out right quick."

"Lakewalkers is strange folk. Black magicians, they say."

Fawn struggled up on one elbow to say hotly, "You should be grateful if they are. Because blight bogles are blacker ones. I *saw* one, yesterday. Closer than you are to me now. Anything patrollers have to do to put them down is all right by me!"

Petti's thoughts seemed to darken. "Was that what—did the blight bogle . . . blight you?"

"Make me miscarry?"

"Aye. Because girls don't usually miscarry just from being knocked around, or falling down stairs, or the like. Though I've seen some try for it. They just end up being bruised mothers, usually."

"Yes," said Fawn shortly, scrunching back down. "It was the bogle." Were these too-close questions? Not yet, she decided. Even Dag had offered some explanations, just enough to satisfy without begging more questions. "It was ugly. Uglier than the mud-men, even. Bogles kill everything they touch, seemingly. You should go look at its lair, later. The woods are all dead for a mile around. I don't know how long it will take for them to grow back."

"Hm." Petti busied herself unsealing jars, sniffing for wholesomeness and fishing out the broken wax to be rinsed and remelted, later. "Them mud-men was ugly enough. The day before we was brought to the digging camp, seems there was a woman had a sick child, who went to them and insisted on being let go to get him help. She tried carrying on, weeping and wailing, to force them. Instead, they killed her little boy. And ate him. She was in a state by the time we got there. Everybody was. Even them bandits, who I don't think was in their right minds either, wasn't too easy about that one."

Fawn shuddered. "Dag said the mud-men ate folks. I wasn't sure I believed him. Till after . . . afterwards." She hitched her shoulders. "Lakewalkers hunt those things. They go *looking* for them."

"Hm." The woman frowned as she kept trying to assemble the meal by her normal routine and coming up short against missing tools and vessels. But she improvised and went on, much as Fawn had. She added from across the room after a while, "They say Lakewalkers can beguile folk's minds."

"Look, you." Fawn lurched back up on her elbow, scowling. "*I* say, *that* Lakewalker saved my life yesterday. At least twice. No, three times, because I'd have bled to death in the woods trying to walk out if he'd died in the fight. He fought off five of those mud-men! He took care of me all last night when I couldn't move for the pain, and carried out my bloody clouts with never a word of complaint, *and* he cleaned up your kitchen *and* he fixed your fence *and* he buried your dogs nice in the shady woods, and he didn't have to do *any* of that." *And his heart breaks for the memory of water lilies.* "I've seen that man do more good with one hand in a day than I've seen any other man do with two in a week. Or ever. If he's beguiled *my* mind, he sure has done it the hard way!"

The farmwife had both her hands raised as if to ward off this hot, pelting defense, half-laughing. "Stop, stop, I surrender, girl!"

"Huh!" Fawn flopped back again. "Just don't you give me any more *they says*."

"Hm." Petti's smile dwindled to bleakness, but whatever shadowed her thoughts now, she did not confide to Fawn.

Fawn lay quietly on her pallet till dusk drove the men indoors. At that point, Tad was made to carry off the feather tick, and the space was used for a trestle table. Makeshift benches—boards placed across sawed-off logs—were brought in to serve for the missing chairs. Petti allowed to Dag as how she thought it all right for Fawn to sit up long enough to take the meal with the family. Since the alternative appeared to be having Petti bring her something in bed in some lonely nook of the house, Fawn agreed decisively to this.

The meal was abundant, if makeshift and simple, eaten by the limited light of candle stubs and the fire at the end of the long summer day. Everyone would be going to bed right after, not just her, Fawn thought. The room was hot and the conversation, at first, scant and practical. All were exhausted, their minds filled with the recent disruptions in their lives. Since everyone was mostly eating with their hands anyhow, Dag's slight awkwardness did not stick out, Fawn observed with satisfaction. You wouldn't think his missing hand bothered him a bit, unless you noticed how he never raised his left wrist into sight above the table edge. He spoke only to encourage Fawn, next to him, to eat up, though about that he was quite firm.

"Kind o' you to help Tad with all that busted glass," the farmwife said to Dag.

"No trouble, ma'am. You should all be able to step safe now, leastways."

Sassa offered, "I'll help you to get new windows in, Petti, soon as things are settled a bit."

She gave her brother-in-law a grateful look. "Thankee, Sassa."

Grandfather Horseford grumbled, "Oiled cloth stretched on the frames was good enough in *my* day," to which his gray-haired son responded only, "Have some more pan bread, Pa." The land might still be the old man's, in name at least, but it was plain that the house was Petti's.

Inevitably, Fawn supposed, the talk turned to picking over the past days' disasters. Dag, who looked to Fawn's eye as though he was growing tired, and no wonder, was not expansive; she watched him successfully use his diversion trick of answering a question with a question four times running. Until Sassa remarked to him, sighing, "Too bad your patrol didn't get there a day sooner. They might've saved that poor little boy who got et."

Dag did not exactly wince. It was merely a lowering of his eyelids, a slight, unargumentative tilt of his head. A shift of his features from tired to expressionless. And silence.

Fawn sat up, offended for him. "Careful what you wish after. If Dag's patrol had got there anytime before I—we—before the bogle died and the mud-men ran off, there'd have been a big fight. Lots of folks might have gotten killed, and that little boy, too."

Sassa, brow furrowed, turned to her. "Yes, but—*et*? Doesn't it bother you extra? It sure bothers me."

"It's what mud-men do," murmured Dag.

Sassa eyed him, disconcerted. "Used to it, are you?"

Dag shrugged.

"But it was a *child*."

"Everyone's someone's child."

Petti, who'd been staring wearily at her plate, looked up at that.

In a tone of cheery speculation, Jay said, "If they'd have been *five* days faster, *we'd* not have been raided. And our cows and sheep and dogs would still be alive. Wish for that, while you're at it, why don't you?"

With a grimace that failed to quite pass as a smile, Dag pushed himself up from the table. He gave Petti a nod. "'Scuse me, ma'am."

He closed the kitchen door quietly behind him. His booted steps sounded across the porch, then faded into the night.

"What bit him?" asked Jay.

Petti took a breath. "Jay, some days I think your mama must have dropped you on your head when you was a baby, really I do."

He blinked in bewilderment at her scowl, and said less in inquiry than protest, "What?"

For the first time in hours, Fawn found herself chilled again, chilled and shaking. Her wan droop did not escape the observant Petti. "Here, girl, you should be in bed. Horse, help her."

Horse, mercifully, was much quieter than his younger relations; or perhaps his wife had given him some low-down on their outlandish guests in private. He propelled Fawn through the darkening house. The loss of light was not from her going woozy, this time, though her skull was throbbing again. Petti followed with a candle in a cup for a makeshift holder.

The ground floor of one of the add-ons consisted of two small bedrooms opposite each other. Horse steered Fawn inside to where her feather tick had been laid across a wooden bed frame. The slashed rope webbing had been re-knotted sometime recently, maybe by Dag and Tad. A moist summer night breeze wafted through the small, glassless windows. Fawn decided this must be a daughter's bedchamber; the girls would likely be arriving home tomorrow with the wagon.

As soon as the transport was safely accomplished, Petti shooed Horse out. Awkwardly, Fawn swapped out her dressings, half-hiding under a light blanket that she scarcely needed. Petti made no comment on them, beyond a "Give over, here," and a "There you go, now." A day ago, Fawn reflected, she would have given anything to trade her strange man helper for a strange woman. Tonight, the desire was oddly reversed.

"Horse 'n' me have the room across," said Petti. "You can call out if you need anything in the night."

"Thank you," said Fawn, trying to feel grateful. She supposed it would not be understood if she asked for the kitchen floor back. The floor and Dag. Where would these graceless farmers try to put the patroller? In the barn? The thought made her glower.

Long, unmistakable footfalls sounded in the hall, followed by a sharp double rap against the door. "Come in, Dag," Fawn called, before Petti could say anything.

He eased inside. A stack of dry garments lay over his left arm, the laundry Fawn had seen draped over the pasture fence earlier, Fawn's blue dress and linen drawers; underneath were his own trousers and drawers that had been so spectacularly bloodied yesterday. He had her bedroll tucked under his armpit.

He laid the bedroll down in a swept corner of the room, with her cleaned clothes atop. "There you go, Spark."

"Thank you, Dag," she said simply. His smile flickered across his face like light on water, gone in the instant. Didn't anyone ever just say *thank you* to patrollers? She was really beginning to wonder.

With a wary nod at the watching Petti, he stepped to Fawn's bedside and laid his palm on her brow. "Warm," he commented. He traded the palm for the inside of his wrist. Fawn tried to feel his pulse through their skins, as she had listened to his heartbeat, without success. "But not feverish," he added under his breath.

He stepped back a little, his lips tightening. Fawn remembered those lips breathing in her hair last night, and suddenly wanted nothing more than to kiss and be kissed good night by them. Was that so wrong? Somehow, Petti's frowning presence made it so.

"What did you find outside?" she asked, instead.

"Not my patrol." He sighed. "Not for a mile in any direction, leastways."

"Do you suppose they're all still looking on the wrong side of Glassforge?"

"Could be. It looks like it's fixing to rain; heat lightning off to the west. If I really were stuck in a ditch, I wouldn't be sorry, but I hate to think of them running around in the woods in the dark and wet, in fear for me, when I'm snug inside and safe. I'm going to hear about that later, I expect."

"Oh, dear."

"Don't worry, Spark; another day it will be the other way around. And then it will be my turn to be, ah, humorous." His eyes glinted in a way that made her want to laugh.

"Will we really go to Glassforge tomorrow?"

"We'll see. See how you're doing in the morning, for one."

"I'm doing much better tonight. Bleeding's no worse than a monthly, now."

"Do you want your hot stone again?"

"Really, I don't think I need it anymore."

"Good. Sleep hard, then, you."

She smiled shyly. "I'll try."

His hand made a little move toward her, but then fell back to his side. "Good night."

"G'night, Dag. You sleep hard too."

He gave her a last nod, and withdrew; the farmwife carried the candle out with her, closing the door firmly behind. A faint flash of the heat lightning Dag had mentioned came through the window, too far away even to hear the thunder, but otherwise all was darkness and silence. Fawn rolled over and tried to obey Dag's parting admonishment.

"Hold up," murmured the farmwife, and since she carried the only light, the stub melting down to a puddle in the clay cup, Dag did so. She shouldered past and led him to the kitchen. Another candle, and a last dying flicker from the fireplace, showed the trestle table and benches taken down and stowed by the wall, and the plates and vessels from dinner stacked on the drainboard by the sink, along with the bucket of water refilled.

The farmwife looked around the shadows and sighed. "I'll deal with the rest of this in the morning, I guess." Belying her words, she moved to cover and set aside the scant leftover food, including a stack of pan bread she had apparently cooked up with breakfast in mind.

"Where do you want me to sleep, ma'am?" Dag inquired politely. Not with Fawn, obviously. He tried not to remember the scent of her hair, like summer in his mouth, or the warmth of her breathing young body tucked under his arm.

"You can have one of those ticks that little girl mended; put it down where you will."

"The porch, maybe. I can watch out for my people, if any come out of the woods in the night, and not wake the house. I could pull it into the kitchen if it comes on to rain."

"That'd be good," said the farmwife.

Dag peered through the empty window frame into the darkness, letting his groundsense reach out. The animals, scattered in the pasture, were calm, some grazing, some half-asleep. "That mare isn't actually mine. We found it at the bogle's lair and rode it out. Do you recognize it for anyone's?"

Petti shook her head. "Not ours, anyways."

"If I ride it to Glassforge, it would be nice to not be jumped for horse thieving before I can explain."

"I thought you patrollers claimed a fee for killing a bogle. You could claim it."

Dag shrugged. "I already have a horse. Leastways, I hope so. If no one comes forward for this one, I thought I might have it go to Miss Bluefield. It's sweet-tempered, with easy paces. Which is part of what inclines me to think it wasn't a bandit's horse, or not for long."

Petti paused, staring down at her store of food. "Nice girl, that Miss Bluefield."

"Yes."

"You wonder how she got in this fix."

"Not my tale, ma'am."

"Aye, I noticed that about you."

What? That he told no tales?

"Accidents happen, to the young," she went on. "Twenty, eh?"

"So she says."

"*You* ain't twenty." She moved to kneel by the fire and poke it back for the night.

"No. Not for a long time, now."

"You could take that horse and ride back to your patrol tonight, if you're that worried about them. That girl would be all right, here. I'd take her in till she's mended."

That had been precisely his plan, yesterday. It seemed a very long time ago. "Good of you to offer. But I promised to see her safe to Glassforge, which was where she was bound. Also, I want Mari to look her over. My patrol leader—she'll be able to tell if Fawn's healing all right."

"Aye, figured you'd say something like that. I ain't blind." She sighed, stood, turned to face him with her arms crossed. "And then what?"

"Pardon?"

"Do you even know what you're doing to her? Standing there with them cheekbones up in the air? No, I don't suppose you do."

Dag shifted from cautious to confused. That the farmwife was shrewd and observant, he had certainly noticed; but he did not understand her underlying distress in this matter. "I mean her only good."

"Sure you do." She frowned fiercely. "I had a cousin, once."

Dag tilted his head in faint encouragement, torn between curiosity and an entirely unmagical premonition that wherever she was going with this tale, he didn't want to go along.

"Real nice young fellow; handsome, too," Petti continued. "He got a job as a horse boy at that hotel in Glassforge where your patrols always stay, when they're passing through these parts. There was this patroller girl, young one, came there with her patrol. Very pretty, very tall. Very nice. Very nice to *him,* he thought."

"Patrol leaders try to discourage that sort of thing."

"Aye, so I understood. Too bad they don't succeed. Didn't take too long for him to fall mad in love with the girl. He spent the whole next year just waiting for her patrol to come back. Which it did. And she was nice to him again."

Dag waited. Not comfortably.

"Third year, the patrol came again, but she did not. Seems she was only visiting, and had gone back to her own folks way west of here."

"That's usual, for training up young patrollers. We send them to other camps for a season or two, or more. They learn other ways, make friends; if ever we have to combine forces in a hurry, it makes everything easier if some patrollers already know each other's routes and territories. The ones training up to be leaders, we send 'em around to all seven hinterlands. They say of those that they've walked around the lake."

She eyed him. "You ever walk around the lake?"

"Twice," he admitted.

"Hm." She shook her head, and went on, "He got the notion he would go after her, volunteer to join with you Lakewalkers."

"Ah," said Dag. "That would not work. It's not a matter of pride or ill will, you understand; we just have skills and methods that we cannot share."

"You mean to say, not pride or ill will alone, I think," said the woman, her voice going flat.

Dag shrugged. *Not my tale. Let it go, old patroller.*

"He did find her, eventually. As you say, the Lakewalkers wouldn't have him. Came back after about six months, with his tail between his legs. Bleak and pining. Wouldn't look at no other girl. Drank. It was like, if he couldn't be in love with her, he'd be in love with death instead."

"You don't have to be a farmer for that. Ma'am," Dag said coolly.

She spared him a sharp glance. "That's as may be. He never settled, after that. He finally took a job with the keelboat men, down on the Grace River. After a couple of seasons, we heard he'd fallen off his boat and drowned. I don't think it was deliberate; they said he'd been drunk and had gone to piss over the side in the night. Just careless, but a kind of careless that don't happen to other folks."

Maybe that had been the trouble with his own schemes, Dag thought. He had never been careless enough. If Dag had been twenty instead of thirty-five when the darkness had overtaken him, it might have all worked rather differently . . .

"We never heard back from that patroller girl. He was just a bit of passin' fun to her, I guess. She was the end of the world to him, though."

Dag held his silence.

She inhaled, and drove on: "So if you think it's amusin' to make that girl fall in love with you, I say, it won't seem so funny down the road. I don't know what's in it for you, but there's no future for her. Your people will see to that, if hers won't. You and I both know that—but she don't."

"Ma'am, you're seeing things." Very plausible things, maybe, given that she could not know the true matter of the sharing knife that bound Dag and Fawn so tightly to each other, at least for now. He wasn't about to try to explain the knife to this exhausted, edgy woman.

"I know what I'm seeing, thank you kindly. It ain't the first time, neither."

"I've scarcely known the girl a day!"

"Oh, aye? What'll it be after a week, then? The woods'll catch fire, I guess." She snorted derision. "All I know is, in the long haul, when folks tangle hearts with your folks, they end up dead. Or wishing they was."

Dag unclenched his jaw, and gave her a short nod. "Ma'am . . . in the long haul, all folks end up dead. Or wishing they were."

She just shook her head, lips twisting.

"Good *night*." He touched his hand to his temple and went to haul the tick, stuffed into the next room, out onto the porch. If Little Spark was able to travel at all tomorrow, he decided, they would leave this place as soon as might be.

8

To Dag's discontent, no patrollers emerged from the woods that night, either before or after the rain drove him inside. He did not see Fawn again till they met over the breakfast trestle. They were both back in their own clothes, dry and only faintly stained; in the shabby blue dress she looked almost well, except for a lingering paleness. A check of the insides of her eyelids, and of her fingernails, showed them not as rosy as he thought they ought to be, and she still grew dizzy if she attempted to stand too suddenly, but his hand on her brow felt no fever, good.

He was pressing her to eat more bread and drink more milk when the boy Tad burst through the kitchen door, wide-eyed and gasping. "Ma! Pa! Uncle Sassa! There's one of them mud-men in the pasture, worrying the sheep!"

Dag exhaled wearily; the three farm men around the table leaped up in a panic and scattered to find their tool-weapons. Dag loosened his war knife in its belt sheath and stepped out onto the porch. Fawn and the farmwife followed, peering fearfully around him, Petti clutching a formidable kitchen knife.

At the far end of the pasture, a naked man-form had pounced across the back of a bleating sheep, face buried in its woolly neck. The sheep bucked and threw the creature off. The mud-man fell badly, as if its arms were numb and could not properly catch itself. It rose, shook itself, and half loped, half crawled after the intended prey. The rest of the flock, bewildered, trotted a few yards away, then turned to stare.

"Worried?" Dag murmured to the women. "I'd say those sheep are downright appalled. That mud-man must have been made from a dog or a wolf. See, it's trying to move like one, but nothing works. It can't use its hands like a man, and it can't use its jaws like a wolf. It's trying to tear that silly sheep's throat out, but all it's getting is a mouthful of wool. Yech!"

He shook his head in exasperation and pity, stepped off the porch, and strode toward the pasture; behind him, Petti gasped, and Fawn muffled a squeak.

He jogged to the end of the lane, to circle between the mud-man and the woods, then hopped up and swung his legs over the rail fence. He stretched his shoulders and shook out his right arm, trying to work out the soreness and knots, and drew his knife. The morning air was heavy with moisture, gray on the ground, lilac and pale pink rising to turquoise in the sky beyond the tree line. The grass was wet from the rain, beaded droplets glimmering like scattered silver, and the saturated soil squelched under his boots. He weaved around a few sodden cow flops and eased toward the mud-man. Aptly named— the creature was filthy, smeared with dung, hair matted and falling in its eyes, and it whiffed of nascent rot. Its flesh was already starting to lose tone and color, the skin mottled and yellowish. Its lips drew back as it snarled at Dag and froze, undecided between attack and flight.

Jump me, you clumsy suffering nightmare. Spare me the sweat of chasing you down. "Come along," Dag crooned, crouching a little and bringing his arms in. "End this. I'll get you out of there, I promise."

The creature's hips wriggled as it leaned forward, and Dag braced himself as it sprang. He almost missed his move as it stumbled on the lunge, hands pawing the air, neck twisting and straining in a vain attempt to bring its all-too-human jaw to Dag's neck. Dag blocked one black-clawed hand with his left arm, spun sideways, and slashed hard.

He jumped back as hot blood spurted from the creature's neck, trying to save himself more laundry duty. The mud-man managed three steps away, yowling wordlessly, before it fell to the mucky ground. Dag circled in cautiously, but no further mercy cut was required; the mud-man shuddered and grew still, eyes glazed and half-open. A tuft of dirty wool, stuck to its lips, stopped fluttering. *Absent gods, this is an ugly cleanup chore.* But neatly enough done, this time. He wiped his blade on the grass, making plans to beg a dry rag from the farmwife in a moment.

He stood up and turned to see the farm men, huddled in a terrified knot clutching their tools, staring at him openmouthed. Tad came running from the fence and was caught around the waist by his father as he attempted to approach the corpse. "I told you to stay back!"

"It's dead, Pa!" Tad wriggled free and gazed up with a glowing face at Dag. "He just walked right up to it and took it down slick as anything!"

Ah. The last mud-men these folk had encountered had still been bound by the will of their maker, intelligent and lethal. Not like this forsaken, sick, confused animal trapped in its awkward body. Dag didn't feel any overwhelming need to correct the farm men's misperceptions of his daring. Safer if they remained cautious of the mud-men anyway. His lips curled up in grim amuse-

ment, but he said only, "It's my job. You can have the burying of it, though."
The farm men gathered around the corpse, poking it at tool-handle distance.
Dag strolled past them toward the house, not looking back.

Most of the animals had collected in the upper end of the pasture, away
from the disturbing intruder. The bay mare raised her head and snuffled at him
as he approached. He paused, wiped his knife dry on her warm side, sheathed
it, and scratched her poll, which made her flop her ears sideways, droop her
lip, and sigh contentedly. The farmwife's tart suggestion of last night that he
take the mare and ride off surfaced in his memory. Tempting idea.

Yes. But not alone.

He climbed the fence, crossed the yard, and made his way up onto the
porch. Fawn gazed up at him with nearly as worshipful an expression as Tad,
only with keener understanding. The farmwife had her arms crossed, torn between gratitude and glowering.

Dag was suddenly mortally tired of mistrustful strangers. He missed his
patrol, for all their irritations. He almost missed the irritations, in their comfortable familiarity.

"Hey, Little Spark. I was going to wait for the wagon and take you to
Glassforge lying flat, but I got to thinking. We might double up and ride out
the way we came in the other day, and you wouldn't be jostled around any
worse."

Her face lit. "Better, I should think. That lane would rattle your teeth, in
a wagon."

"Even taking it slowly and carefully, we could reach town in about three
hours' time. If you think it wouldn't overtire you?"

"Leave now, you mean? I'll pack my bedroll. It'll only take a moment!"
She twirled about.

"Put my arm harness in it, will you? Along with the other things." Arm
harness, knife pouch, and the linen bag of shattered bone and dreams—everything else that he'd arrived in, he was wearing; everything he'd borrowed was
put back.

She paused, lips pursing as if following the same inventory, then nodded
vigorously. "Right."

"Don't bounce. Don't *scamper,* either. Gently!" he called after her. The
kitchen door shut on her trailing laugh.

He turned to find Petti giving him a measuring look. He raised his brows
back at her.

She shrugged, and said on a sigh, "Not my business, I suppose."

He bit back rude agreement, converting the impulse to a more polite nod,
and turned to collect the mare.

By the time he'd reaffixed the rope to the halter for reins and led the horse
to the porch, murmuring promises of grain and a nice stall in Glassforge into

the fuzzy flicking ears, Fawn was back out, breathless, with her bedroll slung over her shoulder, pelting Petti with good-byes and thank-yous. The honest warmth of them drew an answering smile from the farmwife seemingly despite herself.

"You be a lot more careful of yourself, now, girl," Petti admonished.

"Dag will look after me," Fawn assured her cheerily.

"Oh, aye." Petti sighed, after a momentary pause, and Dag wondered what comment she'd just bit back. "That's plain."

From the mounting block of the porch, Dag slid readily aboard the mare's bare back. Happily, the horse had wide-sprung ribs and no bony back ridge, and so was as comfortable to sit as a cushion; he needed to beg neither saddle nor pads from the farm. He stiffened his right ankle to make a stirrup of his foot for Fawn, and she scrambled up and sat across his lap as before. Wriggling into place, she smoothed her skirts and slipped her right arm around him. A little to his surprise, Petti shuffled forward and thrust a wrapped packet into Fawn's hands.

"It's only bread and jam. But it'll keep you on the road."

Dag touched his temple. "Thank you, ma'am. For everything." His hand found the rope reins again.

She nodded stiffly. "You, too." And, after a moment, "You just think about what I said, patroller. Or just think, anyways."

This seemed to call for either no answer at all, or a long defensive argument; Dag prudently chose the first, helped Fawn tuck the packet in her bedroll, nodded again, and turned the horse away. He extended his groundsense to its limit in one last check, but nothing resembling an aggravated patroller beating through the bushes stirred for a mile in any direction, nor more distraught dying mud-men either.

The bay mare's hooves scythed through the wiry chicory, its blossoms looking like bits of blue sky fallen and scattered along the ruts, and the nodding daisies. The farm men were dragging the mud-man's corpse into the woods as they rode down the fence line. They all waved, and Sassa trotted over to the end of the lane in time to say, "Off to Glassforge already? I'll be going in soon. If you see any of our folks, tell them we're all right! See you in town?"

"Sure!" said Fawn, and "Maybe," said Dag. He added, "If any of my people turn up here, would you tell them we're all right and that I'll meet them in town too?"

"'Course!" Sassa promised cheerily.

And then the track curved into the woods, and the farm and all its folk fell out of sight behind. Dag breathed relief as the quiet of the humid summer morning closed in, broken only by the gentle thump of the mare's hooves, the liquid trill of a red-crest, and the rain-refreshed gurgle of the creek that the road followed. A striped ground squirrel flickered across the track ahead of them, disappearing with a faint rustle into the weeds.

Fawn cuddled down, her head resting on his chest, and allowed herself to be rocked along, not speaking for a while. Ambushed again by the deep fatigue of her blood loss after the dawn's spate of excitement, Dag judged; like other injured younglings he'd known, she seemed likely to overestimate her capacity, swinging between imprudent activity and collapse. He hoped her recovery would be as swift. She made a warm and comfortable burden, balanced on his lap. The mare's walk was certainly smoother than a wagon would have been in these muddy ruts, and he had no intention of jostling either of them with a trot. A few mosquitoes whined around them in the damp shade, and he gently bumped them away from her fair skin with a flick of his ground against theirs.

The scent of her skin and hair, the moving curve of her breasts as she breathed, and the pressure of her thighs on his stimulated him, but not nearly so much as the light, the contentment, and the flattering sense of safety swirling through her complex ground. She was not herself aroused, but her air of openness, of sheer physical acceptance of his presence, made him unreasonably happy in turn, like a man warmed by a fire. The deep red note of her inmost injury still lurked underneath, and the violet shadings of her bruises clouded her ground as they did her flesh, but the sharp-edged glints of pain were much reduced.

She could not sense his ground in turn; she was unaware of his lingering inspection. A Lakewalker woman would have felt his keen regard, seeing just as deeply into him if he did not close himself off and keep closed, trading blindness for privacy. Feeling guiltily perverse, he indulged his inner senses upon Fawn without excuse of need—or fear of self-revelation.

It was a little like watching water lilies; rather more like smelling a dinner he was not allowed to eat. Was it possible to be starved for so long as to forget the taste of food, for the pangs of hunger to burn out like ash? It seemed so. But both the pleasure and the pain were his heart's secret, here. He was put in mind, suddenly, of the soil at the edge of a recovering blight; the weedy bedraggled look of it, unlovely yet hopeful. Blight was a numb gray thing, without sensation. Did the return of green life *hurt*? Odd thought.

She stirred, opening her eyes to stare into the shadows of the woods, here mostly beech, elm, and red oak, with an occasional towering cottonwood, or, in more open areas around the stream, stubby dogwood or redbud, long past their blooming. Splashes of the climbing sun spangled the leaves of the upper branches, sparking off lingering water drops.

"How will you find your patrol in Glassforge?" she asked.

"There's this hotel patrols stay at—we make it our headquarters when we're in this area. Nice change from sleeping on the ground. It'll also be our medicine tent. I'm pretty sure that more patrollers than my partner Saun took blows when we jumped those bandits the other night, so that's where they'll be holed up. They're used to our ways, there."

"Will you be there long?"

"Not sure. Chato's patrol was on their way south over the Grace River to trade for horses when they got waylaid by this trouble, and my patrol was riding a pattern up northeast, when we broke off to come here. Depends on the injured, I suspect."

She said thoughtfully, "Lakewalkers don't run the hotel, do they? It's Glassforge folks, right?"

"Right."

"What all jobs do they do in a hotel?"

He raised his brows. "Chambermaid, cook, scullion, horse boy, handyman, laundress . . . lots of things."

"I could do some of that. Maybe I could get work there."

Dag tensed. "Did Petti tell you about her cousin?"

"Cousin?" She peered up at him without guile.

Evidently not. "No—never mind. The couple that run the place have owned it for years; it's built on the site of an old inn, I think, which was his father's before. Mari would know. It's brick, three floors high, very fine. They burn brick as well as glass in Glassforge, you know."

She nodded. "I saw some houses in Lumpton Market once, they say were built from Glassforge brick. Must have been quite a job hauling it."

He shifted a little beneath her. "In any case, there'll be no work for you till you stop fainting when you jump up. Some days yet, I expect. *If* you eat up and rest."

"I suppose," she said doubtfully. "But I don't have much money."

"My patrol will put you up," he said firmly. "We owe you for a malice, remember." *We owe you for your sacrifice.*

"Yes, all right, but I need to look ahead, now I'm on my own. I'm glad I met all those Horsefords. Nice folks. Maybe they'll introduce me around, help get me a start."

Would she not go home? Neither the picture of her dragging back to the realm of Stupid Sunny nor the notion of her as a Glassforge chambermaid pleased him much. "Best see what Mari has to say about that knife, before making plans."

"Mm." Her eyes darkened, and she huddled down again.

The peace of the woodland descended again, easing Dag's spirit. The light and air and solitude, the placid mare moving warmly beneath him, and Fawn curled against him with her ground slowly releasing its accumulation of anguish, put him wholly in a present that required nothing more of him, nor he of it. Released, for a moment, from an endless chain of duty and task, tautly pulling him into a weary future not chosen, merely accepted.

"How're you doing?" he murmured into Fawn's hair. "Pain?"

"No worse than when I was sitting up at breakfast, anyhow. Better than last night. This is all right."

"Good."

"Dag . . . " She hesitated.

"Mm?"

"What do Lakewalker women do who get in a fix like mine?"

The question baffled him. "Which fix?"

She gave a small snort. "I suppose I have been collecting troubles, lately. A baby and no husband was the one I was thinking of. Grass widowhood."

He could sense the grating of grief and guilt through her with that reminder. "It doesn't exactly work like that, for us."

She frowned. "Are young Lakewalkers all really, really . . . um . . . virtuous?"

He laughed softly. "No, if by virtuous you just mean keeping their trousers buttoned. Other virtues are more in demand. But young is young, farmer or Lakewalker. Pretty much everyone goes through an awkward period of fumbling around finding things out."

"You said a woman invites a man to her tent."

"If he's a lucky man."

"Then how do . . . " She trailed off in confusion.

He finally figured out what she was asking. "Oh. It's our grounds, again. The time of the month when a woman can conceive shows as a beautiful pattern in her ground. If the time and place are wrong for a child, she and her man just pleasure each other in ways that don't lead to children."

Fawn's silence following this extended for a quite a long time. Then she said, "What?"

"Which what?"

"How do people . . . people can do that? How?"

Dag swallowed uneasily. How much *could* this girl not know? By the evidence so far, quite a lot, he reflected ruefully. How far back did he need to begin?

"Well—hands, for one."

"Hands?"

"Touching each other, till they trade release. Tongues and mouths and other things, too."

She blinked. "Release?"

"Touch each other as you'd touch yourself, only with a better angle and company and, well, just better all around. Less . . . lonely."

Her face screwed up. "Oh. Boys do that, I know. I guess girls could do it for them, too. Do they like it?"

"Um . . . generally," he said cautiously. This unexpected turn of the conversation sped his mind, and his body was following fast. *Calm yourself, old patroller.* Fortunately, she could not sense the heated ripple in him. "Girls like it, too. In my experience."

Another long, digestive silence. "Is this some Lakewalker lady thing? Magic?"

"There are tricks you can do with your grounds to make it better, but no. Lakewalker ladies and farmer girls are equally magical in this. Anyway, farmers have grounds too, they just can't sense them." *Absent gods be thanked.*

Her expression now was intensely cogitative, and a stuttering swirl of arousal had started in her as well. It wasn't, he realized suddenly, just her hurts that blocked its flow. Something that half-blood woman at Tripoint had once told him, that he'd scarcely believed, came back to him now: that some farmer women never learned how to pleasure themselves, or to find release. She'd laughed at his expression. *Come, come, Dag. Boys practically trip over their own parts. Women's are all tucked neatly up inside. They can be just as tricky for us as for the farmer boys to find. Many's the farmwife has me to thank for providing her man with the treasure map, scandalized as she'd be to learn it.* Since he'd had much to thank her for as well, he'd set about it, dismissing the ineptness of farm boys from his mind and, in a short time, from hers.

That had been a long time ago . . .

"What other things?" Fawn said.

"Beg pardon?"

"Besides hands and tongues and mouths."

"Just . . . don't . . . not . . . never mind." And now his arousal had grown to serious physical discomfort. Atop a horse, of all things. There were many things not to try on a horse, even one as good-natured as this mare. He couldn't avoid remembering several of them, which *didn't help.*

Spark couldn't sense his ground. He could stand in front of her rigid with mind-numbing lust, and as long as he kept his trousers on, she wouldn't know. And considering all her recent disastrous experiences, she oughtn't to know. Bad if she laughed . . . no, upon reflection, good if she laughed. *Bad* if she was disgusted or horrified or frightened, taking him for another lout like Stupid Sunny or that poor fool he'd shot in the backside. If it grew too excruciating, he could slip off the horse and disappear into the woods for a spell, pretending to be answering a call of nature. Which he would be; no lie there. *Stop it. You did this to yourself. Suffer in silence. Think of something else. You can control your body. She can't tell.*

She sighed, rustled about, and gazed up into his face. "Your eyes change color with the light," she observed in a tone of new interest. "In the sun they're all bright gold like coins. In the shade they go brown like clear spice tea. In the night, they're black like deep pools." She added after a moment, "They're really dark right now."

"Mm," said Dag. Every breath brought her heady scent to his mouth, to his mind. He could not very well stop breathing.

A flash of motion at treetop height caught both their eyes.

"Look, a red-tailed hawk!" she cried. "Isn't he beautiful!" Her head and body turned to follow the pale clean-cut shape, ruddy translucent tail feathers almost glowing against the washed blue of the sky, and her hot small hand came down to support herself. Directly on Dag's aching erection.

His startled recoil was so abrupt, he fell off the horse.

He landed on his back with a breath-stealing thump. Thankfully, she landed atop him and not underneath. Her weight was soft upon him, her breath accelerated by the shock. Her pupils were too wide for this light, and, as she twisted around and thrust out one hand to support herself, her gaze grew fixed upon his mouth.

Yes! Kiss me, do. His hand spasmed, and he laid it out flat and stiff, palm up upon the grass, lest he lunge at her. He moistened his lips. The damp of the grass and the soil began soaking into the back of his shirt and trousers. He could feel every curve of her body, pressed into his, and every curse of her ground. Absent gods, he was halfway to groundlock all by *himself* . . .

"Are you all right?" she gasped.

Terror shot through him, wilting his arousal, that the fall might have torn something loose inside her to start her bleeding again like the first day. It would take the better part of hour to carry her back to the farm, and in her current depleted state, she might not survive another such draining.

She scrambled off him and plunked herself ungracefully on the ground, panting.

"Are *you* all right?" he asked urgently in turn.

"I guess so." She winced a little, but she rubbed her elbow, not her belly.

He sat up and ran his hand through his hair. *Fool, fool, blight you, pay attention . . . ! You might have killed her.*

"What happened?" she asked.

"I . . . thought I saw something out of the corner of my eye, but it was just a trick of the light. I didn't mean to shy like a horse." Which had to be the weakest excuse for an excuse he'd ever uttered.

The mare, in fact, was less shaken than either of them. She had sidestepped as they'd gone over, but now stood peacefully a few yards off, looking at them in mild astonishment. No further excitement seeming forthcoming, she put her head down and nibbled a weed.

"Yes, well, after that mud-man this morning, it's no wonder you're jumpy," Fawn said kindly. She stared around at the woods in renewed worry, then balanced a hand on his shoulder, pushed herself up, and tried to brush the dirt off her sleeve.

Dag took a few deep breaths, letting his pounding heart slow, then rose as well and went to recapture the mare. A fallen tree a few steps into the woods looked like an adequate mounting block; he led the horse up to it, and Fawn dutifully followed. And if they started this all over again, he feared he would disgrace himself before they ever got to Glassforge.

"To tell the truth," Dag lied, "my left arm was getting a bit tired. Do you think you could sit behind and hang on pillion style, for a while?"

"Oh! I'm sorry. I was so comfortable, I didn't think it might be awkward for you!" she apologized earnestly.

You have no idea how awkward. He grinned to hide his guilt, and to reassure her, but he was afraid it just came out looking demented.

Up they climbed once more. Fawn settled herself with both dainty feet to one side, and both dainty hands wrapped around his waist in a firm, warm grip.

And all Dag's stern resolve melted in the unbidden thought: *Lower. Lower!*

He set his teeth and dug his heels into the blameless mare's sides to urge her to a brisker walk.

Fawn balanced herself, wondering if she laid her head to Dag's back if she could hear his heartbeat again. She'd thought she'd been recovering well this morning, but the little accident reminded her of how tired she yet was, how quickly the least exertion stole her breath. Dag was more tired than he looked, too, it seemed, judging by his long silences.

She was embarrassed by how close she'd come to trying to kiss him, after their clumsy fall. She'd probably landed an elbow in his gut, and he'd been too kind to say anything. He'd even grinned at her, helping her up. His teeth were a trifle crooked, but nothing to signify, strong and sound, with a fascinating little chip out of one of the front ones. His smile was too fleeting, but it was probably safer for her tattered dignity that his grin was even rarer. If he'd grinned at her so kissably while they were still flat on the grass, instead of giving her that peculiar look—maybe it had been suppressed pain?—she'd likely have disgraced herself altogether.

The nasty name that Sunny had called her during their argument over the baby stuck in her craw. With one mocking word, Sunny had somehow turned all her love-in-intent, her breathless curiosity, her timid daring, into something ugly and vile. He'd been happy enough to kiss her and fondle her in the wheatfield in the dark, and call her his pretty thing; the slur came later. Dubious therefore, but still . . . was it typical for men to despise the women who gave them the attention they claimed to want? Judging from some of the rude insults she'd heard here and there, maybe so.

She did not want Dag to despise her, to take her for something low. But then, she would never apply the word *typical* to him.

So . . . was Dag lonely? Or lucky?

He didn't seem the lucky sort, somehow.

So how would you know? Her heart felt as if it knew him better than any man, no, any *person* she'd ever met. The feeling did not stand up to inspection. He could be married, for all he'd said to the contrary. He could have children. He could have children almost as old as her. Or who knew what? He hadn't said. There was a lot he hadn't talked of, when she thought about it.

It was just that . . . what little he'd talked about had seemed so important. As though she'd been dying of thirst, and everyone else had wanted to give her piles of dry gimcrackery, and he'd offered her a cup of plain pure water. Straightforward. Welcome beyond desire or deserving. Unsettling . . .

The valley they were riding down opened out, the creek ran away through broad fields, and the farm lane gave onto the straight road at last. Dag turned the mare left. And whatever opportunity she had just wasted was gone forever.

The straight road was busier today, and grew more so as they neared the town. Either the removal of the bandit threat had brought more people out on the highway, or it was market day. Or both, Fawn decided. They passed sturdy brick-wagons and goods-wagons drawn by teams of big dray horses pulling hard going out, and rode alongside ones returning, not empty, but loaded with firewood or hitchhiking county folk taking produce and handcrafts to sell. She caught snatches of cheerful conversation, the girls flirting with the teamsters when no elders rode with them. Farm carts and haywains and yes, even that manure wagon she'd wished for in vain the other day. The scent of coal smoke and woodsmoke came to Fawn's nose even before they rounded the last curve and the town came into sight.

Nothing about this arrival was like anything she had pictured when she'd started out from home, but at least she'd *got* here. Something that she'd begun, finally finished. It felt like breaking a curse. Glassforge. At last.

9

Fawn leaned precariously around Dag's shoulder and gazed down the main street, lined with older buildings of wood and stone or newer ones of brick. Plank sidewalks kept people's feet out of the churned mud of the road. A block farther on, the mud gave way to cobblestones, and beyond that, brick. A town so rich they paved the street with brick! The road curved away to follow the bend in the river, but she could just glimpse a town square busy with a day market. Most of the smokes that smudged the air seemed to be coming from farther downstream and downwind. Dag turned the mare into a side street, jerking his chin at the brick building rising to their left, blunt and blocky but softened by climbing ivy.

"There's our hotel. Patrols always stay there for free. It was written into the will of the owner's father. Something about the last big malice we took out in these parts, nigh on sixty years ago. Must've been a scary one. Good thinking on someone's part, because it gets the area patrolled more often."

"You looked for sixty years without finding another?"

"Oh, there've been a couple in the interim, I believe. We just got them so small, the farmers never knew. Like, um . . . pulling a weed instead of chopping down a tree. Better for us, better for everyone, except harder to convince folks to chip in some payment. Farsighted man, that old innkeep."

They turned again under a wide brick archway and into the yard between the hotel and its stable. A horse boy polishing harness on a bench glanced up and rose to come forward. He did not reach for the mare's makeshift bridle.

"Sorry, mister, miss." His nod was polite, but his look seemed to sum up the worth of the battered pair riding bareback and find it sadly short. "Hotel's full up. You'll have to find another place." The twist of his lips turned slightly derisive, if not altogether without sympathy. "Doubt you could make the price of a room here anyways."

Only Fawn's hand on Dag's back felt the faint rumble of—anger? no, amusement pass through him. "Doubt I could too. Happily, Miss Bluefield, here, has made the price of all of them."

The boy's face went a little blank, as he tried to work this out to anything that made sense to him. His confusion was interrupted by a pair of Lakewalkers hobbling out of the doorway into the yard, staring hard at Dag.

These two looked more like proper patrollers, neat in leather vests, with their long hair pulled back in decorated braids. One had a face nearly as bruised as Fawn's, with a strip of linen wrapped awkwardly around his head and under his jaw not quite hiding a line of bloody stitches. He leaned on a stick. The other had her left arm, thickened with bandages, supported in a sling. Both were dark-haired and tall, though their eyes were an almost normal sort of clear bright brown.

"Dag Redwing Hickory . . . ?" said the woman cautiously.

Dag swung his right leg over the mare's neck and sat sideways a moment; smiling faintly, he touched his hand to his temple in a gesture of acknowledgment. "Aye. You all from Chato's Log Hollow patrol?"

Both patrollers stood straighter, despite their evident hurts. "Yes, sir!" said the man, while the woman hissed at the hotel servant, "Boy, take the patroller's horse!"

The boy jumped as though goosed and took the halter rope, his stare growing wide-eyed. Dag slid down and turned to help Fawn, who swung her legs over.

"Ah! Don't you dare jump," he said sternly, and she nodded and slid off into his arm, collecting something pleasantly like a hug as he eased her feet to the ground. She stifled her longing to lean her head into his chest and just stand there for, oh, say, about a week. He turned to the other patrollers, but his left arm stayed behind her back, a solid, anchoring weight.

"Where is everyone?" Dag asked.

The man grinned, then winced, his hand going to his jaw. "Out looking for you, mostly."

"Ah, I was afraid of that."

"Yeah," said the woman. "Your patrol all kept swearing you'd turn up like a cat, and then went running out again anyway without hardly stopping to eat or sleep. Looks like the cat fanciers had the right of it. There's a fellow upstairs name of Saun's been fretting his heart out for you. Every time we go in, he badgers for news."

Dag's lips pursed in a breath of relief. "On medicine tent duty, are you?"

"Yep," said the man.

"How many carrying-wounded have we got?"

"Just two—your Saun and our Reela. She got her leg broke when some mud-men spooked her horse over a drop."

"Bad?"

"Not good, but she'll get to keep it."

Dag nodded. "Good enough, then."

The man blinked in belated realization of Dag's stump, but he added nothing more awkward. "I don't know how tired you are, but it would be kindly done if you could step up and put Saun's mind at ease first thing. He really has been fretting something awful. I think he'd rest better for seeing you with his own eyes."

"Of course," said Dag.

"Ah . . . " said the woman, looking at Fawn and then, inquiringly, at Dag.

"This here's Miss Fawn Bluefield," said Dag.

Fawn dipped her knees. "How de' do?"

"And she is . . . ?" said the man dubiously.

"She's with me." Something distinctly firm in Dag's voice discouraged further questions, and the two patrollers, after civil if still curious nods at Fawn, led the way inside.

Fawn had only a glimpse of the entry hall, featuring a tall wooden counter and archways leading off to some big rooms, before she followed the patrollers up a staircase with a time-polished banister, cool and smooth under her hesitant fingertips. One flight up, they turned into a hallway lined with doors on either side and a glass window set in the end for light.

"You partner's mostly lucid today, although he still keeps claiming you brought him back from the dead," said the man over his shoulder.

"He wasn't dead," said Dag.

The man shot a look at the woman. "Told you."

"His heart had stopped and he'd quit breathing, was all."

Fawn blinked in bafflement. And, she was heartened to see, she wasn't the only one.

"Er . . . " The man stopped outside a door with a brass number 6 on it. "Pardon, sir? I'd always been taught it was too risky to match grounds with someone mortally injured, and unworkable to block the pain at speed."

"Likely." Dag shrugged. "I just skipped the extras and went in and out fast."

"*Oh,*" said the woman in a voice of enlightenment that Fawn did not share.

The man blurted, "Didn't it hurt?"

Dag gave him a long, slow look. Fawn was very glad it wasn't her at the focus, because that look could surely reduce people to grease spots on the floor. Dag gave the other patroller a moment more to melt—precisely timed, she was suddenly certain—then nodded at the door. The woman hastened to open it.

Dag passed in. If the two patrollers had been respectful before, the look they now exchanged behind his back was downright daunted. The woman glanced at Fawn doubtfully but did not attempt to exclude her as she slipped through the door in Dag's wake.

The room had cutwork linen curtains, pushed open and moving gently in the summer air, and flanking the window two beds with feather ticks atop straw ticks. One was empty, though it had gear and saddlebags piled on the floor at its foot. So did the other, but in it lay an—inevitably—tall young man. His hair was light brown, unbraided, and spread out upon his pillow. A rumpled sheet was pulled up to his chest, where his torso was wrapped around with bandages. He stared listlessly at the ceiling, his pale brow wrinkled. When he turned his head at the sound of steps and recognized his visitor, the pain in his face transformed to joy so fast it looked like a flash flood washing over him.

"Dag! You made it!" He laughed, coughed, grimaced, and moaned. "Ow. Knew you would!"

The patroller woman raised her eyebrows at this broad claim but grinned indulgently.

Dag walked to the bedside and smiled down, adopting a cheerful tone. "Now, I know you had six broken ribs at least. I ask you, *is* this the time for speeches?"

"Only a short one," wheezed the young man. His hand found Dag's and grasped it. "Thank you."

Dag's brows twitched, but he didn't argue. Such sincere gratitude shone in the young man's eyes, Fawn warmed to him at once. Finally, somebody seemed to be taking Dag at his worth. Saun turned his head to peer somewhat blearily at her, and she smiled at him with all her heart. He blinked rapidly and smiled back, looking a bit flummoxed.

Dag gave the hand a little shake from side to side, and asked more softly, "How're you doing, Saun?"

"It only hurts when I laugh."

"Oh? Don't let the patrol know that." The dry light in Dag's eyes was mirth, Fawn realized.

Saun sputtered and coughed. "Ow! Blast you, Dag!"

"See what I mean?" He added more sternly, "They tell me you haven't been sleeping. I said, couldn't be—this is the patroller we have to roll out of his blankets by force in camp in the morning. Feather beds too soft for you now? Shall I bring you a few rocks to make it more homelike?"

Saun held a hand to his bandaged chest and carefully refrained from chuckling. "Naw. All *I* want is your tale. They said" —his face grew grave in memory, and he moistened his lips—"they found your horse yesterday miles from the lair, found the lair, found half your gear and your bow abandoned in a pile. Your *bow*. Didn't think you'd ever leave *that* on purpose. Two rotting mud-men and a pile of something Mari swore was the dead malice, and a trail of blood leading off to nothing. What were we supposed to think?"

"I was rather hoping someone would think I'd found shelter at the nearest farm," Dag said ruefully. "I begin to suspect I'm not exciting enough for you all."

Saun's eyes narrowed. "There's more than that," he said positively.

"Quite a bit, but it's for Mari's ears first." Dag glanced at Fawn.

Saun slumped in apparent acceptance of this. "As long as I get more sometime."

"Sometime." Dag hesitated, then added diffidently, "So . . . did they also find the body I'd left in the tree?"

Three faces turned to stare.

"Evidently not yet," Dag murmured.

"See what I told you? See?" said Saun to his companions in a voice of vindication. He added to Dag through slightly gritted teeth, "Sometime soon, all right?"

"As I can." Dag nodded at the two from the other patrol. "Did Mari say when she'd be back?"

They shook their heads. "She left at dawn," the woman offered.

"Need anything more right now, Saun?" asked the patroller man.

"You just brought me what I wanted most," said Saun. "Take a break, eh?"

"I think I will." With a barely audible grunt of pain, the patroller man sat down on the other bed, evidently his own, shed his boots, and used his hands to swing the stiff leg inboard. "Ah."

Dag nodded in farewell. "Sleep hard, Saun. Try and wake up smarter, eh?"

A faint snort and a muffled *Ow!* followed the three out. Dag's face, turning away, softened like a man finding grace in an unexpected hour. "Yeah, he'll be all right," he muttered in satisfaction.

The patroller woman closed the door quietly behind them.

"So, was that Saun the Sheep?" asked Fawn.

"Aye, the very lamb," said Dag. "If he lives long enough to trade in some of that enthusiasm for brains, he'll be a good patroller. He's made it to twenty, so far. Must be luck." His smile took a twist. "Same as you, Little Spark."

As they started down the hall, a woman's voice called weakly from a room with an open door.

"That's Reela," said the patroller woman quickly. "Do you have all you need, sir?"

"If not, I'll find it." Dag gave a dismissing wave. "I've known this place for years."

"Then if you'll excuse me, I'll go see what she wants." She nodded and stepped away.

As they made their way down the stairs, Fawn heard Dag mutter under his breath, "Stop sir-ing me, you dreadful puppies!" He paused at the bottom, his hand on the rail, and looked back upward, his face going distant.

"Now what are you thinking?" Fawn asked softly.

"I'm thinking . . . that when our walking wounded are set to look after our carrying-wounded, it's a sure sign we're too short-rostered. Mari's patrol is sixteen, four by four. It should be twenty-five, five by five. I wonder how many Chato's patrol is down by? Ah, well." He vented a sigh. "Let's rustle us up some food, Spark."

Dag led her to a rather astonishing little commode chamber, where she was able to swap out her dressings and wash up in the pretty painted tin basin provided. When she emerged, he escorted her in turn to one of the big downstairs rooms, full of tables with benches or chairs but, at this hour, empty of other people. In a few minutes, a serving girl came out of the kitchen in back with a tray of ham, cheese, two kinds of bread, cream-and-rhubarb pie, and strawberries, with a pitcher of beer and a jug of milk, fresh, the girl informed them, from the hotel's own cows kept out back. Fawn mentally added *serving girl* to her list of potential Glassforge jobs, as well as *milkmaid,* and set to under Dag's benign eye. More relaxed than she'd ever seen him, he plowed in heartily, she noted with satisfaction.

They were contesting the last strawberry, each trying to press it on the other, when Dag's head came up, and he said "Ah." In a moment, Fawn could hear through the open windows the clatter of horses and echo of voices in the stable yard. In another minute, the door slammed open and booted footsteps rapped across the floorboards. Mari, trailed by two other patrollers, swept into the dining room, halted by their table, planted her fists on her hips, and glowered at Dag.

"*You,*" she uttered, and never had Fawn heard one syllable carry so much freight.

Deadpan, Dag topped up his beer glass and handed it to her. Not taking her exasperated eyes from him, she raised it to her lips and gulped down half. The other two patrollers were grinning broadly.

"Were you *trying* to give me the fright of my life, boy?" she demanded, plunking the glass back down almost hard enough to crack it.

"No," Dag drawled, rescuing the glass and filling it again, "I suspect that was just a bonus. Sit down and catch your breath, Aunt Mari."

"Don't you *Aunt Mari* me till I'm done reaming you out," she said, but much more mildly. One of the patrollers at her shoulder, catching Dag's eye, pulled out a chair for her, and she sat anyhow. By the time she'd blown out her breath and stretched her back, her posture had grown much less alarming.

Except for the underlying exhaustion creeping to the surface; Dag's brows drew down at that.

He reached across the table and gripped her hand. "Sorry for any false scares. Saun told me about you finding my messes yesterday. I kind of had my hand full, though."

"Aye, so I heard."

"Oh, did you find the Horsefords' farm, finally?"

"About two hours ago. Now, there was a garbled tale and a half." She glanced speculatively at Fawn, and her frown at Dag deepened.

Dag said, "Mari, may I present Miss Fawn Bluefield. Spark, this is my patrol leader, Mari Redwing Hickory. Mari's her personal name, Redwing is our tent name, and the Hickory is for Hickory Lake Camp, which is our patrol's home base."

Fawn ducked her head politely. Mari returned an extremely provisional nod.

Gesturing, Dag continued, "Utau and Razi, also of Hickory Camp." The two other patrollers made friendly salutes of greeting to her not unlike Dag's. Utau was older, shorter, and burlier, and wore his thinning hair in a knot like Mari's. Razi was younger, taller, and gawkier; his hair hung down his back in a single plait almost to his waist, with dark red and green cords woven in.

The older one, Utau, said, "Congratulations on the malice, Dag. The youngsters were all hopping mad that they'd missed their first kill, though. I'd suggested we have you take them all out to the lair and walk them through it, for consolation, and to show them how it's done."

Dag shook his head, caught between a low laugh and a wince. "I don't think that would be all that useful to them, really."

"So just how much of a foul-up was it?" Mari inquired tartly.

The residue of amusement drained from Dag's eyes. "Foul enough. The short tale is, Miss Bluefield, here, was kidnapped off the road by the pair I'd trailed from the bandit camp. When I caught up with them all at the lair, I was outmatched by the mud-men, who got a good way into taking me apart. But I noticed that the malice, mud-men, and all, were making the interesting mistake of ignoring Miss Bluefield in the scuffle. So I tossed my sharing knives to her, and she got one into the malice. Took it down. Saved my life. World too, for the usual bonus."

"*She* got that close to a malice?" asked Razi, in a voice somewhere between disbelief and amazement. "How?"

For answer, Dag leaned over and, after a glance at her for permission, gently folded back the collar of her dress. His finger traced over numb spots of flesh around her neck that Fawn realized belatedly must be the bruises from the malice's great hands, and she shuddered involuntarily despite the summer warmth of the room. "Closer than that, Razi."

The two patrollers' lips parted. Mari leaned back in her chair, her hand going to her mouth. Fawn had not seen a mirror for days. Whatever did the marks look like?

"The malice misjudged her," Dag continued. "I trust you all will not. But if you want to repeat those congratulations to the right person, Utau, feel free."

Under Dag's cool eye, Utau unscrewed his face and slowly brought his hand to his temple. After groping a moment for his voice, he managed, "Miss Bluefield."

"Aye," Razi seconded, after a stunned moment.

"Wildly demonstrative bunch, you know, we patrollers," Dag murmured in Fawn's ear, his dry amusement flickering again.

"I can see that," she murmured back, making his lip twitch.

Mari rubbed her forehead. "And the long tale, Dag? Do I even want to hear it?"

The grim look he gave her locked all her attention. "Yes," he said. "As soon as may be. But in private. Then Miss Bluefield needs to rest." He turned to Fawn. "Or do you want to rest up first?"

Fawn shook her head. "Talk first, please."

Mari braced her hands on her trousered knees and rolled her shoulders. "Ah. All right." She peered around, eyes narrowing. "My room?"

"That would do."

She pushed to her feet. "Utau, you were up all night. You're now off duty. Razi, get some food in you, then ride out to Tailor's Point and let them know Dag's been found. Or shown up, anyway." The patrollers nodded and turned away.

Dad murmured to Fawn, "Bring your bedroll."

Mari's room proved to be on the third floor. Fawn found herself dizzy and shaky by the time she'd climbed the second flight of stairs, and she was grateful for Dag's supporting hand. Mari led them into a narrower room than Saun's, with only one bed, though otherwise similar right down to the messy pile of gear and saddlebags at the foot. Dag gestured for Fawn to lay her bedroll across the bed. Fawn untied the bindings and unrolled it; the contents clinked.

Mari's brows rose. She picked up Dag's ruptured hand harness and held it out like the sad carcass of some dead animal. "*That* took some doing. I see now why you didn't bother to take your bow along. You still got your arm?"

"Just barely," said Dag. "I need to get that thing restitched with stronger thread, this time."

"I'd rethink that idea if I were you. Which do you want to have come apart first, you or it?"

Dag paused a moment, then said, "Ah. You have a point, there. Maybe I'll get it fixed just the same."

"Better." Mari set the harness back down and picked up the makeshift linen bag and let it drift through her hand, feeling the contents shift within. Her expression grew sad, almost remote. "Kauneo's heart's knife, wasn't it?"

Dag nodded shortly.

"I know how long you've kept it aside. This fate was worthy."

Dag shook his head. "They're all the same, really, I've come to believe." He took a breath and advanced to the bed, motioning Fawn to sit.

She perched cross-legged on the bed's head, smoothing her skirt over her knees, and watched the two patrollers. Mari had gold eyes much like Dag's, if a shade more bronze, and she wondered if she really was his aunt and his use of the title not, as she'd first thought, just a joke or a respectful endearment.

Mari set the bag back down. "Do you plan to send it up to be buried with the rest of her uncle's bones? Or burn it here?"

"Not sure yet. It will keep with me; it has so far." Dag drew a deeper breath, staring down at the other knife. "Now we come to the long story."

Mari sat down at the bed's foot and crossed her arms, listening closely as Dag began his tale again, this time starting with the night raid on the bandit camp. His descriptions of his actions were succinct but very exact, Fawn noticed, as though certain details might matter more, though she was not sure how he sorted which to leave in or out. Until he came to, "I believe the mud-man lifted Miss Bluefield from the road because she was two months pregnant. And came back and took her from the farm for the same reason."

Mari's lips moved involuntarily, *Was?*, then compressed. "Go on."

Dag's voice stiffened as he described his risky raid on the malice's cave. "I was just too late. When I hit the entrance and the mud-men, the malice was already taking her child."

Mari leaned forward, her brows drawing down. "Separately?"

"So it seems."

"Huh . . . '' Mari leaned back, shook her head, and peered at Fawn. "Excuse me. I am so sorry for your loss. But this is new to me. We knew malices took pregnant women, but then, they take anyone they can catch. Rarely, the women's bodies are recovered. I did not know the malice didn't always take both grounds together."

"I don't think," said Fawn distantly, "it would have kept me around very long. It was about to break my neck when I finally got the right knife into it."

Mari blinked, glanced down at the blue-hilted bone knife lying on the bedroll, and stared up again at Dag. "What?"

Carefully, Dag explained Fawn's mix-up with his knives. He was very kind, Fawn thought, to excuse her from any blame in the matter.

"The knife had been unprimed. You know what I was saving it for."

Mari nodded.

"But now it's primed. With the death of Spark's—of Miss Bluefield's daughter, I believe. What I don't know is if that's all it drew from the malice. Or whether it will even work as a sharing knife. Or . . . well, I don't know much, I'm afraid. But with Miss Bluefield's permission, I thought you could examine it too."

"Dag, I'm no more a maker than you are."

"No, but you are more . . . you are less . . . I could use another opinion."

Mari glanced at Fawn. "Miss Bluefield, may I?"

"Please. I want to understand, and . . . and I don't, really."

Mari leaned over and picked up the bone knife. She cradled it, ran her hand along its smooth pale length, and finally, much as Dag had, held it to her lips with her eyes closed. When she set it down again, her mouth stayed tight for a moment.

"Well" —she took a breath—"it's certainly primed."

"That, I could tell," said Dag.

"It feels . . . hm. Oddly pure. It's not that souls go into the knives—you did explain that to her, yes?" she demanded of Dag.

"Yes. She's clear on that part."

"But different people's heart's knives do have different feels to them. Some echo of the donor lingers, though they all seem to work alike. Perhaps it's that the lives are different, but the deaths are all the same, I don't know. I'm a pa-troller, not a lore-master. I think"—she tapped her lips with a forefinger— "you had better take it to a maker. The most experienced you can find."

"Miss Bluefield and I," said Dag. "The knife is properly hers, now."

"This isn't any business for a farmer to be mixed up in."

Dag scowled. "What would you have me do? Take it from her? *You?*"

"Explain, please?" Fawn said tightly. "Everyone is talking past me again. That's all right mostly, I'm used to it, but not for *this.*"

"Show her your knives, Mari," Dag said, a rasp of challenge in his voice, for all that it was soft.

She looked at him, then slowly unbuttoned her shirt partway down and drew out a dual knife pouch much like Dag's, though of softer leather. She pulled the strap over her head, pushed the bedroll aside, and laid out two bone knives side by side on the quilt. They were nearly identical, except for different-colored dye daubed on the lightly carved hilts, red and brown this time.

"These are a true pair, both bones from the same donor," she said, caress-ing the red one. "My youngest son, as it happens. It was his third year patrol-ling, up Sparford way, and I'd just got to thinking he was getting over the riskiest part of the learning . . . well." She touched the brown one. "This one is primed. His father's aunt Palai gave her death to it. Tough, tough old woman—absent gods, we loved her. Preferably from a safe distance, but there's one like that in every family, I think." Her hand drifted again to the red one. "This one is unprimed, bonded to me. I keep it by me in case."

"So what would happen," said Dag dryly, "to anyone who tried to take them from you?"

Mari's smile grew grim. "I'd outstrip the worst wrath of Great-aunt Palai." She sat up and slipped the knives away, then nodded at Fawn. "But I think it's different for her."

"It's all strange to me." Fawn frowned, staring at the blue-hilted knife. "I have no happy memories about this to balance the sorrows. But they're my memories, all the same. I'd rather they weren't . . . wasted."

Mari raised both hands in a gesture of frustrated neutrality.

"So could I have leave from the patrol to travel on this matter?" asked Dag.

Mari grimaced. "You know how short we are, but once this Glassforge business is settled, I can't very well refuse you. Have you ever drawn leave? Ever? You don't even get sick!"

Dag thought a moment. "Death of my father," he said at last. "Eleven years ago."

"Before my time. Eh! Ask again when we're ready to decamp. If there's no new trouble landed in our laps by then."

He nodded. "Miss Bluefield's not fit to travel far yet anyway. You can see by her eyelids and nails she's lost too much blood, even without how her knees give way. No fever yet, though. Please, Mari, I did all I could, but could you look her over?" His hand touched his belly, making his meaning clear.

Mari sighed. "Yes, yes, Dag."

He stood expectantly for a moment; she grimaced and sat up, waving to a set of saddlebags leaning in the corner. "There's your gear, by the by. Luckily your fool horse hadn't got round to scraping it off in the woods. Go on, now."

"But will you . . . can't I . . . I mean, it's not as though you have to undress her."

"Women's business," she said firmly.

Reluctantly, he made for the door, though he did scoop up his arm harness and recovered belongings. "I'll see about getting you a room, Spark."

Fawn smiled gratefully at him.

"Good," said Mari. "Scat."

He bit his lip and nodded farewell. His boot steps faded down the hall.

Fawn tried not to be too unnerved by being left alone with Mari. Scary old lady or not, the patrol leader seemed to share some of Dag's straightforward quality. She had Fawn sit quietly on the bed while she ran her hands over her. She then sat behind Fawn and hugged her in close for several silent minutes, her hands wrapped across Fawn's lower belly. If she was doing something with her groundsense, Fawn could not feel it, and wondered if this was what being deaf among hearing people was like. When she released Fawn, her face was cool but not unkind.

"You'll do," she said. "It's clear you were ripped up unnatural, which accounts for the suddenness of the bleeding, but you're healing about as quick as could be expected for someone so depleted, and your womb's not hot. Fever's a commoner killer in these things than bleeding, though less showy. You'll have some blight-scarring in there, I guess, slow to heal like the ones on your neck, but not enough to stop you having other children, so you be more careful in future, *Miss* Bluefield."

"Oh." Fawn, looking back through clouds of regret, had not even thought ahead to her future fertility. "Does that happen to some women, after a miscarriage?"

"Sometimes. Or after a bad birth. Delicate parts in there. It amazes me the process works at all, when I think about all the things I've seen can go wrong."

Fawn nodded, then reached to put away Dag's blue-hilted knife, still lying on her bedroll atop her spare clothes.

"So," said Mari in a carefully bland tone, "who's the other half owner 'sides you of that knife's priming? Some farm lout?"

Fawn's jaw set. "Just me. The lout made it very clear he was giving it all to me. Which was why I was out on the road in the first place."

"Farmers. I'll never understand 'em."

"There are no Lakewalker louts?"

"Well . . . '' Mari's long, embarrassed drawl conceded the point.

Fawn reread the faded brown lettering on the bone blade. "Dag meant to drive this into his own heart someday. Didn't he." This Kauneo had intended that he should.

"Aye."

Now he couldn't. That was something, at least. "You have one, too."

"Someone has to prime. Not everyone, but enough. Patrollers understand the need better."

"Was Kauneo a patroller?"

"Didn't Dag say?"

"He said she was a woman who'd died twenty years ago up northwest someplace."

"That's a bit close-mouthed even for him." Mari sighed. "It's not my place to tell his tales, but if you are to have the holding of that knife, farmer girl, you'd better understand what it is and where it comes from."

"Yes," said Fawn firmly, "please. I'm so tired of making stupid mistakes."

Mari twitched a—provisionally—approving eyebrow at this. "Very well. I'll give you what Dag would call the short tale." Her long inhalation suggested it wasn't going to be as short as all that, and Fawn sat cross-legged again, intent.

"Kauneo was Dag's wife."

A tremor of shock ran through Fawn. Shock, but not surprise, she realized. "I see."

"She died at Wolf Ridge."

"He hadn't mentioned any Wolf Ridge to me. He just called it a bad malice war." Though there could be no such thing as a good malice war, Fawn suspected.

"Farmer girl, Dag doesn't talk about Wolf Ridge to anyone. One of his several little quirks you have to get used to. You have to understand, Luthlia is the biggest, wildest hinterland of the seven, with the thinnest population of Lakewalkers to try to patrol it. Terrible patrolling—cold swamps and trackless woods and killing winters. The other hinterlands lend more young patrollers to Luthlia than to anywhere, but they still can't keep up.

"Kauneo came from a tent of famously fierce patrollers up that way. She was very beautiful I guess—courted by everyone. Then this quiet, unassuming young patrol leader from the east, walking around the lake on his second training tour, stole her heart right out from under all of them." A hint of pride colored her voice, and Fawn thought, *Yes, she's really his aunt.* "He made plans to stay. They were string-bound—you farmers would say, married—and he got promoted to company captain."

"Dag wasn't always a patroller?" said Fawn.

Mari snorted. "That boy should have been a hinterland lieutenant by now, if he hadn't . . . agh, anyway. Most of our patrols are more like hunts, and most turn up nothing. In fact, it's possible to patrol all your life and never be in on a malice kill, by one chance or another. Dag has his ways of improving those odds for himself. But when a malice gets entrenched, when it goes to real war . . . then we're all making it up as we go along."

She rose, stalked across the bedchamber to her washstand, poured a glass of water, and drank it down. She fell to pacing as she continued.

"Big malice slipped through the patrol patterns. It didn't have many people to enslave up that way, no bandits like the malice you slew here. There are no farmers in Luthlia, nor anywhere north of the Dead Lake, save now and then some trapper or trader slips in that we escort out. But the malice did find wolves. It *did* things to wolves. Wolf-men, man-wolves, dire wolves as big as ponies, with man-wits. By the time the thing was found, it had grown itself an army of wolves. The Luthlian patrollers sent out a call-up for help from neighbor hinterlands, but meanwhile, they were on their own.

"Dag's company, fifty patrollers including Kauneo and a couple of her brothers, was sent to hold a ridge to cover the flank of another party trying to strike up the valley at the lair. The scouts led them to expect an attack of maybe fifty dire wolves. What they got was more like five hundred."

Fawn's breath drew in.

"In one hour Dag lost his hand, his wife, his company all but three, and the ridge. What he didn't lose was the war, because in the hour they'd bought, the other group made it all the way through to the lair. When he woke up in the medicine tent, his whole life was burned up like a pyre, I guess. He didn't take it well.

"In due course his dead wife's tent folk despaired of him and sent him home. Where he didn't take it well some more. Then Fairbolt Crow, bless his bones—our camp captain, though he was just a company captain back then—got smart, or desperate, or furious, and dragged him off to Tripoint. Got some clever farmer artificer he knew there to make up the arm harness, and they went round and round on it till they hit on devices that worked. Dag practiced with his new bow till his fingers bled, pulled himself together to meet Fairbolt's terms, and let me tell you Fairbolt didn't cut him any slack, and was let back on patrol. Where he has been ever since.

"Some ten or twelve sharing knives have passed through Dag's hand since—people keep giving them to him because they're pretty sure to get used—but he always kept that pair aside. The only mementos of Kauneo I know of that he didn't shove away like they scorched him. So that's the knife now in your keeping, farmer girl."

Fawn held it up and drew it through her fingers. "You'd think it would be heavier." *Did I really want to know all this?*

"Aye." Mari sighed.

Fawn glanced curiously at Mari's gray head. "Will you ever be a company captain? You must have been patrolling for a long time."

"I've had far less time in the field than Dag, actually, for all I'm twenty years older. I walked the woman's path. I spent four or five years training as a girl—we *must* train up the girls, for all that fellows like Dag disapprove, because if ever our camps are attacked, it'll be us and the old men defending them. I got string-bound, got blood-bound—had my children, that is—and then went back to patrolling. I expect to keep walking till my luck or my legs give out, five more years or ten, but I don't care to deal with anything more fractious than a patrol, thank you. Then back to camp and play with my grandchildren and their children till it's time to share. It will do, as a life."

Fawn's brow wrinkled. "Did you ever imagine another?" Or being thrown into another, as Fawn had been?

Mari cocked her head. "Can't say as I ever did. Though I'd have my boy back first if I were given wishes."

"How many children did you have?"

"Five," Mari replied, with distinct maternal pride that sounded plenty farmerish to Fawn, for all she suspected Mari would deny any such thing.

A rap on the door was followed by Dag's plaintive voice: "Mari, can I please come back in now?"

Mari rolled her eyes. "All right."

Dag eased himself around the door. "How is she doing? Is she healing at all? Could you match grounds? Or do a little reinforcement, even?"

"She's healing as well as could be expected. I did nothing with my ground, because time and rest will do the job every bit as well."

Dag took this in, seeming a bit disappointed, but resigned. "I have you a room, Spark, down one floor. Tired?"

Exhausted, she realized. She nodded.

"Well, I'll take you down and you can start in on the resting part, least-ways."

Mari rubbed her lips and studied her nephew through narrowed eyes. Groundsense. Fawn wondered what the patrol leader had seen with hers that she wasn't saying. Did closed mouths run in the Redwing family like golden eyes? Fawn rolled up her bedroll and let Dag shoo her out.

"Don't let Mari scare you," Dag said, letting his left arm drift along at her back, whether protectively or for subtle concealment Fawn could not tell, as they descended the stairs. They turned into the adjoining corridor.

"She didn't, much. I liked her." Fawn took a breath. Some secrets took up too much space to keep tiptoeing around. "She told me a little more about your wife, and Wolf Ridge. She thought I needed to know."

Silence stretched for three long footfalls. "She's right."

And that, evidently, was all Fawn was going to get for now.

Fawn's new room was narrow like Mari's, except this one overlooked the main street instead of the stable yard. A washstand with ewer already filled, piecework curtains and a quilt in a matching pattern, and rag rugs on the floor made it fine and homey to Fawn's eyes. A door in the side wall apparently led into the next chamber. Dag swung the bar across and shoved it down into its brackets.

"Where is your room?" Fawn asked.

Dag gestured at the closed door. "Through there."

"Oh, good. Will you take a rest? Don't tell me you aren't owed some heal-ing too. I saw your bruises."

He shook his head. "I'm going out to find a harnessmaker. I'll come back and take you down to dinner later, if you'd like."

"I'd like that fine."

He smiled a little at that and backed himself out. "Seems all I do in this place is tell folks to go to sleep."

"Yes, but I'm actually going to do it."

He grinned—*that grin should be illegal*—and shut the door softly.

On the wall beside the washstand hung a shaving mirror, fine flat Glass-forge glass. Reminded, Fawn slid up to it and turned down the collar of her blue dress.

The bruise masking most of the left side of her face was purple going greenish around the edges, with four dark scabs from the mud-man's claws mounting to her cheekbone, still tender but not hot with infection. The pattern of the malice's hand on her neck, four blots on one side and one on the other, stood out in sharp contrast to her fair skin. The marks had a peculiar black tint and an ugly raised texture unlike any other contusion Fawn had ever seen. Well, if there was any special trick to their healing, Dag would know it. Or might have experienced it himself, if he had got close enough to as many malices as Mari's inventory of his past knives suggested.

Fawn went to the window and just caught a glimpse of Dag's tall form passing below, arm harness tossed over his shoulder, striding up the street toward the town square. She gazed out at Glassforge after he'd made his way out of sight along the boardwalk, but not for long; yawning uncontrollably, she slipped off her dress and shoes and crawled into the bed.

10

Dag returned at dinnertime as promised. Fawn had put on her good dress, the green cotton that her aunt Nattie had spun and woven; she followed him downstairs. The raucous noises coming out of the room where they'd eaten their quiet lunch gave her pause.

Seeing her hesitate, Dag smiled and bent his head to murmur, "Patrollers can be a rowdy bunch when we all get together, but you'll be all right. You don't have to answer any questions you don't want. We can make out you're still too shaken by our fight with the malice and don't want to talk about it. They'll accept that." His hand drifted to her collar as if to arrange it more tidily, and Fawn realized he was not covering up the strange marks on her neck, but rather, making sure they showed. "I think we don't need to mention what happened with the second knife to anyone besides Mari."

"Good," said Fawn, relieved, and allowed him to take her in, his arm protective at her back.

The tables this evening were indeed full of tall, alarming patrollers, twenty-five or so, variously layered with road dirt. Given Dag's warning, Fawn managed not to jump when their entrance was greeted with whoops, cheers, table pounding, and flying jibes about Dag's three-day vanishing. The roughness of some of the jests was undercut by the real joy in the voices, and Dag, smiling crookedly, gave back: "Some trackers! I swear you lot couldn't find a drink in a rain barrel!"

"Beer barrel, Dag!" someone hooted in return. "What's wrong with you?"

Dag surveyed the room and guided Fawn toward a square table on the far side where only two patrollers sat, the Utau and Razi she'd met earlier. The two waved encouragement as they approached, and Razi shoved out a spare chair invitingly with his boot.

Fawn was not sure which patrollers were Mari's and which were Chato's; the two patrols seemed to be mingled, not quite at random. Any sorting seemed to be more by age, as there was one table with half a dozen gray heads at it, including Mari; also two other older women Fawn had not seen at the well-house, so presumably from the Log Hollow patrol. The young woman with her arm in the sling was at a table with three young men, all vying to cut her meat for her; she was presently holding them off with jabs of her fork and laughing. The men patrollers seemed all ages, but the women were only young or much older, Fawn noticed, and remembered Mari's account of her life's course. In the home camps would the proportions be reversed?

Breathless serving maids and boys weaved among the tables lugging trays laden with platters and pitchers, rapidly relieved by reaching hands. The patrollers seemed more interested in speed and quantity than in decorum, an attitude shared with farmhouse kitchens that made Fawn feel nearly comfortable.

They sat and exchanged greetings with Razi and Utau; Razi leaped up and acquired more plates, cutlery, and glasses, and both united to snag passing food and drink to fill them. They did ply Dag with questions about his adventures although, with cautious glances, spared Fawn. His answers were either unexcitingly factual, vague, or took the form that Fawn recognized from the Horsefords' table of effectively diverting counterquestions. They finally desisted and let Dag catch up with his chewing.

Utau glanced around the room, and remarked, "Everyone's a lot happier tonight. Especially Mari. Fortunately for all of us downstream of her."

Razi said wistfully, "Do you suppose she and Chato will let us all have a bow-down before we go back out?"

"Chato looks pretty cheerful," said Utau, nodding across the room at another table of patrollers, although which was the leader Fawn could not tell. "We might get lucky."

"What's a bow-down?" asked Fawn.

Razi smiled eagerly. "It's a party, patroller-style. They happen sometimes, to celebrate a kill, or when two or more patrols chance to get together. Having another patrol to talk to is a treat. Not that we don't all love one another" — Utau rolled his eyes at this—"but weeks on end of our own company can get pretty old. A bow-down has music. Dancing. Beer if we can get it . . ."

"We could get lots of beer, here," Utau observed distantly.

"Lingerrrring in dark corners—" Razi trilled, catching up the tail of his braid and twirling it.

"Enough—she gets the idea," said Dag, but he smiled. Fawn wondered if it was in memory. "Could happen, but I guarantee it won't be till Mari thinks the cleanup is all done. Or as done as it ever gets." His eye was caught by something over Fawn's shoulder. "I feel prophetic. I predict chores before cheer."

"Dag, you're such a morbid crow——" Razi began.

"Well, gentlemen," said Mari's voice. "Do your feet hurt?"

Fawn turned her head and smiled diffidently at the patrol leader, who had drifted up to their table.

Razi opened his mouth, but Dag cut in, "Don't answer that, Razi. It's a trick question. The safe response is, 'I can't say, Mari, but why do you ask?'"

Mari's lips twitched, and she returned in a sugary voice, "I'm *so* glad you asked that question, Dag!"

"Maybe not so safe," murmured Utau, grinning.

"How's the arm-harness repair coming?" Mari continued to Dag.

Dag grimaced. "Done tomorrow afternoon, maybe. I had to stop at two places before I found one that would do it for free. Or rather, in exchange for us saving his life, family, town, territory, and everyone in it."

Utau said dryly, "Naturally, you forgot to mention it was you personally who took their malice down."

Dag shrugged this off in irritation. "Firstly, that wasn't so. Secondly, none of us could do the job without the rest of us, so all are owed. I shouldn't . . . none of us should have to *beg*."

"It so happens," said Mari, letting this slide by, "that I have a sitting-down job for a one-handed man tomorrow morning. In the storeroom here is a trunkful of patrol logs and maps for this region that need a good going-over. The usual. I want someone with an eye for it to see if we can figure how this malice slipped through, and stop up the crack in future. Also, I want a listing of the nearby sectors that have been especially neglected. We're going to stay here a few extra days while the injured recover, and to repair gear and fur-bish up."

Utau and Razi both brightened at this news.

"We'll do some local search-pattern catch-up at the same time," Mari continued. "And let the Glassforge folk see us doing so," she added, with dour emphasis and a nod at Dag. "Give 'em a show."

Dag snorted. "Better we should offer them double their blight bogles back if they're not happy with our work."

Razi choked on the beer he was just swallowing, and Utau kindly if unhelpfully thumped his back. "Oh, how I wish we could!" Razi wheezed when he'd caught his breath again. "Love to see the looks on their stupid farmer faces, just once!"

Fawn congealed, her beginning ease and enjoyment of the patrollers' banter abruptly quenched. Dag stiffened.

Mari cast them both an enigmatic look, but moved off without comment, and Fawn remembered their exchange earlier on the universal nature of lout-ishness. *So.*

Razi burbled on obliviously, "Patrolling out of Glassforge is like a holiday.

Sure, you ride all day, but when you come back there are real beds. Real baths! Food you don't have to fix, not burned over a campfire. Little comforts to bargain for up in the town."

"And yet farmers built this place," Fawn murmured, and she was sure by his wince that Dag heard clearly the missing *stupid* she'd clipped out.

Razi shrugged. "Farmers plant crops, but who planted farmers? We did."

What? Fawn thought.

Utau, perhaps not quite as oblivious as his comrade, glanced at her, and countered, "You mean our ancestors did. Pretty broad claim of credit, there."

"Why shouldn't we get the credit?" said Razi.

"And the blame as well?" said Dag.

Razi made a face. "I thought we did. Fair's fair."

Dag smiled tightly, drew a breath, and pushed himself up. "Well. If I'm to spend tomorrow peering at a bunch of ill-penned, misspelled, and undoubtedly incomplete patrol logs, I'd better get my eyes some rest now. If everyone else is as short on sleep as I am, it'll be a good quiet night for catching up."

"Find us lots of local patrols, Dag," urged Razi. "*Weeks'* worth."

"I'll see what I can do."

Fawn rose too, and Dag shepherded her out. He made no attempt to apologize for Razi, but an odd look darkened his eyes, and Fawn did not like her sense of his thoughts receding to someplace barred to her. Outside, the late-summer dusk was closing in. He bade her good night at her door with studied courtesy.

The next morning Dag woke at dawn, but Fawn, to his approval, still slept. He went quietly downstairs and nabbed two patrollers from their breakfast to lug the records trunk upstairs to his room. In a short time he had logs, maps, and charts spread out on the room's writing table, bed, and, soon after, the floor.

He heard the muffled creak of the bed and Fawn's footsteps through the adjoining wall as she finally arose and rattled around her room getting dressed. At length, she poked her head cautiously around the frame of his door open to the hall, and he jumped up to escort her down to a breakfast much quieter than last night's dinner, as a last few sleepy patrollers drifted out singly or in pairs.

After the meal, she followed him back upstairs to stare with interest at the paper and parchment drifting across his room. "Can I help?"

He remembered her susceptibility to boredom and itchy hands, but mostly he heard the underlying, *Can I stay?* He obligingly set her to mending pens, or fetching a paper or logbook from across the room from time to time—make-work, but it kept her quietly occupied and pleasantly near. She grew fascinated with the maps, charts, and logs, and fell to reading them, or trying to. It was not just the faded and often questionable handwriting that made this a slow process for her. Her claim to be able to read proved true, but it was plain from her moving finger and lips and the tension in her body that she was not fluent, probably due to never having had enough text to practice on. But when he scratched out a grid on a fresh sheet to turn the muddled log entries into a record visible at a glance, she followed the logic swiftly enough.

Around noon, Mari appeared in the open doorway. She raised an eyebrow at Fawn, perched on the bed poring over a contour map annotated with hand corrections, but said only, "How goes it?"

"Almost done," said Dag. "There is no point going back more than ten years, I think. Quiet around here this morning. What are folks up to?"

"Mending, cleaning gear, gone uptown. Working with the horses. We found a blacksmith whose sister was among those we rescued from the mine, who's been very willing to help out in the stable." She wandered in and peered over his shoulder, then leaned back against the wall with her arms folded. "So. How did this malice slip past us?"

Dag tapped his grid, laid out on the table before him. "That section was last walked three years ago by a patrol from Hope Lake Camp. They were trying to run a sixteen-man pattern with just thirteen. Three short. Because if they'd dropped it down to a twelve-pattern, they'd have had to make two more passes to clear the area, and they were already three weeks behind schedule for the season. Even so, there's no telling they missed anything; that malice might well not have been hatched out yet."

"I'm not looking to lay blame," said Mari mildly.

"I know." Dag sighed. "Now, as for neglected sections . . . " His lips peeled back in a dry smile. "That was more revealing. Turns out all sections within a day's ride of Glassforge that can be patrolled from horseback are up-to-date, or as up-to-date as anything, meaning no more than a year overdue. What's left are some swampy areas to the west and rocky ravines to the east that you can't take a horse through." He added reflectively, "Lazy whelps."

Mari smiled sourly. "I see." She scratched her nose. "Chato and I figured he'd lend me two men, and we'd both send out sixteen-groups, dividing up the neglected sections between us. He and I are both going to be stuck here arguing with Glassforgers about what we're due for our recent work on their behalf, so I'd thought to put you in charge of our patrol. Give you first pick of sections, though."

"You're so sweet, Mari. Waist-deep wading through smelly muck, with leeches, or sudden falls onto sharp rocks? They both sound so charming, I don't know how I can decide."

"Alternatively, you can roll up your sleeves and come help me arm wrestle with Glassforgers. That works exceptionally well, I've noticed."

Fawn, who had set down the map and was following the talk closely, blinked at this.

Dag grimaced in distaste. In his list of personal joys, parading their wounded to shame farmers into pitching in ranked well below frolicking with leeches and barely above lancing oozing saddle boils. "I swore the last time I put on that show for you, it would be the last." He added after a reflective moment, "And the time before. You have no shame, Mari."

"I have no *resources*," she returned, her face twisting in frustration. "Fairbolt once figured it takes at least ten folks back in the camps, not counting the children, to support one patroller in the field. Every bit of help we fail to pull in from outside puts us that bit more behind."

"Then why don't we pull in more? Isn't that why farmers were planted in the first place?" The argument was an old one, and Dag still didn't know the right answer.

"Shall we become lords again?" said Mari softly. "I think not."

"What's the alternative? Let the world drift to destruction because we're too ashamed to call for help?"

"Keep the balance," said Mari firmly. "As we always have. We cannot ever let ourselves become dependent upon outsiders." Her glance slid over Fawn. "Not us."

A little silence fell, and Dag finally said, "I'll take swamps."

Her nod was a bit too satisfied, and Dag wondered if he'd just made a mistake. He added after a moment, "But if you let us take along a few horse boys from the stables here to watch the mounts, we won't have to leave a patroller with the horse lines while we slog."

Mari frowned, but said at last, reluctantly, "All right. Makes sense for the day-trips, anyway. You'll start tomorrow."

Fawn's brown eyes widened in mild alarm, and Dag realized the source of Mari's muffled triumph. "Wait," he said. "Who will look after Miss Bluefield while I'm gone?"

"I can. She won't be alone. We have four other injured recovering here, and Chato and I will be in and out."

"I'm sure I'll be fine, Dag," Fawn offered, although a faint doubt colored her voice.

"But can you keep her from trying to overdo?" Dag said gruffly. "What if she starts bleeding again? Or gets chilled and throws a fever?"

Even Fawn's brow wrinkled at that last one. Her lips moved on a voiceless protest, *But it's midsummer.*

"Then I'll be better fit to deal with that than you would," said Mari, watching him.

Watching him flail, he suspected glumly. He drew back from making more of a show of himself than he already had. He'd had his groundsense closed down tight since they'd hit the outskirts of Glassforge yesterday, but Mari clearly didn't need to read his ground to draw her own shrewd conclusions, even without the way Fawn glowed like a rock-oil lamp in his presence.

He rolled up his chart and handed it to Mari. "You can have that to tack on the wall downstairs, and we can mark it off as we go. For whatever amusement it will provide folks. If you hint there could be a bow-down when we reach the end, it might go more briskly."

She nodded affably and withdrew, and Dag put Fawn to work helping him restack the contents of the trunk in rather better order than he'd found it.

As she brought him an armload of stained and tattered logbooks, she asked, "That's twice now you've talked about *planting farmers*. What do you mean?"

He sat back on his heels, surprised. "Don't you know where your family comes from?"

"Sure I do. It's written down in the family book that goes with the farm accounts. My great-great-great-grandfather"—she paused to check the generations on her fingers, and nodded—"came north to the river ridge from Lumpton with his brother almost two hundred years ago to clear land. A few years later, Great-great-great got married and crossed the western river branch to start our place. Bluefields have been there ever since. That's why the nearest village is named West Blue."

"And where were they before Lumpton Market?"

She hesitated. "I'm not sure. Except that it was just Lumpton back then, because Lumpton Crossroads and Upper Lumpton weren't around yet."

"Six hundred years ago," said Dag, "this whole region from the Dead Lake to nearly the southern seacoast was all unpeopled wilderness. Some Lakewalkers from this hinterland went down to the coasts, east and south, where there were some enclaves of folks—your ancestors—surviving. They persuaded several groups to come up here and carve out homes for themselves. The idea was that this area, south of a certain line, had been cleared enough of malices to be safe again. Which proved to be not quite the case, although it was still much better than it had once been. Promises were exchanged . . . fortunately, my people still remember what they were. There were two more main plantations, one east at Tripoint and one west around Farmer's Flats, besides the one south of the Grace at Silver Shoals that most folks around here eventually came from. The homesteaders' descendants have been slowly spreading out ever since.

"There were two notions about this scheme among the Lakewalkers—still are, in fact. One faction figured that the more eyes we had looking for malice outbreaks, the better. The other figured we were just setting out malice food. I've seen malices develop in both peopled and unpeopled places, and I don't see much to choose between the horrors, so I don't get too excited about that argument anymore."

"So Lakewalkers were here before farmers," said Fawn slowly.

"Yes."

"What was here before Lakewalkers?"

"What, you know nothing?"

"You don't have to sound so shocked," she said, obviously stung, and he made a gesture of apology. "I know plenty, I just don't know what's true and what's tall tales and bedtime stories. Once upon a time, there was supposed to have been a chain of lakes, not just the big dead one. With a league of seven beautiful cities around them, commanded by great sorcerer-lords, and a sorcerer king, and princesses and bold warriors and sailors and captains and who knows what all. With tall towers and beautiful gardens and jeweled singing birds and magical animals and holy whatnot, and the gods' blessings flowing like the fountains, and gods popping in and out of people's lives in a way that I would find downright unnerving, I'm pretty sure. Oh, and ships on the lakes with silver sails. I think maybe they were plain white cloth sails, and just looked silver in the moonlight, because it stands to reason that much metal would capsize a boat. What I *know* is the tall tale is where they say some of the cities were five miles across, which is impossible."

"Actually" —Dag cleared his throat—"that part I know to be true. The ruins of Ogachi Strand are only a few miles out from shore. When I was a young patroller up that way, some friends and I took an outrigger to look at them. On a clear, quiet day you can see down to the tops of stone wreckage along the old shoreline, in places. Ogachi really was five miles across, and more. These were the people who built the straight roads, after all. Which were thousands of miles long, some of them, before they got so broken up."

Fawn stood up and dusted her skirt, and sat on the edge of his bed, her face tight with thought. "So—where'd they all go? Those builders."

"Most died. A remnant survived. Their descendants are still here."

"Where?"

"Here. In this room. You and me."

She stared at him in real surprise, then looked down at her hands in doubt. "Me?"

"Lakewalker tales say . . . " He paused, sorting and suppressing. "That Lakewalkers are descended from some of those sorcerer-lords who got away from the wreck of everything. And farmers are descended from ordinary folks on the far edges of the hinterlands, who somehow survived the original malice wars, the first great one, and the two that came after, that killed the lakes and left the Western Levels." Also dubbed the Dead Levels, by those who'd skirted them, and Dag could understand why.

"There was more than one war? I never heard that," she said.

He nodded. "In a sense. Or maybe there's always only been one. The question you didn't ask is, where do the malices come from?"

"Out of the ground. They always have. Only"— she hesitated, then went on in a rush—"I suppose you're going to say, not always, and tell me how they got into the ground in the first place, right?"

"I'm actually a little vague on that myself. What we do know is that all malices are descendants of the first great one. Except not descended like we are, with marriage and birth and the passing of generations. More like some monstrous insect that laid ten thousand eggs that hatch up out of the ground at intervals."

"I saw that thing," said Fawn lowly. "I don't know what it was, but it sure wasn't a bug."

He shrugged. "It's just a way of trying to think about them. I've seen a few dozen of them in my life, so far. I could as well say the first was like a mirror that shattered into ten thousand splinters to make ten thousand little mirrors. Malices aren't material at all, in their inner nature. They just pull matter in from around them to make themselves a house, a shell. They seem to feed on ground itself, really."

"How did it shatter?"

"It lost the first war. They say."

"Did the gods help?"

Dag snorted. "Lakewalker legends say the gods abandoned the world when the first malice came. And that they will return when the earth is entirely cleansed of its spawn. If you believe in gods."

"Do you?"

"I believe they are not here, yes. It's a faith of sorts."

"Huh." She rolled up the last maps and tied their strings before handing them to him. He settled them in place and closed the trunk.

He sat with his hand on the latch a moment. "Whatever their part really was," he said finally, "I don't think it was just the sorcerer-lords who built all those towers and laid those roads and sailed those ships. Your ancestors did, too."

She blinked at this, but what she was thinking, he could not guess.

"And the lords didn't come from nowhere, or elsewhere, either," Dag continued tenaciously. "One line of thought says there was just one people, once, and that the sorcerers rose out of them. Except that then they bred up for their skills and senses, and then used their magic to make themselves more magical, and lordly, and powerful, and so grew away from their kin. Which may have been the first mistake."

She tilted her head, and her lips parted as if to speak, but at that point a pair of footsteps echoed from the hall. Razi stuck his head through the doorframe.

"Ah, Dag, there you are. You should smell this." He thrust out a small glass bottle and pulled off the leather stopper plugging its neck. "Dirla found this medicine shop up in town that sells the stuff."

Dirla smiled proudly over his shoulder.

"What is it?" asked Fawn, leaning in and sniffing as the patroller waved the bottle past her. "Oh, pretty! It smells like chamomile and clover flowers."

"Scented oil," he answered. "They have seven or eight kinds."

"What do you use it for?" Fawn asked innocently.

Dag mentally consigned his comrade to the middle of the Dead Levels. "Sore muscles," he said repressively.

"Well, I suppose you could," said Razi thoughtfully.

"Scented back rubs," breathed Dirla in a warm voice. "Mm, nice idea."

"How *useful* of you two to stop by," Dag overrode this before it could grow more interesting still, either to himself, who didn't hanker after a repeat of the discomforts of his ride from the Horsefords', or to Fawn, who would undoubtedly *ask more questions.* "Happens I need this trunk taken back downstairs to the storeroom." He stood up and pointed. "Lug."

They grumbled, if lightheartedly, and lugged.

Dag closed the door behind them, shooed Fawn to her own room, and followed. Wondering if he dared ask just where that shop was located, and if it might be on the way to the harnessmaker's.

Walking the patterns in the marshes west of Glassforge took six days.

Dag chose the closest section first, and so was able to bring the patrol back to the hotel's comforts that night, and to check on Fawn. After an increasingly worried search of the premises, he found her shelling peas in the kitchen and making friends with the cooks and scullions. With some relief, he gave over his vision of her as distressed and lonely among condescending Lakewalker strangers although not his fear of her imprudently overtaxing her strength.

For the next section he chose the most distant, of necessity a three-day outing, to get it out of the way. Dag met the complaints of the younger patrollers with a few choice tales of swamp sweeps north of Farmer's Flats in late winter, icily gruesome enough to silence all but the most determined grumblers. The patrol was able to leave most of their gear with the horses, but the need for skin protection meant that boots, shirts, and trousers took the brunt of the muck and mire. When they draggled back to Glassforge late the following night, they were greeted by the attendants of the hotel's pleasant bathhouse, conveniently sited with its own well between the stable and the main building, with a marked lack of joy; the laundresses were growing downright surly at the sight of them. This time Dag found Fawn waiting up for him, filling the time and her hands by helping to mend hotel linens and coaxing stories from a pair of seamstresses.

He returned the next night to exchange tales with her over a late supper. He held her fascinated with his account of a roughly circular and distinctively flat stretch of marsh some six miles across that he was certain was a former patch of blight, recovering and again supporting life—most of it noxious, not to mention ravenous, but without question thriving. He thought the slaying of that malice must have predated the arrival of farmer settlers in this region by well over a century. She entertained him in turn with a long, involved account of her day's adventures in the town. Sassa the Horseford brother-in-law, now home again, had stopped by and made good on his promise to show her his glassworks. They had capped the tour with a visit to his brother's papermaking shop, and for extras, the back premises of the ink maker's next door.

"There are more kinds of work to do here than I ever dreamed," she confided in a tone of thoughtful speculation.

She had also, clearly, overdone; when he escorted her to her door, she was drooping and yawning so hard she could scarcely say good night. He spent a little time persuading her ground against an incipient cold, then checked the healing flesh beneath the ugly malice scabs for necrosis or infection and made her promise to rest on the morrow.

The next day's pattern walk was truncated for Dag in the early afternoon when one patroller managed to trade up from mere muck and leeches to a willow root tangle, water over his head, and a nest of cottonmouths. Leaving the patrol to Utau, Dag rode back to town supporting the very sick and shaken man in front of him. Dag was not, happily, called upon to do anything unadvised and perilous with their grounds on the way, though he was grimly aware Utau had urged the escort upon him against just that chance. But the snakebit man survived not only the ride, but also being dipped briskly in the bathhouse, dried, and carried up and slung into bed. By that time, Chato and Mari had been found, allowing Dag to turn the responsibility for further remedies over to them.

Some news Mari imparted sent Dag in search of Fawn even before a visit to the bathhouse on his own behalf. The sound of Fawn's voice raised in, what else, a question, tugged his ear as he was passing down the end stairs, and he about-faced into the second-floor corridor. A door stood open—Saun's—and he paused outside it as Saun's voice returned:

"My *first* impression of him was as one of those grumpy old fellows who never talks except to criticize you. You know the sort?"

"Oh, yes."

"He rode or walked in the back and never spoke much. The light began to dawn for me when Mari set him at the cap—that's the patroller in the end or edge position of a grid with no one beyond. We don't spread out to the limits of our vision, d'you see, but to the limits of our groundsenses. If you and the patrollers to your sides can just sense each other, you know you aren't missing any malice sign between you. Mari sent him out a *mile*. That's more than double the best range of my groundsense."

Fawn made an encouraging noise.

Saun, suitably rewarded, continued, "Then I got to noticing that whenever Mari wanted something done out of the ordinary way, she'd send him. Or that it was his idea. He didn't tell tales often, but when he did, they were from all over, I mean everywhere. I'd start to add up all the people and places in my head, and think, *How?* I'd thought he had no humor, but finally figured out it was just maddening-dry. He didn't seem like much at first, but he sure accumulated. And you?"

"Different than yours, I'll say. He just *arrived*. All at once. Very . . . definitely there. I feel like I've been unpacking him ever since and am nowhere near the bottom yet."

"Huh. He's like that on patrol, in a way."

"Is he good?"

"It's like he's more there than anyone . . . no, that's not right. It's like he's so nowhere-else. If you see?"

"Mm, maybe. How old is he really? I've had trouble figuring that out—"

Suppressed ground or no, someone was bound to notice the swamp reek wafting from the hall on the humid summer air pretty soon. Dag unquirked his lips, knocked on the doorframe, and stepped inside.

Saun lay abed wearing, above, only his bandages; the rest, however clothed, was covered by a sheet. Fawn, in her blue dress, sat leaning back in a chair with her bare feet up on the bed edge, catching, presumably with her wriggling toes, whatever faint breeze might carry from the window. For once, her hands were empty, but Saun's brown hair showed signs of being recently combed and rebraided into two neat, workmanlike plaits.

Dag was greeted with broad smiles on two faces equally fresh with youth and pale with recent injury. Both hurt near-fatally on his watch—now, there was a thought to cringe from—but their expressions showed only trust and affection. He tried to muster a twinge of generational jealousy, but their beauty just made him want to weep. Not good. Six days on patrol with nary a malice sign shouldn't leave him this tired and strange.

"How de', Spark. Lookin' for you. Hello, Saun. How're the ribs?"

"Better." Saun sat up eagerly, his flinch belying his words. "They have me walking up and down the hall now. Fawn here's been keeping me company."

"Good!" said Dag genially. "And what have you two found to talk about?"

Saun looked embarrassed. "Oh, this and that."

Fawn returned more nimbly, "Why were you looking for me?"

"I have something to show you. In the stable, so find your shoes."

"All right," she said agreeably, and rose.

Her bare feet thumped away up the hallway, and he called after her, "Slow down!" He did not consider himself a wit, but this fetched her usual float-ing laugh. In her natural state, did she ever travel at any pace other than a scamper?

He studied Saun, wondering if any warning-off might be in order here. That the broad-shouldered youth was attractive to women, he'd had occasion to note, if never before with concern. But in Saun's current bashed state, he was no menace to curious farmer girls, Dag decided. And cautions might draw counterquestions Dag was ill equipped to answer, such as, *What business is it of yours?* He settled on a friendly wave farewell and started to withdraw into the hall again.

"Oh, Dag?" called Saun. "Old patroller?" He grinned from his propping pillows.

"Yes?" Blight it, when had the boy picked up on that catchphrase? Saun must have paid closer attention to Dag's occasional mutters than he would have guessed.

"No need for the fishy glower. All your pet Spark wants to hear are Dag tales." He settled back with a snicker, no, a snigger.

Dag shook his head and retreated. At least he managed to stop wincing before he exited the stairs.

Dag arrived in the stable, its stalls crowded with the horses of the two patrols, barely before Fawn did. He led her to the straight stall housing the placid bay mare, and pointed.

"Congratulations, Spark. Mari's made it official. You now own this nice horse. Your share of our pay from the Glassforge town fathers. I found you that saddle and bridle on the peg, too; should be about the right size for you. Not new, but they're in real good condition." He saw no need to mention that the tack had been part of a private deal with the willing harnessmaker who had done such a fine job repairing his arm-harness.

Fawn's face lit with delight, and she slid into the stall to run her hands over the horse's neck and scratch her star and her ears, which made the mare round her nostrils and drop her poll in pleasure. "Oh, Dag, she's wonderful, but" —Fawn's nose wrinkled in suspicion—"are you sure this isn't your share of the pay? I mean, Mari's been nice to me and all, but I didn't think she'd pro-moted me to patroller."

A little too shrewd, that. "If it had been left to me, there would be a lot more, Spark."

Fawn did not look entirely convinced, but the horse nudged her for more scratches, and she turned back to the task. "She needs a name. She can't go on being *that mare*." Fawn bit her lip in thought. "I'll name her Grace, after the river. Because it's a pretty name and she's a pretty horse, and because she carried us so smoothly. Do you want to be Grace, sweet lady, hm?" She carried on with the petting and making-much; the mare signified her acceptance of the affection, the name, or both by cocking her hips, easing one hind hoof, and blowing out her breath, which made Fawn laugh. Dag leaned on the stall partition and smiled.

At length, Fawn's face sobered in some new thought. She wandered back out of the stall and stood with her arms folded a moment. "Except . . . I'm not sure if I'll be able to keep her on a milkmaid's pay, or whatever."

"She's yours absolutely; you could sell her," Dag said neutrally.

Fawn shook her head, but her expression did not lighten.

"In any case," Dag continued, "it's too early for you to be thinking of taking on work. You're going to need this mare to ride, first."

"I'm feeling much better. The bleeding stopped two days ago, if I were going to get a fever I think I would have by now, and I don't get dizzy anymore."

"Yes, but . . . Mari has given me leave to take the sharing knife back to camp and have it looked at by a maker. I know the best. I was thinking, since Lumpton Market and West Blue are more or less on the way to Hickory Lake from here, we ought to stop in at your farm on the way and put your folks out of their cruel suspense."

Her eyes flashed up at him with an unreadable look. "I don't want to go back." Her voice wavered. "I don't want my whole stupid story to come out." And firmed: "I don't want to be within a hundred miles of Stupid Sunny."

Dag took a breath. "You don't have to stay. Well, you can't stay; your testimony will be needed on the matter of the knife. Once that's done, the choice of where to go next is yours."

She sucked on her lower lip, eyes downcast. "They'll try to make me stay. I know them. They won't believe I can be a grown . . . " Her voice grew more urgent. "Only if you promise to go with me, *promise* not to leave me there!"

His hand found its way to her shoulder in attempted reassurance of this odd distress. "And yet I might with your goodwill leave you here?"

"Mm . . ."

"Just trying to figure out if it's the here or the there or the me leaving that's being objected to."

Her eyes were wide and dark, and her moist lips parted as her face rose at these words. Dag felt his head dipping, his spine bending, as his hand slipped around her back, as if he were falling from some great height, falling soft . . .

A throat cleared dryly behind him, and he straightened abruptly.

"There you are," said Mari. "Thought I might find you here." Her voice was cordial but her eyes were narrowed.

"Oh, Mari!" said Fawn, a bit breathlessly. "Thank you for getting me this nice horse. I wasn't expecting it." She made her little knee-dip.

Mari smiled at her, managing to give Dag an ironic eyebrow-cock at the same time. "You've earned much more, but it was what I could do. I am not *entirely* without a sense of obligation."

This crushed conversation briefly. Mari continued blandly, "Fawn, would you excuse us for a while? I have some patrol business to discuss with Dag, here."

"Oh. Of course." Fawn brightened. "I'll go tell Saun about Grace." And she was off again at a scamper, flashing a grin over her shoulder at Dag.

Mari leaned against the end post of the stall and crossed her arms, staring up at Dag, till Fawn had vanished through the stable door and out of earshot. The aisle was cool and shady compared to the white afternoon outside, redolent with horses, quiet but for the occasional champing and shifting of the heat-lazy animals and the faint humming of the flies. Dag raised his chin and clasped his hand and hand replacement behind his back, winding his thumb around the hook-with-spring-clamp presently seated in the wooden cuff, and waited. Not hopefully.

It wasn't long in coming. "What are you about, boy?" Mari growled.

Any sort of response that came to, *Whatever do you mean, Mari?* seemed a waste of time and breath. Dag lowered his eyelids and waited some more.

"Do I need to list everything that's wrong with this infatuation?" she said, exasperation plain in her voice. "I daresay you could give the blighted lecture yourself. I daresay you have."

"A time or two," he granted.

"So what are you thinking? Or are you thinking?"

He inhaled. "I know you want to tell me to back away from Fawn, but I can't. Not yet anyway. The knife binds us, till I get it up to camp. We're going to have to travel together for a time yet; you can't argue with that."

"It's not the traveling that worries me. It's what's going to happen when you stop."

"I'm not sleeping with her."

"Aye, yet. You've had your groundsense locked down tight in my presence ever since you got in. Well, that's partly just you—it's such a habit with you, you stay veiled in your *sleep*. But this—you're like a cat who thinks it's hiding because it's got its head stuck in a sack."

"Ah, mental privacy. Now, there's a farmer concept that could stand to catch on."

She snorted. "Fine chance."

"I'm taking her up to camp," Dag said mulishly. "That's a given."

In a sweetly cordial voice, Mari murmured, "Going to show her off to your mother? Oh, how lovely."

Dag's shoulders hunched. "We'll go by her farm, first."

"Oh, and you'll meet *her* mother. Wonderful. That'll be a success. Can't you two just hold hands and jump off a cliff together? It'd be faster and less painful."

His lips twitched at this, involuntarily. "Likely. But it has to be done."

"Does it?" Mari pushed off the post and stalked back and forth across the stable aisle. "Now, if you were a young patroller lout looking to dip his wick in the strange, I'd just thump him on the side of the head and end this thing here and now. I can't tell if you're trying to fool me, or yourself!"

Dag set his teeth and went on saying nothing. It seemed wisest.

She fetched up at her post again, leaned back, scuffed her boot, and sighed. "Look, Dag. I've been watching you for a long time, now. Out on patrol, you'd never neglect your gear or your food or your sleep or your feet. Not like the youngsters who get heroic delusions about their stamina, till they crash into a rock wall. You pace your body for the long haul."

Dag tilted his head in acknowledgment, not certain where she was going with this.

"But though you'd never starve your body to wasting and still expect to go on, you starve your heart, yet act as though you can still draw on it forever without the debt ever coming due. If you fall—*when* you fall, you're going to fall like a starving man. I'm standing here watching you start to topple now, and I don't know if any words of mine are strong enough to catch you. I don't know why, blast and blight it"—her voice shifted in renewed aggravation— "you haven't let yourself get string-bound with any one of the nice widows that your mother—well, all right, not your mother—that one of your friends or other kin used to introduce you to, till they gave up in despair. If you had, I daresay you'd be immune to this foolishness now, knife or no."

Dag hunched tighter. "It would not have been fair to the woman. I can't have what I had with Kauneo over again. Not because of any lack on the woman's part. It's me. I can't *give* what I gave to Kauneo." *Used up, emptied out, dry.*

"Nobody expected that, except maybe you. Most people don't have what you had with Kauneo, if half of what I've heard is true. Yet they contrive to rub along tolerably well just the same."

"She'd die of thirst, trying to draw from that well."

Mari shook her head, mouth flat with disapproval. "Dramatic, Dag."

He shrugged. "Don't push for answers you don't want to hear, then."

She looked away, pursed her lips, stared up at the rafters stuck about with dusty cobwebs and wisps of hay, and tried another tack. "Now, all things considered, I can't object to your indulging yourself. Not you. And after all, this farmer girl has no relatives here to kick up a fuss for me."

Dag's eyes narrowed, and a fool's hope rose in his heart. Was Mari about to say she wouldn't interfere? Surely not . . .

"If you can't be turned or reasoned with, well, these things happen, eh?" The sarcasm tingeing her voice quenched the hope. "But if you are so bound and determined to get in, you'd better have a plan for how you're going to get out, and I want to hear it."

I don't want to get out. I don't want an end. Unsettling realization, and Dag wasn't sure where to put it. Blight it, he hadn't even *begun* . . . anything. This argument was moving too fast for him, no doubt Mari's intent. "All the great plans I ever made for my life ended in horrible surprises, Mari. I swore off plans sometime back."

She shook her head in scorn. "I halfway wish you were some lout I could just thump. Well . . . no, I don't. But you're you. If she's cut up at the end— and I don't see how this can be anything other than a real short ride—so will you be. Double disaster. I can see it coming, and so can you. So what *are* you going to do?"

Dag said tightly, "What do you suggest, seeress?"

"That there's no way you can end this well. So *don't start.*"

I haven't started, Dag wanted to point out. A truth on his lips and a lie in his ground, perhaps? Endurance had been his last remaining virtue for a long, long time, now; he hugged his patience to him and stood, just stood.

In the face of his stubborn silence, Mari shifted her stance and her attack once more. "There are two great duties given to those born of our blood. The first is to carry on the long war, with resolute fortitude, in living and in dying, in hope or out of it. In that duty you have not ever failed."

"Once."

"Not ever," she contradicted this. "Overwhelming defeat is not failure; it's just defeat. It happens sometimes. I never heard that you ran from that ridge, Dag."

"No," he admitted. "I didn't have the chance. *Surrounded* makes running away a bit of a puzzle, which I did not get time to solve."

"Aye, well. But then there's the other great duty, the second duty, without which the first is futile, dross and delusion. The duty you have so far failed al-together."

His head came up, stung and wary. "I've given blood and sweat and all the years of my life so far. I still owe my bones and my heart's death, which I mean to give, which I *will* give in their due time if chance permits, but suicide is a self-indulgence and a desertion of duty no one will ever accuse me of, I decided that years ago, so I don't know what else you want."

Her lips compressed; her gaze went intent with conviction. "The *other* duty is to create the next generation to hand on the war *to.* Because all we do, the miles and years we walk, all that we bleed and sweat and sacrifice, will come to nothing if we do not also pass on our bodies' legacy. And that's a task on which you have turned your back for the past twenty years."

Behind his back, his right hand gripped the arm cuff till he could hear the wood creak, and he forced his clench to loosen lest he break what had been so recently mended. He tried clamping his teeth down just as tight on any response, but one leaked out nonetheless: "Borrow my mother's jawbone, did you?"

"I expect I could do her whole speech by rote, I've had to listen to her complaints often enough, but no. This is my own, hard-won with my life's blood. Look, I know your mother pushed you too soon and too hard after Kauneo and set your back up good and stiff, I know you needed more time to get over it all. But time's gone by, Dag, time and past time. That little farmer girl's the proof of it, if you needed any. And I don't want to be caught underneath when you come crashing down."

"You won't be; we're leaving."

"Not good enough. I want your word."

You can't have it. And was that, itself, some decision? He knew he wavered, but had he already gone beyond some point of no return? *And what would that point be?* He scarcely knew, but his head was pounding with the heat, and a bone-deep exhaustion gripped him. His drying clothing itched and stank. He longed for a cold bath. If he held his head under for long enough, would the pain stop? Ten or fifteen minutes ought to do it.

"If I had died at Wolf Ridge, I would be childless now just the same," he snarled at Mari. *And not even my kin could complain. Or leastways, I wouldn't have to listen.* "I have a plan. Why don't you just pretend that I'm dead?"

He turned on his heel and marched out.

Which would have made a grander exit if she hadn't shouted so furiously and so accurately after him, "Oh, certainly—why not? You do!"

11

Dag thought he'd had his groundsense strapped down tight, but whatever of his vile mood still leaked through the cracks was enough to clear the bathhouse of the three convalescent patrollers idling there within five minutes of his entry. Still, at length both his body and his wits cooled, and he went off to find some useful task to occupy himself, preferably away from his comrades. He found it in taking a saddle with a broken tree uptown to the harness-maker's to trade in for a replacement, and retrieving some other mended gear there, which filled the time till dinner and the arrival of the anxious Utau and the rest of his swamp-slimed patrol.

Mari's arguments were not, any of them, wrong, exactly. *Or at all,* Dag admitted glumly to himself. Ashamed, he dutifully set his mind to the upholding of a self-restraint that had once been more routine than breathing . . . which had somehow grown as heavy as a stone cairn upon his chest. *Dead men don't need air, eh?*

At dinner that night he behaved toward Fawn with meticulous courtesy, no more. Her eyes watched him curiously, wary. But there were enough other patrollers at the table for her to pelt with her questions, tonight mostly about how patrol patterns were arranged and walked, that his silence passed unremarked.

Never had rectitude seemed less rewarding.

The next day was officially devoted to rest and the preparations for the bow-down, and Dag allowed himself to be made mule to help carry in supplies from uptown gathered by the more eager. He crossed paths with Mari only long enough to volunteer for evening watch and door duty, and be briskly refused.

"I can't put the patroller who slew the malice onto guard duty during the celebration of his own deed," she said shortly. "I'd have a revolt on my hands—and rightly, too." She added after a reluctant moment, stopping his protest, "Make sure that little farmer girl knows she's invited, too."

Shortly after, he ran into the enthusiast from Log Hollow who was nabbing the volunteer musicians from the combined patrols for *practice,* a novelty in the experience of most involved, and did not escape till almost time to collect Fawn.

Fawn peered at her hair in the shaving mirror and decided that the green ribbons, loaned by Reela of the broken leg, matched her good dress very well. Reela had been teaching her how to do Lakewalker hair braids, which had turned out to have various meanings; the knot at the nape, Fawn had found out, was a sign of mourning, except when it was a prudent arrangement for going into a fight. Knowing this made the mob of patrollers look different to Fawn's eyes, and gave her a strange feeling, as though the world had shifted under her feet, if only a little, and could never shift back. In any case she could be certain that tonight's style, with her hair tied up high on the back of her head by a jaunty bow and allowed to swing like a horsetail, curls bouncing, didn't say anything she didn't intend in patroller.

Dag came to her door, seeming more relaxed this evening; Fawn wondered if Mari had imparted some bad news to him in the stable yesterday, to so depress his spirits last night. But now his eyes were bright. His simple white shirt made his coppery skin seem to glow. Yesterday's reek of swamp and horse and emergency was replaced with lavender soap and something warm underneath that was just Dag. His hair was clean and soft and already escaping whatever order a stern combing had imposed upon it, looking very touchable, if only she could reach that high. Tiptoes. A stepladder. Something . . .

The atmosphere in the dining room was not too different from other nights, ravenous and raucous, except more crowded because for once everyone was there at the same time. They were all notably cleaned up, and many seemed to have obtained, or shared, scent water. Party clothes seemed to be everyone's same clothes, except laundered. Fawn supposed saddlebags didn't really have room for many changes; the women were all still wearing trousers. Did they ever wear skirts? Hairstyles seemed more elaborate, though. Some of the younger patrollers even wore bells in their braids.

Food and drink, especially drink, overflowed through the entry hall into the next room, where chairs were pushed to the walls and rugs rolled up to make a space to dance. Fawn found herself a seat with the rest of the convalescents, Saun and Reela and the man from Chato's patrol with the game knee and stitches in his jaw, and that poor subdued fellow who'd managed to get snakebit yesterday and was now good-naturedly enduring some pretty merciless ribbing about it. The teasers also distributed fresh beer to all the chair-bound, however, and seemed dedicated to keeping it coming. Fawn sipped hers and smiled shy thanks.

Dag had vanished briefly, but now he returned, screwing something into his wrist cap. Fawn blinked in astonishment to recognize a tambourine, fitted with a wooden peg so he might hold it securely.

"My goodness! I didn't know you played anything."

He grinned at her, giving the frame a last adjustment and drumming his fingers over the stretched skin. The staccato sound made her sit up.

"How clever. What did you play before you lost your hand?"

"Tambourine," he replied cheerily. "I tried the flute, but it tangled my fingers up even when I had twice as many, and when I tackled the fiddle, I was accused of tormenting cats. With this, I can never strike a wrong note. Besides"—he lowered his voice conspiratorially—"it gets me off the hook for the dancing." He winked at her and drifted up to the head of the room, where some other patrollers were collecting.

Their array of instruments seemed a bit random, but mostly small, as would fit in a spare corner of a saddlebag. There were several flutes, of wood, clay, or bone, two fiddles, and a makeshift collection of overturned tubs for thumping on, obviously filched from around the hotel. The room filled and quieted.

A gray-haired man with a bone flute stepped forward into the hush and began a melody Fawn found haunting; it made the hairs stir on her arms. Disturbed, she studied that pale length of bone, its surface burned about with writing, and was suddenly certain it was someone's relative. Because thighbones came in pairs, but hearts came one by one, so what *did* Lakewalker makers do with the leftovers, in all honor? The tune was so elegiac, it had be some prayer or hymn or memorial; Fawn could see a few people's lips moving on words they obviously knew by heart. A hush followed for a full minute, with everyone's eyes downcast.

A rattle like a snake from the tambourine, and a sudden spatter of drumming, broke the sorrow to bits as if trying to blow it out the windows. The fiddlers and flute players and tub-thumpers struck up a lively dance tune, and patrollers swung out onto the floor. They did not dance in couples but in groups, weaving complex patterns around one another. Except for the shifting about of partners in blithe disregard of anyone's sex, it reminded Fawn a lot of farmer barn dances, although the patrollers seemed to do without a caller. She wondered if they were doing something with their groundsenses to take the place of that outside coordination. Intensely complex as the patterns seemed, the dancers seldom missed a step, although when someone did, it was greeted with much hooting and laughter as the whole bunch rearranged themselves, picked up the pulse, and started again. The bells rang merrily. Dag stood at the back of the musicians, keeping steady time, punctuating his rhythms with well-placed spurts of jingling, watching it all and looking unusually happy; he didn't talk or sing, but he smiled a bit as the jokes flew by.

The younger patrollers' appetites for fast dances seemed insatiable, but at length the wheezing musicians traded out for a couple of singers. Outside, the long summer sun had gone down, and the room was hot with candles and lamps and sweaty bodies. Dag unscrewed his tambourine and came to sit at Fawn's feet, catching up on his beer-drinking with the aid of what seemed a bucket brigade of well-wishers.

One song was new to Fawn, another to a known tune but with different words, and a third she'd heard her aunt Nattie croon as she spun thread, and she wondered if it had originated with farmers or Lakewalkers. The singers were a man and a woman from Chato's patrol, and their voices blended beguilingly, hers pure and fair, his low and resonant. By this time, Fawn wasn't sure if the song about a lost patroller dancing in the woods with magical bears was fantasy or not.

The man with the bone flute joined them, making a trio; when he sent a preamble of notes into the air for the next song, Dag set his half-full glass rather abruptly on the floor. His smile over his shoulder at Fawn more resembled a grimace. "Privy run. Beer, eh," he excused himself, and levered to his feet.

Three sets of eyes marked his movement in concern: Mari's, Utau's, and one other older comrade's; Mari made a gesture of query, *Should I . . . ?* to which Dag returned a small headshake. He trod out without looking back.

"Fifty folk walked out that day," the song began, and Fawn quickly twigged to Dag's sudden retreat, because it turned out to be a long, involved ballad about the battle of Wolf Ridge. It named no names in its weaving of poetry and tune, of woe, gallantry, sacrifice, and victory, subtly inviting all to identify with its various heroes, and under any other circumstances Fawn would have found it thrilling. Most of the patrollers, truly, seemed variously thrilled or moved; Reela swiped away a tear, and Saun hung openmouthed in the intensity of his listening.

They do not know, Fawn realized. Saun, who had patrolled with Dag for a year and claimed to know him well, did not know. Utau did, listening with his hand over his mouth, eyes dark; Mari, of course, did, with her glances at the archway out which Dag had quietly vanished, and through which he did not return. The song finished at last, and another, more cheerful one started.

When Dag still did not return, Fawn slipped out herself. Someone else was exiting the commode chamber, so she tried outside. It was blessedly cooler out here, the blue shadows relieved by yellow light from the cheery windows, from the lanterns flanking the porch door, and, across the yard, from above the stable doors. Dag was sitting on the bench outside the stable, head back against the wall, staring up at the summer stars.

She sat down beside him and just let the silence hang for a time, for it was not uncomfortable, cloaking them like the night. The stars burned bright and seeming-close despite the lanterns; the sky was cloudless. "You all right?" she asked at last.

"Oh, yeah." He ran his hand through his hair, and added reflectively, "When I was a boy, I used to just love all those heroic ballads. I memorized dozens. I wonder if all those other old battle songs would have seemed as obscene to their survivors?"

Yet he claims not to sing. Unable to answer this, Fawn offered, "At least it helps people remember."

"Yes. Alas."

"It wasn't a *bad* song. In fact, I thought it was awfully good. As a song, I mean."

"I don't deny it. Not the fault of the song-maker—whoever it was did a fine job. If it were less effective, it wouldn't make me want to weep or rage so bad, I suppose. Which was why I left the room. My groundsense was a little open, in aid of the music-making. I didn't want to blight the mood. Pack thirty-eight tired, battle-nervy patrollers into one building for a week, and moods start to get around fast."

"Do you often make music, when you're out on patrol?" She tried to picture patroller song and dance around a campfire; the weather likely didn't always cooperate.

"Only sometimes. Camps can be pretty busy in the evenings. Curing hides and meat, preserving medicinal plants we pick up while patrolling, keeping logs and maps up to date. If it's a mounted patrol, a lot of horse care. Weapons training for the youngsters and practice for everyone. Mending, of clothes and boots and gear. Cooking, washing. All simple tasks, but they do go on."

His voice slowed in reminiscence. "Patrols vary in size—in the north they send out companies of a hundred and fifty or two hundred for the great seasonal wilderness sweeps—but south of the lake, patrols are usually smaller and shorter. Even so, you're like to be in each other's hair for weeks on end with no entertainment *but* each other. After a while, everyone knows all the songs. So there's gossip. And factions. And jokes. And practical jokes. And revenge for practical jokes. And fistfights over revenge for practical jokes. And knife fights over—well, you get the idea. Although if the emotions are allowed to melt down into that sour a soup, you can bet the patrol leader will be having a very memorable talk with Fairbolt Crow about it, later."

"Have you ever?"

"Not about that. Although all talks with Fairbolt tend to be memorable." In the shadows, he scratched his nose and smiled, then leaned his head back and let his eyes rest on the mellow windows across the yard. The singing had stopped, and dance tunes had begun again; feet thumping on the floor made the whole building pulse like a drum.

"Let's see, what else? On warm summer nights, gathering firewood is always a popular activity."

Fawn considered this, and the amusement underlying his voice. "Should think that would be wanted on cold nights, more."

"Mm, but you see, on warm nights, no one complains if folks are gone for two hours and come back having forgotten the firewood. Bathing in the river, that's another good one."

"In the dark?" said Fawn doubtfully.

"In the river is even more the question. Especially when the season's turned frosty. Walks, oh sure, that's believable, when everyone's been out slogging since dawn. Scouting around, too—that draws many selfless volunteers. Some dangerous squirrels out in those woods, they could mount an attack at any time. You can't be too prepared." A rumbling chuckle escaped his chest.

"Oh," said Fawn, finally understanding. Her lips curled up, if only for the rare sight of the laugh lines at the corners of his eyes.

"Followed by the breakups and the makeups and the people not talking to each other, or worse, going over it all *again* till you're ready to stuff your head in your blanket and scream for the listening to it. Ah, well." He vented a tolerant sigh. "The older patrollers generally have things worked out smooth, but the younger ones can be downright restive. It's not as though folks' lives stop for patrol. Walking the patterns isn't some emergency where you can drop everything, deal heroically, and then go home for good and all. It all starts again tomorrow at dawn. And you'll have to get up and walk your share just the same." He stretched, joints creaking a bit, as if in contemplation of such an early start.

"It's not that we're all mad, you know, although sometimes it seems like it," he went on in a lower voice. "Groundsense makes our moods very contagious. Not just by speech and gestures; it's like it gets in the air." His hand traced an upward spiral. "Now, for instance. Once a certain number of people open their grounds to each other, there starts to be . . . leakage. Bow-downs are really good for that. That building over there's downright awash, right now. All *sorts* of things can start to seem like a good idea. Absent gods be thanked for the beer."

"The beer?"

"Beer, I have concluded" —he held up an edifying finger, and Fawn began to realize that he was slightly drunk; people had kept the musicians well supplied with encouraging refreshment, earlier—"*exists* for the purpose of being blamed the next day. Very regrettable beverage, beer."

"Farmers use it for that, too," Fawn observed.

"A universal need." He blinked. "I think I need some more."

"Are you thirsty?"

"No." He slumped down, staring at her sidelong. His eyes were dark pools in this light, like night condensed. The lanternlight made glimmering orange halos around his hair, and slid across his faintly sweat-sheened features like a caress. "Just considering the potential of regret . . ."

He leaned toward her, and Fawn froze in hope so strong it felt like terror. Did he mean to kiss her? His breath was tinged with beer and exertion and Dag. Hers stopped altogether.

Stillness. Heartbeats.

"No," he sighed. "No. Mari was right." He sat up again. Fawn nearly burst into unfathomable tears. Nearly reached for him.

No, you can't. Daren't. He'll think you're that . . . that awful word Sunny used. It burned in her memory like an infected gash, *Slut.* It was an ugly word that had somehow turned her into an ugly thing, like a splash of ink or blood or poison discoloring water. *For Dag, I would be only beautiful.* And tall. She wished herself taller. If she were taller, no one could call her names just for, for *wanting* so much.

He sighed, smiled, rose. Gave her a hand up. They went back inside.

In the entry hall Dag's head turned, listening. "Good, someone's using the tambourine. They can get along without me for what's left of this." Truly, the music coming through the archway seemed slower and sleepier. He made for the staircase.

Fawn found her voice. "You going up?"

"Yeah. It was good, but it's been enough for one night. You?"

"I'm a little tired, too." She followed after him. What had happened, or not happened, out on the bench felt a lot like that moment on the road, some turn she had somehow missed.

As they exited the staircase on the second floor, bumping and laughter echoed up behind them. Dirla and two young patrollers from Chato's group burst out giggling, saluted Dag with cheerful hellos, and swung down the adjoining hallway. Fawn stopped and stared as they paused at Dirla's door, for one fellow looped his arm around her neck and kissed her, but she was still holding the other's hand to her . . . chest. Dirla—tall Dirla—extended one booted foot and pushed the door open, and they all fell through; it closed, cutting off some jest.

"Dag," Fawn said hesitantly, "what was that?"

He cocked an amused eyebrow at her. "What did it look like to you?"

"Is Dirla taking that . . . I mean, them . . . is she going to *bed* with those fellows?"

"Seems likely."

Likely? If his groundsense did half what he said, he *likely* knew very well. "*Both* of them?"

"Well, numbers are generally uneven, out on patrol. People make adjustments. Dirla is very . . . um . . . generous."

Fawn swallowed. "Oh."

She followed him up their hallway. Razi and Utau were just unlocking the door to their room; Utau looked, and smelled, distinctly the worse for beer, and Razi's hair, escaping his long braid, hung plastered in sweaty strands across his forehead from the dancing. They both bade Dag a civil good night and disappeared within.

"Well," said Fawn, determined to be fair, "it's too bad they weren't lucky enough to find ladies, too. They're too nice to be lonely." She added after a suspicious glance upward, "Dag, why are you biting your wrist?"

He cleared his throat. "Sometime when I am either a lot more sober or a lot more drunk, Spark, I shall attempt to explain the exceedingly complicated story of how those two came to both be married to the same accommodating woman back at Hickory Lake Camp. Let's just say, they look out for each other."

"Lakewalker ladies can marry more than one fellow? At a time? You're gulling me!"

"Not normally, and no, I'm not. I said it was complicated."

They fetched up before his door. He gave her a slightly strained smile.

"Well, *I* think Dirla is greedy," Fawn decided. "Or else those fellows are awfully pushy."

"Ah, no. Among Lakewalkers of the civil sort, which you know we all are, the woman invites. The man accepts, or not, and let me tell you, saying no gracefully without giving offense is a burden. I guarantee, whatever is going on back there was her idea."

"Among farmers, that would be thought too forward. Only bad girls, or, or" *stupid* "foolish ones would, well. Good girls wait to be asked." *And even then they're supposed to say no unless he comes with land in hand.*

He stretched his right arm out, supporting himself on the wall, half sheltering her. He stared down at her. After a long, long, thoughtful pause, he breathed, "Do they, now?" He scraped his teeth over his lower lip, the chip catching briefly. His eyes were lakes of darkness to fall into, going down for fathoms. "So, um, Spark . . . how many nights would you say we have wasted, here?"

She turned her face upward, swallowed, and said tremulously, "Way too many?"

They did not exactly fall into each other's arms. It was more of a mutual lunge.

He kicked his door open and kicked it closed again after them, because his arms were too full of her. Her feet did not touch the floor, but that was not the only reason she felt as though she was flying. Half his kisses missed her mouth, but that was all right, almost any part of his skin sliding beneath her lips was joy. He set her down, reached for the door bar, and stopped himself, wheezing slightly. *No, don't stop now . . .*

His voice recaptured seriousness. "If you mean this, Spark, bar the door."

Not taking her eyes from his dear, bony, faintly frenzied face, she did so. The oak board fell into place in its brackets with a solid, satisfying *clunk.* It seemed a sufficient compromise of customs.

His hand, reluctantly, slid from her shoulder and let her go just long enough for him to stride over and turn up the oil lamp on the table beside his bed. Dull orange glow became yellow flare within the glass chimney, filling the room with light and shadow. He sat rather abruptly on the edge of his bed, as if his knees had given way, and stared at her, holding out his hand. It was shaking. She climbed up into the circle of his arm, then folded her knees under her to raise her face to his again. His kisses slowed, as if tasting her lips, then, startlingly, tasting in truth, his tongue slipping inside her mouth. Odd, but nice, she decided, and earnestly tried to do it back. His hand wound in her hair, undid her ribbon, and let her curls fall down to her shoulders.

How did people get rid of their clothes, at times like these? Sunny had merely lifted her skirts and shoved down her drawers; so had the malice, come to think.

"Sh, now, what dark thought went past just now?" Dag chided. "Be here. With me."

"How did you know what I thought?" she said, trying not to be unnerved.

"I don't. I read grounds, not minds, Spark. Sometimes, all groundsense does is give you more to be confused about." His hand hesitated on the top button of her dress. "May I?"

"Please," she said, relieved of a procedural worry. Of course Dag would know how to do this. She had only to watch and copy.

He undid a few more fastenings, gently pulled down one sleeve, and kissed her bared shoulder. She gathered her courage and went after the buttons of his shirt. Mutual confidence established, things went faster after that, cloth tumbling to the floor over the side of the bed. The last thing he undid, after a hesitation and a glance at her from under his lashes, was his arm harness, unbuckling the straps around his lower arm and above his elbow, and setting it on the table. His hand rubbed the red marks left by the leather. For him, she realized dimly, it was a greater gesture of vulnerability and trust than removing his trousers had just been.

"Light," Dag muttered, hesitating. "Light? Farmers are supposed to like it dark, I've heard."

"Leave it on," Fawn whispered, and he smiled and lay back. When all that height was laid out flat, it stretched a long way. His bed was not as narrow as hers in the next room, but still he filled it from corner to corner. She felt like an explorer facing a mountain range that crossed her whole horizon. "I want to look at you."

"I'm no rose, Spark."

"Maybe not. But you make my eyes happy."

The corners of his eyes crinkled up enchantingly at that, and she had to stretch up and kiss them. Skin slid on skin for the length of her body. His muscles were long and tapering, and the skin of his torso was unevenly tanned where his shirts had been on or off, paler still below his waist along his lean flank. A faint dusting of dark hair across his chest narrowed and thickened, going down in a vee below his belly. Her fingers twined in it, brushing with and against the grain. So, with his odd Lakewalker senses, what more of her did he touch?

She swallowed, and dared to say, "You said you could tell."

"Hm?" His hand spiraled around her breast, and how could such a soft caress make it suddenly ache so sweetly?

"The time of the month a woman can get a child, you said you could tell." Or wait, no, was that only Lakewalker ladies? "A beautiful pattern in her ground, you said." Yes, and she'd believed Sunny, hadn't she, on a piece of bed lore that, if not a mean lie, had turned out to be a costly untruth, and Sunny's tale had seemed a lot less unlikely than this. A shiver of unease, *Am I being stupid again . . . ?* was interrupted when Dag propped himself up on his left elbow and looked at her with a serious smile.

His hand traced her belly, crossing the malice marks there that had turned to thin black scabs. "You're not at risk tonight, Spark. But I should be right terrified to try to make love to you that way so soon after your injuries. You're so dainty, and I'm, um, well, there are other things I'd very much like to show you."

She risked a peek down, but her eye caught on the parallel black lines beneath his beautiful hand, and a flash of sorrow and guilt shook her. Would she ever be able to lie down with anyone without these cascades of unwelcome memory washing through her? And then she wondered if Dag—with, it seemed, so many more accumulated memories—had a similar problem.

"Sh," he soothed, and his thumb crossed her lips, though she had not spoken. "Reach for lightness, bright Spark. You do not betray your sorrow to set it aside for an hour. It'll be waiting patiently for you to pick it up again on the other side."

"How long?"

"Time wears grief smooth like a river stone. The weight will always be there, but it'll stop scraping you raw at the slightest touch. But you have to let the time flow by; you can't rush it. We wear our hair knotted for a year for our losses, and it is not too long a while."

She reached up and ran her hand through his dark tousle, petting and winding it through her fingers. Gratified fingers. She gave a lock a little tug. "So what was this supposed to mean?"

"Shaved for head lice?" he offered, breaking the bleakness as she giggled, no doubt his intent.

"Go on, you did not either have head lice!"

"Not lately. They're another story, but I have better things to do with my lips right now . . . " He began kissing his way down her body, and she wondered what magic was in his tongue, not just for his kisses and how they seemed to lay trails of cool fire across her skin, but for how, with his words, he seemed to lift stones from her heart.

Her breath caught as his tongue reached the tip of her breast and did exhilarating things there. Sunny had merely pinched her through her dress, and, and *blight* Sunny for haunting her head like this, *now.* Dag's hand drifted up, his thumb caressing her forehead, then he sat up.

"Roll over," he murmured. "Let give you a back rub. Think I can bring your body and ground into better tune."

"Do you—if you want—"

"I won't say, *trust me.* I will say, *try me,*" he whispered into her curls. "Try me."

For a one-handed man, he did this *awfully* well, she thought muzzily a few minutes later, her face pressed into the pillow. Memory seemed to melt out of her brain altogether. The bed creaked as he moved off it briefly, and she opened one eye, *don't let him get away,* but he returned in a moment. A slight gurgle, a cool splash pooling on the inward curve of her back, the scent of chamomile and clover . . .

"Oh, you got some of that nice oil." She thought a moment. "When?"

"Seven days ago."

She muffled a snicker.

"Hey, a patroller should be prepared for any emergency."

"Is this an emergency?"

"Just give me a bit more time, Spark, and we'll see . . . Besides, it's good for my hand, which tends to get rough. You don't want hangnails catching in tender places, trust me on that."

The oil did change the texture of his touch as he worked his way smoothly down to her toes, turned her over, and started back up.

Hand. Soon supplemented with tongue, in very tender and surprising places indeed. His touch was like silk, there, there, *there?* ah! She jerked in surprise, but eased back. So, this was *making love.* It was all very nice, but it seemed a bit one-sided.

"Shouldn't it be your turn?" she asked anxiously.

"Not yet," he said, rather muffled. "'M pretty happy where I am. And your ground is flowing almost right, now. Let me, let me just . . ."

Minutes flew. *Something* was swirling through her, like some astonishingly sweet emergency. His touch grew firmer, swifter, surer. Her eyes closed, her breath came faster, and her spine began to arch. Then her breath caught, and she went rigid, silent, openmouthed, as the sensation burst from her, climbing up to white out her brain, to rush like a tide to her fingers and toes, and ebb.

Her back eased, and she lay shaking and amazed. *"Oh."* When she could, she raised her head and stared down over her body, strange new landscape that it had become. Dag was up on one elbow, watching her in return, eyes black and bright, with a grin on his face bordering on smug.

"Better?" he inquired, as if he didn't know.

"Was that some . . . some Lakewalker magic?" No wonder folks tried to follow these people to the ends of the world.

"Nope. That was Little Spark magic. All your own."

A hundred mysteries seemed to fly up and away like a flock of startled birds into the night. "No *wonder* people want to do this. It all makes much more sense now . . ."

"Indeed." He crawled up the bed to kiss her again. The taste of herself on his lips, mixed with the scent of chamomile and clover, was a little disturbing, but she valiantly kissed him back. Then brushed her lips across his enthralling cheekbones, his eyelids, definite chin, and back to his mouth, as she giggled helplessly. She could feel an answering rumble from deep in his chest as she lay across him.

She had brushed against him, but she had not yet *touched* him. It was surely his turn now. Hands should work two ways. She sat up, blinking against dizziness.

He stretched out straight and smiled up, his crinkling eyes now resting inquiringly on her, downright inviting, in an unhurried sort of way. He lay open to her, to her gaze, in a way that astonished her anew. All but his mysterious ground, of course. That was beginning to seem an unfair advantage. Where to begin, *how* to begin? She recalled how he had started.

"May I . . . touch you too?"

"Please," he breathed.

It might be mere mimicry, but it was a start, and once started, acquired its own momentum. She kissed her way down and up his body, and arrived back at the middle.

Her first tentative touch made him jerk and catch his breath, and she shied back.

"No, it's all right, go on," he huffed. "I'm a little, um, sensitized just at the moment. It's good. Almost anything you can do is good."

"Sensitized. Is that what you call it?" Her lips curled up.

"I'm trying to be *polite,* Spark."

She tried various touches, strokes, and grips, wondering if she was doing this right. Her hands felt clumsy and rather too small. The occasional catches of his breath were not very informative, she thought, though once in a while his hand covered hers to squeeze some silent suggestion. Was that gasp pleasure or pain? His apparent endurance for pain was a bit frightening, when she thought about it. "Can I try your oil on *my* hands?"

"Certainly! Although . . . this may be over rather quickly if you do."

She hesitated. "Couldn't we . . . do it again? Sometime?"

"*Oh* yes. I'm very renewable. Just not very fast. Not" —he sighed—"as quick as when I was younger, anyway. Though that's mostly been to my advantage, tonight."

And mine. His patience humbled her. "Well, then . . ."

The oil made her hands slip and slide in ways that intrigued her and seemed to please him, too. She grew more daring. *That,* for example, made him jerk, no, convulse, much as he'd done to her a while ago.

"Brave Spark!" he gasped.

"Is that good?"

"*Yes* . . ."

"Figured if you thought it would please me, it might be something that pleased you, too."

"Clever girl," he crooned, his eyes closing again.

She chilled. "Please don't make fun of me."

His eyes opened, and his brows drew in; he raised his head from the pillow and frowned down over his torso at her. "Wasn't. You have one of the hungriest minds it's ever been my pleasure to meet. You may have been starved of information, but your wits are as sharp as a blade."

She caught her breath, lest it escape as a sudden surprised sob. His words could not be true, but *oh* they sounded so nice to hear!

At her shocked look, he added a little impatiently, "Come, child, you can't be that bright and not know it."

"Papa said I must be a fool to ask so many questions all the time."

"Never that." His head tilted, and his eyes took on that uncanny inward look. "There's a deep, dark place in your ground just there. Major fissure and blockage. I . . . it's not going to be the work of an hour to find the bottom of that one, I'm afraid."

She gulped. "Then let's set it aside with the rest of the stones, for now. It'll wait." She bent her head. "I'm neglecting you."

"I won't argue with that . . ."

Tongues, she discovered, worked like fingers on fellows quite as well, if differently, as they worked on ladies. Well, then. What would happen if she did *this* and also *this* and *that* at the same time . . .

She found out. It was fascinating to watch. Even from the oblique angle of view down here she could see his expression grow so inward it might have been a trance. For a moment, she wondered if levitation were a Lakewalker magical skill, for he seemed about to rise off the bed.

"Are you all right?" she asked anxiously, when his body stopped shuddering. "Your forehead got all wrinkled up funny there for a minute, when your, um, back curved up like that."

His hand waved while he regained his breath; his eyes stayed squeezed shut, but finally opened again. "Sorry, what? Sorry. Was waiting for all those white sparks on the insides of my eyelids to finish exploding. *That* wasn't something to miss."

"Does that often happen?"

"No. No, indeed."

"Are you all right?" she repeated.

His grin lit his face like a streak of fire. "All right? I think I'm downright *astounding*." From an angle of attack that would seem to allow, at best, a wallow, he lunged up and wrapped both arms around her, and dragged her back down to his chest, heedless of the mess they'd made. It was his turn to kiss her face all over. Laughter turned to accidental touching, to—

"Dag, you're *ticklish*."

"No, I'm not. Or only in certain *aiee*!" When he got his breath back, he added, "You're fiendish, Spark. I like that in a woman. Gods. I haven't laughed this much in . . . I can't remember."

"I like how you giggle."

"I was not *giggling*. That would be undignified in a man of my years."

"What was that noise, then?"

"Chortling. Yes, definitely. Chortling."

"Well," she decided, "it looks good on you. Everything looks good on you." She sat up on her elbow and let her gaze travel the long route down his body and back. "*Nothing* looks good on you, too. It's most unfair."

"Oh, as if *you* aren't sitting there looking, looking . . ."

"What?" she breathed, sinking back into his grip.

"Naked. Edible. Beautiful. Like spring rain and star fire."

He drew her in again; their kisses grew longer, lazier. Sleepier. He made a great effort, and reached out and turned off the lamp. Soft summer-night air stirred the curtains. He flung the sheet up and let it settle over them. She cuddled into his arm, pressing her ear to his chest, and closed her eyes.

To the ends of the world, she thought, melting into deeper darkness.

12

Dag spent the radiant summer dawn proving beyond doubt to Fawn that her last night's first-in-a-lifetime experience needn't be a once-in-a-lifetime experience. When they woke from the ensuing sated nap, it was mid-morning. Dag seriously considered the merits of lying low till the patrols had taken their planned departure, but unexpectedly sharp hunger drove both him and Fawn to rise, wash, dress, and go see if breakfast was still to be had downstairs.

Fawn entered the staircase ahead of Dag and turned sideways to let Utau, clumping up to collect more gear to load, pass her by. Dag smiled brightly at his sometime-linker. Utau's head cranked over his shoulder in astonishment, and he walked into the far wall with a muffled thud, righted himself, and wheeled to stare. Prudently deciding to ignore that, Dag followed Fawn before Utau could speak. Dag suspected he needed to get better control of his stretching mouth, as well as of his sparking ground. A responsible, mature, respected patroller should not walk about grinning and glowing like some dementedly carved pumpkin. It was like to frighten the horses.

Mari's patrol was slated to ride north and pick up their pattern again where it had been broken off almost two weeks ago by the call for aid. With his patrol's purse newly topped off by the Glassforgers, Chato planned to continue on his mission to purchase horses from the limestone country south of the Grace. He would be slowed on the first leg by a wagon to carry Saun and Reela, neither quite ready to ride yet; the pair were to finish convalescing at a Lakewalker camp that controlled a ferry crossing down on the river, and be picked up again on the return journey. Both patrols had planned their removals for the crack of noon, a merciful hour. Dag sensed Chato's moderating influence at work. Mari was perfectly capable of ordering a dawn departure after a bow-down, then concealing her evil hilarity behind a rod-straight face as her bleary troop stumbled out. Mari was far and away Dag's favorite relative, but that was a pretty low fence to get over, and he prayed to the absent gods that he might avoid her altogether this morning.

After breakfast Dag helped lug the last of Saun's gear to the wagon, and turned to find his prayers, as usual, unanswered. Mari stood holding the reins of her horse, staring at him in mute exasperation.

He let his eyebrows rise, trying desperately not to smile. Or worse, chortle. "What?"

She drew a long breath, but then just let it out. "Besotted fool. There's no more use trying to talk to you this morning than to those twittering wrens in that elm across the yard. I said my piece. I'll see you back in camp in a few weeks. Maybe the novelty will have worn off by then, and you'll have your wits back, I don't know. You can do your own blighted explaining to Fairbolt, is all I can say."

Dag's back straightened. "That I will."

"Eh!" She turned to gather her reins, but then turned back, seriousness replacing the aggravation in her eyes. "Be careful of yourself in farmer country, Dag."

He would have preferred a tart dressing-down to this true concern, against which he had no defense. "I'm always careful."

"Not so's I ever noticed," she said dryly. Silently, Dag offered her a leg up, which she accepted with a nod, settling in her saddle with a tired sigh. She was growing thinner, he thought, these last couple of years. He gave her a smile of farewell, but it only made her lean on her pommel and lower her voice to him. "I've seen you in a score of moods, including foul. I've never before seen you so plain happy. Enough to make an old woman weep, you are . . . Take care of that little girl, too, then."

"I plan to."

"Huh. Do you, now." She shook her head and clucked her horse forward, and Dag belatedly recalled his last statement to her on the subject of plans.

But he could almost watch himself being displaced in her head with the hundred details a patrol leader on duty must track—as well he remembered. Her gaze turned to sweep over the rest of her charges, checking their gear, their horses, their faces; judging their readiness, finding it enough to go on with. This day. Again.

Fawn had been helping Reela, apparently one of the several dozen people, or so it seemed to Dag, that Fawn had managed to make friends of in this past week. The two young women bade each other cheery good-byes, and Fawn popped down off the wagon to come stand with him as he watched his patrol form up and trot out through the gateway. At least as many riders gave a parting wave to her as to him. In a few minutes, Chato's patrol too mounted up and wheeled out, at a slower pace for the rumbling wagon. Saun waved as enthusiastic a farewell as his injuries permitted. Silence settled in the stable yard.

Dag sighed, caught as usual between relief to be rid of the whole maddening lot of them, and the disconcerting loneliness that always set in when he was parted from his people. He told himself that it made no sense to be shaken by both feelings simultaneously. Anyway, there were more practical reasons to be wary when one was the only Lakewalker in a townful of farmers, and he struggled to wrap his usual guarded courtesy back about himself. Except now with Fawn also inside.

The horse boys disbanded toward the tack room or the back door to the kitchen, walking slowly in the humidity and chatting with each other.

"Your patrollers weren't so bad," said Fawn, staring thoughtfully out the gate. "I didn't think they'd accept me, but they did."

"This is patrol. Camp is different," said Dag absently.

"How?"

"Eh . . . " Weak platitudes rose to his mind, *Time will tell, Don't borrow trouble.* "You'll see." He felt curiously loath to explain to her, on this bright morning, why his personal war on malices wasn't the sole reason that he volunteered for more extra duty than any other patroller in Hickory Lake Camp. His record had been seventeen straight months in the field without returning there, though he'd had to switch patrols several times to do it.

"Must we leave today, too?" asked Fawn.

Dag came to himself with a start and wrapped his arm around her, snugging her to his hip. "No, in fact. It's a two-day hard ride to Lumpton from here, but we've no need to ride hard. We can make an easy start tomorrow, take it in gentle stages." Or even later, the seductive thought occurred.

"I was wondering if I ought to give my room back to the hotel. Since I'm not really a patroller and all."

"What? No! That room is yours for as long as you want it, Spark!" Dag said indignantly.

"Um, well, that's sort of the point, I thought." She bit her lip, but her eyes, he realized, were sparkling. "I was wondering if I could sleep in with you? For . . . frugality."

"Of course, frugality! Yes, that's the thing. You are a thoughtful girl, Spark."

She cast him a merry smirk. She flashed an entrancing dimple when she smirked, which made his heart melt like a block of butter left in the summer sun. She said, "I'll go move my things."

He followed, feeling as utterly scatter-witted as Mari had accused him of being. He could not, could *not* run up and down the streets of Glassforge, leaping and shouting to the blue sky and the entire population, *She says I make her eyes happy!*

He really wanted to, though.

&

They did not leave the next day, for it was raining. Nor the next either, for rain threatened then, too. On the following morning, Dag declared Fawn too sore from the previous night's successfully concluded bed experiments to ride comfortably, although by midafternoon she was hopping around as happily as a flea and *he* was limping as the pulled muscle in his back seized up. Which provided the next day's excuse for lingering, as well. He pictured the conversation with Fairbolt, *Why are you late, Dag? Sorry, sir, I crippled myself making passionate love to a farmer girl.* Yeah, that'd go over well.

Watching Fawn discover the delights that her own body could provide her was an enchantment to Dag as endlessly beguiling as water lilies. He had to cast his mind far back for comparisons, as he'd made those discoveries at a much younger age. He could indeed remember being a little crazed with it all for a while. He found he really didn't need to rack his brains to provide variety in his lovemaking, for she was still overwhelmed by the marvel of repeatability. So he probably hadn't created anything he couldn't handle, quite.

Dag also discovered in himself a previously unsuspected weakness for foot rubs. If ever Fawn wanted to fix him in one place, she didn't need to hog-tie him with ropes; when her small firm hands worked their way down past his ankles, he slumped like a man poleaxed and just lay there paralyzed, trying not to drool too unattractively into his pillow. In those moments, never getting out of bed again for the rest of his life seemed the very definition of paradise. As long as Spark was in the bed with him.

The short summer nights filled themselves, but Dag was unsettled by how swiftly the long days also slipped by. A gentle ride out for Fawn to try her new mare and riding trousers, with a picnic by the river, turned into an afternoon under a curtaining willow tree that lasted till sundown. Sassa the Horseford kinsman popped up again, and Dag found in Fawn an apparently bottomless appetite for tours of Glassforge crafters. Her endless curiosity and passion for questions was by no means limited to patrollers and sex, flattering as that had been, but seemed to extend to the whole wide world. Sassa's willing, nay, proud escort and array of family connections guided them through the complex back premises of a brick burner, a silversmith, a saddler, three kinds of mills, a potter—Fawn cast a simple pot under the woman's enthusiastic tutelage, becoming cheerfully muddied—and a repeat of the visit to Sassa's own glassworks, because Dag had missed it before on account of being up to his waist in swamp.

Dag at first mustered a mere polite interest—he seldom paid close attention anymore to the details of anything he wasn't being asked to track and slay—but found himself drawn in along the trail of Fawn's fascination. With studied and sweating intensity, the glass workers brought together sand and fire and meticulous timing to effect transformations of the very ground of their materials into fragile, frozen brilliance. *This is farmer magic, and they don't even realize it,* Dag thought, completely taken by their system of blowing glass into molds to make rapid, reliable replicas. Sassa gave to Fawn a bowl that she had seen being made the other day, now annealed, and she determined to take it home to her mother. Dag was doubtful about getting it to West Blue intact in a saddlebag, but Sassa provided a slat box padded with straw and hope. Which was going to be bulky and awkward; Dag steeled himself to deal with it.

Later, Fawn unpacked the bowl to set on the table beside their bed to catch the evening light. Dag sat on the bed and stared with nearly equal interest at the way the patterns pressed into it made wavering rainbows.

"All things have grounds, except where a malice has drained them," he commented. "The grounds of living things are always moving and changing, but even rocks have a sort of low, steady hum. When Sassa made that batch of glass and cast it, it was almost as if its ground came alive, it transformed so. Now it's become still again, but changed. It's like it" —his hand reached out as if grasping for the right word—"sings a brighter tune."

Fawn stood back with her hands on her hips and gave him a slightly frustrated look; as if, for all her questions, he walked in a place she could not follow.

"So," she said slowly, "if things move their grounds, can pushing on grounds move things?"

Dag blinked in faint shock. Was it chance or keen logic that brought her question so close to the heart of Lakewalker secrets? He hesitated. "That's the theory," he said at last. "But would you like to see how a Lakewalker would move the ground in that bowl from one side of the table to the other?"

Her eyes widened. "Show me!"

Gravely, he leaned over, reached out with his hand, and shoved the bowl about six inches.

"Dag!" Fawn wailed in exasperation. "I thought you were going to show me magic."

He grinned briefly, although mostly because he could scarcely look at her and *not* smile. "Trying to move anything through its ground is like pushing on the short end of a long lever. It's always easier to do it by hand. Although it's said . . . " He hesitated again. "It's said the old sorcerer-lords linked together in groups to do their greater magics. Like matching grounds for healing, or a lovers' groundlock, only with some lost difference."

"Don't you do that now?"

"No. We are too reduced—maybe our bloodlines were adulterated in the dark times, no one knows. Anyway, it's forbidden."

"I mean for your pattern walking."

"That's just simple perception. Like the difference between feeling with your hand and pushing with your hand, perhaps."

"Why is pushing forbidden? Or was that linking up in bunches to push that's not allowed?"

He should have known that the last remark would elicit more questions. Throwing one fact to Fawn was like throwing one piece of meat to a pack of starving dogs; it just caused a riot. "Bad experiences," he replied in a quelling tone. All right, by the pursing of her lips and wrinkling of her brow, quelling wasn't going to work; try for distraction. "Let me tell you, though, not a patroller up Luthlia way survives the lake country without learning how to bounce mosquitoes through their grounds. Ferocious little pests— they'll drain you dry, they will."

"You use magic to repel *mosquitoes*?" she said, sounding as though she couldn't decide whether to be impressed or offended. "We just have recipes for horrible stuff to rub on our skins. Once you know what's in them, you'd almost rather be bit."

He snickered, then sighed. "They say we are a fallen folk, and I for one believe it. The ancient lords built great cities, ships, and roads, transformed their bodies, sought longevity, and brought the whole world crashing down at the last. Though I suspect it was a really good run for a while, till then. Me—I bounce mosquitoes. Oh, and I can summon and dismiss my horse, once I get him trained up to it. And help settle another's hurting body, if I'm lucky. And see the world double, down to the ground. That's about it for Dag magic, I'm afraid."

Her eyes lifted to his face. "And kill malices," she said slowly.

"Aye. That mainly."

He reached for her, swallowing her next question with a kiss.

It took the better part of a week for Dag's boat anchor of a conscience to drag him out of the clouds and back onto the road. He wished he could just jettison the blighted deadweight. But one morning he turned back from shaving to find Fawn, half-dressed and with her bedroll open on the bed, frowning down at the sharing knife that lay there.

He came and wrapped her in his arms, her bare back to his bare torso.

"It's time, I guess," she said.

"I guess so, too." He sighed. "Not that you couldn't count my unused camp-time by years, but Mari gave me leave to solve the mystery of that thing, not to linger here in this brick-and-clapboard paradise. The hirelings have been giving me squinty looks for days."

"They've been real nice to *me*," she observed accurately.

"You're good at finding friends." In fact, everyone from the cooks, scullions, chambermaids, and horse boys up to the owner and his wife had grown downright defensive of Fawn, farmer heroine as she was. To the point where Dag suspected that if she demanded, *Throw this lanky fellow into the street!* he'd shortly find himself sitting in the dust clutching his saddlebags. The Glassforgers who worked here were used to patrollers and their odd ways with each other, but it was clear enough to Dag that they just barely tolerated this mismatch, and that only for the sake of Fawn's obvious delight. Other patrons now drifting in, drovers and drivers and traveling families and boatmen up from the river to secure cargoes, looked askance at the odd pair, and even more askance after collecting whatever garbled gossip was circulating about them.

Dag wondered how askance he would be looked at in West Blue. Fawn had gradually grown reconciled to the planned stop at her home, partly from guilt at his word picture of her parents' probable anxiety, and partly by his pledge not to abandon her there. It was the only promise she'd ever asked him to repeat.

He dropped a kiss on the top of her head, letting his finger snake around and drift over the healing wounds on her left cheek. "Your bruises are fading now. I figure if I bring you back to your family claiming to be your protector, it'll be more convincing if you don't look like you just lost a drunken brawl."

Her lips twitched up as she caught his hand and kissed it, but then her fingers drifted to the malice marks on her neck. "Except for these."

"Don't pick."

"They itch. Are they ever going to drop off? The other scabs did already."

"Soon enough, I judge. It'll leave these deep bitter-red dents underneath for a time, but they'll fade almost like other scars. They'll turn silvery when they're old."

"Oh—that long shiny groove on your leg that starts behind your knee and goes around up your thigh—was that a malice-clawing, then?" She had mapped every mark upon him as assiduously as a pattern-grid surveyor, these past days and nights, and demanded annotations for most of them, too.

"Just a touch. I got away, and my linker put his knife in a moment later."

She turned to hug him around the waist. "I'm glad it didn't grab any higher," she said seriously.

Dag choked a laugh. "Me too, Spark!"

They were on the straight road north by noon.

They rode slowly, in part for their dual disinclination for their destinations, but mostly because of the dog-breath humidity that had set in after the last rain. The horses plodded beneath a brassy sun. Their riders talked or fell silent with, it seemed to Dag, equal ease. They spent the next afternoon—rainy again—in the loft of the barn at the well-house where they'd first glimpsed each other, picnicking on farm fare and listening to the soothing sounds of the drops on the roof and the horses champing hay below, didn't notice when the storm stopped, and lingered there overnight.

The next day was brighter and clearer, the hot white haze blown away east, and they reluctantly rode on. On the fifth night of the two-day ride they stopped a short leg from Lumpton Market to camp one last time. Fawn had figured an early start from Lumpton would bring them to West Blue before dark. It was hard for Dag to guess what would happen then, though her slowly unfolding tales of her family had at least given him a better sense of who he would encounter.

They found a campsite by a winding creek, out of view of the road, beneath a scattered stand of leatherpod trees. Later in the fall, the seedpods would hang down beneath the big spade-shaped leaves like hundreds of leather straps, but now the trees were in full bloom. Spikes stood up from crowns of leaves with dozens of linen-white blossoms the size of egg cups clustered on them, breathing sweet perfume into the evening air. As the moonless night fell, fireflies rose up along the creek and from the meadow beyond it, twinkling in the mist. Beneath the leatherpod tree, the shadows grew black.

"Wish I could see you better," Fawn murmured, as they lay down across their combined blankets and commenced a desultory fiddling with each other's buttons. No one wanted a blanket atop, in this heat.

"Hm." Dag sat up on one elbow and smiled in the dark. "Give me a minute, Spark, and I might be able to do something about that."

"No, don't put more wood on the fire. 'S too hot now."

"Wasn't going to. Just wait and see. In fact, close your eyes."

He extended his groundsense to its full range and found no menace for a mile, just the small nesting life of the grass: mice and shrews and rabbits and sleepy meadowlarks; above, a few fluttering bats, and the silent ghostly passage of an owl. He drew his net finer still, filling it with tinier life. Not a bounce, but a persuasion . . . yes. This still worked. The tree began to throng with his invited visitors, more and more. Beside him, Fawn's face slowly emerged from the gloom as though rising from deep water.

"Can I open them yet?" she asked, her eyes dutifully scrunched up.

"Just a moment more . . . yes. Now."

He kept his eyes on her face as she looked up, so as not to miss the best wonder of all. Her eyes opened, then shot wide; her lips parted in a gasp.

Above them, the leatherpod tree was filled with hundreds, perhaps thousands, of—in Dag's wide-open perception, slightly bewildered—fireflies, so dense the lighter branches bent with their load. Many of them crawled inside the white blossoms, and when they lit, the clusters of petal cups glowed like pale lanterns. The cool, shadowless radiance bathed them both. Her breath drew in. "Oh," she said, rising on one elbow and staring upward. "Oh . . ."

"Wait. I can do more." He concentrated, and drew down a lambent swirl of insects to spiral around and land in her dark hair, lighting it like a coronet of candles.

"Dag . . . !" She gave a wild laugh, half delight, half indignation, her hands rising to gently prod her curls. "You put bugs in my hair!"

"I happen to know you like bugs."

"I do," she admitted fairly. "Some kinds, anyhow. But how . . . ? Did you learn to do this up in the woods of Luthlia, too?"

"No, actually. I learned it in camp, back when my groundsense first came in—I was about twelve, I guess. The children learn it from each other; no adult ever teaches it, but I think most everyone knows how to catch fireflies this way. We just forget. Grow up and get busy and all. Though I admit, I never collected more than a handful at one time before."

She was smiling helplessly. "It's a bit eerie. But I like it. Not sure about the hair—eh! Dag, they're tickling my ears!"

"Lucky bugs." He leaned in and blew off the wanderers from the curve of her ear, kissing the tickle away. "You should be crowned with light like the rising moon."

"Well," she said, in a gruff little voice, and sniffed. Her gaze traced the bending lantern-flowers above, and returned to his face. "What do you want to go and do a thing like that for anyhow? I'm already as full of joy for you as my body can hold, and there you go and put *more* in. Downright wasteful, I say. It's just going to spill over . . . " The light shimmered in her swimming eyes.

He pulled her up and across him, and let the warm drops spatter across his chest like summer rain. "Spill on me," he whispered.

He released her twinkling tiara and let the tiny creatures fly up into the tree again. In the scintillant glow, they made slow love till midnight brought silence and sleep.

Lumpton Market was a smaller town than Glassforge, but lively nonetheless. It lay at the confluence of two rocky rivers, which flanked a long shale-and-limestone ridge running northward. Two old straight roads crossed there, and it had surely been the site of a hinterland city when the lords ruled. As it was, much of the new town was made of ancient building blocks mined out of the encroaching woods, and drystone walls of both ordinary fieldstone and much less identifiable rubble abounded around both outlying fields and house yards. Now that Dag's eye was alerted to it, however, he noticed a few newer, finer houses on the outskirts built of brick. The bridges were timber, recent, and wide and sturdy enough for big wagons.

The hostelry familiar and friendly to patrollers for which Dag was aiming lay on the north side of Lumpton, so he and Fawn found themselves in early afternoon riding through the town square, where the day market was in full swing. Fawn turned in her saddle, looking over the booths and carts and tarps as they passed around the edge of the busy scene.

"I have that glass bowl for Mama," she said. "I wish I had something to bring Aunt Nattie. She hardly ever gets taken along when my parents come down here." A yearly ritual, Dag had been given to understand.

Aunt Nattie was Fawn's mother's much older sister, blind since a childhood infection had stolen her sight at age ten. She had come along with Fawn's mother when she'd married years ago, in some sort of dowry deal. Semi-invalid but not idle, she did all the spinning and weaving for the farm, with extra to sell for cash money sometimes. And was the only member of her family Fawn spoke of without hidden strain in her voice and ground.

Obligingly, now that he understood her purpose, Dag followed Fawn's gaze. One would not, presumably, carry food to a farm. The cloth and clothing for sale, new and used, likewise would seem foolish. His eye ran over the more permanent shops lining the square. "Tools? Scissors, needles? Something for her weaving or sewing?"

"She has a lot of those." Fawn sighed.

"Something that gets used up, then. Dyes?" His voice faded in doubt. "Ah. Likely not."

"Mama did most of the coloring, though I do it nowadays. Wish I could get her something just for her." Her gaze narrowed. "Furs . . . ?"

"Well, let's look." They dismounted, and Fawn looked over the tarp where a farmwoman offered some, in Dag's expert view, rather inferior pelts; all common local beasts, raccoon and possum and deerhide.

"I can get her something much better, later," Dag murmured, and with a grimace of agreement Fawn gave over poking through the sad piles. They strolled onward side by side, leading their horses.

Fawn stopped and wheeled, lips pursing, as they passed a narrow medicine shop tucked between a shoemaker and a barber-toothdrawer-scribe—it was unclear if the latter was all one man. The medicine shop had a broad window, with small square glass panes set in a bowed-out wooden frame to make a larger view. "I wonder if they sell scent water like what your patroller girls found in Glassforge?"

Or oil, Dag could not help wondering. They could stand to restock for future use, although the likelihood of immediate future use at the Bluefield homestead seemed remote. Whatever gratitude her family might feel for his bringing their only daughter back alive was unlikely to extend to letting them sleep together there. In any case, they tied their horses to one of the hitching rails conveniently lining the cobblestone sidewalk and went inside.

The shop had four kinds of scent water but only plain oil, which made Dag's selection immediate. He occupied himself looking over the shop's actually impressive stock of herbals, several of which he recognized as of high quality and coming from Lakewalker sources, while Fawn made herself redolent with happy indecision. Her choice finally made, they waited while their small purchases were wrapped. Or not so small in proportion to Fawn's thin purse, Dag noted as she braced herself to trade out some of her few coins for the little luxury.

Outside, Dag tucked the packets away in his saddlebags and turned to give Fawn a leg up on the bay mare. She was standing staring at her saddle in dismay.

"My bedroll's gone!" Her hand went to the dangling rawhide strings behind her cantle. "Did it drop on the road? I know I tied it on better than . . ."

His hand followed hers, and his voice tightened. "These are cut. See, the knots are still tied. Sneak thief."

"Dag, the knife was in my bedroll!" she gasped.

He snapped open his groundsense, flinching as it was battered by the uproar pouring from all the people nearby. He searched through the noise for a faint, familiar chime. Just . . . there. His head came up, and he looked along the square to where a slight figure was disappearing between two buildings, the roll cast casually over his shoulder as though he owned it.

"I see it," he said thickly. "Wait here!" His legs stretched as he followed after, not quite running. Behind him, he could hear Fawn demanding of passersby, *Did you see anyone fooling around by our horses?*

Dag tamped outrage down to annoyance, mostly at himself. If he'd been traveling through here with a group of patrollers, someone would always have been left with the horses as a routine precaution. So what had made him drop his guard? Some misplaced sense of anonymity? The fact that if only he'd bothered to glance out the window, he could have kept an eye on the horses himself? If he'd left his groundsense more open, he might have picked up some restive response from Copperhead as a stranger came too near. Too late, never mind.

In an alley in back of the buildings he closed with his quarry. The boy was crouched behind a woodpile, and not alone; a much larger and older companion—brother, friend, thief-boss?—knelt with him as they spread open the bedroll to examine their prize.

The big man was saying disgustedly, "This is just some girl's clothes. Why didn't you pinch those saddlebags, you fool?"

"That red brute of a horse tried to kick me, and people were looking," the boy replied in a surly tone. "Wait, what's that?"

The big man lifted the sharing knife sheath by its broken strap; the pouch swung, and his hand went toward the bone hilt.

"Your death, if you touch it," Dag snarled, coming up on them. "I'll see to that."

The boy took one look at him, yelped, and sprang away, casting a panicked glance over his shoulder as he ran. The big man, his eyes widening, shoved to his feet, hand closing on a stout log from the pile. It was plain that they were far past the point of lame explanations and apologies, sir, about mistaken ownership, even if the burly thief had possessed the wits and nerve to try to escape that way. He came around already swinging.

Dag flung up his arm to protect his face from a blow that would have caved it in. As it was, the oak log connected with his forearm with a sickening thud, and he was bashed by his own arm-plus-log so hard as to be knocked half off his feet. Hot agony burst in his forearm. No chance to go for his knife, but the hook-and-spring presently attached to his left arm cuff doubled as a weapon of no small menace; the big man ducked back in fright as Dag's return swing grazed his throat. Rapidly revising his chances against this unexpected unhanded reprisal—brighter than he looked?—the would-be thief dropped both knife pouch and log and galloped after his smaller partner.

Fawn and a party of three or four Lumpton locals rounded the corner as Dag staggered upright again. Quietly, he flipped a corner of the blanket over the leather pouch with a booted toe.

"Dag, are you all right?" Fawn cried in alarm. "Your nose is bleeding!"

Dag could feel a wet trickle over his lip, and licked at it, unmistakable iron tang. He tried to raise his hand to touch his throbbing face but found it would not work properly. Drawing breath through his teeth in a long hiss at the flaring pain, he searched his mind for curses and found none strong enough. His groundsense, turned in upon himself, left him in no doubt. He wheeled away, bent over, and spat blood and fury on the ground before turning back to her. "Nose is all right," he mumbled in frustrated wrath. "Right arm's broken. *Blight* it!"

13

Their hostelry in Lumpton Market turned out to be an elderly inn just off the straight road north from town. Fawn thought it a sad comedown from the fine hotel in Glassforge, for it was small and grubby, if not without a certain air of shabby comfort. Further, it demanded cash money even from patrollers. In summer, however, patrons were sent out back of the kitchen to eat their dinners on plank tables and benches under some graceful old black walnut trees overlooking the side road, much better than the dank common room. Looking around curiously, Fawn saw no other Lakewalkers here tonight, just a quartet of teamsters at one table intent on their beer and, beyond them, a farm couple busy with a pack of noisy young children. Even with his height, striking looks, and splinted arm in a sling, Dag drew only brief stares, and Fawn felt reassuringly unnoticed in his shadow.

Dag slumped onto his bench with an understandably tired grunt, and Fawn slid in at his right. She plucked loose the ties of the lumpy leather wrap he'd directed she bring from his saddlebag, unrolling it to find it contained an array of extra devices for his wrist cuff. "Goodness, what are all these?"

"This and that. Experiments, or things I don't use every day." As she stared in bewilderment and held up a wooden bolt anchoring a curved and edged metal piece looking like a small stirrup, he added, "That's a scraper. I spend a lot of time in the evening scraping hides, out on patrol. Boring as all get out, but one of the first jobs I took on after I got the arm harness. Forced me to strengthen the arm, which was good when I took up the bow."

The scullion who doubled as servingwoman plunked down mugs of beer and trotted back inside. With hook and splinted hand, Dag clumsily reached, winced, and fell back, and Fawn said, "Ah! The bonesetter *told* you not to try and use your hand. Five times when I was listening, and I don't know how many more while I was out of the room. I thought he was going to slap you at one point." The man had hardly needed Fawn's encouragement to bind Dag's arm with quelling thoroughness, having taken the measure of his aggravated patient very quickly. The barest tips of Dag's fingers stuck out beyond the cotton wrappings. "You just keep it down in that sling there. We need to figure out how we're to get along with all this."

Hurriedly, she held the mug to his lips; he grimaced, but drank thirstily. She managed not to splash him too badly when he nodded he was done, and whisked her handkerchief from her pocket to overtake his right arm up to mop his lips. "And if you use your bandages for a napkin they're going to stink long before six weeks are up, so don't."

He scowled sideways at her, ferociously.

"*And* if you keep looking at me like that, you're going to make me break out in giggles, and then you'll be throwing your boots at my head, and then where will we be?"

"No, I won't," he growled. "I need you to get the blasted boots off in the first place."

But the corner of his mouth curled up nonetheless. Fawn was so relieved she got up on one knee and kissed the curl, which made it curve up more.

He vented a long, apologetic sigh for his touchiness. "Third from the left, there" —he nodded to the leather wrap—"should be a sort of fork-spoon thing."

She pulled it out and examined it, an iron spoon with four short tines on the tip. "Ah, clever."

"I don't use it too often. A knife's usually better, if I have anything at the table but my hook or the social hand." That last was Dag's name for the wooden hand-in-glove, which seemed to have little use but disguise among strangers, and not a very effective one at that.

With a slight *clunk,* Dag set his wooden cuff against the table edge. "Try swapping it out."

Dag's most commonly used device, the hook with the clever little spring strip, was set in tight. Fawn, leaning in, had to take a better grip before she was able to twist it out. The eating tool replaced it more readily. "Oh, that's not too hard."

Their plates arrived, piled with carrots and mashed potatoes with cream gravy and a generous portion of pork chops. After an exchange of silent looks— Fawn could see Dag working to keep his frayed temper—she leaned over and efficiently cut his meat, leaving the rest to him. The fork-spoon worked tolerably well, although it did involve his extending his elbow awkwardly. Thoughtfully, she kept the beer coming. It might just have been getting a good hot meal into him after a too-long day, but he slowly relaxed. The stout scullion then brought thick wedges of cherry pie, which threatened to push relaxation into sleep right there on the benches.

Fawn said, "So . . . should we stay here and rest up tomorrow, or push on and rest at West Blue? Will you be able to ride so far?" He had ridden from the bonesetter's, his reins wrapped around his hook, but that had only been a mile.

"I've done more with worse. The powder will help." He'd prudently picked up what he said was a Lakewalker remedy for pain from the medicine shop before they'd left the town square. Fawn wasn't sure if the faint glaze in his eyes was from the drug or the ache in his arm; but on reflection, it was just as well the medicine didn't work better, or there would be no slowing him down at all. Confirming this, he stretched, and said, "I wouldn't mind pushing on. There's folks at Hickory Lake who can do things to help this heal faster."

"Is it set all right?" she asked anxiously.

"Oh, yes. That bonesetter might have been a ham-handed torturer, but he knew his trade. It'll heal straight."

Dag had called him much worse things than that during the setting, but the fellow had just grinned, evidently used to colorful invective from his patients. Possibly, Fawn thought, he collected the choice bits.

"If you don't knock it around." Fawn felt a little sick with anticipation of her homecoming. But if she had to do it at all, better to get it over with. Dag clearly thought it her duty, the right thing to do; and not even for Stupid Sunny and all her brothers put together would she risk Dag thinking her craven. *Even if I am.* "All right. We'll ride on."

Dag rubbed his chin with his left sleeve. "In that case, we'd best get our tales straight. I want to leave out the primed knife in front of your family, just as we did for my patrol all but Mari."

That seemed both fair and prudent. Fawn nodded.

"Anything else is up to you, but you have to tell me what you want."

She stared down at the red streaks and crumbs on her empty plate. "They don't know about me and Sunny. So they're going to be mad that I scared them for seemingly nothing, running off like that."

He leaned over and touched his lips to a red dent in her neck where one of the malice scabs had finally flaked off. "Not for nothing, Spark."

"Yeah, but they don't know much about malices, either."

"So," he said slowly, as if feeling his way, "if your Sunny has 'fessed up, you will have one situation, and if he hasn't, you'll have another."

"He's not my Sunny," Fawn said grumpily. "We were both real clear on that."

"Hm. Well, if you don't tell your folks why you really left, you'll have to make up some lie. This creates a tension and darkness in your ground that weakens a person, in my experience. I really don't see why you feel any need to protect Sunny. Seems to me he benefits more from you keeping this secret than you do."

Fawn's eyebrows rose. "The shame of the thing goes on the girl. *Used goods,* they call you. You can't get another suitor with good land, if word gets around you're no virgin. Though . . . I think a lot of girls do anyhow, so you really have to wonder."

"Farmers, eh." Dag pursed his lips. "Does the same apply to widows, then? Real ones, not grass ones."

Fawn colored at this reminder, though she had to smile a little. "Oh, no. Widows are a whole different matter. Widows, now . . . well, nobody can do as they please, really, there might be children, there might be no money, but widows hold their heads up fine and make their own way. Better if they're not poor, to be sure."

"So, ah . . . do you hanker after a suitor with good land, Spark?"

She sat up, startled. "Of course not! I want you."

He cocked an eyebrow at her. "So why are you worrying about this, again? Habit?"

"No!" She hesitated; her heart and voice fell. "I suppose . . . I thought we were a midsummer dream. I just keep trying real hard not to wake up. Stupid, I guess. Somewhere, sometime . . . someone will come along who won't let me keep you. Not for always."

He looked away, through the deep shade of the walnut trees and down the side road where dust from the recent passage of a pony cart still hung golden in the westering sun. "However difficult your family is, mine is going to be worse, and I expect to stand up to them. I won't lie, Spark; there are things that can take me from you, things I can't control. Death is always one." He paused. "Can't think of anything else right at the moment, though."

She gave a short, shaken nod, turning her face into his shoulder till she got her breath back.

He sighed. "Well, what you'll say to your people is not my choice. It's yours. But my recommendation is to tell as much truth as you can, save for the knife priming."

"How will we explain my going to your camp?"

"Your testimony to my captain is required in the death of the malice. Which is true. If they ask for more, I'll get up on my tall horse and say it's Lakewalker business."

Fawn shook her head. "They won't want to let me go off with you."

"We'll see. You can't plan other people's actions; only your own. If you try, you just end up facing the wrong way for the trouble you actually get. Hey." He bent down and kissed her hair. "If they chain you to the wall with iron bolts, I undertake to break you out."

"With no hands?"

"I'm very ingenious. And if they don't chain you, then you can walk away. All it takes is courage, and I know you have that."

She smiled, comforted, but admitted, "Not in my heart, not really. They . . . I don't know how to explain this. They have ways of making me smaller."

"I don't know how they'll be, but you are not the same as you were. One way or another, things will be different than you expect."

Truly.

Exhausted, hurting, and uneasy, they did not make love that night, but held each other close in the stuffy inn chamber. Sleep was slow in coming.

The summer sun was again slanting west when Fawn halted her mare and sat staring up the hill where a descending farm lane intersected the road. It had been a twenty-mile ride from Lumpton Market, and Dag had to admit, if only to himself, that his right arm was swollen and aching more than he cared for, and that his left, picking up an unaccustomed load, was not at its best either. They had taken the straight road north along the spreading ridge between the rivers for almost fifteen miles before turning west. Descending into the valley of the western branch, they'd crossed at a stony ford before turning north once more along the winding river road. A shortcut, Fawn claimed, to avoid doubling back a mile to the village of West Blue with its wagon bridge and mill.

And now she was home. Her ground was a complicated swirl at the moment, but it hardly took groundsense to see that her foremost emotion was not joy.

He kneed his horse up next to hers. "I think I'd like my social hand, to start," he murmured.

She nodded, and leaned over to open his belt pouch and swap out his hook for the less useful but less startling false hand. She paused to recomb her own hair and retie it in the curly horsetail with the bright ribbon, then stood up in her stirrups to take the comb to him as well; he lowered his head for the, in his unvoiced opinion, useless attempt to make him look his best. He perfectly understood her determination to walk back into her home looking proud and fine, not beaten and bedraggled. He just wished for her sake that he could look more the part of a valiant protector instead of something the cat had dragged in. *You've looked worse, old patroller. Go on.*

Fawn swallowed and turned Grace into the lane, which wound up the slope for almost a quarter mile, lined on both sides with the ubiquitous dry-stone walls. Past a grove of sugar maple, walnut, and hickory trees, a dilapidated old barn appeared on the right, and a larger, newer barn on the left. Above the new barn lay a couple of outbuildings, including a smokehouse; faint gray curls of smoke leaked from its eaves, and Dag's nose caught the pleasant tang of smoldering hickory. A covered well sat at the top of the yard, and, on around to the right, the large old farmhouse loomed.

The central core of it was a two-story rectangle of blocky yellowish stone, with a porch and front door in the middle overlooking the river valley. On the far north end, a single-story add-on looked as though it contained two rooms. On the near end, an excavation was in progress, with piles of new stone waiting, evidently an addition planned to match the other. On the west, another add-on girdled with a long, covered porch ran the length of the house, clearly the kitchen. No one was in sight.

"Suppertime," said Fawn. "They must all be in the kitchen."

"Eight people," said Dag, whose groundsense left him in no doubt.

Fawn took a long, long breath, and dismounted. She tied both their horses to the back porch rail and led Dag around to the steps. Her lighter and his heavier tread echoed briefly on the porch floor. Top and bottom halves of a double door were open wide and hooked to bolts in the wall, but beyond them was another, lighter doorframe with a gauze screen. Fawn pushed the screen door open and slipped in, holding it for him. He let his wooden hand rest briefly on her shoulder before dropping it to his side.

At a long table filling most of the right-hand half of the room, eight people turned and stared. Dag swiftly tried to match faces with the names and stories he'd been given. Aunt Nattie could be instantly identified, a very short, stout woman with disordered curly gray locks and eyes as milky as pearls, her head now cocked with listening. The four brothers were harder to sort, but he thought he could determine Fletch, bulky and oldest, Reed and Rush, the nonidentical twins, brown-haired and brown-eyed, and ash-haired and blue-eyed respectively, and Whit, black-haired like Fawn, skinny, and youngest but for her. A plump young woman seated next to Fletch defeated his tutorial. Fawn's parents, Sorrel and Tril Bluefield, were no hardship to identify, a graying man at the table's head who'd stood up so fast his chair had banged over, and on the near end a short, middle-aged woman stumbling out of her seat shrieking.

Fawn's parents descended upon her in such a whirl of joy, relief, and rage that Dag had to close off his groundsense lest he be overwhelmed. The brothers, behind, were mostly grinning with relief, and Aunt Nattie was asking urgently, "What? Is that Fawn, you say? Told you she wasn't dead! About time!"

Fawn, her face nearly unreadable, endured being hugged, kissed, and shaken in equal measure; the dampness in her blinking eyes was not, Dag thought, caught only from the emotions around her. Dag stiffened a little when her father, after hugging her off her feet, put her down and then threatened to beat her; but while his paternal relief was very real, it seemed his threats were not, for Fawn didn't flinch in the least from them.

"Where have you *been*, girl?" her mother's voice finally rose over the babble to demand.

Fawn backed up a trifle, raised her chin, and said in a rush, "I went to

Glassforge to look for work, and I may have found some too, but first I have to go with Dag, here, to Hickory Lake to help make his report to his captain about the blight bogle we killed."

Her family gazed at Fawn as though she'd started raving in a fever; Dag suspected the only part they'd really caught was *Glassforge*.

Fawn went on a bit breathlessly, before they could start up again, "Mama, Papa, this here is my friend, Dag Redwing Hickory." She gave her characteristic little knee-dip, and pulled Dag forward. He nodded, trying to find some pleasantly neutral expression for his face. "He's a Lakewalker patroller."

"How de' do," said Dag politely and generally.

A silence greeted this, and a lot more staring, necks cranked back. Short stature ran in Fawn's family, evidently.

Confirming Dag's guess, Fawn's mother, Tril, said, "Glassforge? Why would you want to go there to look for work? There's plenty of work right here!"

"*Which* you left on all of us," Fletch put in unhelpfully.

"And wouldn't Lumpton Market have been a lot closer?" said Whit in a tone of judicious critique.

"Do you *know* how much trouble you caused, girl?" said Papa Bluefield.

"Yeah," said Reed, or maybe Rush—no, Rush, ash-headed, check—"when you didn't show for dinner market-day night, we figured you were out dawdling and daydreaming in the woods as usual, but when you didn't show by bedtime, Papa made us all go out with torches and look and call. The barn, the privy, the woods, down by the river—it would have saved a deal of stumbling around in the dark and yelling if Mama had counted your clothes a day sooner!"

Fawn's lip had given an odd twitch at something in this, which Dag determined to ask about later. "I am sorry you were troubled," she said, in a carefully formal tone. "I should have written a note, so's you needn't have worried I'd met with an accident."

"How would *that* have helped for worrying, fool girl!" Fawn's mother wept a bit more. "Thoughtless, selfish . . ."

"Papa made *me* ride all the way to Aunt Wren's, in the idea you might have gone there, and he made Rush ride to Lumpton asking after you," Reed said.

A spate more of complaint and venting from all parties followed this. Fawn endured without argument, and Dag held his tongue. The ill words were not ill meant, and Fawn, apparently a native speaker of this strange family dialect, seemed to take them in their spirit and let the barbs roll off, mostly. Her eyes flashed resentment only once, when the plump girl beside Fletch chimed in with some support of one of his more snappish comments. But Fawn said only, "Hello, Clover. Nice to see you, too," which reduced the girl to nonplussed silence.

Notably missing was any word about Sunny Sawman. So Fawn's judgment on that score was proven shrewd. Too early to guess at the consequences . . .

Dag was not sure how long the uproar would have continued in this vein, except that Aunt Nattie levered herself up, grasped a walking stick, and stumped around the table to Fawn's side. "Let me see you, girl," she said quietly, and Fawn hugged her—the first hug Dag had seen going the other way—and let the blind woman run her hands over her face. "Huh," said Aunt Nattie. "Huh. Now introduce me to your patroller friend. It's been a long time since I've met a Lakewalker."

"Dag," said Fawn, reverting to her breathless, anxious formality, "This is my aunt Nattie that I've told you about. She'd like to touch you, if that's all right."

"Of course," said Dag.

The little woman stumped nearer, reached up, and bounced her fingers uncertainly off his collarbone. "Goodness, boy, where *are* you?"

"Say something," Fawn whispered urgently.

"Um . . . up here, Aunt Nattie."

Her hand went higher, to touch his chin; he obligingly bent his head. "Way up there!" she marveled. The knobby, dry fingers brushed firmly over his features, pausing at the slight heat of the bruises on his face from yesterday, circling his cheekbones and chin in inexplicable approval, tracing his lips and eyelids. Dag realized with a slight shock that this woman possessed a rudimentary groundsense, possibly developed in the shadow of her lifelong blindness, and he let his reach out to touch hers.

Her breath drew in. "Ah, Lakewalker, right enough."

"Ma'am," Dag responded, not knowing what else to say.

"Good voice, too," Nattie observed, Dag wasn't sure who to. She stopped short of checking his teeth like a horse's, although by this time Dag would scarcely have blinked at it. She felt down his body, her touch hesitating briefly at the splints and sling; her eyebrows went up as she felt his arm harness through his shirt and briefly gripped his wooden hand. But she added only, "Nice deep voice."

"Have you eaten?" asked Tril Bluefield, and when Fawn explained no, they'd ridden all day from Lumpton, shifted to what Dag guessed was her more normal motherly mode, driving a couple of her sons to set chairs and places. She put Fawn next to herself, and Fawn insisted Dag be placed on her own right, "On account of I promised to help him out with his broken arm." They settled at last. Clover, finally introduced as Fletch's betrothed, was also drafted to help, plopping plates and cups of what smelled like cider down in front of them. Dag, by this time very thirsty, was most interested in the drink. The food was a well-cooked stew, and Dag silently rejoiced at being confronted with something he could handle by himself, though he wondered who in the household had bad teeth.

"The fork-spoon, I think," he murmured in Fawn's ear, and she nodded and rummaged it out of his belt pouch.

"What happened to your arm?" asked Rush, across from them.

"Which one?" asked Dag. And endured the inevitable moment of rustling, craning, and stunned stares as Fawn calmly unscrewed his hand and replaced it with the more useful tool. "Thank you, Spark. Drink?" He smiled down at her as she lifted the cup to his lips. It was fresh cider, very tart from new summer apples. "And thanks again."

"You're welcome, Dag."

He licked the spare drop off his lower lip, so she didn't have to chase it with her napkin, yet.

Rush finally found his voice, more or less. "Er . . . I was going to ask about the, er, sling . . ."

Fawn answered briskly, "A sneak thief at Lumpton Market lifted my bedroll yesterday. Dag got it back, but his arm was broken in the fight before the thieves got scared and ran off. Dag gave a real good description to the Lumpton folks, though, so they might catch the fellows." Her jaw set just a trifle. "So I kind of owe him for the arm."

"Oh," said Rush. Reed and Whit stared across the table with renewed, if daunted, interest.

Tril Bluefield, looking hungrily and now more carefully at her restored daughter, frowned and let her hand drift to Fawn's cheek where the four parallel gouges were now paling pink scars. "What are those marks?"

She glanced sidelong at Dag; he shrugged, *Go on*. She said, "That's where the mud-man hit me."

"The what?" said her mother, face screwing up.

"A . . . sort of bandit," Fawn revised this. "Two bandits grabbed me off the road near Glassforge."

"What? What happened?" her mother gasped. The assorted brothers, too, sat up; on Dag's right, he could feel Fletch tense.

"Not too much," said Fawn. "They roughed me up, but Dag, who was tracking them, came up just then and, um. Ran them off." She glanced at him again, and he lowered his eyelids in thanks. He did not especially wish to begin his acquaintance with her family with a listing of all the dead bodies he'd left around Glassforge, the human ones at least. Far too many human ones, this last round. "That's how we first met. His patrol had been called to Glassforge to deal with the bandits and the blight bogle."

Rush asked, "What happened to the bandits after that?"

Fawn turned to Dag, who answered simply, "They were dealt with." He applied himself to his stew, good plain farm food, in the hope of avoiding further expansion on this subject.

Fawn's mother bent her head, eyes narrowing; her hand went out again, this time to the left side of Fawn's neck and the deep red dent and three ugly black scabs. "Then what are those nasty-looking things?"

"Um . . . well, that was later."

"*What* was later?"

In a desperately bright voice, Fawn replied, "That's where the blight bogle lifted me up. They make those sorts of marks—their touch is deadly. It was big. How big, would you say, Dag? Eight feet tall, maybe?"

"Seven and a half, I'd guess," he said blandly. "About four hundred pounds. Though I didn't have the best vantage. Or light."

Reed said, in a tone of growing disbelief, "So what happened to this supposed blight bogle, if it was so deadly?"

Fawn's look begged help, so Dag replied, "It was dealt with, too."

"Go on, Fawn," said Fletch scornfully. "You can't expect *us* to swallow your tall tales!"

Dag let his voice go very soft. "Are you calling your sister a liar . . . sir?" He let the *and me?* hang in implication.

Fletch's thick brows wrinkled in honest bewilderment; he was not a man sensitive to implication, either, Dag guessed. "She's my sister. I can call her anything I want!"

Dag drew breath, but Fawn whispered, "Dag, let it go. It doesn't matter."

He did not yet speak this family dialect, he reminded himself. He had worried about how to conceal the strange accident with the sharing knife; he'd not imagined such feeble curiosity or outright disbelief. It was not in his present interest—or capacity—to bang Bluefield heads together and bellow, *Your sister's courage saved my life, and dozens, maybe thousands, more. Honor her!* He let it go and nodded for more cider.

Blatantly changing the subject, Fawn asked Clover after the progress of her wedding plans, listening to the lengthy reply with well-feigned interest. The addition in progress on the south end of the house, it appeared, was intended for the soon-to-be-newlyweds. The true purpose of the question—camouflage—was revealed to Dag when Fawn added casually, "Anyone hear from the Sawmans since Saree's wedding?"

"Not too much," said Reed. "Sunny's spent a lot of time at his brother-in-law's place, helping clear stumps from the new field."

Fawn's mother gave her a narrow-eyed look. "His mama tells me Sunny's betrothed to Violet Stonecrop as of midsummer. Hope you're not disappointed. I thought you might be getting kind of sweet on him at one point."

Whit piped up, in a whiny, practiced brotherly chant, "Fawn is sweet on Suh-nee, Fawn is sweet on Suh-nee . . ."

Dag cringed at the spate of deathly blackness that ran through Fawn's ground. *He does not know,* he reminded himself. *None of them do.* Although he would not have cast bets on Tril Bluefield's unvoiced suspicions, because she now said in a flat voice unlike any he'd yet heard from her, brooking no argument, "Stop that, Whit. You'd think you were twelve."

Dag could see the little ripple in Fawn's jaw as she unset her teeth. "Not sweet in the least. I think Violet deserves better."

Whit looked disappointed at not having drawn a more spectacular rise out of his sister from his expert lure but, glancing at his mother, did not resume his heckling.

"Perhaps," Dag suggested gently, "we should go see to Grace and Copperhead."

"Who?" asked Rush.

"Miss Bluefield's horse, and mine. They've been waiting patiently out there."

"What?" said Reed. "Fawn doesn't have a horse!"

"Hey, Fawn, where'd *you* get a horse?"

"Can I ride your horse?"

"No." Fawn thrust back her chair. Dag rose more quietly with her.

"Where *did* you get a horse, Fawn?" asked Papa Bluefield curiously, staring anew at Dag.

Fawn stood very straight. "She was my share for helping deal with the blight bogle. Which Fletch here doesn't believe in. I must have ridden all the way from Glassforge on a wish horse, huh?"

She tossed her head and marched out. Dag cast a polite nod of farewell in the general direction of the table, thought to add a spoken, "Good evening, Aunt Nattie," and followed. Behind him, he could hear her father's growl, "Reed, go help your sister and that fellow with their horses." Which in fact launched a general migration of Bluefields onto the porch to examine the new horse.

Grace was exhaustively discussed. At last Dag swapped back for his hook and led his own horse in an escape to the old barn, where spare stalls were to be found. He lingered looking over the stall partition, keeping a light contact with his groundsense so the gelding wouldn't snake around and attempt to savage Reed, his unfamiliar groom. Copperhead was not named for his chestnut color, despite appearances. When both horses were at last safely rubbed down, watered, and fed, Dag walked back to the house through the sunset light with Fawn, temporarily out of earshot of the rest of her relations.

"Well," she said under her breath, "that could have gone worse."

"Really?" said Dag.

"Really."

"I'll take your word. Truth to tell, I'm finding your family a bit strange. My nearest kin don't often like what I have to say, but they certainly *hear* what I have to say, and not something else altogether."

"They're better one at a time than in a bunch like that."

"Hm. So . . . what was that about market-day night?"

"What?"

"When Rush said they'd missed you market-day night."

"Oh. Nothing much. Except that I left market-day morning while it was still dark. Wonder where they thought I was all day?"

A number of Bluefields had collected in the front parlor, including Aunt Nattie, now plying a drop spindle, and Fawn's mother. Dag set down his saddlebags and let Fawn unpack her gifts. Fletch, about to escort his betrothed home to her nearby farm, paused to watch as well.

Tril held the sparkling glass bowl up to the light of an oil lamp in astonishment. "You really did go to Glassforge!"

Fawn, who had wobbled all evening between trying to put on a good show and what seemed to Dag a most unfamiliar silent shrinking, said only, "That's what I told you, Mama."

Fawn pressed the corked scent bottle into her aunt's hands and urged her to splash some on her wrists, which, smiling agreeably, she did. "Very pretty, lovie, but this sort of foolery is for courtin' girls to entice their boys, not for lumpy old women like me. Better you should give it to Clover."

"That's Fletcher's job," said Fawn, with a more Spark-like edged grin at her brother. "Anyhow, all sorts of folks wear it in Glassforge—patroller men and women both, for some."

Reed, hovering, snorted at the idea of men wearing scent, but Nattie showed willing and eased Dag's heart by splashing a bit more on both herself and her younger sister Tril, and some on Fawn as well. "There! Sweet of you to think of me, lovie."

It was growing dark outside. The boys dispersed to various evening chores, and Clover made farewells to her prospective in-laws. The two young women, Fawn and Clover, eyed each other a little stiffly as Clover made more congratulations on Fawn's safe return, and Dag wondered anew at the strangeness of farmer customs. A Lakewalker only-girlchild would have been the chief inheritor of her family's tent, but that position here was apparently held by Fletch; and not Fawn but Clover would take Tril Bluefield's place as female head of this household in due time. Leaving Fawn to go . . . where?

"I suppose," said Papa Bluefield a trifle grudgingly, "if your friend here has a bedroll, he could lay it in the loft. Keep an eye on his horse."

"Don't be daft, Sorrel," Aunt Nattie spoke up unexpectedly. "The man can't climb the loft ladder with that broken arm."

"He needs to be close by me, so's I can help him," said Fawn firmly. "Dag can lay his bedroll in Nattie's weaving room."

"Good idea, Fawn," said Nattie cheerily.

Fawn slept in with her aunt; the boys shared rooms upstairs, as did their parents. Papa Bluefield looked as though he was thinking hard, suddenly, about the implications of leaving Fawn and Dag downstairs with a blind chaperone. And then—inevitably—of the implications of how long Dag and Fawn had been on the road together. Did he know anything about his aging sister-in-law's groundsense?

"I'll try harder not to cut your throat with your razor tomorrow, Dag," Fawn said.

"I've lost more blood for less," he assured her.

"We should likely try to get on the road early."

"What?" said Papa Bluefield, coming out of his frowning cogitation. "You're not going anywhere, girl!"

She turned to him, stiffening up tight. "I told you first thing, Papa. I have an obligation to give witness."

"Are you stupid, Fawn!"

Dag caught his breath at the hard black rip through Fawn's ground; his eyes went to Nattie, but she gave no visible reaction, though her face was turned toward the pair.

Papa Bluefield went on, "Your obligations are here, for all you've run off and turned your back on them this past month! You've had enough gallivanting for a while, believe you me!"

Dag interposed quietly and quite truthfully, "Actually, Spark, my arm's not doing all that well tonight. I wouldn't mind a day or two to rest up."

She turned anxious eyes up at him, as if not sure whether she was hearing support or betrayal. He gave her a small, reassuring nod.

Papa Bluefield gave Dag a sideways look. "You'd be welcome to go on, if you've a need."

"*Papa!*" snapped Fawn, gyrating back to something not strained show, but blazingly sincere. "The idea! Dag saved my life *three* times, twice at great risk to his own, once from the bandits, once from the malice—the bogle—and once again the night after the bogle . . . hurt me, because I would have bled to death right there in the woods if he hadn't helped me. I will *not* have him turned out on the road by himself with two bad arms! For shame! Shame on this house if you dare!" She actually stamped her foot; the parlor floor sounded like a drum.

Papa Bluefield had stepped backward. His wife was staring at Dag with eyes wide, holding the glass bowl tightly. Nattie . . . was amazingly hard to read, but she had a strange little smile on her lips.

"Oh." Papa Bluefield cleared his throat. "You hadn't exactly made that plain, Fawn."

Fawn said wearily, "How could I? No one would let me finish a story without telling me I must be making things up."

Her father glanced at Dag. "*He's* a quiet one."

Dag could not touch his temple; he had to settle for a short nod. "Thinking. Sir."

"Are you, now?"

It was not, in the Bluefield household, apparently possible to *finish* a debate. But when the squabbling finally died into assorted mumblings, drifting away up stairs or down halls in the dark, Dag ended up with his bedroll set down beside Aunt Nattie's loom, with an impressive pile of quilts and pillows arranged for his ease. He could hear the shortest two women of the family rustling around in the bedroom beyond in low-voiced preparation for bed, and then the creak of the bed frames as they settled down.

Dag disposed his throbbing arm awkwardly, grateful for the pillows. Save for the night on the Horsefords' kitchen floor, he had never slept inside a farmer's house, certainly not as an invited guest, though his patrols had sometimes been put up, by arrangement, in farmers' barns. This beat a drafty hayloft with snow sifting in all hollow. Before he'd met Fawn's family, he would scarcely have understood why she would want to leave such comforts.

He wasn't sure if it was worse to be loved yet not valued than valued but not loved, but surely it was better to be both. For the first time, he began to think a farm's brightest treasure need not be furtively stolen; it might be honestly won. But the hopes forming in his mind would have to wait on tomorrow for their testing.

14

The next morning passed quietly. To Fawn's eye Dag looked tired, moved slowly, and said little, and she thought his arm was probably troubling him more than he let on. She found herself caught up, will or nil, in the never-ending rhythm of farm chores; cows took no holidays even for homecomings. She and Dag did take a walk around the place in the midmorning, and she pointed out the scenes and sites from her tales of childhood. But her guess about his arm was confirmed when, after lunch, he took some more of the pain powder that had helped him through yesterday's long ride. He slipped out—wordlessly—to the front porch overlooking the river valley and sat leaning against the house wall, nursing the arm and thinking . . . whatever he was thinking about all this. Fawn found herself assigned to stirring apple butter in the kitchen, and while you are about it, dear, why don't you make up some pies for supper?

She was fluting the edge of the second one and reluctantly contemplating building up the fire under the hearth oven, which would make the hot room hotter still, when Dag came in.

"Drink?" she guessed.

"Please . . ."

She held the water ladle to his lips; when he'd drained it, he added, "There's a young fellow who's tethered his horse in your front woods. I believe he imagines he's sneaking up the hill in secret. His ground seems pretty un-settled, but I don't think he's a house robber."

"Did you see him?" she asked, then halted, considering what an absurd question that sounded if you didn't know Dag. And then how well she *had* come to know Dag, that it should fall so readily from her lips.

"Just a glimpse."

"Was he bright blond?"

"Yes."

She sighed. "Sunny Sawman. I'll bet Clover told folks that I'm back, and he's come to see for himself if it's true."

"Why not ride openly up the lane?"

She flushed a little, not that he'd likely notice in this heat, and admitted, "He used to sneak up to steal kisses from me that way, from time to time. He was afraid of my brothers finding out, I think."

"Well, he's afraid of something." He hesitated. "Do you want me to stay?"

She tilted her head, frowning. "I better talk to him alone. He won't be truthful if he's in front of anyone." She glanced up uneasily at him. "Maybe . . . don't go far?"

He nodded; she didn't seem to need to explain further. He stepped into Aunt Nattie's weaving room, flanking the kitchen, and set the door open. She heard him dragging a chair behind it, and the creak of wood and possibly of Dag as he settled into it.

A few moments later, footsteps sounded on the porch, attempted tiptoe; they paused outside the kitchen window above the drainboard. She stepped up and stared without pleasure at Sunny's face, craning around and peering in. He jerked back as he saw her, then whispered, "Are you alone?"

"For now."

He nodded and nipped in through the back door. She regarded him, testing her feelings. Straw-gold hair still curled around his head in soft locks, his eyes were still bright blue, his skin fair and fine and summer-flushed, his shoulders broad, his muscular arms, tanned where his sleeves were rolled up, coated with a shimmer of gold hairs that had always seemed to make him gleam in sunlight. His physical charm was unchanged, and she wondered how it was that she was now so wholly unmoved by it, who had once trembled beneath it in a wheatfield in such wild, flattered elation.

His daughter would have been a pretty girl. The thought twisted in her like a knife, and she fought to set it aside.

"Where is everyone?" he asked cautiously, looking around again.

"Papa and the boys are up cutting hay, Mama is out giving the chickens a dusting with that antilice powder she got from your uncle, and Aunt Nattie's bad knee hurt so she went to lie down after lunch."

"Nattie's blind, she won't see me anyhow. Good." He loomed nearer, staring hard at her. No—just at her belly. She resisted an impulse to slump and push it out.

His head cocked. "As little as you are, I'd have thought you'd be popping out by now. Clover sure would have bleated about it if she'd noticed."

"You talk to her?"

"Saw her at noon, down in the village." He shifted restlessly. "It's all the talk there, you turning up again." He turned again, scowling. "So, did you come back to fuss at me some more? It won't do you any good. I'm betrothed to Violet now."

"So I heard," said Fawn, in a flat voice. "I actually hadn't planned to see you at all. We wouldn't have stayed on today except for Dag's broken arm."

"Yeah, Clover said you had some Lakewalker fellow trailing you. Tall as a flagpole, with one arm wooden and the other broke, who didn't hardly say boo. Sounds about useless. You been running around alone with him for three or four weeks, seemingly." He wet his lips. "So, what's your plan? Switching horses in the middle of the river? Going to tell him the baby is his and hope he can't count too good?"

A cast-iron frying pan was sitting on the drainboard. Swung in an appropriate arc, it would just fit Sunny's round face, Fawn thought through a red haze. "No."

"I'm not playing your little game, Fawn," said Sunny tightly. "You won't pin this on me. I meant what I said." His hands were trembling slightly. But then, so were hers.

Her voice went, if possible, even flatter. "Well, you can put your mind and your nasty tongue to rest. I miscarried down near Glassforge the day the blight bogle nearly killed me. So there's nothing left to pin on anyone, except bad memories."

His breath of relief was visible and audible; he squeezed his eyes shut with it. The tension in the room seemed to drop by half. She thought Sunny must have gone into a flying panic when he'd heard of her return, watching his comfortable little world teeter, and felt grimly recompensed. *Her* world had been turned upside down. But if she could now turn it back upright, make all her misery not have been, at the cost of losing all she'd learned on the road to Glassforge—would she?

She could not, she thought, in all fairness judge Sunny for acting as though his daughter weren't real to him; she'd scarcely seemed real to Fawn a deal of the time either, after all. She asked instead, "So where did you think I'd gone?"

He shrugged. "I thought at first you might have thrown yourself in the river. Gave me a turn, for a while."

She tossed her head. "But not enough of one to do anything about it, seemingly."

"What would there have been to do at that point? It seemed like the sort of stupid thing you'd do when you get a mad on. You always did have a temper. I remember how your brothers'd get you so wound up you could scarcely breathe for screaming, sometimes, till your pa'd tear his hair and come beat you for making such awful noise. Then the word got around that some of your clothes had gone missing, which made it seem you'd run off, since not even you would take three changes to go drowning. Your folks all looked, but I guess not far enough."

"You didn't help look then, either, I take it."

"Do *I* look stupid? I didn't want to find you! You got yourself into this fix, you could get yourself out."

"Yeah, that's what I figured." Fawn bit her lip.

Silence. More staring.

Just go away, you awful lout. "I haven't forgotten what you said to me that night, Sunny Sawman. You aren't welcome in my sight. In case you'd any doubt."

He shrugged irritably. His golden brows drew together over his snub nose. "I figured the blight bogle was a tall tale. What really happened?"

"Bogles are real enough. One touched me. Here and there." She fingered her neck where the dents glowed an angry red, and, reluctantly, laid her palm over her belly. "Lakewalkers make special knives to kill malices—that's their name for blight bogles. Dag had one. Between us, we did for the bogle, but it was too late for the child. It was almost too late for the two of us, but not quite."

"Oh, magic knives, now, as well as magic monsters? Sure, I believe that. Or maybe some of those secret Lakewalker medicines did the job, and the rest is a nice tale to cover it, make you look good in front of your family, eh?" He moved closer to her. She moved back.

"They don't even know I was pregnant. I didn't tell them that part." She drew a long breath. "Do you really care which, so long as it's not on you? Feh!" She gripped her hair, then drew her hands down hard over her face. "You know, I really don't give two pennies what you think as long as you go think it somewhere else." Aunt Nattie had once remarked that the opposite of love was not hate, but indifference. Fawn felt she was beginning to see the point of that.

Sunny edged closer again; she could feel his breath stir the sweat-dampened hairs on her neck. "So . . . have you been letting that patroller fellow poke you? Does your family know *that*?"

Fawn's breath clogged in rage. She would *not* scream . . . "After a *miscarriage*? You got no brains at all, Sunny Sawman!"

He did hesitate at that, doubt flickering in his blue eyes.

"Besides," she went on, "you're marrying Violet Stonecrop. Are you poking her yet?"

His lips drew back in something like a smile, except that it was devoid of humor. He stepped closer still. "I was right. You *are* a little slut." And grinned in countertriumph at the fury she knew was reddening her face. "Don't give me that scowl," he added, lifting a hand to squeeze her breast. "I *know* how easy you are."

Her fingers groped for the frying-pan handle.

Long footsteps sounded from the weaving room; Sunny jumped back hurriedly.

"Hello, Spark," said Dag. "Any more of that cider around?"

"Sure, Dag," she said, backing away from Sunny and escaping across the room to the crock on the shelf. She shifted the lid and drew a cup, willing her hands to stop shaking.

Somehow, Dag was now standing between her and Sunny. "Caller?" he inquired, with a nod at Sunny. Sunny looked as though he was furiously wondering whether Dag had just come in, if they had been overheard, and if the latter, how incriminatingly much.

"This here's Sunny Sawman," said Fawn. "He's leaving. Dag Redwing Hickory, a Lakewalker patroller. He's staying."

Sunny, looking unaccustomedly up, gave a wary nod. Dag looked back down without a whole lot of expression one way or another.

"Interestin' to meet you at last, Sunny," said Dag. "I've heard a lot about you. All true, seemingly."

Sunny's mouth opened and closed—shocked that his slanderous threats had failed to silence Fawn? Well, he had only his own mouth to blame now. He looked toward the weaving room, which had no other exit except into Nattie and Fawn's bedroom, and did not come up with a reply.

Dag continued coolly, "So . . . Sunny . . . has anyone ever offered to cut out your tongue and feed it to you?"

Sunny swallowed. "No." He might have been trying for a bold tone, but it came out rather a croak.

"I'm surprised," said Dag. He gently scratched the side of his nose with his hook, a quiet warning, Fawn thought, if both unobserved and unheeded by Sunny.

"Are you trying to start something?" asked Sunny, recovering his belligerence.

"Alas." Dag indicated his broken arm with a slight movement of the sling. "I'll have to take you up later."

Sunny's eyes brightened as the apparent helplessness of the patroller dawned on him. "Then maybe you'd better keep a still tongue in *your* head till then, Lakewalker. Ha! Only Fawn would be fool enough to pick a cripple for a bullyboy!"

Dag's eyes thinned to gold slits as Fawn cringed. In that same level, affable tone, he murmured, "Changed my mind. I'll take you up now. Spark, you said this fellow was leaving. Open the door for him, would you?"

Plainly unable to imagine what Dag could possibly do to him, Sunny set his teeth, planted his legs, and glowered. Dag stood quite still. Confused, Fawn hastily set down the cup, slopping cider on the table; she swung the screen door inward and held it.

When Dag moved, his speed was shocking. She caught only a glimpse of him swerving half-around Sunny, his leg coming up hard behind Sunny's knees, and his left arm whipping around with a wicked whir and glint of his hook.

Suddenly Sunny was flailing forward, mouth agape, lifted by Dag's hook through the seat of his trousers. His feet churned but barely touched the floor; he looked like someone tumbling on ice. Three long Dag-strides, a loud ripping noise, and Sunny was sailing through the air in truth, headfirst all the way over the porch boards to land beyond the steps in an awkward heap, haunches up, face scraping the dirt.

It was partly terrorized relief that Dag hadn't just torn Sunny's throat out with his hook as calmly as he'd slain that mud-man, but Fawn burst into a shriek of laughter. She clapped her hand across her mouth and stared at the ridiculously cheering sight of Sunny's drawers flapping through the new vent in his britches.

Sunny twisted around and glared up, his face flushing a dull, mottled red, then scrambled to his feet, fists clenching. Between the dirt and the curses filling his mouth his spluttering was nearly incoherent, but the general sense of *I'll get you, Lakewalker! I'll get you both!* came through clearly enough, and Fawn's breath caught in new alarm.

"Best bring a few friends," Dag recommended dryly. "If you have any." Aside from the flaring of his nostrils, he seemed barely winded.

Sunny took two steps up onto the porch, but then veered back uncertainly as that hook came quietly to the fore. Fawn darted for the frying pan. As Sunny hovered in doubt, his head jerked up at a thumping and shuffling sounding from the weaving room—blind Aunt Nattie with her cane. She had risen from her nap at last. Sunny stared wildly around, tripped backward down the steps, turned, and fled around the side of the house.

"You're right, Spark," Dag said, closing the screen door again. "He doesn't much care for witnesses. You can sort of see why."

Nattie wandered into the kitchen. "Hello, Fawn, lovie. Hello, Dag. My, that apple butter smells good." Her face turned, following the retreating footsteps rounding the house and fading. "Young fool," she added reflectively. "Sunny always thinks if I can't see him, I can't hear him. You have to wonder, really you do."

Fawn gulped, dropped the pan on the table, and flew into Dag's embrace. He wrapped his left arm around her in a reassuring hug. Aunt Nattie's head tilted toward them, a smile touching her lips. "Thank you kindly for that bit o' housecleaning, patroller."

"My pleasure, Aunt Nattie. Here, now." Dag folded Fawn closer. "For what it's worth, Spark, he was more afraid of you than you were of him." He added reflectively, "Sort of like a snake, that way."

She gave a shaken giggle, and his grip eased. "I was about to hit him with the frying pan, just before you came in."

"Thought something like that might be up. I was having a few daydreams along that line myself."

"Too bad you couldn't really have cut his tongue out . . . " She paused. "Was that a joke or not? I'm not too sure sometimes about patroller humor."

"Eh," he said, sounding faintly wistful. "Not, in any case, currently practical. Though I suppose I'm right glad to see Sunny doesn't believe any of those ugly rumors about Lakewalkers being black sorcerers."

Her trembling diminished, but her brows pinched as she thought back. "I'm so glad you were there. Though I wish your arm wasn't broken. Is it all right?" She touched the sling in worry.

"That wasn't especially good for it, but I haven't unset it. We're lucky for your aunt Nattie and Sunny's, ah, sudden shyness."

She drew back to stare up at his serious face, her eyes questioning, and he went on, "See, despite whatever hog butchering he's done, Sunny's never been in a lethal fight. I've been in no other kind since I was younger than him. He's used to puppy scraps, the sort you have with brothers or cousins or friends or, in any case, folks you're going to have to go on living with. Age, weight, youth, muscle, would all count against me in that sort of scuffle, even without a broken arm. If you truly want him dead, I'm your man; if you want less, it's trickier."

She sighed and leaned her head against his chest. "I don't want him dead. I just want him behind me. Miles and years. I suppose I just have to wait for the years. I still think of him every day, and I don't *want* to. Dead would be even worse, for that."

"Wise Spark," he murmured.

Her nose wrinkled in doubt. How seriously had he *meant* that lethal offer, to be so relieved that she hadn't taken him up on it? Remembering, she fetched him his drink, which he accepted with a smile of thanks.

Nattie had drifted to the hearth to stir the apple butter which, by the smell, was on the verge of scorching. Now she tapped the wooden spoon on the pot rim to shake off the excess, set it aside, turned back, and said, "You're a smart man, patroller."

"Oh, Nattie," said Fawn dolefully. "How much of that awfulness did you hear?"

"Pretty much all, lovie." She sighed. "Is Sunny gone yet?"

That funny look Dag got when consulting his groundsense flitted over his face. "Long gone, Aunt Nattie."

Fawn breathed relief.

"Dag, you're a good fellow, but I need to talk with my niece. Why don't you take a walk?"

He looked down to Fawn, who nodded reluctantly. He said, "I expect I could stand to go check on Copperhead, make sure he hasn't bitten anybody yet."

"I 'spect so," Nattie agreed.

He gave Fawn a last hug, bent down to touch his cider-scented lips to hers, smiled in encouragement, and left. She heard his steps wend through the house to the front door, and out.

Fawn wanted to put her head down in Nattie's lap and bawl; instead, she busied herself raking the coals under the oven for the pies. Nattie sat on a kitchen chair and rested her hands on her cane. Haltingly at first, then less so, the story came out, from Fawn's foolish tumble at the spring wedding to her growing realization and fear of the consequences to the initial horrid talk with Sunny.

"Tch." Nattie sighed in regret. "I knew you were troubled, lovie. I tried to get you to talk to me, but you wouldn't."

"I know. I don't know if I'm sorry now or not. I figured it was a problem I'd bought all on my own, so it was a problem to pay for all on my own. And then I thought my nerve would fail if I didn't plunge in."

For Nattie today, Fawn resolved to leave out nothing of her journey except the uncanny accident with Dag's sharing knife—partly because she was daunted by the complicated explanations that would have to go with, partly because it made no difference to the fate of her pregnancy, but mostly because Lakewalker secrets were so clearly not hers to give away. No, not just Lakewalker secrets—Dag's privacy. She grasped, now, what an intimate and personal possession his dead wife's bone had been. It was the only confidence he'd asked her to keep.

Taking a breath, Fawn plunged in anew. She described her lonely trudge to Glassforge, her terrifying encounter with the young bandit and the strange mud-man. Her first flying view of the startled Dag, even more frightening, but in retrospect almost funny. The Horsefords' eerie abandoned farm, the second abduction. The whole new measure for terror she'd learned at the malice's hands. Dag at the cave, Dag that night at the farm.

She did end up with her head in Nattie's lap then, though she managed to keep her tears down to a choked sniffling. Nattie petted her hair in the old way she hadn't done since Fawn had been small and weeping in pain for some minor hurt to her body, or in fury for some greater wound to her spirit. "Sh. Sh, lovie."

Fawn inhaled, wiped her eyes and nose on her apron, and sat up again on the floor next to Nattie's chair. "Please don't tell Mama and Papa any of this. They're going to have to go on living with the Sawmans. There's no point in making bad blood between the families now."

"Eh, lovie. But it gars me to see Sunny get off free of all this."

"Yes, but I couldn't stand for my brothers to know. They'd either try to do something to Sunny and cause trouble, or they'd make a mock of me for being so stupid, and I don't think I could bear that about this." She added after a moment of consideration, "Or both."

"I'm not sure even your brothers are thoughtless enough to make mock of *this*." Nattie hesitated, then conceded reluctantly, "Well, perhaps half-Whit."

Fawn managed a watery smile at the old jibe. "Poor Whit, maybe it's that old joke on his name that drives him to be such an awful thorn to everyone. Maybe I should start calling him Whitesmith instead, see if it helps."

"There's a thought." Nattie sat up, staring into her personal dark. "I think maybe you're right about the bad blood, though. Oh my, yes. All right. This story will stop with me unless some other problem comes from it."

Fawn breathed relief at this promise. "Thank you. Talking with you eases me, more than I expected." She thought over Nattie's last words, then said more firmly, "You have to understand, I'm going away with Dag. One way or another."

Nattie did not immediately burst into objections and dire warnings, but said only, "Huh." And then, after a moment, "Curious fellow, that Lakewalker. Tell me more."

Fawn, busying herself once more about the kitchen, was only too glad to expand on her new favorite subject to an unexpectedly sympathetic, or at least not immediately outraged, ear. "I met his patrol in Glassforge . . . " She described Mari and Saun and Reela—if touching only lightly on Dirla and Razi and Utau—and Sassa's proud tours to show off his town, and all the fascinating things folks found for work there that did not involve cows, sheep, or pigs. The bow-down, and Dag's unexpected talents with a tambourine—a word picture that made Nattie laugh along with Fawn. At that point, Fawn came to a sudden stop.

"You're heels-up in love with him, then," Nattie said calmly. And, at Fawn's gasp, "Come, girl, I'm not *that* blind."

In love. It seemed too weak a term. She'd imagined herself *in love* back when she was mooning over Sunny. "More than that. I trust him . . . right down to the ground."

"Oh, aye? After all that tale, I think I'm half in love with him myself." Nattie added after a thoughtful moment, "Haven't heard such joy in your voice for a long, long time, lovie. Years."

Fawn's heart sprang up as though weights had been shifted from it, and she laughed aloud and gave Nattie a hug and a kiss that made the old woman smile foolishly. "Now, now. There's still some provin' to be done, you know."

But then the pies were baked, and Fawn's mother returned to start the rest of supper, sending Fawn to milk the cows so the boys could keep cutting hay while the light lasted. She went by the front porch on the way, but Dag had not yet returned to his thinking seat there.

Dag made his way back to the house after a stroll around the lower perimeter of the farm, in part to stretch his legs and mind and in part to be certain Sunny had indeed packed off. Resentful and ripe for trouble, that boy, and his abrupt and satisfying removal from Fawn's presence had likely been dangerously self-indulgent for a Lakewalker alone in farmer country, but Dag could not regret the act, despite the renewed throbbing of his jostled arm. Dag's last veiled fear that, once back in the safety of her home, Fawn might repent her patroller and double back to her first love, faded altogether.

Once upon a time, Sunny had held star fire in his hand, and thrown it away in the mud of the road. He wouldn't be getting that fortune back, ever. There seemed nothing in the wide green world Dag could do to him worse than what he had already done to himself. Smiling crookedly, Dag dismissed Sunny from his thoughts in favor of more urgent personal concerns.

In the kitchen, he found Fawn gone but her mother, Tril, buzzing about putting together supper for eight. A clicking and whirring from the next chamber proved to be Nattie at her spinning wheel, within sight and call of her sister, and he made sure to say *how de'*; she returned a friendly but unenlightening, "Evening, patroller," and carried on. Evidently the incident with Sunny was not to be discussed. On the whole, Dag was relieved.

He greeted Tril amiably and attempted to make himself useful hooking pots on and off the fire for her, while trying to think his way to other possibilities for a half-handed man to show his worth to the female who was, in Lakewalker terms, the head of Tent Bluefield. Tril watched him in such deep alarm, he began to fear he was looming, too tall for the room, and he finally just sat down and watched, which seemed to ease her. His comment about the weather fell flat, as did a leading question about her chickens; alas, Dag knew little about farm animals beyond horses. But a few questions about Fletch's upcoming wedding led by a short route to West Blue marriage customs generally, which was exactly where Dag wanted her to go. The best way to keep her going, he quickly discovered, was to respond with comments on Lakewalker customs on the same head.

Tril paused in kneading biscuit dough to sigh. "I was afraid last spring Fawn was yearning after the Sawman boy, but that was never a hope. His papa and Jas Stonecrop had had it fixed between them for years that Sunny would marry Violet and the two farms would come together in the next generation. It's going to be a rich spread, that one. If Violet has more than one boy, there may be enough to divide among them without the younger ones having to go off homesteading the way Reed and Rush keep talking of."

The twins spoke of going to the edge of the cultivated zone, twenty miles or so west, and breaking new land between them, after Fletch married. It was a plan much discussed but so far little acted upon, Dag was given to understand. "Fathers arrange marriages, among farmers?"

"Sometimes." Tril smiled. "Sometimes they just think they do. Sometimes the fathers have to be arranged. The land, though, or the family due-share for children who aren't getting land—that has to be understood and written out and kept by the village clerk, or you risk bad blood later."

Land again; farmers were all about land. Other wealth was thought of as land's equivalent, it seemed. He offered, "Lakewalker couples usually choose each other, but the man is expected to bring bride-gifts to her family, which he is considered to be joining. Horses and furs, traditionally, though it depends on what he has accumulated." Dag added, as if casually, "I have eight horses at the moment. The other geldings are on loan to the camp pool, except for Copperhead, who is too evil-tempered to foist on anyone else. The three mares I keep in foal. My brother's wife looks after them along with her mares."

"Camp pool?" Tril said, after a puzzled moment.

"If a man has more than he needs, he can't just sit on it and let it rot. So it goes to the camp pool, usually to outfit a young patroller, and the camp scribe keeps a record of it. It's very handy if you go to switch camps, because you can carry a letter of record and draw for your needs when you get there, instead of carrying all that burden along. At the hinterland meetings every two years, one of the jobs for the camp scribes is to meet and settle up any lingering differences. I have a long credit at Stores." How to translate that into acreage temporarily defeated him, but he hoped she understood he was not by any measure destitute, despite his present road-worn appearance. He rubbed his nose reflectively with the side of his hook. "They tried me as a camp scribe for a while after I lost my hand, but I didn't take to the fiddly work and all the writing. I wanted to be moving, out in the field."

"You can read and write?" Tril looked as though this was a point in Dag's favor—good.

"Pretty much all Lakewalkers can."

"Hm. Are you the oldest in your family, or what?"

"Youngest by ten years, but I've only the one brother living. It was a great sorrow to my mother that she had no daughter to carry on her tent, but my brother married a younger sister of the Waterstriders—they had six—and she took our tent name so's it wouldn't be lost, and moved in so's my mother wouldn't be alone." *See, I'm a nice tame fellow, I have a family too. Of a sort.* "My brother is a very gifted maker at our camp." He decided not to say of what. The production of sharing knives was the most demanding of Lakewalker makings, and Dar was highly respected, but it seemed premature to introduce this to the Bluefields.

"Doesn't he patrol?"

"He did when he was younger—nearly everyone does—but his making skills are too valuable to waste on patrolling." Dag's, needless to say, weren't.

"So what of your father? Was he a maker or a patroller?"

"Patroller. He died on patrol, actually."

"Killed by one of those bogles Fawn talks of?" It was not entirely clear to Dag if Tril had believed in bogles before, but on the whole he thought she'd come to now, and was rendered very uncomfortable thereby.

"No. He went in after a younger patroller who was swept away in a bad river crossing, late in the winter. I wasn't there—I was patrolling in a different sector of the hinterland, and didn't hear for some days."

"Drowned? Seems an odd fate for a Lakewalker."

"No. Or not just then. He took a fever of the lungs and died about four nights later. Drowned in a sense, I suppose." Actually, he'd died of sharing; the two comrades who were trying to fetch him home in his dire illness had entered the tent to find him rolled over on his knife. Whether he'd chosen that end in shrewd judgment or delirium or despair or just plain exhaustion from the struggle, Dag would never know. The knife had come to him, anyway, and he'd used it three years later on a malice up near Cat Lick.

"Oh, aye, lung fever is nasty," Tril said sympathetically. "One of Sorrel's aunts was carried off by that just last winter. I'm so sorry."

Dag shrugged. "It was eleven years ago."

"Were you close?"

"Not really. He was away when I was smaller, and then I was away. I knew his father well, though; Grandfather had a bad knee by then, like Nattie" — Nattie, listening through the doorway as she spun, lifted up her head and smiled at her name—"and he stayed in camp and helped look after me, among other things. If I'd lost a foot instead of a hand, I might have ended like that, Uncle Dag to my brother's pack." *Or I might have shared early.* "So, um . . . are there any one-handed farmers?"

"Oh, yes, accidents happen on farms. Folks deal with it, I expect. I knew a man with a wooden leg, once. I've never heard tell of anything like that rig of yours, though."

Fawn's mother was relaxing nicely in his presence now and didn't jump at all anymore when he moved. On the whole, Dag suspected that it was easier to coax wild animals to take food from his hand than to lull Bluefields. But he was clearly making progress. He wondered if his Lakewalker habits were betraying him, and if he ought to have started with Fawn's papa instead of with the women. Well, it hardly mattered where he started; he was eventually going to have to beguile the whole lot of them in order to get his way.

And in they clumped, sweaty and ravenous. Fawn followed, smelling of cows, with two covered buckets slung on a yoke, which she set aside to deal with later. The crowd, minus Clover tonight, settled down happily to heaping portions of ham, beans, corn bread, summer squash, assorted pickled things, biscuits, butter, jams, fresh apple butter, cider, and milk. Conversation lagged for a little. Dag ignored the covert glances as he dealt with biscuits by stabbing them whole with his fork-spoon; Tril, if he read her aright, was simply pleased that he seemed to like them. Happily, he did not need to feign this flattery although he would have if necessary.

"Where did you go while I was milking?" Fawn finally asked him.

"Took a walk down to the river and back around. I am pleased to say there's no malice sign within a mile of here, although I wouldn't expect any. This area gets patrolled regularly."

"Really?" said Fawn. "I've never seen patrollers around here."

"We cross settled land at night, mostly, to avoid disturbing folks. You wouldn't notice us."

Papa Bluefield looked up curiously at this. It was quite possible, over the years, that not all patrols had passed as invisibly to him as all that.

"Did you ever patrol West Blue?" Fawn asked.

"Not lately. When I was a boy just starting, from about age fifteen, I walked a lot in this area, so I might have. Don't remember now."

"We might have passed each other all unknowing." She looked thoughtful at this notion.

"Um . . . no. Not then." He added, "When I was twenty I was sent on exchange to a camp north of Farmer's Flats, and started my first walk around the lake. I didn't get back for eighteen years."

"Oh," she said.

"I've been all over this hinterland since, but not just here. It's a big territory."

Papa Bluefield sat back at the table's head and eyed Dag narrowly. "Just how old are you, Lakewalker? A deal older than Fawn, I daresay."

"I daresay," Dag agreed.

Papa Bluefield continued to stare expectantly. The sound of forks scraping plates was suddenly obtrusive.

Cornered. Must this come out here? Perhaps it was better to get it on the table sooner than later. Dag cleared his throat, so that his voice would come out neither squeaking like a mouse's nor too loud, and said, "Fifty-five."

Fawn choked on her cider. He probably should have glanced aside first to see she wasn't trying to swallow anything. His fork-spoon hand was no good for patting her on the back, but she recovered her breath in a moment. "Sorry," she wheezed. "Down the wrong pipe." She looked up sideways at him in muffled, possibly, alarm. Or dismay. He hoped it wasn't horror.

"Papa," she muttered, "is fifty-three."

All right, a little horror. They would deal with it.

Tril was staring. "You look forty, if that."

Dag lowered his eyelids in nonargument.

"Fawn," Papa Bluefield announced grimly, "is eighteen."

Beside him, Fawn's breath drew in, sharply aggravated.

Dag tried, almost successfully, to keep his lips from curling up. It was hard, when she was clearly boiling so much inside she was ready to pop. "Really?" He eyed her blandly. "She told me she was twenty. Although from my vantage, it scarcely makes a difference."

She hunched her shoulders sheepishly. But their eyes connected, and then she had trouble not laughing too, and all was well.

Papa Bluefield said in an aggravated tone, "Fawn had an old bad habit of telling tall tales. I tried to beat it out of her. I should have beat her more, maybe."

Or less, Dag did not say aloud.

"As it happens, I come from a very long-lived kin," Dag said, by way of attempted repair. "My grandfather I told you of was still spry till his death at well over a hundred." One hundred twenty-six, but there was more than enough mental arithmetic going on around the table right now. The brothers, particularly, seemed to be floundering, staring at him in renewed wariness.

"It all works out," Dag went on into the too-long pause. "If, for example, Fawn and I were to marry, we would actually arrive at old age tolerably close together. Barring accidents."

All right, he'd said the magic word, *marry*. It wasn't as if he hadn't done something like this before, long ago. Well, all right, it had been nothing at all like this. Kauneo's kin had been overpowering in an entirely different manner. The terror rippling through him felt the same, though.

Papa Bluefield growled, "Lakewalkers don't marry farmer girls."

He couldn't grip Fawn's hand below the table for reassurance; all he could do was dig his fork into her thigh, with unpredictable but probably unhelpful results at the moment. He did glance down at her. Was he about to jump off this cliff alone or with her? Her eyes were wide. And lovely. And terrified. And . . . thrilled. He drew a long breath.

"I would. I will. I wish to. Marry Fawn. Please?"

Seven stunned Bluefields created the loudest silence Dag had ever heard.

15

In the airless moment while everyone else around the table was still inhaling, Fawn said quickly, "I'd like that fine, Dag. I would and will and wish, too. Yes. Thank you kindly." *Then* she drew breath.

And then the storm broke, of course.

As the babble rose, Fawn thought Dag should have tackled her family one at a time instead of all together like this. But then she noticed that neither Mama nor Aunt Nattie was adding to the rain of objections, and truly, whenever Papa turned to Mama for support he received instead a solemn silent stare that seemed to unnerve him. Aunt Nattie said nothing at all, but she was smiling dryly. So maybe Dag had been doing more than just thinking, all this day.

Fletch, possibly in imitation of Papa's earlier and successful attempt to embarrass Dag about his age, came up with, "We don't take kindly to cradle robbing around these parts, Lakewalker."

Whit, his tone mock-thoughtful but his eyes bright with the excitement of battle, put in, "Actually, I'm not sure if *he's* robbing cradles, or *she's* robbing graves!"

Which made Dag wince, but also offer a wry headshake and a low murmur of, "Good one, Whit."

It also made Fawn so furious that she threatened to serve Whit's pie on his head instead of his plate, or better still his head on his plate instead of his pie, which drew Mama into the side fray to chide Fawn, so Whit won twice, and smirked fit to make Fawn explode. She hated how easily they all could make her feel and act twelve, then treat her so and feel justified about it; if they kept this up much longer, she was afraid they'd succeed in dropping her back to age two and screaming tantrums right on the floor. Which would do just about nothing for her cause. She caught her breath and sat again, simmering.

"I hear Lakewalker men are landless, and do no work 'cept maybe hunting," said Fletch, determinedly returning to the attack. "If it's Fawn's portion you're after, let me tell you, she gets no land."

"Do you think I could carry farm fields away in my saddlebags, Fletch?" said Dag mildly.

"You could stuff in a couple o' chickens, maybe," Whit put in so helpfully.

Dag's eyes crinkled. "Be a bit noisy, don't you think? Copperhead would take such offense. And picture the mess of eggs breaking in my gear."

Which made Whit snicker unwillingly in turn. Whit, Fawn decided, didn't care which side he argued for, as long as he could stir the pot and keep it boiling. And he preened when folks laughed at his jokes. Dag had him half-wrapped around his thumb already.

"So what *do* you want, eh?" asked Reed aggressively, frowning.

Dag leaned back, face growing serious; and somehow, she was not sure how, commanding attention all around the table. It was as if he suddenly grew taller just sitting there. "Fletch brings up some very real concerns," Dag said, with a nod of approval at Fawn's eldest brother that puffed him up a bit despite himself. "As I understand it, if Fawn married a local lad, she would be due clothing, some furniture, animals, seed, tools, and a deal of labor to help set up her new house. Except for her personal gear, it's not Lakewalker custom or expectation that I should have any of that. Nor could I use it. But neither should I like to see her deprived of her rights and due-share. I have an alternate plan for the puzzle."

Papa and Mama were both listening seriously too, as if they were all three speaking the same language of a sudden. "And what would that be, patroller?" said Papa, brows now pinched more in thought than in antagonism and not nearly as red in the face as he'd been at first.

Dag tilted his head as if in thanks, incidentally emphasizing his permission to speak without interruptions from juniors. "I *of course* undertake to care for and protect Fawn for as long as I live. But it's a plain fact that I don't lead a safe life." A slight, emphatic tick of his wrist cuff on the table edge was no accident, Fawn thought. "For now, I would have her leave her marriage portion here, intact, but defined—written out square in the family book and in the clerk's record, witnessed just as is right. No man knows the hour of his shari—of his end. But if ever Fawn has to come back here, I would have it be as a real widow, not a grass one." He tilted his head just enough toward Fawn that only she saw his slight wink, and she was as cheered by the wink as chilled by the words, so that her heart seemed to spin unanchored. "She—and her children, if any— would then have something to fall back on wholly separate from my fate."

Mama, face scrunched up in concentration, nodded thoughtfully at this.

"In the hope that such a day would be long from now or never, it would have to be attested by Fletch and Clover as well. Can't help thinking that Clover would be just as glad to put off paying out that due-share, with all the work she'll have here starting up."

Fletch, opening his mouth, shut it abruptly, as it finally dawned that not only would he not be required to disgorge any family resources right away, but also that Fawn would be out of the house when he brought his new bride home. And only by the slightest brightening of Dag's eyes did Fawn realize that Dag had hit Fletch precisely where he was aiming, and knew it.

A blessed silence fell just long enough to finish consuming pie. Fawn was reattaching Dag's hook before Whit wiped his lips, and said in brotherly bewilderment, "But why ever would you want to marry Fawn in the first place?"

The tone of his voice alone threw Fawn back into a pit of unwelcome memories of youthful mockery. As if she were the most unlikely candidate for courtship in the whole of West Blue and for a hundred miles beyond in any direction, as if she were a cross between a village idiot and a freak of nature. What was that stupid phrase that had worked so well, *repeatedly,* to rile her up? *Hey, Runt! You must have been drinking ugly juice this morning!* And how those words had made her feel like it.

"Need I say?" asked Dag calmly.

"Yes!" said Fletch, in his stern I-am-so-paternal voice that made Fawn long to kick him even more than she longed to kick Whit, and even made Papa cock a bemused eyebrow at him.

"Yeah, old man," said Rush, scowling. Of all at the table but Nattie, the twins had said the least so far, but none of it had been favorable. "Give us three good reasons!"

Dag's eyelids lowered briefly in a cool yet strangely dangerous assent; but his side glance at Fawn felt like a caress after a beating. "Only that? Very well." He held their attention while he appeared to think, deliberately clearing a silence in which to speak. "For the courage of her heart, which I saw face down the greatest horrors I know without breaking. For the high and hungry intelligence of her mind, which never stops asking questions, nor thinking about the answers. For the spark of her spirit, which could teach bonfires how to burn. That's three. Enough for going on with."

He rose from the table, his hook hand briefly touching her shoulder. "All this is set beside me, and you ask me instead if I want *dirt?* I do not understand farmers." He excused himself with a polite nod all around, and a murmured, "Evening, Aunt Nattie," and strode out.

Fawn wasn't sure if she was more thrilled with his words or with his *timing.* He had indeed figured out the only way to get in the last word in a bunch of Bluefields—shoot it into the target and run.

And whatever comment, mockery, or insult might have risen in his wake was undercut to shamed silence by the sound of Mama, weeping quietly into the apron clutched up to her face.

The debate didn't end there, naturally. It mostly broke up into smaller parts, as they took on family members in ones or twos, although Fawn gave Dag credit for trying for efficiency, that first night. The twins cornered her the next afternoon in the old barn, where she had gone to give Grace and Copperhead some treats and a good brushing.

Rush leaned on the stall partition and spoke in a voice of disgust. "Fawn, that fellow is *way* too old for you. He's older than Papa, and Papa's older than rocks. And he's all so banged up. If you were married, you'd have to look at that stump he hides, I bet. Or touch it, *ew*."

"I've seen it," she said shortly, brushing bay hairs into the air in a cloud. "I help him with his arm harness, now his other arm's broke." And a great deal of other assistance that she was not inclined to bring to the twins' attention. "You should see his poor gnarly feet if you want to see banged up."

Reed sat on a barrel of oats across the aisle with his knees drawn up and his arms wrapped around them, rocking uneasily. He said in a thin tone, "He's a Lakewalker. He's *evil*."

This brought Fawn's irritated and vigorous brushing to an abrupt halt; Grace twitched her ears in protest. Fawn turned to stare. "No, he's not. What are you going on about?"

"They say Lakewalkers eat their own dead to make their sorcery. What if he makes you have to eat corpses? Or worse? What does he really want you for?"

"His wife, Reed," said Fawn with grim patience. "Is that so very hard to believe?"

Reed's voice hushed. "What if it's to make magic?"

He already does that would likely not be a useful answer. "What, are you afraid I'll be made a human sacrifice? How sweet of you, Reed. Sort of."

Reed unfolded indignantly. "Don't you laugh. It's true. I saw a Lakewalker once who'd stopped to eat in the alehouse in West Blue. Sunny Sawman dared me to peek in her saddlebags. She had bones in them—human bones!"

"Tell me, was she wearing her hair in a knot at the nape of her neck?"

Reed stared. "How'd you know?"

"You're lucky you weren't caught."

"I was. She took me and shook me and told me I'd be cursed if I ever touched anything of a Lakewalker's again. She scowled so—she told me she'd catch and eat me!"

Fawn's brows drew down. "How old were you, again?"

"Ten."

"Reed, for pity's sake!" said Fawn in utter exasperation. "What would you tell a little boy you caught rifling your bags so as to scare him enough never to do it again? You're just lucky you didn't run into Dag's aunt Mari—I bet she could have come up with a tall tale that would have made you pee yourself into the next week." She was suddenly glad the sharing knife was stored with her own things, and wondered if she ought to warn Dag to watch his saddlebags.

Reed looked a bit taken aback, as if this point had never before occurred to him, but he went on anyhow. "Fawn, those bones were real. They were *fresh*."

Fawn had no doubt of it. She also had no desire to start down some slippery slope of explanation with the twins, who would only ask her how she knew and badger her endlessly when her answers didn't fit their notions. She finished brushing Grace's flanks and turned her attention to her mane and forelock.

Rush was still mired in the age difference. "It's sickening to think of a fellow that old pawing you. What if he got you pregnant?"

She was definitely not ready for that again so soon, but it was hardly a prospect that filled her with horror. Perhaps her and Dag's future children, if any, wouldn't be saddled with being so blasted short—now, there was a heartening thought. She smiled softly to herself as Grace nudged her velvety nose into her hand and whuffled.

Rush went on, "He as much as said it was his plan to keep you till you were and then send you back to batten on us."

"Only if he *dies*, Rush!"

"Yeah, well, how much longer can that be?"

"And what does it matter to you anyhow? You and Reed are going to go west and break land. You won't even be here." She let herself out of the stall and latched the door.

"On Fletch and Clover, then."

"You two are so, so, so"— she groped for a sufficient word—"howling *stupid*."

"Oh, yeah?" Rush shot back. "He claimed he wanted to marry you because you were smart, and how dumb do you have to be to believe that? You know it's just so's he can get his old hands on your young . . . self."

"Hand," she corrected coldly. And how she missed its touch on her young . . . everything. Escape from West Blue, with or without a wedding, could not happen soon enough.

Rush imitated upchucking, with realistic noises. Fawn supposed stabbing him with the pitchfork was out, but maybe she could at least whack him over the head with it . . . ? He added, "And how d'you think we'll feel in front of *our* friends, stuck with that fellow in the family?"

"Considering your friends, I can't say as I'm real moved by that plea."

"I can't see as you've much considered anybody but yourself, lately!"

Reed said, more urgently and with a peculiar fearful tinge in his voice, "I see what it is. He's magicked you up some way already, hasn't he?"

"I don't want to hear another word out of you two."

"Or what?" said Rush. "You'll never speak to us again?"

"I'm working on that one," snarled Fawn, and stalked out of the barn.

Not all of the encounters were so aggravating. Fawn found an unexpected ally in Clover, with whom she'd never before much gotten along, and Clover brought Fletch right into line. The two girls were now in great charity with each other, feeling they could have been best friends forever and mistaken in all their prior judgments; Fletch was a bit dizzied. Dag made undaunted use of the news about his age to put himself rather above it all, and he mainly talked privately with Mama and Papa or Nattie. Whit continued to fire off barbs in blithe disregard for their aim, with the result that *everybody* grew furious with him except for Dag, who continued patient and determined.

"I've dealt with dissolving patrols down to and including breaking up knife fights," he assured Fawn at one especially distraught moment. "No one here's tried to stab each other yet."

"It's been a near thing," Fawn growled.

By supper of the second night after Dag's proposal, Fawn's parents had gone so far as to forbid discussion of the topic at the table, somewhat to Dag's relief. It did render the meal uncharacteristically quiet. Dag thought his plan to extract Fawn gracefully from the clutches of her kin was not going as well as he'd hoped. Whether it took two days or twenty or two hundred, he was determined to persevere, but it was plain Fawn was close to melting in this family crucible, and her strain communicated itself to him, open to her ground as he could not help being.

They'd taken too long on this journey already. Much more tarrying in West Blue, and he'd risk not beating Mari's patrol back to Hickory Lake, and they would panic and think him missing again. And this time, he wouldn't be dragging back in with another malice kill in his bag to buy forgiveness.

Bluefields were falling to him, slowly. Fletch and Clover were openly agreeable, Nattie quietly agreeable, and Tril mainly just quiet. Whit didn't greatly care, and Papa Bluefield still sat on the fence.

Sorrel and Tril Bluefield reminded Dag a bit of patrol leaders, their heads stuffed with too many duties and details, too many people's conflicting desires and needs. An unsolvable dilemma had a good chance of being invited to go away; he thought they might break simply because they could not afford to spend all their time and energy on one problem when so many more crowded upon them. Dag felt almost cruelly ruthless, but he steeled himself to keep up the blandishments and subtle pressure. Fawn took care of the unsubtle pressure.

Reed and Rush remained a stubborn reservoir of resistance. Dag was not sure why, as neither would talk to him despite several friendly lures. Separately, he thought he might have gotten somewhere, but together they stayed locked in a knot of disapproval. Fawn, when he asked her for guidance into their objections, just went tight-lipped. But their more hotheaded remarks at least served to drive their papa further and faster toward conciliation than he would have gone on his own, if only from sheer embarrassment. Some opposition was its own worst enemy.

Still . . . I should have liked to have made some real tent-brothers. Now, *there* was an unreasonable hope to flush from hiding. Dag frowned at himself. The gift of comradeship he'd once found with Kauneo's brothers in Luthlia, so fine in the having, was all the more painful in the loss. Maybe it was better this way.

After the postsupper chores the family usually gathered in the parlor, cooler than the kitchen, to share the lamplight. Dag had walked out with Fawn to feed scraps to the chickens; as they came through the kitchen door and into the central hall, he heard raised voices from the parlor. By this time Dag cringed at opening his groundsense in this raucous company, not a one of them capable of a decent veiling; but he did prick his ears to hear Reed's voice, rumbling, hostile, and indistinct, and then Tril's, raised in sharp fear: "Reed! Put that down! Fawn brought me that all the way from Glassforge!"

Beside him, Fawn drew in her breath and hurried forward. Dag strode after, bracing himself.

In the parlor, Reed and Rush had more or less cornered their parents. Tril was sitting beside the table that held the bright oil lamp, some sewing in her lap; Nattie sat across the room in the shadows with the drop spindle that was rarely out of her hands, now stilled. Whit crouched by Nattie, a spectator on the fringe, for once not heckling. Sorrel stood facing Reed, with Rush pacing nervously around them.

Reed was holding up the glass bowl and declaiming, overdramatically in Dag's view, "—sell your daughter to some bloody-handed corpse-eater for the sake of a piece of glass?"

"Reed!" Fawn cried furiously, dashing forward. "You give that back! It's not yours!"

Dag thought it was sheer force of habit; when confronted with that familiar sisterly rise, Reed quite unthinkingly raised the bowl high out of Fawn's hopping reach. At her enraged squeal, he tossed it to Rush, who just as unthinkingly caught it.

Tears of fury sprang in Fawn's eyes. "You two are just a pair of yard dogs—"

"If you hadn't dragged Useless here home with you—" Rush began defensively.

Ah, yet another new nickname for himself, Dag realized. He was collecting quite a set of them here. But his own fraying temper was not nearly such a grating goad to him as Fawn's humiliated helplessness.

Sorrel glanced at his distraught wife, whose hands had flown to her mouth, and barked angrily, "Boys, that's enough!" He strode forward and started to pull the bowl out of Rush's grasp. Sorrel, unwilling to snatch, let go just as Rush, afraid to resist, did likewise.

It was no one's fault, exactly, or at least no one's intention. Dag saw it coming as did Fawn, and a desolate little wail broke from her lips even before the bowl hit the wooden floor edge on and burst, falling into three large pieces and a sparkling spray of splinters.

Everyone froze in equal horror. Whit opened his lips, looked around, and then closed them flat.

Sorrel recovered his voice first, hoarse and low. "Whit, don't move. You got no shoes on."

Tril cried, "Reed! Rush! How *could* you!" And began sobbing into her sewing.

Their mother's anger might have rolled right off the pair, Dag thought, but the genuine heartbreak in her voice seemed to cut them off at the knees. They both began incoherent apologies.

"Sorry does no mending!" she cried, tossing the scrap of cloth aside. It was flecked with blood where she had inadvertently driven her needle into her palm in the shock of the crash. "I've had it with the whole pack of you—!"

The Bluefield uproar was so painful in Dag's ground, which he tried to close but could not for the strength of his link to Fawn, that he found himself dropping to his knees. He stared at the pieces of glass on the floor in front of him as the angry and anguished voices continued overhead. He could not shut them out, but he could redirect his attention; it was an old, old method of dealing with the unbearable.

He slipped his splinted right arm from its sling, and with it and his hook he clumsily pushed the large pieces of the bowl as close together as he could. Those splinters, now—most of those glass splinters were no bigger than mosquitoes. If he could bounce a mosquito, he could move one splinter, and if he could move one, he could move two and four and more . . . He remembered the sweet song of this bowl's ground as it had rested in the sunset light of their refuge in Glassforge, gifting rainbows, and he began a low humming, searching up and down for the right note, just . . . there.

The glass splinters began to wink, then shift, then rise and flow over the boards of the parlor floor. He shifted them not with his hand, but with the ground of his hand. The ground of his left hand, the hand that was not there, and the very thought was so terrifying he shied from it.

But even that terror did not break his concentration. The splinters flew up, circling and swirling like fireflies around the bowl to find their places once more. The bowl glowed golden along all the spider-lines of its fractures, like kiln fire, like star fire, like nothing earthly Dag had ever seen. It scintillated, reflecting off his draining, chilling skin. He held the pure note faintly through his rounded lips. The lines of light seemed to melt into rivulets, streams, rivers of pale gold running all through the glass, then spread out like a still lake under a winter sunrise.

The light faded. And was gone.

Dag came back to himself bent over on his knees, his hair hanging around his face like a curtaining fringe, mouth slack, staring down at the intact glass bowl. His skin felt as cold and clammy as lard on a winter morning, and he was shivering, shuddering so hard his stomach hurt. He pressed his teeth together so that they would not chatter.

The only sounds in the room were of eight people breathing: some heavily, some rapidly, some choked with tears, some wheezing with shock. He thought he could pick out each one's pattern with his ears alone. He could not force himself to look up.

Someone—Fawn—thumped down on her knees before him. "Dag . . . ?" she said uncertainly. Her small hand reached out to touch his chin, to tilt his face upward to meet her wide, wide eyes.

He pushed the bowl forward with his left arm. It was hot to the touch but not dangerously so. It did not melt or disappear or explode or fall apart again into a thousand pieces. It just sang slightly as it scraped across the floor, the ordinary song of ordinary glass that had never been slain or resurrected. He found his voice, or at least a close imitation of his voice; it sounded utterly unfamiliar in his own ears, as though it was coming from underwater or underground. "Give that back to your mama."

He pressed his wrist cuff to her shoulder and levered himself upright. The room wavered around him, and he was suddenly afraid he was going to vomit, making a mess right there on the middle of the parlor floor in front of everyone. Fawn clutched the bowl to her breast and rose after him, her eyes never leaving his face.

"Are you all right?" she asked.

He gave her a short headshake, wet his cold lips, and stumbled for the parlor door to the central hall. He hoped he could make it out onto the front porch before his stomach heaved. Tril, on her feet, was hovering nearby, and she stepped back as he passed. Fawn followed, pausing only long enough to thrust the bowl into her mother's hands.

Dag heard Fawn's voice behind him, low and fierce: "He does that for hearts, too, you know."

And she marched forthrightly after him.

16

Fawn followed Dag onto the front porch and watched in worry as he sat heavily on the step, his left elbow on his knee and his head down. In the west behind the house, the sky was draining of sunset colors; to the east, above the river valley, the first stars were pricking through the darkening turquoise vault. The air grew soft as the day's heat eased. Fawn settled down to Dag's right and raised her hand uncertainly to his face. His skin was icy, and she could feel the shudders coursing through his body.

"You've gone all cold."

He shook his head, swallowing. "Give me a little . . . " In a few moments he straightened up, taking a deep breath. "Thought I was going to spew my nice dinner on my feet, but now I think not."

"Is that usual? For after doing things like that?"

"No—I don't know. I'm not a maker. We'd determined that by the time I was sixteen. Hadn't the concentration for it. I needed to be moving all the time. I am *not* a maker, but *that* . . ."

"Was?" she prompted when he stayed stopped.

"That was a *making*. Absent gods." He raised his left arm and rubbed his forehead on his sleeve.

She tucked her arm around him, trying to share warmth; she wasn't sure how much good it did, but he smiled shakily for the attempt. His body was chilled all down his side. "We should go into the kitchen by the hearth. I could fix you a hot drink."

"When I can stand up." He added, "Maybe go around the outside of the house."

Where they would not have to hazard her family. She nodded understanding.

"Groundwork," he began, and trailed off. "You have to understand. Lakewalker groundwork—magic, you might say—involves taking something and making it more so, more itself, through reinforcing its ground. There's a woman at Hickory Lake who works with leather, makes it repel rain. She has a sister who can make leather that turns arrows. She can make maybe two coats a month. I had one once."

"Did it work?"

"Never had occasion to find out while I had it. I saw another turn a mud-man's spear, though. Iron tip left nothing but a scratch in the hide. Of the coat, not of the patroller," he clarified.

"Had? What happened to it?"

"Lent it to my oldest nephew when he began patrolling. He handed it on to his sister when she started. Last I knew my brother's youngest took it with him when he went out of the hinterland. I'm not sure the coats are all that useful, for they're like to make you careless, and they don't protect the face and legs. But, you know . . . you worry for the youngsters." His shudders were easing, but his expression remained strained and distant. "That bowl just now, though . . . I pushed its ground back to purest bowl-ness, and the glass just followed. I felt it so clear. Except that, except that . . . " He leaned his forehead down against hers, and whispered fearfully, "I pushed with the ground of my left hand, and I have no left hand and it *has* no ground. Whatever was there, for that minute, is gone again now. I've never heard of anything like that. But the best makers don't speak of their craft much except to their own. So I don't know. Don't . . . know."

The door swung open; Whit edged out into the shadows of the porch. "Um . . . Fawn . . . ?"

"What, Whit?" she said impatiently.

"Um. Aunt Nattie says. Um. Aunt Nattie says she's had enough of this nonsense and she'll see you and the patroller in her rooms and be having the end of it one way or another as soon as the patroller is up to it. Um. Sir."

Behind the fringe of his hair, Dag's lips twitched slightly. He raised his face. "Thank you, Whit," he said gravely. "Tell Aunt Nattie we'll be along soon."

Whit gulped, ducked his head, and fled back indoors.

They rose and went around the north side of the house to the kitchen, Dag resting his left arm heavily across Fawn's shoulders. He stumbled twice. She made him sit by the hearth while she fixed him a cup of hot water with some peppermint leaves crushed in, holding it to his lips while he drank it down. By then he'd stopped shivering, and his clammy skin had dried and warmed again. She saw her parents and Fletch peeking timidly from the darkness of the hall, but they said nothing and did not venture in.

Aunt Nattie appeared at the door to her shadowed weaving room. "Well, patroller. You were flyin' there for a bit, I guess."

"Yes, ma'am, I was," Dag agreed wryly.

"Fawn, you fetch in the patroller and what lights you want." She turned back into the dark, scuffing feet and cane over the floorboards, not wearily, but just for the company of the sound, as she sometimes did.

Fawn looked anxiously at Dag. The firelight she'd poked up glimmered red-orange over his skin, yellow on his coarse white shirt and the sling, and his eyes were dark and wide. He looked tired, and confused, and as if his arm was hurting, but he smiled reassuringly at her, and she smiled back. "You ready?" she asked.

"Not sure, but I'm too curious to care. Possibly not a trait helpful to longevity in a patroller, but there you go."

She took down the candle lamp with the chipped glass sleeve from the mantel and lit it, grabbing the unlit iron holder with the three stubs while she was at it, and led off. With a muffled *eh,* he levered himself up out of his chair and paced after her.

Nattie called from their bedroom, "Close both doors, lovie. It will keep the noise out."

And in, Fawn reflected. She pushed the door to the kitchen closed with her foot and picked her way around the loom and the piles of Dag's gear. In the bedroom, Nattie seated herself on the side of her narrow bed and motioned to the one across from it. Fawn set the lamp and the iron ring on the table between and lit the other candles, and went back and closed the bedroom door. Dag glanced at her and sat down facing Nattie, the bed ropes creaking under his weight, and Fawn eased down at his left. "Here we are, Aunt Nattie," she announced, to which Dag added, "Ma'am."

Nattie stretched her back and grimaced, then leaned forward on her cane, her pearly eyes seeming to stare at them in a disturbingly penetrating fashion. "Well, patroller. I'm going to tell you a story. And then I'm going to ask you a question. And then we'll see where we're goin' on to."

"I'm at your disposal," Dag said, with that studied courtesy Fawn had learned concealed caution.

"That's to be seen." She sniffed. "You know, you're not the first Lakewalker I've met."

"I sensed that."

"I lead a dull life, mostly. Lived in this house since Tril married Sorrel nigh on thirty years ago. I hardly get off this farm 'cept down to West Blue for the market day or a little sewing bee now and then."

Actually, Nattie did both regularly, being a chief supplier of fine cloth and having a deep ear for village gossip, but Fawn forbore to intrude on the stream of . . . whatever this was going to be. Reminiscence?

Apparently so, for Nattie went on, "Now, the summer before Fawn was born was a tough time. Her mama was sick, and the boys were rambunctious, and her papa was overworked as usual. I wasn't sleeping so good myself, so I did my gathering in the north woods at night after they'd all gone to bed. The boys being less help than more in the woods at that stage of their lives."

Ages three to ten, roughly; Fawn could picture it, and shuddered.

"Roots and herbs and plants for remedies and dyes, you know. Night's not only more peaceful, the scents are sharper. I especially wanted some wild ginger for Tril, thought I might make a tea to settle her poor stomach. Anyhow, I was sorry for the peaceful that night, because I fell and twisted my ankle something fierce. I tried callin' for a bit, but I was too far from the house to be heard."

Truly, the woods on the steep valley slope to the north of their place extended for three miles before the next farm. Fawn made an encouraging noise in lieu of a nod.

"I figured I was doomed to lie in the dew till morning when I'd be missed, but then I heard a sound in the leaves—I was afraid it was a wolf or bear come to eat me, but instead it was a Lakewalker patroller. I was thinking at first I'd rather a bear, but he turned out to be a nice young fellow.

"He laid hands on my foot and eased me amazingly, and picked me up and carried me back to the house. I was skinnier back then, mind, bit of a dab, really. He was not near so tall as you" —she nodded in Dag's general direction—"but right stout. Nice voice, almost as deep as yours. He explained all about how he was on exchange from some camp way out east, and this was his first patrol in these parts—lonely and homesick, I was thinking. Anyhow, I fed him quiet in the kitchen, and he did a real fine job bandaging my ankle up nice and firm.

"I don't know if he decided I was his adopted aunt, or if he was more like a boy picking up a bird with an injured wing and making a pet of it, but late the next night there came a tapping on my window. He was back with some medicine, some for my foot and some for Tril's tummy, which he handed in—he wouldn't stay that time, though. The powders worked wonderful well, I must say." She sighed in fond recollection.

"Off he went and I thought no more of it, but next summer, about the same time of year, there came that tapping at my window again. We had a bit of a picnic on the back porch in the dark, and talked. He was glad to hear Tril had delivered you safe, Fawn. He gave me some little presents and I gave him some food and cloth. The next summer the same; I got to looking out for him.

"The next year he came back one more time, but not alone. He brought his new bride, just to show her off to me I think, he was that proud of her. He showed me their Lakewalker marriage-bracelets, string-bindings they called 'em, knowin' I had a maker's interest in all things to do with the craft, thread and cords and braids as well as the weaving and knitting.

They let me hold them in my hands and feel them. Gave me a turn, they did. They weren't just fancy cord. They were *magical*."

"Yes," said Dag cautiously, and at Fawn's curious look expanded, "Each betrothed puts a tiny bit of their ground into their own cord. The string-binding ceremony tangles the two grounds, then they exchange, his for hers."

"Really?" said Fawn, fascinated, trying to remember if she'd noticed such bracelets on the patrollers at Glassforge. Yes, for Mari'd had one, and so had a couple of other older patrollers. She had thought them merely decorative. "Do they do anything? Can you send messages?"

"No. Well, only that if one spouse dies, the other can feel it, for the ground drains out of their binding cord. They're often put safe away to save wear, although they can be remade if they're damaged. But if one spouse is out on patrol, the other back in camp usually wears theirs. Just . . . to know. To the one out on patrol, it comes as more of a shock, because you don't expect . . . I've seen that happen twice. It's not good. The patroller is dismissed at once to ride home if it's at all possible. There's a special terror to knowing what but not how, except that you are *too late,* and a thought that, you know, *maybe* the string just got burned up in a tent fire or some freak thing—enough hope for agony but not enough for ease. When I woke up in the medicine tent after . . ."

The room grew so quiet, Fawn thought she could hear the candles burning.

She lifted her face to his and said a little wryly, "You know, you've either got to finish those sorts of sentences or not start them."

He sighed and nodded. "I think I can say this to you. If I can't I've no business . . . anyway. I was about to say, when I woke up in the medicine tent after Wolf Ridge with my hand gone, so was Kauneo's binding string, which I wore on that side. Lost on the ridge. I guess I made some difficulties trying to find it, being fairly mixed up in the head right about then. They hadn't wanted to tell me she was gone till I was stronger, but they pretty much had to, and then I wouldn't believe them. It was like, if I could just find that binding string, I could prove them wrong. I got over it in due course."

He was looking away from her as he said this. Fawn drew her breath in and let it out gently between her teeth. He looked back down at her and smiled, sort of, and tried to move his hand to grasp hers in reassurance, wincing as the sling brought him up short in painful reminder. "It was a long time ago," he murmured.

"Before I was born."

"Indeed." He added after a moment, "I don't know why I find that an easing thought, but I do."

Nattie had her head cocked to one side with the intensity of her listening; when he did not go on, she put in, "Now, I do know this, patroller. Without those binding strings, you aren't married in Lakewalker eyes."

He nodded cautiously, then remembered to say aloud, "Yes. That is to say, they are a visible proof of a valid marriage, like your village clerk's record and writing your name in the family book with all the witnesses' signatures below. The string-binding is the heart and center of a wedding. The food and the music and the dancing and the arguments among the relatives are all extra."

"Uh-huh," said Nattie. "And there's the problem, patroller. Because if Fawn and you stand up in the parlor before the family and all like you say you want, and sign your names and make your promises, seems to me *she'd* be getting married, but *you* wouldn't. I said I had a question, and this is it. I want to know exactly what you are about, that you think this won't twist around somehow and leave her cryin'."

Fawn wondered for a moment why he was being held responsible for her future tears but not her for his. She supposed it was the, the *blighted* age thing again. It seemed unfairly unbalanced, somehow.

Dag was silent for several long breaths. He finally raised his chin, and said, "When I first rode in here, I had no thought of a farmer wedding. But it didn't take long to see how little her family valued Spark. Present company excepted," he added hastily. Nattie nodded grimly, not disagreeing. "Not that they don't love her and try to look out for her, in a sort of backhanded, absentminded way. But they don't seem to see her, not as she is. Not as I see her. Of course, they don't have groundsense, but still. Maybe the past fogs the present, maybe they just haven't looked lately, maybe they never have looked, I don't know. But marriage seems to raise a woman's standing in a farmer family. I thought I could give her that, in an easy way. Well, it seemed easy at the time. Not so sure now." He sighed. "I was real clear about the widowhood business, though."

"Seems like a hollow gift, patroller."

"Yes, but I can't do a string-binding here. I can't make the string, for one; it takes two hands and I've got none, and I'm not sure Fawn can make one at all, and we've no one to do the blessing and the tying. I was thinking that when we reached Hickory Lake I might try for a string-binding there, despite the difficulties."

"Think your family will favor this idea?"

"No," he said frankly. "I expect trouble about it. But I've outstubborned everything my life has thrown at me so far."

"He's got a point there, Aunt Nattie," Fawn dared to say.

"Mm," said Aunt Nattie. "So what happens if they pitch her out on her ear? Which Lakewalkers have done to farmer suitors before, I do believe."

Dag fell very quiet for a little, then said, "I'd walk with her."

Nattie's brows went up. "You'd break with your people? *Can* you?"

"Not by choice." His shrug failed to conceal deep unease. "But if they chose to break with me, I couldn't very well stop them."

Fawn blinked, suddenly disquieted. She'd dreamed only of what joy they might bring to each other. But that keelboat seemed to be towing a whole string of barges she hadn't yet peeked into. Dag had, it seemed.

"Huh-huh-hm," said Nattie. She tapped her cane gently on the floorboards. "I'm thinkin' too, patroller. I got two hands. So does Fawn, actually."

Dag seemed to freeze, staring at Nattie sharply. "I'm . . . not at all sure that would work." He added after a longer moment, "I'm not at all sure it wouldn't. I have some know-how. Fawn knows this land, she can help gather the necessaries. Hair from each of us, other things. Mine's a bit short."

"I have tricks for dealing with short fibers," said Nattie equitably.

"You have more than that, I think. Spark . . . " He turned to her. "Give me a piece your aunt has made. I want to hold something of her making. Something especially fine, you know?"

"I think I know what he's wanting. Look in that trunk at the foot of my bed, lovie," said Nattie. "Fletch's wedding shirt."

Fawn hopped up, went around to the wooden trunk, and lifted the lid. The shirt was right on top. She picked it up by the shoulders, letting the white fabric fall open. It was almost finished, except for the cuffs. The smocking around the tops of the sleeves and across the yoke in back was soft under her touch, and the buttons, already sewn down the front placket, were carved of iridescent mussel shell, cool and smooth.

She brought it to Dag, who laid it out in his lap, touching it clumsily and gingerly with his right fingertips and, more hesitantly, letting his hook hand drift above it, careful not to snag. "This isn't just one fiber, is it?"

"Linen for strength, cotton for softness, a bit of nettle flax for the shimmer," Nattie said. "I spun the thread special."

"Lakewalker women never spin or weave thread so fine. It takes too much time, and we never have enough of that."

Fawn glanced at his coarse shirt, which she had thought shoddy, with a new eye. "I remember helping Nattie and Mama set up the loom for that cloth, last winter. It took three days, and was so tedious and finicky I thought I'd scream."

"Lakewalker looms are little hanging things, which can be taken down and carried easy when we move camp. We could never shift that big wooden frame of your aunt's. That's a farmer tool. Sessile, as bad as barns and houses. Targets . . . " He lowered his gaze to the cloth again. "This is good ground, in this. It used to be plants, and . . . and creatures. Now its ground is wholly transformed. All shirt, whole. That's a good making, that is." He raised his face and stared at Nattie with a new and keen curiosity. "There's a blessing worked in."

Fawn would have sworn Nattie's lips twitched in a proud smirk, but the expression fleeted away too fast to be sure. "I tried," Nattie said modestly. "It's a wedding shirt, after all."

"Huh." Dag sat up, indicating with a nod that Fawn should take the shirt back. She folded it away again carefully and sat on the trunk. A tension hung between Nattie and Dag, and she hesitated to walk between them, lest something delicate tear and snap like a spiderweb.

Dag said, "I'm willing to try for the binding strings if you are, Aunt Nattie. It sure would change the argument, up home. If it doesn't work, we're no worse off than we were, except for the disappointment, and if it does . . . we're that much farther along."

"Farther along to where?" asked Nattie.

Dag gave a wry snort. "We'll all find out when we arrive, I expect."

"That's a fair saying," allowed Nattie amiably. "All right, patroller. You got yourself a bargain."

"You mean you'll speak for us to Mama and Papa?" Fawn wanted to jump up and squeal. She stopped it down to a more demure squeak, and leaped to the bed to give Nattie a hug and a kiss.

Nattie fought her off, unconvincingly. "Now, now, lovie, don't carry on so. You'll be giving me the heebie-jeebies." She sat up straight and turned her face once more toward the man across from her. "One other thing . . . Dag. If you'd be willing to hear me out."

His brows twitched up at the unaccustomed use of his name. "I'm a good listener."

"Yeah, I noticed that about you." But then Nattie fell silent. She shifted a little, as if embarrassed, or . . . or shy? Surely not . . . "Before that young Lakewalker fellow left, he gave me one last present. Because I said I was sorry to part never having seen his face. Well, actually, his lady gave it me, I suppose. She was something of a hand at Lakewalker healings, it seemed, of the sort he did for my poor ankle when first we met."

"Matching grounds," Dag interpreted this. "Yes? It's a bit intimate. Actually, it's a lot intimate."

Nattie's voice fell to almost a whisper, as if confiding dark secrets. "It was like she lent me her eyes for a spell. Now, he wasn't too different from what I'd pictured, sort of homely-handsome. Hadn't expected the red hair and the shiny suntan, though, on a fellow who'd been sleeping all day and running around all night. Touch of a shock, that." She went quiet for a long stretch. "I've never seen Fawn's face, you know." The offhand tone of her voice would have fooled no one present, Fawn thought, even without the little quaver at the end.

Dag sat back, blinking.

In the silence, Nattie said uncertainly, "Maybe you're too tired. Maybe it's . . . too hard. Too much."

"Um . . . " Dag swallowed, then cleared his throat. "I am mightily tired this night, I admit. But I'm willing to try for you. Not sure it'll work, is all. Wouldn't want to disappoint."

"If it don't work, we're no worse off than we were. As you say."

"I did," he agreed. He shot a bleak smile at Fawn. "Change places with me, Spark?"

She scrambled off Nattie's bed and took his spot on her own, as he sat down beside Nattie. He hitched his shoulders and slipped his arm out of his sling.

"You be careful with that arm," warned Fawn anxiously.

"I think I can lift it from the shoulder all right now, if I don't try to wriggle my fingers too much or put any pressure on it. Nattie, I'm going to try to touch your temples, here. I can use my fingers for the right side, but I'm afraid I'll have to touch you with the backside of my hook on the left, if only for the balance. Don't jump around, eh?"

"Whatever you say, patroller." Nattie sat bolt upright, very still. She nervously wet her lips. Her pearl eyes were wide, staring hard into space. Dag eased up close to her, lifting his hands to either side of her head. Except for a somewhat inward expression on his face, there was nothing whatsoever to see.

Fawn caught the moment only because Nattie blinked and gasped, shifting her eyes sideways to Dag. *"Oh."* And then, more impatiently, "No, don't look at that dumpy old woman. I don't want to see her anyhow, and besides, it isn't true. Look over *there.*"

Obligingly, Dag turned his head, parallel with Nattie's if rather above it. He smiled at Fawn. She grinned back, her breath coming faster with the thrill shivering about the room.

"My word," breathed Nattie. "My word." The timeless moment stretched. Then she said, "Come on, patroller. There isn't hardly nothing human in the wide green world could be as pretty as that."

"That's what I thought," said Dag. "You're seeing her ground as well as her face, you know. Seeing her as I do."

"Do you, now," whispered Nattie. "Do you. That explains a lot." Her eyes locked hungrily on Fawn, as if seeking to memorize the sightless vision. Her lids welled with water, which glimmered in the candlelight.

"Nattie," said Dag, his voice a mix of strain and amusement and regret, "I can't keep this up much longer. I'm sorry."

"It's all right, patroller. It's enough. Well, not that. But you know."

"Yes." Dag sighed and sat back, slumping. Awkwardly, he slipped his splinted arm back in its sling, then bent over, staring at the floor.

"Are you sick again?" asked Fawn, wondering if she should dash for a basin.

"No. Bit of a headache, though. There are things floating in my vision. There, they're fading now." He blinked rapidly and straightened again. "Ow. You people do take it out of me. I feel as though I'd just come off walking patterns for ten days straight. In the worst weather. Over crags."

Nattie sat up, her tears smearing in tracks like water trickling down a cliff face. She scrubbed at her cheeks and glared around the room that she could no longer see. "My word, this is a grubby hole we've been stuffed in all this time, Fawn, lovie. Why didn't you ever say? I'm going to make the boys whitewash the walls, I am."

"Sounds like a good idea to me," said Fawn. "But I won't be here."

"No, but *I* will." Nattie sniffed resolutely.

After a few more minutes to recover her stability, Nattie planted her cane and hoisted herself up. "Well, come on, you two. Let's get this started."

Fawn and Dag followed her out past the weaving room; once through the door to the kitchen, Fawn cuddled in close to Dag's left side, and he let his arm drift around behind her back and anchor her there, and maybe himself as well. The whole family was seated around the lamplit table, Papa and Mama and Fletch on the near end, Reed and Rush and Whit beyond. They looked up warily. Whatever conference they were having, they'd kept their voices remarkably low; or else they hadn't been daring to talk to one another at all.

"Are they all there?" muttered Nattie.

"Yes, Aunt Nattie."

Nattie stepped up to the center of the kitchen and thumped the floor with her cane, drawing herself up in full Pronouncement Mode such as Fawn had very seldom seen, not since the time Nattie had so-finally settled the argument for damages with the irate Bowyers over the twins' and Whit's cow-racing episode, years ago. Nattie drew a long breath; everyone else held theirs.

"*I'm* satisfied," Nattie announced loudly. "Fawn shall have her patroller. Dag shall have his Spark. See to it, Tril and Sorrel. The rest of you lot" —she glared to remarkable effect, when she put her mind to it, the focused blankness making her eyes seem quite uncanny—"behave yourselves, for once!"

And she turned and walked, very briskly, back into her weaving room. Just in case anyone was foolish enough to try to challenge that last word, she gave her cane a jaunty twirl and knocked the door closed behind her.

17

ag woke late from a sodden sleep to find that his next duty in this dance was to ride with Fawn and her parents to West Blue to register their intentions with the village clerk, and to beg his official attendance on the wedding. Fawn was fussed and nervous getting Dag shaved, washed up, and dressed, which confused him at first, because she'd had the help down to a fairly straightforward routine, and despite his fatigue he wasn't being gracelessly cranky this morning. He finally realized that at last they would be seeing people outside of her family—ones she'd known all her life. And vice versa. It would be the first view most of West Blue would have of Dag the Lakewalker, *that lanky fellow Fawn Bluefield dragged home* or however he was now known to local gossip.

He tried not to let his imagination descend too far into the disagreeable possibilities, but he couldn't help reflecting that the only resident of West Blue who had met him so far was Stupid Sunny. It seemed too much to hope that Sunny was not given to gossip, and it was already proven he'd a habit of altering the facts to his own favor. His humiliation was more likely to make him sly than contrite. The Bluefields could well be Dag's only allies in the farmer community; it seemed a thin thread to hang from. So he let Fawn carry on in her efforts to turn him out presentably, futile as they seemed.

The hamlet, three miles south via the shade-dappled river road, appeared peaceful and serene as Sorrel drove the family horse cart down the main, and seemingly only, street. It was a day for fluffy white clouds against a bright blue sky utterly innocent of any intent to rain, which added to the illusion of good cheer. The principal reasons for the village's existence seemed to be a grain mill, a small sawmill, and the timber wagon bridge, which showed signs of having been recently widened. Around the little market square, presently largely idle, were a smithy, an alehouse, and a number of other houses, mostly built of the native river stone. Sorrel brought the cart to a halt before one such and led the way inside. Dag ducked his head under an excessively low stone lintel, just missing braining himself.

He straightened cautiously and found the ceiling sufficient. The front room seemed a cross between a farmhouse parlor and a camp lore-tent, with benches, a table, and shelves stuffed with papers, rolled parchments, and bound record books. The litter of records flooded on into the rooms beyond. In through the back hall bustled the clerk himself, who seemed, by the way he dusted the knees of his trousers, to have been interrupted in the midst of gardening. He was on the high side of middle age, sharp-nosed, potbellied, and perky, and was introduced to Dag by the very farmerly name of Shep Sower.

He greeted the Bluefields as old friends and neighbors, but he was clearly taken aback by Dag. "Well, well, well!" he said, when Sorrel, with determined help from Fawn, explained the reason for the visit. "So it's true!" His stout but equally perky wife arrived, gaped at Dag, dipped her knees rather like Fawn upon introduction, smiled a bit frantically, and dragged Tril away out of earshot.

The registry process was not complex. It consisted of the clerk's first finding the right record book, tall and thick and bound in leather, dumping it open on the table, thumbing through to the most recent page, and affixing the date and penning a few lines under some similar entries. He required the place and date of birth and parents' names of both members of the couple—he didn't even ask before jotting down Fawn's, although his hand hesitated and the pen sputtered when Dag recited his own birth date; after a doubtful stare upward, he blotted hastily and asked Dag to repeat it. Sorrel handed him the rough notes of the marriage agreement, to be written out properly in a fair hand, and Sower read it quickly and asked a few clarifying questions.

It was only at this point that Dag discovered there was a fee for this service, and it was customary for the would-be husband to pay it. Fortunately, he had not left his purse with his other things at the farm, and doubly fortunately, because they had been far longer about this journey than he'd planned, he still had some Silver Shoals copper crays, which sufficed. He had Fawn fish the little leather bag from his pocket and pay up. Apparently, arrangements could also be made for payment in kind, for the coinless.

"There always come some here who can't sign their own names," Sower informed Dag, with a nod at his sling. "I sign for them, and they make their X, and the witnesses sign to confirm it."

"It's been six days since I busted the arm," said Dag a little tightly. "For this, I think I can manage." He did let Fawn go first, watching her closely. He then had her dip the quill again and help push it into his fingers. The grip was painful but not impossible. The signature was not his best, but at least it was clearly legible. The clerk's brows went up at this proof of literacy.

The clerk's wife and Fawn's mother returned. Missus Sower's gaze on Dag had become rather wide-eyed. Craning her neck curiously, she read out, "Dag Redwing Hickory Oleana."

"Oleana?" said Fawn. "First I heard of that part."

"So you'll be Missus Fawn Oleana, eh?" said Sower.

"Actually, that's my hinterland name," Dag put in. "Redwing is what you would call my family name."

"Fawn Redwing," Fawn muttered experimentally, brows drawing down in concentration. "Huh."

Dag scratched his forehead with the side of his hook. "It's more confusing than that. Lakewalker custom has the fellow taking the name of his bride's tent, by which I would become, er . . . Dag Bluefield West Blue Oleana, I suppose."

Sorrel looked horrified.

"What do we do, then, swap names?" asked Fawn in a tone of great puzzlement. "Or take both? Redwing-Bluefield. Er. Redfield? Bluewing?"

"You two could be purple-something," Sower suggested genially, with a wheezing laugh.

"I can't think of anything purple that doesn't sound stupid!" Fawn protested. "Well . . . Elderberry, I suppose. That's lake-ish."

"Already taken," Dag informed her blandly.

"Well . . . well, we have a few days to think it over," said Fawn valiantly.

Sorrel and Tril glanced at each other, seemed to inhale for strength, and bent to sign below. The day and time for the wedding was set for the earliest moment after the customary three days at which the clerk would be available to lend his official presence, which to Fawn's obvious relief was the afternoon of the third day hence.

"In a hurry, are you?" Sower inquired mildly, and while Dag did not at first catch his covert glance at Fawn's belly, she did, and stiffened.

"Unfortunately, I have duties waiting at home," Dag put in quellingly, letting his wrist cuff rest on her shoulder. Actually, aside from averting panic by beating Mari back to camp, till this blighted arm healed he was going to be just as useless at Hickory Lake as he was here at West Blue. It hardly mattered at which spot he sat around grinding his teeth in frustration, although West Blue at least had more novelty. But the disturbing mystery of the sharing knife was an itch at the back of his mind, well buried under the new distractions yet never fading altogether.

Three people jerked away from the Sowers' front window and pretended to have been walking up the street when Dag, Fawn, and her parents made their way out the front door. Across the street, a couple of young women clutched each other and bent their heads together, giggling. A group of young men loitering in front of the alehouse undraped themselves from the wall and went back inside, two of them hastily.

"Wasn't that Sunny Sawman just went into Millerson's?" Sorrel said, squinting.

"Wasn't that Reed with him?" said Fawn, in a more curious tone.

"So that's where Reed got off to this morning!" said Tril indignantly. "I'll skin that boy."

"Sawman's place is the second farm south of the village," Fawn informed Dag in an undervoice.

He nodded understanding. It would make the West Blue alehouse a convenient haunt, not that it wasn't a gathering place for the whole community, by the descriptions Dag had garnered. Sunny must realize that his secrets had been kept, or his standing with the Bluefield twins would be very different by now; if not grateful, the relief might at least render him circumspect. So, were any of those loiterers the friends Sunny had threatened to persuade to help slander Fawn? Or had that been an empty threat, and Fawn had merely fallen for the lie? No telling now. The boys were unlikely to cast slurs on her in her brother's presence, surely.

They all climbed back into the cart, and Sorrel, clucking, backed his horse and turned the vehicle around. He slapped the reins against the horse's rump, and it obligingly broke into a trot. West Blue fell behind.

Three days. There was no particular reason that simple phrase should make his stomach feel as though it wanted to flip over, Dag thought, but . . . *three days.*

After the noon dinner, Dag dismissed the obscurities of farmer customs from his mind for a time in favor of his own. He and Fawn went out together on a gathering trip around the farm.

"What are we looking for, really?" she asked him, as he led off first toward the old barn below the house.

"There's no set recipe. Spinnable things with some personal meaning to help catch our grounds upon. A person's own hair is always good, but mine's not long enough to use pure, and a few more hooks never hurt. The horsehair will give length and strength, I figure. It's often used, and not just for wedding cords."

In the cool shade of the barn, Fawn culled two collections of long sturdy hairs from the tails and manes of Grace and Copperhead. Dag hung on the stall partition, eyes half-shut, gently reminding Copperhead of their agreement that the gelding would treat Fawn with the tender concern of a mare for her foal or

become wolf-bait. Horses did not reason by consequences so much as by asso-
ciations, and the rangy chestnut had fewer wits than many, but by dint of repeated groundwork Dag had at length put this idea across. Copperhead
nickered and nuzzled and lipped at Fawn, endured having hairs pulled out
while scarcely flinching, ate apple slices from her hand without nipping, and
eyed Dag warily.

There were no water lilies to be had on the Bluefield acres, and Dag was
uncertain that their stems would yield up flax the way the ones at Hickory
Lake did anyway, but to his delight they discovered a cattail-crowded drainage
ditch up beyond the high fields that sheltered some red-winged blackbird nests.
He held Fawn's shoes on his hook and murmured encouragement, grinning at
her expression of revulsion and determination, as she waded out in the muck
and gathered some goodly handfuls of both cattail fluff and feathers. After that,
they tramped all around the margins and crossed and recrossed the fallow
fields. It was not the season for milkweed silk, as the redolent flowers were just
blooming, and the stems were useless, but at length they discovered a few
dried brown sticks lingering from last fall whose pods hadn't broken open, and
Dag pronounced the catch sufficient.

They took it all back to Nattie's weaving room, where Fawn stripped
feathers and picked out milkweed seeds, and Nattie set out her own chosen
mix of fibers: linen for strength, a bit of precious purchased cotton brought
from south of the Grace River for softness and something she called *catch,*
nettle flax for shine, all dyed dark with walnut stain. Fawn bit her lip and undertook the hair trimming, taking special care with Dag, not so much to avoid
stabbing him with the scissors, he eventually realized, as to be sure his head
wouldn't look like a scarecrow's on the day after tomorrow. She set up a small
mirror to cautiously clip out some of her own curly strands. Dag sat quietly,
enjoying watching her contort, counting the hours backward to when they'd
last been able to lie together, and forward to the next chance. *Three days . . .*

Under her aunt's close supervision Fawn then mixed the ingredients in
two baskets until Nattie, plunging her arms in and feeling while frowning judiciously in a way that had Fawn holding her breath, pronounced them ready
for the next step. Shaping such a disparate mass of fibers into the long rolls for
spinning could only be done by the gentlest carding and a lot of handwork, and
even Fawn's willing fingers looked to be tiring by the end.

They went on to the spinning itself after supper. The male members of the
family had some dim idea that the three were up to some outlandish Lakewalker project to please Dag, but they were well trained not to intrude upon
Nattie's domain, and Dag doubted they suspected magic, so subtle and invisible a one as this was. They went off about their own usual pursuits. Tril drifted
in and out from labors in the kitchen, watching but saying little.

After some debate, it was decided Fawn would be the spinner after all; she was certain Nattie would do it better, but Dag was certain that the more making she put into the task with her own hands, the better the faint chance of tangling her ground in the cord would be. She chose to spin on the wheel, a device Dag had never seen in operation before coming here, saying she was better at it than at the drop spindle. Once she'd finally settled and gathered up her materials and her confidence, the task went much more quickly than Dag had expected. At length she triumphantly handed over for Nattie's inspection two hanks of sturdy if rather hirsute two-ply thread something between yarn and string in texture.

"Nattie could have spun it smoother and more even." Fawn sighed.

"Mm," said Nattie, feeling the bundles. She didn't disagree, but she did say, "This'll do."

"Shall we go on now?" Fawn asked eagerly. Full night had fallen, and they had been working by candlelight for the past hour.

"We'll be more rested in the morning," said Dag.

"I'm all right."

"*I'll* be more rested in the morning, Spark. Have some pity on an old patroller, eh?"

"Oh. That's right. Groundwork drains you pretty dry." She added after a cautious moment, "Will this be as bad as the bowl?"

"No. This is a lot more natural. Besides, I've done this before. Well . . . Kauneo's mother actually did the spinning that time, because neither of us had the skill. Each of us had to do our own braiding, though, to catch our grounds."

Fawn sighed. "I'm never going to be able to sleep tonight."

In fact, she did, although not before Dag had heard through the closed door Nattie telling her to settle, it was worse than sleeping with a bedbug. Fawn's soft giggle was his last memory of the night.

They met again in the weaving room right after breakfast, as soon as the rest of the family had cleared off. This time, Dag closed the door firmly. They'd set up a backless bench, filched from the porch, so that Fawn could sit astride it with Dag directly behind her. Nattie took a seat in a chair just beyond Fawn's knee, listening with her head cocked, her weak groundsense trying to strain beyond its normal limit of the reach of her skin. Dag watched while Fawn practiced on some spare string; it was a four-stranded braiding that produced an extremely strong cord, a pattern called by Lakewalkers *mint-stem* for its square cross section, and by farmers, Dag was bemused to learn, the same.

"We'll start with my cord," he told her. "The main thing is, once I catch my ground in the braiding, don't stop, or the ground-casting will break, and we'll have to undo it all and start again from the beginning. Which, actually, we can do right enough, but it's a bit frustrating to get almost to the end and then sneeze."

She nodded earnestly and finished setting up, knotting the four strands to a simple nail driven into the bench in front of her. She spread out the wound-up balls that kept the loose ends under control, gulped, and said, "All right. Tell me when to start."

Dag straightened and slipped his right arm from its sling, scooting up behind her close enough to touch, kissing her ear for encouragement and to make her smile, succeeding perhaps in the first but not the second. He looked over her head and brought both arms around and over hers, letting his hand and hook touch first the fiber, then her fingers, then hover over her hands. His ground, flowing out through his right hand, caught at once in the thick threads. "Good. Got it anchored. Begin."

Her nimble hands began to pull, flip, twist, repeat. The tug as the thin stream from his ground threaded beneath her touch was palpable to him, and he recalled anew how very strange it had felt the first time, in a quiet tent in wooded Luthlia. It was still very strange, if not unpleasant. The room became exceedingly still, and he thought he could almost mark the shift of the light and shadows beyond the windows as the morning sun crept up the eastern sky.

His right arm was shaking and his shoulders aching by the time she had produced a bit over two feet of cord. "Good," he whispered in her ear. "Enough. Tie off."

She nodded, tied the locking end knot, and held the strands tight. "Nattie? Ready?"

Nattie leaned over with the scissors and, guided by Fawn's touch, cut below the knot. Dag felt the snap-back in his ground, and controlled a gasp.

Fawn straightened and jumped up from the bench. Anxiously, she turned and held out the cord to Dag.

He nodded for her to run it through his fingertips below the increasingly grubby splint wrappings. The sensation was bizarre, like looking at a bit of himself in a distorted mirror, but the anchoring was sound and sweet. "Good! Done! We did it, Spark, Aunt Nattie!"

Fawn smiled like a burst of sunlight and pressed the cord into her aunt's hands. Nattie fingered it and smiled too. "My word. Yes. Even I can feel that. Takes me back, it does. Well done, child!"

"And the next?" she said eagerly.

"Catch your breath," Dag advised. "Walk around, shake out the kinks. The next will be a bit trickier." The next might well be impossible, he admitted bleakly to himself, but he wasn't going to tell Spark that; confidence mattered in these subtle things.

"Oh, yes, your poor shoulders must hurt after all that!" she exclaimed, and ran around to climb up on the bench behind him and knead them with her small strong hands, an exercise he could not bring himself to object to, although he did manage not to fall forward onto the bench and melt. He remembered what else those hands could do, then tried not to. He would need his concentration. Two days, now . . .

"That's enough, rest your fingers," he heroically choked out after a bit. He stood up and walked around the room himself, wondering what else he could do, or should do, or hadn't done, to make the next and most critical task succeed. He was about to step into the unaccustomed and worrisome territory of things he'd never done before—of things no one had ever done before, to his knowledge. Not even in ballads.

They sat on the bench again, and Fawn secured the four strands of her own string on the nail. "Ready when you are."

Dag lowered his face and breathed the scent of her hair, trying to calm himself. He ran his stiff hand and hook gently down and up her arms a couple of times, trying to pick up some fragment, some opening on the ground he could sense swirling, so alive, beneath her skin. Wait, there was something coming . . . "Begin."

Her hands started moving. After only about three turns, he said, "Wait, no. Stop. That isn't your ground, that's mine again. Sorry, sorry."

She blew out her breath, straightened her back, wriggled, and undid her work back to the beginning.

Dag sat for a moment with his head bent, eyes closed. His mind picked at the uncomfortable memory of the left-handed groundwork he'd done on the bowl two nights ago. The break in his right arm did weaken his very dominant ground on that side; maybe the left now tried to compensate for the right as the right had long done for the maimed left. This time, he concentrated hard on trying to snag Fawn's ground from her left hand. He stroked the back of her hand with his hook, pinched with ghostly fingers that were not there, just . . . there! He had something fastened in, fragile and fine, and it wasn't him this time. "Go."

Again, her hands began flying. They were a dozen turns into the braid when he felt the delicate link snap. "Stop." He sighed. "It's gone again."

"Ngh!" Fawn cried in frustration.

"Sh, now. We almost had something, there."

She unknotted, and hitched her shoulders, and rubbed the back of her head against his chest; he could almost feel her scowl, although from this angle of view he could only see her hair and nose. And then he could feel it when her scowl turned thoughtful.

"What?" he said.

"You said. You said, people put their hair in the cords because it was once part of their ground, and so it was easy to pick up again, to hitch on to. Because it was once part of their body, right? Your living body makes its ground."

"Right . . ."

"You also once said, one night when I was asking you all about ground, that people's blood stays alive for a little while even after it leaves their bodies, right?"

"What are you," he began uneasily, but was cut off when she abruptly seized his hook hand and drew it around close in front of her. He felt pressure and a jerk, then another, through his arm harness. "Wait, stop, Spark, what are you—" He leaned forward and saw to his horror that she'd gouged open the pads of both of her index fingers on the not especially sharp point of the hook. She squeezed each hand with the other in turn to make the blood drip, and took up the strands again.

"Try again," she said in an utterly determined little growl. "Come on, quick, before the bleeding stops. *Try.*"

He could not spurn a demand so astonishing. With a fierceness that almost matched hers, he ran his hands, real and ghostly, down her arms once more. This time, her ground fairly leaped out into the blood-smeared string, anchoring firmly. "Go," he whispered. And her hands began to twist and flip and pull.

"You are scaring the piss out of me, Spark, but it's working. Don't stop."

She nodded. And didn't stop. She finished her cord, of about the length of the one they'd done for him, just about the time her fingers ceased bleeding. "Nattie, I'm ready for you."

Nattie leaned in and snipped below the end knot. Dag felt it as Fawn's ground snapped back the way his had.

"Perfect," he assured her. "Absent gods, it's fine."

"Was it?" She twisted around to look up at him, her face tight. "I couldn't feel anything. I couldn't feel anything any of the times. Really?"

"It was . . . you were . . . " He groped for the right words. "That was *smart,* Spark. That was beyond smart. That was brilliant."

The tightness turned to a blaze of glory, shining in her eyes. *"Really?"*

"*I* would not have made that mental leap."

"Well, of course *you* wouldn't have." She sniffed. "You'd have gone all protective or tried to argue with me."

He gave her a hug, and a shake, and felt a strange new sympathy for her parents and their mixed reaction to her homecoming that first night. "You're probably right."

"I am certainly right." She gave a more Spark-like giggle.

He sat back, releasing her, and slipped his aching splinted arm back into its sling. "For pity's sake, go wash your fingers at once. With strong soap and plenty of it. You don't know where that hook has been."

"Everywhere, hasn't it?" She shot a merry grin over her shoulder, stroked her cord once more, and danced out to the kitchen.

Nattie leaned over and picked up the new cord from the bench, running it thoughtfully through her fingers.

"I didn't know she was going to do that," Dag apologized weakly.

"You never do, with her," Nattie said. "She'll be keeping you alert, I expect, patroller. Maybe more than you bargained for. Funny thing is, *you* think you know what you're doing."

"I used to." He sighed. "Though that may have been because I was only doing the same things over and over."

Spark returned from the kitchen, towing her mother to see their finished work. Dag trusted Fawn wouldn't mention the last wrinkle about the blood. Tril and Nattie handed the cords back and forth; Tril gave one a tug, nodding thoughtfully at its strength. She squared her shoulders and dug in her apron pocket.

"Nattie, do you remember that necklace Mama had with the six real gold beads, one for every child, that broke that time the cart went over in the snow, and she never found all the bits and never had it fixed?"

"Oh, yes," said her sister.

"The piece came to me, and I never did anything with it either. It's been in the back of a drawer for years and years. I thought you might could use the beads to finish off the end knots of these cords of Fawn's."

Fawn, excited, looked into her mother's palm and picked up one of the four oblong gold beads, peering through the hole. "Nattie, can we? Dag, would it work all right?"

"I think it would be a fine gift," Dag said, taking one that Fawn pressed upon him to examine. Actually, he wasn't altogether certain it wasn't a prayer. He glanced at Tril, who gave him a short, nearly expressionless nod. "Very beautiful. They would look really good against that dark braid and make the ends hang better, too. I'd be honored to accept."

Beads and cords were put into Nattie's clever hands, and she made short work of affixing the old gold to the ends, trimming the last bit of cord below the anchoring knots into neat fringes. When she finished, the two lengths— one a little darker, one with a coppery glint—lay glimmering in her lap like live things. Which they were, in a sense.

"That'll look well, when Fawn goes up to your country," said Tril. "They'll know we're . . . we're respectable folks. Don't you think, patroller?"

"Yes," he said, hearing the plea in her voice and hoping he didn't lie.

"Good." She nodded again.

Nattie took charge of the cords, putting them away until the day after tomorrow when she undertook to bind them about the unlikely pair. Tangled and blessed, the cords would complete the ground link, if both hearts willed it, sign and signifier of a valid union that any Lakewalker with groundsense must witness. Faithfully made. Dag was certain he would remember this hour of making as long as he lived, as long as he wore the cord curled around his arm, and how Spark had poured her heart's blood so furiously into it. *And if her true heart stops, I'll know.*

18

*O*ne day was Dag's first thought upon awakening the next morning.

He'd expected this wedding-eve day to be one of quiet preparation for the small family ceremony, with perhaps time to meditate with proper seriousness on the step he was about to take—also to calm the tiny voice screeching in the back of his mind, *What are you doing? How did you end up here? This wasn't in your plans! Do you have any idea what's going to happen when you get home?* To the last question a simple *No* seemed to Dag a sufficient answer. More complicated questions, such as, *How are you going to protect Spark when you can't even protect yourself?* or *What about half-blood children?* he tried to ignore, although the last thought led directly to, *Would they be sawed-off and fiery?* and kept on going from there.

But after breakfast there descended upon the Bluefield farm not the one or two neighbor girlfriends of Fawn's he'd been led dimly to expect, but two girlfriends, five of their sisters, four sisters-in-law, a few mutual cousins, and an indeterminate number of mothers and grandmothers. They were like a plague of locusts in reverse, bringing quantities of food with hands that produced and put in order instead of consuming and laying waste. They talked, they laughed, they sang, they—or at least the younger ones—giggled, and they filled the house to bursting. The male Bluefields promptly fled to the far corners of the farm. Dag, fascinated, lingered. For a time.

Being introduced to the young women wasn't too bad, even though he mainly garnered either intimidated silences or nervous titters in return. The bolder ones, however, observing Fawn's aid to him, wanted to try their hands at it too, and he was shortly ducking being fed and watered like some strange new pet. *Fattened for the slaughter,* he tried not to think. An even more giggly troop, albeit led by a sterner matron, along with Fawn, who refused to explain anything, cornered him with strings and proceeded to measure various parts of his body—happily for his shredding equanimity, not *that* one—and floated away again in gales of laughter. Nattie's weaving room, ordinarily a quiet refuge, was jammed, and the kitchen was not only crowded but intolerably overheated from the busy hearth. By noon, Dag followed the men into self-imposed exile, although he lurked close enough to listen to the singing floating out through the open windows. With all the males gone, some of the songs grew unsurprisingly rowdy; this was to be a wedding party, after all. He was glad Fawn was not to be deprived of these flourishes due to her strange choice of partner.

The female help left before supper, although with plans to return again in the morning for the final push, but it wasn't till afterward that Dag found his thinking time. He settled by himself on the front porch, dangling his legs over the edge and watching the quiet river valley turn from gold-green to muted gray as the sun set. In the eaves of the old barn, the soft, tawny mourning doves called in their soft, tawny voices. It was Dag's favorite view on the whole farm, and he thought whoever had originally sited this house must have shared the pleasure. He felt strangely unanchored, all his old certainties falling behind, and no new ones to replace them. Except for Spark. And she made an unlikely fixed point in his spinning world, because she moved so fast he feared he'd miss her if he blinked.

He caught sight of Rush walking down the lane in the gathering shadows. After the bowl episode, the twins had stopped aiming barbs at him, but only because they now avoided talking to him at all. If he couldn't make friends, perhaps intimidation would do instead? Whit by contrast had become rather fascinated with Dag, following him about as though afraid he'd miss another magic show. Dag tried treating him as a particularly feckless young patroller, which seemed to work. If only his arm hadn't been broken he might have offered to teach Whit archery, which would have made a good way to move them along amiably. As it was, his idle comment about it made Whit say, showing willing to a degree that surprised him, "When you come back, maybe?"

Which made him wonder: were they ever coming back? Half of Dag's original intent for the marriage proposal had been to repair Fawn's bridges here in case of some dire need—in case of his death, bluntly. A Lakewalker would be trying to join his bride's family, to fit in as a new tent-brother; and the family in turn would expect to receive him as one. Farmer kin took in new sisters, not new brothers, and they weren't trained up to the reverse. It had taken Dag some time to realize that the only members of the family he really needed to please in order to carry off Fawn were the elders, and they had quite expected her to be carried off sometime by someone in any case. Dag was a stretch of custom, but not a reversal. The questions this begged for Dag's own homecoming niggled hard, the more so since Fawn could not anticipate most of them.

And here came Rush again, walking back up the lane. He spied Dag on the porch and angled toward him between the house and the old barn, a grassy area the sheep were sometimes turned out to crop. What the sheep refused to eat was scythed once a year to keep the space from turning back to woods and blocking the view. Rush, Dag realized as he approached, was tense, and Dag considered opening his groundsense wider, unpleasant as it was likely to prove.

"Hey, patroller," said Rush. "Fawn wants you. Down by the road at the end of the lane."

Dag blinked once, slowly, to cover the fact that he'd just snapped open his groundsense to its full range. Fawn, he determined first, was not down by the end of the lane, but nearly out of his perceptions to the west, up over the ridge. Not alone—with Reed?—she seemed not to be in any special distress, however. So why was Rush lying? Ah. The woods below were not unpeopled. Concealed among the trees near the road were the smudges of four horses, standing still—tied? Four persons accompanied them. Three blurred grounds he did not know, but the fourth he recognized as Stupid Sunny. Was it so wild a guess to think that the other three were also husky young farm boys? Dag thought not.

"Did she say why?" Dag asked, to buy a moment more to think.

Rush took a couple of breaths to invent an answer, apparently having expected Dag to leap up without delay. "Some wedding thing or other," he replied. "She didn't say, but she wants you right now."

Dag scratched his temple gently with his hook, glad that he had mostly stuck to the deeply ingrained habit of not discussing Lakewalker abilities with anyone here, Fawn and Nattie excepted. He was now one move ahead in this game; he tried to figure how not to squander that advantage, because he suspected it was the only one he had. It would be amusing to just sit here and watch Rush dig himself deeper concocting more desperate reasons for Dag to walk down the hill into what was shaping up to be a neat little ambush. But that would leave the whole pack of them running around loose all night to evolve other plans. As little as Dag wanted to deal with this tonight, still less did he want to deal with it in the morning. And most especially did he not want it to impinge on Spark in any way. His brotherly enemies, it seemed, were looking after that angle for him just now. So.

He let his groundsense play lightly over the lower woods, which he had crossed several times on foot in the past days, looking for . . . yes. Just exactly that. A flush, not of excitement, but of that very peculiar calm that came over him when facing a bandit camp or a malice lair jerked his mind up to another level. Targets, eh. He knew what to do with targets. But would targets know what to do with him? His lips drew back. If not, he would teach them.

"Um . . . Dag?" said Rush uncertainly.

He wasn't wearing his war knife. That was fine; he had no hand to wield it. He stood up and shook out his left arm. "Sure, Rush. Where did you say, again?"

"Down by the road," said Rush, both relieved and the reverse. Absent gods, but the boy was a poor liar. On the whole, that was a point in his favor.

"You coming with me, Rush?"

"In a minute. You go along. I have to get something in the house."

"All right," said Dag amiably, and trod off down the hill to the lane. He descended it for a few hundred paces, then cut over to the wooded hillside, plotting his routes. He needed to surprise his ambushers on the correct side for his purpose. He wondered how fast they could run. His legs were long; theirs were young. Best not to cut it too close.

Mari would beat me for trying this fool stunt. It was an oddly comforting thought. Familiar.

Dag ghosted down the hill at an angle until he was about fifteen feet behind the four young men hiding in the shadows of the trees and keeping watch on the lane. *Looks like Sunny took my advice.* It was still early twilight; Dag's groundsense would give him considerable advantage in the dark, but he wanted his quarry to be able to see him. "Evening, boys," he said. "Looking for me?"

They jumped and whirled. Sunny's gold head was bright even in the shadows. The others were more nondescript: one stout, one as muscular as Sunny, and one skinny; young enough to be foolish and big enough to be dangerous. It was an unpleasant combination. Three were armed with cudgels, for which Dag had a new respect. Sunny had both a stick and a big hunting knife, the latter still in the sheath at his belt. For now.

Sunny got his breath back and growled, "Hello, patroller. Let me tell you how it's going to be."

Dag tilted his head as if in curiosity.

"You're not wanted here. In a few minutes Rush is going to bring down your horse and your gear, and you're going to get on and ride north. And you don't come back."

"Amazing!" Dag marveled. "How do you figure you're going to make that happen, son?"

"If you don't, you get the beating of your life. And we'll tie you on your horse and you'll still ride north. Only without your teeth." Sunny's grin showed white in the shadows, to emphasize this threat. His friends shifted, a little too tense and worried to quite share the amusement, although one tried a huffy sort of laugh to show support.

"Not to find fault, but I see a few problems with your plan. First would be a notable absence of horse. I 'spect Rush is going to have a trifle of difficulty handling Copperhead." Dag let his groundsense spread briefly as far as the old barn. Rush's troubles were indeed beginning. He decided he did not have the attention to spare on managing his horse at this distance, and withdrew the link. The entire family had been told, at the dinner table in front of Sorrel and Tril, to leave Copperhead alone unless Dag was there. Rush was on his own. Dag tried not to smile too much.

"Patroller, *Fawn* can handle your horse."

"Indeed she can. But, you know, you sent Rush. Unfortunate, that."

"Then you can start walking."

"After a beating? You have a high opinion of my stamina." He let his voice go softer. "Think the four of you can take me?"

They glanced at his sling, at his handless left arm, at each other. Dag was flattered that they didn't all burst into laughter at this point. He thought they should have, but he wasn't about to say so. The stout one, in fact, looked just a shade ashamed. Sunny, granted, was more guarded. That hunting knife was a new ornament.

"Just to make it clear, I decline your invitation to the road. I don't care to miss my wedding. Now, it does look as if you have the numbers on your side. Are you prepared to kill me tonight? How many of you are ready to die to make that happen? Have you thought how your parents and families will feel about it tomorrow? How the survivors are going to explain to them what happened? Killing gets a lot messier than you'd think, and the mess doesn't end with burying the corpses. I speak from long experience."

He had to stop this; by their uncertain expressions, his words were getting through to at least two of them, and that hadn't exactly been his intent when he'd started babbling, here. Run and chase, that was the game plan. Fortunately, Sunny and the other muscular one were starting to try to stalk him, moving apart and around to get into position for a rush. To encourage them, he started to back up. And called, "No wonder Fawn calls you Stupid Sunny."

Sunny's head jerked up. From the side, one of his friends muffled a guffaw; Sunny shot a glare at him and snapped to Dag, "Fawn's a slut. But you know that. Don't you, patroller."

Right, that's done it. "You'll have to catch me first, boys. If you're as slow-footed as you are slow-witted, I shouldn't have a problem—"

Sunny lunged, his stick whistling through the air. Dag was not there.

Dag stretched his legs, driving up the hill, dodging around trees, boots slipping on old leaves and damp limestone lumps and green-black rolling round hickory husks. By the thump and pained grunt, at least one of his pursuers was finding the footing equally foul. He didn't actually want to lose the boys in the woods, but he wanted a good head start by the time he arrived . . .

Here.

Ah. Hm.

His chosen tree turned out to be a shagbark hickory with a trunk a bit less than a foot and a half wide. And no side branches for twenty feet straight up. This was a mixed blessing. It would certainly be a challenge for the boys to follow him up it. If he could get up it. He pulled his right arm from the sling and let it swing out of his way, reached up with his left, jammed in his hook, clapped his knees around the trunk, and began shinnying. Yanked the hook out again, reached, jammed, shinnied. Again. Again. He was about fifteen feet in the air when the pursuit arrived, winded and swearing and waving their cudgels. It occurred to him, in a meditative sort of way as he dragged his body skyward, that even without the unpleasant searing feeling in his left shoulder muscles, he was putting an awful lot of trust in a small wooden bolt and some stitching *designed* to pull out. The rough bark strips crackled and split beneath his gripping knees, small bits raining down in an aromatic shower. If his hook gave way and he slid down, the bark would have an interesting serrated effect between his legs, too.

He made it to the first sturdy side branch, put an arm and a leg over, winched himself up, and stood. He searched for his objective. Absent gods, another fifteen feet to go. Up, then.

A dry branch gave way under one foot, which was partly useful, for he was then able to kick it free and drop it on the upturned face of the skinny fellow who was being urged up the tree in Dag's wake by his friends. He yelped and fell back, discouraged for a moment. Dag didn't need too many more moments.

To his delight, a rock whistled up past him, then another. "Ow!" he cried realistically, to lure more of them. A couple more missiles rose and fell, followed by a meaty *clunk* and an entirely authentic "*OW!*" from below. Dag made sure they could hear his evil laugh, even though he was wheezing like a smithy's bellows by now.

Almost to goal. Absent gods, the blighted thing was well out on that side branch. He extended himself, gripping the branch he was half-lying across under his right armpit, feet sliding along the wobbly bough below it, wishing for almost the first time in his life for more height and reach. Overbalance at this elevation, and he could swiftly prove himself stupider than Stupid Sunny. A little more, a little more, get his hook around that attachment . . . and a good yank.

Dag clung hard as the rough gray paper-wasp nest the size of a watermelon parted from the branch and began its thirty-five foot-drop. Most of the nest's residents were home for the evening, his groundsense told him, settling down for the night. *Wake up! You're under attack!* His feeble effort to stir up the wasps with his ground seemed redundant when the plummeting object hit the dirt and ruptured with a loud and satisfying *thwack*. Followed by a deep angry whine he could hear all the way up here.

The first screams were a deal more satisfying, though.

He cuddled back against the trunk of the tree, feet braced on some less flexible side branches, gasping for breath and applying himself to a few refinements. Persuading the furious wasps to advance up trouser legs and down collars proved not as difficult as he'd feared, although he could not simply bounce them like mosquitoes, and they were much less tractable than fireflies. A matter of practice, Dag decided. He set to it with a will.

"Ah! Ah! They're in my hair, they're in my hair, they're *stinging meee!*" came a wail from below, voice too high-pitched to identify.

"Augh, my *ears!* Ow, my hands! Get them off, *get them off!*"

"Run for the river, Sunny!"

The shuffling sounds of retreat filtered up through the leaves; the pell-mell flight wouldn't help them much, for Dag made sure they left under full guard. Even without groundsense, though, he could tell when his trouser-explorers made it all the way to target by the earsplitting shrieks that went up and up until breath was gone.

"*Limp* for the river, Sunny," Dag muttered savagely, as the frantic cries trailed away to the east.

Then came the matter of getting down.

Dag took it slowly, at least till the last ten feet when his hook slipped free and scored a long slash down the trunk in the wake of the flying bark bits from under his knees. But he did manage to land on his feet and avoid banging his splint very much on anything on the way. He staggered upright, gasping. "It was easier . . . when I could just . . . gut them . . ."

No. Not really.

He sighed, and did his best to tidy himself up a trifle, brushing bark and sticks and wide papery leaves from his clothing and hair with the back of his hook, and gratefully slipping his throbbing right arm back into its sling. A few stray wasps buzzed near in investigative menace; he sent them off after their nest mates and slithered back down the slope to where the horses were tied.

He picked apart their ties and did his best to loop up their reins so they wouldn't step on them, led them out onto the road, and pointed them south, trying to plant horsey suggestions about barns and grain and home into their limited minds. They would either find their way, or Sunny and his friends could have a fine time over the next few days looking for them. Once the boys could get their swollen selves out of bed, that is. A couple of the would-be bullies, including Sunny—Dag had made quite sure of Sunny on that score—would *definitely* not be wishing to ride home tonight. Or for many nights to come.

As he was wearily climbing back up the lane, he met Sorrel hastening down. Sorrel gripped a pitchfork and looked thoroughly alarmed.

"What in thunder was that awful screeching, patroller?" he demanded.

"Some fool young fellows trespassing in your woods thought it would be a grand idea to chuck rocks at a wasp nest. It didn't work out the way they'd pictured."

Sorrel snorted in half-amused vexation, the tension draining out of his body, then paused. "Really?"

"I think that would be the best story all around, yes."

Sorrel gave a little growl that reminded Dag suddenly of Fawn. "Plain enough there's more to it. Have it in hand, do you?" He turned again to walk up the lane side by side with Dag.

"That part, yes." Dag extended his groundsense again, this time toward the old barn. His future brother-in-law was still alive, though his ground was decidedly agitated at the moment. "There's another part. Which I think is your place and not mine to deal with." It was not one patrol leader's job to correct another patrol leader's people. On the other hand, teaming up could sometimes be remarkably effective. "But I think we might get forward faster if you'd be willing to take some direction from me."

"About what?"

"In this case, Reed and Rush."

Sorrel muttered something about, ". . . ready to knock their fool heads together." Then added, "What about them?"

"I think we ought to let Rush tell us. Then see."

"Huh," said Sorrel dubiously, but he followed as Dag turned aside from the lane at the old barn.

The sliding door onto the lane was open, and a soft yellow light spilled out from an oil lantern hung on a nail in a rafter. Grace, in a box stall by the door, snorted uneasily as they entered. The packed-dirt aisle smelled not unpleasantly of horses and straw and manure and dove droppings and dry rot. From Copperhead's box sounded an angry squeal. Dag held out a restraining hand as Sorrel started to surge forward. *Wait,* Dag mouthed.

It was hard for Dag not to laugh out loud as the scene revealed itself, although the sight of half his gear strewn across the stall floor being well trampled by Copperhead did quite a lot to help him keep a straight face. On the far wall of the stall, some wooden slats were nailed to make a crude manger, and above it a square was cut in the ceiling to allow hay to be tossed down directly from the loft above. Although the hole was big enough to stuff down an armload of hay, it wasn't quite big enough for Rush's broad shoulders to make the reverse trip. At the moment, having scrambled off the top of the manger as a partial ladder, Rush had one leg and both arms awkwardly jammed through the hole, and was attempting to twist the rest of his body out of range of Copperhead's snapping yellow teeth. Copperhead, ears flat back and neck snaking, squealed and snapped again, apparently for the pure evil pleasure of watching Rush squirm harder.

"Patroller!" Rush cried as he saw them come up to the stall partition. "Help me! Call off your horse!"

Sorrel shot Dag a worried look; Dag returned a small headshake and draped his arms over the partition, leaning comfortably.

"Now, Rush," said Dag in a conversational voice, "I distinctly remember telling you and your brothers that Copperhead was a warhorse, and to leave him alone. Do you remember that, Sorrel?"

"Yes, I do, patroller," said Sorrel, matching his tone, also resting his elbows on the boards.

"I know you magic him in some way! Get him off me!"

"Well, we'll have to see about that. Now, what I'm mightily curious about is just how you happened to be in his stall, without my leave, but with my saddlebags and bedroll and all my gear, which I had left in Aunt Nattie's weaving room. I think your pa would like to hear that story, too." And then Dag fell silent.

The silence stretched. Rush made a tentative move to swing down. Copperhead, excited, stamped and snapped and made a most peculiar noise, halfway between whipsaw menace and a horselaugh, Dag thought. Rush swung up again hastily.

"Your brute of a horse savaged me!" Rush complained. His shirt was ripped on one shoulder, and some blood leaked through, but it was clear to Dag's eye by the way Rush moved that there was nothing broken.

"Now, now," said Dag in a mock-soothing tone. "That was just a love bite, that was. If Copper'd really savaged you, you'd be over there, and your arm would be over here. Speaking from experience and all."

Rush's eyes widened as it dawned on him that if he'd wanted sympathy, he'd gone to the wrong store with the wrong coin.

Dag didn't say anything some more.

"What do you want to know?" Rush finally asked, in a surly tone.

"I'm sure you'll think of something," Dag drawled.

"Pa, make him let me down!"

Sorrel vented an exasperated sigh. "You know, Rush, I've drawn you and your brother out of wells of your own digging more than once when you were younger, because every boy's got to survive his share of foolishness. But as you're both so fond of telling me, you're not youngsters anymore. Seems to me you got yourself up there. You can get yourself down."

Rush looked appalled at this unexpected parental betrayal. He started blurting a somewhat garbled account for his predicament involving an imaginary request relayed from Fawn.

Dag gave Sorrel another small headshake. Sorrel looked increasingly grim.

"No," Dag interrupted in a bored voice, "That's not it. Think harder, Rush." After a moment, he said, "I should also mention, I suppose, that Sunny

Sawman and his three strapping friends are now on their way downriver to West Blue. Under escort. Underwater, mostly. I don't think they'll be back for some several days."

"How did you—I don't know what you're talking about!"

More silence.

Rush added in a smaller voice, "Are they all right?"

"They'll live," said Dag indifferently. "You can remember to thank me kindly for that, later." And fell silent again.

After a couple more false starts, Rush at last began to 'fess up. It was more or less the story Dag expected, of alehouse conspiracy and youthful bravado. In Rush's version, Reed was the ringleader, valiantly horrified at the thought of his only sister marrying a Lakewalker corpse-eater and thus making him brother-in-law to one, and Rush's motivations were lost in a mumble; Dag wasn't sure whether this was strict truth or blame-casting, nor did he greatly care, as it was clear enough both boys were in it together. They had found a strangely enthusiastic helper in Sunny, fresh from a summer of stump-pulling and happy to show off his muscle. Unsurprisingly, it appeared Sunny had not seen fit to mention to the twins his prior encounter with Dag. Dag chose not to either. Sorrel looked grimmer and grimmer.

Rush at last stuttered to a halt. A cool silence fell in the warm barn. Rush began to sag down; Copperhead lunged again. Rush tightened up once more, clinging like a possum to a branch. Dag could see that his arms were shaking.

"Now, Rush," said Dag. "I'm going to tell *you* how it's going to be. I am actually prepared to forgive and forget your brotherly plan to beat me crippled or dead and buried in your pa's woods on the night before my wedding. The fact that you also seriously endangered the lives of your friends—because I would not, facing that death, have held back in defending myself—I leave to your pa to take up with you two. I'll even forgive your lies to me." Dag's voice dropped to a deadly register that made Sorrel glance aside in alarm. "What I do not forgive is the *malice* of your lies to Fawn. You'd planned for her to wake up joyful on her wedding morning and then tell her I'd scunnered out in the night, make her believe herself shamed and betrayed, humiliate her before her friends and kin, set her to weeping—although I think her real response might have surprised you." He glanced aside. "You like that picture, Sorrel? No? Good." Dag took a long breath. "Whatever reasons your parents tolerated your torment of your sister in the past, it stops tomorrow. You claim Reed was afraid of me? He wasn't near afraid enough. Either of you so much as look cross-eyed at Fawn tomorrow, or anytime thereafter, I will give you reason to regret it every day for the rest of your lives. You hear me, Rush? *Look at me.*" Dag hadn't used that voice since he was a company captain. He was pleased to note it still worked; Rush nearly fell from his perch. Copperhead shied. Even Sorrel stepped backward. Dag hissed, "You hear me?"

Rush nodded frantically.

"All right. I will halter Copperhead, and you will climb down from there. Then you will pick up every bit of my gear and put it back where you found it. What's broken, you and your brother can fix, what's been rolled through the manure you can scrub—which will keep you two out of further mischief for the rest of the evening, I think—what can't be fixed, you'll replace, what can't be replaced, I leave you to work out with your pa."

"You heard the patroller, Rush," said Sorrel, in a deeply paternal snarl. Really, it was almost as good as the company-captain voice.

Dag extended his ground to his horse, a familiar reach long practiced; he'd been saddled with this chestnut idiot for about eight years, now. Disappointed at the loss of his toy, Copperhead lowered his head to the stall floor and began lipping straw, pretending that it all never happened. Dag thought he had a lot in common with Rush, that way. "You can get down," said Dag.

"He isn't haltered," said Rush nervously.

"Yes, he is," said Dag, "now." Sorrel's eyebrows climbed, but he didn't say anything. Cautiously, Rush climbed down. Red-faced, his eyes wary on Copperhead, he began collecting Dag's strewn possessions: clothing and saddlebags and ripped bedroll, knocked-about saddle and pummeled saddle blanket. The adapted bow, though kicked into a corner, was undamaged; Dag was glad. Only the reasonably benign outcome was keeping him from utter fury right now—that, plus not thinking too hard about Spark. But he had to think about Spark.

"Now," Dag said, as Rush made his way out of the stall with his arms loaded, and Dag closed the stall door after him. Rush set the tangled gear down very carefully. "We come to the other question. What of all this would you have me tell Fawn?"

The place had been quiet like a barn; for a moment, it grew quiet like a tomb.

Sorrel's face screwed up. He said cautiously, "Seems to me she'd be near as distressed for the word of this as for the thing itself. I mean, with respect to Reed and Rush," he added, visions of Fawn weeping over Dag's battered corpse evidently presenting themselves to his mind's eye, as indeed they did to Dag's. Rush, who had been rather red, turned rather white.

"Seems that way to me, too," said Dag. "But, you know, there's eight people who know the truth about what happened tonight. Granted, four of them will be telling lies when they drag home tonight, though I doubt even those will all be the same lies. Some kind of word's going to get around."

Dag let them both dwell on this ugly vision for a little, then said, "I'm not Reed's and Rush's linker, though I should have been. I will not lie to *her* for *them*. But I'll give you this much, and no more: I'll not speak first."

Sorrel took this in almost without expression for a moment, clearly thinking through the deeply unpleasant family ramifications. Then he nodded shortly. "Fair enough, patroller."

Dag extended his groundsense briefly, for all that the proximity of the two shaken Bluefields made it painful. He said, "Reed is coming back to the house with Fawn, now. I'd prefer to leave him to you, Sorrel."

"Send him down here to the barn," said Sorrel, somewhat through his teeth.

"That I will, sir." Dag gave a nod in place of his usual salute.

"Thank you—sir." Sorrel nodded back.

Fawn returned to the kitchen with Reed in some annoyance with him for dragging her out in the dark. She lit a few candle stubs on the mantel to lighten both the room and her mood. Better still for the latter was the sound of Dag's long footfalls coming through from the front hall. Reed, who had ducked into Nattie's weaving room for some reason, came out with an inexplicable triumphant smile on his face. She was about to ask why he was so happy all of a sudden when the look was wiped clean at the sight of Dag entering the kitchen. Fawn bit back yet more irritation with her brother. She had better things to do than fuss at Reed; hugging Dag hello was on the top of that list.

He gave her a quick return embrace with his left arm and turned to Reed. "Ah, Reed. Your papa wants to see you in the old barn. Now."

Reed looked at Dag as though he were a poisonous snake surprised in some place he'd been about to put his hand. "Why?" he asked in a suspicious voice.

"I believe he and Rush have quite a lot to say to you." Dag tilted his head and gave Reed a little smile, which had to be one of the least friendly expressions to go by that name Fawn had ever seen. Reed's mouth flattened in return, but he didn't argue; to Fawn's relief, he took himself off. She heard the front door slam behind him.

Fawn pushed back her unruly curls. "Well, *that* was a fool's errand."

"Where did you two go off to?" Dag asked.

"He dragged me all the way to the back pasture to help rescue a calf stuck in a fence. If the brainless thing had got itself in, it had got itself out by the time we made it there. And then he wanted to walk the fence line while we were out there. I didn't mind the walk, but I have things to do." She stood back and looked Dag over. He was often not especially tidy, but at the moment he looked downright rumpled. "Did you have your quiet think?"

"Yes, I just spent a very enlightening hour. Useful, too, I hope."

"Oh, you. I bet you never sat still." She brushed at a few stray bits of bark and leaf stuck to his shirt, and observed with disfavor a new rip in his trouser knee stained with blood from a scrape. "Walking in the woods, I think. I swear, you been walking so long you don't know how to stop. What, were you climbing trees?"

"Just one."

"Well, that was a fool thing to try with that arm!" she scolded fondly. "Did you fall down?"

"No, not quite."

"That's a blessing. You be more careful. Climbing trees, indeed! I thought I was joking. I don't want my bridegroom broken, I'll have you know."

"I know." He smiled, glancing around. Fawn realized that, miraculously, they were actually alone for a moment. He seemed to realize this at the same time, for he sat in the big wooden chair by the hearth and pulled her toward him. She climbed happily into his lap and raised her face for a kiss. The kiss went urgent, and they were both out of breath when their lips parted again.

She said gruffly, "They won't be able to keep us apart much longer."

"Not even with ropes and wild horses," he agreed, his eyes glinting. His smile grew more serious. "Have you decided yet where you want us to be tomorrow night? Ride or bide?"

She sighed and sat up. "Do you have a partiality?"

He brushed her hair from her forehead with his lips, likely because he had a notable reluctance for touching her about the face with his hook. It turned into a small trail of kisses along the arches of her eyebrows before he, too, sat back thoughtfully. "Here would be physically easier. We won't get to Hickory Lake in a day, still less in a couple of hours tomorrow evening. If we camped, you'd have to do most everything."

"I don't mind the work." She tossed her head.

"There is this. We won't just be making love, we'll be making memories. It's the sort of day you remember all your life, when other days fade. Real question, then, the only really important one, is what memories of this do you want to bear away into your future?"

Now, there was a voice of experience, she thought. Best listen to it. "It's farmer custom for the couple to go off to their new house, sleep under the new roof. The party goes on. If we stay, I swear I'll end up washing dishes at midnight, which is not what I want to be doing at midnight."

"I have no house for you. I don't even have a tent with me. It'll be a roof of stars, if it's not a roof of rain."

"It doesn't look like rain. This high blue weather this time of year usually holds for three or four days. I admit I prefer inn chambers to wheatfields, but at least with you there's no mosquitoes."

"I think we might do better than a wheatfield."

She added more seriously, thinking about his words, "This place is chockfull of memories for me. Some are good, but a lot of them hurt, and the hurtful ones have this way of jostling into first place. And this house'll be full of my family. Tomorrow night, I'd like to be someplace with no memories at all." *And no family.*

He ducked his head in understanding. "That's what we'll do, then."

Her spine straightened. "Besides, I'm marrying a patroller. We should go patroller-style. Bedroll under the stars, right." She grinned and nuzzled his neck, and said seductively, "We could bathe in the river . . ."

He was looking immensely seduceable, eyes crinkling in the way she so loved to see. "Bathing in the river is always good. A clean patroller is, um . . ."

"Unusual?" she suggested.

And she also loved the way his chest rumbled under her when he laughed deep down in it. Like a quiet earthquake. "A happy patroller," he finished firmly.

"We could gather firewood," she went on, her lips working upward.

His worked downward. He murmured around his kiss, "Big, big bonfire."

"Scout for rowdy squirrels . . ."

"Those squirrels are a right menace." He looked down over his nose at her, though she didn't see how he could focus his eyes at this distance. "All three? Optimistic, Spark!"

She giggled, joyful to see his eyes so alight. He'd seemed so moody when he'd first come in.

To her aggravation, she could hear heavy footsteps coming down the stairs, Fletch or Whit, heading this way. She sighed and sat up. "Ride, then."

"Unless we have a barker of a thunderstorm."

"Thunder and lightning couldn't keep me in this house one more day," she said fervently. "It's time for me to go on. Do you see?"

He nodded. "I'm beginning to, farmer girl. This is right for you."

She stole one last kiss before sliding off his lap, thinking, *Tomorrow we'll be buying these kisses fair and square.* Her heart melted in the tenderness of the look he gave her as, reluctantly, he let her slip out of his arm. All storms might be weathered in the safe harbor of that smile.

—

19

Fawn flew through the irreducible farm chores the next morning. The milking fell to her; afterwards, waving a stick with resolute vigor, she sent the bewildered cows off to pasture at a brisk and unaccustomed trot. For practical reasons the rule about the marrying couple's not seeing each other before the wedding was put aside till after the family breakfast, when Aunt Rose Bluefield arrived to help Mama with the food and the house, along with Fawn's closest cousins and girlfriends Filly Bluefield and Ginger Roper to start the primping.

First came proper baths. The women went off to the well; the men were dispatched to the river. Fawn had grave doubts about leaving Dag to the mercies of her father, Fletch, and Whit for such a vulnerable enterprise, although at least the twins weren't to follow till a long list of dirty chores had been completed. Filly and Ginger dragged her away as she was still yelling strict orders down the hill after the men about not letting Dag's splints get wet. There followed a naked, wet, silly, and sudsy half hour by the well; Mama brought out her best scented soap for the task. Once they were back in the bedroom with Ginger and Filly starting on her hair, Fawn was relieved to hear footsteps and men's voices through the closed door to the weaving room, Dag giving some calm instruction to Whit.

Filly and Ginger did their best, from Fawn's dimly remembered description of what Reela had told her, to imitate Lakewalker wedding braids, although Fawn was glumly aware that her own hair was too curly and unruly to cooperate the way Lakewalkers' long locks no doubt did. The result was creditable, anyhow, with the hair drawn up in neat thick ropes from her temples to meet at her crown, and from there allowed to spin down loose behind after its own turbulent fashion. In the little hand mirror, held out at arm's length, Fawn's face looked startlingly refined and grown-up, and she blinked at the strangeness. Ginger's brother had ridden all the way to Mirror Pond this morning, four miles upriver, to get the flowers Fawn had begged of him: three not-too-crumpled white water lilies, which Ginger now bound into the knot of hair on the crown of her head.

"Mama said you could have had all of her roses you wanted," Filly observed, tilting her head to examine the effect.

"These are more lake-ish," said Fawn. "Dag will like them. The poor man doesn't have any family or friends here, and is pretty much having to borrow everything farmer. I know he was pining that he couldn't send down his Lakewalker bride-gifts till after the wedding; they're supposed to be given beforehand, I guess."

Filly said, "Mama wondered if no women of his own people would marry him because of his hand being maimed like that."

Fawn, choosing to ignore the implied reflection upon herself, said only, "I shouldn't think so. A lot of patrollers seem to get banged up, over time. Anyhow, he's a widower."

Ginger said, "My brother said the twins said his horse talks human to him when there's no one around."

Fawn snorted. "If no one's around, how do they know?"

Ginger, considering this, conceded reluctantly, "That's a point."

"Besides, it's the *twins*."

Filly granted, "That's another." She added in regret, "So I guess they made up that story about him magicking together that glass bowl they broke, too?"

"Um. No. That one's true," Fawn admitted. "Mama put it away upstairs for today, so it wouldn't risk getting knocked down again."

A thoughtful silence followed this, while Filly poked at the curls in back to fluff them, and pushed away Fawn's hands trying to smooth them.

"He's so tall," said Ginger in a newly speculative tone, "and you're *so* short. I'd think he'd squash you flatter than a bug. Plus both his arms bein' hurt. However are you two going to manage, tonight?"

"Dag's very ingenious," said Fawn firmly.

Filly poked her and giggled. "How would you know, eh?"

Ginger snickered. "Someone's been samplin', I think. What *were* you two doin', out on the road together for a month like that?"

Fawn tossed her head and sniffed. "None of your business." She couldn't help adding smugly after a moment, "I will say, there's no going back to farmer boys, after." Which won some hoots, quickly muted as Nattie bustled back in.

Ginger set her a chair by Fawn's bench, and Nattie laid out the cloth in which she'd wrapped the braided cords; she'd just delivered Dag's to him, together with the other, surprise present.

"Did he like his wedding shirt?" Fawn asked, a bit wistful because she couldn't very well ask Nattie *How did it look on him?*

"Oh, yes, lovie, he was very pleased. I'd say, even moved. He said he'd never had anything so fine in his life, and was in a wonder that we got it together so quick and secret. Though he said he was relieved for the explanation of you girls with your measurin' strings yesterday, which had evidently been worryin' him a bit." She unrolled the wrap; the dark cord lay coiled in her lap, the gold beads firm and rich-looking upon the ends.

"Where is he wearing his cord? Where should I wear mine?"

"He says folks mostly wear them on the left wrist if they're right-handed. T'other way around if not, naturally. He's put his around his left arm above the harness, for now. He says when the time comes for the binding, he can sit down and you can stand facing him, left side to left side, and I should be able to do the tyin' between you without too much trouble."

"All right," said Fawn doubtfully, trying to picture this. She stuck out her left arm and let Nattie wrap the cord several times around her wrist like a bracelet, tying the ends in a bow knot for now. The beads dangled prettily, and she twisted her hand to make them bounce on her skin. A little of her most secret self was in it, Dag said, bound in with her blood; she had to take his word.

Then it was time to get her dress on, the good green cotton, washed and carefully ironed for this; her other good dress being warm wool for winter. That Dag would remember this dress from that night in Glassforge when he had so gently and urgently removed it, unwrapping her like a gift, must be a secret between them; but she hoped he would find it a heartening sight. Ginger and Filly together lowered the fabric carefully over her head so as not to muss her hair or crush the lilies.

A knock sounded at the door, from someone who did not wait for permission to enter; Whit, who looked at Fawn and blinked. He opened his mouth as if to fire off one of his usual quip-insults, then appeared to think better of it and just smiled uneasily.

"Dag says, what about the weapons?" he recited, revealing himself as a messenger sent. "He seems to want to put them all on. He means, *all* of them, at once. He says it's to show off what a patroller is bringing to his bride's tent. Fletch says, no one wears weapons to a wedding, it just ain't done. Papa says, he don't know what should be done. So Dag says, ask Spark, and he'll abide."

Fawn started to answer *Yes, it's his wedding too, he should have some of his own customs,* then instead said more cautiously, "Just how many weapons are we talking about, here?"

"Well, there's that great pigsticker that he calls his war knife, for starters. Then there's one he slips down in his boot, and another he straps on his thigh sometimes, evidently. What he wants with three knives when he only has one hand, I don't know. Then there's that funny bow of his, and the quiver of arrows, which also has some little knives stuck in it. He seemed a bit put out that he didn't have a sword by him—seems there's one he inherited from his pa back at his camp, and some ash spear or another for fighting from horseback, which he also doesn't have here. Fortunately."

Ginger and Filly listened to this lengthening catalog with their faces screwing up.

Whit, nodding silent agreement at them, finished, "You'd think the man would clank when he walked. You wouldn't want a patroller to fall into water over his head on his way to his wedding, I'll say." His own brows rose in grue-some enthusiasm. "You suppose he's killed anybody with that arsenal? 'Spect he must have, sometime or another. That's a right sobering collection of scars he has, I saw when we were down washing up. Though I suppose he's had a long time to accumulate 'em." He added after another contemplative moment, "Do you think he's getting nervous 'bout the wedding? He don't hardly show it, but with him, how would you tell?"

With Whit as a helper, it was a wonder Dag wasn't frenzied by now, Fawn thought tartly. "Tell him"—Fawn's tongue hovered between *yes* and *no,* remembering just what all she *had* seen Dag kill with those weapons—"tell him just the war knife." In case it *was* nerves and the weapons a consola-tion. "Tell him it can *stand for* the rest of them, all right? We'll know."

"All right." Whit did not take himself off at once, but stood scratching his head.

"Did the shirt fit him good?" Fawn asked.

"Oh, yeah, I guess."

"You guess? Didn't you look? Agh! Useless to ask *you,* I suppose."

"He liked it fine. Kept touchin' it with his fingertips peekin' out of those bandages, anyhow, like he liked the feel. But what *I* want explained is—you know, I had to help him button and unbutton his trousers. So how in the green world has he been managing them for the past week? 'Cause I haven't never seen him going around undone. And I don't care how much of a sorcerer he is, he has to have been doin' the necessary *some* time . . ."

"Whit," said Fawn, "go *away.*"

Ginger and Filly, thinking this through, looked at Fawn's flushing face and began to giggle like steam kettles.

"Because," Whit, never one to take a hint, forged on, "I know it wasn't me or Fletch or Pa, and it couldn't have been the twins, who didn't warm to him a bit. Suppose it could have been Nattie, but really, I think it must have been you, and how—ow!" He ended in a yelp as Nattie smacked him firmly and ac-curately across the knees with her cane.

"Whit, if you don't go find yourself a chore, I'll find you one," she told him. "Don't you go embarrassin' Fawn's patroller with all your supposin', or you'll have me to answer to, and I *will* be here tomorrow."

Whit, daunted at last, took himself out, saying placatingly, "I'll say *just the knife,* right."

Outside, Fawn could hear the sounds of hoofbeats and creaking carts coming up the lane, and calls of greeting, more folks arriving. It felt very peculiar to sit still in this room waiting, instead of being out bustling around doing.

Mama came in, wiping her hands on a towel, to say, "Shep Sower and his wife just got here. They were the last. The sun's as close to noon as makes no never mind. We could start most any time."

"Is Dag ready? Is he all right?"

"He's clean, and dressed neat and plain. He looks very calm and above it all, except that he's had Whit switch out his wooden hand for his hook and back again twice now."

Fawn considered this. "Which did he end up with?"

"Hook, last I seen."

"Hm." So did that mean he was getting more relaxed, to let himself be seen so by strangers, or less, to have the most useful tool and maybe-weapon ready, as it were, to hand? "Well, it'll be over soon. I didn't mean to put him through such an ordeal when I agreed to stop back here."

Mama nodded to Fawn's cousins. "You girls give us a minute."

Nattie rose to her feet, endorsing this. "Come along, chickies, give the bride a breather with her mama." She shepherded Fawn's helpers out to her weaving room and closed the door quietly behind them.

Mama said, "In a few minutes, you'll be a married woman." Her voice was stretched somewhere between anxious and bewildered. "Sooner than I expected. Well, I *never* expected anything like this. We always meant to do right by you, for your wedding. This is all so quick. We've done more preparing for *Fletch*." She frowned at this felt injustice.

"I'm glad it's no more. This is making me nervous enough."

"You sure about this, Fawn?"

"Today, no. All my tomorrows, yes."

"Nattie's kept your confidences. But, you know, if you want to change your mind, we can stop this right now. Whatever trouble you think you're in, we could manage it somehow."

"Mama, we've had this conversation. Twice. I'm not pregnant. Really and truly."

"There are other kinds of troubles."

"For girls, that's the only one folks seem to care about." She sighed. "So how many out there are saying I must be, for you to let this go forward?"

"A few," Mama admitted.

A bunch, I'll bet. Fawn growled. "Well, time'll prove 'em wrong, and I hope you'll make them eat their words when it does, 'cause I won't be here to."

Mama went around behind her and fussed with her hair, which needed nothing. "I admit Dag seems a fine fellow, no, I'll go farther, a good man, but what about his kin? Even he doesn't vouch for your welcome where you're going. What if they treat you bad?"

I'll feel right at home. Fawn bit down on that one before it escaped. "I'll deal. I dealt with bandits and mud-men and blight bogles. I can deal with relatives." *As long as they're not my relatives.*

"Is this *sensible*?"

"If folks were sensible, would anyone ever get married?"

Mama snorted. "I suppose not." She added in a lower voice, "But if you start down a road you can't see the end of, there's a chance you'll find some dark things along it."

About to defend her choice for the hundredth time, Fawn paused, and said simply, "That's true." She stood up. "But it's my road. Our road. I can't stand still and keep breathin'. I'm ready." She kissed her mama on the cheek. "Let's go."

Mama got in one last, inarguable maternal sigh, but followed Fawn out. They collected Nattie and Ginger and Filly along the way. Mama made a quick circuit of the kitchen, finally set aside her towel, straightened her dress, and led the way into the parlor.

The parlor was jammed, the crowd spilling over into the hall. Papa's brother Uncle Hawk Bluefield and Aunt Rose and their son still at home; Uncle and Aunt Roper and their two youngest boys, including the successful water-lily finder; Shep Sower and his cheery wife, always up for a free feed; Fletch and Clover and Clover's folks and sisters and the twins, inexplicably well behaved, and Whit and Papa.

And Dag, a head above everyone but still looking very surrounded. The white shirt fit him well. There hadn't been time for smocking or embroidery, but Nattie and Aunt Roper had come up with some dark green piping to set off the collar and cuffs and button placket. The sleeves were made generous enough to fit over his splints, and over his arm harness on the other side, with second buttons set over to tighten the cuffs later. There had been just enough of the shell buttons left to do the job. Fawn had whisked his sling away from him yesterday long enough to wash and iron it, so it didn't look so grubby even though it was growing a bit tattered. He was wearing the tan trousers with fewer old stains and mends, also forcibly washed yesterday. His worn knife sheath, riding on his left hip, looked so much a part of him as to be almost unnoticeable despite its wicked size.

A bit of spontaneous applause broke out when Fawn appeared, which made her blush. And then Dag wasn't looking at anything else but her, and it all made sense again. She went and stood beside him. His right arm twitched in its sling, as though he desperately wanted to hold her hand but could not. Fawn settled for sliding her foot and hip over, so that they touched along the side, a reassuring pressure. The sense of strain in the room, of everyone trying to pretend this was all right and be nice for Fawn's sake, almost made her want them all to revert back to their normal relaxed horribleness, but not quite.

Shep Sower stepped forth, smiled, cleared his throat, and called them all to attention with a few brief, practiced words. To Fawn's relief, he glanced at Dag and skipped over his usual dire wedding jokes, which everyone else here had likely heard often enough to recite themselves anyhow. He then read out the marriage contract; the older generation listened with attention, nodding judiciously or raising eyebrows and exchanging glances now and then. Dag, Fawn, her parents, the three adult couples, and Fletch and Clover all signed it, Nattie made her mark, and Shep signed and sealed it all.

Then Papa brought out the family book and laid it open on the table, and much the same exercise was repeated. Dag stared curiously over Fawn's shoulder at the pages, and she thumbed back a bit through the entries of births, deaths, and marriages and land swaps, purchases, or inheritances to silently point out her own birth note and, several pages earlier, the note of her own parents' wedding, with the names and countersigned marks of the witnesses— many long dead, a few still right here in this same room doing this same task.

Then Dag and Fawn, coached by Shep, said their promises. There had been a bit of a debate about them, yesterday. Dag had shied at the wording, all the farmer pledges to plow and plant and harvest in due season, since he said he wasn't likely to be doing any of those things and for a wedding vow he ought to be speaking strict truth if ever he did. And as for guarding the land for his children, he'd been doing that all his life for everybody's children. But Nattie had explained the declarations as a poetical way of talking about a couple taking care of each other and having babies and growing old together, and he'd calmed right down. The words did sound odd in his mouth, here in this hot, crowded parlor, but his deep, careful voice somehow gave them such weight it felt as if they might be used to anchor ships in a thunderstorm. They seemed to linger in the air, and all the married adults looked queerly introspective, as if hearing them resonating in their own memories. Fawn's own voice seemed faint and gruff in her ears by comparison, as though she were a silly little girl playing at being a grown-up, convincing no one.

At this point in the usual ceremony it would be time to kiss each other and go eat, but now came the string-binding, about which most everyone had been warned in carefully casual terms. *Something to please Fawn's patroller,* and in case that seemed too alarming, *Nattie will be doing it for them.* Papa brought out a chair and set it in the middle of the room, and Dag sat in it with a nod of thanks. Fawn rolled up Dag's left sleeve; she wondered what was going through his head that he chose to so expose his arm harness to view. But the dark cord with the copper glints was revealed, circling his biceps, Fawn's own cord having been out in plain sight all along.

Papa then escorted Nattie up, and she felt along and found everything, cords and arm and wrist. She pulled loose the bow knots and collected both cords in her hands, winding them about one another, murmuring half-voiced blessings of her own devising. She then rewrapped the combined cords in a figure eight around Dag's arm and Fawn's, and tied them with a single bow. She held her hand on it, and chanted:

"Side by side or far apart,
intertwined may these hearts
walk together."

Which were the words Dag had given Nattie to say, and reminded Fawn disturbingly of the words on Kauneo's thighbone-knife that Dag had carried for so long aimed at his own heart. Possibly the burned script had been meant to recall just such a wedding chant, or charm.

The words, the cords, and the two hearts willing: all had to be present to make a valid marriage in Lakewalker . . . not eyes, but groundsense, that subtle, invisible, powerful perceiving. Fawn wondered desperately how it was people made their assent work the strings' grounds that way. Thinking really hard about it seemed, for her, about as effective as being a five-year-old wishing hard for a pony, eyes scrunched up in futile effort, because a child had no other power by which to move the world.

Doing has no need of wishing.

She would *do* her marriage then, hour by hour and day by day with the work of her hands, and let the wishing fall where it would.

Dag had his head cocked as though he were listening to something Fawn could not hear; his eyelids lowered in satisfaction, and he smiled. With some difficulty, he lifted his right arm and positioned the fingers of his hand about one end of the knot, gathering up the two gold beads from the two different cords; Fawn, at his nod, grasped the other pair. Together, they pulled the knot apart, and Fawn let the cords unwind from around each other. Fawn then tied her cord on Dag's arm, and Dag, with Nattie's help, or rather Nattie with Dag's hindrance, tied his cord around Fawn's wrist, this time with square knots. Dag glanced up under his lids at her with a muted expression, joy and terror and triumph compounded, with just a touch of wild unholy glee. It reminded Fawn of the loopy look on his face right after they'd slain the malice, actually. He leaned his forehead against Fawn's and whispered, "It's good. It's *done.*"

Lakewalker ground magic of a most profound sort. Worked in front of twenty people. And not one of them had seen it. *What have we done?*

Still sitting, Dag snaked his left arm around her and snugged her in for a proper kiss, though it felt disorienting to be lowering her face toward his instead of raising it. With an effort, they both broke off before the kiss continued at improper length. She thought he just barely refrained from pulling her into his lap and ravishing her right there. She was way overdue for a good ravish. *Later,* his bright eyes promised.

And *then* it was time to go eat.

The boys had set up trestle tables in the west yard under the trees, so there would be room for everyone to sit down who wanted to. One whole table was devoted to the food and drink, which people circled and descended upon like stooping hawks, carrying loaded plates away to the other tables. Women banged in and out of the kitchen after things forgotten or belatedly wanted. With only the four families plus the Sowers present, it was literally a quiet wedding, with no music or dancing attempted, and as it chanced, there were no little ones present to fall down the well or out of trees or stable lofts and keep the parents alert, or crazed.

There followed eating, drinking, eating, talking, and eating. When Fawn hauled Dag and his plate to the food trestle for the third time, he bent and whispered fearfully, "How much more of this do I have to get down so as not to offend any of those formidable women I'm now related to?"

"Well, there's Aunt Roper's cream-and-honey pie," said Fawn judiciously, "and Aunt Bluefield's butter-walnut cake, and Mama's maple-hickory nut bars, and my apple pies."

"*All* of them?"

"Ideally. Or you could just pick one and let the rest be offended."

Dag appeared to cogitate for a moment, then said gravely, "Slap on a big chunk of that apple pie, then."

"I do like a man who thinks on his feet," said Fawn, scooping up a generous portion.

"Yeah, while I can still see them."

She smirked.

He added plaintively, "That dimple's going to be the death of me, you know?"

"Never," she said firmly, and led him back to their seats.

She slipped away soon after to her bedroom to change into her riding trousers and shoes and the sturdier shirt that went with them. She left the lilies in her hair, though. When she came back out to Nattie's weaving room, Dag stood up from his neatly packed saddlebags.

"You say when, Spark."

"Now," she replied fervently, "while they're still working through the desserts. They'll be less inclined to follow along."

"Not being able to move? I begin to see your clever plan." He grinned and went to get Whit and Fletch to help him with the horses.

She met them in the lane to the south of the house, where Dag was watching with keen attention as his new brothers-in-law tied on the assorted gear. "I don't think they'll try any tricks on you," she whispered up to him.

"If they were Lakewalkers," he murmured back, "there would be no end of tricks at this point. Patroller humor. Sometimes, people are allowed to live, after."

Fawn made a wry face. Then added thoughtfully, "Do you miss it?"

"Not *that* part," he said, shaking his head.

Despite the cooks' best efforts, the relatives did drag themselves from the trestle tables to see them off. Clover, with a glance at the addition rising on this side of the house, bade Fawn the very best of luck. Mama hugged her and cried, Papa hugged her and looked grim, and Nattie just hugged her. Filly and Ginger flung rose petals at them, most of which missed; Copperhead seemed briefly inclined to spook at this, just to stay in practice evidently, but Dag gave him an evil eye, and he desisted and stood quietly.

"I hate to see you going out on the road with nothing," Mama sniffled.

Fawn glanced at her bulging saddlebags and all the extra bundles, mostly stuffed with packed-up food, tied about patient Grace; Fawn had barely been able to fight off the pressing offer of a hamper to be tied atop. Dag, citing Copperhead's tricksiness, had been more successful at resisting the last-minute provisions and gifts. After a brief struggle with her tongue, she said only, "We'll manage somehow, Mama."

And then Papa boosted her aboard Grace, and Dag, wrapping his reins around his hook, got himself up on tall Copperhead in one smooth lunge despite his sling.

"Take care of her, patroller," Papa said gruffly.

Dag nodded. "I intend to, sir."

Nattie gripped Fawn's knee, and whispered, "You take care o' him, too, lovie. The way that fellow sheds pieces, it may be the thornier task."

Fawn bent down toward Nattie's ear. "I intend to."

And then they were off, to a rain of good-byes but no other sort; the afternoon was warm and fair, and only half-spent. They would be well away from West Blue by time to camp tonight. The farmstead fell behind as they wended down the lane, and was soon obscured by the trees.

"We did it," Fawn said in relief. "We got away again. For a while I never thought I would."

"I did say I wouldn't abandon you," Dag observed, his eyes a brighter gold in this light than the beads on the ends of her marriage cord.

Fawn turned back in her saddle for one last look up the hill. "You didn't have to do it this way."

"No. I didn't." The eyes crinkled. "Think about it, Spark."

Attempting to exchange a kiss from the backs of two variously tall and differently paced horses resulted in a sort of promissory sideswipe, but it was fully satisfactory in intent. They turned their mounts onto the river road.

It was all a perfect opposite to her first flight from home. Then she had gone in secret, in the dark, alone, afraid, angry, afoot, all her meager possessions in a thin blanket rolled on her back. Even the direction was reversed: south, instead of north as now.

In only one aspect were the journeys the same. Each felt like a leap into the utterly unknown.

LEGACY

1

Dag had been married for a whole two hours, and was still light-headed with wonder. The weighted ends of the wedding cord coiling around his upper arm danced in time with the lazy trot of his horse. Riding by his side, Fawn—*my new bride,* now there was a phrase to set a man's mind melting—met his smile with happy eyes.

My farmer bride. It should have been impossible. There would be trouble about that, later.

Trouble yesterday, trouble tomorrow. But no trouble now. Now, in the light of the loveliest summer afternoon he ever did see, was only a boundless contentment.

Once the first half dozen miles were behind them, Dag found both his and Fawn's urgency to be gone from the wedding party easing. They passed through the last village on the northern river road, after which the wagon way became more of a two-rut track, and the remaining farms grew farther apart, with more woods between them. He let a few more miles pass, till he was sure they were out of range of any potential retribution or practical jokers, then began keeping an eye out for a spot to make camp. If a Lakewalker patroller with this much woods to choose from couldn't hide from farmers, something was wrong. *Secluded,* he decided, was a better watchword still.

At length, he led Fawn down to the river at a rocky ford, then upstream for a time till they came to where a clear creek, gurgling down from the eastern ridge, joined the flow. He turned Copperhead up it for a good quarter mile till he found a pretty glade, all mossy by the stream and surrounded by tall trees and plenty of them; and, his groundsense guaranteed, no other person for a mile in any direction. Of necessity, he had to let Fawn unsaddle the horses and set up the site. It was a simple enough task, merely laying out their bedrolls and making just enough of a fire to boil water for tea. Still, she cast an obser-

vant eye at him as he lay with his back against a broad beech bole and plucked
irritably at the sling supporting his right arm with the hook replacing his left
hand.

"You have a job," she told him encouragingly. "You're on guard against the
mosquitoes, ticks, chiggers, and blackflies."

"And squirrels," he added hopefully.

"We'll get to them."

Food did not have to be caught or skinned or cooked, just unwrapped and
eaten till they couldn't hold any more, although Fawn tried his limits. Dag
wondered if this new mania for feeding him was a Bluefield custom no one had
mentioned, or just a lingering effect of the excitement of the day, as she tried
to find her way into her farmwifely tasks without, actually, a farm in which to
set them. But when he compared this to many a cold, wet, hungry, lonely, exhausted night on some of the more dire patrols in his memory, he thought perhaps he'd wandered by strange accident into some paradise out of a song, and
bears would come out tonight to dance around their fire in celebration.

He looked up to find Fawn inching nearer, without, for a change, provender in her hands. "It's not dark yet," she sighed.

He cast her a slow blink, to tease. "And dark is needed for what?"

"Bedtime!"

"Well, I admit it's a help for sleeping. Are you that sleepy? It's been a tiring
day. We could just roll over and . . ."

She caught on, and poked him in reproof. "Ha! Are you sleepy?"

"No chance." Despite the sling he managed a pounce that drew her into his
lap. The prey did not precisely struggle, though it did wriggle enchantingly.
Once she was within kissing range, they found occupation for a little. But then
she grew grave and sat up to touch the cord wrapping her left wrist.

"How odd that this all should feel harder, now."

He kissed her hair beneath his chin. "There's a weight of expectation that
wasn't there before, I suppose. I didn't . . ." He hesitated.

"Hm?"

"I rode into West Blue, onto your family's farm, last week thinking . . . I
don't know. That I would be a clever Lakewalker persuader and get my way. I
expected to change their lives. I didn't expect them to change my life right
back. I didn't used to be *Fawn's patroller,* still less *Fawn's husband,* but now I am.
That's a ground transformation, in case you didn't realize. It doesn't just happen in the cords. It happens in our deep selves." He gave a nod toward his left
sleeve hiding the loop binding his own arm. "Maybe the hard feeling is just
shyness for the two new people we've become."

"Hm." She settled down, briefly reassured. But then sat up again, biting
her lip the way she did when about to tackle some difficult subject, usually
head-on. "Dag. About my ground."

"I love your ground."

Her lips twitched in a smile, but then returned to seriousness. "It's been over four weeks since . . . since the malice. I'm healing up pretty good inside, I think."

"I think so, too."

"Do you suppose we could . . . I mean, tonight because . . . we haven't ever yet . . . not that I'm *complaining*, mind you. Erm. That pattern in their ground you said women get when they can have babies. Do I have it tonight?"

"Not yet. I don't think it'll be much longer till your body's back to its usual phases, though."

"So we could. I mean. Do it in the usual way. Tonight."

"Tonight, Spark, we can do it any way you want. Within the range of the physically possible, that is," he added prudently.

She snickered. "I do wonder how you *learned* all those tricks."

"Well, not all at once, absent gods forfend. You pick up this and that over the years. I suspect people everywhere keep reinventing all the basics. There's only so much you can do with a body. Successfully and comfortably, that is. Leaving aside stunts."

"Stunts?" she said curiously.

"We're leaving them aside," he said definitely. "One broken arm is enough."

"One too many, I think." Her brows drew down in new worry. "Um. I was envisioning you up on your elbows, but really, I think maybe not. It doesn't exactly sound comfortable, and I wouldn't want you to hurt your arm and have to start healing all over, and besides, if you slipped, you really would squash me like a bug."

It took him a moment to puzzle out her concern. "Ah, not a problem. We just switch sides, top to bottom. If you can ride a horse, which I note you do quite well, you can ride me. And you can squash me all you want."

She thought this through. "I'm not sure I can do this right."

"If you do something really wrong, I promise I'll scream in pain and let you know."

She grinned, if with a slight tinge of dismay.

Kissing blended into undressing, and again, to his mixed regret and entertainment, Fawn had to do most of the work. He thought she was much too brisk and businesslike in getting her own clothes off, although the view when she finished was splendid. The setting sun reached fingers of golden light into the glade that caressed her body as she flickered in and out of the leaf shadows; she might well have been one of those legendary female spirits who were supposed to step out of trees and beguile the unwary traveler. The way her sweet breasts moved not *quite* in time with the rest of her was fair riveting to his eye, too. She folded up his astonishing wedding shirt with fully the care he would have wished, tucking it away. He lay back on his bedroll and let her pull off his trousers and drawers with all her considerable determination. She folded them up too, and came and sat, no, plunked, again beside him. The after-wobble was delightful.

"Arm harness. On or off?"

"Hm. Off, I think. Don't want to risk jabbing you in a distracted moment." The disquieting memory of her bleeding fingers weaving her wedding cord flitted through his mind, and he became conscious again of it wound around his upper arm, and the tiny hum of its live ground. *Her* live ground.

With practiced hands, she whisked the hook harness away onto the top of the clothes pile, and he marveled anew at how easy it was all becoming with her.

Except for, blight it all again, having no working hand. The sling had gone west just before the shirt, and he shifted his right arm and attempted to wriggle his fingers. *Ouch.* No. Not enough useful motion there yet. Inside his splints and wrappings, his skin, damp from the sweat of the warm day, was itching. He couldn't *touch.* All right, there was a certain amount he could do with his tongue—especially right now, as she returned and nuzzled up to him—but getting it to the right place at the right time was going to be an insurmountable challenge, in this position.

She withdrew her lips from his and began working her way down his body. It was lovely but almost redundant; it had been well over a week, after all, and . . . *It used to be years, and I scarcely blinked.* He tried to relax and let himself be made love to. Relaxation wasn't exactly what was happening. His hips twitched as Fawn's full attention arrived at his nether regions. She swung her leg over, turned to face him, reached down, and began to try to position herself. Stopped.

"Urk?" he inquired politely. Some such noise, anyway.

Her face was a little pinched. "This should be working better."

"Oil?" he croaked.

"I shouldn't need oil for *this,* should I?"

Not if I had a hand to ready you nicely. "Hang *should,* do what works. You shouldn't have that uncomfortable look on your face, either."

"Hm." She extracted herself, padded over to his saddlebags, and rummaged within. Good view from the back, too, as she bent over . . . A mutter of mild triumph, "Ah." She padded back, pausing to frown and rub the sole of one bare foot on her other shin after stepping on a pebble. *Was* this a time to stop for pebbles . . . ?

Back she came, sliding over him. Small hands slicked him, which made him jolt. He did not allow himself to plunge upward. Let her find her way in her own time. She attempted to do so.

She was getting a very determined look again. "Maidenheads don't *regrow,* do they . . . ?"

"Shouldn't think so."

"I didn't think it was supposed to hurt the second time."

"Probably just unaccustomed muscles. Not in condition. Need more exercise." It was driving him just short of mad to have no hands to grasp her hips and guide her home.

She blinked, taking in this thought. "Is that true, or more of your slick patroller persuasion?"

"Can't it be both?"

She grinned, shifted her angle, then looked brighter, and said, "Ah! There we go."

Indeed, we do. He gasped, as she slid slowly and very, very tightly down upon him. "Yes . . . that's . . . very . . . nice."

She muttered, "They get whole babies through these parts. Surely it's supposed to stretch more."

"Time. Give it." Blight it, at this point in the usual proceedings, *she* would be the one who couldn't form words anymore. They were out of rhythm tonight. He was losing his wits, and she was getting chatty. "Fine now."

Her brows drew down in puzzlement. "Should this be like taking turns, or not?"

"Uhthink . . ." He swallowed to find speech. "Hope it's good for you. Suspect it's better for me. 'S *exquisite* for me right now."

"Oh, that's all right, then." She sat for a moment, adjusting. It would likely not be a good idea at this point to screech and convulse and beg for motion; that would just alarm her. He didn't want her alarmed. She might jump up and run off, which would be tragic. He wanted her relaxed and confident and . . . there, she was starting to smile again. She observed, "You have a funny look on your face."

"I'll bet."

Her smile widened. Too gently and tentatively, she at last began to move. *Absent gods be praised.* "After all," she said, continuing a line of thought of which he had long lost track, "Mama had *twins,* and she isn't that much taller than me. Though Aunt Nattie said she was pretty alarmin' toward the end."

"What?" said Dag, confused.

"Twins. Run in Mama's side of the family. Which made it really unfair of her to blame Papa, Aunt Nattie said, but I guess she wasn't too reasonable by then."

Which remark, of course, immediately made his reeling mind jump to the previously unimagined idea of Spark bearing twins, *his,* which made his eyes cross. Further. He really hadn't even wrapped his mind around the notion of their having one child, yet. *Considering just what you're doing right now, perhaps you should, old patroller.*

Whatever this peculiar digression did to him—his spine felt like an over-drawn bow with its string about to snap—it seemed to relax Fawn. Her eyes darkening, she commenced to rock with more assurance. Her ground, blocked earlier by the discomfort and uncertainty, began to flow again. *Finally.* But he wasn't going to last much longer at this rate. He let his hips start to keep time with hers.

"If I only had a working hand to get down there, we *would* share this turn . . ." His fingers twitched in frustration.

"Another good reason to leave it be to heal faster," she gasped. "Put that poor busted arm back on the blanket."

"Ngh!" He wanted to touch her *so much.* Groundwork? A mosquito's worth was not likely to be enough. *Left-handed groundwork?* He remembered the glass bowl, sliding and swirling back together. That had been no mere mosquito. Would she find it perverse, frightening, horrifying, to be touched so? Could he even . . . ? This was her *wedding night.* She must not recall it with disappointment. He laid his left arm down across his belly, pointed at their juncture. *Consider it a strengthening exercise for the ghost hand. Beats scraping hides all hollow, doesn't it?* Just . . . *there.*

"Oh!" Her eyes shot wide, and she leaned forward to stare into his face. "What did you just *do?*"

"Experiment," he gritted out. Surely his eyes were as wide and wild as hers. "Think the broken right has been doing something to stir up my left ground. Like, not like?"

"Not sure. More . . . ?"

"Oh, *yeah* . . ."

"Oh. *Yeah.* That's . . ."

"Good?"

Her only reply was a wordless huff. And a rocking that grew frantic, then froze. Which was fine because now he did drive up, as that bowstring snapped at last, and everything unwound in white fire.

He didn't think he'd passed out, but he seemed to come to with her draped across his chest wheezing and laughing wildly. "Dag! That was, that was . . . could you do that all along? Were you just saving it for a wedding present, or what?"

"I have no idea," he confessed. "Never done anything like that before. I'm not even sure what I *did* do."

"Well, it was quite . . . quite nice." She sat up and pushed back her hair to deliver this in a judicious tone, but then dissolved into helpless laughter again.

"I'm dizzy. Feel like I'm about to fall down."

"You *are* lying down."

"Very fortunate."

She tumbled down into the cradle of his left arm and snuggled in for a wordless time. Dag didn't quite nap, but he wouldn't have called it being awake, either. Bludgeoned, perhaps. Eventually, she roused herself enough to get them cleaned up and dressed in clothes to sleep in, because the blue twilight shadows were cooling as night slid in, seeping through the woods from the east. By the time she cuddled down again beside him, under the blanket this time, he was fully awake, staring up through the leaves at the first stars.

Her slim little fingers traced the furrows above his brows. "Are you all right? *I'm* all right."

He managed a smile and kissed the fingers in passing. "I admit, I've unsettled myself a bit. You know how shaken I was after that episode with the glass bowl."

"Oh, you haven't made yourself sick again with this, have you?"

"No, in fact. Although this wasn't near such a draining effort. Pretty, um, stimulating, actually. Thing is . . . that night I mended the bowl, that was the first time I experienced that, that, call it a ghost hand. I tried several times after, secretly, to make it emerge again, but nothing happened. Couldn't figure it out. In the parlor, you were upset, I was upset, I wanted to, I don't know. Fix things. I wasn't upset just now, but I sure was in, um, a heightened mood. *Flying,* your aunt Nattie called it. Except now I've fallen back down, and the ghost hand's gone again."

He glanced over to find her up on one elbow, looking at him with the same interested expression as ever. Happy eyes. Not shocked or scared or repelled. He said, "You don't mind that it's, well, strange? You think this is just the same as all the other things I do, don't you?"

Her brows rose in consideration. "Well, you summon horses and bounce mosquitoes and make firefly lamps and kill malices and you know where everyone is for a country mile all around, and I don't know what you did to Reed and Rush last night, but the effect was sure magical today. And what you do for me I can't hardly begin to describe, not decently anyhow. How do you know it isn't?"

He opened his mouth, then closed it, squinting at his question turned upside down.

She cocked her head, and continued, "You said Lakewalker folks' ground-sense doesn't come in all at once, and not at all when they're younger. Maybe this is just something you should have had all along, that got delayed. Or maybe it's something you should have now, growing right on time."

"There's a new thought." He lay back, frowning at the blameless evening sky. His life was full of new things, lately. Some of them were new problems, but he had to admit, a lot of the tired, dreary, old problems had been thoroughly shaken out. He began to suspect that it wasn't only the breaking of his right arm that was triggering this bizarre development. The farmer girl was plowing his ground, it seemed. What was that phrase? *Breaking new land.* A very literal form of ground transformation. He blinked to chase away these twisting notions before his head started to ache.

"So, that's twice," said Fawn, pursuing the thought. "So it can happen, um, more than once, anyhow. And it seems you don't have to be unhappy for it to work. That's real promising."

"I'm not sure I can do it again."

"That'd be a shame," she said in a meditative tone. But her eyes were merry. "So, try it again next time and we'll see, eh? And if not, as it seems you have no end of ingenuity in a bedroll, we'll just do something else, and that'll be good, too." She gave a short, decisive nod.

"Well," he said in a bemused voice. "That's settled."

She flopped down again, nestling in close, hugging him tight. "You'd best believe it."

To Fawn's gladness they lingered late in the glade the next morning, attempting to repeat some of last night's trials; some were successful, some not. Dag couldn't seem to induce his ghost hand again—maybe he was too relaxed?—which appeared to leave him someplace between disappointment and relief. As Fawn had guessed, he found other ways to please her, although she thought he was trying a bit too hard, which made her worry for him, which didn't help *her* relax.

She fed him a right fine breakfast, though, and they mounted up and found their way back to the river road by noon. In the late afternoon, they at last left the valley, Dag taking an unmarked track off to the west. They passed through a wide stretch of wooded country, sometimes in single file on twisty trails, sometimes side by side on broader tracks. Fawn was soon lost—well, if she struck east, she'd be sure to find the river again sometime, so she supposed she was only out of her reckoning for going forward, not back—but Dag seemed not to be.

For two days they pushed through similar woodland. *Pushed* might be too strong a term, with their early stops and late starts. Twice Dag persuaded his ghost hand to return, to her startled delight, twice he didn't, for no obvious reason either way, which plainly puzzled him deeply. She wondered at his spooky choice of name for this ground ability. He worried over it equally afterwards whether or not he succeeded, and Fawn finally decided that it had been so long since he hadn't known exactly what he was doing all the time, he'd forgotten what it felt like to be blundering around in the dark, which made her sniff with a certain lack of sympathy.

She gradually became aware that he was dragging his feet on this journey, despite his worries about beating his patrol back to Hickory Lake, and not only for the obvious reason of extending their bedroll time together. Fawn herself was growing intensely curious about what lay ahead, and inclined to move along more briskly, but it wasn't till the third morning that they did so, and that only because of a threatened change in the weather. The high wispy clouds that both farmers and Lakewalkers called horsefeathers had moved in from the west last night, making fabulous pink streaks in the sunset indigo, and the air today was close and hazy, both signs of a broad storm brewing. When it blew through, it would bring a sparkling day in its wake, but was like to be violent before then. Dag said they might beat it to the lake by late afternoon.

Around noon the woods opened out in some flat meadowlands bordering a creek, with a dual track, and Fawn found herself riding alongside Dag again. "You once said you'd tell me the tale of Utau and Razi if you were either more drunk or more sober. You look pretty sober now."

He smiled briefly. "Do I? Well, then."

"Whenever I can get you to talk about your people, it helps me form up some better idea what I'm heading into."

"I'm not sure Utau's tale will help much, that way."

"Maybe not, but at least I won't say something stupid through not knowing any better."

He shrugged, though he amended, "Unknowing, maybe. Never stupid."

"Either way, I'd still end up red-faced."

"You blush prettily, but I give you the point. Well. Utau was string-bound for a good ten years to Sarri Otter, but they had no children. It happens that way, sometimes, and even Lakewalker groundsense can't tell why. Both his family and hers were pressuring them to cut their strings and try again with different mates—"

"Wait, what? People can cut their marriage strings? What does that mean, and how does it work?" Fawn wrapped a protective right hand around her left wrist, then put her palm hastily back on her thigh, kicking Grace's plump sides to encourage her to step along and keep up with Copperhead's longer legs.

"What leads up to a string-cutting varies pretty wildly with the couple, but lack of children after a good long time trying is considered a reason to part without dishonor to either side. More difficult if only one partner assents to the cutting; then the argument can spread out to both their families' tents and get very divisive. Or tedious, if you have to listen to them all go on. But if both partners agree to it, the ceremony is much like string-binding, in reverse. The wedding cords are taken off and rewrapped around both partners' arms, only with the opposite twist, and knotted, but then the string-blesser takes a knife and cuts the knot apart, and each takes back the pieces of their own."

Fawn wondered if that knife was carved of bone.

"The grounds drain out back to their sources, and, well, it's done. People usually burn the dead strings, after." He glanced aside at her deepening frown. "Don't farmer marriages ever come apart?"

"I think sometimes, but not often. The land and the families hold them together. And there's considered to be a shame in the failure. People do up and leave, sometimes, men or women, but it's more like chewing off your leg to escape a trap. You have to leave so much behind, so much work. So much hope, too, I suppose." She added, "Though I heard tell of one marriage down south of the village that came apart again in two weeks. The bride and all her things just got carted right back to her family, being hardly settled in yet, and the entry was scratched out in the family book. Nobody would ever explain to me why, although the twins and Fletch were snickering over it, so I suppose it might have had to do with bed problems, though she wasn't pregnant by someone else or anything. It was all undone right quick with no argument, though, so someone must have had something pretty big to apologize for, I'd guess."

"Sounds like." His brows rose as he considered this in curiosity, possibly of the more idle sort. "Anyway. Utau and Sarri loved each other despite their sorrow, and didn't want to part. And they were both good friends with Utau's cousin Razi. I'm not just sure who persuaded who to what, but one day Razi up and moved all his things into Sarri's tent with the pair of them. And a few months later Sarri was pregnant. And, to top the matter, not only did Razi get string-bound with Sarri, Razi and Utau got string-bound with each other, so the circle went all the way around and each ended up wearing the strings of both the others. All Otters now. And everyone's families went around for a while looking like their heads ached, but then there came this beautiful girl baby, and a while after, this bright little boy, that all three just dote on, and everyone else pretty much gave up the worrying. Although not the lewd speculation, naturally."

Fawn laughed. "Naturally." Her mind started to drift off in a little lewd speculating of its own, abruptly jerked back to attention when Dag continued in his thoughtful-voice.

"I've never made a child, myself. I was always very careful, if not always for the same reasons. There's not a few who have trouble when they switch over from trying to miss that target to trying to hit it. All their prior care seeming a great waste of a sudden. The sort of useless thing you wonder about late at night."

Had Dag been doing so, staring up at the stars? Fawn said, "You'd think, with that pattern showing in women's grounds, it would be easier rather than harder to get a baby just when you wanted." She was still appalled at how easy it had been for her.

"So you would. Yet so often people miss, and no one knows why. Kauneo and I—" His voice jerked to a halt in that now-familiar way.

She held her peace, and her breath.

"Here's one I never told anyone ever—"

"You need not," she said quietly. "Some people are in favor of spitting out hurts, but poking at them too much doesn't let them heal, either."

"This one's ridden in my memory for a long, long time. Maybe it would look a different size if I got it outside my head rather than in it, for once."

"Then I'm listenin'." Was he about to uncork another horror-tale?

"Indeed." He stared ahead between Copperhead's ears. "We'd been string-bound upwards of a year, and I felt I was getting astride my duties as a company captain, and we decided it was time to start a child. This was in the months just before the wolf war broke. We tried two months running, and missed. Third month, I was away on my duties at the vital time; for the life of me I can't now remember what seemed so important about them. I can't even re-member what they *were*. Riding out and checking on something or other. And in the fourth month, the wolf war was starting up, and we were both caught up in the rush." He drew a long, long breath. "But if I could have made Kauneo pregnant by then, she would have stayed in camp, and not led out her patrol to Wolf Ridge. And whatever else had happened, she and the child would both have lived. If not for that lost month."

Fawn's heart felt hot and strange, as if his old wound were being shared through the very ground of his words. *Not a good secret to lug around, that one.* She tried the obvious patch. "You can't know that."

"I know I can't. I don't think there's a second thought I can have about this that I haven't worn out by now. Maybe Kauneo's leadership, down at the an-chor end of the line, was what held the ridge that extra time after I went down. Maybe . . . A patroller friend of mine, his first wife died in childbed. I know he harbors regrets just as ferocious for the exact opposite cause. There is no knowing. You just have to grow used to the not knowing, I guess."

He fell quiet for a time, and Fawn, daunted, said nothing. Though maybe the listening had been all he'd needed. She wondered, suddenly, if Dag was doubting whether he could sire children. Fifty-five years was a long time to go without doing so, for a man, although she had the impression that it wasn't that he'd been with so many women, before or after Kauneo, as that he'd paid really good atten-tion when he had. In the light of her own history, if no child appeared when finally wanted, it would seem clear who was responsible. Did he fear to disappoint?

But his mind had turned down another path now, apparently, for he said, "My immediate family's not so large as yours. Just my mother, my brother, and his wife at present. All my brother's children are out of the tent, on patrol or apprenticed to makers. One son's string-bound, so far."

Dag's nephews and nieces were just about the same age range as Fawn and her brothers, from his descriptions. She nodded.

He went on, "I hope to slip into camp quietly. I'm of two minds whether to report to Fairbolt or my family first. It's likely rumors have trickled back about the Glassforge malice kill ahead of Mari's return, in which case Fairbolt will want the news in full. And I have to tell him about the knife. But I'd like to introduce you to my brother and mother in my own way, before they hear anything from anyone else."

"Well, which one would be less offended to be put second?" asked Fawn.

"Hard to say." He smiled dryly. "Mama can hold a grudge longer, but Fairbolt has a keen memory for lapses as well."

"I should not like to begin by offending my new mama-in-law."

"Spark, I'm afraid some people are going to be offended no matter what you and I do. What we've done . . . isn't done, though it was done in all honor."

"Well," she said, trying for optimism, "some people are like that among farmers, too. No pleasing them. You just try, or at least try not to be the first to break." She considered the problem. "Makes sense to put the worst one first. Then, if you have to, you can get away by saying you need to go off and see the second."

He laughed. "Good thinking. Perhaps I will."

But he didn't say which he believed was which.

They rode on through the afternoon without stopping. Fawn thought she could tell when they were nearing the lake by a certain lightness growing in the sky and a certain darkness growing in Dag. At any rate, he got quieter and quieter, though his gaze ahead seemed to sharpen. Finally, his head came up, and he murmured, "The bridge guard and I just bumped grounds. Only another mile."

They came off the lesser track they'd been following onto a wider road, which ran in a sweeping curve. The land here was very flat; the woods, mixed beech and oak and hickory, gave way to another broad meadow. On the far side, someone lying on the back of what looked to be a grazing cart horse, his legs dangling down over the horse's barrel, sat up and waved. He kicked the horse into a canter and approached.

The horse wore neither saddle nor bridle, and the young man aboard it was scarcely more dressed. He wore boots, some rather damp-looking linen drawers, a leather belt with a scabbard for a knife, and his sun-darkened skin. As he approached, he yanked the grass stem he'd been chewing from his mouth and threw it aside. "Dag! You're alive!" He pulled up his horse and stared at the sling, and at Fawn trailing shyly behind. "Aren't you a sight, now! Nobody said anything about a broken bone! Your right arm, too, absent gods, how have you been managing anything at all?"

Dag returned an uninformative nod of greeting, although he smiled faintly. "I've had a little help."

"Is *that* your farmer girl?" The guard stared at Fawn as though farmer girls were a novelty out of song, like dancing bears. "Mari Redwing thought you'd been gelded by a mob of furious farmers. Fairbolt's fuming, your mama thinks you're dead and blames Mari, and your brother's complaining he can't work in the din."

"Ah," said Dag in a hollow voice. "Mari's patrol get back early, did it?"

"Yesterday afternoon."

"Lots of time for everyone to get home and gossip, I see."

"You're the talk of the lake. Again." The guard squinted and urged his horse closer, which made Copperhead squeal in warning, or at least in ill manners. The man was trying to get a clear look at Fawn's left wrist, she realized. "All day, people have been giving me urgent messages to pass on the instant I saw you. Fairbolt, Mari, your mama—despite the fact she insists you're dead, mind—and your brother all want to see you first thing." He grinned, delivering this impossible demand.

Dag came very close, Fawn thought, to just laying his head down on his horse's mane and not moving. "Welcome home, Dag," he muttered. But he straightened up instead and kicked Copperhead around head to tail beside Grace. He leaned over leftward to Fawn, and said, "Roll up my sleeve, Spark. Looks like it's going to be a hot afternoon.

2

The bridge the young man guarded was crudely cut timber, long and low, wide enough for two horses to cross abreast. Fawn craned her neck eagerly as she and Dag passed over. The murky water beneath was obscured with lily pads and drifting pond weed; farther along, a few green-headed ducks paddled desultorily in and out of the cattails bordering the banks. "Is this a river or an arm of the lake?"

"A bit of both," said Dag. "One of the tributary creeks comes in just up the way. But the water widens out around both curves. Welcome to Two Bridge Island."

"Are there two bridges?"

"Really three, but the third goes to Mare Island. The other bridge to the mainland is on the western end, about two miles thataway. This is the narrowest separation."

"Like a moat?"

"In summer, very like a moat. All of the island chain backing up behind could be defended right here, if it wanted defending. After the hard freeze, this is more like an ice causeway, but the most of us will be gone to winter camp at Bearsford by then. Which, while it does have a ford, is mostly lacking in bears. Camp's set on some low hills, as much as we have hills in these parts. People who haven't walked out of this hinterland think they're hills."

"Were you born here, or there?"

"Here. Very late in the season. We should have been gone to winter camp, but my arrival made delays. The first of my many offenses." His smile at this was faint.

Flat land and thin woods gave little to view at first as the road wound inward, although around a curve Copperhead snorted and pretended to shy as a flock of a dozen or so wild turkeys crossed in front of them. The turkeys returned apparent disdain and wandered away into the undergrowth. Around the next curve Dag twitched his horse aside into the verge, and Fawn paused with him, as a caravan passed. A gray-headed man rode ahead; following him, on no lead, were a dozen horses loaded with heavy basket panniers piled high with dark, round, lumpy objects covered in turn with crude rope nets to keep the loads from tumbling out. A boy brought up the rear.

Fawn stared. "I don't suppose that's a load of severed heads going somewhere, but it sure looks like it at a distance. No wonder folks think you're cannibals."

Dag laughed, turning to look after the retreating string. "You know, you're right! That, my love, is a load of plunkins, on their way to winter store. This is their season. In late summer, it is every Lakewalker's duty to eat up his or her share of fresh plunkins. You are going to learn *all about* plunkins."

From his tone Fawn wasn't sure if that was a threat or a promise, but she liked the wry grin that went along-with. "I hope to learn all about everything."

He gave her a warmly encouraging nod and led off once more. Fawn wondered when she was going to at last see tents, and especially Dag's tent.

A shimmering light through the screen of trees, mostly hickory, marked the shoreline to the right. Fawn stood up in her stirrups, trying for a glimpse of the water. She said in surprise, "Cabins!"

"Tents," Dag corrected.

"Cabins with awnings." She gazed avidly as the road swung nearer. Half a dozen log buildings in a cluster hugged the shore. Most seemed to have single central fireplaces, probably double-sided, judging from the fieldstone chimneys she saw jutting from the roof ridgelines. Windows were few and doors nonexistent, for most of the log houses were open on one side, sheltered by deerhide canopies raised on poles seeming almost like long porches. She glimpsed a few shadowy people moving within, and, crossing the yard, a Lakewalker woman wearing a skirt and shepherding a toddler. So did only patrolling women wear trousers?

"If it's missing one full side, it's still a tent, not a permanent structure, and therefore does not have to be burned down every ten years." Dag sounded as if he was reciting.

Fawn's nose wrinkled in bafflement. "What?"

"You could call it a religious belief, although usually it's more of a religious argument. In theory, Lakewalkers are not supposed to build permanent structures. Towns are targets. So are farms, for that matter. So is anything so big and heavy or that you've invested so much in you can't drop it and run if you have to. Farmers would defend to the death. Lakewalkers would retreat and regroup. If we all lived in theory instead of on Two Bridge Island, that is. The only buildings that seem to get burned in the Ten-year Rededication these days are ones the termites have got to. Certain stodgy parties predict dire retribution for our lapses. In my experience, retribution turns up all on its own regardless, so I don't worry about it much."

Fawn shook her head. *I may have more to learn than I thought.*

They passed a couple more such clusters of near buildings. Each seemed to have a dock leading out into the water, or perhaps that was a raft tied to the shore; one had a strange boat tied to it in turn, long and narrow. Smoke rose from chimneys, and Fawn could see homely washing strung on lines to dry. Kitchen gardens occupied sunny patches, and small groves of fruit trees bordered the clearings, with a few beehives set amongst them. "How many Lakewalkers are there on this island?"

"Here, about three thousand in high summer. There are two more island chains around the lake too separated to connect to us by bridge, with maybe another four thousand folks total. If we want to visit, we can either paddle across two miles or ride around for twenty. Probably another thousand or so still back maintaining Bearsford, same as about a thousand folks stay here all winter. Hickory Lake Camp is one of the largest in Oleana. With the biggest territory to patrol, as a penalty for our success. We still send out twice as many exchange patrollers as we ever get in return." A hint of pride tinged his voice, even though his last remarks ought to have sounded more complaint than brag. He nodded ahead toward something Fawn did not yet see, and at a jingle of harness and thud of many hooves gestured her into the weeds to make way, turning Copperhead alongside.

It was a patrol, trotting in double file, very much as Fawn had first seen Mari and Dag's troop ride into the well-house farm what was beginning to seem a lifetime ago. This bunch looked fresh and rested and unusually tidy, however, so she guessed they were outward bound, on their way to whatever patch of hinterland they were assigned to search for their nightmare prey. Most of them seemed to recognize Dag and cried surprised greetings; with his reins wrapped around his hook and his other arm in a sling, he could not return their waves, but he did nod and smile. They didn't pause, but not a few of them turned in their saddles to stare back at the pair.

"Barie's lot," said Dag, looking after them. "Twenty-two."

He'd counted them? "Is that good or bad, twenty-two?"

"Not too bad, for this time of year. It's a busy season." He chirped to Copperhead, and they took to the road once more.

Fawn wondered anew what the shape of her life was going to be, tucked in around Dag's. On a farm, a couple might work together or apart, long hours and hard, but they would still meet for meals three times a day and sleep together every night. Dag would not, presumably, take her patrolling. Therefore, she must stay here, in long, scary separations punctuated by brief reunions, at least till Dag grew too old to patrol. Or too injured, *or didn't come back one day,* but her mind shied from thinking too hard about that one. If she was to be left here with these people and no Dag, she'd best try to fit in. Hardworking hands were needed everywhere all the time; surely hers could win her a place.

Dag pulled up Copperhead and hesitated at a fork in the road. The rightward, eastern branch followed the shoreline, and Fawn eyed it with interest; she could hear voices echoing over the water farther along it, a few cheery shouts and calls and some singing too distant to make out the words. Dag straightened his shoulders, grimaced, and led left instead. Half a mile on, the woods thinned again, and the distinctive silvery light reflecting from the water glimmered between the shaggy boles. The road ended at another that ran along the northern shore, unless it was just rejoining the same one circling the perimeter of the island. Dag led left again.

A brief ride brought them to a broad cleared section with several long log buildings, many of which had walls all the way around, with wooden porches and lots of rails for tying horses. No kitchen gardens or washing, although a few fruit trees were dotted here and there, broad apple and tall, graceful pear. On the woodland side of the road was an actual barn, if built rather low, the first Fawn had seen here, and a couple of split-rail paddocks for horses, though only a few horses idled in them at the moment. A trio of small, lean, black pigs rooted among the trees for fallen fruit or nuts. On the lakeside a larger dock jutted out into the water.

Dag edged Copperhead up to one of the hitching rails outside a log building, dropped his reins, and stretched his back. He cast Fawn an afterthought of a smile. "Well, here we are."

Fawn thought this a bit too close-mouthed, even for Dag in a mood. "This isn't your house, is it?"

"Ah. No. Patroller headquarters."

"So we're seeing Fairbolt Crow first?"

"If he's in. If I'm lucky, he will have gone off somewhere." Dag dismounted, and Fawn followed, tying both horses to the rail. She trailed him up onto the porch and through a plank door.

They entered a long room lined with shelves stuffed with piles of papers, rolled parchments, and thick books, and Fawn was reminded at once of Shep Sower's crammed house. At a table at one end, a woman with her hair in iron-gray braids, but wearing a skirt, sat writing in a large ledger book. She was quite as tall as Mari, but more heavily built, almost stout. She was looking up and setting aside her quill even as their steps sounded. Her face lit with pleasure.

"Woo-ee! Look what just dragged in!"

Dag gave her a wry nod. "How de', Massape. Is, um . . . Fairbolt here?"
"Oh, aye."

"Is he busy?" Dag asked, in a most unpressing tone.

"He's in there talking with Mari. About you, I expect, judging from the yelps. Fairbolt's been telling her not to panic. She says she prefers to start panicking as soon as you're out of her sight, just to get beforehand on things. Looks like they're both in the right. What in the world have you done to yourself this time?" She nodded at his sling, then sat up, her eyes narrowing as they fell on the braid circling his left arm. She said again, in an entirely altered tone, "Dag, what in the wide green world have you *done?*"

Fawn, awash in this conversation, gave Dag a poke and a look of desperate inquiry.

"Ah," he said. "Fawn, meet Massape Crow, who is captain to Third Company—Barie's patrol that we passed going out is in her charge, among others. She's also Fairbolt's wife. Massape, this is Missus Fawn Bluefield. My wife." His chin did not so much rise in challenge as set in stubbornness.

Fawn smiled brightly, clutched her hands together making sure her left wrist showed, and gave a polite dip of her knees. "How de', ma'am."

Massape just stared, her lower lip drawn in over her teeth. "You . . ." She held up a finger for a long, uncertain moment, drawling out the word, then swung and pointed past the room's fireplace, central to the inner wall, to a door beyond. "See Fairbolt."

Dag returned her a dry nod and shepherded Fawn to the door, opening it for her. From the room beyond, Fawn heard Mari's voice saying, "If he's stuck to his route, he should be somewhere along the line here."

A man's rumbling tones answered: "If he'd stuck to his route, would he be three weeks overdue? You haven't got a line, there, you've got a huge circle, and the edges run off the blighted map."

"If you've no one else to spare, I'll go."

"You just got back. Cattagus would have words with me till he ran out of breath and turned blue, and then *you'd* be mad. Look, we'll put out the call to every patroller who leaves camp to keep groundsense and both eyes peeled . . ."

Both patrollers, Fawn realized, must have their groundsenses locked down tight in the heat of their argument not to be flying to the door by now. No—she glanced at Dag's stony face—all three. She grabbed Dag by the belt and pushed him through ahead of her, peeking cautiously around him.

This room was a mirror to the first, at least as far as the shelving packed to the ceiling went. A plank table in the middle, its several chairs kicked back to the wall, seemed to be spread with maps. A thickset man was standing with his arms crossed, a frown on his furrowed face. Iron-colored hair was drawn back from his retreating hairline into a single plait down his back; he wore patroller-style trousers and shirt but no leather vest. Only one knife hung from his belt, but Fawn noticed a long, unstrung bow propped against the cold fireplace, together with a quiver of arrows.

Mari, similarly clad, had her back to the door and was leaning over the table pointing at something. The man glanced up, and his gray brows climbed toward what was left of his hairline. His leathery lips twisted in a half grin. "Got that coin, Mari?"

She looked up at him, exasperation in the set of her neck. "What coin?"

"The one you said we'd flip to see who got to skin him first."

Mari, taking in his expression, wheeled. "Dag! You . . . ! Finally! *Where have you been?*" Her eyes, raking him up and down, caught as usual first on the sling. "Ye gods."

Dag offered a short, apologetic nod, seemingly split between both officers. "I was a bit delayed." He motioned with his sling by way of indicating reasonable causes. "Sorry for the worry."

"I left you in Glassforge pretty near four weeks ago!" said Mari. "You were supposed to go straight home! Shouldn't have taken you more than a week at most!"

"No," Dag said in a tone of judicious correction, "I told you we'd be stopping off at the Bluefield farm on the way, to put them at ease about Fawn, here. I admit that took longer than I'd planned. Though once the arm was busted there seemed no rush, as I figured I wouldn't be able to patrol again for nigh on six weeks anyway."

Fairbolt scowled at this dodgy argument. "Mari said that if your luck was good, you'd come to your senses and dump the farmer girl back on her family, but if it ran to your usual form, they'd beat you to death and hide the body. Did her kin bust your bone?"

"If I'd been her kin, I'd have broken *more* of them," Mari muttered. "You still got all your parts, boy?"

Dag's smile thinned. "I had a run-in with a sneak thief in Lumpton Market, actually. Got our gear back, for the price of the arm. My visit to West Blue went very pleasantly."

Fawn decided not to offer any adjustment to this bald-faced assertion. She didn't quite like the way the patrollers—all three of them—kept looking right at her and talking right over her, but they were on Dag's land here; she waited for guidance, or at least a hint. Though she thought he could stand to speed up, in that regard. Conscious of the officers' eyes upon her—Fairbolt was leaning sideways slightly to get a view around Dag—she crept out from behind her husband. She gave Mari a friendly little wave, and the camp captain a respectful knee-dip. "Hello again, Mari. How de' do, sir?"

Dag drew breath and repeated his blunt introduction: "Fairbolt, meet Missus Fawn Bluefield. My wife."

Fairbolt squinted and rubbed the back of his neck, his face screwed up. The silence stretched as he and Mari looked over the wedding cords with, Fawn felt, more than just their eyes. Both officers had their sleeves rolled up in the heat of the day, and both had similar cords winding around their left wrists, worn thin and frayed and faded. Her own cord and Dag's looked bright and bold and thick by comparison, the gold beads anchoring the ends seeming very solid.

Fairbolt glanced aside at Mari, his eyes narrowing still further. "Did you suspect this?"

"This? No! This isn't—how could—but I told you he'd likely done some fool thing no one could anticipate."

"You did," Fairbolt conceded. "And I didn't. I thought he was just . . ." He focused his gaze on Dag, and Fawn shrank even though she was not at its center. "I won't say *that's impossible* because it's plain you found a way. I will ask, what Lakewalker maker helped you to this?"

"None, sir," said Dag steadily. "None but me, Fawn's aunt Nattie, who is a spinner and natural maker, and Fawn. Together."

Though not so tall as Dag, Fairbolt was still a formidably big man. He frowned down at Fawn; she had to force her spine straight. "Lakewalkers do not recognize marriages to farmers. Did Dag tell you that?"

She held out her wrist. "That's why this, I understood." She gripped the cord tight, for courage. If they couldn't be bothered to be polite to her, she needn't return any better. "Now, I guess you could look at this with your fancy groundsense and say we weren't married if you wanted. But you'd be lying. Wouldn't you."

Fairbolt rocked back. Dag didn't flinch. If anything, he looked satisfied, if a bit fey. Mari rubbed her forehead.

Dag said quietly, "Did Mari tell you about my other knife?"

Fairbolt turned to him, not quite in relief, but tacitly accepting the shift of subject. Backing off for the moment; Fawn was not sure why. Fairbolt said, "As much as you told her, I suppose. Congratulations on your malice kill, by the way. What number was that? And don't tell me you don't keep count."

Dag gave a little conceding nod. "It would have been twenty-seven, if it had been my kill. It was Fawn's."

"It was both ours," Fawn put in. "Dag had the knife, I had the chance to use it. Either of us would have been lost without the other."

"Huh." Fairbolt walked slowly around Fawn, as if looking, *really* looking, at her for the first time. "Excuse me," he said, and reached out to tilt her head and study the deep red scars on her neck. He stepped back and sighed. "Let's see this other knife, then."

Fawn fished in her shirt. After the scare at Lumpton Market she had fashioned a new sheath for the blade, single and of softer leather, with a cord for her neck to carry it the way Lakewalkers did. It was undecorated, but she'd sewn it with care. Hesitantly, she pulled the cord over her curls, glanced at Dag, who gave her a nod of reassurance, and handed it over to the camp captain.

Fairbolt took it and sat down in one of the chairs near a window, drawing the bone blade out. He examined it much the way Dag and Mari had, even to touching it to his lips. He sat frowning a moment, cradling it in his thick hands. "Who made this for you, Dag? Not Dar?"

"No. A maker up in Luthlia, a few months after Wolf Ridge."

"Kauneo's bone, yes?"

"Yes."

"Did you ever have reason before to think the making might be defective?"

"No. I don't think it was."

"But if the making was sound, no one but you should have been able to prime it."

"I am very aware of that. And if the making was unsound, no one should have been able to prime it at all. But there it sits."

"That it does. So tell me exactly what happened in that cave, again . . . ?"

First Dag, and then Fawn, had to repeat the tale for Fairbolt, each in their own words. They touched but lightly on how Dag had come upon Fawn, kidnapped off the road by bandits in the thrall of the malice. How he'd tracked her to the malice's cave. And come—Dag bit his lip—just too late to stop the monster from ripping the ground of her two-months-child from her womb. Fawn did not volunteer, nor did Fairbolt ask, how she came to be alone, pregnant—and unwed—on the road in the first place; perhaps Mari, who'd had the tale from Fawn back in Glassforge, had given him the gist.

Fairbolt's attention and questions grew keener when they described the mix-up with Dag's malice-killing sharing knives. How Dag, going down under the malice's guard of mud-men, had tossed the knife pouch to Fawn, how she'd stuck the monster first with the wrong, unprimed knife, then with the right one, shattering it in its use. How the terrifying creature had dissolved, leaving the first knife so strangely charged with the mortality of Fawn's unborn daughter.

By the time they were half-through, Mari had pulled up a chair, and Dag leaned against the table. Fawn found she preferred to stand, though she had to lock her knees against an unwelcome trembling. Fairbolt did not, to Fawn's relief, inquire into the messy aftermath of that fight; his interest seemed to end with the mortal knives.

"You are planning to show this to Dar," Fairbolt said when they'd finished, nodding to the knife still in his lap; from his tone Fawn wasn't sure if this was query or command.

"Yes."

"Let me know what he says." He hesitated. "Assuming the other matter doesn't affect his judgment?" He jerked his head toward Dag's left arm.

"I have no idea what Dar will think of my marriage" —Dag's tone seemed to add, *nor do I care,* but he didn't say it aloud—"but I would expect him to speak straight on his craft, regardless. If I have doubts after, I can always seek another opinion. There are half a dozen knife makers around this lake."

"Of lesser skill," said Fairbolt, watching him closely.

"That's why I'm going to Dar first. Or at all."

Fairbolt started to hand the knife back to Dag but, at Dag's gesture, returned it to Fawn. She put the cord back over her head and hid the sheath away again between her breasts.

Fairbolt, almost eye to eye with her, watched this coolly. "That knife doesn't make you some sort of honorary Lakewalker, you know, girl."

Dag frowned. But before he could say anything, Fawn, despite the heat flushing through her, replied calmly, "I know that, sir." She leaned in toward him, and deepened her voice. "I'm a farmer girl and proud of it, and if that's good enough for Dag, the rest of you can go jump in your lake. Just so *you* know this thing I have slung around my neck wasn't an *honorary* death." She nodded curtly and stood straight.

A little to her surprise, he did not grow offended, merely thoughtful, if that was what rubbing his lips that way signified. He stood up with a grunt that reminded her of a tired Dag, and strode across the room to the far side of the fireplace.

Covering the whole surface between the chimney stone and the outer wall and nearly floor to ceiling was a panel made of some very soft wood. It was painted with a large grid pattern, each marked with a place name. Fawn realized, looking at the names she recognized, that it was a sort of map, if lines on a map could be pulled about and squared off, of parts of the hinterland—all the parts, she suspected. To the left-hand side was a separate column of squares, labeled *Two Bridge Island, Heron Island, Beaver Sigh, Bearsford,* and *Sick List.* And, above them all, a smaller circle in red paint labeled *Missing.*

About a third of the squares had hard wooden pegs stuck in them. Most of them were in groups of sixteen to twenty-five, and Fawn realized she was looking at patrols—some squares were full of little holes as though they might have been lately emptied. Each peg had a name inked onto the side in tiny, meticulous writing, and a number on its end. Some of the pegs had wooden buttons, like coins with holes bored in the middle, hung on them by twisted wires, one or two or sometimes more threaded in a stack. The buttons, too, were numbered.

"Oh!" she said in surprise. "These are all your patrollers!" There must have been five or six hundred pegs in all. She leaned closer to search for names she recognized.

Fairbolt raised his brows. "That's right. A patrol leader can keep a patrol in mind, but once you get to be a company or camp captain, well, one head can't hold them all. Or at least, mine can't."

"That's clever! You can see everything all at once, pretty nearly." She realized she needed to look more closely at Two Bridge Island for names. "Ah, there's Mari. And Razi and Utau, they're home with Sarri, oh good. Where's Dirla?"

"Beaver Sigh," said Dag, watching her pore over the display. "That's another island."

"Mm? Oh, yes, there she is, too. I hope she's happy. Does she have a regular sweetheart? Or sweethearts? What are the little buttons for?"

Mari answered. "For the patrollers who are carrying sharing knives. Not everyone has one, but every patrol that goes out needs to have two or more."

"Oh. Yes, that makes sense. Because it wouldn't do a bit of good to find a malice and have no knife on hand. And you might find another malice, after. Or have an accident." Dag had spoken with a shudder of the ignominy of accidentally breaking a sharing knife, and now she understood. She hesitated, thinking of her own spectacular, if peculiar, sharing knife accident. "Why are they numbered?"

Dag said, "The camp captain keeps a book with records of the owners and donors, for if a knife is used. To send the acknowledgments to the kinfolk, or know where to send the pieces if they chance to be recovered."

Fawn frowned. "Is that why the patrollers are numbered, too?"

"Very like. There's another set of books with all the names and next of kin, and other details someone might want to know about any particular patroller in an emergency. Or when the emergency is over."

"Mm," said Fawn, her frown deepening as she pictured this. She set her hands on her hips and peered at the board, imagining all those lives—and deaths—moving over the landscape. "Do you connect the pegs to people's grounds, like marriage cords? Could you?"

"No," said Dag.

"Does she always go on like this?" asked Fairbolt. She glanced up to find him staring at her rather as she'd been staring at the patroller board.

"More or less, yes," said Dag.

"I'm sorry!" Fawn clapped her hand to her mouth in apology. "Did I ask too many questions?"

Fairbolt gave her a funny look. "No." He reached up and took a peg out of the *Missing* circle, one of two jutting there. He held it out at arm's length, squinting briefly at the fine print on the side, and grunted satisfaction. "I suppose this comes off, now." With surprising delicacy, his thick fingers unwound its wire and teased off one numbered button. The second he frowned at, but twisted back into place. "I never met the Luthlia folks; never got up that way. You be taking care of the honors on this one, Dag?"

"Yes."

"Good. Thanks." He held the peg in his palm as if weighing it.

Dag reached up and touched the remaining peg in the red circle. "Still no word of Thel." It didn't sound like a question.

"No," sighed Fairbolt.

"It's been near two years, Fairbolt," Mari observed dispassionately. "You could likely take it down."

"It's not like the board's out of room up there, now is it?" Fairbolt sniffed, stared unreadably at Dag, gave the peg in his hand a toss, and bent down and thrust it decisively into the square marked *Sick List*.

He straightened up and turned back to Dag. "Stop in at the medicine tent. Let me know what they say about the arm. Come see me after you have that talk with Dar." He made a vague gesture of dismissal, but then added, "Where are you going next?"

"Dar." Dag added more reluctantly, "Mother."

Mari snorted. "What are you going to say to Cumbia about that?" She nodded at his arm cord.

Dag shrugged. "What's to say? I'm not ashamed, I'm not sorry, and I'm not backing down."

"She'll spit."

"Likely." He smiled grimly. "Want to come watch?"

Mari rolled her eyes. "I think I want to go back out on patrol. Fairbolt, you need volunteers?"

"Always, but not you today. Go along home to Cattagus. Your stray has turned up; you've no more excuse to loiter here harassing me."

"Eh," she said, whether in agreement or disagreement Fawn could not tell. She cast a vague sort of salute at Fairbolt and Dag, murmured, "Good luck, child," at Fawn, in a rather-too-ironical voice, and took herself out.

Dag made to follow, but stopped with a look of inquiry when Fairbolt said, "Dag."

"Sir?"

"Eighteen years ago," said Fairbolt, "you persuaded me to take a chance on you. I never had cause to regret it."

Till now? Fawn wondered if he meant to imply.

"I don't care to defend this in the camp council. See that it doesn't boil up that high, eh?"

"I'll try not," said Dag.

Fairbolt returned a provisional sort of nod, and Fawn followed Dag out.

Missus Captain Crow was gone from the outer room. Outside, the sky had turned a flat gray, the water of the lake a pewter color, and the humidity had become oppressive. As they made their way down the porch steps to where the horses were tied, Dag sighed. "Well. That could have gone worse."

Fawn recognized her own words tossed back to her, and remembered Dag's. "Really?"

His lips twitched; it wasn't much of a smile, but at least it was a real one, and not one of those grimaces with the emphasis on the *grim* he'd mostly had inside. "Really. Fairbolt could have pulled my peg and chucked it in the fire. Then all my problems would have been not his problems anymore."

"What, he could have made you not a patroller?"

"That's right."

Fawn gasped. "Oh, no! And I said all those mouthy things to him! You should have warned me! But he made me mad, talking over the top of my head." She added after a moment's reflection, "You all three did."

"Mm," said Dag. He pulled her into his left arm and rested his chin on her curls for a moment. "I imagine so. Things were moving pretty fast there for a while."

She wondered if the patrollers had all been saying things to one another through their groundsenses that she hadn't caught. For sure, she felt there was a good deal back there she hadn't caught.

"As for Fairbolt, you won't offend him by standing up to him, even if you're wrong, but especially if you're right. His back's broad enough to bear correction. He doesn't much care for folks who go belly-up to him to his face then whine about it behind his back, though."

"Well . . . stands to reason, that."

"Indeed. You didn't make a bad impression on him, Spark. In fact, judging from the results, you made a pretty good impression."

"Well, that's a relief." She paused in puzzlement. "What results?"

"He put my peg in the sick box. Still a patroller. The camp council deals with any arguments the families can't solve, or arguments that come up between clan heads. But any active patroller, the council has to go through the camp captain to deal with. It's like he's clan head to all of us. I won't say Fairbolt will or even can protect me from any consequences of this"—he shrugged his left arm to indicate his marriage cord—"but leastways he's keeping that possibility open for now."

Fawn turned to untie the horses, considering this. The tailpiece seemed to be that it was Dag's job—and hers?—to keep the consequences from getting too out of hand. As she scrambled up on Grace, she saw under some pear trees at a little distance Mari sitting on a trestle table swinging her legs, and Massape

Crow on the bench beside her. Mari seemed to be talking heatedly, by the way she was waving her arms, and Massape had her head cocked in apparent fascination. Fawn didn't think she needed groundsense to guess the subject under discussion, even without the curious glances the pair cast their way.

Dag had wrapped Copperhead's reins around his hook. Now he led the horse beside the porch and used the steps for a mounting block, settling into the saddle with a tired grunt. He jerked his chin by way of a *come-along* gesture and led them onto the shore road, heading back east.

3

Fawn turned in her saddle to look as they passed the woodland road they'd come in on, and turned again as the shore road bent out toward a wooden bridge spanning a channel about sixty feet across. The next island spread west, bounding the arm of the lake across from the patroller headquarters. Past the bridge, its farther shoreline curved north and the lake beyond opened out for a square mile. In the distance she could see a few narrow boats being paddled, and another with a small triangular sail. The island reached by the bridge had only a scattering of trees; between them horses and goats and a few sheep grazed, and beneath them more black pigs dozed.

"Mare Island?" Fawn guessed.

"Yep. It and Foal Island, which you can't see beyond the far end over there" —Dag waved vaguely northwest—"are our main pastures. No need to build fences, you see."

"I do. Clever. Is there a Stallion Island?"

Dag smiled. "More or less. Most of the studs are kept over on Walnut Island" —he pointed to a low green bump across the open lake patch—"which works fine until one of the fellows gets excited and ambitious and tries to swim across in the night. Then there's some sorting out to do."

The shore road swung back into the trees, passing behind the clusters of log buildings along the lake bank. After a scant quarter mile, Dag pulled up Copperhead and frowned at a clearing enclosing just two buildings. The lake glimmered dully beyond in the hot afternoon's flat light. "Tent Redwing," Dag said.

"Well" —Fawn took a breath—"this is it, I guess."

"Not quite. Everyone seems to be out. But leastways we can drop off our saddles and bags and take the horses back to pasture."

They rode into the clearing. The two buildings were set facing each other at an angle opening toward the lake, both with long sides gaping under deer-hide awnings. Other deerhide rolls along the eaves looked as though they could be dropped down to provide more wall at need. Houses and porches seemed to be floored with planks, not dirt, at least. Fawn tried to think *simple,* not *squalid.* A stone-lined fire pit lay in the clearing between the two structures—Fawn still could not make herself think of them as tents—in addition to the central fireplaces that could apparently heat both the outer and the enclosed inner chambers. Seats of stumps or sawn-off logs were dotted about; in summer, no doubt almost all work was done outdoors.

She hopped down and helped unsaddle, dealing with the straps and buckles; Dag with his hook hauled the gear from the horses' backs and dumped it on the plank porch of the house on the right. He scratched the back of his head gently.

"Not sure where Mama's got off to. Dar's likely at the bone shack. And if Omba's not out on Mare Island, it'll be a first. Dig down in the bottom of my saddlebags, Spark, and find those strings of horseshoes."

Fawn did so, discovering two bunches of new horseshoes tied together, a dozen each. "My word, no wonder your bags were so heavy! How long have you been carting these around in there?"

"Since we left Glassforge. Present for Omba. Hickory Lake's a rich camp in some ways, but we have few metals in these parts, except for a little copper-working near Bearsford. All our iron has to be traded for from other camps, mostly around Tripoint. Though we've been getting more from farmer sources in the hills beyond Glassforge, lately." He grinned briefly. "When a certain young exchange patroller from Tripoint walking the hinterlands arrived at Massape Crow and said, *That's far enough,* it's told his bride-gift string of horses came in from back home staggering under loads of iron. It made the Crows rich and Fairbolt famous, back in the day."

Fawn led Grace to a log seat and climbed up bareback, and Dag hooked her up the horseshoe bundles, which she twisted about each other and laid over her lap. He climbed up on Copperhead in turn, and they went back out to the road and returned to the bridge.

At the far end of the span he dismounted again to unhook a rope loop from the board gate, open it for Fawn, and shut it again behind them. He did not bother remounting, but led them instead toward a long shed that lay a hundred paces or so away. Fawn slid off Grace, managing not to drop the horseshoes, and Dag hooked off both bridles, flopping them over his shoulder. Copperhead scooted away at once, and after a moment's doubt, Grace followed, soon putting her head down to crop grass.

Of all of his relatives, Dag had talked most freely about his brother's wife, the Waterstrider sister who'd changed her name for her mother-in-law's sake. In order of increasing reticence came his grandfather, remembered with nostalgia from scenes of Dag's youth; Dar, of whom Dag spoke with cool respect; his father, tinged with distance and regret; and, in a pool of silence at the center, his mother. Every conversation Fawn had tried to lead toward her, Dag had led away. About Omba—horse trainer, mare midwife, maker of harness, and, it appeared, farrier—there had been no such problem.

As they rounded the corner of the shed and stepped under its wooden overhang, Fawn had no trouble recognizing Omba, for she came striding out of a door crying, "Dag! Finally!" She was not so thin as Mari, and quite a bit shorter, though still as tall as any man in Fawn's family; Fawn would have guessed her age at fifty or so, which meant she was likely fifteen years older than that. She was dressed much like a patroller woman, and Fawn finally decided that the trousers were just Lakewalker riding garb, period. Her skin, though tanned and weathered, was paler than Dag's, and her eyes a pretty silvery blue. Her dark hair, shot with a few white streaks, ran down her back in a single swift plait, without ornament. She caught sight of the sling, planted her hands on her hips, and said, "Absent gods, brother, what have you done to your right arm!" And then, after a momentary pause, "Absent gods, Dag, what have you done to your *left* arm?"

Dag gave her a nod of greeting, his smile lopsided. "Hello, Omba. Brought you something." He gestured Fawn forward; she held out the horseshoes.

Omba's face lit, and she pounced on the prize. "Do I need those!" She came to a dead halt again at the sight of the cord on Fawn's wrist, and made a choked noise down in her throat. Her gaze rose to Fawn's face, her eyes widening in something between disbelief and dismay. "You're a farmer! You're *that* farmer!"

For an instant, Fawn wondered if there was some Lakewalker significance to Dag's tricking Omba into accepting this gift from Fawn's hands, but she had no time or way to ask. She dipped her knees, and said breathlessly, "Hello, Omba. I'm Fawn. Dag's wife." She wasn't about to make some broader claim such as, *I'm your new sister*; that would be for Omba to decide.

Omba wheeled toward Dag, her eyebrows climbing. "And what does that make you, Dag Redwing Hickory? Besides head down in the slit trench."

"Fawn's husband. Dag Bluefield . . . To-Be-Determined, at this point."

Or would the effect instead be to make Dag not Omba's brother anymore? Lakewalker tent customs continued to confuse Fawn.

"You seen Fairbolt yet?" asked Omba.

"Just came from there. Saw Mari there, too."

"You told him about this?" She jerked her head toward Fawn.

"Certainly."

"What did he do to you?"

"Put me on sick list." Dag wriggled his sling. "That was the To-Be-Determined part, or so I took it."

Omba blew out her breath in unflattering wonder. But not, Fawn thought, in hostility; she hung on tight to that realization. It did not seem as though Dag had taken her advice to start with the hardest ones first. By later today, *not hostile* might yet look pretty good.

"What did Mari say to you all, last night?" asked Dag.

"Oh, *there* was a scene. She came in asking if we'd heard from you, which was a jolt to start, since you were supposed to be with her. Then she said she'd sent you home from Glassforge weeks ago, and everyone was worried you'd been injured, but she said not. Is that right?" She stared at the sling.

"Was at the time. I collected this on the way. Go on."

"Then she had this wild tale about some cutie farmer girl being mixed up in your latest malice kill" —her eyes went curiously to Fawn—"which I barely believed, but now, hm. And that you'd jumped the cliff with her, which your mama hotly denied the possibility of, while simultaneously yelling at Mari for letting it happen. I kept my mouth shut during that part. Though I did wish you well of it."

"Thank you," said Dag blandly.

"Ha. Though I never imagined . . . anyway. Mari said that you'd gone off with the farmer girl, supposed to deliver her home or something. She was afraid you'd met some mishap at the hands of her kin—she said she was picturing gelding. That must have been some cliff. When Mari and your mama got down to arguing over lapses from twenty-five years back, I slipped out. But Mari took Dar down to the dock after, to talk private. He wouldn't say what she'd added, except that it was about bone craft, which even your mama knows by now is the sign she'll get no more from him."

It seemed Mari was still keeping the tale of the accident to the second sharing knife close. Nor had the term *pregnant* turned up in relation to Fawn, at least in front of Dag's mama. Fawn felt suddenly more charitable to Mari.

"Oh, Dag," sighed Omba. "This is going to top anything you've done ever."

"Look on the bright side. Nothing you can do ever after will top this. The effect might even be retroactive."

She gave a bemused nod. "I'll grant you that." She slung the horseshoes onto some pegs on the nearest post, and held up her hands palm out in a warding gesture. "I think I'll just stay out of this one altogether if you don't mind."

"You're welcome to try," said Dag amiably. "We were just over to the tent to drop our things, but it was empty. Where is everyone?"

"Dar went to the shack to work, or hide out. Mari was worried sick for you, and that shook him more than he was willing to let on, I think. She actually said *I'm sorry* to your mother at one point last night."

"And Mama?" said Dag.

"Out on raft duty. Rationing plunkins."

Dag snorted. "I'll bet."

"They tried to convince her to stay ashore with her bad back, but she denied the back and went. There will be no vile plunkin ear chucking today."

Now Fawn was lost. "Rationing plunkins? Is there a shortage?"

"No," said Dag. "This time of year, they're worse than in season—they're in glut."

Omba grinned. "Dar still waxes bitter about how she'd nurse her supply through the Bearsford camp, like there was some sort of prize for arriving at spring with the most winter store still in hand. And then make you all eat up the old ones before allowing any fresh ones."

Dag's lips quirked. "Oh, yeah."

"Did she ever go through a famine?" Fawn asked. "That makes people funny about food, I hear tell."

"Not as far as I know," said Omba.

She's speaking to me, oh good! Though people wishful to vent about their in-laws would bend the ear of anyone who'd listen, so it might not signify much.

"Not that the choices don't get a bit narrow for everyone by late winter," Omba continued. "She's just like that. Always has been. I still remember the first summer Dar and I were courting, when you grew so tall, Dag. We thought you were going to starve. Half the camp conspired to slip you food on the sly."

Dag laughed. "I was about ready to wrestle the goats for the splits and the mishaps. Those are feed plunkins," he added to Fawn aside. "Can't think why I didn't. I wouldn't be so shy nowadays."

"It is a known fact that patrollers will eat anything." Omba twitched a speculative eyebrow at Fawn that made her wonder if she ought to blush.

To quell that thought, Fawn asked instead, "Plunkin ear chucking?"

Dag explained, "When the plunkin heads are dredged up out of the lake bottom, they have two to six little cloves growing up the sides, about half the size of my hand. These are broken off and put back down in the mud to become next year's crop. Plunked in, hence the name. There are always more ears than needed, so the excess gets fed to the goats and pigs. And there are always a lot of youngsters swimming and splashing around the harvesting rafts, and, well, excess plunkin ears make good projectiles, in a reasonably nonlethal sort of way. Especially if you have a good slingshot," he added in a suddenly warmly reminiscent tone. He paused and cleared his throat. "The grown-ups disapprove of the waste, of course."

"Well, some do," said Omba. "Some remember their slingshots. Someone should have given one to your mother when she was a girl, maybe."

"At her age, she's not going to change."

"You've made a change."

Dag shrugged, and asked instead, "How're Swallow and Darkling?"

Omba's face brightened. "Wonderful well. That black colt's going to be fit to go for a stud when he's grown, I think. He'll fetch you a good price. Or if you finally want to trade in Snakebrain over there for dog meat, you could ride him yourself. I'd train him up for you. You two'd look mighty fine, patrolling."

"Mm, thanks, but no. Sometime tomorrow or the next day, soon as I have a chance, I want to pull them out of the herd. I'll get a packsaddle for Swallow, and Darkling can trot at her heels. Send them down to West Blue with my bride-gifts to Fawn's mama, which I am fearsome late presenting."

"Your best horses!" said Omba in dismay.

Dag smiled a slow smile. "Why not? They gave me their best daughter."

"But I'm their only daughter," said Fawn.

"Saves argument there, eh?" said Dag.

Omba caught up her braid and rubbed the end. "To farmers! What do they know about Lakewalker horses? What if they try to make Swallow pull a plow? Or cut Darkling? Or . . ." Her face screwed up, as she evidently pictured even worse farmer misuse of the precious horses.

"My family takes good care of our horses," said Fawn stiffly. "Of all our animals."

"They won't *understand*," said Omba.

"I will," said Dag. He gave her a nod. "See you at dinner. Who's cookin'?"

"Cumbia. You might want to grab a plunkin off the goats on the way, to fortify yourselves."

"Thanks, but I guess we'll survive." He gestured Fawn away. She gave Omba another knee-dip and smile by way of farewell; the Lakewalker woman just shook her head and returned a sardonic wave. *But not hostile,* Fawn reminded herself.

As they reached the bridge again, Dag held the gate aside for a girl leading a couple of horses with pannier baskets piled high with plunkins; she gave him a nod of thanks. These plunkins did indeed seem to be mostly broken or weirdly misshapen or with odd discolorations. Fawn glanced back to see her walking along chirping and tossing out plunkins along her path, and a general movement among the goats and pigs toward this feast.

"Lakewalker animals eat plunkins too, do they?"

"Horses and cows and sheep can't. The pigs and goats chomp them down. So will dogs."

"I haven't seen many dogs. I'd think you'd have more, for hunting and such. For hunting malices, even."

"We don't keep many. Dogs are more hazard than help on patrol. The malices snap them right up, and they have no defense. Except us, and if you're trying to bring down a malice, it'd be no use to be distracted trying to protect a dog, especially if it's turning on you itself."

As they strolled back along the shore road, Fawn asked curiously, "Was your mother ever a patroller?"

"I think she had the training, way back when. All the youngsters at least get taken out on short trips around the camps. Patrollers are chosen for two things, mainly. General health and strength, and groundsense range. Not everyone can project their groundsense out far enough to be useful on patrol. The lack's not considered a defect, necessarily; many's the quite competent maker who can't reach out much beyond his arm's length."

"Is Dar like that?"

"No, his range is almost as long as mine. He's just even better at what he does with bones. What my mother always wanted, now . . ." He trailed off.

Volunteering useful information at last? No, evidently not. Fawn sighed and prompted, "Was what?"

"More children. Just didn't work out that way for her, whether because Father was out on patrol too much, or they were just unlucky, or what, I don't know. I should have been a girl. That was my immediate next lapse after arriving late. Or been eight other children. Or had eight other children, in a pinch, and not off in Luthlia or someplace, but here at Hickory Camp. My mother had a second chance with Dar and Omba's children. She kind of commandeered them from Omba to raise; which I gather caused some friction at first, till Omba gave up and went to concentrate on her horses. They'd worked it all out by the time I got back from Luthlia minus the hand, anyway. There's still just a little . . . I won't call it bad feeling, but feeling, there over that."

Mother-in-law versus daughter-in-law friction was common coin in Fawn's world; she had no trouble following this. She wondered if Cumbia's thwarted thirst for daughters would extend itself to a little farmer girl, dragged in off patrol like some awkward souvenir. She had taken in one daughter-in-law, quite against custom, after all. Some hope there?

"Dag," she said suddenly, "where am I going to live?"

He looked over and raised his eyebrows at her. "With me."

"Yes, but when you're gone on patrol?"

Silence. It stretched rather too long.

"Dag?"

He sighed. "We'll just have to see, Spark."

They were nearly back to his family tent-cabins when Dag paused at a path leading into the woods. If he was checking anything with his groundsense, Fawn could not tell, but he jerked his chin in a come-along gesture and led right. The high straight boles, mostly hickory, gave a pale green shade in the shadowless light, as though they were walking into some underwater domain. The scrub was scant and low on the flat terrain. Fawn eyed the poison ivy and stuck to the center of the well-trodden path, lined here and there with whitewashed rocks.

About a hundred paces in, they came to a clearing. In the center was a small cabin, a real one with four sides, and, to Fawn's surprise, glass windows. Even the patrol headquarters had only had parchment stretched on window frames. More disturbingly, human thighbones hung from the eaves, singly or in pairs, swaying gently in the air that soughed in the papery hickory leaves overhead. She tried not to imagine ghostly whispering voices in the branches.

Dag followed her wide gaze. "Those are curing."

"Those folks look well beyond cure to me," she muttered, which at least made his lips twitch.

"If Dar's busy with something, don't speak till he speaks to us," Dag warned in a quiet voice. "Actually, the same applies even if it looks like he's doing nothing."

Fawn nodded vigorously. Putting the picture together from Dag's oblique descriptions, she figured Dar was the closest thing to a real Lakewalker necromancer that existed. She could not picture being foolish enough to interrupt him in the midst of some sorcery.

A hickory husk, falling from above, made a *clack* and a *clatter* as it hit the shingle roof and rolled off, and Fawn jumped and grabbed Dag's left arm tightly. He smiled reassuringly and led her around the building. On the narrower south side was a porch shading a wedged-open door. But the man they sought was outside, at the edge of the clearing. Working a simple sapling lathe, so ordinary and unsorcerous-looking as to make Fawn blink.

Dar was shorter and stockier than Dag, a solid middle-aged build, with a more rectangular face and broader jaw. He had his shirt off as he labored; his skin was coppery like Dag's but not so varied in its sun-burnishing. His dark hair was drawn back in a Lakewalker-style mourning knot, which made Fawn wonder who for, since his wife Omba's hadn't been. If there was gray in it, she wasn't close enough to see. One leg worked the lathe; the rope to the sapling turned a clamp holding a greenwood blank. Both hands held a curved knife and bore it inward, and pale yellow shavings peeled away to join a kicked-about pile below. Two finished bowls sat on a nearby stump. In the shavings pile lay discarded a partially carved, cracked blank, and another finished bowl that looked to Fawn perfectly fine.

His hands most drew her eye: strong and long-fingered like Dag's, quick and careful. And what a very odd thing it was that it should *feel* so odd to see them in a pair, working together that way.

He glanced up from his carving. His eyes were a clear bronze-brown. He looked back down, evidently trying to keep working, but after another spin muttered something short under his breath and straightened up with a scowl, allowing the blank to wind down, then unclamped it and dropped it into the shavings pile. He tossed the knife in the general direction of the stump and turned to Dag.

"Sorry to interrupt," said Dag, nodding to the half bowl. "I was told you wanted to see me immediately."

"Yes! Dag, where have you been?"

"Been getting here. I had a few delays." He made the sling-gesture.

For once, it did not divert his interrogator's eye. Dar's voice sharpened as his gaze locked on his brother's left arm. "What fool thing have you gone and done? Or have you finally done something right?" He let his breath out in a hiss as his eyes raked over Fawn. "No. Too much to hope for." His brow wrinkled as he frowned at her left wrist. "*How* did you do that?"

"Very well," said Dag, earning an exasperated look.

Dar walked closer, staring down at Fawn in consternation. "So there really was a farmer-piglet."

"Actually"—Dag's voice suddenly went bone dry—"that would be my wife. Missus Fawn Bluefield. Fawn, meet Dar Redwing."

Fawn attempted a tremulous smile. Her knees felt too weak to dip.

Dar stepped half a pace back. "Ye gods, you're serious about this!"

Dag's voice dropped still further. "Deadly."

They locked eyes for a moment, and Fawn had the maddening sense that some exchange had passed or was passing that, once again, she hadn't caught, although it had seemed to spin off the rather insulting term *piglet*. Or, from the heated look in Dag's eye, very insulting term, although she couldn't see exactly why; *chickie* and *filly* and *piglet* and all such baby-animal terms being used interchangeably for little endearments, in Fawn's experience. Perhaps it was the tone of voice that made the difference. Whatever it was, it was Dar who backed down, not apologizing but changing tack: "Fairbolt will explode."

"I've seen Fairbolt. I left him in one piece. Mari, too."

"You can't tell me he's happy about this!"

"I don't. But neither was he stupid." Another hint of warning, that? Perhaps, for Dar ceased his protests, although with a frustrated gesture. Dag continued, "Omba says Mari spoke to you alone last night, after the others."

"Oh, and wasn't that an uproar. Mama always pictures you dead in a ditch, not that she hasn't been close to right now and then just by chance, but I don't expect that of Mari."

"Did she tell you what happened to my sharing knife?"

"Yes. I didn't believe half of it."

"Which half?"

"Well, that would be the problem to decide, now, wouldn't it?" Dar glanced up. "Did you bring it along?"

"That's why we came here."

To Dar's work shack? Or to Hickory Lake Camp generally? The meaning seemed open.

"You seen Mama yet?"

"That will be next."

"I suppose," Dar sighed, "I'd best see it here, then. Before the real din starts."

"That's what I was thinking, too."

Dar gestured them toward the cabin steps. Fawn sat beside Dag, scrunching up to him for solace, and Dar took a seat near the steps on a broad stump.

"Give Dar the knife," said Dag. At her troubled look, he dropped a reassuring kiss atop her head, which made Dar's face screw up as though he was smelling something rank. Fawn frowned but fished the sheath out of her shirt once more. She would have preferred to give it to Dag to hand to his brother, but that wasn't possible. Reluctantly, she extended it across to Dar, who almost as reluctantly took it.

Dar did not unsheathe it immediately, but sat with it in his lap a moment. He took in a long breath, as though centering himself somehow; half the expression seemed to drop from his face. Since it was mostly the sour, disapproving half, Fawn didn't altogether mind. What was left seemed distant and emotionless.

Dar's examination seemed much like that of the other Lakewalkers: cradling the knife, holding it to his lips, but also cheek and forehead, eyes open and closed in turn. He took rather longer about it.

He looked up at last, and in a colorless voice asked Dag to explain, once again, the exact sequence of events in the malice's cave, with close guesses as to the time each movement had taken. He did not ask anything of Fawn. He sat a little more, then the distant expression went away, and he looked up again.

"So what do you make of it?" asked Dag. "What happened?"

"Dag, you can't expect me to discuss the inner workings of my craft in front of some farmer."

"No, I expect you to discuss them—fully—in front of that donor's mother."

Dar grimaced, but counterattacked, unexpectedly speaking to Fawn directly for the very first time: "Yes, and how *did* you get pregnant?"

Did she have to confess the whole stupid episode with Stupid Sunny? She looked up beseechingly at Dag, who shook his head slightly. She gathered her courage and replied coolly, "In the usual way, I believe."

Dar growled, but did not pursue the matter. Instead, he protested to Dag, "She won't understand."

"Then you won't actually be giving away any secrets, will you? Begin at the beginning. She knows what ground is, for starters."

"I doubt that," said Dar sourly.

Dag shifted his splinted hand to touch his marriage cord. "Dar, she made this. The other as well."

"She couldn't . . ." Dar went quiet for a time, brow furrowing. "All right. Flukes happen. But I still think she won't understand."

"Try. She might surprise you." Dag smiled faintly. "You might be a better teacher than you think."

"All right, all right! All right." Dar turned his glower on Fawn. "A knife . . . that is, a dying body that . . . agh. Go all the way back. Ground is in everything, you understand that?"

Fawn nodded anxiously.

"Living things build up ground and alter its essence. Concentrate it. They are always making, but they are making themselves. Man eats food, the food's ground doesn't vanish, it goes into the man and is transformed. When a man—or any living thing—dies, that ground is released. The ground associated with material parts dissipates slowly with the decaying body, but the nonmaterial part, the most complex inner essence, it goes all at once. Are you following this?" he demanded abruptly.

Fawn nodded.

His look said, *I don't think so,* but he went on. "Anyway. That's how living things help a blight recover, by building up ground slowly around the edges and constantly releasing it again. That's how blight kills, by draining ground away too fast from anything caught away from the edge too long. A malice consumes ground directly, ripping it out of the living like a wolf disemboweling its prey."

Dag did not wince at this comparison, although he went a little stony. Actually, that was a brief nod of agreement, Fawn decided. She shivered and concentrated on Dar, because she didn't think he'd respond well to being stopped for questions, at least not by her.

"Sharing knives . . ." He touched the curve of hers. "The inner surface of a thighbone has a natural affinity for blood, which can be persuaded to grow stronger by the maker shaping the knife. That's what I do, in addition to . . . to encouraging it to dwell on its fate. I meet with the pledged heart's-death donor, and he or she shares their blood into the knife in the making. Because their live blood bears their ground."

"Oh!" said Fawn in a voice of surprise, then closed her mouth abruptly.

"Oh what?" said Dar in aggravation.

She looked at Dag; he raised an unhelpful eyebrow. "Should I say?" she asked.

"Certainly."

She glanced sideways at the frowning and—even shirtless—thoroughly intimidating maker. "Maybe you'd better explain, Dag."

Dag smiled a trifle too ironically at his brother. "Fawn reinvented the technique herself, to persuade her ground into my marriage cord. Took me by surprise. In fact, when I recognized it, I nearly fell off the bench. So I'd say she understands it intimately."

"You used a *knife-making* technique on a *marriage* cord?" Dar sounded aghast.

Dag hitched up his left shoulder. "Worked. The only clue I gave her was to mention—days earlier, in another conversation altogether—that blood held a person's ground for a while after leaving the body."

"Fluke," muttered Dar, though more faintly. Craning anew at the cord.

"Yeah, that's life with Spark. Just one fluke after another. Seems no end to them. You were halfway through explaining a making. Go on."

Dag, Fawn realized, had been through the process from the donor's side at least once, if with some maker up in Luthlia and not with Dar. In addition to whatever he had learned from being around his brother, however intermittently.

Dar took a breath and went on. "So at the end of the knife-making, we have a little of the pledged donor's ground in the knife, and that ground is . . . well, you could say it's hungry for the rest. It wants to be reunited with its source. And the other way around. So then we come to the priming itself." His face was stern, contemplating this, for reasons that had nothing to do with her, Fawn thought.

"When the knife is"—he hesitated, then chose the plain word—"driven into the donor's heart, killing him, his essential ground begins to break up. At this very point of dissolution, the ground is drawn into the knife. And held there."

"Why doesn't it just all dissolve then?" Fawn couldn't help asking, then mentally kicked herself for interrupting.

"That's another aspect of my making. If you can fluke it out, good luck to you. I'm not just a bone-carver, you know." His smile was astringent. "When someone—like Dag, for example—then manages to bring the primed knife up to a malice and plunge it in, the malice, which eats ground and cannot stop doing so, draws in the dissolving ground released by the breaking of the knife. You could say the mortal ground acts as a poison to the malice's ground, or as a stroke of lightning to a tree, or . . . well, there are a number of ways to say it, all slightly wrong. But the malice's ground shares in the dissolution of the mortal ground, and since a malice is made of nothing *but* ground, all the material elements it is holding in place fall with it."

Fawn touched the scars on her neck. "That, I've seen."

Dar's brows drew down. "How close were you, really?"

Fawn held out her arm and squinted. "About half my arm's length, maybe." And her arms weren't all that long.

"Dar," said Dag gently, "if you haven't grasped this, I'll say it again; she drove my primed knife into the Glassforge malice. And I speak from repeated personal experience when I tell you, that's way, way closer than any sane person would ever want to be to one of those things."

Dar cleared his throat uncomfortably, staring down at the knife in his lap.

It popped out before she could help herself: "Why can't you just use dying animals' grounds to poison malices?"

Dag smiled a little, but Dar scowled in deep offense. Dar said stiffly, "They haven't the power. Only the ground of a Lakewalker donor will kill a malice."

"Couldn't you use a lot of animals?"

"No."

"Has it been tried?"

Dar frowned harder. "Animals don't work. Farmers don't work either." His lips drew back unkindly. "I'll leave you to make the connection."

Fawn set her teeth, beginning to have an inkling about the *piglet* insult.

Dag gave his brother a grim warning look, but put in, "It's not just a question of power, although that's part of it. It's also a question of affinity."

"Affinity?" Fawn wrinkled her nose. "Never mind. What happened to my—to Dag's other knife?" She nodded to it.

Dar sighed, as if he was not quite sure of what he was about to say. "You have to understand, a malice is a mage. It comes out of the ground, sessile and still in its first molt, a more powerful mage than any of us alone will ever be, and just gets stronger after. So. First, this malice snatched the ground of your unborn child."

Fawn's spirits darkened in memory. "Yes. Mari said no one had known malices could do that separately. Is that important?" It would be consoling if that horror had at least bought some key bit of knowledge that might help someone later.

Dar shrugged. "It's not immediately clear to me that it makes any practical difference."

"Why do malices want babies?"

He held out his hand and turned it over. "It's the inverse of what the sharing knives share. Children unborn, and to a lesser extent, young, are in the most intense possible period of self-making of the most complex of grounds.

Malices building up to a molt—to a major self-making, or self-remaking—
seem to crave that food."

"Couldn't it steal from pregnant animals?"

Dar raised a brow. "If it wanted to molt into an animal body instead of a
human one, perhaps."

"They can and do," Dag put in. "The Wolf Ridge malice couldn't get
enough humans, so it partly used wolves as well. I was told by patrollers who
were in on the knifing of it that its form was pretty . . . pretty strange, at the
end, and it was well past its first molt."

Fawn made a disturbed face. So, she noticed, did Dar.

Dar continued, "Anyway. Secondly, you drove Dag's unprimed knife into
the thing."

Fawn nodded. "Its thigh. He said, anywhere. I didn't know."

"Then—leaving that knife in place, right . . . ?"

"Yes. That was when the bogle—the malice—picked me up the second
time, by the neck. I thought it was going to shake me apart like a chicken."

Dar glanced at her scars, and away. "Then you drove in the actual primed
knife."

"I figured I'd better be quick. It broke." Fawn shivered in the remembered
terror, and Dag's left arm tightened around her. "I thought I'd ruined it. But
then the malice dropped me and . . . and sort of melted. It stank."

"Simplest explanation," said Dar crisply. "A person carrying something
very valuable to them who trips and falls, tries to fall so as to protect their
treasure, even at the cost of hurting themselves. Malice snatches rich ground.
Seconds later, before the malice has assimilated or stored that ground, it's hit
with a dose of mortality. In its fall, it blindly tries to shove that ground into a
safe spot for it: the unprimed knife. A malice certainly has the power to do so
by force and not persuasion. End result, one dissolved malice, one knife with
an unintended ground jammed into it." Dar sucked his lip. "More complicated
explanations might be possible, but I haven't heard anything in your testimony
that would require them."

"Hm," said Dag. "So will it still work as a sharing knife, or not?"

"The ground in it is . . . strange. It was caught and bound at a point of
most intense self-making *and* most absolute self-dissolution, simultaneously.
But still, only a farmer's ground after all." He glanced up sharply. "Unless
there's something about the child no one is telling me. Mixed blood, for example?" His look at his brother was coolly inquiring and not especially
respectful.

"It was a farmer child," Fawn said quietly, looking at the soil. It was bare
at the base of the steps, with a few broken hickory husks flattened into the old
mud. Dag's arm tightened silently around her again.

"Then it will have no affinity, and is useless. An unprimed knife that gets contaminated can be boiled clean and rededicated, sometimes, but not this. My recommendation is that you break it to release that worthless farmer ground, burn it—or send the pieces back to Kauneo's kin with whatever explanation you can concoct that won't embarrass you—and start over with a new knife." His voice softened. "I'm sorry, Dag. I know you didn't carry this for twenty years for such a futile end. But, you know, it happens that way sometimes."

Fawn looked up at Dar. "I'll have that back, now," she said sturdily. She held out her hand.

Dar gave Dag an inquiring look, found no support, and reluctantly handed the sheathed knife back to Fawn.

"A lot of knives never get used," said Dag, in a would-be casual tone. "I see no special need of rushing to dispose of this one. If it serves no purpose intact, it serves no more destroyed."

Dar grimaced. "What will you keep it for, then? A wall decoration? A gruesome memento of your little adventure?"

Dag smiled down at Fawn; she wondered what her own face looked like just now. It felt cold. He said, "It had one use, leastways. It brought us together."

"All the more reason to break it," said Dar grimly.

Fawn thought back on Dag's offer of the same act, way back at the Horsefords' farmhouse. *We could have saved a lot of steps.* How could two such apparently identical suggestions feel like utter opposites? *Trust and untrust.* She hoped she could get Dag alone soon, and ask him whether he accepted his brother's judgment, or only some part of it, or none, or if they should seek another maker. There was no clue in his face. She hid the knife away again in her shirt.

Dag stood and stretched, rolling his shoulders. "It's about dinnertime, I expect. You want to come watch, Dar, or hide out here?"

Fawn began to wish she and Dag could hide out here. Well—she eyed the bones hung from the eaves swinging in the freshening breeze—maybe not just here. But somewhere.

"Oh, I'll come," said Dar, rising to collect his carving knife and the finished bowls and take them inside. "Might as well get it over with."

"Optimist," said Dag, stepping aside for him as he trod up the steps.

Fawn caught a glimpse of a tidy workroom, a very orderly bench with carving tools hung above it, and a small fieldstone fireplace in the wall opposite the door. Dar came back out fastening his shirt, entirely insensible of the ease with which his buttons cooperated with his fingers, latched the door, and passed efficiently around the shack closing the shutters.

The green light of the woods was growing somber as scudding dark clouds from the northwest filled the sky above. The staccato pop of falling nuts sounded like Dag's joints on a bad morning. Fawn clung to Dag's left arm as they started back up the path. His muscles were tight. She lengthened her steps to match his, and was surprised to find she didn't have to lengthen them very much.

4

eyond the clearing with the two tent-cabins, the gray of the lake was darkening, waves starting to spin off white tails of spume. Fawn could hear them slapping the shore beneath the nearby bank, where a stand of cattails bent and hissed in the rising wind. Only a single narrow boat was still in view, with two men paddling like mad for a farther shore. In the slate-colored air to the north, dazzling forks of lightning snaked from sky to earth, their thunder still laggard in arriving. The pearl of the sun, sinking toward Mare Island, disappeared behind a darker cloud even as she watched, turning the light gloomy.

Under the awning of the cabin on the right, a thin, straight, rigid figure in a skirt stood beside their piles of saddles and gear, watching anxiously up the path they were descending. Omba in her riding trousers lurked in the shadows behind, leaning against a support post with her arms crossed.

"What are you going to say?" Fawn whispered urgently to Dag.

"Depends."

"On what?"

"On what she says. If the rumors have run ahead of me, she'll have had time to get over being happy I'm alive and move on to other concerns. Depending on who all 'sides Omba got to her with the rumors, she could be pretty well stirred up."

"You left our gear in plain sight—she'd have to know you're back even without Omba."

"There is that."

Did he even have a plan? Fawn was beginning to wonder.

As they neared, the woman in the skirt stood bolt upright. Her hands twitched out once, then she planted them firmly on her hips. Cumbia Redwing wore her silvery-gray hair pulled back in the simple mourning knot. Her skin had less of the burnished copper in it than Dag's—darker, more leathery, more worn—if striking in contrast with the hair. Fawn might have guessed her age as a healthy seventy, though she knew she was two decades beyond that. Her eyes were the clear tea color, narrowing under pinched-in streaks of silver brows as they swept over Fawn; in a better light, Fawn suspected they would be bright gold like Dag's.

As they came up to the edge of the awning, Cumbia thrust out her chin, and snapped, "Dag Redwing Hickory, I'm speechless!"

Behind them, Dar muttered, "Bet not." Dag's brows barely twitched acknowledgment of this.

Proving Dar right, she went on, "Whatever you patrollers do out on the road, the rule is, you don't bring it home. You can't be bringing your farmer whore into my tent."

As if he hadn't heard her, Dag pulled the shrinking Fawn forward, and said, "Mama, this is my wife, Fawn Bluefield."

"How de' do, ma'am." Fawn dipped her knees, frantically searching amongst the hundred rehearsed speeches in her mind for something to follow. She hadn't imagined doing this in a thunderstorm. She hadn't imagined most of this.

Dag forestalled her. Now standing behind her, he slid his hook, carefully turned downward, under her left wrist and elevated it. "See? Wife." He shrugged his left shoulder to display his own marriage cord.

Cumbia's eyes widened in horror. "You can't have—" With a hiccough of breath, she choked out, "Cut those things."

"No, ma'am," said Dag in a weirdly affable tone. *Flying*, Fawn thought. Off in that other place he went to when things turned deadly sour, when action moved too fast for thought, and he turned it all over to some other part of himself that could keep up. Or not . . .

"Dag, if you do not burn those abominations and take that girl right back where you found her, you are never entering my tent again." Had Cumbia been rehearsing too? Coached by excited rumormongers? There seemed something deeply awkward about her, as if her mouth and eyes were trying to say two different things. Dag might know with his groundsense, if he hadn't obviously closed it down as hard as a hickory shell.

Dag smiled, or at any rate, his mouth curved sunnily, though his eyes stayed tight, making him look, for a moment, oddly like his mother. "Very good, ma'am." He turned to his stunned listeners. "Omba, Dar, good to see you again. Fawn, get your bags and bedroll. We'll send someone back for the saddles tomorrow. Omba, if she throws them out in the rain, could you put them under cover for me?"

Omba, staring wide-eyed, nodded.

Wait, what? "But Dag—"

He bent and hooked up Fawn's saddlebags and handed them to her, then hooked his own over his shoulder. She clutched the heavy load awkwardly to her chest as he put his arm around her back and turned her toward the clearing. The first big raindrops spattered down, batting the hickory leaves and hitting the dirt with audible plops.

"But Dag, no one—she hasn't—I haven't—"

Reversing herself abruptly, Cumbia said, "Dag, you can't go out there now, it's coming on to storm!"

"Come along, Spark." He hustled her out.

A few fat drops plunked onto the top of her head like hard finger-taps, soaking cold down to her scalp. "But Dag, she's not hardly—I didn't even get a chance to—" Fawn turned back to dip her knees again and call a desperate, "Nice to meet you, ma'am!" over her shoulder.

"Where are you going?" cried Cumbia, echoing Fawn's thoughts exactly. "Come back out of the rain, you fool!"

"Keep walking," Dag muttered out of the corner of his mouth. "Don't look back, or it'll be all to do over again." As they passed a big basket leaning against a stump, piled high with dark round shapes, he thunked his hook into one, snatching it up in passing. His stride lengthened. Fawn scurried to keep up.

As they reached the road, Dag hesitated, and Fawn panted, "Where *are* we going?"

He glanced over his shoulder. Through the trees, the far shore of the lake had disappeared behind a thick gray curtain of rain; Fawn could hear the oncoming hiss of it. "I have some folks who owe me favors, but that'll best be for tomorrow, I think. Right now we just need shelter. This way."

To Fawn's considerable dismay, he turned down the path leading to the bone shack. She grappled her saddlebags around over her shoulder and trotted after. The fat raindrops gave way, in a cold gust, to little hailstones, slicing down through the leaves and bouncing off the path, and, more painfully, off her. The pebble-sized ice triggered a heavier and even more alarming hail of hickory husks as the trees creaked in the wind, and Fawn pictured heavy branches coming down on them like huge hammers. Both she and Dag ducked and ran through the ominous shadows.

She was gasping and even Dag was out of breath when they arrived back at Dar's work-cabin. Along the eaves, the bones spun and knocked against one another in the gusts like dreadful wind chimes. Hail and hickory husks rattled off the roof shingles, sometimes sailing up again in high arcs before plopping to earth that was rapidly turning to mud. She and Dag thumped up the steps and huddled under the little porch roof.

With his wet hair plastered to his forehead and his jaw set, Dag attempted to free his hook from the plunkin by grasping the round root under his sling-arm, which made his saddlebags in turn slide off his shoulder and land on his feet. He cursed.

"Here," said Fawn in exasperation. "Let me."

She dumped her own bags, wriggled the plunkin free of his hook, set it down, then turned to pluck the latchstring out of its slot and pull the door open. The shuttered cabin was dark, and she peered in doubtfully.

Dag bent down to hook futilely at his bootlaces. "Undo these for me, would you, Spark?" he muttered. "Dar doesn't like his floor dirtied."

She knocked the hook aside before he could snarl the laces into inextricable wet knots, undid first his, then hers, and set both pairs beside the door. She wiped her hands in aggravation on her riding trousers and followed him inside. He bent over a workbench; a welcome light flared from a good beeswax candle in a clay holder. He lit a second from the first, and with that and the faint gray light leaking through the shutters and from the door, she was finally able to see clearly.

The space was a bare dozen feet long by ten or so wide, lined with shelves and a couple of scarred but cleared-off workbenches. Stools of various heights made from upended logs, cut away beneath for legs and above for short backrests, were thrust under the benches. The space smelled of old wood and fresh wood, herbs and solvents, the honeyed warmth of the candles, oil, leather, and time. And under it all, something undefinable; she tried not to think, *death*.

Dag dragged their bags just inside the door, rolling the plunkin along after with his foot. He closed the door against the gusts. Minus the rattling of bones and clatter of ice and nuts on the roof, the threatening creak of the trees in the wind, the howling storm, the interminable day, the harrowing scene, or half scene, they'd just been through, and both their moods, it might have been almost cozy. As it was, Fawn would have burst into tears if she hadn't been so close to just bursting.

"So," she said tightly, "what happened to all your smooth Lakewalker persuadin', back there?"

Dag sighed and stretched his back. "There were only two ways it could go, Spark. Slow and excruciating, or fast and excruciating. Like yanking a tooth, I prefer my pain to go fast."

"You didn't even give her a chance to say her piece!"

He cocked an eyebrow at her. "Fewest unforgivable things we had the time to say to each other the better, I'd say."

"I didn't get a chance to say *my* piece! I didn't even get to try with her! I'm not saying I would have got anywhere either, but at least I'd have known I tried!"

"I know that trying. Spark, it would've near broke my heart to watch you turning yourself inside out with it. I couldn't have stood it."

He turned to attempt to undo their bedroll strings with his hook; after watching him for a frustrated moment, Fawn reached past and plucked the knots apart, helping him unroll their blankets across the floor. He sat down on his with a weary grunt. She sat down opposite, cross-legged, frowning up at him, and raked her hands through her damp distracted curls.

"Sometimes, once folks have a chance to vent, they'll calm down and talk more reasonable." Cumbia had already advanced as far as promoting Fawn from *farmer whore* to *that girl* just in the short time she'd been given, scarcely worse than the *that fellow* that was Dag's common name in West Blue. Who knew where they might have ended up if they'd just kept at it a bit?

He shrugged. "She won. It's done."

"If she won, what was her prize?" Fawn demanded. "I don't see how anyone won anything much, back there."

"Look—I didn't leave, she threw me out. Either she means it, and she'll never speak to me again, or else it'll be up to her to apologize."

"So what you're actually saying is, you won. Some tactics, Dag!"

He grimaced. "Learned 'em at my mother's knee."

"*What* has got into you? I've seen you in some moods, but I never saw you in a mood like this one! Can't say as I much like it."

He lay back and stared up at the peeled-log ridgepole. None of the support timbers for the roof were squared off or dressed, being just slim bare trunks of the right length fitted into triangles. "I don't much like the way I get here, either. It's like I lose myself when I get mixed up with my closest kin. Dar and Mama mostly—my father when he was alive less so, but some. Mari I can stand. It's part of why I touch down here lightly, or not at all if I can help it. A mile away, or better yet a hundred, I can go back to being me."

"Huh," said Fawn, mulling this over. She didn't find it nearly as inexplicable as she might once have, remembering how vast new possibilities had seemed to open for her in Glassforge, and close down chokingly when she returned to West Blue. It was just that at Dag's age she figured folks ought to be long over that sort of thing. Or maybe they'd just had more time to work down into a rut. Deep, deep rut. "Funny sort of exile."

"Indeed it is." But he wasn't laughing.

The air was chilling fast as the storm rumbled through. The small stone fireplace was clearly there more for warming pots of work supplies than for heating the far from tight building, presumably not used in winter, but Dag bestirred them to lay a fire. "Have to replace that in the morning," he muttered at the neat pile of deadfall standing ready on the porch just outside the door. But once the flames caught—Dag did seem to have a peculiar lucky knack for getting fires going—the yellow light, the scent of woodsmoke, and the occasional orange spark popping out onto the slate hearth lent some much-needed cheer to the room. Their hair and clothes began to dry, and Fawn's skin lost its clamminess.

Fawn set a pot of rain-barrel water on an iron hook to boil for tea, swung it over the fire, and poked at the new coals with a stick, pushing more underneath her pot. "So," she said, in what she hoped did not sound too desperate a tone, "where do we go tomorrow?"

"I figure to draw our own tent from Stores."

They owned a tent? "Where will we set it up?"

"I have an idea or two. If they don't work out, I'll find a third."

Which seemed to be all she was going to get right now. Was this clash with his family over, or not? It wasn't that she thought Dag was lying to her, so much as that she was beginning to suspect his idea of a comfortable outcome did not match hers. If Lakewalkers didn't marry farmers—or at least, didn't do so and then take the farmers home—she wouldn't expect the feeling here against her to be trifling or easily set aside. If this was something no one had successfully done before, her faith that *Dag will know what to do* was . . . if not misplaced, more hope than certainty. She wasn't afraid of hard, but when did *hard* shade over into *insurmountable*?

Her stomach growled. If Dag was half as fatigued as she was, it was no wonder nobody seemed able to think straight. Food would help everything. She rolled the mysterious plunkin across in front of the hearth and stared at it. It still looked disconcertingly like a severed head. "What do we do with this?"

Dag sat cross-legged and smiled—not much of a smile, but a start. "Lots of choices. They all come down to plunkin. You can eat it raw in slices, peel it and cut it up and cook it alone or in a stew, boil it whole, wrap it in leaves and cook it in campfire coals, stick a sword through it and turn it on a spit, or, very popular, feed it to the pigs and eat the pigs. It's very sustaining. Some say you could live forever on plunkin and rainwater. Others say it would just seem like forever." He gestured to her belt knife, one of his spares that he'd insisted she wear since they'd left West Blue. "Try a slice."

Dubiously, she captured the rolling globe between her knees and stabbed it. The brown rind was rather hard, but once opened revealed a dense, pale yellow fruit, solid all the way through, without a core or pit or seeds. She nibbled out a bite as if from a melon slice.

It was crunchy, not as sweet as an apple, not as starchy as a raw potato . . . "A bit parsnippy. Actually, quite a bit nicer than parsnip. Huh." It seemed the problem was not in the quality, but in the quantity.

For simplicity, and because she really didn't feel comfortable cooking over Dar's fireplace, used for who knew what sorcerous processes, they ate it raw in slices. Although Fawn did draw the line at Dag's attempt simply to stab his portion with his hook and gnaw around the edges; she peeled his piece and made him get out his fork-spoon. The plunkin was surprisingly satisfying. Hungry as they both were, they only disposed of half a head, or root, or whatever it was.

"Why don't farmers have this?" Fawn wondered. "Food gets around. Flowers, too. Animals, too, really. We could grow it in ponds."

Dag gestured with his slice, stuck on his fork-spoon. All right, so the official eating tool hadn't made that much difference; it still made it all seem more like a real meal. "The ears need a little tickle in their grounds to germinate. If farmers planted them, they'd just go down in the mud and rot. It's a trick most every Lakewalker here learns. I hated raft duty when I was young, thought it was the dullest thing possible. Now I understand why the old patrollers didn't mind taking their turns, and laughed at me. Soothing, y'know."

Fawn crunched valiantly and tried to picture a young, impatient Dag sitting out on a raft, mostly undressed, coppery skin gleaming in the sun, grouchily tickling plunkin ears, one after another after another. She had to smile. With two hands, scarless and unmarred. Her smile faded.

"They say the old high lords of the lake league made wonderful magical plants, and animals too," Dag said thoughtfully. "Not many seemed to have survived the disasters. Plunkins have tricky growing conditions. Not too deep, not too shallow, mud bottoms. They won't take in those deep, clear, rocky-bottomed lakes east or north. Makes them a regional, er, delicacy. And, of course, they need Lakewalkers, year after year after year. Makes me wonder how far back this camp goes, really."

Fawn considered the continuity of plunkins. When all their world was falling apart around them, some Lakewalker ancestors must have kept the crop going. For hope? For habit? For sheer stubbornness? Eyeing Dag, she was inclined to bet on stubbornness.

They burned the rinds on the fire, and Fawn set the spare half aside for breakfast. Outside, the green dark of the storm had given way to the blue dark of night, and the rain had slowed to a steady drizzle. Dag hooked their bedrolls closer together.

Fawn felt her knife sheath shift between her breasts as she crawled across to sit again on her blanket, and reached up to touch it. "Do you think Dar was telling the truth about the knife?"

Dag leaned back against his saddlebags, damp bare feet to the fire, and frowned thoughtfully. "I think everything Dar said was truth. As far as it went."

"So . . . what does that mean? Do you think he was holding something back?"

"Not sure. It's not that . . . I'd say, the knife is a problem he wants to have go away, not explore."

"If he's as good a knife maker as you say, I'd think he'd be more curious."

Dag shrugged. "Folks are at first. Like Saun the Sheep, or me at Saun's age—it's all new and exciting. But then it becomes the same task over and over, and the new becomes rare. Whether you then find novelty to be exciting or something to resent . . . Thing, is, Dar has spent thirty and more years, all day most every day, making weapons for his relatives and best friends to go kill themselves with. Whatever Dar is doing that lets him go on, I'm not inclined to fool with it."

"Maybe we should ask after a younger knife maker, then." Fawn shoved her own saddlebags around, trying for a more comfortable prop, and lay down next to Dag. "So . . . what did he—and you—mean when you said the ground had to have affinity? You used that word two or three times, like it meant something special."

"Ah. Hm." Dag rubbed his nose with his hook. His features were outlined in the orange glow from the fire, lapped by the light with the rest of him falling into shadow. The walls of the shack seemed to recede into a fathomless darkness. "Well, simply that malice ground takes up Lakewalker mortality readily, as the ground of bone takes up that of blood."

Fawn frowned. "You have to figure, bones take up blood because they were once both together."

"That's right."

"So . . ." She suddenly wasn't sure she liked where this was going. "So . . . ?"

"Legend would have it—*legend* is just like *they say,* only more dried up, you know?"

She nodded cautiously.

"In fact, no one alive now knows for sure. Those who knew died in the knowing, one, two thousand years ago. Chronicles were lost, time was lost— was it two centuries or five or ten that dropped out, how many generations disappeared in the dark?"

"They kept the plunkins going, anyhow."

His lips curved briefly. "There is that."

"So what is this thing that's known or not known?"

"Well, there is more than one version of how malices came into the world. We know they didn't used to be here."

"You've seen, what, twenty-seven of them? Up close? I don't want to know what other people say. What do you believe?"

He sighed. "*They say* is all I have to go on, for most of it. They say the old lords of the lake league worked great magics in great groups. They combined up under the mastery of the high king. One king, the last king, greater and more cunning than any before, at the apex of the greatest array of mages ever assembled, reached beyond the bounds of the world for . . . something. Some say immortality. Some say power. The king stories mostly assume evil intent because of evil results—if there is punishment, there must have been a crime. They blame pride and selfishness, or whatever vice they're especially miffed with. I'm not so sure. Maybe he was attempting to capture some imagined good to share, and it all went horribly wrong.

"You know I said the old lords used their magic to alter plants, animals, and themselves. And their children." He tapped his temple with the backside of his hook, and Fawn realized he thought his eye color was a relic of those efforts. "Extended life, improved groundsense and ability to move the world through its ground." He glanced, briefly and uneasily, at his left arm held up, and she knew he was thinking about his ghost hand again. He let it drop again to his side. "We Lakewalkers, we think, are the descendants of lesser hinterland lords—what must the great ones have been like?

"Anyway. In their attempt to enhance themselves, the high lords drew in *something* from outside the world. God, demon, other. If they'd kidnapped a god, it would explain why the gods shun us. And the king *combined* with it, or it with him. And became something that was neither. Vast, distorted, powerful, insane, and consuming ground instead of . . . of whatever they'd intended."

"Wait, are you saying your own *king* became the first malice?" Fawn rolled up on her elbow to stare in astonishment.

Dag tilted his head in doubt. "He became something. Some lords fell under his power—legend says—and some broke away. A war of matter and magic followed, which sank the lakes and left the Dead Lake and the Western Levels. Whether the malice-king's enemies discovered how to destroy him, or it was another accident, any who knew died in the finding out. *Someone* back then must have discovered how to share mortality. It must have been a great sharing, is all I can say. *Our* malices came from some cataclysmic ground transformation when he, or it, was at last destroyed, and blew up into those ten thousand—or however many—shards or seeds or eggs. But that's what we think the malices are all trying to do, clumsily, when they come out of the ground. Become kings again.

"Hence—to return roundabout to your original question—affinity. Malices take up Lakewalker mortality because they are, or were, partly us."

Along the eaves, bones clanked in a breath of night wind. Fawn found herself trying to shrink under her blankets, which had crept, during this reciting, from her feet to her waist to her nose. This was worse than any tall tale her brothers had ever tormented her with. "Are you saying all those malices are your *relatives?*"

He lay back and, infuriatingly, laughed. "Don't you just hate those family squabbles? Absent gods." The chuckles died down before she got up the nerve to poke him in reproof. "Collateral ancestors at most, Spark. But I suggest you not share that insight around. Some folks are like to be offended."

What have I married into, really? The revelations dismayed her. She thought back to her malice's tormented, merciless eyes. They might have been tea-brown, with a certain now-familiar iridescence.

He let out the last of his black humor in a sigh. "If not relatives, they are certainly our legacy. Our joint inheritance. Not sure what my share is." His hook drifted up to touch his heart. "One, I reckon."

A chill shook Fawn at this vision of his mortal fate. "And you all so proud. Riding by us like lords." And yet Lakewalkers lived, at home, in worse poverty than most farmers, unless the Bearsford camp was any more elaborate than this. She was beginning to suspect not. Noble grandeur was sadly lacking all around. *Squalid scramble* seemed a more apt description.

Dag shrugged. "We have to tell ourselves some flattering stories to keep ourselves going. Day after year after decade. What else? Lie down and die for the endless despair of it all?"

She lay back and followed his stare up into the dim rafters. "Is there an end?"

"Perhaps. If we just keep on. We think there were not an infinite number of malices planted. They don't come up under water or ice or above the tree line, or on old blight. Our maps of the lairs we've destroyed show them thicker toward the Dead Lake, but fewer and farther apart going out. And we say they are immortal, but in fact all that have hatched have been slain. So maybe they wouldn't live forever, but what they destroy betimes is more than enough. Maybe they'll stop hatching out someday just for sheer age, but that'd be a bad hope to count on or dwell on. Like to make a man impatient, and this is no war for the impatient. Yet if all things end, even despair must, too. Not in my life-time. But sometime." He blinked up into the shadows. "I don't believe in much, but I'll believe that."

That despair must end? Or, not in his lifetime? Both, likely.

He sat up and stretched his back, wincing, and, after a desultory futile prod at his arm-harness buckles with his splinted hand, extended it to Fawn to free him for the night. She unbuckled it and set it aside as usual, decided they weren't going to do better than to sleep in their clothes, and, after a brief hesi-tation, cuddled down in her accustomed spot under his left arm, where she could press her ear to his heart. She pulled the blanket up over them both. Dag did not, by word or gesture, suggest lovemaking here tonight, and, relieved, neither did she. The fire died to embers before either of them slept.

5

Dag left on a mumbled errand soon after it was light, leaving Fawn to pack up. She had the bags and bedrolls stacked tidily on the porch, the cabin swept out, and even the fireplace ashes hauled away and scattered in the wet woods, with no sign of his return. She collected from the abundant new deadfall to replace the pile they'd burned last night, and then some, and finally sat on the porch steps with her chin in her hand, waiting. The flock of wild turkeys—or another flock, as there seemed to be a lot more of them this morning, upwards of forty—stalked through the clearing, and Fawn and they eyed each other gloomily.

A figure appeared on the path, and the turkeys ambled off. Fawn sat up eagerly, only to slump in disappointment. It was Dar, not Dag.

He glowered at her without approval but without surprise; likely his groundsense had told him where she and Dag had gone to hole up last night.

"Morning," she tried cautiously.

She received a grunt and a grudging nod in return. "Where's Dag?" he asked.

"He went off." She added warily, "He told me to wait here for him till he got back."

Another grunt. Dar inspected his lathe, wet but undamaged by the storm, and went around the cabin fastening open the shutters. He trod up the steps, stared down at her, slipped off his muddy shoes, and went inside; he came back out in a few minutes looking faintly frustrated, perhaps because she'd left nothing to complain of.

He asked abruptly, "You didn't couple in there last night, did you?"

Fawn stared up in offense. "No, but what business is that of yours?"

"I'd have to do a ground cleansing if you did." He stared at the firewood stack. "Did you collect that, or Dag?"

"I did, of course."

He looked as though he was reaching for a reason to reject it, but couldn't come up with one. Fortunately, at that point Dag came striding up the path. He looked reasonably cheerful; perhaps his errand had prospered?

"Ah." He paused when he saw his brother; they exchanged equally laconic nods.

Dar waited a moment as if for Dag to speak, then when nothing was forthcoming, said, "That was a clever retreat last night. *You* didn't have to listen to the complaints."

"You could've gone for a walk."

"In the rain? Anyway, I thought that was your trick—patroller."

Dag lowered his eyelids. "As you say." He nodded to Fawn and hooked his saddlebags and hers up over his shoulder. "Come along, Spark. G'day, Dar."

Fawn found herself trotting at his heels, casting a farewell nod over her shoulder at Dar, who by the opening and tight closing of his mouth clearly had wanted to say more.

"Were you all right?" Dag asked, as soon as they were out of earshot. "With Dar, I mean."

"I guess. Except that he asked one really rude question."

"Which was?"

Fawn flushed. "He asked if we'd made love in his cabin."

"Ah. Well, he actually does have a legitimate reason for wanting to know that, but he should have asked me. If he really couldn't trust me to know better."

"I hadn't worked round yet to asking him if your mama had softened any overnight. Didn't you want to ask?"

"If she had," Dag said distantly, "I'm sure Dar was able to stiffen her up again."

Fawn asked more quietly, looking down at her feet pacing along the muddy, leaf-and-stick-strewn path, "Did this—marrying me—mess things up any between you and your brother?"

"No."

"Because he seems pretty angry at you. At us."

"He's always annoyed at me for something. It's a habit. Don't worry about it, Spark."

They reached the road and turned right. Dag barely glanced aside as they passed his family's clearing. He made no move to turn in there. The road followed the shoreline around the island and curved south, running between the woods and more groups of cabins hugging the bank. The dripping trees sparkled in the morning light, and the sun, now well up above the farther shore, sent golden beams between the boles through the cool, moist air, which smelled of rain and moss.

Not a quarter mile along, Dag turned left into a clearing featuring three tent-cabins and a dock much like all the others. It was set a little apart from its neighbors by a stand of tall black walnut trees to its north and an orchard of stubbier fruit trees to its south; Fawn could see a few beehives tucked away among the latter. On a stump in front of one of the cabins sat an aging man dressed only in trousers cut off above the knees and held up by a rope belt, and leather sandals. His gray hair was knotted at his nape. He was carving away with long strokes on what looked to be some sort of oar or paddle in the making, but when he saw them he waved the knife in amiable greeting.

Dag dumped their saddlebags atop another stump and led Fawn over to the fellow. By his gnarly feet, she suspected he was an old patroller. He'd clearly been a big man once, now going a little stringy with age, except around his—for a Lakewalker—ample middle. He eyed Fawn as curiously as she eyed him.

Dag said, "Fawn, this is Cattagus Redwing, Mari's husband."

Making him Dag's uncle, then. So, this marriage hadn't estranged Dag from quite all his family. Fawn dipped her knees and smiled anxiously, looking around covertly for Mari. It would be wonderful to see a familiar face. She saw no one else, but heard cheery voices coming from down over the bank.

Cattagus tilted his head in dry greeting. "So, this is what all the fuss is about. Cute as a kitten, I'll grant you that." His voice was wheezy, with a sharp whistling running through it. He looked her up and down, a little smile playing around his lips, shook his head wryly, drew breath again, and added, "Absent gods, boy. I'd never have got away with something like this. Not even when I was thirty years younger."

Dag snorted, sounding more amused than offended. " 'Course not. Aunt Mari would've have had your hide for a tent flap."

Cattagus chuckled and coughed. "That's a fact." He waved aside with his knife. "The girls from Stores brought your tent by."

"Already?" said Dag. "That was quick."

Fawn tracked their gazes to a large handcart set at the side of one cabin, piled high with what appeared to be old hides, with a stack of long poles sticking out the back.

"They said, bring back their cart soon as you get it empty."

"That I can do. Where do Mari and Sarri want me to set up?"

"Better go ask 'em." Cattagus gestured toward the shore.

Fawn followed Dag to peek over the bank. To the left of the dock, at which two narrow boats were tied, a sort of wooden cradle lay in the water, perhaps ten feet long and six feet wide. A woman wearing long black hair to her hips and nothing else, and a black-haired girl-child, were tromping vigorously up and down in it. Marching with them, Razi, equally nude, was clapping his hands and calling to the little girl, who looked to be about four, "Jump,

Tesy! Jump!" She squealed with laughter and hopped like a frog, splashing the woman, who ducked and grinned. The cradle was apparently for retting some sort of long-stemmed plant, and the treaders were engaged in kicking off the rotting matter to clean the fibers. Beyond them, Utau, standing in water to his waist, was supporting the clutching fists of a small boy of perhaps two, whose fat little legs kicked up a fountain of foam. Mari, dressed in only a simple sleeveless shift hemmed at the calf and sandals like her husband's, stood on the dock with her hands on her hips watching them, smiling. She seemed to be halfway through either loading or unloading a couple dozen coils of rough-looking rope from one of the boats, much like the rope netting Fawn had seen on the plunkin panniers.

Dag called down over the bank, "Hey, Mari! We're back."

Indicating that he'd been here once already this morning, likely to arrange this. Fawn wondered if this had been his first idea, or his third, and just how he had gone about explaining his needs. His ability to persuade had not entirely deserted him, it seemed.

Mari waved back. "Be right with you!"

Steps laid from flat stones made a stairway down the steep bank to the dock. In a few moments, Fawn was treated to the somewhat startling sight of a whole family of nude, wet Lakewalkers climbing up from the shore. They seemed quite unconscious of their undress. Fawn, who had never done more than wade in the shallows of the river with her skirts rolled up, supposed it made sense, given that these people were likely in and out of the water a dozen times a day for various purposes. She was nonetheless relieved when they streamed past her with only the briefest greetings and emerged a few minutes later from the cabin on the north of the clearing dressed, if simply: Razi and Utau in truncated trousers like Cattagus's, and Sarri and her daughter in shifts. The little boy, escaping, streaked past still in his skin in a beeline for the water, only to be scooped up and tickled into distraction from his purpose by Utau.

Mari followed up the steps and stopped by Dag. "Morning, Fawn." Her expression today was ironic but not unsympathetic. "Dag, Sarri thought you could set up under the apple tree over there. There's a bit of rising ground there, though you can hardly see it. It'll be the driest spot."

Utau, with the boy now riding atop his shoulders, small hands pulling his hair from its knot, came up with the long-haired woman. To Fawn's eyes, she looked to be about thirty; Fawn added the accustomed fifteen years to her guess. "Hello, Fawn," Utau greeted her, without surprise. Clearly, he'd been given the whole tale by now. "This is our wife, Sarri Otter." A nod at Razi, who had been inspecting the cart and now strode over to join them, confirmed the other part of that *our*.

Fawn had twigged that they were on Sarri's territory, and maybe Mari's;

she gave her knee-dip, and said to the women, "Thank you for having us here."

Sarri folded her arms and nodded shortly, face not unfriendly, eyes curious. "Dag . . . well, Dag," she said, as if that explained something.

Dag, Razi, Utau, and Mari, with Cattagus following along and supplying wheezing commentary, then turned their attention to the alleged tent. The men hauled the cart to the orchard and swiftly unloaded it. The bewildering mess of poles and ropes was transformed with startling speed into a square frame with hides over its arching top and hanging down for walls, neatly staked to the earth. It had a sort of miniature porch, more hides raised up on poles, for an awning in front, which they arranged facing the lakeshore, canted so that the rising sun would not shine in directly. They rolled up and tied the front walls beneath the awning, leaving the little room open to the air much like the more solid structures.

"There!" said Dag in a satisfied voice, standing back and regarding the results. "Tent Bluefield!"

Fawn thought it looked more like Pup-Tent Bluefield; it made the other cabins seem positively palatial. She ventured near and peered in dubiously. *It's all right, I'm just temporary,* the tent seemed to say of itself. But temporary on the way to what?

Dag followed, looking down at her a shade anxiously. "Many's the young couple who starts with no more," he said.

Likely, but you aren't young. "Mm," said Fawn, and nodded to show willing. There was space inside for a double bedroll and a few possessions, but little else. At least the stubby apple tree was not likely to drop lethal branches atop.

"Don't lay anything out in it yet—let the ground dry a while more," said Dag. "We'll get reeds for bedding, rocks for a fire pit, maybe do something for flooring." He strode back to the clearing and collected a pair of short logs, hooking up the smaller and rolling the larger along with his foot, and set them upright beneath the awning for seats. "There."

Excited by this novelty, the little girl Tesy went inside and pranced and danced about, singing to herself. Truly, the tent seemed more playhouse-sized than Dag-sized, though the curved roof would allow him to stand upright, barely. Sarri made to call her daughter back out, but Fawn said, "No—let her. It's a sort of house blessing, I guess," which earned her a grateful and suddenly shrewd look from Sarri.

"If I might borrow your husbands once more," said Dag to Sarri, "I thought we'd go get my things before I take the cart back."

"Sure thing, Dag."

"Mari"—his gaze seemed to test his patrol-leader-and-relative's willingness—"maybe you could show Fawn around while we're gone?"

Implying, among other things, that Fawn was not invited on this expedition. But Mari nodded readily enough. It seemed Fawn was to be accepted by this branch of Dag's family, at least. If temporarily, like the tent. The three men went off with the cart, not altogether unloaded, as both children immediately scrambled atop for the ride. Or rather, Tesy scrambled up, and her little brother wailed in dismay till Razi popped him aboard with her.

"It's normally a bit livelier than this," Mari told Fawn, who was gazing around the clearing. "But as soon as I got back from patrol and could take charge of Cattagus, my daughter took her family across to Heron Island to visit with her husband's folks. They're building a new boat for her." A wave of her hand indicated the third cabin as belonging to this absent family. Was the daughter Mari's name-heiress? What else did Lakewalkers inherit, if they did not own land? Besides their fair share of malices. Was this site apportioned out like tents and horses from some camp pool?

Mari, with Sarri trailing in silent curiosity, took Fawn out back and showed her where the privy was hidden among the trees: not a shed but a slit trench with a hide blind, very tentlike. Water was drawn from the lake, and kettles kept permanently on the hob to boil that intended for drinking. Inside Mari's cabin, Fawn saw that the fireplace had a real oven, which she eyed enviously. Lakewalker women were not limited to pan bread cooked over an open fire, evidently. Though it seemed futile to ask to borrow the oven when Fawn owned no flour, baking pans, lard, butter, eggs, milk, or yeast.

Against the wall in Sarri's cabin stood a simple vertical loom loaded with work in progress, some tough-looking tight-woven fabric Fawn recognized from Lakewalker riding trousers. Fawn wondered at the thread; Sarri explained it was from the ever-useful plunkin, the stems of which, when retted, yielded up a long, strong, durable fiber, which accounted for the retting cradle in the lake. Fawn didn't see a spinning wheel. Little furniture met her eye, apart from some trestle tables and the common upended-log seats. There were no bed frames inside at all; by the bundles of bedding stacked along a wall, it seemed Lakewalkers slept in bedrolls even at home, and Fawn realized why Dag had taken so happily to the floor of Aunt Nattie's weaving room.

They went outside again to find that Dag and the cart had returned. Besides their saddles and bridles, a sword in a worn leather sheath, and a spear, it held only one trunk.

"Is this all you have?" Fawn asked him, as he set it all in a pile beside the tent for later stowage. The trunk hardly seemed large enough to contain, for example, surprise kitchen tackle. It barely seemed large enough for spare boots.

Dag stretched his back and grimaced. "My winter gear's in storage at Bearsford."

Fawn suspected it amounted to little more.

He added, "I also have my camp credit. You'll see tomorrow how that works."

And he was off again, dragging the emptied cart with his hook.

"What shall I do?" Fawn asked rather desperately after him.

"Take a rest!" he called unhelpfully over his shoulder, and turned onto the road.

Rest? She'd been resting, or at least, traveling, which while not restful was certainly not useful work. Her hand traced her wrist cord, and she looked up at the two Lakewalker women, looking down—dubiously?—at her. Sarri's cord, she saw, was two cords wrapped around each other.

"I aim to be a good wife to Dag," Fawn said resolutely, then her voice wavered. "But I don't know what that *means* here. Mama trained me up. If this were a farm, I could run it. I could make soap and candles, but I have no tallow or anything to make lye in. I can cook and preserve, but there's no jars and no storage cellars. If I had a cow, I could milk her, and make cheese and butter, if I had a churn. Aunt Nattie gave me spindles and knitting needles and scissors and needles and pins. Never saw a man more in need of socks than Dag, and I could make good ones, but I have no *fiber*. I can keep accounts, and make a fair ink, but there's no paper nor anything to record." Although those turkeys, she considered, could be forced to yield up quills. "I have knowing hands, but no *tools*. There must be more for me to do here than sit and eat plunkin!"

Mari smiled. "Let me tell you, farmer child, when you come back from weeks out on patrol, you're right glad to sit and eat plunkin for a time. Even Dag is." She added after a moment's reflection, "For about three days, then he's back badgering Fairbolt for a place in the next patrol going out. Fairbolt figures that the reason he has three times the malice kills of anyone else is that he spends twice the time looking for 'em."

Sarri said curiously, "What accounts for the rest?"

"Fairbolt wishes he knew." Mari scratched her head and regarded Fawn in bemusement. "Yeah, Dag said you'd get resty-testy if anyone tried to make you sit still. You two may have more in common than you look."

Fawn said plaintively, "Can you show me how to go on? Please, I'll do anything. I'll even crack nuts." One of her most hated tedious chores back home.

"We're a bit between on that one," said Sarri, with a lopsided smile. "The old falls are rotten and the new ones are too green. We leave 'em for the pigs to clean up, just this season. In a month, now, when the elderberries and the fruit trees come on, we'll all be busy. Cattagus and his wine-making, and nuts in plenty. Rope and baskets, now, that's for doing."

"I know how to make baskets," said Fawn eagerly, "if I had something to make them of."

"When that next batch of retting's done, I'll be glad for help with the spinning," said Sarri judiciously.

"Good! When?"

"Next week."

Fawn sighed. Razi and Utau were just finishing digging a fire pit in front of their tent, and Tesy and her brother were being kept usefully busy hauling stones to line it. Maybe Fawn could at least go gather more deadfall for their future fire. While her back was turned, she noticed, a split-wood basket with three fresh plunkins in it had appeared under her awning.

"Go along, fire-eater," said Mari, sounding amused. "Take a rest till Dag gets back from the medicine tent. Go for a swim."

Fawn hesitated. "In that big lake?" *Naked?*

Mari and Sarri stared at each other. "Where else?" said Sarri. "It's safe to dive off the end of the dock; the water's well over your head there."

This sounded the opposite of safe to Fawn.

Mari added, "Don't dive off the sides, though, or we'll have to pull your head out of the mud like a plunkin."

"I, um . . ." Fawn swallowed, and continued in a much smaller voice, "don't know how to swim."

Mari's brows shot up; Sarri pursed her lips. Both of them gazed at Fawn as though she were a freak of nature like a two-headed calf. That is, even more than most Lakewalkers looked at her that way. Fawn reddened.

"Does Dag know this?" demanded Sarri.

"I . . . I don't know." Would being so readily drownable disqualify one from being a Lakewalker's spouse? When she'd said she wanted to be taught how to go on here, she hadn't imagined swimming lessons being at the top of anyone's list.

"Dag," said Mari in a definite voice, "needs to know this." And added, to Fawn's increasing alarm, "Right away!"

The Two Bridge Island medicine tent was in fact three cabins with its own dock a few hundred paces past patroller headquarters. It seemed not very busy this morning, Dag saw as he neared after dropping the cart at Stores. Only a couple of horses were hitched to the rails out front. Good. No pestilence this week, no patrols dragging home too many smashed-up comrades.

As he mounted the porch to the main building, he met Saun coming out. Ah, one smashed-up comrade, then—if clearly on the path to recovery. The boy looked well, standing up straight and moving only a little stiffly, although he was looking down and touching his chest gingerly. Saun's face lit with delight as he glanced up and saw Dag, which turned to the usual consternation as he took in the sling.

"Dag, man! They said you were missing, then there was a crazy rumor going around you'd come back with the little farmer girl—married, if you can believe! Some people!" His voice trailed off in an *oh* as he took in the cord wrapping Dag's left arm, just visible below his rolled-up sleeve and above his arm-harness strap.

"We got back yesterday afternoon," said Dag, letting the last remark pass. "And you? Last I saw, you were bundled up in a wagon heading south from Glassforge."

"When I could ride again, one of the Log Hollow fellows brought me up to rendezvous with Mari's patrol, and they brought me home. Medicine maker says I can go out again when the patrol does if I rest up good the next couple of weeks. I'm still a little ouchy, but nothing too bad." His stare returned to Dag's left arm. "How did you . . . I mean, Fawn was cute and all, and she sure cheered you up, but . . . all right, there was the malice, maybe she . . . Dag, is your family going to accept this?"

"No."

"Oh." Saun fell silent in dismay. "If . . . what . . . where will you go?"

"That's to be seen. We've set up our tent at Mari's place for the moment."

"I suppose that makes sense. Mari's bound to defend her own . . . um." Saun shook his head, looking wary and confused. "I never heard tell of anything like this. Well, there was a fellow they told me about down at Log Hollow. He got into big trouble a few years back for secretly passing goods and coin along to his farmer lover and her half-blood child, or children—I guess it had been going on for some time when they caught up with him. He argued the goods were his, but the camp council maintained they were the camp's, and it was theft. He wouldn't back down, and they banished him."

Dag tilted his head.

"It was no joke, Dag," Saun said earnestly. "They stripped him to his skin before they turned him out. In the middle of winter. Nobody seemed to know what had happened to him after that, if he made it back to her, or . . . or what."

He was staring at Dag in deep alarm, as if picturing his mentor so used. Was Saun's hero worship of Dag finally to be called into question? Dag thought it a good thing if so, but not for this reason.

"Hardly the same situation, Saun." *For one thing, it's summer.* "In any case, I'll handle it."

Taking this heavy hint—anything lighter would not have penetrated, Dag thought—Saun managed an embarrassed laugh. "Yeah, I suppose you will." After a moment he added in a more chipper tone, turning the subject, "I'm something in the same line myself. Well, of course not with a . . . I'm thinking of asking Fairbolt for a transfer to Log Hollow this fall. Reela"—Saun's voice went suddenly shy—"said she'd wait for me."

Dag recognized that sappy look; he'd seen it in his own shaving mirror. "Congratulations."

"Nothing is *fixed* yet, you understand," Saun said hastily. "Some people think I'm too young to be, well. Thinking about anything permanent. But how can you not, when . . . you know?"

Dag nodded sympathetically. Because either snickering or pity would be a tad hypocritical, coming from him just now. *Was I ever that feckless?* Dag was very much afraid the answer was *yes*. Possibly even without the rider *at his age*.

Saun brightened still further. "Well. Looks like you need the makers more than I did. I won't hold you up. Maybe I'll stop by and say hi to Fawn, later on."

"I expect she'd be glad for a familiar face," Dag allowed. "She's had a rough welcome, I'm afraid."

Saun gave a short nod and took himself off. When in camp, Saun stayed with a family farther down the shore who had a couple of their own children out on exchange patrol at present; Dag gathered that the boy, away from home for the first time, did not lack for mothering.

Dag pushed open the door and made his way into the anteroom. The familiar smell of herbs—sharp, musty, deep, pungent—was strong today, and he glanced through the open door to the next room on this side to see two apprentices processing medicines. Pots bubbled on the fire, piles of dried greenery were laid out on the big table in the room's center, and one girl busied herself with a mortar. They were making up packets: for patrols, or to be sold to farmers for coin or trade goods. Dag didn't doubt that some of what he smelled would end up in that shop at Lumpton Market, at double the price the Lakewalkers received for them.

Another apprentice looked up from the table crammed up to the anteroom's window, where he was writing. He smiled at the patroller, regarding Dag's sling with professional interest. But before he could speak, the door to the other chamber opened and a slight, middle-aged woman stepped out, her summer shift cinched at the waist by a belt holding half a dozen tools of her trade. She was rubbing her chest and frowning.

The medicine maker looked up. "Ah! Dag! I've been expecting you."

"Hello, Hoharie. I saw Saun coming out just now. Is he going to be all right?"

"Yes, he's coming along nicely. Thanks to you, he says. I understand you did some impressive emergency groundwork on him." She eyed Dag in speculation, but at least she refrained from comment on his marriage cord.

"Nothing special. In and out for a quick match at a moment he needed it, was all."

Her brows twitched, but she didn't pursue the point further. "Well, come on in, let's have a look at this." She gestured at his sling. "How in the world have you managed?"

"I've had help."

Dag followed her into her workroom, closing the door behind them. A tall bed, onto which he'd helped lift more than one hurt comrade over the years, stood out in the room's center, but Hoharie gestured him to a chair beside a table, taking another around the corner from it. He slipped his arm out of its sling and laid it out, and she pulled a pair of sharp scissors from her belt and began undoing the wrappings. Upon inquiry, he favored her with a much-shortened tale of how he'd come by the injury back in Lumpton Market. She ran her hands up and down the bared forearm, and he could feel the press of her ground on his own, more invasive than the long probing fingers.

"Well, this is a clean break and a straight setting," she reported. "Doing well, for what, two weeks?"

"Nearer three." It seemed a lot more than that.

"If not for that"—she nodded at his hook—"I'd send you home to heal on your own, but you'd like these splints off sooner, I'd imagine."

"Oh, yes."

She smiled at his heartfelt drawl. "I've done all the groundwork I can for today on your young friend Saun, but my apprentice will be pleased to try."

Dag gave this the grimace it deserved; she grinned back unrepentantly. "Come, Dag, they have to practice on someone. Youth to experience, experience to youth." She tapped his arm cuff. "How's the stump? Giving you any trouble?"

"No. Well . . . no."

She sat back, eyeing him shrewdly. "In other words, yes. Off with the harness, let me see."

"Not the stump itself," he said, but let her unbuckle the harness and lay it aside, and run her experienced hands down his arm and over its callused end. "Well, it's sometimes a little sore, but it's not bad today."

"I've seen it worse. So, go on . . . ?"

He said cautiously, "Have you ever heard of a missing limb still having . . . ground?"

She rubbed her bony nose. "Phantom limbs?"

"Yes, just like that," he said eagerly.

"Itching, pain, sensations? I've heard of it. It's apparently very maddening, to have an itch that can't be scratched."

"No, not that. I knew about that. Met a man up in Luthlia once, must be twenty-five years back, who'd lost most of both feet to frostbite. Poor fellow used to complain bitterly about the itching, and his toes that he didn't have anymore cramping. A little groundwork on the nerves of his legs usually cleared it right up. I mean the *ground* of missing limbs."

"If something doesn't exist, it can't *have* a ground. I don't know if someone could have an illusion of ground, like the illusion of an itch; folks have hallucinations about all sorts of bizarre things, though, so I don't see why not."

"A hallucination shouldn't be able to do real groundwork."

"Of course not."

"Well, mine did. I did."

"What's this tale?" She sat back, staring.

He took a breath and described the incident with the glass bowl in the Bluefield parlor, leaving out the ruckus that had led up to it and concentrating on the mending itself. "The most of it was done, I swear, with the ground of my left hand." He thumped his left arm on the table. "Which isn't there. I was deathly sick after, though, and cold all through for an hour."

She scowled in thought. "It sounds as though you drew ground from your whole body. Which would be reasonable. Why it should take that form to project itself, well, your theory about your right arm being lost to use forcing a, um"—she waved her hands—"some sort of compensation seems like a fair one. Sounds like a pretty spectacular one, I admit. Has it happened again?"

"Couple of times." Dag wasn't about to explain the circumstances. "But I can't make it happen at will. It's not even reliably driven by my own tension. It's just random, or so it seems to me."

"Can you do it now?"

Dag tried, concentrating so hard his brow furrowed. Nothing. He shook his head.

Hoharie bit her lip. "A funny form of ground projection, yes, maybe. Ground without matter, no."

Dag finally said what he hadn't wanted to say, even to himself. "Malices are pure ground. Ground without matter."

The medicine maker stared at him. "You'd know more about that than I would. I've never seen a malice."

"All a malice's material appearance is pure theft. They snatch ground itself, and matter through its ground, to shape at will. Or misshape."

"I don't know, Dag." She shook her head. "I'll have to think about this one."

"I wish you would. I'm"—he cut off the word *afraid*—"very puzzled."

She nodded shortly and rose to fetch her apprentice from the anteroom, introducing him as Othan. The lad looked thrilled, whether at being allowed to do a ground treatment upon the very interesting patroller, or simply at being allowed to do one at all, Dag couldn't quite tell. Hoharie gave up her seat and stood observing with her arms folded. The apprentice sat down and determinedly began tracing his hands up and down Dag's right arm.

"Hoharie," he said after a moment, "I can't get through the patroller's ground veil."

"Ease up, Dag," Hoharie advised.

Dag had held himself close and tight ever since he'd crossed the bridge to the island yesterday. He really, really didn't want to open himself up here. But it was going to be necessary. He tried.

Othan shook his head. "Still can't get in." The lad was starting to look distressed, as though he imagined the failure was his fault. He looked up. "Maybe you'd better try, ma'am?"

"I'm spent. Won't be able to do a thing till tomorrow at the earliest. Ease up, Dag!"

"I can't . . ."

"You *are* in a mood today." She circled the table and frowned at them both; the apprentice cringed. "All right, try swapping it around. You reach, Dag. That should force you open."

He nodded, and tried to reach into the lad's ground. The strain of his own distaste for the task warred with his frantic desire, now that the opportunity was so provokingly close, of getting the blighted splints off for good. The apprentice was looking at him with the air of a whipped puppy, bewildered but still eager to please. He held his arm lightly atop Dag's, face earnest, ground open as any gate.

On impulse, Dag shifted his stump across and slammed it down beside both their arms. Something flashed in his groundsense, strong and sharp. Othan cried out and recoiled.

"Oh!" said Hoharie.

"A ghost hand," said Dag grimly. "A ground hand. Like *that*." His whole forearm was hot with new ground, snatched from the boy. His ghost hand, so briefly perceptible, was gone again. He was shaking, but if he put his arms out of sight below the table, it would only draw more attention to his trembling. He forced himself to sit still.

The apprentice was holding his own right arm to his chest, rubbing it and looking wide-eyed. "*Ow*," he said simply. "What was that? I mean—I didn't do—did I do anything?"

"Sorry. I'm sorry," mumbled Dag. "I shouldn't have done that." *That was new.* New and disturbing, and far too much like malice magic for Dag's comfort. Although perhaps there was only one kind of groundwork, after all. Was it theft, to take something someone was trying with all his heart to press upon you?

"My arm is cold," complained Othan. "But—did it help? Did I actually do any healing, Hoharie?"

Hoharie ran her hands over both her apprentice's arm and Dag's, her frown replaced by an oddly expressionless look. "Yes. There's an extremely dense ground reinforcement here."

Othan looked heartened, although he was still chafing his own forearm.

Dag wriggled his fingers; his arm barely ached. "I can feel the heat of it."

Hoharie, watching them both with equal attention, talked her apprentice through a light resplinting of Dag's arm. Othan gave the flaking, smelly skin a wash first, to Dag's intense gratitude. The boy's own right arm was decidedly weak; he fumbled the wrappings twice, and Hoharie had to help him tie off the knots.

"Is he going to be all right?" Dag asked cautiously, nodding at Othan.

"In a few days, I expect," said Hoharie. "That was a much stronger ground reinforcement than I normally let my apprentices attempt."

Othan smiled proudly, although his eyes were still a trifle confused. Hoharie dismissed him with thanks, closed the door behind him, and slid back into the seat across from Dag. She eyed him narrowly.

"Hoharie," said Dag plaintively, "what's happening to me?"

"Not sure." She hesitated. "Have you ever been tested for a maker?"

"Yes, ages ago. I'd no knack nor patience for it, but my groundsense range was a mile, so they let me go for a patroller. Which was what I'd desperately wanted anyway."

"What was that, nigh on forty years ago? Have you been tested lately?"

"No interest, no point. Such talents don't change after youth . . . do they?"

"Nothing alive is unchanging." Her eyes had gone silvery with interest— or was that covetousness? "I will say, that was no ghost, Dag. That was one of the live-est things I've ever seen. Could it do shaped reinforcements, I wonder?"

Did she think of training him as a medicine maker, in the sort of subtle groundwork that she herself did? Dag was taken aback. "*Dar's* the maker in my family."

"So?" Her shrewd look that went with this made him shift uncomfortably.

"I don't control this. It's more like it works me."

"What, you can't remember how wobbly you were when your groundsense first came in? Some days, my apprentices are all over the map. Some days I still am, for that matter."

"Fifty-five's a bit old for an apprentice, don't you think?" Hoharie herself was younger than Dag by a decade. He could remember when *she'd* been an apprentice. "And any road—a maker needs two good hands." He waved his left, by way of a reminder.

She started to speak, but then sat back, frowning over this last.

"Patrolling's what I do. Always have. I'm good at it." A shiver of fear troubled him at the thought of stopping, which was odd, since hunting malices should be the scariest task there was. But he remembered his own words from

Glassforge: *None of us could do the job without all of us, so all of us are owed.* Makers and patrollers alike, all were essential. *All essential, all expendable.*

Hoharie shrugged surrender, and said, "In any case, come back and see me tomorrow. I want to look at that arm again." She added after a moment, "Both of them."

"I'd take it kindly." He gestured with his sling. "Do I really still need this splint, now?"

"Yes, to remind you not to try anything foolish. Speaking of experience. You patrollers are all alike, in some ways. Give that ground reinforcement some time to work, and we'll see."

Dag nodded, rose, and let himself out, conscious of Hoharie's curious gaze following him.

6

$\mathcal{D}$ag returned from the medicine tent reluctant to speak of the unsettling incident with the maker's apprentice, but in any case, no one asked; instead, five persons took the chance to tell him that he needed to teach his wife to swim. Dag thought the idea fine, but Fawn seemed to find the fact that he still wore splints and a sling to be a great relief to her mind.

"Well, you certainly can't go swimming with that rig on," she said firmly. "When will you have it off, did they say?"

"Soon."

She relaxed, and he did not clarify that *soon* could well mean *tomorrow*.

Sarri's little boy, having been coaxed earlier into hauling rocks for their fire pit and warmly praised for his efforts by his fathers, had crept back to the task, toddling across the clearing with stones as big as his little fingers could clutch and flinging them in with great determination. It set off a small crisis when his excess offerings were removed. His outraged tears were diverted by a treat from Fawn's dwindling store of farm fare, and Dag, grinning, hauled him back to his assorted parents. That evening, Dag and Fawn boiled tea water on their first home fire, even if supper was cold plunkin again. Fawn looked as though she was finally beginning to understand all the plunkin jokes.

They burned the rinds and sat together by the crackling flames, watching through the trees as the sunset light faded on the farther shore. For all his weary unease, Dag still found it a pleasure just to look at the play of light and shadow across Fawn's features, the shine and spring of her hair, the gleam of her dark eyes. He wondered if gazing upon her face through time would be like watching sunsets, never quite the same twice yet unfailing in joy.

As the shadows deepened, the tree frogs in the woods piped a raucous descant to the deep croaking of bullfrogs hidden in the rushes. At last it was time to wave good night across the campsite at the others turning in, and drop the tent flap. By the light of a good beeswax candle, a gift from Sarri, they undressed and lay down in their bedroll. A few hours in Fawn's company had soothed Dag's strained nerves, but he must still have looked tense and absent, for she ran her hand along his face, and said, "You look tired. Do you . . . want to . . . ?"

"I could grow less tired." He kissed her curls away from her face and let his ground ease open a trifle. "Hm."

"Hm?"

"Your ground is very pretty tonight. Glittery. I think your days of fertility are starting up."

"Oh!" She sat up on one elbow. "Am I getting better, then?"

"Yes, but . . ." He sat half-up as well. "From what Mari said, you should be healing up inside at about the same rate as outside. Ground and flesh are still deep-damaged, and will recover slowly. From these"—he touched his lips to the carmine dimples in her neck—"my guess is your womb's not ready to risk a child yet, nor will be for some months."

"No. Nor is the rest of me, really." She rolled back and stared up at their hide roof. "I never thought to have a baby in a tent, though I suppose Lakewalker ladies do. We're not prepared for winter or anything, really. Not enough"—her hands waved uncertainly—"things."

"We travel lighter than farmers."

"I saw the inside of Sarri's cabin. Tent. She doesn't travel all that light. Not with children."

"Well, that's so. When all of Dar and Omba's children were home, shifting camp in season was a major undertaking. I usually tried to be out on patrol," he admitted ruefully.

Fawn sighed in uncertainty, and continued, "It's past midsummer. Time to be making and saving. Getting ready for the cold and the dark."

"Believe me, there is a steady stream of plunkins on their way to winter stores in Bearsford even as we speak. I used to ride that route as a horse boy in the summers, before I was old enough to go for patroller. Though in this season, it's easier to move the folks to the food than the food to the folks."

"Only plunkin?"

"The fruit and nuts will be coming on soon. A lot of the pigs we eat here. One per tent per season, so with four tents on this site, that makes four pig-roasts. Fish. Turkey, of course, and the hunters bring in venison from the woods on the mainland. I used to do that as a boy, too, and sometimes I go out with them between patrols. I'll show you how Stores works tomorrow."

She glanced up at him, catching her lower lip with her white teeth. "Dag—what's our plan, here?" One small hand reached out to trace over his splinted arm. "What happens to me when you go back out on patrol? Because Mari and Razi and Utau—everyone I know—will all be gone then, too."

He hardly needed groundsense to feel the apprehension in her. "By then, I figure, you'll be better acquainted with Sarri and Cattagus and Mari's daughter and her family. Cattagus is Sarri's uncle, by the way—he's an Otter by birth, as if you couldn't tell. My plan is to lie up quiet, get folks used to the idea of you. They will in time, I figure, like they grew used to Sarri's having two husbands."

And yet . . . normally, when patrollers went out, they could be sure their spouses would be looked after in their absences, first by their families, then by their patrol comrades, then by the whole community. It was a trust Dag had always taken for granted, as solid as rock under his feet. It was deeply disturbing to imagine that trust instead cracking like misjudged ice.

He went on in a casual voice, "I think I might skip the next patrol going out and take some of my unused camp time. Plenty to do here. Sometimes, between patrols, I help Omba train her young horses, get them used to a big man up. She mostly has a flock of girls for apprentices, see."

Fawn looked unconvinced. "Do you suppose Dar and your mama will be speaking to you again by then?"

Dag shrugged. "The next move is up to them. It's plain Dar doesn't like this marriage, but he detests rows. He'll let it pass unless he's pressed to act. Mama . . . had her warning. She has ways of making me crazy, and I suppose the reverse is true, but she's not stupid. And she'd be the last person on the lake to invite the camp council to tell her what to do. She'll keep it in the family. All we need do is let time go by and not borrow trouble."

She eased back in reassurance, but there remained a dark streak in her spirit, interlaced with the fresh brightness from her recovering body. Dag suspected the strangeness of it all was beginning to accumulate. He'd seen homesickness devastate young patrollers far less dislocated than Fawn, and he resolved to find familiar tasks for her hands tomorrow. Yes, let her be as busy as she was used to being, till her balance grew steadier.

Meanwhile—here inside Tent Bluefield—the task to hand was surely growing less frantic and more familiar, but no less enchanting for all of that. *Back to taking turns.* He sought her tender lips in a kiss, opening his heart to all the intricacy of her ground, dark and light together.

Dag vanished for a couple of hours the next morning, but returned for lunch—plunkin *again,* but he didn't seem to mind. Then, as promised, he took Fawn to the mysterious Stores. This proved to be a set of long sheds tucked into the woods, down the road past the patroller headquarters. Inside one, they found what appeared to be a woman clerk; at any rate, she sat at a table scratching in a ledger with a quill, surrounded by shelves crammed with more ledgers. A toddler lay asleep in a sort of wooden pen next to her. More sets of shelves, ceiling-high, marched back in rows the length of the building. The dim air smelled of leather and herbs and less-identifiable things.

While Fawn walked up and down the rows of shelves, staring at the goods with which they were crammed, Dag engaged the woman in a low-voiced consultation, which involved dragging out several more ledgers and marking off and initialing lists therein. At one point Dag said, "You still have those?" in a voice of surprise, laughed, and dipped the quill to mark some more. His splints, Fawn noticed, hardly seemed to slow him down today, and he was constantly taking his arm out of the sling.

Dag then led Fawn up and down the rows and had her help him collect furs and other leather goods according to some scheme of his own. A half dozen beautiful dark brown pelts looking like the coats of some extraordinary ferret-shaped creature he explained as coming from mink, small woodland predators from north of the Dead Lake; an exquisite white pelt, soft as whipped cream, was from a winter fox, but it was like no fox fur Fawn had ever seen or touched. These, he said, could be bride-gifts for Mama and Aunt Nattie, and Fawn had to agree they were marvelously better than the local hides they'd rejected back at Lumpton Market.

"Every patrol usually brings back something," Dag explained. "It varies with where they've been and what opportunities they've found. Whatever part of his or her share a patroller doesn't want or can't use is turned over to Stores, and the patroller gets a credit for them, either to draw the equivalent item out later or trade for something of use. Excess accumulations are taken down to farmer country to trade for other things we need. After all my years of patrolling, I have a long credit at Stores. You be thinking about what you want, Spark, and chances are we can find something like."

"Cooking ware?" she said hopefully.

"Next building over," he promised.

One at a time, he pulled three more folded hides from dusty back shelves, and Fawn staggered under the weight of each as they took them to the clerk's table to be signed out. He also, after judicious study, selected a sturdy packsaddle in good condition from a rack of such horse gear. They hauled it all out through the double doors onto the end porch.

Dag prodded the three big bundles with his toe. "Now these," he said, "are actually my own. Bit surprised to still find them here. Two were sent down from Luthlia after I came home, and the other I picked up about three years back during a winter season I spent patrolling in the far south. This one, I figure for your papa. Go ahead and unroll it."

Fawn picked apart the stiff, dry rawhide cords and unfolded what appeared to be an enormous wolf skin. "My word, Dag! This thing must have been as big as a horse!"

"Very nearly."

She frowned. "You can't tell me that was a natural beast."

"No. Mud wolf. The very one they found me under at Wolf Ridge, I'm told. My surviving tent-brothers—you'd say brothers-in-law—skinned and tanned it for me. Never had the heart to tell them I didn't want it. I put it in Stores thinking someone would take it off, but there it's sat ever since."

She wondered if this same beast had savaged his left hand. "It would make a rug for our whole parlor, back in West Blue. But it would be rather horrible, knowing how you came by it."

"I admit I've no desire to look at it. Depending on how your papa feels about me by now, he might wish it hadn't stopped gnawing on me so soon, but on the whole I think I won't explain its history. The other two are worth a look as well."

Fawn unfolded the second big pelt, and recoiled. Heavy black leather in a shape altogether too human was scantily covered with long, ratty gray hair; the mask of the thing, which had a manlike look, still had the fanged jaw attached.

"Another mud wolf. Different version. Fast and vicious, and they moved like shadows in the dark. That one for Reed and Rush, I think," said Dag.

"Dag, that's evil." Fawn thought it through. "Good choice."

Dag chuckled. "Give them something to wonder about, I figure."

"It'll give them nightmares, I should imagine!" Or was that, *I hope?* "Did you kill it?" *And for pity's sake, how?*

Dag squinted at the mummified horror. "Probably. If not that one, plenty like it."

Fawn refolded and bound up both old hides, and undid the third. It was thinner and more supple, and hairless. She unrolled and kept unrolling, her brows rising in astonishment, until fully nine feet of . . . of whatever it was lay out on the porch floor. The fine leather had a beautiful pattern, almost like snakeskin magnified, and gleamed smoothly under her hand, bronze green shading to rich red-brown. For all that the animal was as long as a horse, it seemed to have had short, stubby legs; wicked black claws still dangled from their ends. The jaws of this one, too, had been set back in place after tanning, and were frankly unbelievable, like a stretched-out bear trap made of teeth.

"What kind of malice made *that*? And what poor creature was it made from?"

"Not a mud-man at all. It's an alligator—a southern swamp lizard. A real, natural animal. We think. Unless one of our ancestor-mages got really drunk. Malices do not, thank all the absent gods, emerge too often so far south of the Dead Lake, but what happens when they do get hold of these fellows is scarcely to be imagined. The southern wetlands are one of the places you want to do your patrolling in winter, because cold makes the al-ligators, and the alligator-men, sluggish. That one we just caught on an or-dinary hunting and trapping run, though."

"Ordinary? It looks as if it could eat a man in two bites!"

"They're a danger along the shores of the channels. They lie in the water like logs, but they can move fast when they want. They clamp onto their prey and drag it down into the water to drown, and rip it up later, after it rots a bit." He bent and ran his fingers along the shiny hide. "I should think your papa and Whit could both get a pair of boots out of this one, and belts and something for your mama as well."

"Dag," said Fawn curiously, "have you ever seen the sea?"

"Oh, yeah, couple of times. The south shore, that is, around the mouth of the Gray River. I've not seen the eastern sea."

"What's it like?"

He sat back, squatting, fingers still caressing the swamp-lizard skin, and a meditative look came over his face. "First time was almost thirty years ago. Never forget it. West of the Gray, between the river and the Levels, the land is flat and mostly treeless. All mounted patrols in that wide-sky country. Our company commander had us all spread out, half a mile or more apart, in one long line—that sweep must have been fifty miles across. We rode straight south, day after day. Spring it was, the air all soft and blue, and new green coming up all around, and flowers everywhere. Best patrolling I ever did in my life. We even found one sessile, and did for it without hardly pausing. The rest was just riding along in the sunshine, dangling our feet out of the stirrups, scanning the ground, just barely keeping touch with the patrollers to the right and left. End of the week, the color of the sky changed, got all silvery and light, and we came up over these sand dunes, and there it was . . ." His voice trailed off. He swallowed. "The rollers were foaming in over the sand, grum-bling and grumbling, never stopping. I never knew there were so many shades of blue and gray and green. The sea was as wide and flat as the Levels, but *alive*. You could feel with your groundsense how alive it was, as if it was the mother of the whole wide green world. I sat and stared . . . We all dismounted and took off our boots, and got silly for a while, running in and out of that salty water, warm as milk."

"And then what happened?" Fawn asked, almost holding her breath.

Dag shrugged. "Camped for the night on the beach, turned the line around and shifted it fifty miles, and rode back north. It turned cold and rained on the way back, though, and we found nothing for our pains." He added after a mo-ment, "Wood washed up on the beach burns with the most beautiful strange colors. Never saw anything like."

His words were simple and plain, as his words usually were; Fawn scarcely knew why she felt as though she were eavesdropping on a man at prayers, or why water blurred her eyes.

"Dag . . ." she said. "What's beyond the sea?"

His brows twitched up. "No one's sure."

"Could there be other lands?"

"Oh, that. Yes. Or there were, once. The oldest maps show other continents, three of them. The original charts are long gone, so it's anyone's guess how accurate the copies are. But if any ships have gone to see what's still there, they haven't come back that I ever heard. People have different theories. Some say the gods have interdicted us, and that anyone who ventures out too far is destroyed by holy curses. Some guess the other lands got blighted, and are now all dead from shore to shore, and no one's there anymore. I'm not too fond of that picture. But you'd think, if there were other folks across the seas, and they had ships, some might have got blown off course sometime in the last thousand years, and I've never heard tell of any such. Maybe the *people* over there have interdicted us, till our task is done and all's safe again. That would be sensible."

He paused, gazing into some time or distance Fawn could not see, and continued, "Legend has it there is, or once was, another enclave of survivors on our continent, to the west of the Levels and the great mountains that were supposed to be beyond them. Maybe we'll find out if that's true someday, if anyone, us or them, ever tries to sail all around the shore of this land. Wouldn't need such grand ships for hugging the coast."

"With silver sails," Fawn put in.

He smiled. "I think that's got to happen sometime. Don't know if I'll live to see it. If . . ."

"If?"

"If we can keep the malices down long enough for folks to get ahead. The river men are bold enough to try, but it would risk a lot of resources, as well as lives. You'd need a rich man, a prince or a great lord, to fund such a voyage, and they're extinct."

"Or a bunch of well-off men," Fawn suggested. "Or a whole big bunch of quite ordinary men."

"And one fast-talking lunatic to coax the money out of their pockets. Well, maybe." He smiled thoughtfully, considering this vision, but then shook his head and rose. Fawn carefully rerolled the astonishing swamp-lizard skin.

Dag went back inside to cadge paper, ink, and quills from the clerk, then they both sat at the nearest trestle table in the dappled shade to write their letters to West Blue. Fawn didn't miss West Blue—she'd longed to get away, and she hadn't changed her mind on that—but she couldn't say her feet were planted in their new soil yet. Given the way Lakewalkers kept moving around, maybe home would never be a place. It would be Dag. She watched him across the table, scribbling with his quill clutched in his right fingers and holding down the paper, lifting in the warm breeze, with his hook. She bent her head to her own task.

Dear Mama, Papa, and Aunt Nattie. We got here day before yesterday. Had it only been two days? *I am fine. The lake is very* . . . She brushed the quill over her chin, and decided she really ought to say more than *wet.* She wrote *large,* instead. *We met up with Dag's aunt Mari again. She has a nice* . . . Fawn scratched out the start of *cabin* and wrote *tent. Dag's arm is getting better.* And onward in that vein, till she'd filled half the page with unexceptional remarks. Too much blank space left. She decided to describe Sarri's children, and their campsite, which filled the rest with enough cheery word pictures to grow cramped toward the end. There.

So much left out. Patroller headquarters, and Fairbolt Crow's pegboard. Dar, the unnerving bone shack, Dag's angry mama, the futility of the sharing knife after all this journey. Dag's dark, nervy mood. The threat of swimming lessons. Naked swimming lessons, at that. Some things were *best* left out.

Dag, finishing, handed his letter across for her to read. It was very polite and plain, almost like an inventory, making clear which gifts were for which family members. Both horses and the packsaddle were to be Mama's, as well as some of the fine furs. The mud-man skin for the twins was blandly described, entirely without comment. Fawn grinned as she pictured the three alarming hides being unpacked at West Blue.

Dag stepped inside and returned the quills and ink to the clerk, coming out with the letters folded and sealed just in time to greet a girl who rode up, bareback, on a tall, elegant, dappled gray mare. A dark foal about four months old pranced after, flicking his fuzzy ears; he had the most beautifully shaped head and deepest liquid eyes Fawn had ever seen on a colt, and she spent the time while Dag and the girl organized the packsaddle trying to make up to him. He flirted with her in turn, yielding at last to ear scratching just *there.* Fawn couldn't imagine her mother riding that mare, nor any of her family; maybe the dappled beauty could be broken to harness and pull the light cart to the village, though. *That* would turn a few heads.

A man dressed as a patroller came riding from the direction of the headquarters building. He turned out to be a courier on his way south, apparently a trusted comrade; exactly what old favor Dag was calling in was not clear to Fawn, but however dubiously he greeted the farmer bride or raised his brows at Dag, he had undertaken to deliver the bride-gifts. He stopped with them long enough to get a clear description of the Bluefield farm and how to find it, and then he was off, with the silvery mare following meekly on a lead and the colt capering and scampering. The horse girl, trudging back to Mare Island, looked after them with a downright heartbroken expression.

Dag then led Fawn off to the next storehouse, where they found some lightly used cooking gear—not a proper kitchen's worth, but at least a few things to permit more elaborate meals over an open fire than sliced raw plunkin and tea. And, to Fawn's joy, several pounds of cotton from south of the Grace River, cleaned and combed, an equally generous bag of washed wool, and three hanks of good flax. The tools Aunt Nattie had given Fawn for a wedding present would find their proper use. Despite her burdens her steps were lighter turning back toward their campsite, and she made plans for getting Dag to hold still long enough to measure his gnarly feet for socks.

The following day Dag returned from the medicine tent with no sling or splints, but with a smile on his face that would hardly go away. He flexed and stretched his hand gratefully. He reported he'd been instructed to take it easy for another week, which he interpreted liberally as *no weapons practice yet.* Everything else he embraced immediately, including Fawn.

To her muffled alarm, the next thing he did that afternoon was make her put down her spindle and go with him for her first swimming lesson. She was distracted from her fear of the water only by her embarrassment at their lack of clothes, but somehow Dag made both better. They picked their way past the bending cattails into water to his waist and her chest. At least the lake's murkiness gave them a more decent cloak, its greeny-gold translucence turning opaque just a short way down. The top foot of the water was as warm in the sun as a bath; beneath that it grew cooler. The soft mud squelched between Fawn's curling toes. They were accompanied by a dizzy escort of water bugs, flocks of little black ovals that whirled merrily like beads on a string, and agile water striders, their thin legs making dimples in the brown surface as they skated along. Dag promptly made the bead-shaped bugs an example to Fawn, inviting her to spin them down in little whirlpools with her hands and watch them bob right back to the surface.

Dag insisted she was naturally more buoyant than he, taking the opportunity to pat her most buoyant parts. Fawn thought his assertion that *It doesn't matter how deep the water is, Spark, you're only going to use the top two feet* overly optimistic, but under the influence of his confidence and unfailing good cheer, she gradually began to relax in the water. By the second day, to her own astonishment, she floated for the first time in her life; on the third afternoon, she achieved a dog paddle of several yards.

Even Dag had to admit that the lake's muddiness made Hickory Lake residents all tend to smell a bit green by the end of the summer—*sooner than that,* Fawn did not say aloud—but Sarri took Fawn into the woods and showed her where a clear spring ran that not only allowed her to give lake-scrubbed clothes a final rinse, but also to draw water that didn't need to be boiled before drinking. Fawn managed her first laundry day, and sniffed their clothes, drying on a line strung between two trees, with satisfaction at a job well done.

That afternoon, Dag came in with a small turkey to pluck. Fawn happily started a bag to save feathers, looking ahead to pillows and ticks. They roasted the bird over their fire and invited Mari and Cattagus to help eat it up. Fawn ended the evening casting on her first cotton yarn to her double-ended needle set for Dag's socks, and feeling that this place might become home after all.

Two days later, instead of a swimming lesson, Dag took her out in one of the narrow boats. He had a specially shaped hook for his wrist cuff that allowed him to manage his paddle. Fawn, after a brief lesson on the dock, was placed in the front with a paddle of her own. She felt nervous and clumsy at first, looking over all that expanse of water with Dag out of sight behind her, but she soon fell into the rhythm of the task. Around behind Walnut Island, winking water gave way to a surface that was downright glassy, and Fawn relaxed still more. They paused to admire a dead tree reflected in the water, its bare white branches startling against the green of the woods. It was a roosting place for broad-winged hawks, a few circling gracefully overhead or perching on the branches, and Fawn smiled to remember the day they'd been startled by that big red-tail near Glassforge. Any larger predators, Fawn had gathered, were kept off the islands by Lakewalker magic.

Up the back channel, the air grew still and hot, and the water clear. Huge elderberry bushes leaned over the banks, their branches heavy with thick clusters of green fruit slowly acquiring a promising rosy blush; in another month the berries would be black and ripe, and Fawn could easily see how a boy might gather them from a boat like this one. A shiny sunfish jumped right into their boat at Dag's feet; Dag, laughing at Fawn's startled squeal, scooped the flopping creature gently back into the water and denied that he had enticed it by Lakewalker persuasion. "Much too small, Spark!"

Rounding a tangle of wrack and cattails where red-winged blackbirds traded barking chirps and hoarse whistles, they came at last upon a broad open space crowded with flat lily pads, their white flowers wide to the sun. Thin, iridescent blue dragonflies, and thicker scarlet ones, stitched the air above the marsh, and rows of turtles sunned themselves on logs, yellow-striped necks stretched out, brown backs gleaming like polished stones. A blue heron stalked slowly along the farther shore; it froze briefly, then darted its long yellow beak into the water. A silvery minnow flashed as the heron twisted its neck around, gulped, then stood folded for a moment looking smug. Fawn hardly knew whether it made her happier to watch the flowers or the contented look on Dag's face. Dag sighed in satisfaction, but then frowned.

"I thought this was the same place, but it seems smaller. This water is a lot shallower, too. I remember it as being well over my head. Did I take a wrong turn somewhere?"

"It looks plenty deep to me. Um . . . how old were you, again, first time you found this place?"

"Eight."

"And how tall?"

Dag began to open his mouth, then grinned sheepishly. "Shorter than you, Spark."

"Well, then."

"Well, indeed." He laid his paddle across his lap and just gazed around.

The water lilies, though beautiful, were the same common variety Fawn had sometimes seen in quiet backwaters around West Blue, she decided. She had seen cattails, dragonflies, turtles, blackbirds, and herons before. There was nothing new here, and yet . . . *this place is magical.* The silence in the warm, moist air, broken only by the little noises of the marsh, seemed holy in her ears, as if she were hearing a sound beneath all sound. *This is what having ground-sense must be like, all the time.* The thought awed her.

They sat quietly in the narrow boat, beyond all need of words, until the heat of the sun began to grow uncomfortable; with a sigh, Dag took up his paddle once more and turned them around. His stroke left a glossy whirlpool spiraling down into the clear water, and Fawn's eye followed it. *This is where his heart is anchored. I can see why.*

They had almost rounded the corner into the main arm of the lake when Dag paused again. Fawn twisted around; he held his finger to his lips and grinned at her. His eyes half-lidded, he sat there with an absentminded, sleepy look on his face that didn't reassure her a bit. So she didn't *quite* fall out of the boat when a sudden splash and movement resolved into a huge black bass, twisting in the air and trailing sparkling drops. It fell into the bottom of the narrow boat with a resounding thud, flopped and flapped like mad, then at last lay still, bright gills flexing.

"There's a better size for dinner," said Dag in satisfaction, and thrust his paddle into the water once more.

"Now, *that's* persuasion. Is that how you folks fish all the time?" asked Fawn in amazement. "I wondered why I didn't see any poles or lines lying around."

"Something like that. Actually, we usually use hand-nets. You ever see old Cattagus lying on the dock looking as if he's dozing, with one hand trailing over the side, that's what he's likely doing."

"It seems almost like cheating. Why are there any fish left in this lake?"

"Well, not everyone has the knack."

As they pulled into the dock, sunburned and happy, Fawn made plans for begging some herbs from Sarri's garden and grilling Dag's catch worthily. She managed to clamber onto the weathered gray planks from the wobbly boat without taking an inadvertent swimming lesson, and let Dag hand her up his prize before he tied off the boat's lines. Clutching the bass, she turned her face up to Dag for a quick kiss and hug, and they climbed the stone steps up the steep bank.

His arm around her waist gave her an abrupt squeeze, then fell away. She looked up to follow his glance.

Dar waited in the shade at the top of the bank, frowning like a bit of rainy dark detached from winter and walking around. As they crested the rise, he said to Dag, "I need to talk to you."

"Do you? Why?" Dag inquired, but he gestured toward their tent and the log seats around their fire pit.

"Alone, if you please," Dar said stiffly.

"Mm," said Dag, without enthusiasm, but he gave his brother a short nod. He saw Fawn back to the tent and left her to deal with the fish. Fawn watched uneasily as the pair strolled away out of the campsite and turned onto the road, leaning a little away from each other.

7

They turned left onto the shady road between the shore campsites and the woods. Dag was tired enough not to need to shorten his steps to match his brother's, and not yet annoyed enough to lengthen them to his full patroller's stride and make Dar hurry to keep up. On the whole, he wouldn't bet on that remaining the case. *What is he about?* It didn't take groundsense to see that although Dar had come to Dag, conciliation and apology were not strong in his mood.

"And so?" Dag prodded, although it would have been better tactics to wait Dar out, make him start. *This isn't supposed to be a war.*

"You're the talk of the lake, you know," Dar said curtly.

"Talk passes. There will be some other novelty along soon enough." Dag set his jaw to keep himself from asking, *What are they saying?* He was glumly sure Dar was about to tell him anyway.

"It's a pretty unsavory match. Not only is that girl you dragged home a farmer, she's scarcely more than an infant!"

Dag shrugged. "In some ways Fawn's a child; in others not. In grief and guilt, she's fully grown." *And I am surely qualified to judge.* "In knowing how to go on, I'd call her an apprentice adult. Basic tasks aren't yet routine for her, but when all that energy and attention get freed up at last, watch out! She's ferociously bright, and learns fast. Main thing about the age difference, I reckon, is that it hands me a special burden not to betray her trust." His eyebrows pinched. "Except that the same is true of anyone at any age, so maybe it's not so special after all."

"Betrayal? You've shamed our tent! Mama's become a laughingstock to the ill willed over this, and she hates it. You know how she values her dignity."

Dag tilted his head. "Huh. Well, I'm sorry to hear it, but I suspect she brought that on herself. I'm afraid what she calls dignity others see as conceit."

On the other hand, perhaps it was the accident of Cumbia's having so few children that made her insist on their particular value, to hold her head up against women friends who could parade a more numerous get. Although it was plain fact that Dar's skills were rare and extraordinary. Remembering to placate, Dag added, "Some of it is pride in you, to be fair."

"It could have been in you, too, if you'd bestirred yourself," Dar grumbled. "Still just a patroller, after forty years? You should have been a commander by now. Anything that Mama and Mari agree on must be true, or the sky's like to fall."

Dag gritted his teeth and did not reply. His family's ambition had been a plague to him since he'd returned from Luthlia and recovered enough to begin patrolling again. His own fault, perhaps, for letting them learn he'd turned down patrol leadership despite, or perhaps because of, the broad hint that it could soon lead to wider duties. Repeatedly, till Fairbolt had stopped asking. Or had that leaked out through Massape, reflecting her husband's plaints? At this range, he could no longer remember.

Dar's lips compressed, then he said, "It's been suggested—I won't say who by—that if we just wait a year, the problem will solve itself. The farmer girl's too small to birth a Lakewalker child and will die trying. Have you realized that?"

Dag flinched. "Fawn's mama is short, too, and she did just fine." *But her papa wasn't a big man, either.* He fought the shiver that ran through him by the reflection that the size of the infant and the size of the grown person had little relation; Cattagus and Mari's eldest son, who was a bear of a fellow now, was famous in the family for having been born little and sickly.

"That's more or less what I said—don't count on it. Farmers are fecund. But have you even thought it through, Dag? If a child or children survived, let alone their mother, what's the fate of half-bloods here? They couldn't make, they couldn't patrol. All they could do would be eat and breed. They'd be despised."

Dag's jaw set. "There are plenty of other necessary jobs to do in camp, as I recall being told more than once. Ten folks in camp keep one patroller in the field, Fairbolt says. They could be among that ten. Or do you secretly despise everyone else here, and I never knew?"

Dar batted this dart away with a swipe of his hand. "So you're saying your children could grow up to be servants of mine? And you'd be content with that?"

"We would find our way."

"We?" Dar scowled. "So already you put your farmer get ahead of the needs of the whole?"

"If that happens, it won't be by my choosing." Would Dar hear the warning in that? Dag continued, "We actually don't know that all cross-bloods lack groundsense. If anything, the opposite; I've met a couple who have little less than some of us. I've been out in the world a good bit more than you. I've seen raw talent here and there amongst farmers, too, and I don't think it's just the result of some passing Lakewalker in a prior generation leaving a present." Dag frowned. "By rights, we should be sifting the farmers for hidden groundsense. Just like the mages of old must have done."

"And while we're diverting ourselves in that, who fights the malices?" Dar shot back. "*Nearly* good enough to patrol isn't going to do the job. We need the concentration of bloodlines to reach the threshold of function. We're stretched to the breaking point, and everyone knows it. Let me tell you, it's not just Mama who is maddened to see you wasting the talent in your blood."

Dag grimaced. "Yeah, I've heard that song from Aunt Mari, too." He remembered his own reply. "And yet I might have been killed anytime these past four decades, and my blood would have been no less wasted. Pretend I'm dead, if it'll make you feel better."

Dar snorted, declining to rise to that bait. They had reached the point where the road from the bridge split to cut through the woods to the island's north shore. At Dar's gesture, they turned onto it. The earth was dappled golden-green in the late sun, leaf shadows barely flickering in the breathing summer air. Their pacing sandals kicked up little spurts of dirt in the stretches between drying puddles.

Dar gathered himself, and continued, "It's not just your own family you put to shame. This stunt of yours creates disruption and a bad example in the patrol, as well. You've a reputation there, I don't deny. Youngsters like Saun look up to you. How much harder will this make it for patrol leaders to prevent the next ill-fated farmer romance? I swear, you're thinking only of yourself."

"Yes," said Dag, and added meditatively, "it's a new experience." A slow smile turned his lips. "I kind of like it."

"Don't make stupid jokes," snapped Dar.

I wasn't. Absent gods help me. In fact, it grew less funny the longer he thought about it. Dag took a long breath. "What are you after, Dar? I married Fawn for true—mind, body, and ground. That isn't going to change. Sooner or later, you'll have to deal with it."

"Dealing with it is just what I'm trying to avoid." Dar's scowl deepened. "The camp council could force a change. They've ruled on string-cuttings before."

"Only when the couple was divided and their families couldn't negotiate an agreement. No one can force a string-cutting against the will of *both* partners. And no one of sense would tolerate the precedent if the council tried. It would put everyone's marriage at risk—it would fly against the whole meaning of string-binding!"

Dar's voice hardened. "Then you'll just have to be forced to will it, eh?"

Dag let ten steps pass in silence before he replied. "I'm stubborn. My wife is determined. You'll break your knife on that rock, Dar."

"Have you grasped what you risk? Shunning—banishment? No more patrolling?"

"I've a lot of patrol years left in me. We're stretched, you say—and yet you'd throw those years away into a ditch? For mere conceit?"

"I'm *trying* for exactly the reverse." Dar swiped an angry hand across his brow. "You're the one who seems to be galloping blindly for the ditch."

"Not by my will. Nor Fairbolt's. He'll stand up for me." Actually, Fairbolt had said only that he didn't care to defend this before the camp council—not whether he would overcome his understandable distaste if he had to. But Dag was disinclined to confide his doubts to Dar at this point.

"What," scoffed Dar, "with all the trouble this will make for patrol discipline? Think again."

Had Dar and Fairbolt been talking? Dag began to be sorry he had held himself aloof from camp gossip these past days, even though it had seemed wiser not to present his head for drumming on or let himself be drawn into arguments. He countered, "Fawn's a special case anyway. She's not just any farmer, she's the farmer girl who slew a malice. As contrasted with, for example, your malice count. What was it, again? Oh, yes—none?"

Dar's lips thinned in an unfelt smile. "If you like, brother. Or maybe the count is, every malice that any knife of my making slew. Without a sharing knife no patroller is a malice killer. You're just malice food walking around."

Dag drew breath through his nostrils and tried to get a better grip on his temper. "True. And without hands to wield them, your knives are just—what did you call them?—wall decorations. I think we need to cry truce on this one."

Dar nodded shortly. They paced beside each other for a time.

When he could trust himself to speak again, Dag went on, "Without Fawn's hand, I would be dead now, and maybe a good part of my patrol with me. And you'd have spent the past weeks having memorial rites and making tender speeches about what a fine fellow I was."

Dar sighed. "Almost better, that would be. Simpler, at least."

"I appreciate that *almost*. Almost." Dag gathered his wits, or attempted to. "In any case, your bird won't fly. Fairbolt's made it clear he'll tolerate this for the sake of need and won't take it to the council. And neither will Mama. Get used to us, Dar." He let his voice soften to persuasion, almost plea. "Fawn is her own sort of worthy. You'd see it if you'd let yourself look at her straight. Give her a chance, and you won't be sorry."

"You're besotted."

Dag shrugged. "And the sun rises in the east. You're not going to change either fact. Give up the gloom and set your mind to some more open view."

"Aunt Mari was a feckless fool to let this get by."

"She made all the same arguments that you just did." Rather better phrased, but Dar had never been a diplomat. "Dar, let it ride. It'll work out in time. Folks will get used to it. Fawn and I may always be an oddity, but we won't start a stampede any more than Sarri did with her two husbands. Hickory Lake will survive us. Life will go on."

Dar inhaled, staring straight ahead. "I will go to the camp council."

Dag covered the chill in his belly with a slow blink. "Will you, now. What will Mama say? I thought you hated rows."

"I do. But it's come down to me. Someone has to act. Mama cries, you know. It has to be done, and it has to be done soon." Dar grimaced. "Omba says if we wait till you get your farmer girl pregnant, you'll never be shifted."

"She's right," said Dag, far more coolly than he felt.

Dar bore the look of a man determined to do his duty, however repugnant. Yes, Dar would stiffen Cumbia, even against her better judgment. Did both imagine Dag would cave in to these threats—or did they both realize he wouldn't? Or was it one of each?

"So," said Dag, "I'm a sacrifice you're willing to make, am I? Is Mama so willing?"

"Mama knows—we all know—your passion for patrolling. How hard you fought to get back in after you lost your hand. Is dipping your wick in this farmer girl worth casting away your whole life?"

Dar was remembering the brother from eighteen years back, Dag thought. Agonized, exhausted, seeking only to deal death in turn to that which had made him the walking corpse he'd felt himself to be. And then, with luck, to be reunited in death with all that he'd lost, because no other course seemed possible or even imaginable. Something strange and new had happened to that Dag in the malice cave near Glassforge. Or—something that had been happening below the surface had finally been brought to light. *I'm not who you think I am anymore, Dar. You look at me yet don't see me.* Dar seemed curiously like Fawn's kin, in that way. *So who am I?* For the first time in a long time, Dag wasn't sure he knew the answer, and that was a lot more disturbing than Dar's old assumptions.

Dar misinterpreted Dag's uneasy look. "Yeah, that's got you thinking! About time. I'm not going to back off on this. This is your warning."

Dag touched the cord below his rolled-up left sleeve. "Neither am I. That's yours."

They both maintained a stony silence as they reached the shore road again and turned right. Dar managed a nod when he turned off at the Redwing campsite, but he spoke no word of farewell, of further meetings, or of any other indication of his intent. Dag, fuming, returned an equally silent nod and walked on.

On the mere physical level, Dag thought he need have no fear for either Fawn or himself. It wasn't Dar's style to gather a bunch of hotheads like Sunny and his friends to deliver violent rebuke. A formal charge before the camp council was precisely what Dar would do, no question there. His was no idle threat. Dag felt a curious blankness within himself at the thought, in a way like the familiar empty moment before falling into attack on a malice lair.

He considered the current makeup of the camp council. There were normally a representative and an alternate from each island, chosen yearly by rotation from the heads of the various clans and other elders, plus the camp captain as a permanent member on behalf of the patrol and its needs. Cumbia had been on the council herself once, and Dag's grandfather, before he'd grown too fragile, had been an alternate twice. Dag had scarcely paid attention to who was in the barrel on council this year, or to tell the truth any other year, and suddenly it mattered.

The council resolved most conflicts by open discussion and binding mediation. Only in matters involving banishment or a death sentence did they make their votes secret, and then the quorum was not the usual five, but the full seven. There had only been two murders in Hickory Lake Camp in Dag's lifetime, and the council had settled the more ambiguous by ordering a payment between the families; only one had led to an execution. Dag had never yet witnessed a banishment like the one at Log Hollow that Saun had gossiped about. Dag couldn't help feeling that there must have been a more unholy mess backing up behind that incident than Saun's short description suggested. *Like mine?* Maybe not.

Dag had deliberately steered clear of camp gossip in the past days if only to avoid the aggravation, keeping to himself with Fawn—and healing, don't forget that—but in any case he doubted very many of his friends would repeat the most critical remarks to his face. He could think of only one man he could trust to do so without bias in either direction. He made plans to seek Fairbolt after supper.

Fawn glanced up from the perfect coals in the fire pit to see Dag stride back into the clearing, his scowl black. She had never seen so much quiet joy in Dag as this afternoon out in the lily marsh, and she set her teeth in a moment of fury for whatever his brother had done to wreck his happiness. She also bade silent good-bye to her hope, however faint, that Dar had come as a family peacemaker, dismissing the little fantasy she had started to build up about maybe a dinner invitation from Dag's mama, and what Fawn could bring and how she could act to show her worth to that branch of the Redwings.

At her eyebrows raised in question, Dag shook his head, adding an unfelt smile to show his scowl was not for her. He sat on the ground, picked up a stick, and dug it into the dirt, his face drawn in thought.

"So what did Dar want?" Fawn asked. "Is he coming around to us?" She busied herself with the bass, gutted, cleaned, stuffed with herbs begged from Sarri's garden, and ready to grill. It sizzled gently as she laid it on the rack above her coals, and she stirred the pot of mashed plunkin with onions she'd fixed to go with. Dag looked up at the enticing smells pretty soon, his eyes growing less pinched, although he was still a long time answering.

"Not yet, anyway," Dag said at last.

Fawn pursed her lips. "If there's some trouble, don't you think I need to know?"

"Yes," he sighed. "But I need to talk to Fairbolt first. Then I can say more certainly."

Say what? "Sounds a little ominous."

"Maybe not, Spark." Attracted by his supper, he got up and sat again by her, giving her neck a distracting nuzzle as she tried to turn the fish.

She smiled back, to show willing, but thought, *Maybe so, Dag.* If something wasn't a problem, he usually said so, with direct vigor. If it was a problem with a solution, he'd cheerfully explain it, at whatever length necessary. This sort of silence, she had gradually learned, betokened unusual uncertainty. Her vague conviction that Dag knew everything about everything—well, possibly not about farms—did not stand up to sober reflection.

As she'd hoped, feeding him did brighten him up considerably. His mood lightened still further, to a genuine grin, when she came out from their tent after supper with her hands behind her back, and then, with a flourish, presented his new cotton socks.

"You finished them already!"

"I used to have to help make socks for my brothers. I got fast. Try them under your boots," she said eagerly. "See if they help."

He did so at once, walking experimentally around the dying fire, looking pleased, if a little mismatched in the boots with the truncated trousers that Lakewalker men seemed to wear here in hot weather, when they weren't called on to ride.

"These should be better in summer than those awful lumpy old wool things you were wearing—more darns than yarn, I swear. They'll keep your feet dryer. Help those calluses."

"So fine! Such little, smooth stitches. I'll bet my feet won't bleed with these."

"Your feet bleed?" she said, appalled. "Eew!"

"Not often. Just in the worst of summer or the worst of winter."

"I'll spin up some of that wool for winter later. But I thought you could use these first."

"Indeed." He sat again and removed his boots, drawing the socks off carefully, and kissed her hands in thanks. Fawn glowed.

"I'm going to help Sarri start to spin her plunkin stem flax tomorrow, now the retting's all done," she said. "These women need a wheel to speed things up, they really do. Surely a little one wouldn't be so hard to cart back and forth, and we could all share it around the camp. I could teach them how to use it, give something back for all the help Sarri and Mari have been giving me. Do you think you could bring one back next time you patrol around Lumpton or Glassforge—or West Blue, for that matter? Mama and Nattie could make sure you got a good one," she added in a burst of prudence.

"I could sure try, Spark." And won her heart anew by not protesting a bit about the sight he would present hauling such an unwieldy object atop Copperhead.

She drew him into a promissory sort of cuddle for a time, but at length he recalled whatever Dar had brought to trouble him, and stood up with a sigh.

"Will you be gone long?" she asked.

"Depends on where Fairbolt's got off to."

She nodded, struggling to be content with the vague answer and what all it left out. The dark mood seemed to settle over his shoulders again like a cloak as he strode out to the road and vanished beyond the trees.

Dag tracked Fairbolt down at last at the end of a string of several campsites devoted to the extensive Crow clan on the western side of the island. Fairbolt took one look at his face and led him away from the noisy group of tents, crowded with his and Massape's children and grandchildren, and down to the dock. They sat cross-legged on the boards. Fairbolt's leathery skin was turned to blood-copper by the sunset light, which painted the silky wavelets lapping the shore purple and gleaming orange; his eyes were dark and unrevealing.

Dag drummed his fingers on the wood, and began, "I spoke with Dar a bit ago. Or rather, he spoke to me. He's threatening to go to the camp council. What he thinks they can do, I can't imagine. They can't force a string-cutting." He faltered. "He speaks of banishment."

Fairbolt scarcely reacted. Dag continued, "You're on the council. Has he talked to you?"

"Yes, some. I told him that was a bad plan. Though I suppose there could be worse ones."

Dag braced himself. "What are folks saying, behind my back?"

Fairbolt hesitated, whether embarrassed to repeat the gossip or just organizing his speech Dag wasn't sure. Perhaps the latter, for when he did begin, it was blunt enough. "Massape says some are cruelly amused to see Cumbia's pride crack."

"Idle talk," said Dag.

"Maybe. I'd discount that whole line, except the more they make your mother squirm, the more she leans on Dar."

"Ah. And are there other lines? Naming no names."

"Several." Fairbolt shrugged in a *what-would-you?* gesture. "You want a list? Naming no names."

"Yes. Well, no, but . . . yes."

Fairbolt drew breath. "To start, anyone who's ever been part of a patrol that came to grief relying on farmer aid. Or who endured ingratitude rescuing farmers whose panic resulted in unnecessary patroller injuries or deaths."

Dag tilted his head, half-conceding, half-resisting. "Farmers are untrained. The answer is to train them, not to scorn them."

Fairbolt passed on this with a quirk of his lips and continued, ticking off his fingers, "Anyone who has ever had a relative or friend harassed or ambushed and beaten or killed by farmers over misguided fears about Lakewalker sorcery."

"If we kept less to ourselves, there wouldn't be such misunderstandings. Folks would know better."

Fairbolt ignored this, too. "More closely still, any patroller or ex-patroller who has ever been made to give up a farmer lover themselves. Some pretty bitter anger, there. A few wish you well, but more wonder how you're getting away with it. Those who have had the ugly job of enforcing the rules aren't best pleased with you, either. These people have made real sacrifices, and feel justifiably betrayed."

Dag rubbed his fingers gently back and forth along the wood grain, polished smooth by the passage of many feet. "Fawn slew a malice. She shared a death. She's . . . different."

"I know you think so. Thing is, everyone thinks their own situation was special, too. Which it was, to them. If the rules aren't for everyone, a system for finishing arguments turns into a morass of argument that never ends. And we don't have the time."

Dag looked away from Fairbolt's stern gaze and into the orange disk of the sun, now being gnawed by the black-silhouetted trees across the lake. "I don't know what Dar imagines he can make me do. I made an oath in my ground."

"Aye," said Fairbolt dryly, "in conflict with your prior duty and known responsibilities. You sure did. I swear you look like a man trying to stunt-ride two horses, standing with one foot on the back of each. Fine if he can keep 'em together, but if they gallop up two separate paths, he has to choose, fall, or be torn apart."

"I meant—mean—to keep my duties yoked. If I can."

"And if you can't? Where will you fall?"

Dag shook his head.

Fairbolt frowned at the shimmering water, gone luminous in the twilight to match the sky. A few last swallows swooped and wheeled, then made away for their nests. "The rules issue cuts another way. If it's seen that even so notable a patroller as Dag Redwing can't evade discipline, it makes it that much easier to block the next besotted idiot."

"Am I notable?"

Fairbolt cast him a peculiar look. "Yes."

"Dag Bluefield," Dag corrected belatedly.

"Mm."

Dag sighed and shifted to another tack. "You know the council. Will they cooperate with Dar? How much has he put to them privately already? Was his talk today a first probing threat, or my final chance?"

Fairbolt shrugged. "I know he's been talking to folks. How fast would you think he'll move?"

Dag shook his head once more. "He hates disputes. Hates getting his knife-work interrupted. It takes all his concentration, I know. By choice, I don't think he'd involve himself at all, but if he has to, he'll try to get it all over with as quickly as possible. So he can get back to work. He'll be furious—not so much with me, but about that. He'll push."

"I read him that way as well."

"Has he spoken to you? Fairbolt, don't let me get blindsided, here."

This won another fishy look. "And would you have me repeat my confidential talks with you to him?"

"Um." Dag trusted the fading light concealed his flush. He leaned his back, which was beginning to ache, against a dock post. "Another question, then. Is anyone but Dar like to try to bring this to a head?"

"Formally, with the council? I can think of a few. They'll leave it to your family if they can, but if the Redwing clan fails in its task, they might be moved to step forward."

"So even if I smooth down Dar, it won't be over. Another challenge and another will pop up. Like malices."

Fairbolt raised his eyebrows at this comparison, but said nothing.

Dag continued slowly, "That suggests the road to go down is to settle it, publicly and soon. Once the council has ruled, the same charge can't be brought again. Stop 'em all." *One way or another.* He grimaced in distaste.

"You and your brother are more alike than you seem," said Fairbolt, turning wry.

"Dar doesn't think so," Dag said shortly. He added after a thoughtful pause, "He hasn't been out in the world as much as I have. I wonder if banishment seems a more frightening fate to him?"

Fairbolt rubbed his lips. "How's the arm?"

"Much better." Dag flexed his hand. "Splints have been off near a week. Hoharie says I can start weapons practice again."

Fairbolt leaned back. "I'm planning to send Mari's patrol back out soon. A lot of time lost at Glassforge to make up, plus her patrol isn't the only one that's run late this season. When will you be ready to ride again?"

Dag shifted, unfolding his legs to disguise his unease. "Actually, I was thinking of taking some of my unused camp time, till Fawn's more settled in."

"So when will that be? Leaving aside the matter of the council."

Dag shrugged. "For her part alone, not long. I don't think there's a camp task she can't do, if she's properly taught. I have no doubt in her." His hesitation this time stretched out uncomfortably. "I have doubt in us."

"Oh?"

He said quietly, "Betrayal cuts two ways as well, Fairbolt. Sure, when you go out on patrol you worry for your family in camp—sickness, the accidents of daily life, maybe even a malice attack—there's a residue of danger, but not, not . . . *untrust*. But once you start to wonder, it spreads like a stain. Who can I trust to stand by my wife in her need, and who will fold and leave her to take the brunt alone? My mother, my brother? Clearly not. Cattagus, Sarri? Cattagus is weak and ill, and Sarri has her own troubles. You?" He stared hard at Fairbolt.

To Fairbolt's credit, he did not drop his gaze. "I suppose the only way you'll find out is to test it."

"Yeah, but it won't exactly be a test of Fawn, now, will it."

"You'll have to sooner or later. Unless you mean to quit the patrol." The look that went with this remark reminded Dag of Hoharie's surgical knives.

Dag sighed. "There's soon and there's too soon. You can cripple a young horse, which would have done fine with another year to let its bones grow into themselves, by loading it too soon. Young patrollers, too." *And young wives?*

Fairbolt, after a long pause, gave a nod at this. "So when is not-too-soon, Dag? I need to know where I can put your peg. And when."

"You do," Dag conceded. "Can you give me a bit more time to answer? Because I don't think I can leave the council aside."

Fairbolt nodded again.

"Mind, I can only answer for myself and Fawn. I don't control the acts of anyone else."

"You can persuade," said Fairbolt. "You can shape. You can, dare I suggest, not be a stubborn fool."

Too late for that. This man, Dag was reminded, had six hundred other patrollers to track. Enough for tonight. The frogs were starting their serenade, the mosquitoes were out in companies, and the fat double-winged dragonflies darting over the lake were giving way to the night patrol of flitting bats. He levered himself to his feet, bade Fairbolt a polite good evening, and walked into the gathering dark.

8

They were making ready to lie down in their bedroll before Dag reported his conversations with his brother and Fairbolt to Fawn. From the brevity of his descriptions, compared to the time he'd been gone, Fawn suspected he was leaving a good bit out; more than these clipped essentials had cast him into his dark mood. *Brothers can do that.* But his explanation of the camp council was frightening enough.

In the light of their candle stub atop Dag's trunk, which did for their bedside table, Fawn sat cross-legged, and said, "Seven people can just vote you—us—to be banished? Just like that?"

"Not quite. They have to sit and hear arguments from both sides. And they'll each speak with other folks around their islands, gather opinions, before delivering a ruling of this . . . this gravity."

"Huh." She frowned. "Somehow I thought your people not liking me being here would take the form of . . . I don't know. Leaving dead rotten animals outside our door to step on in the morning, nasty tricks like that. Fellows in masks setting fire to our tent, or sneaking from the bushes and beating you up, or shaving my head, or something."

Dag raised quizzical brows. "Is that the form it would take in farmer country?"

"Sometimes." Sometimes worse, from tales she'd heard.

"A mask won't hide who you are from groundsense. Anyone wants to do something that ugly around here, they sure can't do it in secret."

"That would slow 'em up some, I guess," allowed Fawn.

"Yes, and . . . this isn't a matter for boys' tricks. Our marriage cords, if nothing else, draw it up to another level altogether. Serious dilemmas take serious thought from serious folks."

"Shouldn't we be making a push to talk to those serious folks, too? Dar shouldn't have it all his own way, seems to me."

"Yes—no . . . *blight* Dar," he added, in a burst of aggravation. "This shoves me into exactly the worst actions to ease you in here smoothly. Drawing attention, forcing folks to choose sides. I wanted to lie low, and while everyone was waiting for someone else to do something, let the time for choosing just slip on by. I figured a year would do it."

Fawn blinked in astonishment at his timetable. Perhaps a year didn't seem like such a long time to him? "This isn't exactly your favorite sort of arguin', is it?"

He snorted. "Not hardly. It's the wrong thing at the wrong time, and . . . and I'm not very smooth at it, anyway. Fairbolt is. Twenty minutes talking with him, and your head's turned around. Good camp captain. But he's made it clear this is my own bed to lie in." He added in a lower voice, "And I hate begging for favors. Figured I used up a life's supply long before this." A slight thump of his left arm on the bedroll indicated what favors he was thinking of, which made Fawn huff in turn. Whatever special treatment had won him his arm harness and let him back on patrol must, it seemed to her, have been paid back in full a good long time ago.

Nevertheless, Dag began the next morning to show their presence more openly by taking Fawn out in the narrow boat for plunkin delivery duty. The first step was to paddle out to a gathering raft, which over the season had worked its way nearly to the end of their arm of the lake and would shortly start back up the other side. A dozen Lakewalkers of various ages, sexes, and states of undress manned the ten-foot-square lashing of tree trunks, which seemed to be munching its way down a long stretch of water lilies. This variety had big, almost leathery leaves that stuck up out of the water like curled fans, and small, simple, unappealing yellow flowers, which also stood up on stalks. The crew worked steadily to dig, then trim and separate the stems, roots, and ears, and then replant. Churned-up mud and plant bits left a messy trail in the raft's inching wake.

Dag saluted an older woman who seemed to be in charge. A couple of naked boys rolled a load of plunkins into the narrow boat that made it ride alarmingly low in the water, and after polite farewells, Dag and Fawn paddled off again, a good bit more sluggishly. Fawn was intensely conscious of the stares following them.

Delivery consisted of coasting along the lakeshore, pulling up to each campsite in turn, and tossing plunkins into big baskets affixed to the ends of their docks, which at least showed Fawn where their daily plunkins had been coming from all this time. She hated the way the boat wobbled as she scrambled around at this task, and was terrified of dropping a plunkin overboard and having to go after it, especially in water over her head, but at length they'd emptied their boat out again. And then went back for another load and did it all over again, twice.

Dag waved or called a *how de'* to folks in other boats or along the shore, seemingly the custom here, and exchanged short greetings with anyone working on the docks as their boat pulled up, introducing Fawn to enough new folks that she quickly lost track of the names. No one was spiteful, though some looked bemused; but few of the return stares or greetings seemed really warm to her. After a while she thought she would have preferred rude, or at least blunt, questions to this silent appraisal. But the little ordeal came to an end at noon, when they climbed wearily back up the bank to Tent Bluefield. Where lunch, Fawn reflected glumly, would be plunkin.

They repeated the exercise on the next four mornings, until the raft-folk and dock-folk stopped looking at them in surprise. In the afternoons, Fawn began to help Sarri with the task of spinning up her new plunkin flax, and, for more novelty, aid Cattagus with his rope-braiding, one of his several sitting-down camp chores that did not strain his laboring lungs. His breathing, he explained between wheezes, was permanent damage left from a bad bout of lung fever a few years back that had nearly led him to share, and had forced him finally to give up patrolling and grow, he claimed, fat.

Fawn found she liked working with Cattagus more than with any other of the campsite's denizens. Sarri was stiff and wary, or distracted by her children, and Mari wryly dubious, but Cattagus seemed to regard *Dag's farmer girl* with grim amusement. It was daunting to reflect that his detachment might stem from how close he stood to death—Mari, for one, was very worried about leaving him come bad weather—but Fawn finally decided that he'd likely always had a rude sense of humor. Further, though not as patient a teacher as Dag, he was nearly as willing, introducing her to the mysteries of arrow-making. He produced arrows not only for his patroller wife, but for Razi and Utau as well. It was very much a two-handed chore; Dar, it seemed, had used to make Dag's for him, in his spare time. It didn't need, nor did Cattagus make, any comment that Dag now needed a new source. Fawn found in herself a knack for balance and a sure and steady hand at fletching, and shortly grew conversant with the advantages and disadvantages of turkey, hawk, and crow quills.

Dag trudged off several times to, as he said, *scout the territory,* returning looking variously worried, pleased, or head-down furious. Fawn and Cattagus were sitting beneath a walnut tree having a fletching session when he stalked back from one of the latter sort, ducked into the tent without a word, returned with his bow and quiver, grabbed a plunkin from the basket by the tent flap, and set it up on a stump in the walnut grove. Within fifteen minutes he had reduced the plunkin to something resembling a porcupine smashed by a boulder and was breathing almost steadily again as he tried to unwedge his deeply buried near misses from the tree behind the stump. There were no wider misses to retrieve from the grove beyond.

"That one sure ain't gettin' away," Cattagus observed, with a nod at the remains of the plunkin. "Anybody I know?"

Dag, treading over to them, smiled a bit sheepishly. "Doesn't matter now." He sat down with a sigh, unlatched and set aside his short bow, then picked up one of the new arrows and examined it with a judicious eye. "Better and better, Spark."

She decided this was deliberate diversion. "You know, you keep saying I shouldn't come with you so's folks'll talk frank and free, but it seems to me you might get further with some if they were to talk a little less frank and free."

"That's a point," he conceded. "Maybe tomorrow."

But the next morning ended up being dedicated to some overdue weapons practice, with an eye to the fact that Mari's patrol would be going out again soon. Saun turned up, invited by Razi and Utau, and Fawn grew conscious for the first time of how few visitors had come to the campsite. If she and Dag were indeed a wonder of the lake, she would have thought curiosity, if not friendliness, should have brought a steady stream of neighbors making excuses to get a peek at her. She wasn't sure how to interpret their absence: politeness, or shunning? But Saun was as nice to her as ever.

The session began with archery, and Fawn, fascinated, made herself useful trotting into the walnut grove after misses, or tossing plunkin rinds up into the air for moving targets. Her arrows seemed to work as well as her mentor's, she saw with satisfaction. Cattagus sat on a stump and appraised the archers' skills as freely as his breathlessness would allow. Saun was inclined to be daunted by him, but Mari gave him back as good as she got; Dag just smiled. The five patrollers moved on to blade practice with wooden knives and swords. Mari was clever and fast, but outmatched in strength and endurance, not a surprise in a woman of seventy-five, and soon promoted herself to a seat beside Cattagus to shrewdly critique the others.

The action grew hotter then, with what seemed to Fawn a great many very dirty moves, not to mention uncertainty of whether she was watching sword fighting or wrestling. The clunk and clatter of the wooden blades was laced with cries of *Ow!*, *Blight it!*, or, to Saun's occasional gratification, *Good one!* Dag pushed the others on far past breathlessness, on the gasped-out but convincing theory that the real thing didn't come with rest breaks, so's you'd better know how to move when you couldn't hardly move at all.

The sweat-soaked and filthy combatants then took a swim in the lake, emerging smelling no worse than usual, and assembled in the clearing to munch plunkin and try, without success, to persuade Cattagus to uncork one of his last carefully hoarded jugs of elderberry wine from the prior fall. Dag, slouched against a stump and smiling at the banter, suddenly frowned and sat up, his head turning toward the road.

"What is it?" Fawn, sitting beside him, asked quietly.

"Fairbolt. Not happy about something."

She lowered her voice further. "Think it's our summons from the camp council, finally?" She had lived in increasing dread of the threat.

"Could be . . . no. I'm not sure." Dag's eyes narrowed.

By the time Fairbolt's trotting horse swung into the clearing, all the patrollers had quieted and were sitting up watching him. He was riding bareback, and his face was as grim as Fawn had ever seen. She found her heart beating faster, even though she was sitting still.

Fairbolt pulled up his horse and gave them all a vague sort of salute. "Good, you're all here. I'm looking for Saun, first."

Saun, startled, stood up from his stump. "Me, sir?"

"Yep. Courier just rode in from Raintree."

Saun's home hinterland. Bad news from there? Saun's face drained, and Fawn could imagine his thoughts suddenly racing down a roster of family and friends.

"They've got themselves a bad malice outbreak north of Farmer's Flats, and are calling for help."

Everyone straightened in shock at this. Even Fawn knew by now that to call for aid outside one's own hinterland was a sign of things going very badly indeed.

"Seems the blighted thing came up practically under a farmer town, and grew like crazy before it was spotted," Fairbolt said.

Saun's gnawed plunkin rind fell from his hand. "I'll ride—I have to get home at once!" he said, and lurched forward. He caught himself, breathless, and looked beseechingly at Fairbolt. "Sir, may I have leave to go?"

"No."

Saun flushed, but before he could speak, Fairbolt went on, "I want you to ride with the rest tomorrow morning as pathfinder."

"Oh. Yes, of course." Saun subsided, but stayed on his flexing feet, like a dog straining on the end of a chain.

"Being the high season, almost three-quarters of our patrols are out right now," Fairbolt continued, his gaze sweeping over the suddenly grave patrollers in front of him. "For our first answer, I figure I can pull up the next three patrols due to go out. Which includes yours, Mari."

Mari nodded. Cattagus scowled unhappily, his right hand rubbing on his knee, but he said nothing.

"Being out of the hinterland, it's on a volunteer basis as usual—you folks all in?"

"Of course," murmured Mari. Razi and Utau, after a glance at each other, nodded as well. Fawn hardly dared move. Her breath felt constricted. Dag said nothing, his face oddly blank.

Saun wheeled to him. "You'll come, won't you, Dag? I know you meant to sit out our next patrol in camp, and you've earned some time off your feet, but, but—!"

"I want to speak to Dag private-like," said Fairbolt, watching him. "The rest of you can start to collect your gear. I figure to send the first company west at dawn."

"Couldn't we start tonight? If everyone pulled themselves together?" said Saun earnestly. "Time—you never know how much difference a little time could make."

Dag grimaced at that one, not, Fawn thought, in disagreement.

Fairbolt shook his head, although his glance was sympathetic. "Folks are spread all over the lake right now. It'll take all afternoon just to get the word out. You can't outpace the company you're leading, pathfinder."

Saun gulped and nodded.

Fairbolt gave a gesture of dismissal, and everyone scattered, Razi and Utau for their tent, where Sarri had come to the awning post with her little boy on her hip, staring hard at the scene, Mari and Cattagus to theirs. Saun waved and started jogging up the road back to his own campsite on the island's other end.

Fairbolt slid down from his horse and left it to trail its reins and browse. Dag motioned toward Tent Bluefield, sheltered in the orchard, and Fairbolt nodded. Fawn hurried after their matched patrollers' strides. Fairbolt eyed her, neither inviting nor excluding, so when each man took a seat on an up-ended log in the shade of her tent flap, she did, too. Dag gave her an acknowledging nod before turning his full attention on his commander.

"With three patrols sent out in a bunch, they're going to need an experienced company captain," Fairbolt began.

"Rig Crow. Or Iwassa Muskrat," said Dag, watching him warily.

"My first two choices exactly," Fairbolt said. "If they weren't both a hundred and fifty miles away right now."

"Ah." Dag hesitated. "Surely you're not looking to me for this."

"You've been a company captain. Further, you're the only patroller in camp right now who's been in on a real large-group action."

"And so successfully, too," murmured Dag sourly. "Just ask the survivors. Oh, that's right—there weren't any. That'll give folks lots of confidence in my leadership, sure enough."

Fairbolt made an impatient chopping motion. "Your habit of picking up extra duty means you've worked, at one time or another, with almost every other patroller in camp. No problem with unfamiliar grounds, or not knowing your people pretty much through and through. Weaknesses, strengths, who can be relied on for what."

Dag's slow blink didn't deny this.

Fairbolt lowered his voice. "Another angle. I shouldn't be saying this, but your summons to stand before the camp council is due out in a very few more days. But they can't set a hearing if you're not here to receive the order. You wanted delay? Here's your chance. Do a good job on this, and if you're still called to stand before the council, you'll do so with that much more clout."

"And if I do badly?" Dag inquired, his voice very dry.

Fairbolt scratched his nose and grinned without humor. "Then we are all going to be having much more pressing problems than one patroller's personal lapses."

"And if I'm killed in the field, the problem goes away, too," said Dag with false brightness.

"Now you're thinking like a captain," said Fairbolt affably. "Knew you could."

Dag huffed a very short laugh.

Patroller humor, Fawn realized. *Yeep.*

Fairbolt sat back more seriously. "Not my first pick of solutions, though. Dag, when it comes to malices you're known as about the most volunteerin' fellow in camp. This is your chance to show 'em all nothing's changed."

Dag shook his head. "I don't know what's changed. Changing. More than . . . I sometimes think." His hand touched his left arm, and while Fairbolt might take it to mean his marriage cord, Fawn wondered how much the gesture was for his ghost hand.

Fairbolt glanced at Fawn. "Aye, it's a hard thing to ask a patroller newly string-bound to go out in the field under any circumstances. But this one's bad, Dag. I didn't want to give more details in front of Saun right off, but word from the courier is that they've already lost hundreds of people, farmers and Lakewalkers both. The malice has shifted from its first lair under that poor farmer town to attack Bonemarsh Camp. Most everyone got away, but there's no question the malice captured some. Once our first company is dispatched, I'm going to start scraping up a second—absent gods know from where—because I have an ugly hunch they'll be wanted."

Dag rubbed his brow. "Raintree folks will be off-balance, then. Focusing on the wrong things, defense and refugees and the wounded. People will get frantic for each other, and lose sight of the main chance. Get a knife in the malice. Everything else is a distraction."

"An outsider might be better at keeping his head," said Fairbolt suggestively.

"Not necessarily. It's been thirty years since I patrolled in north Raintree, but I still remember friends."

"And the terrain?"

"Some," Dag admitted reluctantly.

"Exactly. Never been out that way, myself. I figured, by the by, that I'll pair Saun as pathfinder with the company captain."

Dag did not respond directly to this, but touched his throat. "I don't have a primed knife right now. First time I've walked bare in decades. I usually carried two, sometimes three. You wondered how I took out so many malices, besides the extra patrolling? Folks gave me more knives. It was that simple."

"Not the captain's job to place the knife. It's his job to place the knife-wielders."

"I know," Dag sighed.

"And I know you know. So." Fairbolt stood up. "I'm going to finish passing the word up this side of the island. I'll ride back this way. You can give me your answer then." He didn't say *Talk it over with each other,* but the invitation was plain. He stared a moment at Fawn, as if thinking of making some plea to her, but then just shook his head. His horse came wandering over in a way that she suspected was not by chance, and he stepped up on his log seat and swung his leg over. He was back on the road in moments, setting the animal into a lope.

Dag had risen when Fairbolt had; he stood staring after him, but his face was drawn and inward-looking, as if contemplating quite another view. Her own face feeling as stiff and congealed as cold dough, Fawn rose too, and went to him. They walked into each other's arms and held on tight.

"Too soon," whispered Dag. He set her a little from him, looking down in anxiety. Fawn wondered whatever was the use of putting on a brave face when he could see right through to whatever wild roil her ground was in right now. She stiffened her spine anyhow, fighting to keep her breathing even and her lips firm.

"Fairbolt's right about the experience, though," he continued, his voice finding its volume again. "This sort of thing is different from hunting sessiles, or even from that mess we had near Glassforge. I run down the patrol lists in my head and think, *They don't know.* Especially the youngsters. How far north of Farmer's Flats was that town, anyway? Farmer settlements aren't supposed to be allowed above the old cleared line . . ." He shook his head abruptly, and grasped her hands. His gold eyes glittered with an expression she'd never seen in them before; she thought it might be *frantic.*

She swallowed, and said, "You did this once. So the question isn't, Can you do it? but, Can you do it better than someone doing it for the first time ever?"

"No—yes—maybe . . . It's been a while. Still—if not me, who am I condemning to go in my place? Someone has to—"

She reached up and pressed her fingers to his lips, which stilled. She said simply, "Who are you arguin' with, Dag?"

He was silent for the space of several heartbeats, though at length a faint wry smile turned his mouth, just a little.

Fawn took a deeper breath. "When I married a patroller instead of a farmer, I figured I must be signing up for something like this. You for the leaving . . . me for the being left." His hand found her shoulder, and tightened. "It's come on sooner than we thought, but . . . there has to be a first time." She raised her arms to catch his beloved cheekbones between her hands, pressing hard, and gave his head a stern little shake. "Just you make sure it's not the last, you hear?"

He gathered her in. She could feel his heartbeat slow. The scent of him, as she turned and buried her face in his shirt, overwhelmed her: sweat and summer and sun and just plain Dag. She opened her mouth and widened her nostrils as though she could breathe him in and store him up. *Forever. And a day.* Well, there wasn't any forever. *Then I'll take the day.*

"You're not afraid to be left alone here?" he murmured into her curls.

"On the list of things I'm afraid of, that one's just dropped down. Quite a ways."

She could feel his smile. "You have to grant, I've always come back so far."

"Yeah, the other patrollers in Glassforge said you were like a cat, that way." *But they all went out looking for you anyhow.* "Papa used to say to me, when I got all upset about one of our barn cats that had got its fool self in a fix and was crying all woeful, *Lovie, you ever seen a cat skeleton in a tree?*"

That deep chuckle she so loved, too seldom felt lately, rumbled through his chest. They stood there wrapped in each other until the unwelcome sound of trotting hoofbeats echoed from the road. "Right, then," muttered Fawn. She backed off and stared up.

He was looking down with a curious smile. He returned her nod. Squeezed and released her, all but her hand. Turned to face Fairbolt, looking down from his horse.

Fairbolt didn't speak, merely raising his brows in question.

"I'll want to talk to that courier," said Dag. "And have a fresh look at whatever large-scale maps we have of the northern Raintree region."

Fairbolt accepted this with no more comment than a short jerk of his chin. "Get up behind me, then. I'll give you a lift to headquarters." He kneed his horse around, and Dag stepped up on a stump and slid aboard. The burdened beast took to the road again at a rapid walk.

Fawn's eyes were hot but dry. Mostly. Blinking, she ducked inside her tent flap to see what she could do to help get Dag's saddlebags in order.

9

It was midnight before Dag returned to Tent Bluefield. Fawn raised her head at the sound of his steps, falling slower than usual out of the dark, and poked up their campfire coals with a stick, lighting their candle stub from it. In the weak flare of golden light his lips gave her a smile, but his eyes seemed abstracted.

"I was wonderin' if you were going to get any chance to sleep," she said quietly, rising.

"Some. Not much. We'll be saddling the horses just before dawn."

"That's no way to start out, all tired. Should I stay awake to get you up?" It wouldn't be that many more hours at this point.

"No. Someone will come for me. I'll try to go out quiet."

"Don't you dare go sneaking off without waking me," she said, a little fiercely, and led him inside, where the contents of his saddlebags were laid out in neat stacks. His bow lay next to them, its quiver stuffed with arrows. "I was going to pack up your gear, but then I thought I'd better have you check first, see if I got everything right."

He nodded, knelt, and began handing her stacks, briefly inspected; she tucked them into the bags as tidily as she could. The only thing he set aside was his tambourine in its leather case. Fawn wanted to ask *Won't you need that to celebrate the kill?* but then thought perhaps he wanted to protect it, this riding-out being out of the routine. The other possibilities she refused to contemplate. She closed the flaps, buckled them, and turned to pick up the last item, laid out on the trunk beside the flickering stub.

"You've got no sharing knife. You want to take this one?" She held her—their—knife out to him, tentatively.

His face grew grave. Still kneeling, he took it from her and drew it from its sheath, frowning at the faded writing on the bone blade. "Dar thinks it won't work," he said at last.

"I wasn't thinking of it for your first pick. Only to keep by you just . . . just in case. If there were no other choices."

"There will be a dozen and more other knives among my company."

"How many patrollers are going?"

"Seventy."

"Will it be enough?"

"Who knows? One is enough, but it can take all the rest to get that one to the right place at the right time. Fairbolt will hold all the regular patrols going out, and fold in the ones coming home, but he has to think not only of sending help, but of defense."

"I'd think sending help would *be* the best defense."

"To a point. Things might go badly in Raintree, but also another malice could pop up here in Oleana. Since this commotion will put everyone behind schedule—again—it's just that more likely. That's the problem with malices emerging so randomly. Nice when we go months and months at a time without one, but when they come up in a bunch, we can get overwhelmed." His brows drew in; slowly, he resheathed the knife, handing it back to her with a some-what apologetic grimace. "Better not. I have an old bad habit of jumping into things feetfirst, and that's not my job this time."

She accepted his words, and the knife, with a little nod, although her heart ached.

"I have some ideas," he went on, his mind clearly elsewhere. Or perhaps several elsewheres. "But I'm going to need more recent news than what that courier brought. She near rode her horse to death, but she was still two days getting here. Part of what went wrong at Wolf Ridge was due to, hm, not so much bad, as old information. Though for whatever consolation, I'm not sure but what we'd have done just the same if we had known what was coming down on us. If we'd spared a few more to the ridge, it would just have been that many more dead. And a few was all we had." His mouth set in irony. "The help from out of the hinterland not having arrived yet."

Fawn didn't think Dag's company would be dawdling on their road tomorrow.

There seemed so little she could do for him. Socks. Arrows. Packing. It all felt so trivial. All things he had accomplished perfectly well for himself for years before she'd come along to so disrupt his life. She might help by putting him to bed and sitting on him, maybe; it was clear his body needed its rest, and equally clear his mind would scarcely allow it. She raised her hands and began tenderly unbuttoning his shirt. As her wrist moved, her eye was caught by the gold beads of her marriage cord. *He needs to be thinking about his task, not about me.* But time was growing desperately short.

"Dag . . ."

"Mm, Spark?" His fingers in turn gently twisted themselves in the curls of her hair, letting the locks flow over and between them.

"You can feel me through your wedding cord, right? And all the other married Lakewalkers, Mari and Cattagus and all, they can do the same for each other?"

He nodded. She drew his shirt off that long, strappy-muscled torso, folding it up atop his clean and mended riding trousers for morning. Later in the night. Whatever that grim predawn hour was.

She went on, "Well, I can't. I've taken your word that our cords work the same as everyone else's, but I can't feel it for myself."

"Others can tell. And tell you."

"Yeah, well, except I can't be all the time asking, twenty times a day. Cattagus for one doesn't take to being pestered. And besides, he'll have his own worries about Mari."

"True," he conceded, eyeing her.

She slipped out of her own shirt, his hand helping not so much for need, as to trail over her skin in passing. The light touch made her shiver. "I want to know in my own heart. Isn't there anything at all you can do to, to *make* me feel you? The way all the others can?"

He said after a moment, "Not the way the others can, no. You're no Lakewalker."

Nor ever would be, but his wording caught her attention. "Some other way?"

"Let me . . . think about that for a little, Spark. It would take some unusual groundwork."

Stripped for sleep, he was altogether unaroused. If he felt half as distracted as she did right now, that was no surprise. She felt obscurely that she ought to send him off having been thoroughly made love to, but for the first time ever, such intimacy felt forced and unhappy. That was no good either.

"You're all tense. How if you lie down and I give you a back rub? Might help you sleep."

"Spark, you don't have to—"

"And a real good foot rub," she added prudently.

He rolled over into their bedroll with a muffled noise indicating abject surrender, and she smiled a little. She started at his neck. His muscles there were plenty hard and tense, though this seemed poor compensation for the limpness elsewhere. The corded unease gave itself up but slowly as her hands pressed, slid, caressed. Unhurriedly, she worked her way from tousled top to gnarly toe, not making love, just loving.

Perhaps the lack of expectation paid off; in any case, when he at length rolled over again a more alert interest had clearly returned to him. There might yet be sleep for him tonight, if the long way around. She slid down against him to capture his mouth in a deep kiss; his own hand snaked around her shoulder and began tracing lazily over her. She tried to soak up every sensation, hold them like painted patterns on her skin, but racing time washed them constantly beyond her reach.

He arched above her like a clouded night sky, lowering, entering her; if not easily, far more easily than their first urgent fumbles on their wedding night. *Exercise, indeed* she thought, and smiled in memory. She felt a pang of regret that tonight was bound to be futile for trying to catch a child, both too late for this month and too soon for her healing. In these hurried, frightening circumstances, she might have been tempted to take a chance on the healing. Still . . . surely it would be ill omened to conceive their first child out of fear and despair. *Dag'll come back. He must come back.*

He slipped his left arm behind her back, clutched her, and heaved them both over. She adjusted herself with a wriggle and sat up, looking down at him curiously. His face held a different abstraction, and she feared for a moment that they would again lose their intimate impetus to the creeping chill of tomorrow's worries.

No, evidently not. But he watched her though half-lidded eyes as his left arm began a peculiar circuit, briefly touching the cord bound on her left wrist, then her forehead, heart, belly, groin, and wrist again.

"What are you doing?"

"Not sure. Something by feel. A little left-handed groundwork, maybe."

What he'd called his left-handed groundwork hadn't appeared in their lovemaking since he'd recovered the use of his right hand. She had missed his eerie caresses, though she supposed it wasn't to her credit that they'd made her feel so downright smug for marrying a black sorcerer instead of a mere farmer. But that seemed not to be what he was about, this time.

"I'm trying to patch a bit of ground reinforcement into you that will dance with my ground in your cord. Shaped inside your own ground—pretty ground! If you—as you—grow open to me, I think I can coax it in through natural channels. Not sure exactly what the effect will be. Just . . ."

She opened eyes, heart, and body to him, wide and vulnerable. "Need blood?" she asked breathlessly.

She wasn't sure if his huff was a laugh or a sob. "Don't think so. Just . . . just love me . . ."

She found their rhythm again, taking over the lovemaking, abandoning the magic-making to him. His eyes were as wide and black as she'd ever seen them, pools of night with liquid stars in their depths. His left arm continued its rounds, more slowly but somehow more intensely. It ended laid diagonally across his belly just as his back began to arch. Her eyes squeezed shut as the wonderful, increasingly familiar wave of sensation coursed up from her heated loins, stopping her breath. A stranger, sharper wave of sweet warmth wound with it, rising up through her heart and down her arm in time with the pulse of her blood.

Oh. Oh!

Then, as he sank beneath her, the ecstatic shudders in his own body damping out, she said "Oh!" in quite another voice of surprise. She clapped her right hand to the cord encircling her left wrist. "It—it *tingles*. It feels like winter sparks."

"Too much? Does it hurt?" he wheezed anxiously, opening his eyes again.

"No, not at all. Strange . . . oh! It's fading a bit. Am I losing . . . ?"

"You should be able to call it up to you when you wish. Try."

She bit her lip and concentrated. The warm sensation faded. "No . . . no, oh dear. Am I not doing it right?"

"Instead of concentrating, try relaxing. Make yourself open."

"That," she said after a minute, "is a lot harder than concentrating."

"Yes. Not force, but persuasion. Enticement."

She sat astride him with her eyes closed, right hand wrapping her wrist, and tried again. She imagined herself smiling wordlessly, trying to attract Dag over to her for a kiss and a cuddle. *I love you so much . . .*

A prickling heat around, no, inside her wrist seemed like an answering whisper, *Yes, I'm here.* "That's you? In the cord?"

"That's a bit of me that's been in the cord since that night in your aunt Nattie's weaving room," said Dag, smiling up at her.

"And you can feel a bit of me in your cord like this, too?"

"Yep." He added in caution, "It may not last more than a few weeks, as you absorb the ground reinforcement."

"It'll do fine." She vented a long, elated sigh, and slumped down across his chest. But since he couldn't kiss any more of her than the top of her head in this position, she roused herself and reluctantly parted from him. They cleaned up briefly and lay back down just as the candle guttered out. Dag was asleep before she was.

She woke in the dark and rolled over to clutch an empty bedroll. Her heart lurched in panic. Feeling around frantically, she found Dag's dented pillow still warm. She gripped her cord, calmed her breathing, and tried to sense him. *Alive*, of course, the reassuring prickle told her; just over . . . thataway.

He's just gone out to the slit trench, you fool girl, she scolded herself in relief. She rolled on her side, bringing her hands up to her breasts, and bent her head to kiss the heavy, twice-blessed braid.

The tent flap lifted in a few minutes. The shadows outside were nearly as inky as in here. Dag slipped his bare, chilled body into their bedroll again; they wound their arms around each other, and Fawn did her best to share heat through her skin so that he might ease swiftly into whatever space of sleep was left to him this night. But before his breathing slowed, a slap sounded on the leather of their tent flap, and a low voice called, "Dag?" *Utau,* Fawn thought.

"I'm awake," Dag groaned.

"Omba's girls just brought our horses around."

"Right. Be right with you."

From the middle distance sounded a muffled equine snort, and Copperhead's familiar, irritable squeal. Fawn slipped her shift on in the dark and went out to coax a bit of flame from the gray ashes of their fire, trying to get a last few minutes of light from the melted candle stub in the bottom of its clay cup. Back inside, she found Dag dressed already, running his hand over his gear as if in final inventory. There would be no turning back for forgotten items this trip. His face looked tired and strained, but not, she thought, from fear. At least . . . not physical fear. They shared slices of plunkin, gnawed down quickly and without ceremony. Or, in Fawn's case, appetite.

"Now what?" said Fawn.

"The company will assemble at the headquarters tent. Most folks say good-bye at home."

"Right, then."

He hooked up his saddle, Fawn tottered after with the saddlebags, and they went out to where the horses were tied. Razi, Utau, and Mari were saddling theirs, in the light of a torch held aloft by Cattagus. Sarri stood ready to hand things up. In the east, across this arm of the lake, the black shapes of the trees were just growing distinguishable from the graying sky. Mist shrouded the water, and the grass and weeds underfoot were damp with dew.

Cattagus handed the torch to Sarri long enough to hug Mari, muttering into her knotted gray hair, "Mind your steps, you fool old woman." To which she returned, "You just mind yourself, you fool old man." Despite his wheezing, he gave her a leg up, his hand lingering a moment on her thigh as she settled into her saddle.

Dag gave Copperhead a knee to the belly, ducked the return snap of yellow teeth, and tightened his girth for a second time. He turned to grip Fawn's hands, then embraced her as she flung her arms around him and held hard. He put her from him with a kiss, not on her lips, but on her forehead: not farewell, but blessing. The tenderness and terror of it wrenched her heart as nothing else had this anxious morning.

And then he was heaving himself up on Copperhead. The gelding, clearly refreshed by his holiday in pasture, signified his displeasure at being put back to work so early in the morning by sidling and some halfhearted bucking, firmly checked by his rider. The four patrollers angled onto the road and vanished in the shadows; Fawn saw a few more mounted shapes trotting to catch up. Those left behind turned back silently to their tents, though Cattagus gave his niece Sarri a hug around the shoulders before he went in.

Fawn was entirely unable to contemplate falling back to sleep. She went into her tent and straightened her few belongings—housekeeping was a short task with so little house to keep—and tried to set her mind to the work of the day. Spinning was endless, of course. She was helping Sarri with her weaving in return for share of the tough cloth she was presently making and for teaching Fawn how to sew a pair of Lakewalker riding trousers, but it was too early to go over there. She wasn't hungry enough yet to eat more plunkin.

Instead, she traded her shift for a shirt and skirt, put on her shoes, and walked down the shore road toward the split to the bridge. The gray light was growing, with the faintest tinge of blue; only a few pricking stars still shone down through the leaves. She was not, she discovered, the only person with this notion. A dozen or more Lakewalkers, men and women, old and young, had collected along the main road in small groups, scarcely talking. She tried nodding to some neighbors she recognized from the plunkin delivery chore; at least some nodded back, though none smiled. But nobody was smiling much.

Patience was rewarded in a few minutes by the sound of hoofbeats coming from the woodland road. The cavalcade had already broken into the ground-eating trot of the long-legged patrol horses. Dag was in the lead, riding alongside Saun, listening with a thoughtful frown as the young man spoke; but he swiveled his head and flashed a smile at Fawn in passing, and Saun looked back and managed a surprised salute. Others along the road craned their necks for a glimpse of their own, exchanging a few last waves. One woman ran alongside a young patroller and handed up something folded in a cloth that Fawn thought might be a forgotten medicine kit; in any case, the girl grinned gratefully and twisted in her saddle to thrust it away in her bags.

Fawn wasn't sure how seventy patrollers could seem at once so many and so few. But every one had been well kitted-up: good sturdy gear, fine weapons, good horses. *Good wishes.* And what she'd just seen was only a tenth of Fairbolt's patrollers. It wasn't hard to see where the wealth of this straitened island community was being spent.

As the tail of the company vanished around the bend, the onlookers broke up and began walking back to their tents. Almost at the last, an angular figure emerged from the cover of some straggling, sun-starved honeysuckle bushes across the road. Fawn, startled, recognized Cumbia at the same moment the Lakewalker woman saw her. She gave a nod and a polite knee-dip to her mother-in-law, wondering for a moment if this was a good chance to begin speaking with her again. It occurred to Fawn that this task might actually be easier without Dag and his nervy . . . well, *prickliness* seemed an inadequate word for it. *Pigheadedness* came closer. She mustered up a smile to follow, but Cumbia abruptly turned her head and began walking rapidly down the woodland road, back stiff.

It dawned on Fawn that the preparations for such dark morning departures had for long been Cumbia's task. And Cumbia had once had a husband who hadn't returned from patrol, or only in the form of a deathly bone blade. Was this the first time her son had ridden out without bidding her farewell? Fawn wasn't sure if Cumbia had tried to show herself or hide herself, over there on the other side of the road, but she knew Dag hadn't glanced that way. Dar, Fawn noted, had not come with his mother, and she wondered what it meant.

Face pinched, Fawn turned back onto the shore road. She held her hand over her marriage cord, trying for that reassuring tingle. *Come on, girl, he's not even over the bridge yet.* But *there,* the little prickling answered her silent query nonetheless. *Thataway.* She took a deep breath and walked on.

In the inadequate light of their half dozen campfires flickering across this roadside clearing, Dag walked down the horse lines inspecting, but not with his eyes alone. *Three horses lame.* Not bad for three days of hard pushing. The company had traveled with several packhorses carrying food and precious grain. Patrol horses were normally grass-fed, except now and then in farmer country where grain was easier to come by, but grazing took time and grain gave better strength. The loads of provender were rapidly dwindling; tomorrow morning, they could cache three emptied packsaddles and trade out animals, and leave no one slowing the rest by going double-mounted. *Yet.*

Dag had led his company miles north from Hickory Lake to pick up the straight road west, despite Saun's pleas that he could guide them, once they'd passed the borders of Oleana into Raintree, on a shorter, swifter route. They were now, by Dag's reckoning, a half day's ride due north of Bonemarsh Camp. Not a direction from which relief—or, from the malice's point of view, attack—might be expected. According to the shaken party of Lakewalker refugees, mostly women with children, that they had encountered and questioned late this afternoon, the malice had holed up at Bonemarsh. *Temporarily.* Dag had been waiting for such intelligence. Now he had it, it was time to commit his company to his plan. *No excuses, no delays.*

He sighed and began a roundabout stroll through the settling camp, touching this patroller or that on the shoulder. "Meet by my campfire in a few minutes." Razi and Utau were both among them, and to Dag's deeper regret, Mari and Dirla. Others from other patrols, all with skills known to him; not of bow or sword or spear, though all were proficient enough, but of groundsense control. A few were partnered, but most would be leaving their usual partners behind. *They won't like that.* He wished that might prove the worst of their worries.

The night sky was misty, only a few stars showing through, and the ground was sodden. The company had ridden through miserable rain all day yesterday, blowing east into their faces as they pressed west. The next few days should prove fair, though Dag wondered if that would be more to their advantage or to their quarry's. Hauling logs to keep their haunches out of the damp, the patrollers he'd tapped collected quietly around the dwindling fire, watching attentively as Dag came up. In all, sixteen: his twelve chosen, the other two patrol leaders, Saun, and himself.

"All right"—he drew breath—"this is what we're going to do tomorrow. We're facing a malice not only at its full strength, and mobile, but who now certainly knows what sharing knives are. Getting close enough to kill it will be a lot trickier."

Saun stirred and subsided on his log, and Dag gave him an acknowledging nod. "I know you weren't too happy about not sending word ahead, Saun, but a courier could barely have outpaced us, and I wasn't keen to send a rider alone into woods maybe full of mud-men. We are several days ahead of any other possible reinforcements from the east, and also well ahead of any return messengers. No one knows we're coming, no one knows we're here—including the malice."

Dag controlled an urge to pace, grasping his hook behind his back and rocking slightly instead. "I have—one time—seen a malice this advanced taken down, at Wolf Ridge in Luthlia." The younger patrollers around the fire blinked and sat up; a few older ones nodded knowingly, gazes growing more intent. "The strategy had two pieces, though the way it played out was partly accidental. While the most of us held the malice's mud-men and slaves—and attention—in open battle up on the ridge, by way of diversion, a small group of patrollers good at veiling their grounds slipped up on the lair. There were eight pairs in that group, and each pair carried a sharing knife. Orders were, if anyone went down, their partner didn't stay by them, but was to take the knife and go on. If any pairs went down, the same with their linking pairs." The reverse, Dag and everyone listening to him was aware, of the usual patrol procedure to leave no one behind. "When enough patrollers got close enough to the malice to risk a rush, they did." It had been down to four survivors by then, Dag had been told later. "And that was the end of that malice." But not of the cleanup, which had gone on for months thereafter.

"With a malice that strong, didn't they risk getting their grounds ripped?" asked Dirla. And if it was in fear, none could tell, for her voice did not quaver, and she had her groundsense well locked down.

"Some did," said Dag. Bluntly, without apology. "But I think we can try a similar strike. Whatever resistance is forming up right now south of Bone-marsh Camp, trying to protect Farmer's Flats, gets to play the part of the company on the ridge, overwhelming the malice's concentration. We here"—Dag unlocked his hand and gestured around the campfire—"will be for the sneak attack. You were all picked for your groundsense control."

"Not Saun!" complained Dirla. Saun flushed and glowered at her.

"No, he's our walking map. And someone's going to have to stay with the horses." Dag cast Saun an apologetic look; the boy grimaced but subsided.

"And the rest of the company?" asked Obio Grayheron, one of the remaining patrol leaders.

Dag gave him a short nod. "You'll give us a half-day start. At which point it will either be over—or command will pass to you and you'll be free to try again, try something else, or circle to join forces however you can with the Raintree Lakewalkers."

Obio settled back, digesting this unhappily. "And you're going with . . . well. Yes, of course."

Going with the veiled patrol, Dag finished for him. Because Dag was well-known to be one of the cleverest at that trick in camp. Which begged the question, in his own mind if not theirs, whether he had chosen this strategy because it was the best they could do, or because it played to his personal quirks. Well, if the gamble paid off, the subtle self-doubt would be moot. *And also if it doesn't. You can't lose, old patroller. In a sense.*

Saun was shoving shallow furrows in the drying mud with his boot heel. He looked up. "A little cruel on the folks fighting the retreat toward Farmer's Flats. They don't even get to know they're the bait."

"Neither did most of the folks up on Wolf Ridge," said Dag dryly. And, before Saun could ask *How do you know?* continued, "Saun, Codo, Varleen, you're all familiar with Bonemarsh. Stand up and give us a terrain tutorial."

A customary task; Dag stepped back, the local knowledge stepped forth, and the other patrollers began pelting them with variously shrewd questions as the precious parchment maps were passed around, and annotations scribbled in the dirt with sticks, rubbed out, and redrawn. Dag listened as hard or harder than anyone else, casting and recasting tactical approaches in his head, glumly aware that nine-tenths of the planning would prove useless in the event.

There was enough brains and experience in this bunch that Dag scarcely needed to guide the detailed discussion from here; two bad ideas were knocked down, by Utau and Obio respectively, before Dag could open his mouth, and three better ones that Dag wouldn't even have thought of were spat forth, to be chewed over, altered, and approved with only the barest shaping murmurs on his part. Mari, bless her, took over the problem of coaxing sharing knives from a couple of patrollers who were not going with the veiled patrol, as there were six pairs but only four knives among those here assembled. They even sorted themselves out in new partner-pairs before the group, growing quiet and thoughtful, broke up to seek their bedrolls. Dag hoped they would all sleep better than he seemed likely to.

He rolled on his back in his own bedroll, thin on the cold, damp ground, and searched the hazy sky for stars, trying to quiet the busy noise in his head. There was no point in running over the plans for tomorrow yet again, for the tenth, or was that the twentieth, time. He'd done all he could for tonight, except sleep. But when he forced the roiling concerns for his company out, the ache of missing Fawn crept back in.

He'd grown so accustomed to her companionship in so few weeks, as if she'd always been there, or had slotted into some hollow place within him just her shape that had been waiting for years. He'd come to delight not only in her sweet body, awakening appetites he'd imagined dulled by time, age, and exhaustion, but in the way her shining eyes opened wide in her endless questions, that determined set to her mouth when she faced a new problem, her seemingly boundless world-wonder. And if her hunger for life was a joy to him, his own, renewed, was an astonishment.

He considered the dark side of that bright coin uneasily. Had this marriage also reawakened his fear of death? For long, his inevitable end had seemed neither enemy nor friend, just *there,* accepted, to be worked around like his missing hand. If a fellow had nothing to lose, no risk held much alarm, and fear scarcely clogged thought. If that indifference had given him his noted edge, was that edge becoming blunted?

His right hand crept across his chest to trace the heavy cord wrapping his left arm above the elbow, calling up the reassuring hum of Spark's live ground. Indeed, he had something to lose now. By the shadow of his fear, he began to see the shape of his desire, the stirrings of curiosity for a future not constrained and inevitable but suddenly containing a host of unknowns, places and people altogether unimagined, *unconceived* in all senses. *Blight it, I want to live.* Not the best time to make that discovery, eh? He snorted self-disdain.

Instead of letting his thoughts chase one another back around the circle, he folded his left arm in, rolled over around the absence of Spark, and resolutely closed his eyes. The summer night was short. They would head due south at dawn. *And make sure your body and your wits are riding the same horse, old patroller.*

10

Three days gone, Fawn thought. Today would begin the fourth. Was it over, was it even begun, was Dag's company there yet? Wherever *there* was. Somewhere to the west, yes, and he was still alive; so much her marriage cord now told her. Better than no news, but far, far from enough.

She watched across the campsite as Cattagus settled himself at a log table with knife, awl, and assorted deerhide scraps. His task of the morning was to make a new pair of slippers for his great-niece Tesy, judging by the fascinated way she danced around him, giggling when he tickled her feet after measuring them against his pieces. It might have been mere chance that his right hand rested for a moment on his left wrist before he leaned forward and began cutting.

Fawn stretched her back against the apple tree and forced herself to take up her knitting again. Without Sarri's two children, the campsite would have fallen all too quiet these past days. Although the distraction they'd provided by disappearing for several hours day before yesterday didn't exactly count as a help. They'd been found by a neighbor, pressed into aiding the search, in the woods nearly at the other end of the island—on a quest of their own, looking for their fathers. From their infant points of view, Fawn supposed, Razi and Utau were grand playmates who vanished as mysteriously as they arrived, and Sarri's strained, carefully repeated explanations about *gone on patrol* as baffling as if she'd announced they had gone off to the moon.

Fawn's monthly had begun the day after Dag had left, not a surprise, but an unpleasant reminder of too many regrets. Sarri had shown Fawn how Lake-walker women used cattail fluff as absorbent stuffing for their ragbags, which could be emptied into the slit trench instead of tediously washed out along with the bags, after. The consolation was slight. Fawn had spent two unhappy days sitting, spinning, and cramping, trying without success to decide if this was just a bad one, or some abnormal relic from the malice's mishandling, and wishing Mari were here to ask; but the grinding pain had passed off at last, and her fears eased with her bleeding. Today was much better.

Last row. Fawn cast off neatly and laid the new pair of cotton-yarn socks out on her skirted thigh. They had come out well; the few dropped stitches had been properly recaptured, the heels turned at a natural angle and not something that her brothers would have threatened to dress the rooster in. She grinned in memory of the irate bird stalking around with those misshapen wool bags tied to its feet, though at the time she'd been even madder than it had.

She slipped into her tent and combed her unruly hair, tying it up with a ribbon, then rummaged in her scrap bag for a bit of colored yarn. She folded the socks neatly and made a bow around the bundle with the yarn, to help them look more like a present. Then she straightened up, put her shoulders back, and walked down the road toward Cumbia Redwing's encampment.

Rain had blown through from the west last night, and the tall hickory trees shed sparkling drops as a fresh breeze stirred them. Dag's company must have ridden through the same broad storm, Fawn calculated, though whether it had caught them on the road or in shelter she could not guess. Despite the lingering damp, when Fawn came to the Redwing site she spotted Cumbia working outside, sitting on a leather cushion atop the inevitable upended log seat at one of the crude plank tables. She was wearing the sleeveless calf-length shift that seemed usual for women in summer here, this one a faded bluish-red that spoke of some berry dye. The lean, upright posture was slightly bent, the shining silver head turned down over her task. Skeins of the long-fibered plunkin flax yarn lay out on the table; with a four-pronged lucet, Cumbia was looping them into the strong, light cord Lakewalkers used. As Fawn had hoped, Dar and Omba were nowhere in sight—off to the bone shack and Mare Island, presumably.

Cumbia looked up and scowled as Fawn approached. Her hands, as gnarled with work and age as any farmwife's, went on expertly braiding.

Fawn dipped her knees, and said, "How de'. Nice morning."

Silence.

Unpromising, but Fawn hadn't expected this to be easy. "I knitted Dag a pair of socks to go under his riding boots, very fine. He seemed to like them a lot. So I made a pair for you, too." She thrust out her little bundle. Cumbia made no move to take it. If Fawn had been offering a dead squirrel found rotting in the woods, Cumbia's expression might have been much the same. Fawn set the socks down next to the skeins and stepped back just a little, schooling herself not to turn and flee. She had to hook up some response to build on besides that dead stare. "I was glad to see you come watch Dag ride out the other morning. I know you wanted him to become an officer."

The hands reached the end of some counting turn, stopped, and set the wooden tool on the table with a sharp clack. The scowl deepened. As if the words were jerked from her, Cumbia said, "Not like this."

"How else should it be? It seemed very like Dag."

"It came out all wrong." Cumbia blew out her breath. "It generally does, with that boy. The aggravation and sorrow he has brought me, first to last, can hardly be counted." Her gaze on Fawn left no doubt as to what she considered the latest entry in that tally.

At least she's started talking. "Well, folks we're close to most often do aggravate us. Because otherwise we wouldn't care. He's brought good things as well. Twenty-seven malice kills, to start. You have to be proud of that."

Cumbia grimaced. "Oh, he's proven himself on patrol, right enough, but he'd done that by the time he was twenty-five. It's in camp where he's ducked his duties, as if patrolling got him off responsibility for all else. If he'd married when he should have, years ago, we wouldn't be in this muddle now."

"He did, once," Fawn pointed out, in an attempt at a dignified reply. "Right on time for a Lakewalker man, I guess. It turned into a hurtful tragedy that still haunts him."

"He's not the first nor the last to suffer such. Plenty of others have lost folks in the maw of some malice." And Cumbia was one of them, Fawn was reminded. "He's had twenty years to put it behind him."

"Well, then"—Fawn took a breath—"it looks like he's not going to, doesn't it? You all had your chance with him, and a good long chance it was. Maybe it's someone else's turn now."

Cumbia snorted. "Yours?"

"Seems like. I'd say you haven't lost anything to me that you had in the first place. When I met him, he wasn't betrothed to anything but his own death, near as I could tell. And if he's lost *that* infatuation, well, good!"

Cumbia leaned back, her attention now fully engaged. Which wasn't exactly a comfortable feeling, but at least it was a shift from her attempt to pretend Fawn didn't exist at all.

Fawn went on, "You're both of you stiff-necked. I think Dag must get it from you, to tell the truth. *Somebody* has to bend before things break." *Hearts, for one.* "Can't you please stop Dar from going to the camp council? It's bound to end badly."

"Yes, for you," said Cumbia. More level than venomous, oddly.

Fawn raised her chin. "Do you really believe Dag'll choose to cut strings if he's forced to the edge? That he'd break his word? You have a strange idea of your son, for knowing him so long."

"I believe he'll be secretly relieved to be freed of that ill-chosen oath to you, girl. Embarrassed, sure, and obnoxious about it—men always are, when they're caught in the wrong. But in the long run, glad to be rescued from his own mistakes, and gladder still not to have to do it himself."

Fawn bit her lip. *So you think your son's a coward, as well as a liar?* She didn't say it. Or spit it. She was shaken by a faint undercurrent of plausibility in Cumbia's argument. *I've known him half a summer. She's known him all his life.* She gripped the cord around her left wrist, for solace and courage. "What if he chooses banishment?"

"He won't. No Lakewalker could. He'll remember what he owes, and who to."

In general, Dag tried to keep as much distance between himself and his family as he could, and Fawn was beginning to see why. People left their families all the time—it was as normal for a Lakewalker man as it was for a farmer woman. Sometimes it was the straight path for growing up, like Dag's marriage in Luthlia; he presumably had never intended to return from there once he'd wed Kauneo. Sometimes families were impossible in their own right, and could not be fixed, only fled from, and she was beginning to wonder if a little of that might have been behind Dag's first marriage, too. She chose at last, "Who's pushing this camp council showdown—you, or Dar?"

"The family is united in trying to rescue Dag from this—I grant, self-inflicted—disaster."

"Because I think Dar knows better. And if he's telling you something else, he's lying."

Cumbia looked faintly bemused. "Farmer girl, I'm a Lakewalker. I know when someone is lying."

"Fooling himself, then." Fawn tried another tack. "All this is hurting Dag. I can see the strain in him. It wasn't right to send him off to war with all this mess on his mind."

Cumbia's brows rose. "So whose fault was that? It takes two sides to tear a man apart. The solution is simple. Go back to your farm. You don't belong here. Absent gods, girl, you can't even veil your ground properly. It's as if you're walking around naked all the time, do you even know that? Or did Dag not tell you?"

Fawn flinched, and Cumbia looked briefly triumphant. In sudden panic, Fawn wondered if her mother-in-law was reading her ground the way Dag did. *If so, she'll know how to split me up the middle easy as splitting a log with a wedge and mallet.*

Cumbia's head cocked curiously; her eyes narrowed. As if in direct response to this thought, she said, "What use to him is a wife so stupid and ignorant? You'll always be doing the wrong thing here, a constant source of shame to him. He might be too stiff-necked to admit it, but inside, he'll writhe. You'd bear children with weak grounds, incapable of the simplest tasks. If your blighted womb can bear at all, that is. You're pretty now, I admit, but that won't last, either—you'll age fast, like the rest of your kind, growing as fat and distracted as any other fool of a farmwife, while he goes on, rigid with regret."

She's probing. Shooting not at any facts that could possibly be known to her, and certainly not blind, but at Fawn's fears. A vision of her mama and Aunt Nattie, both grown downright dumpy in their middle age, nonetheless assaulted Fawn's imagination. Half a dozen barbs, half a dozen direct hits—*no, not blind. Still . . . I must have hit her somewhere, too, for her to be counterattacking so cruelly.*

Fawn remembered a description she'd heard down in Glassforge of how the rougher keelboat men fought duels. Their wrists were strapped together with rawhide thongs, and their free hands given knives. So they were forced to circle close, unable to disengage or get out of their enemy's stabbing range. This fight with Cumbia felt like that. Driven to her wits' end by her own family, Fawn had not believed Dag when he'd said his would be worse, but if her people fought to bruise and tumble, his aimed to slice to the bone. Maybe Dag was right about the best contact being none. *I didn't come here to fight this old woman, I came to try for some peace. Why am I letting her have her war?*

Fawn took a deep breath, and said, "Dag is the most truthful man I ever met. If we have a problem, he'll tell me, and we'll fix it."

"Huh." Cumbia sat back. Fawn could sense another shift in her mood, away from the sudden, sharp attack, but it did not reassure her. "Then let me tell you the truth about patrollers, girl. Because I was married to one. Sister, daughter, and mother to the breed—walked with them, too, when I was your age, 'bout a thousand years ago. Men, women, old, young, kind or mean-minded, in one thing they are all the same. Once they've seen their first malice, they don't ever give up patrol unless they're crippled or dead. And they don't ever put anyone else before it. Mari—by all right reason, she should be staying in camp taking care of Cattagus, but off she goes. And he sends her, being just as bad. Dag's father was another. All of 'em, the whole lot. Don't you be thinking I imagine Dag'll choose to cut strings because of any consideration for me, or Dar, or anyone else who has supported him his whole life.

"Here's the fork. If Dag doesn't love you enough, he'll choose the patrol. And if he loves you beyond all sense—he'll choose the patrol. Because you're standing in the center of that world he's sent to save, and if he doesn't save it, he doesn't save you, either. When Fairbolt called on him the other night with the news from Raintree, how long did it take your bridegroom to decide to go off and leave you? All alone, with no friends or kin?"

Not very long, Fawn did not say aloud. Her mouth had grown too dry for speech.

"And it wouldn't make a whit of difference if you were Lakewalker born, or a hundred times prettier, or writhing in birth bed, or crying at his child's deathbed, or in agony on your own. Patrollers turn and go all the same. You can't win this one." She sat back and favored Fawn with a slow blink, cold as any snake. "Neither could I. So take your foolish knitting and go away."

Fawn swallowed. "They're good socks. Maybe Omba would like to have them."

Cumbia set her jaw. "You're a touch hard of listening, aren't you, girl?" And then plucked up the little bundle and tossed it into the fire pit smoldering a few yards away.

Fawn almost screamed aloud. *Three days of work!* She dove after it. It had not yet caught, but the dry cotton smoked against the red coals, and a stray end of the jaunty woolen yarn winked in scarlet sparks, curling up and starting to blacken. She leaned in and snatched it back out, brushing off a smear of soot and glowing bits from the browning edge, drawing in her breath sharply at the burning bite of them. Her blue skirt had muddy patches from where her knees had thumped down, and she scrubbed at them as she rose, glaring uselessly at Cumbia.

It wasn't just the pain of the burn on her fingers that started tears in Fawn's eyes. She choked out, "Dag said it would be useless to try and talk to you."

"Should have listened to him, too, eh?" said Cumbia. Her face was nearly expressionless.

"I guess," returned Fawn shortly. Her bright theory that letting Cumbia vent might clear the air seemed singularly foolish now. She wanted to shoot some devastating last word over her shoulder as she stalked off, hurting as she'd been hurt, but she was far too shaken to think of any. She wanted only to escape.

"Go, then," said Cumbia, as if she could hear her.

Fawn clutched the knit bundle in her unburned hand and marched away. She didn't let her shoulders bow till she was out of sight on the road and having to pick her footfalls among the drying puddles. Her stomach shuddered, and this island seemed abruptly lonely and strange, hostile and pinched, despite the bright morning air. Oppressive, like a house turned prison. She sniffed angrily, feeling *stupid stupid stupid,* and smeared away the drops on her lashes with the back of her hand, then turned it to capture the cooling moisture on her throbbing fingers. A reddening line crossed three of them; she thought one might be starting to blister. Mama or Aunt Nattie would have dabbed the spots with butter, made soothing murmurs, and maybe kissed them. Fawn wasn't too sure about the butter—in any case, she had none in the tiny cache of food that passed for her larder—but the rest of the remedy she missed desperately. *Not to be had. Ever again.* The thought made her want to bawl far more than the little pain in her hand.

She'd gone to Cumbia to try to head off the clash with the camp council at its apparent root. To save Dag. She had not only failed, she might have made it even worse. Cumbia and Dar could have no doubt now of what an easy target Dag's farmer wife was. *Why did I think I could help him? Stupid . . .*

In her home campsite—in Mari's and Sarri's campsite, Fawn corrected this thought—Cattagus was still sitting over his leatherwork, now stitching a diminutive slipper held up nearly to his nose, poking rawhide cords in and out of the holes he'd made with his awl. Tesy had gone off somewhere, though Cattagus was apparently keeping an eye on her brother, presently penned in a little corral and diverted with a pair of alarmed turtles; he was tapping on a shell and calling the creature to come out. As Fawn crossed the clearing, Cattagus put down his work and looked at her shrewdly. She recalled Cumbia's shot about walking around naked and wondered if all her efforts to put on a brave face were useless; if any Lakewalker looking at her could see what a seething mess she really was. *Likely.*

To her surprise, Cattagus beckoned her over. She stopped by his table, and he leaned on one elbow, regarding her rather ironically, and wheezed, "So, where have you been, girlie?"

"Went to talk to Cumbia," Fawn admitted. "Tried, anyhow."

"Burn your fingers, did you?"

Fawn hastily pulled her hand from her licking tongue and hid it behind her back. "She threw the socks I'd brought her for a present in the fire. Should have just let them burn, I guess, but I couldn't stand the waste."

"That what you been crouching over all these past three days?"

"Pretty much."

"Huh. Let's see. No, girlie, the burn," he added impatiently as she thrust out her scorched bundle. She gave him her other hand; he held it in his dry, thick fingers, and his gray head bent slightly. He was dressed as usual in nothing but the short trousers and sandals that were his summer uniform, and she was conscious of the smell of him, a mix of old man and lake green, not unpleasant at this concentration, and very Cattagus. Would Dag smell like that when he grew as old? She thought she could learn to like it.

Fawn stared at her rejected knitting as Cattagus kneaded her palm. "Do you think Mari would like those socks? They're too big for me and too small for Dag, but they're good for under riding boots. If she's not too proud to take work from a stupid farmer," she added bitterly. "Or Cumbia's castoffs."

"That last might actually be a draw," said Cattagus, with his whistling chuckle.

He released her hand, which had stopped throbbing; Fawn peeked at the red marks, which had faded to pink instead of raising blisters as she'd thought they would. *He does healing groundwork like Dag.* "Thank you," she said gratefully. Cattagus nodded, picked up the socks, and set them beyond his leather scraps, signifying acceptance of the gift, and Fawn blinked back eye-fog again.

Fawn turned away, then turned back, blurting, "Cumbia said because I can't veil my ground it's just like walking around naked."

"Well," said Cattagus in a slow, judicious drawl, "Cumbia tends to be a bit on the tight side, herself. Full of things she doesn't want others to see. Most folks our age just give up and be what they are."

Fawn tilted her head, considering this. "Older farm folk can be like that, some of them. Well, not with their grounds, of course, but with clothes, and what they do and say."

"Cumbia's still tryin' to fix the world, I'm afraid. She'd have been a relentless patroller. Thank the absent gods she went for a maker." He appeared to lose himself in a vision of patrolling with a younger Cumbia, and shuddered.

"What does she make? Particularly?"

"Rope and cord that does not break. Very much in demand for folks' boats and sailboats, y'see. And other key uses."

"Oh. So . . . so she was making magic when I, um, interrupted her . . . ?"

"No great thing if you did, she's been doing it for so long. Wouldn't have slowed her a bit if you'd been someone she wanted to see."

"I was not that," Fawn sighed. She blinked, trying to recapture her thought. "So do Lakewalkers go about with their grounds open, too?"

"If they're relaxed, or wishful to take in the world around them at its fullest, aye. Too, lots of folks have short groundsense ranges. So you're out of their sight, so to speak, at any little distance, even if you're flaring."

But everyone in this campsite, the children excepted, had long groundsense ranges. She had a sudden horrible thought. "But when Dag and I, when Dag opens up to me . . . um."

Cutting off her words was no help; Cattagus was chuckling downright evilly. Leaving no doubt that he'd caught her meaning, he said, "Me, I cheer for Dag. Even though Mari hits me. Those Redwing women are a stern sisterhood, I can tell you." He added to her hot blush, "It's this breath-thing, y'see. Puts me out of the action myself, mostly. 'Bout all I can do these days is wave on the luckier ones."

Fawn's blush deepened, but she dimly recognized that he had handed her back this intimate revelation by way of turnabout: even-all. Cruelty and kindness, how could one morning hold so much of both? "Folks is folks, I guess," she said.

Cattagus nodded. "Always have been. Always will be. That's better."

She realized she had grown much calmer; her throat no longer ached. She touched the cord on her left wrist, and nodded to Cattagus's. "Is Mari all right this morning? Too?"

"So far." His eyes narrowed at her cord. "Dag did something to yours, didn't he? Or . . . to you."

Fawn nodded, though she flushed again to recall the exact circumstances.

But Cattagus, while he could be shrewd or crude, was not mean-minded, and seemed unlikely to press her for private details. "I got my ground to go into Dag's cord all right, by a . . . a trick, I guess, when we wove them, but I couldn't sense his. So he did some extra groundwork on mine just before he left. It's good to know I could find him, if I had to. Or he me, I suppose."

Cattagus opened his mouth, stopped. Blinked. "Beg pardon?"

She held up her wrist, closed her eyes, and turned about. Opening them, she found herself facing west into the woods. "That way. It's pretty vague, but I reckon, if I got closer, the sense of just where he is would grow tighter. It did the other morning when he was nearby, anyhow." She turned and looked in surprise at Cattagus's climbing brows. "Don't everyone's cords do that?"

"No."

"Oh."

Cattagus rubbed his nose. "Wasn't exactly the cord he did the work on, I think. Best not to mention that trick to anyone else till he gets back."

"Why not?"

"Um. Well. Let's just say, if Dag wants to add any complications to his argument with the camp council, let him pick and choose them himself."

There was an undercurrent, but in what direction it flowed Fawn could scarcely guess. "All right," she said doubtfully. Wistful, she stared west again. "When do you think they'll come back?"

He shrugged. "No knowing." But his eyes seemed to know too much.

Fawn nodded, not so much in agreement as silent sympathy, and took herself off to her tent. She needed to think of a new project for her hands. Not knitting. The sun was climbing toward noon. She hoped it lit Dag's path, wherever it was now winding.

Dead silence, thought Dag, was never a truer phrase.

The high summer sun beat down on a winter landscape. The marshland open to his gaze looked as if it had suffered a week of killing frost. What should have been high green stands of reeds lay flattened and tangled, browning. The line of planted poplars along which his patrol was ghosting looked ghostly themselves, yellowing leaves spinning down one by one in the breezeless air. The air itself was hot, moist, close as only a Raintree summer could be, but devoid of the whine and whirr of insects, empty of birdcalls. It was a blight indeed when even the mosquitoes lay dead, floating with rafts of miscellaneous pond wrack in long, gray smears atop the blank water. The undersides of a couple of dead turtles made dim yellow patches in the murk. The blue sky reflected there in crooked strips, weird contrast to the scum.

The blighted soil nipped at his feet, yet without the deeper sucking drain on his ground that marked land long occupied by a malice. More; Dag could not feel that dry shock in his midsection, like the reverberation of some great blow to the body, that told him a malice lay near. Cautiously, he stood up for a better view of the ruined Lakewalker village that lay along the shore across a quarter mile of open water.

Crouched down in the dead and dying weeds behind Dag, Mari hissed nervous warning.

"It's not here," he breathed to her.

She frowned, nodded acceptance of this, but whispered back, "Its slaves might still be."

He dared to open his groundsense just a little, swallowing against the nausea induced by so much recent blight beating against him. When he was sure he wasn't going to vomit, he opened himself further. Nothing fluttered in his perception but a few distraught blackbirds, fled from the earlier disruption, returning to search futilely for mates or nests.

"There's nothing alive for a mile—wait." He hunkered down again. A few hundred paces beyond the village, in a boggy stretch along the shore, something swirled in his senses, a familiar concentration of distorted ground. Ground around the patch seemed to seep toward it, creeping through the soil like draining water. He narrowed his eyes, searched more carefully.

"I believe there's a mud-man nursery planted beyond the camp. It doesn't seem to have guards just now, though. But there's something else."

Mari's brows twitched up, and her frown deepened. "You'd think it would be watched. If anything was."

Dag considered the possibility of a cleverly baited trap. That would seem to credit this malice with an unlikely degree of foresight, however. He hand-signaled Mari, who passed the order silently, and the patrol took up its stealthy, painfully slow, veiled approach once more, skirting through the scant cover around the edge of this lakelike section of the larger marsh until it reached the abandoned village, or what was left of it.

Perhaps ninety or a hundred dwellings were strung along the lakeside or back from it in kin clusters, home till lately of a community of over a thousand Lakewalkers, with another thousand souls scattered more widely around Bone-marsh. A dozen tent-cabins were burned to the ground; the recent rain had extinguished all coals. Signs of hasty flight were all around, but aside from the burned tents there was only a little mindless destruction. Dag did not see or smell corpses, only partly reassuring, as ground-ripped bodies were sometimes very slow to rot. Still, he permitted himself the hope that most here had escaped, fleeing southward. Lakewalkers knew how to pick up and run. Then he wondered what that little farmer town the malice was supposed to have come up under looked like right now. *What would Spark have done if* . . . he cut off the wrenching thought.

He reached the log wall of the last tent standing and peered uncertainly toward the boggy patch a couple hundred paces off. Back from it, a thicket of scrubby trees—willow, slim green ash, vicious trithorned honey locust—shaded something dark about their boles that he could barely make out with his eye. He opened his groundsense again, flinched, then snapped it back.

"Mari. Codo. To me," he said over his shoulder.

Mari was at his side at once; Codo, the oldest patroller here but for Mari, slid forward in a moment and joined them.

"There's somebody under those trees," Dag murmured. "Not mud-men, not farmer slaves. I think it's some of us. Something's very wrong."

"Alive?" asked Mari, peering too. The half dozen figures didn't move.

"Yes, but . . . extend your groundsenses. Carefully. Don't get caught up. See if it's anything you recognize." *Because I think I do.*

Codo gave him a dry glance from under gray brows, silent commentary on Dag's earlier repeated insistence that no one open their grounds without a direct order. Both he and Mari stared with eyes opened, then closed.

"Not seen anything like that before," muttered Mari. "Unconscious?"

"Groundlocked . . . ?" said Codo.

"Ah. Yes. That's it," said Mari. "But why are they . . ."

Dag re-counted—six with his eyes, five with his groundsense. Which suggested one was a corpse. "I think they're tied to those trees." He turned to Mari's partner Dirla, hovering anxiously. "The rest of you stay back. Codo, Mari, come with me."

There was no cover between here and the stand of scrub. Dag gave up the fraying pretense of stealth and walked openly forward, Codo and Mari right on his heels.

The Bonemarsh Lakewalkers were indeed bound to the thicker tree boles, slumped or half-hanging. They appeared unconscious. Three men and three women, older for the most part; they seemed makers, not patrollers, if Dag could guess from their look and the remains of their clothing. Some bore signs of physical struggle, bruises and cuts, others did not. One woman was dead, waxy and still; Dag hesitated to touch her to check for the stiffness, or lack of it, that would tell him how long. But not very long, he suspected. *Late again, old patroller.*

Codo hissed and drew his knife, starting for the ropes that bound the prisoners.

"Wait," said Dag.

"Eh?" Codo scowled at him.

"Dag, what *is* this?" asked Mari. "Do you know?"

"Aye, I think so. A new malice has to stay by its mud-man nursery to keep them growing, part of what keeps it tied to its lair even after it's no longer sessile. This malice has gotten strong enough to . . . to farm out the task. It's linked up these makers to make its mud-men for it, while it goes . . . off." Dag glanced southward uneasily.

Codo breathed a silent whistle through pursed lips.

"Can we break them out of their groundlock?" said Mari, eyes narrowing.

"Not sure, but wait. What I don't know is how much of a sense the malice has of them, at whatever distance it's gone now. If we fool with them, with this groundwork, might be an announcement that we're here, behind it."

"Dag, you can't be thinking of leaving them!" said Codo in a shocked voice. Mari looked not so much shocked as grim.

"Wait," Dag repeated, and turned to walk toward the boggy patch. The other two exchanged glances and followed.

Every few feet along he found a shallow pit in the wet soil, looking like a mud pot dug by playing children. At the center of each, a snout broke the surface, usually flexing frantically to draw air. He identified muskrat, raccoon, possum, beaver, even squirrel and slow, cold turtle. All were starting to lose their former shapes, like caterpillars in a chrysalis, but none had yet grown to human size. He counted perhaps fifty.

"Well, that's handy," said Codo, looking over his shoulder with fascinated revulsion. "We can kill them in their holes. Save a lot of grief."

"These aren't going to be ready to come out for days, yet," said Dag. "Maybe weeks. We take the malice down first, they'll die in place."

"What are you thinking, Dag?" said Mari.

I'm thinking of how much I didn't want to be in command of this jaunt. Because of decisions like this. He sighed. "I'm thinking that the rest of the company is half a day behind us. I'm thinking that if we can get some drinking water down those poor folks, they'll last till nightfall, and Obio can cut them loose, instead. And we won't have given away our position to the malice. In fact, the reverse—it'll think any pursuit is still back here."

"How far ahead of us do you think this malice is by now?" said Codo.

Dag shook his head. "We'll scout around for clues, but not more than a day, wouldn't you guess? It's plain the malice has gathered up everything it's got and pressed south. Which says to me it's on the attack. Which also says to me it won't be looking behind it much."

"You mean to follow. Fast as we can," said Mari.

"Anyone here got a better idea?"

They both shook their heads, if not happily.

They returned to the patrol, now gathered warily in the village. Dag dispatched a pair to go get Saun and bring up the horses, sending the rest to scout around the desolation the malice had left. About the time Saun arrived with their mounts, Varleen found the butchering place back in the scrub where the malice's forces had eaten their last meal, bones animal and human mixed, some burned, some gnawed raw. Dag counted perhaps a dozen human individuals in the remains for sure, but not more. He tried hard to hang on to that *not more* as a heartening thought, but failed. Fortunately, there was no way for the three patrollers most recently familiar with Bonemarsh Camp to recognize anyone among the disjointed carcasses. The burying, too, Dag left for Obio and the company following.

His veiled patrol had been keyed up for a desperate attack. Gearing back down for a quiet, hasty lunch instead, especially for the ones who'd seen the butchery, went ill, and Dag had no desire to linger, if only for the certainty that the fierce argument over whether to attempt to release the groundlocked makers would start up again. Saun was particularly unhappy about that one, as he recognized some of them from the two years he'd patrolled out of Bone-marsh before he'd exchanged to Hickory Lake.

"What if Obio chooses another route?" Saun protested. "You left him free to."

"Soon as we take the malice down, tonight or tomorrow, we'll send some-one back," said Dag wearily. "Soon as we take the malice down, they may well be able to free themselves."

This argument was, in Dag's view, even more dodgy, but Saun accepted it, or at least shut up, which was all Dag wanted at this point. His own greatest re-gret was for the time they'd lost in their stealthy on-foot approach; they might have ridden into the village at a canter for all the difference it would have made. Dag suspected they were now going to come up on the malice well after dark, exhausted, at the end of a much too long and disturbing day. Part of a commander's task was to bring his people to the test at the peak of their condi-tion and will. He'd fumbled both time and timing, here.

Tracking the malice south presented no difficulty, at least. Starting just beyond the marsh, it had left a trail of blight a hundred paces wide that a farmer could not have missed, let alone anyone with the least tinge of groundsense. *At the end of this, one malice, guaranteed.* Finding it would be dead easy now.

The malice not finding us first will be the hard part. Dag grimaced and kicked Copperhead forward at a trot, his troubled patrol strung out in his wake.

11

Another night attack—without the aid of groundsense this time. *Gods, I'm as blind in the dark as any farmer.* Dag had feared the flare of their grounds would alert the malice's outlying pickets to his patrol, but blundering bodily into sentries in the murk now seemed as likely a risk. A misshapen moon was well up. When they cleared these trees, he might get a better look at what lay ahead. He glanced right and left at the shadows that were his flankers, Mari and Dirla, and Codo and Hann, and was reassured; if his dark-adapted eyes could scarcely make them out, neither could an enemy's.

He dared another deerlike step forward, and another, trying not to think, *Blight it, we've done this once today already.* His patrol had come up on signs of the malice's massed forces soon after midnight, and again left their horses in favor of this stealthy approach. Through terrain for which, unlike Bonemarsh, they had no maps or plan or prior knowledge. If his own exhaustion was a measure of everyone else's, Dag distrusted his decision to strike at once, without allowing a breather; but it was impossible to rest here, and every delay risked discovery. They had come into a level country, with little farms carved out of the woods becoming more and more common, not unlike the region above West Blue. Little abandoned farms. Dag hoped all the people hereabouts had been warned by the refugees from Bonemarsh and fled to Farmer's Flats.

The open fields allowed a glimpse ahead but equally denied cover. As they reached the scrubby edge of what had been a broad stand of wheat, now flattened and dying, Dirla stole over to him. "See that?" she breathed, pointing.

"Aye."

On the field's other side, wooded land rose—as much as any land rose in these parts—angling up to a low ridge. The red glimmer of a few bobbing torches shone through the trees, then vanished again. Silvered by the sickly moon, a narrow triangular structure crowned the crest. A crude timber tower perhaps twenty feet high, built of logs hastily felled and notched to lock across one another, was briefly silhouetted against a distant milky cloud. Whatever shapes crouched on the plank platform at its top were too far away for Dag to make out with his eyes; but despite his tight closure, the threat of the malice beat in his belly with his every pulse.

"Lookout post?" Dirla whispered.

Dag shook his head. "Worse." *Absent gods help us.* This malice was advanced enough to start building *towers.* Even the Wolf Ridge malice had not developed enough for that compulsion. "Can you see how many on the platform . . . ?" Dirla's younger eyes might be sharper than his own.

"Just one, I think."

"It's up there, then. That's where we're headed. Pass the word."

She nodded and silently withdrew.

Now they had to get next to that tower without being spotted. So near— across a trampled field and up a wooded hillside—so far. Dag guessed that the bulk of the malice's mud-men and mind-slaves were camped on the ridge's far side, probably along a stream. Smoke from hidden campfires rose in thin gray wisps into a high haze, confirming his speculation. There was almost no wind, and he regretted the absence of covering rustles from the branches overhead, but what faint breeze there was moved the haze toward him. He hardly needed his eyes now; he could *smell* the enemy: smoke, manure, piss, the cooking of he-dared-not-guess-what meats.

Dag pushed through clutching blackberry brambles, setting his teeth against the gouge and scrape of sturdy thorns, and crouched by a fieldstone wall lining the high side of the wheatfield. He half crawled forward along its shadowed western side until he reached brambles again, then risked a look back. The moon emerged from a cloud, but the tight shapes of the patrollers following him did not once edge into the thin light. *Good, you folks are so good.* Half the distance down. He slid through more dying brambles into the black shade of the woods at the base of the ridge, the patrol too spreading out to ease from shadow to shadow.

To his horror, a muffled grunt and some thumps sounded from his left. He made his way hastily toward the sound. Codo and Hann were crouching over something half-concealed in a crackling deadfall. Hann had drawn his war knife, but glanced up and froze when Dag's hand fell on his arm.

Codo squatted across the chest of a grizzled man—farmer-slave, guard?— both his hands tight around the struggling fellow's throat. "Hann, hurry!" Codo hissed.

Dag touched Codo's shoulder, eased in, and studied their threat-and-victim. Farmer-slave, yes, clothes ragged, eyes wild and mad. Maybe from this farm, or else picked up along the way to add to the malice's straggling, growing army. He wasn't a big man, or young; he reminded Dag uncomfortably of

Sorrel Bluefield. Dag took aim and landed several hard blows to the man's head, until his eyes rolled back and he stopped bucking. The meaty thumps sounded as loud as drumbeats in Dag's ears.

"Blight it, throat slitting's quieter," muttered Codo, cautiously rising. "Surer."

Dag shook his head and pointed uphill. This was no place for an argument, and the pair did not give him one, but turned to continue the silent climb. Dag could roll the issues over in his head without need of words—Hann's glare, burning through the dark, was enough to make the point. A throat-slit guard couldn't claw his way back to consciousness in a few minutes and raise the alarm.

I hate fighting humans. Of all the vileness in this long struggle, the malices' mind-theft of people who should be the Lakewalkers' friends and allies was the worst. Even when the patrollers won, they lost, in clashes that left farmer corpses in their wake. *We all lose.* Dag shook out his throbbing hand. *That might have been Sorrel.* Somebody's husband, father, father-in-law, friend.

I hate fighting. Oh, Fawn, I'm so tired of this.

The farmer's mad eyes were sign enough of his enslaved state, with no need for Dag's groundsense to trace the malice's grip in his mind. Even though they hadn't slit his throat, his brief alarm could have given little warning, surely? Indeed, Dag decided, the malice would be more likely to notice the shock of a death in its growing web of slaves than what might be mistaken for a sort of sleep. Much depended on how many individuals this malice controlled, at what distance, attempting what tasks. *Please, let it be stretched to its limits.* Whatever it was now doing at the top of that tower, ground was flowing toward it in a great sucking drain; Dag could feel the mortal throb of it passing under his boot soles. He had a wild vision of gripping the streaming power with his ghost hand and just letting it tow him right up the slope.

The patrol reached the edge of the clearing, bristling with stumps from the trees felled to build the tower—within the last day, Dag guessed from the still-pungent smell of the sap. In the faint moonlight he could make out the hulking shapes of at least four mud-man guards at the tower's base. Maybe bear-men or even bull-men; big, lithe, stinking. Without need for orders, he could sense his pairs moving to the front. His stomach clenched, and he fought down a wave of nausea. Time to clear the path.

At some faint *clink* or whisper of a weapon drawn from a sheath, a guardian's head turned toward them; it lifted its snout, sniffing suspiciously.

Now.

Dag did not cry his command, just yanked out his war knife and plunged forward, weaving around stumps. His thoughts narrowed to his task: slay the mud-men, get his knife-wielders past them and up the tower as fast as death. *Faster.* Dag took on the nearest mud-man to hand, ducking as it brought up a rusted sword stolen from who-knew-where and swung violently at his head. Dag's return stroke tore out the creature's throat, and he didn't even bother dodging the spray of blood. Arrows from patrol's archers whispered fiercely past his head to sink into the chest of a mud-man beyond, although the shafts didn't drop it; the mud-man staggered forward, roaring. Mari, her sharing knife clenched between her teeth, reached the tower and began to climb. Codo darted past her around the tower's corner and swung himself upward too. Another patroller reached the tower, and another, all in that same intent silence. The rest turned to protect their climbing comrades. Dag could hear them engaging new mud-men reaching the clearing, as yet more came crashing up the hill yowling in alarm.

The dark shape at the top of the tower moved, standing up against a cobalt sky scattered with stars and luminous with moon-washed cloud. The four climbers had almost reached the top. Suddenly the figure crouched, leaped—descended as if floating the full twenty feet to land upon its folding legs and spring again upright. As if it were light as a dancer, and not seven solid feet of corded muscle, sinew, and bone. It wheeled, coming face-to-face with Dag.

This malice was lean, almost graceful, and Dag was shocked by its beauty in the moonlight. Fair skin moved naturally over a face of sculpted bone; hair swept back from its high brow to flow like a river of night down its back. Its androgynous body was clothed in stolen oddments—trousers, a shirt, boots, a Lakewalker leather vest—which it somehow endowed with the air of some ancient high lord's attire. How many molts must it have gone through, how quickly, to have achieved such a human—no, superhuman—form? Its glamour wrenched Dag's gaze, and he could feel his ground ripple—he snapped himself closed, tight and hard.

And open again as Utau, sharing knife out, staggered with a sudden cry. Dag could sense the strain in Utau's ground as the malice turned and gripped it, starting to rip it away. Frantic, Dag extended his left arm and stretched out his ghost hand to snatch at the malice's ground in turn. Out of the corner of his eye, Dag saw Mari, clinging to the tower side, drop her sharing knife down in a pale spinning arc to Dirla, who had temporarily broken free of mud-men.

As a fragment of its ground came away in Dag's ghost hand, the malice turned back to him with an astonished scream. Dag recalled that moment in the medicine tent when he'd snatched ground from Hoharie's apprentice, but this time it felt like clutching a live coal. Pain and terror reverberated up his left arm. He tried to cast the fragment into the earth, but it clung to his ground like burning honey. The malice reached two-handed toward Dag, its dark eyes wide and furious. Dag tried again to close himself against it, and failed. He could feel the malice's grip upon his ground tighten, and his breath locked at the surge of astounding pain that seemed to start from his marrow and strike outward to his skin, as if all his bones were being shattered in place simultaneously.

And Dirla lunged forward onto a stump and plunged Mari's sharing knife into the malice's back.

Dag felt the dying enter his own shredding ground, cloudy and turbulent as blood poured into roiling water. For a moment, he shared the malice's full awareness. The world's ground stretched away from their center for miles, glowing like fire, with slaves and mud-men moving across it in scattered, blazing ranks. The confusing din of their several hundred, no, thousand anguished minds battered his failing consciousness. The malice's vast will seemed to drain from them as Dag watched, leaving blackness and dismay. The irrational intelligence of the great being snatched at his own mind, hungry above all for understanding of its plight, and Dag knew that if this malice took him in, it would have nearly all it needed, and yet still not be saved from its own cravings and desires. *It is quite mad. And the more intelligent it grows, the more agonizing its own madness becomes to it.* It seemed a curious but useless insight to gain, here at the end of breath and light.

The malice screamed again, its voice rising strangely like a song, wavering upward into unexpected purity. Its beautiful body ruptured, caught by its clothing, and it fell in a welter of blood and fluid.

The earth rose up and struck Dag cruelly in the back. Stars spun overhead, and went out.

Fawn shot awake in the dark and sat up in her lonely bedroll with a gasp. Shock shuddered through her body, then a wash of fear. A noise, a nightmare? No echoes pulsed in her ears, no visions faded in her mind. Her heart pounding unaccountably, she slapped her right hand over her left wrist. This panic was surely the opposite of relaxed persuasion and openness, but beneath her marriage cord her whole arm was throbbing.

Something's happened to Dag. Hurt? Hurt *bad* . . . ?

She scrambled up and pushed through her tent flap into the milky light of a partial moon, seeming bright compared to the inky shadows inside. Not stopping to throw anything over her sleeping shift, she picked her way across the clearing, wincing at the twigs and stones that bit her bare feet. It was all that kept her from breaking into a run.

She hesitated outside Cattagus and Mari's tent. The night was cool after the recent rains, and Cattagus had dropped the porch flap down. She slapped it as Utau had theirs on the dark morning he'd come to wake Dag. She tried to guess the time from the moon passing over the lake—two hours after midnight, maybe? There was no sound from within, and she pounded the leather again, then shifted from foot to foot, trying to gather the nerve to go inside and shake the old man by the shoulder.

Before she did, the flap moved on Sarri's tent, and the dark-haired woman emerged. She had paused for sandals, but no robe either, and her feet slapped quickly across the stretch between the two tent-cabins.

"Did you feel that?" Fawn asked her anxiously, keeping her voice low for fear of waking the children. And then felt utterly stupid, for of course Sarri would not feel anything from a marriage cord wrapped around someone else's wrist. "Did you feel anything just now?"

Sarri shook her head. "Something woke me. Whatever it was, was gone by the time I'd gathered my wits." Her right hand too gripped her left wrist, kneading.

"Razi and Utau . . . ?"

"Alive. Alive. At least that." She shot Fawn a curious look. "Did you feel something? Surely you couldn't have . . ."

She was interrupted by a grunt from the tent. Cattagus shouldered through the flap, tying up his shorts around his stout middle and scowling. "What's all this too-roo in the moonlight, girlies?"

"Fawn says she felt something in her cord. Woke her up." Sarri added, as if reluctant to endorse this, "I woke up too, but there wasn't . . . anything. Mari?"

The same gesture, right hand over left, although by putting on an expression of exasperation Cattagus tried, unsuccessfully, to make it not look anxious. He shook his head. "Mari's all right." He added after a moment of reflection, "Alive, at least. What in the wide green world can all those galloping fools be about over there at this time of night?" He glanced west, as if his eyes could somehow penetrate a hundred and more miles and see the answer, but that feat was beyond even his Lakewalker powers, a fact his dry snort seemed to acknowledge.

The two women followed his stare uneasily.

"Look, now," he said, as if in persuasion, "if Utau, Razi, Mari, and Dag are all still alive, the company can't be in that much trouble. Because you know that bunch'd find the manure pile first."

Sarri blew out her breath in not quite a laugh, accepting the thin reassurance as much, Fawn guessed, for his sake as her own.

" 'Specially Dag," Cattagus added under his breath. "You wonder what Fairbolt thought he was about, to put . . ."

"Cattagus." Fawn took a deep breath and thrust out her arm. "My cord feels funny. Can you figure out anything from it?"

His gray brows rose. "Not likely." But he took her wrist gently in his hand anyway. His lips moved briefly as if in surprise, but then schooled away a scowl to some more guarded line. "Well, he's alive. There's that. Can't have got himself ground-ripped if he's alive."

More Lakewalker secrets no one had bothered to mention? "What's ground-ripped?"

Cattagus exchanged a look with Sarri, but before Fawn could grit her teeth in frustration, relented, and said, "Same as what that malice down in Glassforge did to your childie, I take it. 'Cept Lakewalkers-grown can resist, close their grounds against it. If the malice is a sessile, or is not too strong yet."

"What if it *is* strong?" Fawn asked in worry.

"Well . . . they say it's a quick death. No chance to share, though." Cattagus frowned sternly. "But, see here, girlie, don't you go imagining things all night. Your boy's alive, isn't he now, eh?"

Fawn had trouble thinking of Dag as a boy, but the *your* part she clutched hard to her heart, her wrists crossed over her chest. *Dag's mine, yes. Not some blighting malice's.*

"Maybe it's over," said Sarri in a low voice. "I hope it's over."

"When would we know?" asked Fawn.

Cattagus shrugged his ropy shoulders. "From the middle of Raintree, good news could get here in three days. Bad news in two. Very bad news . . . well, we won't worry about that. Ah, go back to bed, girlies!" He shook his head and set the example by ducking back inside, wheezing. Pointedly, Fawn thought.

Sarri shook her head in unwitting echo of her testy uncle, sighed deeply, and made her way back to her tent and her sleeping children. Fawn picked her way slowly back to little Tent Bluefield.

She dutifully lay down, but returning to sleep was beyond futile. After tossing for a time, she rose again and took out her drop spindle and a bundle of plunkin flax, and went out in the moonlight to clamber up on her favorite tall spinning-stump. At least she might have something to show for her night-restlessness. The tap of the gold beads flicking on her wrist as she spun was normally cheerful and soothing, but tonight felt more like fingers drumming. Flick, spin, shape.

She wished she could put spells for protection into her trouser cloth, the way a Lakewalker wife likely could. She could spin her thread strong, weave it tight, sew it soundly, double-stitched and secure. She could make with all her heart, but it would only give the ordinary expected armoring of cloth on skin. *Not enough.* Flick, spin, shape.

Three days till any news, huh. *I don't like this waiting part. Not one bit.* The helpless anxiety was worse than she'd expected it to be, and she felt pushed off-balance. *No more do Sarri or Cattagus like it, either, that's plain enough, but you don't catch them carrying on about it, do you?* Her own unease wasn't special just for being new to her. She felt she suddenly had more insight into Lakewalker moodiness. Her assurances to Dag before he'd ridden off seemed in retrospect unduly blithe and—well, if not *stupid,* a word he'd tried to forbid her, certainly ignorant. *I'm learning now. Again.* Flick, spin, shape.

If Dag died on patrol—her eyes went to her wrist cord, *still alive,* yes, it was a safely theoretical thought. She could dare to think it. *If something happened to him out there, what would become of me?* Despite Hickory Lake's fascinations, without Dag she knew she had no roots here. While these Lakewalkers seemed unlikely to cast her out naked, she had no doubt Fairbolt would whisk her back to West Blue in two shakes of a lamb's tail, likely with a patroller to make sure she arrived. Seemed like his idea of responsible. But she had no roots in West Blue now either; she'd cut them off, if not without a pang, without compunction. Twice. Cutting them a third time wasn't a task she wished to face. If she couldn't stay here, and she wouldn't go back . . .

It was a measure, perhaps, of what this sometimes-horrendous year had done for her that she found this thought curiously undaunting. There was Glassforge. There was Silver Shoals, beyond on the Grace River, an even finer town by Dag's descriptions. There was a world of possibility for an un—grass widow with determination and her wits held close about her. She was practical. She knew how to walk down strange roads, now. She'd come this far. She didn't have to cling to Dag like a drowning woman clutching the only branch in the torrent.

Everybody, it seemed, wanted Dag for something. Fairbolt Crow wanted him for a patroller. His mother wanted him to demonstrate the high value of her bloodline, maybe, to prove her worth through his. His brother Dar wanted him to not make a fuss or be a distraction—to stay quiet, safe inside the rules, ignorable. Fawn wasn't sure but what she should add herself into that tally, because she certainly wanted Dag for the father of her children someday, except Dag seemed to be thinking along those lines himself, so maybe that one was mutual and didn't count. Didn't anyone want Dag just for *Dag?* Without justification, like a milkweed or a water lily or, or . . . a summer night with fireflies.

Because later, in some very dry places, the memory of that hour was enough for going on with.

She had to stop spinning then, because she couldn't see through the silver light blurring in her eyes. She dashed her hand against her hot eyelids to clear her vision. Twice. Then just let the tears run down, sitting bent to her knees with her wrist cord pressed to her forehead. It took a long time to make her breathing stop hitching.

My heart's prize my best friend my true consolation . . . what trouble have you gone and found this time?

Her arm was still throbbing, though more faintly. *Alive,* yes, but . . . she might be just a farmer girl, without a speck of groundsense in her body, she might be any one of a hundred kinds of fool. She might be ignorant of a thousand Lakewalkerish things, but of this she was increasingly certain. *This is not good. This is something very wrong.*

❦

The insides of his eyelids were red. Not black. There was light out there somewhere, warm dawn or warm fire. His curiosity as to which was not enough to make him drag open the heavy weights his lids had become.

He remembered panicked voices, and thinking he should get up and fix the cause, whatever it was. He should. Someone had been shouting about Utau, and Razi—of course it would be Razi—trying to match grounds. Mari's voice, sharp and scared, *Try to get in! Blight it, I'm not losing our captain after all that!* Fairbolt was here? When had that happened? Someone else, *I can't! His ground's too tight!* and later, *Can't, oh gods that hurts!* And, *So if it does that to you, what do you figure it's doing to him?*—Mari's tart voice at its least sympathetic; Dag felt for her victim, whoever he was. More gasping, *I can't, I can't, I'm sorry . . .* The panicked voices had faded then, and Dag had been glad. Maybe they would all go away and leave him be. *I'm so tired . . .*

He breathed, twitched; his gluey eyes opened on their own. Half-dead tree branches laced the paling blue of a new dawn. On one side, orange flames crackled up from a roaring campfire, deliciously warm. Dawn and fire both, ah, that solved the mystery. On his other side, Mari's face wavered into view between him and the sky.

Her dry voice spoke: " 'Bout time you reported for duty again, patroller."

He tried to move his lips.

Her hand pressed his brow. "That was a joke, Dag. You just lie there." Her hand went to his, under blankets it seemed. "Finally warming up, too. Good."

He swallowed and found his lost voice. "How many?"

"Eh?"

"How many died? Last night?" Assuming the malice kill *was* last night. He had mislaid days before, under unpleasantly similar conditions.

"Now you've seen fit to grace us with your gloomy face again—none."

That couldn't be right. Saun, what of Saun, left with the horses? Dag pictured the youth attacked in the dark by mud-men, alone, bloodied, overwhelmed . . . "Saun!"

"Here, Captain." Saun's anxiously smiling face loomed over Mari's shoulder.

That must have been a dream or a hallucination. Or this was. Did he get to pick which? He drew breath enough to get out, "What's happened?"

"Dirla took the malice—" Mari began.

"I got that far. Saw you drop your knife to her." Mari's son's bone. He managed to moisten his lips. "Didn't think you'd ever let that out of your hand."

"Aye, well, I remembered your tale of how you and the little farmer girl got the Glassforge malice. Dirla was closer, and the malice was intent on Utau. I saw the chance and took it."

"Utau?" he repeated urgently. Yes, the malice had been about to rip the ground from his body . . .

Mari gripped his shoulder through the blankets. "Malice grazed him, no question, but Razi brought him home. You, now—that's the closest I've ever heard tell of anyone getting his ground ripped without actually dying. Never seen a man look more like a corpse and still breathe."

"Drink?" said Saun, putting an arm under Dag's shoulders to lift him a bit.

Oh, good idea. It was only stale water from a skin, but it was wonderfully *wet* water. Wettest he'd ever drunk, Dag decided. "Thankee'." And after a moment, "How many of us lost . . . ?"

"None, Dag," said Saun eagerly. Mari frowned.

"Go on."

"Eh, after that, it was all over but the shoutin', of which there was the usual," said Mari. "Sent two pairs to retrieve Saun and the horses, and kept the rest close to guard our camp from hazard. Let four off to sleep a bit ago." She nodded across the fire toward some sodden unmoving bundles stretched on bedrolls. Dag raised his head to look. Beside one of them, Razi sat cross-legged; he smiled tiredly at Dag and sent him a vague salute.

"What of the farmer-slaves?"

"There weren't as many right by here as we'd thought. Seems the malice had sent most of its slaves and mud-men marching off through the woods for some dawn attack on a town just northwest of Farmer's Flats. I imagine they're having a right mess down there this morning. Gods know what those poor farmers thought when the malice fog lifted from their minds and their mud-men scampered. I haven't much tried to herd the folks we found here, though we did check out their camp, and suggest no one try to travel home alone. Most of 'em have gone off by now to try and find friends and family."

Understandable; welcome, even. It might be cowardice, but Dag didn't want to try to deal with distraught farmers this morning, atop everything else. Let the Raintree Lakewalkers take care of their own.

Dag's brow wrinkled. "*How* many did we lose last night?"

Mari drew a long breath and leaned forward to peer into his face. "Dag, are you tracking me at all?"

" 'Course I'm tracking you." Dag unwound his left arm from his blankets and waved his hook at her. "How many fingers am I holding up?" Except it occurred to him that, on some very disturbing level, he did not know the answer.

Mari rolled her eyes in exasperation. Saun, bless him, looked adorably confused.

"Well, we still don't know about those makers we left at Bonemarsh," Saun offered hesitantly.

Mari turned to glare at him. "Saun, don't you dare start that up again with him now."

Yes, *that* was his missing piece, the thing he'd been trying so desperately to remember. Dag sighed, if not exactly in satisfaction.

"We haven't heard from Obio and the company yet," said Mari, "but there's scarcely been time. They might have reached there hours ago."

"They might have taken some other route," said Saun stubbornly.

It looked to turn into a bright day. People tied up outdoors in such heat without drink or food could die of exposure in a surprisingly short time, even without the added stress of whatever the malice's groundlock—or ground link—had done to them. If even one prisoner could release himself, he'd surely free the rest, but suppose none could . . . ? The throbbing headache of nightmare crept back up the base of Dag's skull. "We have to go back to Bonemarsh."

Saun nodded in eagerness. "I'll ride ahead."

"Not alone you won't!" said Mari sharply.

Dag got out, "I left them . . . yesterday. Because I could count. But today I can go back." Yes, as quickly as might be. "There was something wrong, and I knew it, but there was no time, and I knew that too. I have to get back there." *Enough human sacrifice for one malice, enough.*

Mari sat back, dubious. "Make you a deal, Dag. If you can get your fool self up on your fool horse all by yourself, I'll let you ride it. If not, you're staying right here."

Dag grinned wanly. "You'll lose that bet. Saun, help me sit up."

The boy slid an arm under his shoulders again. Dag's head drained nearly to blackness as he came upright, but he kept his blinking eyes open somehow. "See, Mari? I wager there's not a mark on me."

"Your ground's so tight it's cramping. You can't tell me you didn't take hurt under there."

"What does it feel like?" asked Saun diffidently. "A ground rip, that is?"

Dag squinted, deciding Saun was due an honest answer. "Right now, a lot like blood loss, truth to tell. It doesn't hurt anywhere in particular"—*just everywhere generally*—"but I admit I'm not my best."

Mari snorted.

If he ate, perhaps he would gain strength enough to . . . eat. Hm.

Mari went off to deal with less intractable people, and Saun, as anxious for the Bonemarsh makers as Dag, made it his business to get Dag ready to ride. While Saun fed him, Dag took counsel with Mari and Codo to split the patrol, sending six south to find the Raintree Lakewalkers and report on the malice kill, and the rest north with him to, with luck, rendezvous with the rest of the company at Bonemarsh.

In the event, Dag half cheated and used a stump to mount Copperhead. Mari, mounting from another stump, eyed him narrowly but let it pass. The horse was too tired to fight him, which was fortunate, because he was way too tired to fight back. He let Saun take the lead in the ride back north, swifter for the daylight, the lack of need for stealth, and the knowing where they were going, but slower for everyone's exhaustion. Dag sat his horse and wavered in and out of awareness, pretending to be dozing while riding like any good old patroller. Utau, slumping in his saddle and closely shepherded by Razi, looked almost as laid waste as Dag felt.

Dag let his groundsense stay shut, as it seemed to want; it reminded him of the way a man might walk tilted to guard a wound. Maybe, as for blood loss, time and rest would provide the remedy. He tried once to sneak out his ghost hand, but nothing occurred.

The thought of the tree-bound makers he had so ruthlessly abandoned yesterday haunted his hazy thoughts. He searched the memory of his glimpse of the malice's mind for a hint of them, but could recover only a sense of overwhelming confusion. The makers' fate seemed to hang in the air like some absent god's cruel revenge upon his wild hope, scarcely admitted even to himself. If only . . .

If only I could get through this *captaincy without losing anyone, I could stop.*

If only he could balance the long weight of Wolf Ridge? Would it? Dag was dubious of his mortal arithmetic. *In the long run no one gets out alive, you know that.*

They passed into, and out of, a slate-lined ravine, letting the horses drink as they crossed the creek. He could swear they'd passed this same ford not twelve hours ago, pointed the other way. Dizzied, he pressed Copperhead forward into the hot summer morning.

12

Dag knew they were approaching Bonemarsh again by the growing dampness of the soil and air, and a brightening in the corner of his eye as the flat woods opened out into flatter water meadows. He had been staring at nothing but the coarse rusty hairs of Copperhead's mane for the past hour, but looked up as Saun muffled an oath and kicked his tired horse into a canter. Above the Bonemarsh shore, life of a sort had returned: a flock of turkey vultures, the fingerlike fringes of their wing tips unmistakable on their black silhouettes as they wheeled. His impulse to canter after Saun was easily resisted, as neither he nor Copperhead was capable of more than a trot right now, the jolting of which would have tormented his sagging back. And . . . he didn't want to look. He let his horse walk on.

As they neared the south margin of the marsh, Dag straightened, squinting in guarded hope. The vultures were circling over the woods back behind the village, not over the boggy patch along the shore. Maybe they'd merely found the unburied carcasses from the mud-men's feast. Maybe . . .

The rest of his veiled patrol turned onto the shore track, and Dag craned his neck, heart thumping. There were several horses tethered around the scrubby trees, Saun's now among them. The rest of the company had made it, good! Some of them, at least. Enough. Dag could see figures moving in the shade, then his heart clenched again at the glimpse of several long lumps on the ground. He couldn't tell if the faces were covered or not. *Bedrolls, please, let it be bedrolls and not shrouds* . . . Had the company only just arrived? Because surely the next task would be to move the rescued makers off this half-blighted ground to some healthier campsite. But Obio was here, thank all the absent gods, striding out to wave greeting as they rode up.

"Dag!" Obio cried. "You're here—absent gods be praised!" His voice seemed to hold more than just relief to see Dag alive. It had the shaken timbre of a man with a crisis desperately seeking someone else to hand it to. *One of us is thanking the absent gods too soon, I think.*

Dag tried to get both eyes open at once and brace his spine. At least enough to dismount, after which he was determined not to climb back into that saddle again for a long, long time. He slid down and clung to his stirrup leather for a moment, partly for support as he woozily adjusted to standing again, partly because he could barely remember what he was trying to do.

Saun's anxious voice brought him back to the moment. "You have to see this, Captain!"

He turned, moistened his lips. Got out, "How many? Did we lose." He felt too close to weeping, and he feared frightening Saun with his fragility. He wanted to explain, reassure: *Fellows get like this after, sometimes. You'll see it, if you're around long enough.*

But Saun was babbling on: "Everyone's alive that was yesterday. Except now there's a new problem."

In a dim effort to fend it all off for just a moment longer, like a man pulling his blanket over his head when called from his bedroll by raucous comrades, Dag blinked at Obio, and asked in a voice raspy with fatigue, "When did you get here?"

"Last night."

"Where is everyone?"

"We've set up a camp about a mile east, just off the blight." Obio waved toward a distant, greener tree line. "I rested the company yesterday morning, then sent scouts out after you. I started us all toward here at midafternoon, closing up the distance in case, you know. We were getting pretty worried toward dusk, when my scouts hadn't come back and my flankers ran into a couple of mud-men. They did for them pretty quick, but it was plain you hadn't got the malice when you'd planned."

"No. Later. Couple hours after midnight, about twenty miles south."

"So Saun just said. But if—well, here's Griff, my scout who found this. Let him tell."

A worried-looking fellow of about Dirla's age came up and gave Dag a nod. Griff had been walking for ten years, and in Dag's experience was level-headed and reliable. Which made his current rumpled, wild-eyed appearance just that much more disturbing.

"Gods, Dag, I'm so glad you're here!"

Dag controlled a wince, leaning his arm along Copperhead's back for secret support. "What happened?" And added prudently, as Griff's distraught look deepened, "From the beginning."

Griff gulped and nodded. "The two pairs of us scouts came down here to Bonemarsh late yesterday afternoon. We could track where your veiled patrol had passed through, right enough. We figured—well, hoped—that the malice had moved off and you all had moved after it. Then we found these makers tied to the trees"—he glanced over his shoulder—"and then we thought maybe you must have been captured, instead."

Because good patrollers don't abandon their own? Charitable, Griff. "No. We left them tied, passed them by," Dag admitted.

Griff straightened; to Dag's surprise, the look on his face was not horror or contempt, but respect. He asked earnestly, "How did you know it was a trap?"

Trap? What? Dag shook his head. "I didn't. They were a sacrifice to pure tactics. I didn't want to chance warning the malice there were patrollers coming up this close behind it."

"You said there was something really wrong," Saun corrected this, frowning. "And to keep our grounds shut tight when we were touching them."

"That wasn't exactly a stretch of my wits by that point, Saun. Go on, Griff."

"We could see they were groundlocked. Seemed to be. So Mallora did what you do to someone groundlocked, reached in and bumped grounds to break them out of the trance. Except—instead of her waking them up, the groundlock just seemed to, to reach out and suck her in. Her eyes rolled back, and she crumpled up in a heap. The mud-puppies all out in their pots over there"—Griff waved toward the bog—"made these strange bubbling noises and flopped around when it happened. Made us jump, in the dusk. I didn't notice how silent it all really was, till then. Mallora's partner Bryn panicked, I think—she reached out for her, tried to drag her back. And she got sucked in after. I grabbed my partner Ornig before he could reach for Bryn."

Dag nodded, provisionally, but Griff's face was tightening in something like despair. Dag murmured, "It used to happen up in Luthlia sometimes in the winter, someone would fall through rotten ice. And their friends or their kin would try to pull them out, and instead be pulled in after. One after another. Instead of running for help or a rope—though the smart patrollers there always wore a length of rope wrapped around their waists in the cold season. Except if someone's slipped under the ice—well, never mind. The hardest thing . . . the hardest thing in such a string of tragedy was to be the one who stopped. But you bet the older folks understood."

Griff blinked back tears, ducking his head in thanks. He swallowed for control of his voice, and went on, "Ornig and I agreed he would stay, and I would go for help. And I rode hard! But I think I should have stayed, because when we made it back"—he swallowed again—"the makers were all cut down from the trees, as if Ornig had tried to make them more comfortable, but Ornig was all in a heap. He must have . . . tried something." He added after a moment, "He's sweet on Bryn, see."

Dag nodded understanding, and stepped away from Copperhead to get a closer look at what was going on in the grove. If only he could find a tree to lean against—not that honey locust, bole and branches bristling with clusters of nasty triple-headed spines—his hand found a low branch from a young wild cherry, and he gripped it and peered. Three or four patrollers, at least one of whom Dag recognized as one of the company's better medicine makers, moved among bedrolls laid out where space permitted. He counted eight. *More and more at risk.* Someone had a campfire going, though, and something heating in pots—drinking water, medicine?

All good, but there was something deeply wrong with the picture . . . oh. "Why haven't you moved them off this blighted ground?"

Mari, Dirla, and Razi had dismounted during Griff's recitation, moving closer to listen. Razi still held the reins of Utau's horse; Utau drooped over his saddlebow, squinting. Dag wasn't sure how much of this he was taking in.

"We tried," said Obio. "Soon as you carry someone more than about a hundred paces away, they stop breathing."

"Must have been a thrill finding *that* out," Mari said.

"Oh, aye," agreed Obio, fervent. "In the middle of the night last night."

"And if you kill one of the mud-men in their mudholes," Griff added morosely, "the people scream in their sleep. It's pretty blighted unnerving. So we stopped that, too."

"I figured," said Obio, "that if—when—someone caught up with the malice, the groundlock would break on its own. I intended to detail a few folks to look after them and take the company on, as soon as enough scouts came back to give me a guess what we ought to try next. Except . . . you say you all did for the malice, but that ugly groundlock's still holding tight."

"Dirla did," said Dag. "With Mari's sharing knife. Your first personal kill, I believe, Dirla?" It was a shame that the congratulations and celebration that should have been hers were being overwhelmed in this new crisis.

Dirla nodded absently. She frowned past Dag at the unmoving figures in the shaded bedrolls. "Could there be more than one malice? And that's why this link didn't break last night?"

Dag tried to think this utterly horrible idea through logically, but his brains seemed to be slowly turning to porridge. His gut said *no,* right enough, but he couldn't for the life of him say why, not in words.

Mari came to his rescue: "No. Because our malice would have turned all it had toward fighting the second, instead of chasing after farmers and Lakewalkers. Malices don't team up—they eat each other."

Well, that was true, too. *But that's not it.*

"That's what I thought," said Dirla. "But then why didn't this stop when the malice died, like what it does to the farmers and the mud-men?"

Maddening question. Lakewalkers, it must have to do with Lakewalkers . . . "All right," sighed Dag. "I'm thinking . . . we got water down those folks yesterday. If we can get more water and some sort of food—gruel, soup, I don't know—down them again, we can buy a little time, maybe."

"Been doing that," said Obio.

Bless your wits. Dag nodded. "Buy time to think. Keep a close eye, wait for the scouts—then decide. Depending, I'm thinking we might split the company—send some volunteers to help the Raintree folks with the cleanup, and the rest home maybe as early as tomorrow morning." So that Oleana might not, due to Fairbolt's robbed pegboard, find itself facing a similar runaway malice war next season.

The creeping alarm of this unnatural groundlock upon a bunch of already-nervy patrollers was clearly contagious. At this point, Dag could scarcely tell if his own sick unease was from the makers or their distraught caretakers. "Blight it, I wish I had Hoharie here. She works with people's grounds all the time. Maybe she'd have an idea." He might as well wish for that flock of turkey vultures to spiral down, grab him, and fly him away home, while he was at it. He sighed and cast an eye over his exhausted, bleary comrades. "Everyone who was with my veiled patrol is now off duty. Ride on over to the camp—get food, sleep, a wash, whatever you want. Utau, you're on the sick list till I say otherwise." Speaking of reasons to wish for the medicine maker.

Utau roused himself enough to growl, "I like that! If that malice scored me, it scored you a lot worse. I know what I feel like. Why are you still walking around?"

A question Dag didn't care to probe just now, even if his wits had been working. Utau, it occurred to him, had been the only other patroller with his groundsense open, if involuntarily, in those moments of confused terror last night when Dag and the malice had closed on each other. What had he perceived? Evidently not Dag's disastrous attempt to rip the malice in return. Dag temporized, "Until Razi says otherwise, then." Razi grinned and cast him an appreciative half salute; Utau snorted. Dag added, "I'm going to lay me a bedroll down here, shortly."

"On this blight?" said Saun doubtfully.

"I don't want to be a mile away if something changes suddenly."

Mari tugged Saun's sleeve, and murmured, "If that one's actually volunteerin' for a bedroll, don't argue the details." She gave him a significant jerk of her head, and his eyes widened in enlightenment; he stepped over to Dirla.

"I had more sleep last night than you did, Mari," said Dag.

"Dag, I don't know what that was last night after you went down, but it sure wasn't sleep. Sleeping men can be waked up, for one."

"Wait, what's all this?" said Obio.

Utau pushed up on his saddlebow and looked down at Dag a tad ironically. "Malice nearly ripped my ground last night. Dag jumped in and persuaded it to go after him, instead."

"Did it rip you?" Obio asked Dag, eyebrows climbing.

"A little bit," Dag admitted.

"Isn't that something like being a little bit dead?"

"Seemingly."

Obio smiled uncertainly, making Dag wonder just how corpselike he did look at the moment. He was not lovely, that was certain. Would he make Spark's eyes happy all the same? *I bet so.* A bright picture came into his head of the thrill that would flower in her face when he walked into their campsite, when this was all over. Would she drop her handwork and run to his arms? It was the first heartening thought he'd had for hours. Days.

Dag wondered if he'd started to fall asleep standing when a voice broke up this vision, which ran away like water though his hands. He almost cried to have the dream back. Instead, he forced himself to breathe deeply and pay attention.

". . . can send couriers with the news, now," Obio was saying. "I'd like to catch Fairbolt before he sends off the next round of reinforcements."

"Yes, of course," murmured Dag.

Dirla had been talking closely with Mari; at this, she lifted her face, and called, "I'd like to volunteer for that, sir."

You're off duty, Dag started to object, then realized this task would certainly get Dirla home first. Better—she was eyewitness to the malice kill, none closer. If he sent her, Dag wouldn't have to try to pen a report in his present groggy state. She could just *tell* Fairbolt all about it. "You took the malice. You can do any blighted thing you please, Dirla."

She nodded cheerfully. "Then I will."

Obio, his eyes narrowing, said, "In that case, I've a fellow in mind to send with her for partner. His wife was about to have a baby when we left. Absent gods willing, she might still be about to."

Which would cover events from the other part of the company for Fairbolt, too. Good.

"Excellent," agreed Mari. "That's a courier who won't dawdle, eh?"

"You'll need to trade out for fresher horses——" Dag began.

"We'll take care of it, Dag," Razi promised.

"Right. Right." This was all routine. "Dirla. Tell Spark—tell everyone we'll be home soon, eh?"

"Sure thing, Captain."

Obio boosted Mari back on her horse, and she led the rest of the patrol, save Saun and Dirla, off east toward the promised camp. To reassure Obio and Griff, Dag pretended to make an inspection tour of the grove and the bog, for as much good as his eyes could do with his groundsense still clamped down tight.

"There was a dead woman, yesterday," Dag began to Obio.

Obio grunted understanding. "We cut her down and wrapped her, and put her in one of the tents in the village. I'm hoping some of the Bonemarsh folk might come back and identify her before we have to bury her. In this heat, that'll have to be by tomorrow, though."

Dag nodded and trudged on.

The distorting animals trapped in their mud pots were much the same repellent sight as yesterday. The five surviving makers and three patrollers, more inexplicably trapped, were at least physically supported now, as comfortable as they might be made in bedrolls on the ground in the warm summer shade. The other patrollers taking turns to lift them and spoon liquids into them must also be ground-closed and walking blind, Dag realized.

Even apart from the hazard of this peculiar sticky ground-snare, he had the irrational apprehension that opening his ground would be like a man pulling a dressing from a gut wound; that all his insides might spill out. He found that while his back was turned, Saun and Dirla had unsaddled Copperhead and set up Dag's possessions and bedroll in a flat, dry spot raked clear of debris. They'd been awake as long as he had, blight it, why were they so blighted perky? Blighted children . . . The moment his haunches hit his blanket, Dag knew he wasn't getting up again. He sat staring blankly at his bootlaces, transported in memory back to the night after his last malice kill, with Spark on the feather tick in that farmhouse kitchen.

He was still staring when Saun knelt to undo one boot, and Dirla the other. It was surely a measure of . . . something, that he let them.

"Can I bring you anything to eat? Drink?" asked Dirla.

Dag shook his head. While riding he had gnawed down a number of leathery strips of dried plunkin, on the theory that he might so dispose of two tedious chores at the same time. He wasn't hungry. He wasn't anything.

Saun set his boots aside and squinted out into the afternoon light upon the silent, wasted marsh. "How long do you suppose till this place recovers? Centuries?"

"It looks bad now," said Dag, "but the malice was only here a few days, and the blight's not deep. Decades at most. Maybe not in my life, but in yours, I'd say."

Saun's eyes pinched, and he traded an unreadable look with Dirla. "Can I get—do you want anything at all, Captain?"

I want Spark. A mistake to allow himself the thought, because it bloomed instantly into a near-physical ache. In his heart, yes—as if there were any part of him not hurting already. Instead, he said, "Why am I *captain* all at once, here? You call me *Dag,* I call you *Hey, you, boy.* It's always worked before."

Saun grinned sheepishly, but didn't answer. He and Dirla scrambled up; Dag was asleep before the pair left the grove.

Fawn, who hadn't been able to fall to sleep till nearly dawn, woke in the midmorning feeling as though she had been beaten with sticks. Mint tea and plunkin did little to revive her. She turned to her next hand task, weaving string from her spun plunkin flax to make wicks for a batch of beeswax candles Sarri was planning. An hour into it her eyes were blurring, and the throbbing in her left hand and arm was a maddening distraction that matched the throbbing in her head. Was it her heartbeat or Dag's that kept the time? *At least his heart's still beating.* She set down her work, walked up the road to where the path to Dar's bone shack led off, and stood in doubt.

Dag's his brother. Dar has to care. Fawn considered this proposition in light of her own brothers. No matter how furious she might be with them, would she drop her gripe if they were hurt and needed help? *Yes.* Because that's what family was all about, in her experience. They pulled together in a crisis; it was just too bad about the rest of the time. She set her shoulders and walked down the path into the green shade.

She hesitated again at the edge of the sun-dappled glade. If she was truly parading about ground-naked, as Cumbia accused, Dar must know she was here. Voices carried around the corner of the shack. He wasn't, then, deep in concentration upon some necromantic spell. She continued around to find Dar sitting on the top porch step with an older woman dressed in the usual summer shift, her hair in a knot. Dar was holding a sharing knife. He drew a peeved breath and looked up, reluctantly acknowledging Fawn.

Fawn clenched her left wrist protectively to her breast. "Mornin', Dar. I had a question for you."

Dar grunted and rose; the woman, with a curious glance at Fawn, rose too.

"So what is it?" Dar asked.

"It's kind of private. I can come back."

"We were just finishing. Wait, then." He turned to the woman and hefted the knife. "I can deconsecrate this in the afternoon. Do you want to come back tonight?"

"Could. Or tomorrow morning."

"I have another binding tomorrow morning."

"I'll make it tonight, then. After supper?"

"That would do."

The woman nodded briskly and started away, then paused by Fawn, looking her up and down. Her brows rose. "So you're the famous farmer bride, eh?"

Fawn, unable to figure her tone, gave a safe little knee-dip.

She shook her head. "Well, Dar. Your brother." With this opaque pronouncement, she strode off up the path.

By the bitter twisting of Dar's lips, he drew more information from this than Fawn could. Fawn let it go; she had much more urgent worries right now. She approached Dar cautiously, as if he might bite. He set the knife on the porch boards and eyed her ironically.

Too nervous to plunge straight in, Fawn said instead, "What was that woman here for?"

"Her grandfather died unexpectedly in his sleep a few weeks ago, without getting the chance to share. She brought his knife back to be rededicated."

"Oh." Yes, that had to happen now and then. She wondered how Dar did that, took an old knife and bound it to the heart of someone new. She wished he and she could have been friends—*or even relatives*—then she could have asked.

Never mind that now. She gulped and stuck out her left arm. "Before Dag rode off to Raintree, I asked him if he couldn't fix it so's I could feel him through my marriage cord the way he feels me. And he did." She prayed Dar would not ask how. "Last night about two hours after midnight, I woke up— there was this hurting all up my arm. Sarri, she woke up about the same time, but all she said was that Razi and Utau were still alive. Mari, too, Cattagus says. It didn't do this before—I was afraid that—I think Dag's hurt. Can you tell? Anything more?"

Dar's face was not especially revealing, but Fawn thought a flash of alarm did flicker through his eyes. In any case, he did not snipe at her, but merely took her arm and let his fingers drift up and down it. His lips moved, tightened. He shook his head, not, seemingly, in defeat, but in a kind of exasperation. "Gods, Dag," he murmured. "Can you do worse?"

"Well?" said Fawn apprehensively.

Dar dropped her arm; she clutched it to herself again. "Well . . . yes, I think Dag has probably taken some injury. No, I can't be sure how much."

Offended by his level tone, Fawn said, "Don't you care?"

Dar turned his hands out. "If it's so, it won't be the first time he's been brought home on a plank. I've been down this road with Dag too many times. I admit, the fact that he's company captain is a bit . . ."

"Worrisome?"

"If you like. I can't figure what Fairbolt . . . eh. But you say the others are all right, so they must be taking care of him. The patrol looks after its own."

"If he's not lost or separated or something." Fawn could imagine a hundred somethings, each more dire than the last. "He's my husband. If he's hurt, I should be lookin' after him."

"What are you going to do? Jump on your horse and ride off into a war zone? To lose yourself in the woods, drown in a bog or a river, be eaten by the first wolf—or malice—whose path you cross? Come to think, maybe I should have Omba saddle up your horse and put you on it. It would certainly solve my brother's problems for him."

And it was *extremely* aggravating that just such panicked thoughts had been galloping through her mind all morning. She scowled. "Maybe I wouldn't be as lost as all that. When Dag fixed my cord, he fixed it so's I can tell where he is. Generally, anyhow," she added scrupulously.

Dar squinted down at her for a long, silent, unnerving moment; his frown deepened. "It has nothing to do with your marriage cord. Dag has enslaved some of your ground to his." He seemed about to say more, but then fell silent, his face drawn in doubt. He added after a moment, "I had no idea that he . . . it's potent groundwork, I admit, but it's not a good kind."

"I don't understand."

"Naturally not."

Fawn clenched her teeth. "That means, you have to explain more."

"Do I?" The ironic look returned.

"Yes," said Fawn, very definitely.

A little to her surprise, he shrugged acquiescence. "It's malice magic. Forbidden to Lakewalkers for very good reasons. Malices mind-enslave farmers through their grounds. It's part of what makes farmers as useless on patrol as dogs—a powerful enough malice can take them away and use them against us."

"So why doesn't that happen to Lakewalkers?" she shot back.

"Because we can close our grounds against the attack."

Reluctantly, she decided Dar was telling the truth. So would the Glassforge malice have stolen her mind and will from her if it had been given a bit more time? Or would it simply have ripped out her ground on the spot as it had her child's? No telling now. It did cast a disturbing new light on what she had assumed to be farmer slander against Lakewalkers and their beguilements. But if—

Cattagus's oblique warning about the camp council returned to her mind with a jerk. "How, forbidden?" *How fiercely forbidden, with what penalties?* Had she just handed Dag's brotherly enemy another weapon against him? *Oh, gods, I can't do anything right with these people!*

"Well, it's discouraged, certainly. A Lakewalker couldn't use the technique on another Lakewalker, but farmers are wide-open, to a sufficiently powerful"—he hesitated—"maker," he finished, puzzlement suddenly tingeing his voice. He shook it off. His eyes narrowed; Fawn suddenly did not like his sly smile. "It does rather explain how Dag has you following him around like a motherless puppy, eh?"

Dismay shook her, but she narrowed her eyes right back. "What does *that* mean?" she demanded.

"I should think it was obvious. If not, alas, to my brother's credit."

She strove to quell her temper. "If you're tryin' to say you think your brother put some kind of love spell on me, well, it won't wash. Dag didn't fix my cord, or my ground, or whatever, till the night before he left with his company."

Dar tilted his head, and asked dryly, "How would you know?"

It was a *horrible* question. Was he reading her ground the way Cumbia had, to so narrowly target her most appalling possible fears? Doubt swept through her like a torrent, to smack to a sudden stop against another memory—Sunny Sawman, and his vile threats to slander her about that night at his sister's wedding. That ploy had worked admirably well to stampede Fawn. Once. *I may be just a little farmer girl, but blight it, I do learn. Dag says so.* She raised her face to meet Dar's eye square, and suddenly the look of doubt was reversed from her to him.

She drew a long breath. "I don't know which of you is using malice magic. I do know which of you is the most *malicious*."

His head jerked back.

Yeah, that stings, doesn't it, Dar? Fawn tossed her head, whirled, and stalked out of the clearing. She didn't give him the satisfaction of looking back, either.

Out on the road again, Fawn first turned right, then, in sudden decision, left. In the time it took her to walk the mile down the shore to patroller headquarters, her courage chilled. The building appeared quiet, although there was a deal of activity across the road at the stables and in the paddocks, some patrol either coming in or going out, or maybe folks getting ready to send the next company west to the war. *Maybe Fairbolt won't be here,* she told herself, and climbed the porch.

A strange patroller at the writing table pointed with his free hand without looking up from his scratching quill. "If the door's open, anyone can go in."

Fawn swallowed her rehearsed greetings, nodded, and scuttled past. *Blight this naked-ground business.* She peeked around the doorjamb to the inner chamber.

Fairbolt was sitting across from his pegboard with his feet up on another chair and a shallow wooden box in his lap, stirrings its contents with one thick finger and frowning. A couple more chairs pulled up beside him held more such trays. He squinted up at his board, sighed, and said, "Come in, Fawn."

Emboldened, she stepped to his side. The trays, unsurprisingly, held pegs. He looked, she thought, very much like a man trying to figure out how to fill eight hundred holes with four hundred pegs. "I don't mean to interrupt."

"You're not interrupting much." He looked up at last and gave her a grimace that was possibly intended to be a smile.

"I had a question."

"There's a surprise." He caught her faint wince and shook his head in apology. "Sorry. To answer you: no, I've had no courier from Dag since his company left. I wouldn't expect one yet. It's still early days for any news."

"I figured that. I have a different question."

She didn't think she'd let her voice quaver, but his brows went up, and his feet came down. "Oh?"

"Married Lakewalkers feel each other through their wedding cords—if they're alive, anyhow. Stands to reason you'd be listenin' out for any such news from your patrollers—if any strings went dead—and folks would know to pass it on to you right quick."

He looked at her in some bemusement. "That's true. Dag tell you this?"

"No, I figured it. What I want to know is, couriers or no couriers, have you gotten any such mortal news from Dag's company?"

"No." His gaze sharpened. "Why do you ask?"

This was where it got scary. Fairbolt *was* the camp council, in a way. *But I think he's patrol first.* "Before he left, Dag did some groundwork on my cord, or on me, so's I could feel if he was alive. Same as any other married Lakewalker, just a little different route, I guess." Almost as briefly as she had for Dar, she described waking up hurting last night, and her moonlit talk with Sarri and Cattagus. "So just now I took my cord to Dar, because he's the strongest maker I know of. And he allowed as how I was right, my cord spoke true, Dag was hurt somehow last night." She hardly needed to add, she thought, that for Dar to grant his brother's farmer bride to be right about anything, it had to be pretty inarguable.

All the intent, controlled alarm she'd missed from Dar shone now in Fairbolt's eyes. His hand shot out; he jerked it to a stop. "Excuse me. May I touch?"

Fawn mustered her nerve and held out her left arm. "Yes."

Fairbolt's warm fingers slid up and down her skin and traced her cord. His face tensed in doubt and dismay. "Well, something's there, yes, but . . ." Abruptly, he rose, strode to the doorway, and stuck his head through. His voice had an edge Fawn had not heard before. "Vion. Run over to the medicine tent, see if Hoharie's there. If she's not doing groundwork, ask her step down here. There's something I need her to see. Right now."

The scrape of a chair, some mumble of assent; the outer door banged before Fairbolt turned back. He said to Fawn, somewhat apologetically, "There's reasons I went for patroller and not maker. Hoharie will be able to tell a lot more than I can. Maybe even more than Dar could."

Fawn nodded.

Fairbolt drummed his fingers on his chair back. "Sarri and Cattagus said their spouses were all right, yes?"

"Yes. Well, Sarri wasn't quite sure about Utau, I thought. But all alive."

Fairbolt walked over to the larger table and stared down; Fawn followed. A map of north Raintree was laid out atop an untidy stack of other charts. Fairbolt's finger traced a loop across it. "Dag planned to circle Bonemarsh and drop down on it from the north. My guess was that the earliest they could arrive there was today. I don't know how much that storm might have slowed them. Really, they could be anywhere within fifty miles of Bonemarsh right now."

Fawn let her left hand follow his tracing. The directional urge of her cord, alas, did not seem to respond to marks on maps, only to the live Dag. But she stared down with sudden new interest.

Maps. Maps could keep you from getting lost even in places you'd never been before. This one was thick with a veining of roads, trails, rivers, and streams, and cluttered with jotted remarks about landmarks, fords, and more rarely, bridges. Dar might be right that if she just jumped on her horse and rode west, she would likely plunge into disaster. But if she jumped on her horse with an aid like this . . . she would still be running headlong into a war zone. A mere pair of bandits had been enough to overcome her, before. *I would be more wary, now.* The map was something to think hard about, though.

"What could have happened to Dag, do you think?" she asked Fairbolt. "Dag alone, and no one else?"

He shrugged. "If you want to start with most likely chances, maybe that fool horse of his finally managed to bash him into a tree. The possibilities for freak accidents after that are endless. But they can't have closed in for the malice kill yet."

"Why not?"

His voice went strangely soft. "Because there would be more dead. Dag and I figured, based on Wolf Ridge, to lose up to half the company in this. That's how I expect to know, when . . ." He trailed off, shaking his head. "Obio Grayheron will take command. He's good, even if he doesn't have that edge that . . . ah, gods, I hate this helpless waiting."

"You, too?" said Fawn, her eyes widening.

He nodded simply.

A knock sounded on the doorjamb, and a quiet voice. "Problems, Fairbolt?"

Fairbolt looked up in relief. "Hoharie! Thank you for stopping over. Come on in."

The medicine maker entered, giving Fairbolt a vague wave and Fawn a curious look. Fawn had been introduced to her by Dag and shown the medicine tent, which to Fawn's mind nearly qualified as a building, but they had barely spoken then. Hoharie was an indeterminate age to Fawn's eyes, not as tall as most Lakewalker women. Her summer shift did not flatter a figure like a board, but the protuberant eyes in her bony face were shrewd and not unkind. Like Dag's eyes, they shifted colors in the light, from silver-gilt in the sun to, now, a fine gray.

Fairbolt hastened to set her a chair by the map table, and moved boxes of pegs to free two more. Fawn directed an uncertain knee-dip at her and sat where Fairbolt pointed, just around the table's corner.

"Tell your tale, Fawn," said Fairbolt, settling on her other side.

Fawn gulped. "Sir. Ma'am." Fighting an urge to gabble, Fawn repeated her story, her right hand kneading her left as she spoke. She finished, "Dar accused Dag of making malice magic, but I swear it isn't so! It wasn't Dag's fault—I *asked* him to fix my cord. Dar puts it in the worst possible light on purpose, and it makes me so mad I could spit."

Hoharie had listened to the spate with her head cocked, not interrupting. She said mildly, "Well, let's have a look then, Fawn."

At her encouraging nod, Fawn laid her left arm out on the table for Hoharie's inspection. The medicine maker's lips twisted thoughtfully as she gazed down at it. Her fingers were thin and dry and hardly seemed to press the skin, but Fawn's arm twinged deep inside as they drifted along. Fairbolt watched closely, occasionally remembering to breathe. Hoharie sat back at last with a hard-to-read expression.

"Well. That's a right powerful piece of groundwork for a patroller. You been hoarding talent over here, Fairbolt?"

Fairbolt scratched his head. "If it's so, Dag's been hoarding himself."

"Did he mention that thing about the glass bowl and the ghost hand to you?"

Fairbolt's eyebrows shot up. "No . . . ?"

"Huh."

"*Is* it"—Fawn swallowed—"what Dar said? Bad magic?"

Hoharie shook her head, not so much in negation as caution. "Now, mind you, I've never seen a malice's mind-slave up close. I've just heard about them. Though I have dissected mud-men, and *there's* a tale. This almost reminds me more of matching grounds for healing, truth to tell. Which is like a dance between two grounds that push on each other. As contrasted with a shaped or unshaped ground reinforcement, where the medicine maker actually gives ground away. Could be when a malice matches ground, it's just so powerful it compels rather than dances, pushing the other right over. Though there is a disparity in this as well . . . I wouldn't be able to tell how much unless I had Dag right here."

Fawn sighed wistfully at the notion of having Dag right here, safe.

Fairbolt said in a somewhat choked voice, "Isn't a hundred miles away a bit far for matching grounds, Hoharie? It's usually done skin to skin, in my experience."

"That's where the *almost* comes in. This has both, mixed. Dag's put a bit of worked—rather delicately worked—ground reinforcement into Fawn's left arm and hand, which is what she feels dancing with his ground in the cord. It's all very, um . . . impulsive."

Perhaps taking in the confusion in Fawn's face, Hoharie went on: "It's like this, child. What you farmers call magic, Lakewalker *or* malice, it's all just groundwork of some kind. A maker draws the ground he works with out of himself, and has to recover by growing it back at the speed of life, no more. A malice steals ground from the world around it, insatiably, and puts nothing back. Think of a rivulet and a river in flood. The one'll give you a nice drink on a hot day. The other will wash away your house and drown you. They're both water. But no one sane has any trouble telling one from the other. See?"

Fawn nodded, if a bit uncertainly, to show willing.

"So is my company captain hurt or not?" said Fairbolt, shifting in impatience. "What's going on over there in Raintree, Hoharie?"

Hoharie shook her head again. "You're asking me to tell you what something looks like from a glimpse in a piece of broken mirror held around a corner. In the dark. Am I looking at all of it, or just a fragment? Does it correspond to anything?" She turned to Fawn. "What hurts, exactly?"

Fawn stretched and clenched her fingers. "My left hand, mostly. Up the arm it fades. Except I feel a little shivery all over."

Fairbolt muttered, "But Dag hasn't got a . . ." His face screwed up, and he scowled in a confusion briefly greater than Fawn's.

"It's . . . how shall I put this," said Hoharie in some reluctance. "If the rest of his ground is as stressed as the bit I feel, his body must be in a pretty bad way."

"How bad, *how*?" snapped Fairbolt. Which made Fawn rather glad, because she was much too frightened to yell at the medicine maker herself.

Hoharie opened her hands in a wide, frustrated shrug. "Well, not quite enough to kill him, evidently."

Fairbolt bared his teeth at her, but then sat back in a glum slump. "If I get any sleep at all tonight, Hoharie, it won't be your doing."

Fawn leaned forward and stared at her hand. "I was kind of hoping you would tell me I was a stupid little farmer girl imagining things. Everybody else used to, but now that I want it . . ." She looked up, and added uneasily, "Dag's not going to get in some kind of trouble for this making, is he?"

"Well, if—when he gets back I guarantee *I'll* be asking him a few questions," said Hoharie fervently. "But they won't have anything to do with this argument before the camp council."

"It was all my fault, truly," said Fawn. "Dar made me afraid to tell. But I thought—I thought Fairbolt had a need and a right to know, on account of the company."

Fairbolt pulled himself together, and said gravely, "Thank you, Fawn. You did the right thing. If you feel any changes in this, please tell me or Hoharie, will you?"

Fawn nodded earnestly. "So what do we do now?"

"What we generally have to do, farmer girl," Fairbolt sighed. "We wait."

13

$\mathcal{D}$ ag woke well after dark, to roll his aching body up, pull on his boots without lacing them, and stagger to the slit trench. The night air was chill and dank, but the two patrollers on duty had kept the campfire burning with a cheery orange glow. One waved to Dag as he wandered past, and Dag returned the silent salute. The scene looked deceptively peaceful, as though they watched over comrades merely sleeping.

After relieving himself, Dag considered more sleep. His bone-deep grinding fatigue of earlier seemed scarcely improved. The marsh remained silent—this hour should have been raucous with frogs, insects, and night birds—and eerily odorless. Either the reek of its normal life or the stench of death should have saturated this foggy air. Well, the rot would come in time, a week or a month or six or next spring. Which, while it would doubtless smell repulsive enough to gag anyone for a mile downwind, would be a first sign of life beginning its repair of the blight—rot had a lively ground of its own.

Dag stared at the grove, the campfire seeming like a lantern among the trees, remembering his patrol's first approach . . . only yesterday? If this was after midnight—he glanced at the wheel of the stars—he could call it two days ago, though that seemed scarcely more reasonable. Frowning thoughtfully, he counted a careful two hundred paces away from the grove and found a stump to sit upon. He stretched out his aching legs. If he had opened his groundsense at this distance before without triggering the trap, presumably he might do it again.

He hissed in surprise as he eased his veil apart for the first time in days. *Cramping,* Mari had described his closure, and that seemed barely adequate to describe this shaking agony. Normally, he paid as little attention to his own ground as he did to his body, the two conflating seamlessly. Meaning to examine the groundlocked makers, Dag instead found his inner senses wrenched onto himself.

In the ground of his right arm a faint heat lingered, last vestiges of the healing reinforcement snatched from, or gifted by, Hoharie's apprentice. Over time such a reinforcement was slowly absorbed, converted from the donor's ground into that of the recipient's, not unlike the way his food became Dag. Even this trace would be gone altogether in a few more weeks. In the ground of his left arm . . .

His ghost hand was not there at the moment. The ground of his arm was spattered with a dozen dark spots, black craters seeming like holes burned in a cloth from scattered sparks. A few more throbbed on his neck and down his left side. Surrounding them in gray rings were minute patches of blight. This wasn't just fading reverberation from a malice-handling like Utau's, though that echoed in him too. The spots were the residue, he realized, of the ground he'd ripped from the malice in that desperate night-fight. It was like nothing he'd ever seen before, yet immediately recognizable. *Strangely familiar* seemed the perfect summation, actually.

But then, he'd never before met up with anyone crazed enough to try to ground-rip a malice. Maybe he was seeing why it was not a recommended technique? Injury or healing to a living body injured or healed its ground in turn; ground-ripping or prolonged exposure to blight killed a body through its ravaged ground. What was this peculiar infestation doing to his body now? Nothing good, he suspected. With this map to guide him, he could trace deep aches in his flesh that centered over the splotches, if barely distinguishable from his present general malaise. Pain marked damage, normally. What kind of damage?

So . . . was the pulsating grayness slowly being absorbed by Dag's ground, or . . . or was the blight spreading? He swallowed and stared, but could sense no discernible change.

Stands to reason, he could almost hear Spark say. How would a smart little farmer girl analyze this? What were the possibilities?

Well, his ground could be slowly repairing itself, as in any other wound. Or his ground might be unable to repair itself until the sources of injury were removed, the way an arrow had to be extracted before the flesh around it could start to knit. Sometimes, if more rarely, flesh knitted around a fragment that could not be removed. Sometimes it closed but festered. Or . . . was the blight spreading out faster than his ground could repair it? In which case . . .

In which case, I'm looking at my death wound. A mortality flowing as slowly as honey in winter, as inexorably as time.

Spark, no, how long do we——?

In a spasm of inspiration, he tried to call up his ghost hand to grip a splotch, tear it out, dump it in the soil, anywhere—was it possible to ground-rip *yourself*?—but his odd power remained elusive. He then massaged around a spot on his left ribs with his right hand, willing its ground to reach in, but found it as impossible as to will flesh to penetrate flesh. The effort made his side twinge, however.

An even more horrific possibility occurred to him then. The fragments of the first great malice-king, it was said, grew into the plague of the world. What if each of these fragments had the same potential? *Could I turn into a malice?* Or malice food?

Dag bent his head and huffed through his open mouth, his hand clutching his hair. *Oh, absent gods, do you hate me that much?* Or he might split into a dozen malices—or—no, a dominant one would no doubt conquer and subsume the others, then emerge the lone victor of . . . what? Once the miniature malice had consumed all the ground and the life of the body it lived in, it, too, presumably must die. Unless it could escape . . .

Dag panted for breath in his panic, then swallowed and sat up. *Let's go back to the death-wound idea, please?* What if this was not a spew of malice seed, but more like a spatter of malice blood, carrying the toxic ground but not capable of independent life for long. Indeed—gingerly, he turned his senses inward again—there was not that sense of nascent personality that even the lowliest sessile malice exuded. Poison, yes. He could live with—well, be happy with—well . . .

He sat for several shaken minutes in the silent dark, then peeked again. No change. It seemed he was not dissolving into gray dust on the spot. Which meant he was doomed to wake up to his responsibilities in the morning all the same. So. He'd had a reason for coming out here. What was it . . . ?

He inhaled and, very cautiously, extended his groundsense outward once more. The lingering blight all around nibbled at him, but it was ignorable. He found the dead trees in the grove, the trapped mud-men beyond, the live patrollers on night watch. He steered away from the groundlocked makers, barely letting his senses graze them. Before, he had found a gradient of ground moving through the soil, sucked into the making of the mud-man nursery. Did such a draw sustain it still?

No. The death of the malice had done that much good, at least.

Or . . . maybe not. The mud-men were still alive, even if they'd stopped growing. Therefore, they must still be drawing ground, if slowly. The only source of ground in the system was the locked makers and, now, the three fresh patrollers. And he did not think their depleted bodies could produce new ground fast enough to keep up. What must be the end of it, if this accursed lock could not be broken?

The weakest makers would likely die first. With them gone, increased stress would be thrown onto the survivors, who would not last long, Dag suspected. Death would cascade; the remainder must die very quickly. At which point the mud-men would also die. Would that be the end of it, the problem collapsing into itself and gone? Or were there other elements, hidden elements at work inside the lock?

No one could find out without opening their ground to the lock. No one could open their ground to the lock without being sucked into it, it seemed. Impasse.

My head hurts. My ground *hurts.* But no such collapse was happening now. Dag clutched the thought to himself as if it were hope. Perhaps the morning would bring better counsel, or even better counselors than one battered old patroller so frighteningly out of his depth. Dag sighed, levered himself up, and stumbled back to his bedroll.

What the morning brought was distractions, mainly. A pair of scouts returned from the south to report much the sort of chaos Dag expected—farmer and Lakewalker refugees scattered all over, improvised defenses in disarray—but also encouraging signs of people beginning to sort themselves out with the news of the death of the malice. About midday, some two dozen Bonemarsh exiles cautiously approached. Dag assigned his patrol of cleanup volunteers the initial task of helping them to identify and bury their dead, including the woman maker, and scavenge the village for still-usable supplies that might be carried off to the other north Raintree camps that would be taking in the nearly two thousand homeless. The Raintree Lakewalkers were likely in for a straitened winter, coming up. Bonemarsh casualties, he was glad to learn, had been relatively low. No one seemed to know yet if the same had been the case for that farmer town the malice had taken first.

Three of the Bonemarsh folks agreed to stay and help nurse their ground-locked makers and the hapless would-be rescuers. The makers all had names, now, and life stories that the returned refugees had determinedly pressed on Dag. He wasn't sure if that helped. In any case, he sent the first batch of locals off with a patroller escort and an earnest request to send him back any spare medicine makers or other experts who might be able to get a grip on his lethal puzzle. But he didn't expect much help from that quarter, as every medicine maker in Raintree had to be up to the ears in nearer troubles right now.

He had slightly more hope of the full patrol of twenty-five he sent home that afternoon, carrying both a warning to Hickory Lake of their neighbor's impending winter shortages, and a much more urgently worded plea for Hoharie or some equally adept maker to come to his aid. To stay at Bonemarsh, Dag selected the best medicine makers—for patrollers—his company had, including several veteran mothers or grandmothers, whom he figured for already knowing how to keep alive people who couldn't talk or walk or feed themselves. Small ones, anyway. *They can work up.*

He hadn't expected them to work up to him, however. "Dag," said Mari, with her usual directness, "the bags under your eyes are so black you look like a blighted raccoon. Have you had anybody look *you* over yet?"

He'd been thinking of quietly hauling one of the better field medicine fellows out of range of the grove to examine him. Mari, he realized glumly, was not only at the top of that list by experience and groundsense skill, but would corner any substitute and have the story ripped out of him in minutes anyway. Might as well save steps.

"Come on," he sighed. She nodded in stern satisfaction.

He led off to his stump of last night, or one like it, sat, and cautiously opened himself. It took a couple of minutes, and he ended with his head bent nearly to his knees. *Still hurts.*

He heard a long, slow hiss through her teeth that for Mari was as scary as swearing. In a tone of cool understatement, she observed, "Well, that don't look so good. What *is* that black crap?"

"Some sort of ground contamination. It happened when I . . ." he started to say, *ground-ripped the malice,* but changed it to, "when I tried to draw the malice off from Utau, and it turned on me. It was like bits of it stuck to me, and burned. I couldn't get rid of it. Then I closed up and passed out."

"You sure did. I thought you were just ground-ripped—hah, listen to me, *just* ground-ripped—like Utau. Does that, um . . . hurt? Looks like it ought to."

"Yeah." Dag turned his groundsense on himself, closing his eyes for an instant to feel more clearly. Two of the gray patches on his left arm, separate last night, seemed to have grown together since like two water droplets joining. *I'm losing ground.*

Mari said hesitantly, "You want me to try anything? Think a bit of ground reinforcement might help, or a match?"

"Not sure. I wouldn't want to get this crud stuck to you. I suspect it's"— *lethal*—"not good. Better wait. It's not like I'm falling over."

"It's not like you're dancing a jig, either. This isn't like . . . Utau's ground, it's like it's scraped raw, shivering and won't stop, but you can see it'll come right in its own time. This . . . yeah, this is outside my ken. You need a real medicine maker."

"That's what I figured. Hope one shows up soon. Meantime, well, I can still walk, it seems. If not jig." Dag hesitated. "If you can refrain from gossiping about this all over camp, I'd take it kindly."

Mari snorted. "So if this had happened to any other patroller, how fast would you have slapped him onto the sick list?"

"Privileges of captaincy," Dag said vaguely. "You know that road, patrol leader."

"Yeah? Would that be the privilege to be stupid? Funny, I don't seem to recall that one."

"Look, if anybody with more skill shows up here to hand this mess on to, you bet I'll be on my horse headed east in an hour." Except that he could not ride away from what he carried inside, now, could he? "I have no idea who the Raintree folks can spare or when, but I figure the soonest we could get help from home is six days." He stared around; the afternoon was growing hazy, with a brassy heat in the air that foreboded evening thundershowers.

Mari glanced toward the grove, and said quietly, "Think those folks will last six more days?"

Dag let out a long breath and heaved himself to his feet. "I don't know, Mari. Does look like we need to rustle up some kind of tent covering to gather them under, though. Rain tonight, you think?"

"Looks like," she agreed.

They strolled silently back to the dead grove.

He wasn't sure how much Mari talked, or didn't, but a lot of people in the grove camp that evening seemed to take it as their mission to tell him to go lie down. He was persuadable, except that with nothing to do but sit cross-legged on his bedroll and stare at the groundlocked makers, he found himself drifting into hating them. Without this tangle, he could have gone home with today's patrol. In three days' time, held Spark hard and not let go even for breathing. His earlier weariness of this long war was as nothing to his present choked surfeit. He slept poorly.

By late the following afternoon, two of the older makers had lost the ability to swallow, and one was having trouble breathing. As Carro, one of Mari's cronies from Obio's patrol, held the man up in her lap in an effort to ease him, Dag knelt beside the bedroll and studied his labored gasps. Breathing this bad in a dying man was normally a signal to share, and soon. But was this fellow dying? Need he be? His thinning hair was streaked with gray, but he was hardly elderly; before this horror had fallen on him, Dag judged him to have been hale, lean and wiry. Artin was his name, Dag didn't want to know, an excellent smith and something of a weapons-master. Under his own tracing fingers, Dag could read a lifetime of accumulated knowledge in the subtle calluses of Artin's hands.

Mari blotted the face and hair of the nearby woman she had just spent several fruitless minutes trying to get water down, while the woman had writhed and choked. "If we can't get more drink into them in this heat, they aren't going to last anything like five more days, Dag."

Carro nodded to the man in her lap. "This one, less."

"I see that," murmured Dag.

Saun paced about. Dag had guessed he would volunteer for the patrol lingering in Raintree to assist the refugees, and indeed he'd scorned an offer to ride back to Hickory Lake yesterday; but, taking his partnership with Dag seriously, he'd instead requested assignment to this duty. He slept in the now-reduced camp to the east off the blight, but lived at Dag's left elbow in the daytime. Which would be a fine thing if only Saun acted less like a flea on a griddle in the face of these frustrations.

Now he declared, "We have to try *something*. Dag, you say you think these makers are still supporting the mud-men. If that's so, doesn't it make sense to cut off the load?"

"Obio and Griff said they tried that," said Dag patiently. "The results were pretty alarming, I gathered."

"But no one *died*. It could be like one of Hoharie's cuttings, hurting to heal."

It was a shrewd argument, and it attracted Dag more than the prospect of just sitting here watching while these people suffered and failed. *My company.* He wasn't quite sure how these Raintree makers had become honorary members of it in his mind, but they had. His three unconscious patrollers were the least depleted, so far, but Dag could see that wasn't going to last.

"I admit," Dag said slowly, "I'd like to see what happens for myself." Although how much telling detail he was likely to observe with his groundsense closed was a bitter question. "Maybe . . . do one. And then we'll see."

Saun gave him a quick nod of understanding and went to fetch his sword. It was the same weapon that had put Saun in harm's way back at Glassforge; Dag had heroically refrained from pointing out how useless the deadweight had been to Saun on this trip, too. But for dispatching mud-men in their pots, it would do nearly as well as a spear, and better than a knife.

Sword over his shoulder, Saun trod determinedly back through the grove and out toward the boggy patch, his boots squelching in the mud from last night's rain. He slowed, trying to pick his way more cleanly upon clumps of dead grasses, and peered down into the mud pots with a look of curious revulsion.

The unformed monsters therein were in a revolting enough state, distorted past any hope of returning to their animal lives, and equally far from transformation to their mock-human forms. Innocent but doomed. Dag's brow furrowed. So—if their transformation could somehow be completed, with the malice dead would they switch their slavish allegiance to the Lakewalker makers? It was a disturbing idea, as if Dag's brain didn't teem with enough of those already. The more disturbing for being seductive. Powerful subhuman servants might be used for a multitude of desperately needed tasks. Had the mage-lords of old made something like them? All malices seemed to hatch with the knowledge, not to mention the compulsion, of such makings, which suggested it was an old, old skill. But the mud-slaves presumably would require a continuous supply of ground reinforcement to live, making them lethally expensive to maintain.

Dag was glad to give over this line of thought as Saun called, "Which should I start with? The biggest?"

Mari, her face screwed up in doubt as she stared down at the damp woman maker, said, "The smallest?"

"I'm not sure it matters," Dag called back. "Just pick one."

Saun stepped toward a mud pot, gripped his sword in both hands, braced his shoulders, squinted, and struck. Squalling and splashing rose from the hole, and flying mud; Saun grimaced, pulled back, and struck hastily again.

"What was it?" Mari called.

"Beaver. I think. Or maybe woodchuck." Saun jumped back, looking sick, as the splashing died away.

Carro's cry wrenched Dag's attention around. The makers—all the groundlocked folk—were writhing and moaning in their bedrolls, as if in pain—deep, inarticulate animal sounds. The other two on-duty patrollers hurried to their sides, alarmed. The makers did not seem to be actually convulsing, so Dag stifled a wild look around for something to shove between teeth besides his hook, bad idea, or his fingers.

Artin's breathing passed from labored to choked. Carro pulled down his blanket and pressed her ear to his chest. "Dag, this isn't good."

"No more, Saun!" Dag called urgently over his shoulder, and bent to Artin's other side. The smith's lips were turning a leaden hue, and his eyelids fluttered.

"His heartbeat's going all wrong," said Carro. "Sounds like partridge wings."

Just before the archer shoots the bird out of the air? Dag continued the unspoken thought. *His heart is failing. Blight it, blight it . . .*

Saun hurried back; Dag raised his glance from Saun's muddy boots to his suddenly drained face. Saun's lips parted, but no sound came out. Dag needed no words to interpret that particular appalled look, of a heart going hollow with fear and guilt. *You should not shoulder such a burden, boy. No one should.* But someone had to.

Not today, blight it.

Help might be coming, if the makers could be kept alive till then. *Somehow.* He remembered, for some reason, his impulsive attack on the malice's cave back in Glassforge. *Any way that works, old patroller.*

"I'm going to try a ground match," Dag said abruptly, moving to get a better grip on Artin's shuddering body. "Dance his heart back to the right beat, if I can." As he had once done for Saun.

Mari's voice called sharply, "Dag, no!"

He was already opening his ground. Finding his way into the other's body through his ground. Pain on pain, clashing rhythms, but Dag's dance was the stronger one. The true world rushed back into his awareness, blight and glory and all, and he became aware of how keenly he'd missed his groundsense, as if he'd been walking around for days with the best part of himself bloodily amputated. *Dance with me, Artin.*

Dag breathed satisfaction as he felt the smith's heart and lungs take up a steadier, stronger cadence once more. Dag did not share in such shocking pain as Saun's injuries, but he could feel the fragility in the maker's ground, how close it was to the edge of another such fall into disorder and death. Were the others as weakened? Dag's perceptions widened in increasing fascination.

All the Lakewalkers' grounds were wound about and penetrated by a subtle gray structure like ten thousand tangled threads. The threads combined and darkened, running out like strands of smoke to the mud-men's pots. The mud-men's grounds were the strangest of all: turned black, strong, compellingly human in shape. The fleshly bodies of the animals labored in vain, straining to match that impulsion. Starving in their arrested growth.

The malice spatters on Dag's ground seemed to be shivering in time with the complex ground structure imprisoning the makers, and Dag had a sudden terror that somehow the still-living malice bits lodged within him were what was keeping this thing intact. Would he have to die for it to be broken . . . ? Ah. *No.* Affinity both had with each other, no question, but his spatters were as formless as a ground reinforcement, if an inverted one that was negative and destructive rather than positive and healing.

Dag struggled to understand what he was sensing. In normal persuasive making, the maker pushed and reinforced ground found within the object, striving to make things more themselves, as in Dag's old arrowproof coat where the protection of skin became leather became a shield. In healing, ground was gifted freely, unformed, to be turned into the recipient's ground without resistance. A ground match, such as he had just done for Artin, was a dance in time. The malices' enslavement of farmer minds, Dag realized suddenly, must also be such a ground dance, if enormously powerful to work so compulsively and at such distances. But it had to be continuously maintained, as he had glimpsed from the inside during this last kill, and the match died when the malice did. *It has a limited range, too,* he realized, which was why the malice had been forced to move along with its army.

This groundwork, though . . . had a range of only a hundred paces, but it had most certainly survived its malice maker. Contained, powerful, horrific . . . familiar. Familiar? *So where have I seen anything like this before?* What groundwork both survived its maker's death and retained the nature of its maker, not melding with its recipient, even after it had been released?

Sharing knives do. On a smaller scale, to be sure, but . . . scarcely less complex. The ground of the consecrated knife was shaped by its maker into an involuted container for the donor's future death, and that dissolving ground, once received, was held tight. Altered, if with and not against the donor's will, to something lethal to malices.

Dar must be giving something of himself away with each knife he made, Dag reflected. On some level, folks knew this, which was why they treated their knife makers with such care. How draining was such a making? Again and again and again? *Very.* No wonder Dar had so little left of himself for any other purpose.

Dag turned his inner eye back upon the malice's groundwork. This huge, horrific making was involuted and powerful beyond any scope he would ever have. But—beyond his understanding, as well?

The intuitive leap was effortless, like flying in a dream. *I see how this may be broken!* He grinned and opened his eyes.

Tried to grin. Tried to open his eyes.

Face, eyes, body were gone from him; his mind seemed one with his ground, floating cut off from the outer world. Gray threads wound into him like little searching mouths, like worms, sucking and consuming.

I'm trapped—

Fawn carefully tucked the dozen new beeswax candles that were her share of the afternoon's making into Dag's trunk, closed the lid, drifted out under her tent awning, and stared through the trees at the leaden gleam of the lake under the humid sky. She scratched absently at one of the mosquito bites speckling her bare arms, and pawed at a whine near her ear. Yet another reason to miss Dag, silly and selfish though it seemed. She sighed . . . then tensed.

The heartthrob echo of pain in her left arm and down her side, her constant companion for three days, changed into something racing. A wave of terror swept through her, and she could not tell if the first breath of it was Dag's or her own, though the panting that followed seemed all hers. The rhythm broke up into something chaotic and uneven; then it muted. *No, don't die—*

It didn't, but neither did it return to its former definition. *Absent gods forfend, what was that?* She gulped, flipped down her tent flap behind her, and started walking quickly up the shore road, breaking into a trot till she grew winded, then walking again. She did not want to draw stares by running like a frightened deer.

She passed patroller headquarters, where one of Omba's horse girls was leading off two spent mounts, heads down, lathered, and muddy. Only couriers in a hurry would ride horses in wet like that, but Fawn quelled hope, or fear, of word from Dag's company; Fairbolt had said today would still be too soon. Considering the deathly signals he was waiting for, she could not wish for more speed.

She popped up the steps to Hoharie's medicine cabin—medicine tent, she corrected the thought—and stood for a moment trying to catch her breath, then pushed inside.

Hoharie's apprentice, what was his name, Othan, came out of the herb room and frowned at her. "What do *you* want, farmer girl?"

Fawn ignored his tone. "Hoharie. Said I should come see her. If anything changed in my marriage cord. Something just did."

Othan glanced at the closed door to the inner room. "She's doing some groundwork. You'll have to wait." Reluctantly, he jerked his head toward the empty chair by the writing table, then went back into the herb room. Something pungent was cooking over its small fireplace, making the hot chambers hotter.

Fawn sat and jittered, rubbing her left arm, though her probing fingers made no difference to the sensations. The former throbbing had been a source of fear to her for days, but now she wished for it back. And why should her throat feel as though she was choking?

After what seemed forever, the door to the inner chamber opened, and a buxom woman came out with a boy of maybe three in her arms. He was frowning and feverish, eyes glazed, his head resting against her shoulder and his thumb stuck in his mouth. Hoharie followed, gave Fawn a nod of acknowledgment, and went with them into the herb room. A murmur of low voices, instructions to Othan, then Hoharie returned and gestured Fawn before her into the inner room, closing the door behind them.

Fawn turned and mutely thrust out her arm.

"Sit, girl," Hoharie sighed, pointing to a table in the corner with a pair of chairs. Hoharie winced as she settled across from Fawn, stretching her back, and Fawn wondered what she had just done for that little boy, and how much it had cost her in her ground. Would she even be able to help Fawn just now?

While Hoharie, her eyes half-closed, felt up and down Fawn's arm, Fawn stammered out a description of what had just happened. Her words sounded confused and inadequate in her own ears, and she was afraid they conveyed nothing to the medicine maker except maybe the idea that she was going crazy. But Hoharie listened without comment.

Hoharie at last sat up and shook her head. "Well, this was odd before, and it's odder now, but without any other information I'm blighted if I can guess what's really going on."

"*That's* no help!" It came out something between a bark and a wail, and Fawn bit her lip in fear she had offended the maker, but Hoharie merely shook her head again in something between exasperation and agreement.

Hoharie opened her mouth to say more, but then paused, arrested, her head turning toward the door. In a moment, boot steps sounded on the porch outside, and the squeak of the door opening. "Fairbolt," Hoharie muttered, "and . . . ?"

A rap at the inner door, and Fairbolt's voice: "Hoharie? It's urgent."

"Come in."

Fairbolt shouldered through, followed by—tall Dirla. Fawn gasped and sat up. Dirla was as mud-spattered as the horse she must have ridden in on, braids awry, shirt reeking of dried and new sweat, her face lined with fatigue under sunburn. Her eyes, though, were bright.

"They got the malice," Fairbolt announced, and Hoharie let out her breath with a triumphant hoot that made Dirla smile. Fairbolt cast Fawn a curious look. "About two hours after midnight, three nights back."

Fawn's hand went to her cord. "But that was when . . . *What happened to Dag?* How bad was he hurt?"

Dirla gave her a surprised nod, but replied, "It's, um, hard to say."

"*Why?*"

Fairbolt, his eyes on Hoharie, pulled the patroller forward, and said, "Tell your tale again, Dirla."

As Dirla began a description of the company's hard ride west, Fawn realized the pair must have come to find Hoharie, not her. Why? *Get to the part about Dag, blight you, Dirla!*

". . . we came up on Bonemarsh about noon, but the malice had moved—south twenty miles, we found out later, launching a big attack toward Farmer's Flats. Dag wouldn't let us stop for anything, even those poor makers. I'd never seen anything like it. The malice had enslaved the *grounds* of these Bonemarsh folk, somehow making them cook up a new batch of mud-men for it, or so Dag claimed. It left them tied to trees. The patrol was pretty upset when Dag ordered us to leave them in place, but Mari and Codo came in on his side, and Dag had this look on his face that made us afraid to press him, so we rode on."

Fawn gnawed her knuckles through Dirla's excited description of the veiled patrol slipping through an enemy-occupied farm at night, the breathless scramble up a hill, the rush upon a bizarre crude tower. "My partner Mari had almost made it to the top when the malice jumped down—must have been over twenty feet. Like it was flying. I never knew a malice could look so beautiful . . . Utau went for it. I had my ground shut tight, but later Utau said the malice just peeled his open like popping the husk off a hickory nut. He thought he was done for, but then Dag, who didn't even *have* a sharing knife, went for the thing barehanded. Bare-hooked, anyway. It left Utau and turned on him. Mari shouted for me and threw me down her knife, and I didn't quite see what happened then. Anyway, I drove Mari's knife into the thing, and all its bright flesh . . . burst. Horrible. And I thought it was over, and we were all home alive, and it was a miracle. Utau staggered over and draped himself on me till Razi could get to him—and then we saw Dag."

Fawn rocked, hunched tight with her arms wrapping her waist to keep from interrupting. Or screaming.

Dirla went on, "He was passed out in the dirt, stiff as a corpse, with his ground wrapped up so tight it was stranglin' him, and no one could get through to try to make a match or a reinforcement, though Mari and Codo and Hann all tried. For the next few hours, we all thought he was dying. Half-ground-ripped, like Utau, but worse."

"Wait," said Hoharie. "Wasn't he physically injured at all?"

Dirla shook her head. "Maybe knocked around a bit, but nothing much. But then, around dawn, he just woke up. And got up. He didn't look any too good, mind you, but he made it onto his horse somehow and pushed us all back to Bonemarsh. Seems he was fretting over those makers we'd left, as well he might.

"When we arrived, the rest of the company had made it in, but those makers—their groundlock didn't break when the malice died, and no one could figure out why not. Worse, anyone who tries to open grounds to them gets drawn into their lock, too. Obio lost three patrollers finding that one out. Dag believes they're all dying. Mari couldn't get him to leave them, though she thinks he should be on the sick list—it's like he's obsessed. Though by the time us couriers left that evening, we'd at least got him to sleep for a while. Utau and Mari, they don't like any of it one little bit. So"—Dirla turned her gaze on the medicine maker, her hands clutching each other in unaccustomed plea—"Dag said he wished he had you there, Hoharie, because he needs someone who knows folks' grounds down deep. So I'm asking for you for him, because Dag—he got *us* through. He got us *all* through."

Fairbolt cleared his throat. "Would you be willing to ride to Raintree, Hoharie?"

An appalled look came over the medicine maker's face as she stared wildly around at her workplace. Fawn thought she could just about see the crowded roster of tasks here racing through Hoharie's mind.

"—in an hour?" Fairbolt continued relentlessly.

"Fairbolt!" Hoharie huffed dismay. After a long, long moment she added, "Could you make it two hours?"

Fairbolt returned a short, satisfied nod. "I'll have two patrollers ready to escort you, and whoever you need to take with you."

Fawn blurted, "Can I come with you? Because I think I'm part of Dag's puzzle, too." She nearly held out her left arm in evidence.

The three Lakewalkers stared down at her in uncomplimentary surprise.

Fawn hurried on, "It's not a war zone anymore, and if I went with you, I couldn't get lost, so I wouldn't be being stupid at all. *I* could be ready in an hour. Less."

Dirla said, not scornfully but in a tone of kindness that was somehow even more annoying, "That fat little plow horse of yours couldn't keep up, Fawn."

"Grace is not fat!" said Fawn indignantly. *At least, not very.* "And she may not be a racehorse, but she's *persistent.*" She added after a moment, as her wits caught up with her mouth, "Anyhow, couldn't you put me up on a patrol horse just like Hoharie?"

Fairbolt smiled a little, but shook his head. "No, Fawn. The malice may be gone, but north Raintree is going to be disrupted for weeks yet, in the aftermath of all this. I made a promise to Dag to see you came to no harm while he was gone, and I mean to keep it."

"But—"

Fairbolt's voice firmed in a way that made Fawn think of her father at his most maddening. "Farmer child, you are one more worry I don't need to have right now. Others have to wait for their husbands and wives to return as well."

And what was the counterargument to that? *I am not a child?* Oh, sure, that one had always worked *so well.* "Funny, I ran around out there in the wide world for eighteen years without your protection, and survived." *Barely,* she was depressingly reminded.

A bitter smile bent Fairbolt's lips, and he murmured, "No, farmer child . . . you've always had our protection." Fawn flushed. As she dropped her eyes in shame, he gave a satisfied nod, and went on more kindly, "I imagine Cattagus and Sarri would be glad to learn the news about the malice. Maybe you could run and let them know."

It was a clear dismissal. *Run along.* Fawn looked around and found no allies, not Dirla, and not even Hoharie, despite the curious look in her eyes; the medicine tent might be her realm, but it was plain the road was Fairbolt's, and she would yield to his judgment in the matter.

Fawn swallowed, nodded, and took herself out, as chairs scraped and the conference continued more intently. Without her. Not being a Lakewalker and all.

She stumped up the path between the medicine tent and Fairbolt's headquarters, fuming and rubbing her arm. Its thrumming echoed in her heart and head and gut until she was in a fair way to screaming from it. So was she a

Lakewalker bride or a farmer bride? Because if the first was under Lakewalker disciplines, the other could not be. People couldn't just switch her label back and forth at their convenience. Fair was fair, if not, *hah,* Fairbolt.

In one thing she was surely expert, and that was running away from home. Of which the first well-tested rule was, don't give folks a chance to *argue* with you. How had she forgotten that one? She set her teeth and turned aside at patroller headquarters.

A pair of patrollers conferring over a logbook looked up as she entered. "Fairbolt's not here," said one.

"I know," Fawn replied breezily. "I just talked with him up at Hoharie's." Which was perfectly true, right? No one, later, could say she'd lied. "I need to borrow one of his maps for a bit. I'll bring it back as soon as I can."

The patroller shrugged and nodded, and Fawn whipped into Fairbolt's pegboard chamber, hastily rolled up the map of north Raintree still out on top of the center table, tucked it under her arm, and left, smiling and waving thanks.

She dogtrotted to Mare Island, let herself through the bridge gate, and found one of Omba's girls in the work shed.

"I need my horse," said Fawn. "I want to take her out for some exercise." *A hundred or so miles worth.*

"She could use some," the girl conceded. Then, after a moment, "Oh, that's right. You need *help* summoning her." The girl sniffed, grabbed a halter and line off a nail, and wandered out into the pastures.

While she was gone, Fawn hastily found an old sack and filled it with what she judged to be a three-day supply of oats. Was it stealing, to take the equivalent of what her mare would have eaten anyhow? She decided not to pursue the moral fine point, as the lush grass here grew free and the grain had to be painstakingly brought in from off island. She considered hiding the sack under her skirts, decided it would involve walking funny, then, remembering that sneak thief down in Lumpton Market, just cast it over her shoulder as if she'd a right. The horse girl, when she led Grace in, didn't even ask about it.

Back at Tent Bluefield, Fawn tied Grace to a tree while she went inside, skinned into her riding clothes, and swiftly packed her saddlebags. She pulled her sharing knife from its place in Dag's trunk and slung it around her neck under her shirt, then fastened the steel knife Dag had given her to her belt. Last, she plopped plunkins into her saddlebags opposite the grain sack till they balanced, and fastened the buckles. Food and to spare for one little farmer girl for a three-day ride, and no stopping.

Finally, she fished Dag's spare quill and ink bottle from the bottom of his trunk and knelt beside it, penning a short note on a scrap of cloth. *Dear Cattagus and Sarri. Dag's company killed the malice, but he's hurt, so I'm going to Raintree to meet up with him, because he's my husband, and I have a right. Ask Dirla about the rest.*

Back soon. Love, Fawn. She worked it into the tent-flap ties, where it fluttered discreetly but visibly. Then she stood on a stump to saddle Grace, heaved up and tied on her saddlebags, and climbed aboard. She was over the bridge in ten minutes more.

14

By sunset, Fawn guessed she had covered about twenty-five miles from Hickory Lake. The hours of interspersed trotting and walking, nursing her mare along in what she hoped was the best balance between speed and endurance, had given her plenty of time to think. Unfortunately, by now her thoughts were mainly variations on *Have I taken a wrong turn yet?* Fairbolt's map was not as reassuring as she'd hoped. The Lakewalker notion of roads seemed more Fawn's idea of trails; their trails, paths; and their paths, wilderness. So she wasn't altogether sorry when she heard the hoofbeats coming up behind her.

She turned in her saddle. Rounding the dense greenery of the last curve, a husky patroller rode, followed by Hoharie, her apprentice Othan towing a packhorse and a spare mount in a string, and another patroller. Fawn didn't bother trying to race ahead, but she didn't halt, either. In a moment, the others cantered up to surround her, and she let Grace drop back to a walk.

"Fawn!" cried Hoharie. "What are you doing out here?"

"Riding my fat horse," said Fawn shortly. "They told me she needed exercise."

"Fairbolt didn't give you permission to come with us."

"I'm not with you. I'm by myself."

As Hoharie sucked on her lower lip, eyes narrowed in thought, Othan chimed in. "You have to turn around and go back, farmer girl. You can't follow us."

"I'm ahead of you," Fawn pointed out. She added, "Though you're welcome to pass. Go on, run along."

Hoharie glanced back at her two patrollers, now riding side by side at the rear and watching dubiously. "I really can't spare a man to see you home."

"Nobody's asking you to."

Hoharie drew a deeper breath. "But I will, if you make me."

Fawn halted her mare and glanced back at the two big, earnest fellows. They would do their duty; that was a bit of a mania, with patrollers. If she let herself get cumbered with either one of that grim pair, he would see her back to Hickory Lake, sure enough, and in no good mood about it, likely. Patrollers had objections to leaving their partners.

Fawn tried one more time. "Hoharie, please let me come with you. I won't slow you down, I promise."

"That's not the problem, Fawn. It's your own safety. You don't belong out here."

I know where I belong, thank you very much. By Dag's side. Fawn rubbed her left arm and frowned. "I don't want to cost you your escort. If it's that unsafe, you might need them yourself." She let her shoulders slump, her head droop. "All right, Hoharie. I'm sorry. I'll turn around." She bit her tongue on any further artistic embellishments. *Keep it simple. And short.* Lakewalkers read grounds, not thoughts, Dag claimed, and Fawn's ground had plenty of other reasons to be in a roil besides duplicity.

Hoharie stared at her for a long, uncertain moment, and Fawn held her breath, lest the medicine maker be inspired to detach a guard anyhow. But finally Hoharie nodded. "You've come out a long way. If your horse can't make it back tonight, it should still be safe enough to stop if you get within ten miles of the lake."

"Grace is doing all right," Fawn said distantly, and turned away. Although she had to kick the mare back into a walk, as she was much inclined to turn and follow the other horses.

Dag's groundsense range was a mile; Fawn didn't think any of Hoharie's party had a better range, but she let Grace go on for a mile and a bit before halting, just to be safe. She slid down and let her mare browse for a few minutes before leading her back onto the road. In the summer-damp earth, the hoofprints of the Lakewalker horses showed plain even in the failing light. *No wrong turns now.* Fawn grinned and trailed after them till she could barely see in the shadows, then dismounted again and led Grace off the road to outwait the hours of darkness.

Fawn watered the mare in a nearby stream, then rubbed her down and fed her oats. She washed up herself, swatted mosquitoes, gnawed a plunkin slice, squashed a crawling tick with her knife haft, and rolled up in her blanket. The songs of the small night creatures only made the underlying stillness more profound. It weighed in upon her just how different this desolate darkness was from that of her seemingly equally lonesome trudge through the settled country south of Lumpton Market. These vasty woods did harbor wolves, and bears, and catamounts; she'd seen the skins of all three in the stores back at

Hickory Lake. In the aftermath of the malice, mindless mud-men like the one Dag had slain so deftly at the Horsefords' could also be wandering around out here. She'd hardly given such hazards a thought when she'd camped during the after-wedding trip up to the lake, in woodlands not so very different. But then she'd had Dag by her side. Curling up in his arms each night had seemed like settling into her own private magical fortress. She touched the steel knife he had given her, sheathed at her belt, and sighed.

But by the first gray light of morning, neither she nor Grace had been eaten by catamounts yet. Heartened, Fawn returned to the trail and found Hoharie's tracks once more. An hour into the ride, she was given pause when the tracks seemed to part from her map, turning off onto a path. But a closer dismounted searching found them coming back and continuing; likely the party had just diverted to a campsite for the night. A pile of recent horse droppings reassured Fawn that she remained the right distance behind. She kicked Grace along, glumly confident that she risked no chance of overtaking Hoharie prematurely. On the other hand, Grace was carrying barely half the weight of those big patrollers' mounts. Over time that might add up to more of an edge than anyone thought.

Late in the morning Hoharie's tracks were suddenly confused by those of a much larger cavalcade, going the other way. A patrol, Fawn guessed—Raintree Lakewalkers, or part of Dag's company heading home? The heavy prints turned off on another trail, and Fawn, frowning, unrolled her map and studied it. They could be diverting to visit a small Lakewalker camp marked a few miles to the south, or could be patrolling, or who knew? Their passage rendered the trail they'd come down unmistakable, but also left Hoharie's overlying signs harder to make out in the deeply pocked muddy patches. But at midday, Fawn came to one of the rare timber bridges over a deep-flowing brown river, and was assured of her place on the map once more. From time to time she passed spots where recent deadfalls had been roughly cleared from the road, and she wondered if that was a task patrols undertook as well, when they weren't in a tearing hurry.

By late afternoon, Grace's steps were shortening and stiffening, and Fawn's backside was numb. How did couriers and their horses ever manage such distances at such speed? She dismounted and led the mare up a few of the steeper slopes, insofar as there were any in these parts, fell into resentment at the loss of precious daylight, then finally considered Dirla and ruthlessly cut a switch. This activated Grace again, making Fawn feel equally justified and guilty.

At a close-grown place where the road mud seemed wildly churned, she paused, spooking a couple of turkey vultures and some crows. The former grunted and hissed, reluctantly retreating, and the latter flapped off, yammering complaint. She peeked over the rim of a shallow ravine where the vegetation was trampled down and caught her breath at the sight of half a dozen naked, rotting corpses piled below. She ventured just close enough to be certain they were mud-men and not Lakewalkers, then hastily remounted. She wasn't sure if the patrol had slain them sometime back, or if Hoharie's guards had done for them just recently; the stench was no certain clue. The absence of visible catamounts was suddenly not enough to make her feel safe anymore. She pushed along well past sunset mainly because she was now terrified to stop.

In the deep dark that night she rolled up small and scared, sniveling miserable, stupid tears for the lack of Dag. She buried her face in her blanket edge. With none to see her, she supposed she might bawl to her heart's content, but she really didn't want to make unnecessary noise. She hoped any predator within ten miles would be too replete with scavenged mud-men to hunt farmer girls and plump, tired horses. She slept badly despite her exhaustion.

She'd figured the last morning would be the worst, and truly, she woke hurting just as much as she'd suspected she would. But it would be a much shorter leg than yesterday, and at the end of it, she would find Dag. Her cord still assured her of this; if anything, her arm throbbed more clearly, if more worrisomely, with each passing mile. Barely an hour into the morning's ride she found Hoharie's campsite just off the track, the dirt cast over the campfire ashes still warm. Only the level terrain and Fawn's switch kept Grace plodding forward into the long afternoon.

As the light flattened toward the west, Fawn rode abruptly out of the humid green of the endless woods into an open landscape metallic with heat. *We're here.*

The woods gave way to water meadows, their grasses gone yellow and limp. The sorry shrubs scattered about bore drooping brown leaves, or none. It all looked very sodden and strange. But ahead, she could see a trickle of cook-fire smoke from a stand of skeletal trees along a leaden shoreline. She didn't need her stolen map anymore, hadn't for the past two hours; her aching body bleated to her, *There, there, he's over there.* Hoharie and her little troop were just dismounting.

As Fawn rode up, Mari came striding out of the trees, waving her arms and crying urgently, "Close your grounds! Close your grounds!"

Hoharie looked startled, but waved acknowledgment and turned to check Othan and the patrollers, who apparently also obeyed. She saw Fawn, who brought Grace to a weary halt just a few paces away, and her face set, but before she could say anything, Mari, coming to her stirrup, continued.

"You're here sooner than I dared hope! Dirla fetch you?"

"Yes," said Hoharie.

"Praise the girl. Did you run across the patrol we sent back home?"

"Yes, about a day out of Hickory Lake."

"Ah, good." Mari's eye fell on Fawn, hunched over her saddlebow. "Why'd you bring her?" The tone of the question was not dismissive, but genuinely curious, as though there might be some very good, if obscure, Lakewalkerish reason for Fawn's presence in Hoharie's train.

Hoharie grimaced. "I didn't. She brought herself."

Fawn tossed her head.

Othan leaned over and hissed at her, "You lied, farmer girl! You promised to turn around!"

"I did," said Fawn defiantly. "Twice."

Hoharie looked not-best-pleased, but the shrewd and curious look on Mari's face scarcely changed.

"Did you get a look at Utau, when you passed the patrol?" asked Mari. "We sent him home in Razi's care."

"Oh, yes," said Hoharie. She dismounted and stretched her back. Really, all her party looked as hot and tired and dirty as Fawn felt. So much for Lakewalker conceit about their stamina. "Strangest ground damage I ever saw. I told Utau, six months on the sick list."

"That long?" Mari looked dismayed.

"Likely less, but that'll hold Fairbolt off for three, which should be about right."

They exchanged short laughs of mutual understanding.

Fawn slid off sweaty Grace, who stood head down and flop-eared, liquid eyes reproachful, legs as stiff as Fawn's own. Saun came out of the grove to Mari's shoulder, trailed by a couple of other patrollers, both older women. As the women began to confer with Hoharie and Mari, he strode up to Fawn, looking astonished.

"You shouldn't be out here! Dag would have a fit."

"Where *is* Dag?" She craned past him toward the grove. *So close.* "What's happened to him?"

Saun ran a hand over his head in a harried swipe. "Which time?"

Not a reassuring answer. "Day before yesterday, about the time Dirla rode in to Hickory Lake. Something happened to Dag then, I know it. I *felt* it." *Something terrible?*

His brows drew down in wonder, but he caught her by the arm as she tried to push past him. "Wait! You can't close your ground. I don't know if you'd be drawn in, too—wait!" She wrenched out of his grip and broke into a stumbling run. He pelted after, crying in exasperation, "Blight it, you're as bad as him!"

Among the trees, a number of people seemed to be collected together in bedrolls under makeshift awnings of blankets and hides, four women under one and four men under another. They lay too still for sleep; not still enough for death. A little way off, another bedroll was partly shaded under a blanket hitched to an ash tree's limbs. Fawn fell to her knees beside it and stared in shock.

Dag lay faceup under a light blanket. Someone had removed his arm harness and set it atop his saddlebags at the head of the bedroll. Fawn had watched his beloved face in sleep, and knew its shape in all its subtle movements. This was like no sleep she'd ever seen. The copper of his skin seemed tarnished and dull, and his flesh stretched too tightly over his bones. His sunken eyes were ringed with dark half circles. But his bare chest rose and fell; he breathed, he lived.

Saun slid to his knees beside her and grabbed her hands as she reached for Dag. "No!"

"Why not?" said Fawn furiously, yanking futilely against his strong grip. "What's *happened* to him?"

Saun began to give her a garbled and guilty-sounding account of his trying to help by slaying mud-men in pots—Fawn gazed in bewilderment toward the boggy shoreline where he pointed—that she could only follow at all because of the prior descriptions of the groundlock she'd heard from Dirla. Of Dag, leaping into the eerie danger to save somebody named Artin, which sounded just like Dag, truly. Of Dag being sucked into the lock, or spell, or whatever this was. Of Dag lying unarousable all these three days gone. Fawn stopped fighting, and Saun, with a stern look at her, let her wrists go; she rubbed them and scowled.

"But I'm not a Lakewalker. I'm a farmer," said Fawn. "Maybe it wouldn't work on me."

"Mari says no more experiments," said Saun grimly. "They've already cost us three patrollers and the captain."

"But if you don't . . ." *If you don't poke at things, how can you find anything out?* She sat back on her heels, lips tight. All right: look around first, poke later. Dag's breathing didn't seem to be getting worse right away, anyhow.

Mari, meanwhile, had led Hoharie and Othan out to the mud pots, then back through the grove to examine the other captives. Mari was finishing what sounded to Fawn like a more coherent account of events than Saun's as they came over and knelt on the other side of Dag. Her tale of Dag's ground match with Artin's failing heart had the medicine maker letting out her breath in a faint whistle. Even more frightening to Fawn was Mari's description of the strange blight left on Dag's ground from his fight with the malice.

"Huh." Hoharie scrubbed at her heat-flushed face, smearing road dirt in sweaty streaks, and stared around. "For the love of reason, Mari, what did you drag me here for? In one breath you beg me to break this unholy groundlock, and in the next you insist I don't dare even open my ground to examine it. You can't have it both ways."

"If Dag went into that thing and couldn't get himself out, I know I couldn't. I don't know about you. Hoped you'd have more tricks, Hoharie." Mari's voice fell quiet. "I've been picking at this knot for days, now, till I'm near cross-eyed crazy. I'm starting to wonder when it will be time to cut our losses. Except . . . all of those makers' own bonded knives went missing during the time they were prisoners of the malice. Of the nine people down, only Bryn is carrying an unprimed knife right now. That's not much to salvage, for the price. And I'm not real sure what would happen to someone locked up like that trying to share, or to her knife—or to the others. We had ill luck with those mud-puppies, that's certain."

Saun, now leaning against the barren ash tree with his arms folded, grimaced agreement.

Fawn's belly shuddered as it finally dawned on her what Mari was talking about. The picture of Mari, or Saun, or Hoharie—likely Mari, it seemed her idea of a leader's duty—taking those bone knives and methodically driving them through the hearts of her comrades, going down the rows of bedrolls one after another . . . *No, not Dag!* Fawn touched the knife beneath her shirt, suddenly fiercely glad that her accident with it back at Glassforge had at least blocked this ghastly possibility.

Hoharie was frowning, but it seemed to Fawn more in sorrow than dissent.

"I will say," said Mari, "Dag falling into this lock seemed to give everyone in it new strength—for a little while. But the weaker ones are failing again. If we were to add a new patroller every three days, I don't rightly know how long we could keep them alive—except, of course, the problem would just get bigger and bigger as we strung it out. I'm not volunteerin', note. And I'm not volunteerin' you either, Hoharie, so don't go getting ideas."

Hoharie rubbed the back of her neck. "I'm going to have to get ideas of some sort. But I'm not going to attempt anything at all tonight. Fatigue distorts judgment."

Mari nodded approval, and described the camp off the blight to the east where everyone not tending the enspelled apparently retreated to sleep. When she paused, Fawn motioned at Dag and broke in, "Mari—is it really true I can't touch him?"

Mari said, "It may be. The finding out could be costly."

Or not, thought Fawn. "I rode all this way."

Hoharie said, in a sort of weary sympathy, "We told you to stay home, child. There's nothing for you to do here but grieve."

"And get in the way," muttered Othan, almost inaudibly.

"But I can *feel* Dag. Still!"

Hoharie did not look hopeful, but she rose to her knees, reached across Dag, and took up Fawn's left arm anyway, probing along it. "Has it changed any lately?"

"The ache feels stronger for being closer, but no clearer," Fawn admitted. "It's funny. Dag gave me this for reassurance, but instead it's made me frantic."

"Is that you or him that's frantic?"

"I can't hardly tell the difference."

"Huh." Hoharie let her go and sat back. "This gets us no further that I can see. Yet." With a pained grunt, she rose to her feet, and everyone else did too.

Fawn held out her hands, palms open, to Mari. "Surely there's something I can do!"

Mari looked at her and sighed, but at least it was a sigh of understanding. "There's bedding and catch-rags to be washed."

Fawn's hands clenched. "I can do that, sure." Better: it was a task that would keep her here in the grove, and not exiled a mile away.

"Oh, *that's* important. You rode a long way to do laundry, farmer girl," said Othan, and missed the cool look that the Lakewalker women turned on him. It was no stretch to Fawn to guess who had been doing the washing so far.

Mari said more firmly, "Not that there's a pile. It's so hard to get anything into these people, there's not much coming out. In any case, not tonight, Fawn. You look bushed."

Fawn admitted it with a short nod. When it was all sorted out, the party's horses, including Grace, were led off to the east camp by the patrollers, but Fawn managed to keep her bedroll and saddlebags in the grove by Dag. It was driving her half-mad not to be allowed to touch him, but she set about finding other tasks for her hands, helping with the fire and the batches of broths and thin gruel that these experienced women had cooking.

Hoharie commenced a second, more thorough physical examination of all the silent groundlocked folk, an expression of extreme frustration on her face. "I might as well be some farmer bonesetter," Fawn heard her mutter as she knelt by Dag. The tart thought came to Fawn that really, they might all be better off with one; farmer bonesetters and midwives always had to work by guess and by golly, with indirect clues. They likely grew good at it, over time.

Resolutely, Fawn took on the laundry the following morning as soon as she could rise and move. At least the work abused different muscles than the ones she'd overtaxed the past three days. Riding trousers rolled above her knees, she waded out into the cool water of the marsh towing a makeshift raft of lashed-together deadwood holding the soiled blankets and catch-rags. The water seemed peculiarly clear and odorless, for a marsh, but it was fine for washing. And she could keep an eye on the long lumpy shadow beneath the ash tree that was Dag, and see the silhouettes of the ground-closed helpers moving about the grove.

To her surprise one of the Lakewalker men, not a patroller but a survivor from the ruined village down the shore, came out and joined her in the task, silently taking up the rubbing and scrubbing by her side. He said only, "You're Dag Redwing's farmer bride," not a question but a statement; Fawn could only nod. He had a funny look on his face, drawn and distant, that made Fawn shy of speaking to him, though she murmured thanks as they passed clouts back and forth. He took the main burden of lugging the heavy, wet cloths back to the blighted trees, and, being much taller, of hanging them up on the bare branches after she shook them out. The only other thing he said, rather abruptly as they finished and he turned away, was, "Artin the smith is my father, see."

Hoharie paced around the grove and squinted, or walked out to a distance and stared, or sat on a stump and drew formless lines on the ground with a stick, scowling. She went methodically through an array of more startling actions, yelling at or slapping the sleepers, pricking them with a pin, stirring up the half-formed mud-men in their pots. Mari and Saun, with difficulty, dissuaded her from killing another one by way of a test. Flushed after her futile exertions, she came and sat cross-legged by Dag's bedroll, scowling some more.

Fawn sat across from her nibbling on a raw plunkin slice. She wished she could feed Dag—would the taste of genuine Hickory Lake plunkin be like home cooking to him? But even if she could touch him, he could not chew—he could barely swallow water. She supposed she might try cooking and mashing up some of the root and thinning it down for a gruel, disgusting as that sounded. She asked Hoharie quietly, "What do you figure?"

Hoharie shook her head. "This isn't just a lovers' groundlock enlarged. Something of the malice must linger in it. Has to be an involuted ground reinforcement of some sort, to survive the malice's death; what it's living *on* is a puzzle. Well, not much of a puzzle; it has to be ground, the mud-men's or the people's or both. People's, most likely."

"Like . . . like a tick? Or a belly-worm? Made of ground," Fawn added, to show she wasn't confused about that.

Hoharie gave a vague wave that seemed to allow the comparison without exactly approving it. "It has to be worked ground. Malice-worked. Could be—well, it obviously is—quite complex. I still don't understand the part about it being so anchored in place. Question is, how long can it last? Will it be absorbed like a healing reinforcement? And if so, will it strengthen or slay? Is it just their groundlock paralysis that is weakening these folks, or is there something more eating away at them, inside?"

At Fawn's faint gasp Hoharie's eyes flicked up; she glanced from Dag to Fawn, and murmured, "Oh, sorry. Talking to myself, I'm afraid."

"It's all right. I want to know everything."

"So do I, child," Hoharie sighed. She levered to her feet and wandered off again.

Saun having gone off to the east camp to sleep after taking a night watch, it was Othan who came at noon to feed Dag broth. Fawn watched enviously and critically as he raised Dag's head into his lap, wincing at every harsh *click* of spoon on teeth or muffled choke or dribble lost down over Dag's chin. At least Dag's face wasn't rough with stubble; Saun had shaved it just this morning. Fawn had wondered at the effort, since Dag couldn't feel it—but somehow it did make him look less sick. So maybe the use of it was not for Dag, but for the people who looked so anxiously after him. She had smiled gratefully at Saun, anyhow.

Othan, on the other hand, glowered at her as he worked.

"*What?*" she finally demanded.

"You're hovering. Back off, can't you? Half a mile would do."

"I've a right. He's my husband."

"That hasn't been decided yet."

Fawn touched her marriage cord. "Dag and I decided it. Quite a ways back down the road."

"You'll find out, farmer." Othan coaxed the last spoonful of broth down his patient's throat, which moved just enough to swallow, and laid Dag's head back down on the folded blanket that substituted, poorly, for a pillow. Fawn considered collecting dry grass to stuff it with, later. Othan added, "He was a good patroller. Hoharie says he could be even more. They say you've seduced him from his duty and will be the ruination his life if the camp council doesn't fix things."

Fawn sat up indignantly. "*They say?* So let *them say* it to my face, if they're not cowards." *And anyhow, I think we sort of seduced each other.*

"My uncle who's a patroller says it, and he's no coward!"

Fawn gritted her teeth as Othan—safely ground-closed Othan—stroked a strand of sweat-dampened hair back from Dag's forehead. How dare he act as if he owned Dag, just because he was Lakewalker-born and she wasn't! The, the *stupid* boy was just a wet-behind-the-ears apprentice no older than she was. Younger, likely. Her longing to shut Othan up, make him look nohow, was quelled by her sudden realization that he might be a lead into just the sort of camp gossip Dag had so carefully shielded her from. Also—this was half an argument. Just what all had Dag been saying back to Hickory Lake Camp? She recalled the day he'd made that poor plunkin into a porcupine with his bow and her arrows. Her spinning mind settled on, "I'm not a patch on your malices, for ruination."

"They're not *our* malices."

Fawn smiled blackly. "Oh, yes, they are." She added after a fuming moment, "And there isn't any *was* about it, unless you want to say he *was* a good patroller, and he now *is* a really good captain! He took his company right through that awful Raintree malice like a knife through butter, to hear Dirla tell it. Despite being married to a farmer, so there!"

"Despite, yeah," Othan growled.

Fawn took a grip on her shredding temper as Mari and Hoharie came up. Othan scrambled to his feet, giving over glaring at Fawn in order to look anxiously at the medicine maker. Hoharie looked grim, and Mari grimmer.

"Which one, then?" said Mari.

"Dag," said Hoharie. "I've worked on his ground enough to be most familiar with it, and he's also the most recent to fall into the lock. If that counts for anything. Othan, good, you're here," she continued without a pause. "I'm going to enter this groundlock, and I want you to try to anchor me."

Othan looked alarmed. "Are you sure, Hoharie?"

"No, but I've tried everything else I can think of. And I won't walk away from this."

"No, you're leaving that dirty job to me," muttered Mari irritably. Hoharie returned her the sort of sharp shrug that indicated a lengthy argument concluded.

Hoharie went on, "I'll set up a light link to you, Othan, and try for a glimpse inside the groundlock, then pull back. If I can't disengage, you are to break with me instantly and *not* try to enter in after me, do you hear?" She caught her apprentice's gaze and held it sternly. Othan gulped and nodded.

Fawn scrunched back in the litter of dry grass and dead leaves on Dag's far side, wrapping her arms around her knees and trying to make herself small, so they wouldn't notice and exclude her.

Hoharie paused, then said, "My knife is in my saddlebags, Mari, if it comes to that."

"When should it come to it, Hoharie? Don't leave me with that decision, too."

"When the weakest start to die, I believe it will throw more strain on the rest. So it will go faster toward the end. That poor maker who died before Dag's patrol arrived showed that such deaths won't break the lock; if anything, it may grow more concentrated. I think . . . once two or more of the nine— no, ten—are down, then start the sharing. And you'll just have to see what happens next." She added after a moment, "Start with me, of course."

"That," said Mari distantly, "will be my turn to pick."

Hoharie's lips thinned. "Mm."

"I don't recommend this, Hoharie."

"I hear you."

Evidently not, because the medicine maker lowered herself cross-legged by the head of Dag's bedroll, motioning Othan down beside her. He sat up on his knees. She straightened her spine and shut her eyes for a moment, seeming to center herself. She then took Othan's hand with her left hand; there apparently followed another moment of invisible-to-Fawn ground adjustments. Without further hesitation, Hoharie's right hand reached out and touched Dag's forehead. Fawn thought she saw him grimace in his trance, but it was hard to be sure.

Then Hoharie's eyes opened wide; with a yank, she pulled her hand from Othan's and slammed the heel of it into his chest, pushing him over backward. Her eyes rolled up, her face drained of color and expression, and she slumped across Dag.

With a muted wail, Othan scrambled up and dove for her. Mari cursed and caught Othan from behind, wrapping her arms around his torso and trapping his hands. "No!" she yelled in his ear. "Obey her! Close up! Close up, blight you, boy!"

Othan strained against her briefly, then, with a choke of despair, sprawled back in her grip.

"Ten," snarled Mari. "That's it, that's all we're doing here. Not eleven, you hear?" She shook him.

Othan nodded dully, and she let him free. He leaned on his hands, staring at his unconscious mentor in horror.

"What did you feel?" Mari demanded of him. "Anything?"

He shook his head. "I—nothing useful, I don't think. It was like I could feel her ground being pulled away from me, into the dark . . . !" He turned a distraught face to the patrol leader. "I didn't let go, Mari, I didn't! She pushed me away!"

"I saw, boy," sighed Mari. "You did what you could." Slowly, she stood up, and braced her legs apart and her hands on her hips, staring down at the two enspelled in their heap. "We'll lay her out with the rest. She's in there with them now; maybe she can do something different. If this thing was weakening with age, could we tell? If nothing else, she may have bought three more days of time." Her voice fell to a savage mutter. "Except I don't want more time. I want this to be *over*."

Hoharie's bedroll was placed under the ash tree close to Dag's. Othan took up a cross-legged station of guard, or grief, on the opposite side to Fawn, who sat similarly beyond Dag. They didn't much look at each other.

Toward sunset, Mari came and sat down between the two bedrolls.

"Blight you two," she said conversationally to the unconscious pair, "for leaving this on me. This is company captain work, not patrol leader work. No fair slithering out of it, Dag my boy." She looked up and caught Fawn's eye from where she lay on her side near Dag. Fawn sat up and returned an inquiring look.

"Bryn"—Mari hooked a thumb over her shoulder toward the rank of female sleepers beneath their awning—"will be all of twenty-two next week. If she has a next week. She's young. Good groundsense range. She might yet grow up to have a passel of youngsters. Hoharie, I've known her longer. A medicine maker has valuable skills. She might yet save the lives of a dozen girls like Bryn. So how shall I decide which first? Some choice. Maybe," she sighed, "maybe it won't make any difference. I hardly know which way to wish for.

"Agh! Pay no attention to my maunderings, girl," Mari continued, as Fawn's stare widened. "I think I'm getting too old. I'm going to go sleep off this blight tonight. It drains your wits as well as your strength, blight does. All despair and death. You get into this mood." She clambered back to her feet and gazed blearily down over Dag's supine form at Fawn. "I know you can't feel the blight direct, but it's working on you, too. You should take a break off this deathly ground as well."

Fawn shook her head. "I want to stay here. By Dag." *For whatever time we have left.*

Mari shrugged. "Suit yourself, then." She wandered away into the softening twilight.

⁕

Fawn awoke to moonlight filtering down through the ash tree's bare branches. She lay a moment in her bedroll trying to recapture her dreams, hoping for something usefully prophetic. In ballads, people often had dreams that told them what to do; you were supposed to follow instructions precisely, too, or risk coming to several stanzas of grief. But she remembered no dreams. She doubted they'd reveal anything even if she did.

Farmer dreams. Perhaps if she'd been Lakewalker-born . . . she scowled at Othan, asleep and snoring faintly on the other side of Hoharie. If anyone were to have any useful uncanny visions, it would more likely be him, blight him.

No, not "blight him." That wasn't fair. Reluctantly, she allowed he had courage, as he'd shown this afternoon, and Hoharie would not have favored him out of her other apprentices and brought him along if he didn't have promise as well. It was merely that Fawn would feel better if he were completely stupid, and not just stupid about farmers. Then he wouldn't be able to make her doubt herself so much. She sighed and rose to pick her way out to the slit trench at the far edge of the grove.

Returning, she sat up on her blanket and studied Dag. The stippled moonlight made his unmoving face look disturbingly corpse-colored. The dark night-glitter of his eyes, smiling at her, would have redeemed it all, but they remained sunken and shut. He might die, she thought, without her ever seeing their bright daylight gold again. She swallowed the scared lump in her throat. Would they let her touch him after he was dead? *I could touch him now.* But there was little she could do for him physically that wasn't already being done more safely by others. *Wait on that, then.*

Involuted ground reinforcement. She rolled the phrase over in her mind as if tasting it. It clearly meant something quite specific to Hoharie, and doubtless to Dag and Mari as well. And Othan. A ground reinforcement curling up on itself, which didn't gradually become part of its new owner? She rubbed her arm, and wondered if the ground reinforcement Dag had done on her was involuted or not. If she followed Hoharie's explanation, it seemed that the *involution* was a cut-off bit of malice, like her own was a cut-off bit of Dag. Remembering the Glassforge malice, she was glad she and Dag had stopped it before it had developed such far-flung powers.

Her brows bent. Had Hoharie ever seen a malice up as close as Fawn had? Makers seemed to stay back in camp, mostly. So maybe not. Sharing knives might be complicated to make, but they were so simple to use, a farmer child might do so—as Fawn had proven. She smiled now to remember Dag's wild cry: *Sharp end first!*

Her thoughts fell like water drops into a still pool.

Sharing knives kill malices.

There's a bit of leftover malice in Dag and Artin and these other people.

Maybe it just needs an extra dose of mortality to finish cleaning it out.

. . . I have a sharing knife.

She inhaled, shuddering. It wasn't possible for her to think of something to try that Dag and Mari and Hoharie hadn't, and already dismissed for some good reason that Fawn was simply too ignorant to know. Was it?

There was a lot of Lakewalker emotion and habit tied up in sharing knives. Sacrificial in every sense, *sacred.* Not seen as a fit subject for idle fooling around with. She hunched over, wide-awake now.

It didn't have to be through the heart, did it? That was only for unprimed knives, first collecting their dose of mortality. For discharging the death, anywhere in the malice's groundworked body would apparently do. She might have stabbed the Glassforge malice in the foot, to the same stunning effect. So where were the, the malice bits lodged in the enspelled Lakewalkers? Pooled or diffuse, they all had to be connected, because to touch any of them triggered the same trap.

Her knife, Dar had said, was of dubious potency and value. No affinity. *But it's the only one I have a right to.*

Her eyes turned to Dag. *And he's the only one I have a right to. So.*

Swiftly, before her nerve failed her, she rose and, careful not to touch his skin, delicately drew down his blanket. She lifted it past his ribbed chest, his loose breechclout, his long legs, letting it fall again in folds at his feet. His body was all sculpted shadows in the moonlight, too thin. She'd thought she'd started to put some meat on his bones, but it was all used up again by the past weeks of dire strain, and then some.

Not the heart, not the eye—*eew!*—not the gut. For nonlethal flesh wounds, one was pretty much limited to arms and legs, carefully away from where those big veins and nerves ran down. Under the arm would be bad, she was pretty sure, likewise the back of the knee and the inner thigh. Better the outer thigh, or the arm just below the shoulder. Dag's strappy arm muscles didn't seem all that thick, compared to the length of the bone blade hanging around her neck. Thigh, then. She crouched down.

If Hoharie had been conscious, Fawn could have asked her. But then Fawn would still be waiting for the Lakewalker expert to fix things, and likely would not have conceived this desperate notion at all. Now the medicine maker lay entranced with the rest, leaving only Othan in charge. Fawn wouldn't have asked Othan for a drink in a downpour, nor have expected him to give her one. Still . . .

Am I about to be stupid again?

Think it through.

This might do nothing, in which case she would have to clean the blood off her knife and explain the ugly hole in her husband tomorrow morning. Envisioning which, she scrambled back to her saddlebags and dug out one of her spare clean ragbags stuffed with cattail fluff, and some cord. There, a good bandage.

This might do what she hoped.

This might do something awful. But something awful was going to happen anyhow. She could not make things worse.

Right, then.

She laid out the makeshift swab, dragged her pouch from around her neck, and pulled out the pale knife. The little delay had sapped her courage. She hunkered by Dag's left hip a moment, trying to gather it again. She wished she could pray, but the gods, they said, were absent. She had nothing to trust in now but her own wits.

She swallowed a whimper. *Dag says you're smart. If you can't trust you, trust him.*

Sharp end first. Anywhere. She drew back her hand, took careful aim at what she hoped was all nice thick muscle, then plunged the bone knife in till the tip nicked against Dag's own bone. Still without ever touching him. Dag grunted and jerked in his sleep. She whipped her shaking hand away from the hilt, which stood out from his lean thigh, all indigo blue and ivory in the silver light.

From over her shoulder, Othan's voice screamed, "What are you *doing*, you crazy farmer?"

He reached to clamp her shoulders and drag her roughly back from Dag. But not before she saw Dag's left arm jolt up from his bedroll as though its invisible hand was wrapping itself around the sharing knife's hilt, and heard the faint, familiar *snap* of splintering bone blade.

15

He had floated in an increasingly timeless gray fog, all distinctions fading. It seemed a just consolation that with them faded all fear, want, and pain. But then, inexplicably, something bright and warm troubled his shredding perceptions, as if the north star had torn herself loose from the sky and ventured too near him in naive, luminous, fatal curiosity. *Don't fall, no . . . stay away, Spark!* Longing and horror wrenched him, for to grasp that joy would slay it. *Is it my fate to blight all that I love?*

But the star fire didn't touch him. Later, a bolt of new strength shot through him, and for a short time, coherent thought came back. Some other light had fallen into this prison, also known to him . . . He recognized Hoharie's intense ground in all its ever-astonishing vigor—so strange that such a spring of strength should dwell in such a slight and unassuming body. But the hope it should have brought him turned to ashes as he took in her anger, horror, and frustration.

I thought sure you'd figure the trick of it from out there, as I could not—I'm the blinder one, I had to look to see it.

And the wailing answer, *I had to look to be sure . . . I had to be certain . . . oh, Dag, I am so sorry . . .* before the fog blurred all to voiceless sorrow once more.

He raced to make his watch rounds in this brief, stolen respite, to count his company as every captain should. Artin, yes, barely holding on, his ground so drained as to be translucent at the edges; Bryn and Ornig; Mallora; the other Bonemarsh makers. And now Hoharie. He remembered to count himself. Ten, all dying in place. Again he led those who had trusted in him into the boundless dark. *At least this time I can't desert them.*

More timelessness. Gray mouths leeched him.

The star fire moved too close again, and he breathed dread like cold mist. But the sky-spark held something else, a faint, familiar chime; her fair light and its wordless song wound together. Their intertwined beauty overthrew his heart. *This is surely the magic of the whole wide green world; Lakewalker groundwork has nothing to compare with it . . .*

And then pain and the song pierced him.

He could feel every detail of the roiling ground that stabbed into his thigh: Kauneo's bone, his own blood of old, the involuted and shaped vessel for mortality that was the gift of the Luthlian knife maker. Spark's daughter's death, death without birth, self-making and self-dissolution intermingled in their purest forms.

Too pure. It lay self-contained within the involution, innocent of all taint of desire, motion, and time. *It lacks affinity* seemed too flat a statement to sum up its aloof stillness. Free of all attachment. Free of all pain.

We give best from abundance. I can share pain.

Flying as never before, he raised his arm by its ground, and his ghost hand—pure ground, piebald with blight and malice spatter—wrapped the hilt and the ground of the hilt. His own old blood gave him entry into the involution; he let his blackened ground trace up its ancient, dried path; catch, hold; and he remembered the night Fawn had woven his wedding cord with bloody fingers, and so drawn her own ground into it. And her wide-open eyes and unguarded offer, later, on another night of ground-weaving, *Need blood?* As if she would gladly have opened her veins on the spot and poured all that vivid flood into his cupped hands, sparing nothing. *As she does now.*

Do not waste her gift, old patroller.

His blackened touch seemed a violation, but he twisted the mortal ground between his ghost fingers the way Fawn spun thread. He grinned somewhere inside himself to imagine Dar's outraged voice, *You used a* wedding-cord *technique on a* sharing knife . . . ? The involution uncoiled, giving up its long burden into his hand. Kauneo's bone cracked joyfully, a sound beneath sound heard not with his ears but in his groundsense, and he knew in that moment that Dar's theory of how the farmer babe's death had entered his knife was entirely wrong-headed, but he had no time now to examine it. He held mortality in his hand, and it would not wait.

Within his hand, not upon it; the two were as inextricable as two fibers spun into one strong thread. *Affinity.* Now, at last, he closed his hand upon the malice's dark construction.

His ghost hand twisted, stretched, and tore apart as the mortality flowed from him into the gray mouths, along the lines of draining hunger, and he howled without sound in the agony of that wrenching. The malice spatters on his body were ripped out from their patches of blight as if dragged along on a towline, gashing through his ground and out his arm. The dazzling fire raced, consuming its dark path as it traveled. The gray fog-threads of the malice's involution blazed up in fire all over the grove, leaving a web of red sparks hanging for a moment as if suspended in air. When it reached the mud-men's dense impelling ground-shapes, they exploded in fiery pinwheels, their aching afterimages spinning in Dag's groundsense, weighty as whirlpools peeling off a paddle's trailing edge.

Then—quiet.

Dag had not known that silence could reverberate so; or maybe that was just him. When a long strain was released, the recoil itself could become a new source of pain . . . No, actually, that was just his body. He'd thought he'd missed his body, back when his mind had been set adrift from it in that ground-fog; now he was not so sure. Its pangs were all suddenly very distinctive indeed. Head, neck, back, arm, haunches all cried out, and his bladder definitely clamored for attention. His body was noisy, cranky, and insistent. But he sought something more urgent.

He pried his eyes open, blinking away the glue and sand that seemed to cement his lids together. He was staring up at bare silvered branches and a night sky washed with moonlight strong enough to cast interlaced shadows. Across the grove, voices were moaning in surprise or crying out in shock. Shouts of alarm transmuted to triumph.

In the blue moonlight and red flare of new wood thrown on a nearby fire, a baffling sight met his gaze. Fawn and Hoharie's apprentice Othan seemed to be dancing. Or perhaps wrestling. It was hard to be sure. Othan was breathing hard through his nose; Fawn had both hands wrapped around one of his wrists and was swinging from it, dragging his arm down. His boots stamped in an unbalanced circle as he tried to shake her off, cursing.

Dag cleared his throat and said mildly, albeit in a voice as rusty and plaintive as an old gate hinge, "Othan, quit manhandling my wife. Get your own farmer girl."

The two sprang apart, and Othan gasped, "Sir! I wasn't—"

What he wasn't, Dag didn't hear, because with a sob of joy Fawn threw herself down across his chest and kissed him. He thought his mouth tasted as foul as an old bird's nest, but strangely, she didn't seem to mind. His left arm, deadened, wasn't working. His right weighed far too much, but he hoisted it into the air somehow and, after an uncertain wobble, let it fall across her, fingers clutching contentedly.

He had no idea why or how she was here. It was likely a Fawn-fluke. Her solid wriggling warmth suggested hopefully that she was not a hallucination, not that he was in the best shape to distinguish, just now.

She stopped kissing him long enough to gasp, "Dag, I'm so sorry I had to stab you! I couldn't think of any other way. Does it hurt bad?"

"Mm?" he said vaguely. He was more numb than in pain, but he became aware of a shivering ache in his left thigh. He tried to raise his head, failed, and stirred his leg instead. An utterly familiar knife haft drifted past his focus. He blinked in bemusement. "A foot higher and I'd have thought you were mad at me, Spark."

Her helpless laughter wavered into weeping. The drops fell warm across his chest, and he stroked her shuddering shoulder and murmured wordlessly.

After a moment she gulped and raised her face. "You have to let me go."

"No, I don't," he said amiably.

"We have to get those bone fragments dug out of your leg. I didn't know how far to stick it in, so I pushed it all the way, I'm afraid."

"Thorough as ever, I see."

She shrugged out of his weak grip and escaped, but grinned through her tears, so that was likely all right. He eased open his groundsense a fraction, aware of something deeply awry in his own body's ground just below his perceptions, but managed a head count of the people in the grove before he tightened up again. All alive. Some very weak, but *all* alive. Someone had flung himself onto a horse bareback and was galloping for the east camp. Othan was diverted from his farmer-wrestling to tend on Hoharie, struggling up out of her bedroll. Dag gave up captaining, lay back with a sigh of boundless fatigue, and let them all do whatever they wanted.

In due course Othan came back with Hoharie's kit and some lights and commenced some pretty unpleasant fiddling about down by Dag's side. Weary Hoharie directed, and Fawn hovered. That the blade should hurt worse coming out than going in made some sense, but not that it should do so more *often*. Voices muttered, rose and fell. "It's bleeding so much!" "That's all right. It'll wash the wound out a bit. Now the swab." "Hoharie, do you know what that swab *is*?" "Othan, think. Of course I do. Very clever, Fawn. Now tie the strips down tight. No peeking under it, unless it soaks through." "Did he get it all?" "Yes, look—fit the pieces together like a puzzle, and check for missing chips or fragments. All smooth, see?" "Oh, yes!" "Hoharie, it's like his ground is *shredded*. Hanging off him in strips. I've never felt anything like!" "I saw when it happened. It was spectacular. Get the bleeding stopped, get everyone off this blight and over to the east camp. Get me some *food*. Then we'll tackle it."

The evacuation resembled a torchlight parade, organized by the folks who came pelting over from the east camp, all dressed by guess and riotous with relief. Those freed from the groundlock who could sit a horse were led off two to a mount, holding each other upright, and the rest were carried. Dag was carted eastward feetfirst on a plank; Saun's face, grinning loonlike, drifted past his gaze in the flickering shadows. Mari's voice complained loudly about missing the most exciting part. Dag gripped Fawn's hand for the whole mile and refused to let go.

The east camp didn't settle down till dawn. Fawn woke again near noon, trapped underneath Dag's outflung arm. She just lay there for a while, relishing the lovely weight of it and the slow breath ruffling her curls. Eventually, she gently eased out from under, sat up, and looked around. She thought it a measure of Dag's exhaustion that her motions didn't wake him the way they usually did.

Their bedroll was sheltered under a sort of half tent of bent saplings splinted together supporting a blanket roof. Half-private. The camp extended along the high side of a little creek, well shaded by green, unblighted trees; maybe twenty or twenty-five patrollers seemed to be moving about, some going for water or out to the horse lines, some tending cook fires, several clustered around bedrolls feeding tired-looking folks who nevertheless were doggedly sitting up.

At length, Dag woke too, then it was her turn to help him prop up his shoulders against his saddlebags. Happily, she fed him. He could both chew and swallow, and not choke; halfway through, he revived enough to start capturing the bits of plunkin or roast deer from her with his right hand and feed himself. His hand still trembled too much to manage his water cup without spilling, though. His left arm, more disturbingly, didn't move at all, and she suspected the bandage wrapping his left leg disguised even deeper ills than the knife wound. His eyes were bloodshot and squinty, more glazed than bright, but she reveled in their gold glints nonetheless, and the way they smiled at her as though they'd never quit.

In all, Fawn was glad when Hoharie came by, even if she was trailed by Othan. She was accompanied and supported by Mari, whose general air of relief clouded when her eye fell on Dag. The medicine maker looked fatigued, but not nearly as ravaged as Dag, perhaps because her time in the lock had been the shortest. She had all her formidable wits back about her, anyhow.

Othan unwrapped the leg, and Hoharie pronounced his neat stitches that closed the vertical slit to be good tight work, and the redness only to be expected and not a sign of infection yet, and they would do some groundwork later to prevent adhesions. Othan seemed even more relieved at the chance to rewrap the wound with more usual sorts of patroller bandages.

While this was going on, Mari reported: "Before you ask three times, Dag—everyone made it out of the groundlock alive."

Dag's eyes squeezed shut in thankfulness. "I was pretty sure. Is Artin going to hold on? His heart took hurt, there, I thought."

"Yes, but his son has him well in hand. All the Raintree folks could be carried off by their kin as early as tomorrow, at least as far as the next camp. They'll recover better there than out here in the woods."

Dag nodded.

"Once they're away our folks will be getting anxious to see home again, too. Bryn and Ornig are up already, and I don't think Mallora will be much behind. Young, y'know. I don't know about you, but I'm right tired of this place. With that hole in your leg it's plain you're not walking anywhere. It's up to Hoharie to say how soon you can ride."

"Ask me tomorrow," said Hoharie. "The leg's not really the worst of it."

"So what about the arm, Hoharie?" Dag asked hesitantly. His voice still sounded like something down in a swamp, croaking. "It's a bit worryin', not moving like that. Kind of takes me back to some memories I don't much care to revisit."

Hoharie grimaced understanding. "I can see why." As Othan tied off the new dressing and sat back, she added quietly, "Time to give me a look. You have to open yourself, Dag."

"Yeah," he sighed. He didn't sound at all enthusiastic, Fawn thought. But he lay back against his saddle prop with a faraway look on his face; his lips moved in something deeper than a wince. Mari hissed, Hoharie's lips pursed, and Othan, who had sewn up bleeding flesh without a visible qualm, looked suddenly ill.

"Well, that's a bigger mess than Utau, and I thought he was impressive," allowed Hoharie. "Let me see what I can do with this."

"You can't do a ground reinforcement after all you just went through!" Dag objected.

"I have enough oomph left for one," she replied, her face going intent. "I was saving it for you. Figured . . ."

Fawn tugged at Mari and whispered urgently, "What's going on? What do you all sense?" *That I can't.*

"The ground down his left side's all marked up with blight, like big deep bruises," Mari whispered back. "But those nasty black malice spatters that I felt before seem to be gone now—that's a real good sign, I reckon. The ground of his left arm, though, is hanging in tatters. Hoharie's wrapping it all up with a shaped ground reinforcement—ooh, clever—I think she means to help it grow back together easier as it heals."

Hoharie let out her breath in a long sigh; her back bent. Dag, his expression very inward, stared down at his left arm as it moved in a short jerk. "Better!" he murmured in pleased surprise.

"Time," said Hoharie, and now she sounded down in that swamp, too. Dag gave her a dry look as if to say, *Now who's overdoing?* She ignored it, and continued, "It'll all come back in time as your ground slowly heals. *Slowly*, got that, Dag?"

Dag sighed in regret. "Yeah . . ." His voice fell further. "The ghost hand. It's gone, isn't it? For good. Like the other."

Hoharie said somewhat impatiently, "Gone for *a* good, to be sure, but not necessarily forever. I know it perturbed you, Dag, but I wish you'd stop think-

ing of that hand as some morbid magic! It was a ground projection, a simple . . .
well, it was a ground projection, anyway. As your ground heals up from all this
blight, it should come back with the rest of it. Last, I imagine, so don't go fuming and fretting."

"Oh," said Dag, looking brighter. Fawn could have hit him for winking at
her like *that* just then, because it almost made her laugh out loud, and she'd
never dare explain why to all these stern Lakewalkers.

"Now," said Hoharie, sitting up and rubbing her forehead with the back of
her wrist—Othan, watching her closely, handed her a clean rag, and she repeated the gesture with it and nodded thanks. "It's my chance to ask a few
questions. What I need to know is if a similar act would solve a similar problem. Because I need to write this out for the lore-tent if it does, and maybe pass
it along to the other hinterlands, too."

"I hope there never is a similar problem," said Mari, "because that would
mean another runaway malice like this one, and this one got way too close to
being unstoppable. But write it out all the same, sure. You never know."

"No one can know till it's tried," said Dag, "but my own impression was
that any primed knife, placed in any of the groundlocked people, would have
worked to clean out the malice's involution. It only needed someone to think
of it—and dare."

"It seems a strange way to spend a sacrifice," agreed Hoharie. "Still . . .
ten for one." All the Lakewalkers looked equally pensive, contemplating this
mortal arithmetic. "When did you think of it?"

"Pretty nearly as soon as I was trapped in the groundlock. I could see it,
then."

Hoharie's gaze flicked to Fawn's left wrist. Fawn, by now inured to being
talked past, almost flinched under the suddenly intent stare. "That was also
about the time you felt a change in that peculiar ground reinforcement Dag
gave you, wasn't it, Fawn? Did it seem to come with, say, a compulsion?"

Othan sat up straight. "Oh, of course! That would explain how she knew
what to do!"

Did it? Fawn's brows drew down in doubt. "It didn't seem anything like so
clear. I wish it had been."

"So how did you know?" asked Hoharie patiently. "To use your sharing
knife like that?"

"I . . ." She hesitated, casting her mind back to last night's desperation. "I
figured it."

"How?"

She struggled to express her complex thoughts simply. A lot of it hadn't
even been in words, just in pictures. "Well, you said. That there were cut-off
bits of malice in that groundlock. Sharing knives kill malices. I thought it might
just need an extra dose to finish the job."

"But your knife had no affinity."

"What?" Fawn stared in confusion.

Dag cleared his throat. His voice went gentle. "Dar was right—about that, anyway. The mortality in your knife was too pure to hold affinity with malices, but I was able to break into its involution and add some. A little extra last-minute making, would you say, Hoharie?"

Hoharie eyed him. "Making? I'm not sure that wasn't *magery*, Dag."

Fawn's brow wrinkled in distress. "Is that what tore up your ghost hand? Oh, if I had known—!"

"Sh," soothed Dag. "If you had known, what?"

She stared down at her hands, clutching each other in her lap. After a long pause, she said, "I'd have done it all the same."

"Good," he whispered.

"So," said Othan, clearly struggling with this, "you didn't really *know*. You were just guessing." He nodded in apparent relief. "A real stab in the dark. And in fact, except for Dag saving it all at the last, you were wrong!"

Fawn took a long breath, considering this painful thought. "Sometimes," she said distantly, with all the dignity she could gather, "it isn't about having the right answers. It's about asking the right questions."

Dag gave a slow blink; his face went curiously still. But then he smiled at her again, in a way that made the knot in her heart unwind, and gave her a considering nod. "Yeah—it was what we in Tent Bluefield call a fluke, Othan," he murmured, and the warm look he gave Fawn with *that* made the knot unwind all the way down to her toes.

Later in the afternoon, Saun came back from the woods with a peeled-sapling staff—hickory, he claimed; with that and Saun's shoulder for support, Dag was able to hobble back and forth to the slit trench. That cured Dag of ambition for any further movement. He was quite content to lie propped in his bedroll, occasionally with Fawn tucked up under his arm, and watch the camp go by, and not talk. He was especially content not to talk. A few inquiring noises were enough to persuade Fawn to ripple on about how she'd arrived so astonishingly here. He felt a trifle guilty about giving her so little tale in return, but she had Saun and Mari to cull for more details, and she did.

The next day the last of the company's scouts returned, having hooked up with another gaggle of Bonemarsh refugees returning to check on their quick and their dead. With the extra hands on offer, it was decided to move the recovering makers to better shelter that day, and the Raintree cavalcade moved off in midafternoon. The camp fell quiet. At this point, Dag's remaining patrol realized that the only barrier between them and a ride for home was their convalescent captain. The half dozen patrollers who were capable of giving minor ground reinforcements either volunteered or were volunteered to contribute to his speedier recovery. Dag blithely accepted them all, until his left foot began to twitch, his speech slurred, and he started seeing faint lavender halos around everything, and Hoharie, with some dire muttering about *absorption time, blight it,* cut off the anxious suppliers.

The miasma of homesickness and restlessness that permeated the air was like a fog; by evening, Dag found it easy to persuade Mari and Codo to split the patrol and send most of them home tomorrow with Hoharie, leaving Dag a suitable smaller group of bodyguards, or nursemaids, to follow on as soon as he was cleared to mount a horse again.

Mari, after a consultation with Hoharie out of Dag's earshot, appointed herself chief of their number. "Somebody's got to stand up to you when you get bored and decide to advance Hoharie's timetable by three days," she told Dag bluntly, when he offered a reminder of Cattagus. "If we leave you nothing but the children, you'll ride right over 'em."

Despite his pains and exhaustion, Dag was wholly satisfied to lie with Fawn that night in their little shelter, as if he'd entered some place of perfect balance where all needs were met and no motion was required. He wasn't homesick. On the whole, he had no desire at all to think about Hickory Lake and what awaited him there . . . *no.* He stopped that slide of thought. *Be here. With her.*

He petted her, letting her dark hair wind and slide through his fingers, silky delight. In her saddlebags she had brought candles, of all things, of her own making, and had stuck one upright in a holder made from a smooth dented stone she'd found in the stream. He was unaroused and, in his current condition, likely unarousable, but looking at her in this gilded light he was pierced with a pure desire, as if he were gazing at a running foal, or a wheeling hawk, or a radiant, melting sunset. Wonder caught up in flight that no man could possess, except in the eye and impalpable memory. Where time was the final foe, but the long defeat was not *now, now, now* . . .

Fawn seemed content to cuddle atop the bedroll and trade kisses, but at length she wriggled up to do off her boots and belt. They would sleep in their clothes like patrollers, but she drew the line at unnecessary lumps. With a thoughtful frown, she pulled her sharing knife cord over her head.

"I reckon I can put this away in my saddlebags, now." She slid the haft out of its sheath and spilled the three long shards of the broken blade out on the bedroll, lining them up with her finger.

Dag rolled over and up on his elbow to look. "Huh. So, that explains what Othan was doing down there, fishing all those out of me. I wondered."

"So . . . now what do we do with it?" Fawn asked.

"A spent knife, if it's recovered, is usually given back to the kin of the bone's donor, or if that can't be done, burned on a little pyre. It's been twenty years, but . . . Kauneo should have kin up in Luthlia who remember her. I still have her uncle Kaunear's bone, too, back home in my trunk—hadn't quite got round to arranging for it when this Raintree storm blew in on us. I should send them both up to Luthlia in a courier pouch, with a proper letter telling everyone what their sacrifices have bought. That would be best, I think."

She nodded gravely and extended a finger to gently roll a shard over. "In the end, this *did* do more than just bring us together, despite what Dar said about the farmer ground being worthless. Because of your making that redeemed it. I'm—not glad, exactly, there's not much glad about this—satisfied, I think. Dar said—"

He hoisted himself up and stopped her lips with a kiss. "Don't worry about what Dar says. I don't."

"Don't you?" She frowned. "But—wasn't he right, about the affinity?"

Dag shrugged. "Well . . . it would have been strange if he weren't. Knives are his calling. I'm not at all sure he was right about the other, though."

"Other?"

"About how your babe's ground got into my knife."

Her black eyebrows curved up farther.

He lay back again, raising his hand to hover across from his stump as a man would hold his two hands some judicious distance apart. "It was just a quick impression, you understand, when I was unmaking the knife's involution and releasing the mortal ground. I couldn't prove it. It was all gone in the instant, and only I saw. But . . . there was more than one knife stuck in that malice at that moment back at Glassforge. And there is more than one sort of ground affinity. There was a link, a channel . . . because the one knife was Kauneo's marrowbone, see, and the other was her heart's death. Knives don't take up souls, if there is such a thing, but each one has a, a *flavor* of its donor. I expect she died wanting and regretting, well, a lot of things, but I know a child was one. I wouldn't dare say this to anyone else, but I'll swear it to you. It wasn't the malice pushed that ground into Kauneo's bone. I think it was given *shelter*."

Fawn sat back, her lips parting in wonder. Her eyes were huge and dark, winking liquid that reflected the candlelight in shimmers.

He added very quietly, "If it was a gift from the grave, it's the strangest I ever heard tell of, but . . . she liked youngsters. She would have saved 'em all, if she could."

Fawn whispered, "She's not the only one, seemingly." And rolled over into his arms, and hugged him tight. Then sat up on her elbow, and said, most seriously, "Tell me more about her."

And, to his own profound astonishment, he did.

It came in a spate, when it came. To speak easily of Kauneo at last, to re-possess such a wealth of memory from the far side of pain, was as beyond all expectation as claiming a stolen treasure returned after years. As miraculous as getting back a missing limb. And his tears, when they fell, seemed not sorrow, but grace.

16

For the next couple of days Dag seemed willing to rest as instructed, to Fawn's approval, although she noticed he seemed less fidgety and fretful when she sat by him. Saun had stayed on, with Griff for his partner; Varleen replaced Dirla as Mari's partner. There were not too many camp chores for Fawn's hands, everyone having pretty much caught up with their cleaning and mending in the prior days, though she did spend some time out with the younger patrollers working on, or playing with, the horses. Grace hadn't gone lame, though Fawn thought it had been a near thing. The mare was certainly recovering faster than Dag. Fawn suspected Lakewalkers used their healing magic on their horses; if not officially, certainly on the sly.

On the third day, the heavy heat was pushed on east by a cracking thunderstorm. The tree branches bent and groaned menacingly overhead, and leaves turned inside out and flashed silver. The patrollers ended up combining their tent covers—except for the one hide that blew off into the woods like a mad bat—on Dag and Fawn's sapling frame, and clustering underneath. The nearby creek rose and ran mud-brown and foam-yellow as the blow subsided into a steady vertical downpour. By unspoken mutual assent, they all eased back and just watched it, passing around odd bits of cold food while their cook-fire pit turned into an opaque gray puddle.

Griff produced a wooden flute and instructed Saun on it for a time. Fawn recognized maybe half of the sprightly tunes. In due course Griff took it back and played a long, eerie duet with the rain, Varleen and Saun supplying muted percussion with sticks and whatever pots they had to hand. Dag and Mari seemed satisfied to listen.

Everyone went back to nibbling. Dag, who had been lying slumped against his saddlebags with his eyes closed, pushed himself slightly more upright, adjusted his left leg, and asked Saun suddenly, "You know the name of that farmer town the malice was supposed to have come up under?"

"Greenspring," Saun replied absently, craning his neck through the open, leeward side of their shelter to look, in vain, for a break in the clouds.

"Do you know where it is? Ever been there?"

"Yeah, couple of times. It's about twenty-five miles northwest of Bonemarsh." He sat back on his saddlecloth and gestured vaguely at the opposite shelter wall.

Dag pursed his lips. "That must be, what, pretty nearly fifty miles above the old cleared line?"

"Nearly."

"How was it ever let get started, up so far? It wasn't there in my day."

Saun shrugged. "Some settlement's been there for as long as I've been alive. Three roads meet, and a river. There were a couple of mills, if I remember rightly. Sawmill first. Later, when there got to be more farms around it, they built one for grain. Blacksmith, forge, more. We'd stopped in at the blacksmith a few times, though they weren't too friendly to patrollers."

"Why not?" asked Fawn, willing to be indignant on Saun's behalf.

"Old history. First few times farmers tried to settle up there, the Raintree patrollers ran them off, but they snuck back. Worse than pulling stumps, to try and get farmers off cleared land. On account of all the stumps they had to pull to clear it, I guess. There finally got to be so many of them, and so stubborn, it would have taken bloodshed to shift 'em, and folks gave up and let 'em stay on."

Dag frowned.

Saun pulled his knees up and wrapped his arms around them in the damp chill. "Fellow up there once told me Lakewalkers were just greedy, to keep such prime farming country for a hunting reserve. That his people could win more food from it with a plow than we ever could with bows and traps."

"What we hunt, they could not eat," growled Mari.

"That's the same fellow who told me blight bogles were a fright story made up by Lakewalkers to keep farmers off," Saun added a bit grimly. "You wonder where he is now."

Griff and Varleen shook their heads. Fawn bit her lip.

Dag wound a finger in his hair, pulling gently on a strand. He was overdue for another cut, Fawn thought, unless he meant to grow it out like his comrades. "I want to look at the place before we head home."

Griff's brow furrowed. "That'd be a good three days out of our way, Dag."

"Maybe only two, if we jog up and catch the northern road again." He added after a moment, "We could leave here two days early and be home on schedule all the same."

Mari gave him a fishy look. "Thought it was about time for you to start gettin' resty. Hoharie said, seven days off it for that leg. We all heard her."

"Come on, you know she padded that."

Mari did not exactly deny this, but she did say, "And why would you want to, anyway? You know what blight looks like, without having to go look at more. It's all the same. That's what makes it blight."

"Company captain's duty. Fairbolt will want a report on how this all got started."

"Not his territory, Dag. It's some Raintree camp captain's job to look into it."

Dag's eyelids lowered and rose, in that peculiar I-am-not-arguing-about-this look; his gaze met Fawn's curious one. "Nonetheless, I need to see whatever can be seen. I'm not calling for a debate on this, in case any of you were confused." A faint, rare tinge of iron entered his voice. Not arguing, apparently, but not giving way, either.

Mari's face screwed up. "Why? I could likely give you a tolerably accurate description of it all from right where I sit, and so could you. Depressing, but accurate. What answers are you lookin' for?"

"If I knew, I wouldn't have to go look." More hair-twisting. "I don't think I'm even looking for answers. I'm think I'm looking for new questions." He gave Fawn a slow nod.

The next morning dawned bright blue, and everyone spent it getting their gear spread out in the sun or up on branches to dry out. By noon, Dag judged this task well along, and floated the notion of starting out today—in gentle, easy stages, to counter Mari's exasperated look and mutter of *Told you so*. But since Mari was as sick of this place as everyone else, Dag soon had his way.

With the promise of home dangling in the distance, however roundaboutly, the youngsters had the camp broken down and bundled up in an hour, and Saun led their six mounts and the packhorse northwest. They skirted wide around the dead marsh, flat and dun in a crystalline light that still could not make it sparkle, for all that a shortcut across the blight would have saved several miles.

Halfway around, Mari drew her horse to a halt and turned her face to a vagrant moist breeze.

"What?" Saun called back, alert.

"Smell that?" said Mari.

"Right whiffy," said Varleen, wrinkling her nose.

"Something's starting to rot," Dag explained to Fawn, who rode up beside him and looked anxiously inquiring. "That's good."

She shook her head. "You people."

"Hope is where you find it." He smiled down at her, then pushed Copperhead along. He could feel his weary patrol's mood lighten just a shade.

As he'd promised Mari, they weaved through the woodlands of Raintree at a sedate walk. They rode with groundsenses open, like people trailing their hands through the weeds as they strolled, not formally patrolling, but as routine precaution. You never knew. Dag himself had once found and done for a very early sessile that way, when he was riding courier all alone in the far northeast hinterland of Seagate. Still, their amble put a good twelve miles between them and the Bonemarsh blight by the time they stopped in the early evening. Dag thought everyone slept a bit better that night; even he did, despite the throbbing ache in his healing thigh.

They started off the next day earlier, but no faster. Varleen spotted two mud-man corpses off the trail that appeared to have died naturally, running down at the end of the stolen strength the malice had given them, suggesting the hazard from the rest of their cohort was now much reduced. Even at this slow pace, the little patrol came up on the first noxious pinching of the blight around Greenspring by midafternoon.

In the shade of the last live trees before the trail opened out into cleared fields, Dag held up his hook, and everyone pulled their mounts to a halt.

"We don't all have to go in. We could set up a camp here. You could stay with Varleen and Griff, Fawn. Blight this deep will be draining, even if you can't feel it. Bad for you. And . . . it could be ugly." *Will be ugly.*

Fawn leaned on her pommel and gave him a sharp look. "If it's bad for me, won't it be worse for you? Convalescing as you aren't—at least not any too fast, that I can see."

Mari vented a sour chuckle. "She's got you there."

Fawn took a breath and sat up. "This place—it's something like West Blue, right?"

"Maybe," Dag allowed.

"Then—I need to see it, too." She gave a firm little nod.

They exchanged a long look; her resolve rang true. *Should I be surprised?* "Soonest begun, soonest done, then. We won't linger long." Dag braced himself and waved Saun onward.

They rode first past deserted farms: sickly, then dying, then dead, then dead with a peculiar gray tinge that was quite distinctive. Dag knew it well and furled his groundsense in tight around him, as did the other patrollers. It didn't help quite enough.

"What are we looking for?" asked Griff, as the first buildings of a little town hove into view past a screen of bare and broken buckthorn bushes, someone's scraggly attempt at a hedge.

"I'd like to find the lair, to start," said Dag. "See where the malice started out, try to figure why it wasn't spotted."

It wasn't that hard; they just followed the gradient of blight deeper and deeper. It felt like riding into a dark hollow, for all that the land here was as level as the rest of Raintree. The flattened vegetation grew grayer, and even the clapboard houses, with their fences leaning drunkenly, seemed drained of all color. It all smelled as dry and odorless as cave dust. The town was maybe twice the size of West Blue, Dag gauged. It had three or four streets. A sturdy wharf jutted into a river worthy of the name and not just a jumped-up creek, which seemed to flow deeply enough to float small keelboats up from the Grace, and certainly rafts and flatboats down. A square for a day market; alehouse and smithy and forge; perhaps two hundred houses. A thousand people, formerly. None now.

The pit of the blight seemed to lie in a woodlot at the edge of the town. The horses snorted uneasily as their riders forced them forward. A shallow, shale-lined ravine with a small creek running through it shadowed a near cave partway up one side, not unlike the one they'd seen near Glassforge, if much smaller. It was quite empty now, the shale slumping in a slide to half block the water. Alongside the creek the earth was pocked with man-wide, man-deep pits, so thickly clustered in places as to seem like a wasp nest broken open. The malice's first mud-man nursery, likely.

"With all these people around," said Griff, "it's hard to believe that no one spotted any of the early malice signs."

"Maybe someone did," said Fawn, "and no one paid them any mind. Being too young and short. The woodlot is common for the whole town. You bet the youngsters here played in that creek all the time, and in these woods."

Dag hunched over his saddlebow and inhaled carefully, steadying his shuddering stomach. *Yes.* Malice food indeed, of the richest sort. Delivered up. This was how the malice had started so fast. He remembered its beauty in the silver light. How many molts . . . ? *As many as it liked.*

"Did no one know to run?" asked Varleen. "Or did it just come up too quick?"

"It came up fast, sure, but not that fast," opined Mari. She frowned at Dag's huddle. "Some were killed by ill luck, but I expect more were killed by ignorance."

"Why were—" Fawn began, and stopped.

Dag turned his head and raised his brows at her.

"I was going to say, why were they so ignorant," she said in a lower voice. "But I was just as ignorant myself, not long back. So I guess I know why."

Dag, still wordless with the nightmare images running through his mind, just shook his head and turned Copperhead around. They rode up from the ravine on the widest beaten path.

As they returned down the main street near the wharf, Saun's head suddenly came up. "I swear I hear voices."

Dag eased his groundsense open slightly, snapping it back again almost at once, cringing at the searing sensation. But he'd caught the life-sparks. "Over that way."

They rode on, turning down a side street lined with bare trees and empty houses, some new clapboard, the older ones log-sided. A few had broken glass windows; most still made do with old-fashioned parchment and summer netting, though also split or ripped. The street became a rutted lane, beyond which lay a broad field, its trampled grass and weeds gray-dun. A score or so of human figures milled about on its far end along what used to be a tree line. A few carts with dispirited horses hitched to them stood by.

"They can't be back trying to farm this!" said Saun in dismay.

"No," said Dag, rising in his stirrups and squinting, "it's no crop they're planting today."

"They're digging graves," said Mari quietly. "Must be some refugees who've come back to try and find their kin, same as at Bonemarsh."

Griff shook his head in regret.

Dag hitched his reins into his hook, for all that his left arm was still very weak, to free his hand. He waved the patrol forward, but with a cautioning gesture brought them to a halt again at a little distance from the Greenspring survivors.

The townsmen formed up in a ragged rank, clutching shovels and mattocks in a way that reminded Dag a lot of the Horsefords' first fearful approach to him, sitting so meekly on their porch. If the Horsefords had suffered reason to be nervy, these folks had cause to be half-crazed. Or maybe all-the-way crazed.

After an exchange of looks and low mutters, a single spokesman stepped out of the pack and moved cautiously toward the patrol, stopping a few prudent paces off, but within reasonable hearing distance. Good. Reassurances might work better delivered in a soothing tone, rather than bellowed. Dag touched his temple. "How de'."

The man returned a short, grudging nod. He was middle-aged, careworn, dressed in work clothes due for mending that hadn't been washed for weeks, an almost welcome whiff of something human in this odorless place. His face was so gray with fatigue as to look blighted while alive. Dag thought, unwillingly, of Sorrel Bluefield again.

"You folks shouldn't be on this sick ground," Dag began.

"It's our ground," the man returned, his stare distant.

"It's been poisoned by the blight bogle. It'll go on poisoning you if you linger on it."

The man snorted. "I don't need some Lakewalker corpse-eater to tell me that."

Dag tried a brief, acknowledging nod. "You can bury your dead here if you like, though I wouldn't advise it, but you should not camp here at night, leastways."

"There's shelter still standing." The townsman raised his chin and scowled, and added in a tone of warning, "We'll be guarding this ground tonight. In case you all were thinking of sneaking back."

What did the fellow imagine? That Dag's patrol had come around to try to steal the bodies of their dead? Infuriated protests rose in his mind: *We would not do such a foul thing. We have plenty of corpses of our own just now, thank you all the same. Farmer bones are of no use to us, ground-ripped bones are no use to us, and as for ground-ripped farmer bones . . . !* Teeth tight, he let nothing escape but a flat, "You do that."

Perhaps uneasily realizing he'd given offense, the townsman did not apologize, but at least slid sideways: "And how else will we find each other, if any more come back? The bogle cursed us and marched us off all over the place . . ."

Had he been one of the bewildered mind-slaves? It seemed so. "Did no one know to run for help, when the bogle first came up? To spread a warning?"

"What help?" The man huffed again. "You Lakewalkers on your high horses rode us down. I was there." His voice fell. "We were all mad with the bogle spells, yes, but . . ."

"They had to defend—" Dag began, and stopped. The cluster of nervous townsmen had not put down their tool-weapons, nor dispersed back to their forlorn task. He glanced aside at Fawn, watching in concern from atop Grace, and rubbed his aching forehead. He said instead, abruptly, "How about if I get down from this high horse? Will you step away and talk with me?"

A pause, a stare. A nod.

Dag steeled himself to dismount. Varleen, watching closely, slid down and went to Copperhead's bridle, and Saun dropped from his own mount, unshipped the hickory staff that he'd carted along slotted under his saddle flap, and stepped to Dag's stirrup. Dag's leg did not quite turn under him as he landed on it, and he exchanged an almost-smile with Saun as the youth carefully unhanded his arm, both, he thought, thrown back in memory to their night attack on the bandit camp, ages ago. He gripped the staff and turned to the townsman, who was blinking as if he was just now taking in the details of his interrogator's ragged condition.

Dag pointed to a lone dead tree, blown or fallen down in the field, and the townsman nodded again. As Dag swung the staff and limped toward it, he found Fawn at his left side. Her hand slipped around his arm, not yet in support, but ready if his leg folded again. He wondered if he should chase her back to Grace, spare her what promised to be some grim details. He dismissed his doubts—*too late anyway*—as they arrived at the thick trunk. *She speaks farmer.* With that thought, Dag guided Fawn around to sit between them. Both men could see over her head better than she could see around Dag, and . . . if this fellow's most recent view of a Lakewalker patroller had been looking up the wrong end of a spear, he could likely use a spacer. *We both could.*

Dag breathed a little easier as the mob of townsmen went back to their digging. Now it was the Lakewalkers' turn to stand in a tight cluster, holding their horses and watching Dag uneasily.

"This bogle was bad for everyone," Dag began again. "Raintree Lakewalkers lost folks, too, and homes. Bonemarsh Camp's been blighted—it'll have to be abandoned for the next thirty or more years, I reckon. This place, longer."

The man grunted, whether in agreement or disagreement was hard to tell. Maybe just in pain.

"Have very many people come back? To find each other?" Fawn put in.

The man shrugged. "Some. Most of us here knew we'd be coming as a burial party, but . . . some. I found my wife," he added after a moment.

"That's good, then," said Fawn in a tone of encouragement.

"She's buried over there," the townsman added, pointing to a long mound of turned earth along the tree line. *Mass grave,* Dag thought.

"Oh," said Fawn, more quietly.

"They waited for us to come back," the man continued. "All the wives and daughters. All the boys. The old folks. It was like there was something strange and holy happened to their bodies, because they didn't rot, not even in the heat. It's like they were waiting for us to come back and find them."

Dag swallowed, and decided this was not the moment to explain the more arcane features of deep blight.

"I'm so sorry," said Fawn softly.

The man shrugged. "Could have been worse. Daisy and Cooper over there, they found each other alive just an hour ago." He nodded toward a man and one of the few women, who were both sitting on the tail of a wagon. Staring blankly, with their backs to each other.

Fawn's little hand touched the man's knee; he flinched. "And . . . why worse?" Fawn could ask such things; Dag would not have dared. He was glad she was here.

"Daisy, she'd thought Coop had their youngsters with him. Coop, he thought she'd had them with her. They'd had four." He added after a moment, "We're saving the children for last, see, in case more folks show up. To look." Dag followed his glance to a line of stiff forms lying half-hidden in the distant weeds. Behind it, the men were starting to dig a trench. It was longer than the finished mound.

"Are the orphans being sheltered somewhere off the blight?" Fawn asked.

Thinking absent-gods-knew-what; about someone brokering some bright arrangement to hook up the lost half families with one another, if he knew her.

The man glanced down at her. Likely she looked as young to him as she did to Dag, for he said more gently, "No orphans here, miss."

"But . . ." She sucked on her lower lip, obviously thinking through the implication.

"We've found none alive here under twelve. Nor many over."

Dag said quietly, as she looked up at him as if he could somehow fix this, "Next to pregnant women, children have the richest grounds for a malice building up to a molt. It goes for them first, preferentially. When Bonemarsh was evacuated, the young women would have grabbed up all the youngsters and run at once. The others following as they could, with what animals and supplies they could get at fast, with the off-duty patrollers as rear guard. The children would have been got out in the first quarter hour, and the whole camp in as little more. They did lose folks beyond the range of warning—some of those makers we freed from the groundlock had stayed to try and reach a party of youngsters who'd gone out gathering that day."

Fawn frowned. "I hadn't heard that part of the tale. Did they find them in time?"

Dag sighed. "No. Some of the Bonemarsh folk who came back later recovered the bodies, finally. For a burial not so different than this." He nodded toward the mounds; the townsman, listening, stared down and dug his boot heel into the dry soil, brows pinching in wonder. *Yes*, thought Dag. *Witness her. Farmers can ask, and be answered. Won't you try us?*

"Did they take their—" Fawn shut up abruptly, remembering not to ask about knife-bones in front of farmers, Dag guessed. She just shook her head.

The townsman gave Dag a sidelong look. "You're not from Bonemarsh. Are you."

"No. My company rode over from Oleana to help out. We're on our way home now."

"Dag's patrol killed your blight bogle," Fawn put in, a little proudly. "When the malice's—bogle's curse lifted from your mind, that was when."

"Huh," said the man. And then, after a bleak silence, "Could have been sooner."

Stung to brusqueness, Dag said, "If any of you had owned the wits to run and give warning at the first, it could have been a *lot* sooner. We did all we could with what we had, as soon as we knew."

A stubborn silence stretched between them. There was too much grief and strain here, thick as mire, for argument or apology today. Dag had pretty much pieced together the picture he'd come for. It was maybe time to go.

A trio of townsmen came out of the barren woods, back from some errand there—pissing, searching?—and stopped to gape at the newcomers. One grizzled head came up sharply; staring, the man began to walk toward the fallen tree, faster and faster. His stride turned into a jog, then a run; his face grew wild, and he waved frantically, crying, "Sassy! Sassy!"

Dag stiffened, his hand drifting to his knife haft. The townsman beside Fawn straightened up with a moan and held out his palm in a gesture of negation, shaking his head. The runner slowed as he neared, gasping for breath, rubbing his red-rimmed eyes and peering at Fawn. In a voice gone gray, he said, "You aren't my Sassy."

"No, sir," said Fawn, looking up apologetically. "I'm Dag's Fawn."

He continued to peer. "Are you one of ours? Did those patrollers bring you back?" He waved toward the Lakewalkers still standing warily with their horses. "We can try and find your folks . . ."

"No, sir, I'm from Oleana."

"Why are you with them?"

"I'm married to one."

Taken aback, the man turned his head to squint; his gaze narrowed on Saun, who was standing holding Copperhead's reins, watching them alertly. The man's mouth turned down in a scowl. "If that's what that boy told you, missie, I'm afraid he was lying."

"*He's* not—" She broke off as Dag covered and squeezed her hand in warning.

The grizzled man took a breath. "If you want to stay here, missie, we could find you, find you . . ." He trailed off, looking around dolefully.

"Shelter?" muttered his comrade. "Not hardly." He stood up and squeezed his friend's shoulder. "Give it over. She's not our business. Not today."

With a disappointed glance over his shoulder, the grizzled man dragged off.

"I hope he finds his Sassy," said Fawn. "Who was—is she? His daughter?"

"Granddaughter," replied the townsman.

"Ah."

"We need to get off this blight, Fawn," said Dag, wondering if, had it been some other day, the townsmen would have made Fawn their business. Disquieting thought, but the dangerous moment, if that had been one, was past.

"Oh, of course." She jumped up at once. "You've got to be feeling it. How's your leg doing?"

"It'll be well enough once I'm in the saddle again." He grounded the butt of the hickory stick and levered himself up. He was starting to ache all over, like a fever. The townsman trailed along after them as Dag hobbled back to his horse.

It took Saun and Varleen both to heave Dag aboard Copperhead, this time.

He settled with a sigh, and even let Saun find his left stirrup for him and take away his stick. Varleen gave Fawn a neat boost up on Grace, and Fawn smiled thanks.

"You ready, Dag?" Saun asked, patting the leg.

"As I'll ever be," Dag responded.

As Saun went around to his horse, the townsman's eyebrows rose. "*You're her Dag?*" Surprise and deep disapproval edged his voice.

"Yes," said Dag. They stared mutely at each other. Dag started to add, "Next time, don't—" but then broke off. This was not the hour, the place, or the man. *So when, where, and who will be?*

The townsman's lips tightened. "I doubt you and I have anything much to say to each other, patroller."

"Likely not." Dag raised his hand to his temple and clucked to urge Copperhead forward.

Fawn wheeled Grace around. Dag was afraid she'd caught the darker undercurrents after all, because the struggle was plain in her face between respect for bereavement and a goaded anger. She leaned down, and growled at the townsman, "You might try *thank you.* Somebody should say it, at least once before the end of the world."

Disconcerted, the townsman dropped his eyes before her hot frown, then looked after her with an unsettled expression on his face.

As they left the blighted town and struck east up a wagon road alongside the river, Mari asked dryly, "Satisfied with your look-see, Dag?"

He grunted in response.

Her voice softened. "You can't fix everything in the whole wide green world by yourself, you know."

"Evidently not." And, after a moment, more quietly, "Maybe no one can."

Fawn eyed him with worry as he slumped in his saddle, but he did not suggest stopping. He wanted a lot more miles between him and what lay behind him. Greenspring. Should it be renamed Deadspring on the charts, now? Mari had been right; he'd had no need for a new crop of nightmares, let alone to have gone looking for them. He was justly served. Even Fawn had grown quiet. No answers, no questions, just silence.

He rode in it as they turned north across the river, looking for the road home.

17

Some six days after striking the north road, the little patrol clopped across the increasingly familiar wooden span to Two Bridge Island. Fawn turned in her saddle, watching Dag. His head came up, but unlike everyone else, he didn't break into whoops, and his lopsided smile at their cheers somehow just made him look wearier than ever. Mari had decreed easy stages on the ride home to spare their mounts, though everyone knew it had been to spare Dag. That Mari fretted for him troubled Fawn almost more than this strange un-Dag-like fatigue that gripped him so hard. The last day or two the *easy* part had silently dropped out, as the patrol pressed on more like horses headed for the barn than the horses themselves.

They paused at the split in the island road, and Mari gave a farewell wave to Saun, Griff, and Varleen. She jerked her head at Dag. "I'll be taking this one straight home, I think."

"Right," said Saun. "Need a helper?"

"Razi and Utau should be there. And Cattagus." Her austere face softened in an inward look, then she added, "Yep." Fawn wondered if she'd just bumped grounds with her husband to alert him to her homecoming.

Dag roused himself. "I should see Fairbolt, first."

"Fairbolt's heard all about it by now from Hoharie and the rest," said Mari sternly. "*I* should see Cattagus."

Saun glanced at his two impatient comrades, both with families waiting, and said, "I'll stop in and see Fairbolt on my way down island. Let him know we're back and all."

Dag squinted. "That'd do, I guess."

"Consider it done. Go rest, Dag. You look awful."

"Thankee', Saun," said Dag, the slight dryness in his voice suggesting it was for the latter and not the former statement, though it covered both. Saun grinned back, and the younger patrollers departed at a trot that became a lope before the first curve.

Dag, Mari, and Fawn took the shore branch, and while no one suggested a trot, Mari did kick her horse into a brisker walk. She was standing up in her stirrups peering ahead by the time they turned into her campsite.

Everyone had come out into the clearing. Razi and Utau held a child each, and Sarri waved. Cattagus waved and wheezed, striding forward. In addition there was a mob of new faces—a tall middle-aged woman and a fellow who had to be her spouse, and a stair-step rank of six gangling children ranging from Fawn's age downward to a leaping little girl of eight. The woman was Mari's eldest daughter, obviously, back from the other side of the lake with her family and her new boat. They all surged for Mari, although they stepped aside to give Cattagus first crack as she slid from her saddle. " 'Bout time you got back, old woman," he breathed into her hair, and, "You're still here. Good. Saves thumpin' you," she muttered sternly into his ear as they folded each other in.

Razi dumped his wriggling son off on Sarri, who cocked her hip to receive him, Utau let Tesy loose with admonitions about keeping clear of Copperhead, and the pair of men came to help Dag and Fawn dismount. Utau looked tired but hale enough, Fawn thought. Mari's son-in-law and Razi had all three horses unsaddled and bags off in a blink, and the two volunteered to lead the mounts back to Mare Island, preferably before the snorting Copperhead bit or kicked some bouncing child.

Tent Bluefield was still standing foursquare under the apple tree, and Sarri, smiling, rolled up and tied the tent flaps. Everything inside looked very neat and tidy and welcoming, and Fawn had Utau drop their grubby saddlebags under the outside awning. There would be serious laundry, she decided, before their travel-stained and reeking garments were allowed to consort again with their stay-at-home kin.

Dag eyed their bedroll atop its thick cushion of dried grass rather as a starving dog would contemplate a steak, muttered, "Boots off, leastways," and dropped to a seat on an upended log to tug at his laces. He looked up to add, "Any problems while we were away?"

"Well," said Sarri, sounding a trifle reluctant, "there was that go-round with the girls from Stores."

"They tried to steal your tent, the little—!" said Utau, abruptly indignant. Sarri shushed him in a way that made Fawn think this was an exchange much-repeated.

"What?" said Dag, squinting in bewilderment.

"Not stealing, exactly," said Sarri.

"Yes, it was," muttered Utau. "Blighted sneakery."

"They told me they'd been ordered to bring it back to Stores," Sarri went on, overriding him. "They had it halfway down when I caught them. They wouldn't listen to me, but Cattagus came out and wheezed at them and frightened them off."

"Razi and I were out collecting elderberries for Cattagus," said Utau, "or I'd have been willing to frighten them off myself. The nerve, to make away with a patroller's tent while he was out on patrol!"

Fawn frowned, imagining the startling—shocking—effect it would have had, with her and Dag both so travel-weary, to come back and find everything gone. Dag looked as though he was imagining this, too.

"Uncle Cattagus puffing in outrage was likely more effective," Sarri allowed. "He turns this alarming purple color, and chokes, and you think he's going to collapse onto your feet. The girls were impressed, anyway, and left off."

"Ran, Cattagus tells it," said Utau, brightening.

"When Razi and Utau came back they put your tent up again, and then went down and had some words with the folks in Stores. They claimed it was all a misunderstanding."

Utau snorted. "In a pig's eye it was. It was some crony of Cumbia's down there, with a notion for petty aggravation. Anyway, I spoke to Fairbolt, who spoke with Massape, who spoke with someone, and it didn't happen again." He nodded firmly.

Dag rubbed the back of his neck, looking pinch-browed and abstracted. If he'd had more energy, Fawn thought he might have been as angry as Utau, but just now it merely came out saddened. "I see," was all he said. "Thank you." He nodded up to Sarri as well.

"Fawn, not to tell you your job, but I think you need to get your husband horizontal," said Sarri.

"I'm for it," said Fawn. Together, she and Utau pulled Dag upright and aimed him into the tent.

Utau, releasing Dag's arm from over his shoulder as he sank down onto his bedroll, grunted, "Dag, I swear you're worse off than when I left you in Raintree. That groundlock do this to you? Your leg hasn't turned bad, has it? From what Hoharie said, I'd thought she'd patched you up better 'n this before she left you."

"He was better," said Fawn, "but then we went and visited Greenspring on the way home. It was all really deep-blighted. I think it gave him a relapse of some sort." Except she wasn't so sure it was the blight that had drained him of the ease he'd gained after their triumph over the groundlock. She remembered the look on his face, or rather the absence of any look on his face, when they'd ridden out of the townsmen's burying field past the line of small uncorrupted corpses. He'd *counted* them.

"That was a fool thing to do for a ground-ripped man, to go and expose yourself to more blight," Utau scolded. "You should know better, Dag."

"Yeah," sighed Dag, dutifully lying flat. "Well, we're all home now."

Sarri and Utau took themselves out with an offer of dinner later, which Fawn gratefully accepted. She fussed briefly over Dag, kissed him on the forehead, and left him not so much dozing as glazed while she went to deal with unpacking their gear. She glanced up at the lately contested awning of little Tent Bluefield as she began sorting.

Home again.

Was it?

Fawn brought Dag breakfast in bed the next morning. So it was only plunkin, tea, and concern; the concern, at least, he thought delicious. Though he had no appetite, he let her coax him into eating, and then bustle about getting him propped up comfortably with a nice view out the tent flap at the lakeshore. As the sun climbed he could watch her down on the dock scrubbing their clothes. From time to time she waved up at him, and he waved back. In due course, she shouldered the wet load and climbed up out of sight somewhere, likely to hang it all out to dry.

He was still staring out in benign lassitude when a brisk hand slapped the tent side, and Hoharie ducked in. "There you are. Saun told me you'd made it back," she greeted him.

"Ah, Hoharie. Yeah, yesterday afternoon."

"I also heard you weren't doing so well."

"I've been worse."

Hoharie was back in her summer shift, out of riding gear; indeed, she'd made a questionable-looking patroller. She settled down on her knees and folded her legs under herself, looking Dag over critically.

"How's the leg, after all that abuse?"

"Still healing. Slowly. No sign of infection."

"That's a blessing in a deep puncture, although after all that ground reinforcement I wouldn't expect infection. And the arm?"

He shifted it. "Still very weak." He hadn't even bothered with his arm harness yet this morning, though Fawn had cajoled him into clean trousers and shirt. "No worse."

"Should be better by now. Come on, open up."

Dag sighed and eased open his ground. It no longer gave him sensations akin to pain to do so; the discomfort was more subtle now, diffuse and lingering.

Horarie frowned. "What did you do with all that ground reinforcement you took on last week over in Raintree? It's barely there."

"It helped. But we crossed some more blight on the way back."

"Not smart." Her eyes narrowed. "What's your groundsense range right now?"

"Good question. I haven't . . ." He spread his senses. He hardly needed groundsense to detect Mari's noisy grandchildren, shouting all over the campsite. The half-closed adults were subtler smudges. Fawn was a bright spark in the walnut grove, a hundred paces off. Beyond that . . . nothing. "Very limited." Shockingly so. "Haven't been this weak since I lost my real hand."

"Well, if you want an answer to, *How am I recovering?* there's your test. No patrolling for you for a while, Captain. Not till your range is back to its usual."

Dag waved this away. "I'm not arguin'."

"That tells a tale right there." Hoharie's fingers touched his thigh, his arm, his side; he could feel her keen regard as a passing pressure through his aches. "After my story and Saun's, Fairbolt reckoned he'd be putting your peg back in the sick box. He wanted me to tell him for how long."

"So? How long?"

"Longer than Utau, anyway."

"Fairbolt won't be happy about that."

"Well, we've talked about that. About you. You did rather more in that Bonemarsh groundlock than just take hurt, you know."

Something in her tone brought him up, if not to full alertness, which eluded him still, then to less vague attention. He let his ground ease closed again. Hoharie sat back on the woven mat beside the bedroll and wrapped her arms around her knees, regarding him coolly.

"You've been patrolling for a long time," she observed.

"Upwards of forty years. So? Cattagus walked for almost seventy. My grandfather, longer than that. It's a life."

"Ever think of another? Something more settled?"

"Not lately." Or at least, not until this summer. He wasn't about to try to describe how confused he'd become about his life since Glassforge.

"Anyone ever suggest medicine maker?"

"Yes, you, but you weren't thinking it through."

"I remember you complained about being too old to be an apprentice. May I point out, yours could be about the shortest apprenticeship on record? You already know all the herb-lore, from decades of patrol gathering. You know field aid on the practical side—possibly even more than I do. Your ground-matching skills are astonishing, as Saun has lived to testify to anyone who will listen."

"Saun, you may have noticed, is a bit of an enthusiast. I wouldn't take him too seriously, Hoharie."

She shook her head. "I *saw* you do things with ground projection and manipulation, inside that groundlock, that I can still barely wrap my mind around. I examined Artin, after it was all over. You not only could do it, you could be good, Dag. A lot of people can patrol. Not near as many can do this level of making, fewer still such direct groundwork. I know——I scout for apprentices every year."

"Be reasonable, Hoharie. Groundsense or no, a medicine maker needs two clever hands for, well, all sorts of tasks. You wouldn't want me sewing up your torn trousers, let alone your torn skin. And the list goes on."

"Indeed it does." She smiled and leaned forward. "But——patrollers work in partnered pairs all the time. You're used to it. And I get, from time to time, a youngster mad for medicine-making, and with clever hands, but a bit lacking on the groundsense side. You get along well with youngsters, even if you do scare them at first. I'm thinking——what about pairing you up with someone like that?"

Dag blinked. Then blinked again. *Spark?* She had the cleverest hands of anyone he'd ever met, and, absent gods knew, the wits and nerve for the task. His imagination and heart were both suddenly racing, tossing up pictures of the possibilities. They could work together right here at Hickory Lake, or at Bearsford Camp. Honorable, necessary, respected work, to win her a place here in her own right. He could be by her side every day. And every night. And once she was trained, they might do more . . . would Fawn like the notion? He would ask her at once. He grinned at Hoharie, and she brightened.

"I see you get the idea," she said in a tone of satisfaction. "I'm so glad! As you might guess, I have someone in mind."

"Yes."

"Oh, did Othan talk to you?"

"Beg pardon?"

"It's his younger brother, Osho. He's not quite ready for it yet, mind, but neither are you. But if I knew he'd be pairing with you, I could admit him to training pretty soon."

"Wait, what? No! I was thinking of Fawn."

It was Hoharie's turn to rock back, blinking. "But Dag——even if she's still——she has no groundsense at all! A farmer can't be a medicine maker. Or any kind of a maker."

"Farmers are, in their own way, all the time. Midwives, bonesetters."

"Certainly, but they can't use our ways. I'm sure their skills are valuable, and of course better than nothing, but they just can't."

"I'd do that part. You said."

"Dag . . . the sick and the hurt are vulnerable and touchy. I'm afraid a lot of folks wouldn't trust or accept her. It would be one strange thing too many. There's also the problem of her ground. I like Fawn, but having her ground always open around delicate groundwork, maybe distracting or interfering . . . no."

It wouldn't distract me, he thought of arguing. He settled his shoulders back on his cushion, his little burst of excitement draining away again, leaving his fatigue feeling worse by contrast. Instead, he asked, more slowly, "So why don't we do more for farmers? No, I don't mean the strong makers like you, you're rare and needed here, but all of us. The patrols are out there all the time. We know and use a dozen little tricks amongst ourselves, that we could find ways to share. More than just selling plants and preparations. We could build up goodwill, over time." He remembered Aunt Nattie's tale of her twisted ankle. Just such a good deed had borne some fair fruit, even decades afterwards.

"Oh, Dag." Hoharie shook her head. "Do you think no one's tried it, tempted through pity? Or even friendship? It sounds so fine, but it only works as long as nothing goes wrong, as it inevitably must. That goodwill can turn to bad will in a heartbeat. Lakewalkers who let themselves get in over their heads trying to share such help have been beaten to death, or worse."

"If it were . . ." His voice faltered. He didn't have a counterargument for this one, as it was perfectly true. *There has to be a better way* was easy to say. It was a lot harder to picture exactly how.

Returning to her subject, Hoharie said, "Fairbolt doesn't much want to give you up, but he would for this. He can see a lot of the same things I do. He's watched you for a long time."

"I owe Fairbolt"—Dag lifted his left arm—"everything, pretty much. My arm harness was his doing. He'd spotted something like it in Tripoint, see. A farmer artificer and a farmer bonesetter over there had got together to fix things like it for some folks who'd lost limbs in mining and forge accidents. Neither of them had a speck of groundsense, but they had *ideas*."

Hoharie began to speak, but then turned her head; in a moment, Fawn popped around the tent's open side, looking equally pleased and anxious. "Hoharie! I'm so glad you're here. How is he doing? Mari was worried."

As if Fawn didn't expect her own worry to count with the medicine maker? *And is she so wrong in that?*

Hoharie smiled reassuringly. "He mostly needs time and rest and not to do fool things."

Dag said plaintively, not to mention horizontally, "How can I do fool things when I can't do anything?"

Hoharie gave his query the quelling eyebrow twitch it deserved, and went on to give Fawn a set of sensible instructions and suggestions, which added up to *food, sleep,* and *mild camp chores when ready.* Fawn listened earnestly, nodding. Dag was sure she'd remember every word. And be able to quote them back at him, likely.

Hoharie rose. "I'll send Othan down in a couple of days to pull those stitches out."

"I can do that myself," said Dag.

"Well, *don't*," she returned. She glanced down at him. "Think about what I said, Dag. If your feet—or your heart—ache too much to walk another mile, you could do a world of good right here."

"I will," he said, unsettled. Hoharie waved and took herself out.

Frowning, Fawn flopped down on her knees beside him and ran a small hand over his brow. "Your eyebrows are all scrunched up. Are you in pain?" She smoothed away the furrows.

"No." He caught the hand and kissed it. "Just tired, I guess." He hesitated. "Thinkin'."

"Is that the sort of thinkin' where you sit like a bump for hours, and then jump sideways like a frog?"

He smiled despite himself. "Do I do that?"

"You do."

"Well, I'm not jumping anywhere today."

"Good." She rewarded this resolve with a kiss, and then several more. It unlocked muscles in him that he hadn't known were taut. One muscle, at least, remained limp, which would have disturbed him a lot more if he hadn't been through such convalescences before. *Must rest faster.*

Dag spent the next three days mired in much the same glazed lassitude. He was driven from his bedroll at last not by a return of energy, but by a buildup of boredom. Out and about, he found unexpectedly intense competition for the sitting-down camp chores among the ailing—Utau, Cattagus, and himself. He watched Cattagus, moving at about the same rate he did, and wondered if this was what it was going to feel like to be old.

There being no hides to scrape at the moment, and Utau and Razi having shrewdly been first in line to help Cattagus with his elderberries, Dag defaulted to nut-cracking; he had, after all, a built-in tool for it. He was awkward at first with the fiddly aspects, but grew less so. Fawn, who plainly thought the task the most tedious in the world, wrinkled her nose, but it exactly suited Dag's mood, not requiring any thought beyond a vague philosophical contemplation of the subtle shapes of nuts and their shells. Walnuts. And hickory shells. Over and over, very reliably. They might resist him, but only rarely did they counterattack, the hickory being the more innately vicious.

Fawn kept him company, first spinning, then working on two pairs of new riding trousers, one for him and one for her, made of cloth shared by Sarri. Sitting with him in the shade of their awning one afternoon, she remarked, "I'd make you more arrows, but everyone's quivers are full up."

Dag poked at a particularly intractable nutshell. "Do you like making arrows better than making trousers?"

She shrugged. "It just feels more important. Patrollers *need* arrows."

He sat back and contemplated this. "And we don't need trousers? I think you have that the wrong way round, Spark. It's poison ivy country out there, you know. Not to mention the nettles, thistles, burrs, thorns, and bitey bugs."

She pursed her lips as she poked her needle slowly through the sturdy cloth. "For going into a fight, though. When it counts."

"I still don't agree. I'd want my trousers. In fact, if I were waked up out of my bedroll in a night attack, I think I'd go for them before my boots *or* my bow."

"But patrollers sleep in their trousers, in camp," she objected. "Although not in hotels," she allowed in a tone of pleasurable reminiscence.

"That gives you a measure of importance, then, doesn't it?" He batted his eyes at her. "I can just picture it, a whole patrol riding out armed to the teeth, all bare-assed. Do you have any idea what the jouncing in those saddles would do to all our tender bits? We'd never make it to the malice."

"Agh! Now *I'm* picturing it!' She bent over, laughing. "Stop! I'll allow you the trousers."

"And I'll thank you with all my heart," he assured her. "And with my tender bits." Which made her dissolve into giggles again.

He could not remember when she'd last laughed like this, which sobered him. But he still smiled as he watched her take up her sewing once more. He decided he would very much like to thank her with his tender bits, if only they would get around to reporting for duty again. He sighed and took aim at another hickory shell.

Fortunately, or unfortunately, while he was still recuperating, Fawn's monthly came on—a bad one, it seemed, alarmingly bloody. Dag, concerned, dragged Mari over to Tent Bluefield for a consultation; she was reassuringly unimpressed, and rattled off a gruesome string of what Dag decided were the female equivalent of old-patroller stories, about Much Worse Things She Had Seen.

"I don't recall the young women on patrol having this much trouble," he said nervously, hovering.

Mari eyed him. "That's because girls with these sorts of troubles gener'lly don't choose to become patrollers."

"Oh. Makes sense, I guess . . ."

Softening, Mari allowed as how Fawn was likely still healing up inside, which from the state of the scars on her neck Dag guessed to be exactly the case, and that the problems should improve over the next months, and even unbent enough to give Fawn a tiny ground reinforcement in the afflicted area.

Dag thought back to his too-few years with Kauneo, how a married man's life got all wound about in these intimate rhythms, and how they had sometimes annoyed him—till he'd been left to wish for them back. He dealt serenely, wrapping hot stones, and coaxing some of Cattagus's best elderberry wine out of him and into Fawn, and her pains eased.

At last, one bright, quiet morning, Dag hauled his trunk out under the canopy for a writing desk and took on the task of his letter to Luthlia. At first he thought he would keep it painlessly short, a sentence or two simply locating each bone's malice kill. He was so much in the habit of concealing the complications of the unintended priming; it seemed so impossible to set it out clearly; and the tale of Fawn and her lost babe seemed too inward a hurt to put before strangers' eyes. Silence was easier. And yet . . . silence would seem to deny that a farmer girl had ever had any place in all this. He weighed the smooth shards of Kauneo's bone in his hand one last time before wrapping them up in a square of good cloth that Fawn had hemmed, and changed his mind.

Instead he wrote out as complete an account of the chain of events, focusing on the knives, as he could manage, most especially not leaving out his belief of how the babe's ground had found refuge from the malice. It was still so compressed he wasn't sure but what it sounded incoherent or insane, but it was all the truth as he knew it. When he was done he let Fawn read it before he sealed it with some of Sarri's beeswax. Her face grew solemn; she handed it back with a brief nod. "That'll do for my part."

She helped him wrap up the packet carefully, with an outer cover of deer leather secured by rawhide strings for protection, and he addressed it to Kauneo's kin, ready for Razi to take up to the courier at patroller headquarters. He fingered the finished bundle, and said slowly, "So many memories . . . If souls exist, maybe they lie in the track of time we leave behind us. And not out ahead, and that's why we can't find them, not even with groundsense. We're lookin' in the wrong direction."

Fawn smiled wryly into his eyes, leaned up, and kissed him soft. "Or maybe they're right here," she said.

Fairbolt turned up the next day. Dag had been half-expecting him. They found seats on a pair of stumps out in the walnut grove, out of earshot from the busy campsite.

"Razi says you're feeling better," Fairbolt remarked, looking Dag over keenly.

"My body's moving again, anyway," Dag allowed. "My groundsense range still isn't doing too well. I don't think Hoharie's notion that it has to come all the way back before I patrol again is right, though. Halfway would be good as most."

"It's not about you going back on patrol, for which judgment I'll be relying on Hoharie and not you, thanks. It's about your camp council summons. I've been holding 'em off on the word that you're still too injured and ill after Raintree, which is harder to make stick when it's seen you are up and about. So you can expect it as soon as that Heron Island dredging fracas is sorted out."

Dag hissed through his teeth. "After Raintree—after all Fawn and I did— they're *still* after a camp council ruling against us? Hoharie, and I, and Bryn and Mallora and Ornig would all be dead and buried right now in blighted Bonemarsh if not for Fawn! Not to mention five good makers lost. This, on top of the Glassforge malice—what more could they possibly want from a farmer girl to prove herself worthy?" His outrage was chilled by a ripple of cold reflection—in forty years he had never been able to prove *himself* worthy, in certain eyes. He'd concluded sometime back that the problem was not in him, it was in those eyes, and no doing of his could ever fix it. Why should any doing of Fawn's be different?

Fairbolt scratched his ear. "Yeah, I didn't figure that news would sit too well with you." He hesitated. "I owe an apology to Fawn, for trying to stop her here when you were calling her from out of that groundlock. It seems right cruel, in hindsight. I had no idea it was you behind her restiness that day."

Dag's brows drew down. "You been talking to Othan about the Bonemarsh groundlock?"

"I've been talking to everyone who was there, as I had the chance, trying to piece it all together."

"Well, just for the scribe, it wasn't me who told Fawn to put that knife in my leg, like, like some *malice* riding a farmer slave. She figured it out by her own wits!"

Fairbolt held up both palms in a gesture of surrender. "Be that as it may, how are you planning to handle this council challenge? I've discouraged and delayed it about as much as I can without being bounced off your hearing myself for conflict of interest. And since I don't mean to let myself get excluded from this one, the next move has to fall on you. Which is where it belongs anyway, I might point out."

Dag bent, venting a weary sigh. "I don't know, Fairbolt. My mind's been working pretty slow since I got back. It feels like a bug stuck in honey, truth to tell."

Fairbolt frowned curiously. "An effect of that peculiar blight you took on, do you think?"

"I . . . don't know. It's an effect of something." Accumulation, maybe. He could feel it, building up in him, but he could not put a name to it.

"It wouldn't hurt for you to tell more of your tale around, you know," said Fairbolt. "I don't think everyone rightly understands how much would be lost to this camp, and to Oleana, if you were banished."

"What, brag and boast?" Dag made a face. "I should be let to keep Fawn because I'm special?"

"If you're not willing to say it to your friends, how are you going to stand up in council and say it to your enemies?"

"Not my style, and an insult to boot to everyone who walks their miles all the same, without fanfare or thanks. Now, if you want me to argue that I should be let to keep Fawn because *she's* special, I'm for it."

"Mm," said Fairbolt. If he was picturing this, the vision didn't seem to bring him much joy.

Dag looked down, rubbing his sandal in the dirt. "There is this. If the continued existence of Hickory Lake Camp—or Oleana—or the wide green world—depends on just one man, we've already lost this long war."

"Yet every malice kill comes, at the end, down to one man's hand," Fairbolt said, watching him.

"Not true. There's a world balanced on that knife-edge. The hand of the patroller, yes. But held in it, the bone's donor, and the heart's donor, and the hand and eye and ground of the knife maker. And all the patrol backing up behind who got the patroller to that place. Patrollers, we hunt in packs. Then all the camp and kin behind them, who gave them the horses and the gear and the food to get there. And on and on. Not one man, Fairbolt. One man or another, yes."

Fairbolt gave a slow, conceding nod. He added after a moment, "*Has* anyone said *thank you* for Raintree, company captain?"

"Not as I recollect," Dag said dryly, then was a little sorry for the tone when he caught Fairbolt's wince. He added more wistfully, "Though I do hope Dirla got her bow-down."

"Yes, they had a great party for her over on Beaver Sigh, I heard from the survivors."

Dag's smile tweaked. "Good."

Fairbolt stretched his back, which creaked faintly in the cool silence of the shade. Between the dark tree boles, the lake surface glittered in a passing breeze. "I like Fawn, yet . . . I can't help imagining how much simpler all our lives could be right now if you were to take that nice farmer girl back to her family down in West Blue and tell them to keep the bride-gifts and her."

"Pretty insulting, Fairbolt," Dag observed. He didn't say who to. It would take a list, he decided.

"You could say you'd made a mistake."

"But I didn't."

Fairbolt grimaced. "I didn't think that notion would take. Had to try, though."

Dag's nod of understanding was reserved. Fairbolt spoke as if this was all about Fawn, and indeed, it had all begun with her. Dag wasn't so sure his farmer bride was all it was about now. The *all* part seemed to have grown much larger and more complex, for one. Since Raintree? Since West Blue? Since Glassforge? Or even before that, piling up unnoticed?

"Fairbolt . . ."

"Mm?"

"This was a bad year for the patrol. Did we have more emergences, all told, or just worse ones?"

Fairbolt counted silently on his fingers, then his eyebrows went up. "Actually, fewer than last year or the year before. But Glassforge and Raintree were so much worse, they put us behind, which makes it seem like more."

"Both bad outbreaks were in farmer country."

"Yes?"

"There *is* more farmer country now. More cleared land, and it's spreading. We're bound to see more emergences like those. And not just in Oleana. You're *from* Tripoint, Fairbolt, you know more about farmer artificers than anyone around here. The ones I watched this summer in Glassforge, they're more of that sort"—Dag raised his arm in its harness—"doing more things, more cleverly, better and better. You've heard all about what happened at Greenspring. What if it had been a big town like Tripoint, the way Glassforge is growing to be?"

Fairbolt went still, listening. Listening hard, Dag thought, but what he was thinking didn't show in his face.

Dag pushed on: "Malice takes a town like that, it doesn't just get slaves and ripped grounds, it gets know-how, tools, weapons, boats, forges and mills already built—power, as sure as any stolen groundsense. And the more such towns farmers build, and they will, the more that ill chance becomes a certainty."

Fairbolt's grim headshake did not deny this. "We can't push farmers back south to safety by force. We haven't got it to spare."

"Then they're here to stay, eh? I'm not suggesting force. But what if we had their help, that power, instead of feeding it to the malices?"

"We cannot let ourselves depend. We *must not* become lords again. That was our fathers' sin that near-slew the world."

"Isn't there any other way for Lakewalkers and farmers to be with each other than as lords and servants, malices and slaves?"

"Yes. Live apart. Thus we avert lordship." Fairbolt made a slicing gesture.

Dag fell silent, his throat thick.

"So," said Fairbolt at length. "What *is* your plan for dealing with the camp council?"

Dag shook his head.

Fairbolt sat back in some exasperation, then continued, "It's like this. When I see a good tactician—and I know you are one—sit and wait, instead of moving, as his enemy advances on him, I figure there could be two possible reasons. Either he doesn't know what to do—or his enemy is coming into his hand exactly the way he wants. I've known you for a good long time . . . and looking at you right now, I still don't know which it is you're doing."

Dag looked away. "Maybe I don't either."

After another silence, Fairbolt sighed and rose. "Reasonable enough. I've done what I can. Take care of yourself, Dag. See you at council, I suppose."

"Likely." Dag touched his temple and watched Fairbolt trudge wearily away through the walnut grove.

The next day dawned clear, promising the best kind of dry heat. The lake was glassy. Dag lay up under the awning of Tent Bluefield and watched Fawn finish weaving hats, the result of her finding a batch of reeds of a texture she'd declared comparable to more farmerly straw. She took her scissors and, tongue caught fetchingly between her teeth, carefully trimmed the fringe of reeds sticking out around the brim to an even finger length. "There!" she said, holding it up. "That's yours."

He glanced at its mate lying beside her. "Why isn't it braided up all neat around the rim like the other?"

"Silly, that's a *girl's* hat. This is a *boy's* hat. So's you can tell the difference."

"Not to question your people, but that's not how *I* tell the difference between boys and girls."

This won a giggle, as he'd hoped. "It just *is,* for straw hats, all right? So now I can go out in the sun without my nose coming all over freckles."

"I think your nose looks cute with freckles." *Or without . . .*

"Well, I don't." She gave a decisive nod.

He leaned back, his eyes half-closing. His bone-deep exhaustion was creeping up on him, again. Maybe Hoharie had been right about that appalling recovery time after all. . . .

"That's it." Fawn jumped to her feet.

He opened his eyes to find her frowning down at him.

"We're going on a picnic," she declared roundly.

"What?"

"Just you wait and see. No, don't get up. It's a surprise, so don't look."

He watched anyway, as she bustled about putting a great deal of food and two stone jugs into a basket, bundled up a couple of blankets, then vanished around behind Cattagus and Mari's tent to emerge toting a paddle for the narrow boat. Bemused, he found himself herded down to the dock and instructed to get in and have a nice lie-down, padded and propped in the bottom of the boat facing her.

"You know how to steer this craft?" he inquired mildly, settling.

"Er . . ." She hesitated. "It looked pretty easy when you did it." And then, after a moment, "You'll tell me, won't you?"

"It's a deal, Spark."

The lesson took maybe ten minutes, once they'd pushed off from the dock. Their somewhat-wandering path evened out as she settled into her stroke, and then all he had to do was coax her to slow down and find the rhythm that would last. She found her way to that, too. He pushed back his boy's hat and smiled from under the fringe at her. Her face was made luminous even beneath the shadow of her own neat brim by the light reflecting off the water, all framed against the deep blue sky.

He felt amazingly content not to move. "If your folks could see us now," he remarked, "they really would believe all those tales about the idleness of Lake-walker men."

He'd almost forgotten the blinding charm of her dimple when she smirked. She kept paddling.

They rounded Walnut Island, pausing for a glimpse of some of the stallions prancing elegantly in pasture, then glided up through the elderberry channels. Several boats were out gathering there today; Dag and Fawn mainly received startled stares in return for their waves, except from Razi and Utau, working again on Cattagus's behalf and indirectly their own. Cattagus fermented his wines in large stone crocks buried in the cool soil of the island's woods, which he had inherited from another man before him, and him from another; Dag had no idea how far back the tradition went, but he bet it matched plunkins. They stopped to chat briefly with the pair. A certain hilarity about Dag's hat only made him pull it on more firmly, and Fawn paddle onward, tossing her head but still dimpling.

At length, to no surprise but a deal of pleasure on Dag's part, they slipped into the clear sheltered waters of the lily marsh. He then had the amusement, carefully concealed under his useful hat fringe, of watching Fawn paddle around realizing that her planning had missed an element, namely, where to spread blankets when all the thick grassy hillocks like tiny private islands turned out to be growing from at least two inches of standing water. He listened to as much of her foiled muttering as he thought he would get away with, then surrendered to his better self and pointed out how they might have a nice picnic on board the boat, wedged for stability up into a willow-shaded wrack of old logs. Fawn took aim and, with only a slightly alarming scraping noise, brought them upright into this makeshift dock.

She sat in the bottom of the boat facing him, their legs interlaced, and shared food and wine till she'd succeeded in fulfilling several of Hoharie's recommendations at once by driving him into a dozy nap. He woke at length more overheated than even farmer hats and the flickering yellow-green willow shade could contend with, and hoisted himself up to strip off his shirt and arm harness.

Fawn opened one eye from her own replete slump, then sat up in some alarm as he lifted his hips to slip off his trousers. "I don't think we can do *that* in a narrow boat!"

"Actually, you can," he assured her absently, "but I'm not attempting it now. I'm going into the water to cool off."

"Aren't you supposed to get cramps if you swim too soon after a heavy meal?"

"I'm not going swimming. I'm going floating. I may not move any muscles at all."

He selected a dry log about three feet long from the top of the wrack, wriggled it loose, and slipped into the water after it. The surface of the water was as warm as a bath, but his legs found the chill they sought farther down, flowing over his skin like silk. He hung his arms over his makeshift float, propped his chin in the middle, kicked up some billowing coolness, and relaxed utterly.

In a little while, to his—alas, still purely aesthetic—pleasure, Fawn yanked her shift over her flushed face, unwedged a log of her own, and splashed in after him. He floated on blissfully while she ottered around him with more youthful vigor, daring to wet her hair, then her face, then duck under altogether.

"Hey!" she said in a tone of discovery, partway through this proceeding. "I can't sink!"

"Now you know," he crooned.

She splashed him, got no rise, then eventually settled down beside him. He opened his eyes just far enough to enjoy the sight of her pale bare body, seemingly made liquid by the water-waver, caressed by the long, fringed water weeds as she idly kicked and turned. He looked down meditatively at the yellow willow leaves floating past his nose, harbinger of more soon to come. "The light is changing. And the sounds in the air. I always notice it, when the summer passes its peak and starts down, and the cicadas come on. Makes me . . . not sad, exactly. There should be a word." As though time was sliding away, and not even his ghost hand could catch it.

"Noisy things, cicadas," Fawn murmured, chinned on her own log. "I heard 'em just starting up when I was riding to Raintree."

They were both quiet for a very long time, listening to the chaining counterpoint of bug songs. The brown wedge of a muskrat's head trailed a widening vee across the limpid water, then vanished with a plop as the shy animal sensed their regard. The blue heron floated in, but then just stood folded as though sleeping on one leg. The green-headed ducks, drowsing in the shade across the marsh, didn't move either. The clear light lay breathing like a live thing.

"This place is like the opposite of blight," murmured Fawn after a while. "Thick, dense . . . if you opened up, would its ground just flow in and replenish you?"

"I opened up two hours ago. And yes, I think it may," he sighed.

"That explains something about places like this, then," she muttered in satisfaction.

A much longer time later, they regretfully pulled their wrinkled selves up onto the wrack and back into the boat, dressed, and pushed back to start for home. The sun was sliding behind the western trees as they crossed the wide part of the lake, and had turned into an orange glint by the time they climbed the bank to Tent Bluefield. Dag slept that night better than he had for weeks.

18

Fawn woke late the next morning, she judged by the bright lines of light leaking around the edges of their easterly tent flaps. The air inside was still cool from the night, but would grow hot and stuffy soon. Wrapped around her, Dag sighed and stirred, then hugged her in tighter. Something firm nudged the back of her thigh, and she realized with a slow smirk that it wasn't his hand. *I thought that picnic would be good for him.*

He made a purring noise into her hair, indicating the same satisfying realization, and she wriggled around to turn her face to his. His eyes gleamed from under his half-closed eyelids, and she sank into his sleepy smile as if it were a pillow. He kissed her temple and lips, and bent his head to nuzzle her neck. She let her hand begin to roam and stroke, giving and taking free pleasure from his warm skin for the first time since he'd been called out to Raintree. He pulled her closer still, seeming to revel in her softness pressing tight to him, skin to skin for the length of her body. This needed no words now, no instruction. No questions.

A hand slapped loudly three times against the leather of the tent flap, and a raspy female voice called, "Dag Redwing Hickory?"

Dag's body stiffened, and he swore under his breath. He held Fawn's face close to his chest as if to muffle her, and didn't answer.

The slaps were repeated. "Dag Redwing Hickory! Come on, I know you're in there."

A frustrated hiss leaked between his teeth. All his stiffening, alas, slackened. "No one in here by that name," he called back gruffly.

The voice outside grew exasperated. "Dag, don't fool with me, I'm not in the mood. I dislike this as much as you do, I daresay."

"Not possible," he muttered, but sighed and sat up. He ran his hand through his sleep-bent hair, rolled over, and groped for his short trousers.

"What is it?" Fawn asked apprehensively.

"Dowie Grayheron. She's the alternate for Two Bridge Island on camp council this season."

"Is it the summons?"

"Likely."

Fawn scrambled into her shift and trailed after Dag as he shoved through their tent flap and stood squinting in the bright sun.

An older woman, with streaked hair like Omba's braided up around her head, stood drumming her fingers on her thigh. She eyed Dag's bed-rumpled look in bemusement, Fawn more curiously. "The camp council hearing for you is at noon," she announced.

Dag started. "Today? Short notice!"

"I came around twice yesterday, but you were out. And I know Fairbolt warned you, so don't pretend this is a surprise. Here, let me get through this." She spread her legs a trifle, pulled back her shoulders, and recited, "Dag Redwing Hickory, I summon you to hear and speak to grave complaints brought before the Hickory Lake Camp Summer Council by Dar Redwing Hickory, on behalf of Tent Redwing, noon today in Council Grove. Do you hear and understand?"

"Yes," Dag growled.

"*Thank* you," she said. "That's done."

"But I'm not Dag Redwing," Dag put in. "That fellow no longer exists."

"Save it for the grove. That's where the argumentation belongs." She hesitated, glancing briefly at Fawn and back to Dag. "I will point out, you've been summoned but your child-bride has not. There's no place for a farmer in our councils."

Dag's jaw set. "Is she explicitly excluded? Because if she has been, we have a sticking point before we start."

"No," Dowie admitted reluctantly. "But take it from me, she won't help your cause, Dag. Anyone who believed before that you've let your crotch do your thinking won't be persuaded otherwise by seeing her."

"Thank you," said Dag in a voice of honeyed acid. "I think my wife is pretty, too."

Dowie just shook her head. "I'm going to be so glad when this day is over." Her sandals slapped against her heels as she turned and strode off.

"There's a woman sure knows how to blight a mood," Dag murmured, his jaw unclenching.

Fawn crept to Dag's side; his arm went around her shoulders. She swallowed, and asked, "Is she any relation to Obio Grayheron?"

"He'd be her cousin by marriage. She's head of Tent Grayheron on this island."

"And she has a vote on the council? That's . . . not too encouraging."

"Actually, she's one I count as friendly. I patrolled for a year or so with her back when I was a young man, before I left to exchange and she quit to start her family."

If that was friendly, Fawn wondered what hostile was going to be like. Well, she'd soon find out. Was this all as sudden as it seemed? Maybe not. The camp council question had been a silence in the center of things that Dag had been skirting since they'd returned from Raintree, and she'd let him lead her in that circuit. True, he'd plainly been too ill to be troubled with it those first few days. But after?

He doesn't know what he wants to do, she realized, cold knotting in her belly. *Even now, he does not know.* Because what he wanted was impossible, and always had been, and so was the alternative? What was a man supposed to do then?

They dressed, washed up, ate. Dag did not return to cracking nuts, nor Fawn to spinning. He did get up and walk restlessly around the campsite or into the walnut grove, wherever he might temporarily avoid the other residents moving about their own early chores. When the dock cleared out from the morning swimmers, he went down and sat on it for a time, knees bent under his chin, staring down into the water. Fawn wondered if he was playing at that old child's amusement he'd showed her, of persuading the inedible little sunfish that clustered in the dock's shade to rise up and swim about in simple patterns. The sun crept.

As the shadows narrowed, Dag came up under their awning and sat beside her on his log seat. He propped his right elbow on his knee, neck bent, staring down at his sandals. At length he looked up toward the lake, face far away— Fawn couldn't tell if he was trying to memorize the view or not seeing it at all. She thought of their visits to the lily marsh. *This place nourishes him.* Would he starve in his spirit, exiled? A man might die without a mark on him, from having his ground ripped in half.

She took a breath, sat straight. Began, "Beloved."

His face turned sideways to her in a fleeting smile. He looked tired.

"What are you going to do?"

"I don't know." He seemed for an instant if he wanted to amend that bluntness in some reassuring fashion, but then just let it stand.

She angled her face away. "I wasn't going to tell you this story, but now I think I will. When you were first gone to Raintree, I knitted up another pair of socks like those you'd been so pleased with, and took them to your mother for a present. A peace offering, like."

"Didn't work." It wasn't a guess, nor a chiding; more of a commiseration.

Fawn nodded. "She said—well, we said several things to each other that don't matter now. But one thing she said sticks. She said, once a patroller sees a malice, he or she doesn't ever put another thing—or person—ahead of patrolling."

"I do wonder sometimes how she was betrayed, and who the patroller was. My father, I suspect."

"Did sound like," Fawn conceded. "But not with another woman, I don't guess."

"Me, either. Something Aunt Mari once let slip—Dar and I once may have had a sister who died as an infant in some tragic way. He says he doesn't remember any such thing, so she would have had to be either before or within a few years after he was born. If so, she was buried in a deep, deep silence, because Father never mentioned her, either."

"Huh." Fawn considered this. "Could be . . . Well." She bit her lip. "I'm no patroller, but I *have* seen a malice, and if there's anything your mama was right about, it's that. She said if you didn't love me enough, you'd choose the patrol." She held up a hand to stem his beginning protest. "And that if you loved me beyond all sense—you'd choose the patrol. Because you couldn't protect me for real and true any other way."

He subsided, silenced. She raised her face to meet his beautiful eyes square, and went on, "So I just want you to know, if you have to choose the patrol—I won't die of it. Nor be worse off for having known and loved you for a space. I'll still be richer going down the road than when you met me, by far, if only for the horse and the gear and the knowing. I never knew there was as much knowing as this to be had in the whole world. Maybe, looking back, I'll remember this summer as a dream of wonders . . . even the nightmare parts. If I didn't get to keep you for always, *leastways* I had you for a time. Which ought to be magic enough for any farmer girl."

He listened gravely, not attempting, after his first protest, to interrupt. Trying to sort it out, maybe, for he said, "Are you saying you're too tired to keep up this struggle anymore?"

She eyed him. "No, that's you, I think."

He gave a little self-derisive snort. "Could be."

"Keep it straight. I love you, and I'll walk with you down any path you choose, but . . . this one isn't my choice to make. It's yours."

"True. And wise." He sighed. "I thought we both chose in that scary little parlor back in West Blue. And yet your choice will be honored or betrayed by mine in turn. They don't come separately."

"No. They don't. But they do come in order. And West Blue, well—that was before either you or I saw Greenspring. That town could've been West Blue, those people me and mine. I watched your lips move, counting down that line of dead . . . To keep you, there's a lot of things I'd fight tooth and toenail. Your kin, my kin, another woman, sickness, farmer stupidity, you name it. Can't fight Greenspring. *Won't.*"

He blinked rapidly, and for a moment the gold in his eyes looked molten. He swiped the shiny water tracks from his cheekbones with the back of his hand, leaned forward, and kissed her on the forehead, that terrifying kiss of blessing again. "Thank you," he whispered. "You have no idea how that helps."

She nodded shortly, swallowing down the hot lump in her own throat.

They went into their tent to change, him out of his short trousers and sandals, her out of her somewhat grubby shift. When, on her knees sorting through his trunk, she tried to hand him up his cleanest shirt, he surprised her by saying, "No—my *best* shirt. The good one your Aunt Nattie wove."

He hadn't worn his wedding shirt since their wedding. Wondering, she shook it out, its folds wrapped in other clothes to keep it from creasing—her green cotton dress, as it happened.

"Oh, yes, wear that one," he said, looking over his shoulder. "It's so pretty on you."

"I don't know, Dag. It's awfully farmer-girl. Shouldn't I dress more Lakewalker for this?"

He smiled crookedly down at her. "No."

It was disquieting, in this context, to be all gussied up in their wedding-day clothes again. She adjusted the hang of the cord on her left wrist, and the gold beads knocked cool against her skin. Were they to be unmarried in this new noon hour, as if tracing back over some exact path after they had gotten lost? Maybe they *had* gone astray, somewhere along the way. But fingering the links of events back one by one in her memory, she couldn't see where.

Dag had picked up his hickory stick, so she guessed they were in for a longish walk to this grove, since he'd stopped using it around the campsite a few days back. She brushed her skirts straight, slipped her shoes on, and followed him out of the tent.

Dag realized he'd walked for a mile without seeing a single thing that had passed his eyes, and it wasn't because the route was so familiar. His mind seemed to have come to some still place, but he wasn't sure if it was poised or simply numb. They were passing patroller headquarters when Fawn, uncharacteristically silent till then, asked her first question: "Where is this council grove, anyhow?"

He glanced down at her. The rosy flush from their walk in the noon warmth kept her from being pale, but her face was set. "Not much farther. Just past Hoharie's medicine tent."

She nodded. "Will there be very many people there? Is it like a town council?"

"I don't know town councils. There are nearly eight thousand folks around Hickory Lake; the whole point of having a camp council is so they don't have to all show up for these arguments. Anyone can come listen who's interested, though. It depends on how many people or families or tents are involved in a dispute. It's only Tent Redwing—and Tent Bluefield—today. There'll be Dar and Mama, but not too many friends of theirs, because they wouldn't care to have them watch this. My friends are mostly out on patrol this season. So I don't expect a crowd." He hesitated, swinging his staff along, then shrugged his left shoulder. "Depends on how they take our marriage cords. *That* affects most everyone, and could grow much wider."

"How long will it take?"

"At the start of a session, the council leader lights a session candle. Session lasts as long as it takes to burn down, which is about three hours. They say of a dispute that it's a one-candle or two-candle or ten-candle argument. They can spread over several days, see." He added after a few more paces, "But this one won't." *Not if I can help it.*

"How do you know?" she asked, but then it was time to turn off into the grove.

Grove was a misnomer; it was more of a clearing, a wide circular space at the edge of the woods weeded of poison ivy and other noxious plant life and bordered by huge, flowering bushes people had planted over the years—elderberry, forsythia, lilac—some so old their trunks were thick as trees. Upended log seats were scattered about on grass that a couple of placid sheep were at work nibbling short. To one side rose an open frame nearly the size of patrol headquarters under a shingled roof, for bad weather, but today a small circle of seats was set up in the shade at the clearing's edge. A few more folks were walking in as Dag and Fawn arrived, so apparently they were not late.

Fairbolt Crow, talking head down with Mari, arrived last. They split off from each other, Fairbolt taking the remaining unoccupied log seat at the end of a close-set row of seven backed up to some venerable elderberry bushes, branches hanging heavy with fruit. Mari strode over to the gaggle of patrollers seated to Dag's right. Dag was not surprised to see Saun, Razi, and Utau already there; Saun jumped to his feet and rolled up a log for her. He was a little more surprised to see Dirla—had she paddled all the way over from Beaver Sigh for this?—and Griff from Obio's patrol.

Clustered to the left of the councilor's row were only Dar, Cumbia, and Omba, the latter plainly not too happy to be there. His mother looked up from a bit of cord she was working in her lap for habit or comfort, shot Dag one glance of grim triumph, which he scarcely knew how to interpret—*See what you made me do?* maybe—then looked away. The *looked away* part he had no trouble understanding, since he did the same, like not watching a medicine maker rummage in one's wound. Dar merely appeared as if he had a stomachache, and blamed Dag for it, hardly unusual for Dar.

One log seat waited directly across from the councilors. Utau muttered something to Razi, who hurried to collect another from nearby and set it beside the first. Not ten feet of open space was left in the middle. No one was going to have to bellow . . . at least, not merely to be heard.

Fawn, looking every bit as wary as a young deer, stopped Dag just out of earshot by clutching his arm; he bent his head to her urgent whisper, "Quick! Who are all those new people?"

Fairbolt was seated, perhaps not accidentally, closest to the patrollers, and Dowie Grayheron beside him. Dag whispered back, "Left from Fairbolt and Dowie is Pakona Pike. She's council leader this season. Head of Tent Pike." A woman of ninety or so, as straight-backed as Cumbia and one of her closer friends—Dag did not expect benign neutrality from her, but he didn't say it to Fawn.

"Next to her are Laski Beaver and Rigni Hawk, councilor and alternate from Beaver Sigh." Laski, a woman in her eighties, was head of Tent Beaver on Beaver Sigh, and a leather maker—it was her sister who made the coats that turned arrows. No one would ever have pulled *her* from her making for council duty. Rigni, closer to Dag's age, came from a tent of makers specializing in boats and buildings, though she herself was just emerging from raising a brood of children. She was also one of Dirla's aunts; she might have heard some good of Dag and Fawn.

"Next down from them, Tioca Cattail and her alternate Ogit Muskrat, from Heron Island. I don't know them all that well." Only that Tioca was a medicine maker, and since the recent death of her mother head of Tent Cattail on Heron. Ogit was a retired patroller of about Cumbia's age, curmudgeonly as Cattagus but without the charm; of no special making skills, he liked being on council, Dag had heard. While he was not close friends with Cumbia, the two had certainly known each other for decades. Despite Ogit's patrol connections Dag did not hold much hope for an ally in him.

Fawn blinked and nodded, and Dag wondered if she would remember all this and keep it straight. In any case, she now let him lead her forward. He seated her on his right, to the patroller side of things, and settled himself, laying his hickory staff at his feet and sitting up with a polite nod to the councilors across from him.

On a shorter sawed-off log in front of Pakona sat a beeswax candle. She nodded back grimly, lit the wick, and lowered a square parchment windbreak around it, lanternlike. From beside it she picked up a peeled wooden rod, the speaker's stick, and tapped it three times against the makeshift table. Everyone fell silent and regarded her attentively.

"There's been a deal of talk and gossip about this," she began, "so I don't think anyone here needs more explaining-to. The complaint in the matter comes from Tent Redwing against its member Dag Redwing. Who's speaking for Tent Redwing?"

Dag stirred at his naming, but voiced no protest. *Let that one go for now. You'll find your chance.*

"I do," said Dar, holding up one hand; behind him, Cumbia nodded. Cumbia, as head of Tent Redwing, was more than capable of speaking for herself and everyone else, and Dag wondered at this trade-off. An extension of Dag's shunning? Didn't trust herself to keep her voice and argument steady? She looked like old iron, today. But mostly, she looked old.

"Pass this down to Dar, then," said Pakona. The stick went from hand to hand. "Speak your tent's complaint, Dar."

He took the stick, inhaled, cast Dag a level stare, and began. "It won't take long. As we all know, Dag returned late from a patrol this summer with a farmer paramour in tow that he named his wife, on the basis of a pair of wedding cords that no one had witnessed them make. We say that the cords are counterfeit, produced by trickery. Dag is in simple violation of the longstanding rule against bringing such . . . self-indulgences within the bounds of camp. Tent Redwing requests the camp and the patrol enforce the usual penalties, returning the girl to her people by whatever means required and fining Dag Redwing for his transgression."

Dag, rigid with surprise, exhaled carefully. How *interestingly* clever of Dar—yes, this had to be Dar's idea. He had entirely shifted his argument from the one threatened before Dag had departed for Raintree, of forced stringcutting or banishment. A glance at Fairbolt's rising eyebrows told Dag the camp captain, too, had been taken by surprise; he cast Dag an apologetic glance. Dag wasn't sure how long ago Dar had rethought his attack, but he had been shrewd enough to keep it from Fairbolt.

Dag opened his ground just enough to catch the councilors' sevenfold flicker of ground examination upon him and Fawn. Tioca Cattail tilted her head, and said, "Pardon, but they appear to be perfectly usual cords to me. Can't that girl shut down her—no, I suppose not. How do you think they are false?"

"They were falsified in the making," said Dar. "The exchange of grounds in the cords marks a true marriage, yes, but the making also acts—normally— as a barrier against anyone not bearing Lakewalker bloodlines from contaminating our kinships. It's not a great making, true. It's more like the lowest boundary. We tend to think *everyone can do it,* but that is itself the sign of the value of this custom in the past.

"I say the farmer girl did *not* make her own cord, but that Dag made it for her, with a trick he stole from my knife-making techniques, of using blood to lead live ground into an object. It represents nothing but cunning."

"How do you know this, Dar?" asked Fairbolt, frowning.

Dar said, a trifle reluctantly, "Dag told me himself."

"That's not what I said!" Dag said sharply.

Pakona held up a quelling hand. "Wait for the stick, Dag."

"Hold on," said Rigni Hawk, her nose wrinkling. "We're taking hearsay testimony on a matter when we have two eyewitnesses sitting right in the circle?"

"*Thank* you, Rigni," huffed Fairbolt in relief. "Quite right. Pakona, I think the stick should go to Dag for this tale."

"He has reason to lie," said Dar, looking sullen.

"That'll be for us to sort out," said Rigni firmly.

Pakona waved, and Dar reluctantly handed the stick around via Omba to Dag.

"So how did you make those cords?" asked Tioca in curiosity.

"Fawn and I made both cords together," Dag said tightly. "As *some* of you may remember, my right arm was broken at the time" —he made the old sling-gesture—"and the other is, well, as you see. Lakewalker blood or no, I was quite incapable of weaving any cord at all. Fawn wove the cord she now wears, I sat behind her on the bench with my arms along hers, and I cast my ground into it in the usual way. I don't see how anyone in his right mind can maintain *that* cord is invalid!"

Pakona waved to quell him again, but murmured, "So, go on. What about the other?"

"I admit, I attempted to aid her in catching up her ground to weave into the second cord. We were having no luck at all when suddenly, all on her own, she cut open both her index fingers and wove while bleeding. Her ground welled right up and into the cord. I didn't help her any more than she helped me; less, I'd say."

"You instructed her to do this, then," said Tioca.

"No, she came up with it—"

"A few nights earlier, Dag and I had been talking about ground," Fawn put in breathlessly, "and he'd told me blood held ground after it left the body, because it was, like, alive separately from the person. Which I thought was a right disturbing idea, so I remembered it."

"You've not been given leave to speak here, girl," said Pakona sharply.

Fawn sat back and clapped her hand over her mouth in apology and alarm. Dag set his jaw, but added, "Fawn is exactly right. I recognized it as a technique that any of us here who have been bonded to sharing knives have likewise seen, but I didn't suggest it. Fawn thought of it herself."

"They used a *knife-making* technique on *wedding cords,*" Dar said in a voice of outrage.

"Groundwork is groundwork, Hoharie says," Dag shot back. "I defy you to find a rule anywhere says you can't."

Tioca's eyes narrowed in considerable intrigue. "Medicine-making does have to be a little more . . . adaptable than some other kinds of making," she allowed. *Such as knife-work* hung implied. In a kindly sort of tone. Dag allowed himself an instant of enjoyment, watching Dar's teeth grit.

"One brother's word against t'other's," rumbled Ogit Muskrat from his end of the row. "One's a maker, one's not. Given the matter is making, I know which I'd trust."

Fawn, her lips pressed tight, cast a look up at Dag: *But you're a maker, too!* He gave her a small headshake. He was letting himself get distracted, wound up in side issues. This wasn't about their cords.

Very canny of Dar to try to make it so, though. It dropped the whole smoldering issue of threatened banishment against a, what was that word Fairbolt had used, *notable* patroller, into the lake. Was that part Cumbia's doing— shaken by doubt of her son's allegiance despite her harsh words to Fawn? A reaction to whatever reputation Dag had won in Raintree? It certainly avoided complicated and possibly ferocious campwide debates over the council's right to force a string-cutting. If Dar could make it stick, it made everything simple and the problem go away, without anyone having to change anything.

And if Dar couldn't make it stick, there was still the other strategy to fall back on. But Dag doubted there was a person on council who wouldn't prefer the simpler version, Fairbolt not excepted.

"But if you rule the girl's cord is invalid," said Laski Beaver, scratching her head, "yet Dag's is not, does that mean he's married to her but she's not married to him? Makes no sense."

"Both are invalid," snapped Dar. Pakona, with admirable even-handedness, gave him the same quelling glower and headshake she'd given Dag, and he subsided.

Pakona turned back, and said, "Bring those things up here, Dag. We need a closer look." She added reluctantly, "The girl, too."

Dag had Fawn roll up the soft fine fabric of his left sleeve and dutifully rose to walk slowly down the row of councilors. Fawn followed, silent and scared. The touches, both with fingers and groundsense, were for the most part brief enough to be courteous, although a couple of the women's hands strayed curiously to the fabric of his shirt. Tioca, Dag was almost certain, detected his fading ground reinforcement being slowly absorbed in Fawn's left arm, but she said nothing about it to the others. Fairbolt, at the end of the line, waved them both away: "I've seen 'em. Repeatedly."

Dag and Fawn recrossed the circle and sat once more. He watched her head bend as she straightened her skirts. In the green dress, she looked like some lone flower found in a woodland pool, in a spring-come-late. *Very late. She is not your prize, old patroller, not to be won nor earned. She's her own gift. Lilies always are.* His only-fingers traced her cord on his arm, and fell back, gripping his knee.

"There's our vote, then," said Pakona. "Is this unusual cord-making to be taken as valid, or not?"

"There's this," said Laski, slowly. "Once word gets out, I'd think others could repeat this trick. Acceptance would open the door to more of these mismatches."

"But they're good ground constructions," said Tioca. "As solid as, well, mine." She wriggled her left wrist and the cord circling it. "Are cords not to be proof of marriage anymore?"

"Maybe all cord-makings will have to be witnessed, hereafter," said Laski.

A general, unenthusiastic *hm* as everyone envisioned this.

"I suggest," said Pakona, "that we set the future actions of future folks beyond the scope of this council, or we'll still be arguing as the hundredth candle burns down. We only have to rule on this couple, this day. We've seen all there is to see, heard from the only ones who were there. Whether the idea for the thing was Dag's or the farmer girl's seems to me not to make a great deal of difference. The outcome was the same. A *no* vote will see it finished right now. A *yes* vote will . . . well, it won't. Dar, is this agreeable to Tent Redwing?"

Dar leaned back for a low-voiced exchange with their frowning mother. Cumbia had run out of cord to play with; her hands now kneaded the fabric of her shift along her thin thighs. A grimace, a short nod. Dar turned back. "Yes, we accept," he replied.

"Dag, you?"

"Yes . . . ," said Dag slowly. He glanced aside at Fawn, watching him in trusting bewilderment, and gave her a little nod of reassurance. "Go ahead."

Dar, expecting more argument, looked at him in sharp surprise. Dag remembered Fairbolt's word picture of the sitting tactician. Wise man, Fairbolt. He settled back to watch the candle burn down as Pakona started down the row.

"Ogit?"

"No! No farmer spouses!" Well, that was clear.

"Tioca?"

A slight hesitation. "Yes. I can't reconcile it with my maker's conscience to say that's not a good making."

Rigni, called upon, looked plaintively at Tioca and at last said, "Yes."

Laski, after a bit of a struggle, said, "No."

Pakona herself said, "No," without hesitation, and added, "if we let this in, it's going to be every kind of mess, and it will go on and on. Dowie?"

Dowie looked down the row and made a careful count on her fingers, and looked appalled. A *no* from her would finish the matter. A *yes* would create a tie and throw it onto Fairbolt. After a long, long pause, she cleared her throat, and said, "Yes?"

Fairbolt gave her palpable cowardice a slow, blistering, and ungrateful glare. Then he sighed, sat up, and stared around. A longer silence stretched.

You know they're good cords, Fairbolt, Dag thought. Dag watched the struggle in the captain's face between integrity and practicality, and admired how long it was taking the latter to triumph. In a way, Dag wished the integrity would pull ahead. It wasn't going to make a bit of difference in the end, after all, and Fairbolt would feel better about himself later.

"Fairbolt?" said Pakona, cautiously. "Camp captain always goes last to break the tie votes. It's a duty."

Fairbolt waved this away in a *Yeah, yeah, I know* gesture. He cleared his throat. "Dag? You got anything more to say?"

"A certain amount, yes. It will seem roundabout, but it will go to the center in the end. Makes no never mind to me whether it's before or after you have your say, though."

Fairbolt gave him a little nod. "Go ahead, then. You have the stick."

Pakona looked as though she wanted to override this, but thought better of annoying Fairbolt while his vote hung in the breeze. She crossed her arms and settled back. Dar and Cumbia were frowning in alarm, but Dag certainly had all their attention.

Dag's mind was heavy, his head ached, but his heart felt light, as if it were flying. *Might just be falling. We'll know when we hit the ground.* He set the speaking stick aside, reached down, gripped his hickory staff, and stood up. Full height.

"Excepting the patrollers who just came back from Raintree with me, how many folks here have heard the name of a farmer town called Greenspring?"

An array of blank looks from the center and left, although Dirla's aunt Rigni, after a glance at her patroller niece, hesitantly raised her hand for a moment. Dag returned her a nod.

"I'm not surprised there are so few. It was the town in Raintree where that last malice started up, unchecked. No one told me the name either, when I was called out to ride west. Now, partly that was due to the confusion that always goes with such a scramble, but you know—partly, it wasn't. No one knew, or said, because it didn't seem important to them.

"So how many here—not my patrollers—know the numbers of dead at Bonemarsh?"

Ogit Muskrat said gruffly, "We've all heard them. 'Bout fifty grown-ups and near twenty youngsters."

"Such a horror," sighed Tioca.

Dag nodded. "Nineteen. That's right." Fairbolt was watching him curiously. *No, I'm not taking your advice about boasting, Fairbolt. Maybe the reverse. Just wait.* "So who knows how many died at Greenspring?"

The patrollers to his right looked tight-lipped, holding back the answer. The majority of the councilors just looked baffled. After a stretch, Pakona finally said, "Lots, I imagine. What has this to do with your counterfeit wedding cords, Dag?"

He let that *counterfeit* slide unchallenged, too. "I said it was roundabout. Of a thousand townsfolk—roughly half the population of Bonemarsh—Greenspring lost about three hundred grown-ups and *all*—or nearly all—of their youngsters. I counted not less than one hundred sixty-two such bodies at the Greenspring burying field, and I know there were the bones of at least three more at the Bonemarsh mud-men feast we cleaned up after. Didn't mention those three to the townsmen doing the burying. It wouldn't have helped, at the time."

He glanced down at Fawn, glancing up at him, and knew they were both wondering if some of those scattered bones might have been the missing Sassy. Dag hoped not. He shook his head at Fawn, to say, *no knowing,* and she nodded and hunkered on her seat.

"Does anyone but me see something terribly wrong with those two sets of numbers?"

The return stares held discomfort, more than a twinge of sympathy, even pity, but no enlightenment. Dag sighed and plowed on. "All right, try this.

"Bonemarsh died—people slain, animals slaughtered, that beautiful country blighted for a generation—*because we failed at Greenspring.* If the malice had been recognized and stopped there, it would never have marched as far as Bonemarsh.

"It wasn't lack of patrollers or patrolling that slew Greenspring. Raintree patrol is as stretched as anyone else's, but there would have been enough, if only. It was a lack of . . . something else. Talking. Knowing. Friendships, even. A whole lot of simple things that could have been different, that one man or another might have changed, but didn't."

"Are you blamin' the Raintree patrol?" burst out Mari, unable to contain herself any longer. "Because that isn't the way I saw it. Seems the farmers were told not to settle there, but they didn't *listen.*" Pakona made her hand-wave again, though not with any great conviction.

"I'm not blaming either side more than the other," said Dag, "and *I don't know the answers.* And I know I don't know. And it's stopped me, right cold.

"But you see—once upon a time, I didn't know dirt about patrolling, either. And half of what I thought I did know was wrong. There's a cure for ignorant young patrollers, though—we send 'em for a walk around the lake. Turns 'em into much smarter old patrollers, pretty reliably. Good system. It's worked for generations.

"So I'm thinkin'—maybe it's not enough anymore just to walk around the lake. Maybe we, or some of us, or *one* of us, needs to walk around the world."

The circle had grown very quiet.

Dag took a last breath. "And maybe that fellow is me. Sometimes, when you don't know how to start, you just have to start anyway, and find out movin' what you'd never learn sittin' still. I'm not going to argue and I'm not going to defend, because that's like asking me to tell you the ending before I've begun. There may not even be an ending. So Fairbolt, you can cast that last vote any way you please. But tomorrow, my wife and I are going to be down that road and gone. That's all." He gave a short, sharp nod, and sat back down.

19

Fawn let out her breath as Dag settled again beside her. Her heart was pounding as though she'd been running. She wrapped her arms around herself and rocked, looking around the circle of formidable Lakewalkers.

From the restive pack of patrollers to her right, she heard Utau mutter, "You all were asking me what it felt like to be ground-ripped? Now you know."

To which Mari returned a low-voiced, "Shut up, Utau. You don't have the stick."

Razi said under his breath, "No, I think we've just been hit with it." She motioned him, too, to shush.

Both Pakona and Fairbolt glanced aside, not friendly-like, and the patrollers subsided. Fairbolt sat back with his arms folded and glowered at his boots.

Dag murmured to Fawn, "Give this back to Pakona, will you, Spark? I won't be needing it again." He handed her the little length of wood they'd called the speaking stick.

She nodded, took it carefully, and trod across the circle to the scary old woman who looked even more like Cumbia's sister than Cumbia's sister Mari did. Maybe it was the closer age match. Or maybe they were near-related; these Lakewalkers all seemed to be. Neither of them wishing to get as close to the other as to pass it from hand to hand, Fawn laid the stick down next to the candle-lantern and skittered back to the shelter of Dag. Despite the prohibition on her speaking here, she swallowed, cupped her hand to his ear, and whispered, "Back at the firefly tree, I thought if I loved you any harder, I wouldn't be able to breathe. I was right." Gulping, she sat back down.

His crooked smile was so tender it pierced her like some sweet, sharp blade, saying better than words, *It's all right*. All wrong and all right, mixed together so confusingly. He hugged her once around the shoulders, fiercely, and they both looked up to watch Fairbolt, as did everyone else.

Fairbolt grimaced, scratched his head, sat up. Smiled a little Fairboltish smile that wasn't the sort of thing anybody would want to smile along with. And said, "I abstain."

A ripple of dismay ran along the line of his fellow councilors, punctuated at the end by an outraged cry from Dar, "*What?*"

"You can't do that!" said Dowie. She swiveled to Pakona, beside her. "Can he do that?" And less audibly, "Can I do that?" which made Fairbolt rub his forehead and sigh.

But he answered her, "I can and do, but not often. I generally prefer to see things settled and done. But if Dag is taking his farmer bride away regardless, I fail to see the emergency in this."

"What about Tent Redwing?" demanded Dar. "Where's our redress?"

Fairbolt tilted his head, appearing to be considering this. "Tent Redwing can do as any other disputant can in the event of a locked council decision. Bring the complaint again to the new council next season. It's only two months now to Bearsford Camp."

"But he'll be gone!" wailed Cumbia. It was a measure of her distress, Fawn thought, that she didn't even grab for the stick before this outburst. But for once, Pakona didn't wave her down; she was too busy gripping her own knees, maybe.

Fairbolt shook his head. "This marriage-cord redefinition is too big and complicated a thing for one man to decide, even in an emergency. It's a matter for a campwide meet, separate from the emotions of a particular case. Folks need time to talk and think about this, more careful-like."

Fawn could see that this argument was working on the camp council. And it was plain enough that to some, it didn't matter how Fawn went away, as long as she went. The mob of patrollers was looking downright mulish, though—if not as mulish as Dar.

Dar turned around for a rapid, low-voiced consultation with Cumbia. She shook her head, once in anger, once in something like despair, then finally shrugged.

Dar turned back. "Tent Redwing requests the speaking stick."

Pakona nodded, picked it up, and hesitated. "You can't ask for another vote on the same matter till Bearsford, you know."

"I know. This is . . . different but urgently related."

"That string-cutting idea, that's for a camp meet as well. And as I've told you before, I don't think you'll get it. Especially not if *she's*"—a head jerk toward Fawn—"already gone."

"It's neither," said Dar. She shrugged acceptance and passed the stick along to him.

Dar began, "Tent Redwing has no choice but to accept this delay." He glowered at Fairbolt. "But as is obvious to everyone, by Bearsford season Dag plans to be long gone. Our complaint, if sustained, involves a stiff fine owed to the camp. We ask that Dag Redwing's camp credit be held against that new hearing, lest the camp be left with no recourse if the fine is ordered. Also to assure he'll show up to face the council."

Pakona and Ogit looked instantly approving. Laski and Rigni looked considering, Tioca and Dowie dismayed. Fairbolt had hardly any expression at all.

Pakona said, in a tone of relief, "Well, that at least has plenty of precedent."

Dag was smiling in a weird dry way. Fawn dared to push up on one knee and whisper in his ear again, "What does that mean? Can they make you come back?"

"No," he murmured to her. "See, once in a while, some angry loser receives a council order to make restitution and tries to resist by drawing out his camp credit and hiding it. This stops up that hole, till the settlement is paid. But since Dar will never be able to bring the complaint to Bearsford Council—or anywhere else, since I won't be there to answer it—this would tie up my camp credit indefinitely. Stripping me like a banishment, without actually having to push through a banishment. May work, too, since no one likes to see the camp lose resources. Right clever, except that I was ready to walk away stark naked if I had to. I won't be rising to this bait, Spark."

"Brothers," she muttered, subsiding back to her hard seat.

His lips twitched. "Indeed."

Pakona said, "Tent Redwing's request seems to me reasonable, especially in light of what Dag Redwing said about his intention to leave camp."

"Leave?" said Ogit. "Is that what you call it? I'd call it plain desertion, wrapped up in fancy nonsense! And what are you going to do about that, Fairbolt?" He leaned forward to glare around the council at the camp captain on the other end.

"That will be a matter internal to the patrol," Fairbolt stated. And the iron finality in his voice was enough to daunt even Ogit, who sat back, puffing but not daring to say more.

Breaking his intent to speak no further, Dag gave Fairbolt a short nod. "I'll like to see you after this, sir. It's owed."

Fairbolt returned the nod. "At headquarters. It's on your way."

"Aye."

Pakona knocked her knuckles on the log candle table. "That's our vote, then. Should Dag Redwing's camp credit be held till the Bearsford council? *Yes* will hold it, *no* will release it." It was plain that she struggled not to add something like, *To be taken off and frittered away on farmer paramours,* but her leader's discipline won. Barely, Fawn sensed. "Ogit?"

"Yes." No surprise there. The string of three more yesses, variously firm or reluctant, were more of a disappointment; the vote was lost before it even came to Pakona's firm *Yes.* Dowie looked down the row, seemed to do some mental arithmetic, and murmured a safely useless, "No."

Fairbolt grimaced, and grumbled, "No," as well.

Pakona stated, "Tent Redwing's request is upheld. Camp council rules Dag Redwing's camp credit is held aside until the Bearsford rehearing."

A little silence fell, as it all sank in. Until broken by Saun, surging up to yell, "You blighted *thieves* . . . !" Razi and Griff both tackled him and wrestled him back into his seat. "After Raintree! After *Raintree!*" Mari turned and scowled at him, but seemingly could not force herself to actually *chide.* As she turned back, the look she shot at her nephew Dar would have burned bacon, Fawn thought.

Omba's jaw had been working for quite some time. Now she snatched the speaking stick out of her surprised husband's hand, waved it, and cried out, "*Make him take his horse!* Copperhead is a blighted menace. The beast has bitten three of my girls, kicked two, and torn more hide off his pasture-mates than I ever want to sew up again. I don't care if Dag walks out bare to the skin, but I *demand* his horse go with him!" Which all sounded plenty irate, except that her eye away from Dar and toward Dag shivered in a wink.

"*There's* a mental picture for you, Spark," Dag said out of the corner of his mouth at her. "Me and Copperhead, bareback to bare-backside . . ."

She could have shaken him till his teeth rattled for making her almost laugh aloud in the midst of this mess. As it was, she had to clap her hand over her mouth and look down into her lap until she regained control. "Happy eyes!" she whispered back, and had the sweet revenge of watching him choke back a surprised guffaw.

Dar glowered at them both, furiously impotent against their private jokes. Which was also pretty tasty, amongst the ashes.

"Wherever did you come by that horse, anyhow?" Fawn asked under her breath.

Dag murmured back, "Lost a game of chance with a keelboat man at Silver Shoals, once."

"Lost. Ah. That explains it."

Pakona considered Dag, not in a friendly way. "That does bring up the question of where camp credit leaves off and personal effects begin." And if she was picturing Dag walking out naked, it wasn't with the same emotions Fawn did, by a long shot.

Fairbolt rumbled, "No, it doesn't, Pakona. Unless you want to start a revolt in the patrol."

Saun, still squirming in his seat with Utau's hand heavy on his shoulder, looked as if he was ready to begin an uprising right now. And if steam wasn't billowing from Dirla, Razi, and Griff, it was only because they weren't wet.

Pakona raised an eyebrow at Fairbolt. "Can't you keep your rowdy young-sters under control, Fairbolt?"

"Pakona, I'd be *leading* them."

Her mouth thinned in lack of appreciation of his humor, or whatever that was—black and sincere, anyhow. But she veered off, nonetheless. "Very well. Till the Bearsford rehearing, the . . . *former* patroller can take away his horse Copperhead, its gear, and whatever personal effects it can carry. The farmer girl can leave with whatever she came with; it's no business of ours."

"What about all those bride-gifts he sent off?" said Dar suddenly.

Dag stirred, his eyes narrowing dangerously.

Mari looked up at this one. "Dar, *don't even start.*" Fawn wasn't sure if that was her patrol leader voice or her aunt voice, or some alloy of the two, but Dar subsided, and even Pakona didn't reprimand her.

Pakona straightened her spine and looked around the circle. "Tent Red-wing, do you have anything more to say before I close this session?"

Dar choked out through flat lips, "No, ma'am." The camp-credit ruling had left him looking bitterly satisfied, but Cumbia, behind him, was drawn and quiet.

"Dag Redwing?"

Dag shook his head in silence.

Pakona held out her hand, and the speaking stick was passed back to her. She tapped it three times on the log table, leaned forward, and blew out the session candle.

At the door to his pegboard chamber, Fairbolt excluded Dag's outraged escort of fellow patrollers and their increasingly imaginative and urgent offers to wreak vengeance on Dar. Dag was just as glad. Fairbolt gestured him and Fawn to seats, but Dag shook his head and simply stood, hanging wearily on his hickory stick. *Not fellow patrollers anymore, I suppose.* What was he now, if not Fawn's patroller? He hardly knew. Fawn's Dag, leastways. *Always.* She leaned up under his left arm, looking anxiously at Fairbolt, and Dag let some of his weight rest on her slim shoulders.

"I'm sorry about how that came out back there," said Fairbolt, jerking his head in the general direction of the council grove. "I didn't expect Dar to blindside me. Twice."

"I always said my family was impossible. I never said they were stupid," sighed Dag. "I thought it was a draw between the two of you, myself. I'd made up my mind to it when I walked into that circle that I was going to walk out banished for real, and if they didn't offer it, I was going to take it myself." He added, "You have my resignation, of course. I should have stopped in here before the session and not blindsided you with that, too, but I wasn't just sure how things were going to play out. If you want to call it desertion, I won't argue."

Fairbolt leaned down and plucked Dag's peg from the painted square on the wall labeled *Sick List*. He straightened up and weighed it thoughtfully in his palm. "So what are you going to do out there, walking around farmer country? I just can't picture you plowing dirt."

"Leastways it would involve movin', though right now sitting looks pretty good. That mood'll pass, it always does. I wasn't joking when I said *I do not know*." He had once traveled great distances. For all he knew, the next great journey would be all in one place, but walked the long way, through time, a passage he could barely envision, let alone explain. "No plan I ever made has been of the least use to me, and sometimes—plans keep you from seeing other paths. I want to keep my eyes clear for a space. Find out if you really can teach an old patroller new tricks."

"You've learned quite a few lately, from what Hoharie says."

"Well . . . yes." Dag added, "Give my regrets and thanks to Hoharie, will you? She almost tempted me away from you. But . . . it would have been the wrong road. I don't know much right now, but I know that much."

"No lordship," said Fairbolt, watching him.

"No," Dag concurred. "I mean to find some other road, wide enough for everyone. Someone has to survey it. Could be the new way won't be mine to make, but mine to be given, out there. From someone smarter than me. If I keep my ground open, watch and listen hard enough."

Fairbolt said meditatively, "Not much point for a man to learn new things if he doesn't come back to teach 'em. Pass 'em on."

Dag shook his head. "Change needs to happen. But it won't happen today, here, with these people. Camp council proved that."

Fairbolt held his hand out, palm down, in a judicious rocking gesture. "It wasn't unanimous."

"There's a hope," Dag conceded. "Even if it was mainly due to Dowie Grayheron having a spine of pure custard." Fairbolt barked a laugh, shaking his head in reluctant agreement

Dag said, "This wasn't my first plan. I'd have stayed here with Spark if they'd have let me. Be getting myself ready for the next patrol even now."

"No, you'd still be on the sick list, I assure you," said Fairbolt. He glanced down. "How's the leg? You were favoring it, walking back, I noticed."

"It's coming along. It still twinges when I'm tired. I'm glad I'll be riding Copperhead instead of walking, bless Omba's wits. I'll miss that woman."

Fairbolt stared out the hooked-open window at the glimmer of the lake.

"So . . . if you could have your first plan back—sorry, Fawn, not even what you call Lakewalker magic could make that happen now, but *if*—would you take it?"

It was a testing question, and a good one. Dag tilted his head in the silence, his eyelids lowering, rising; then said simply, "No." As Fawn looked solemnly up at him, he gave her a squeeze around the shoulders. "Go on and chuck my peg in the fireplace. I'm done with it."

Fairbolt gave him a short nod. "Well, if you ever change your mind—or if the world bucks you off again—you know where to find us. I'll still be here."

"You don't ever give up, do you?"

Fairbolt chuckled. "Massape wouldn't let me. Very dangerous woman, Massape. The day I met her, forty-one years gone, all my fine and fancy plans for my life fell into Hickory Lake and never came up again. Hang on to your dangerous woman too, Dag. They're rare, and not easy to come by."

Dag smiled. "I've noticed that."

Fairbolt tossed the peg in his palm once more, then, abruptly, held it out to Fawn. "Here. I think this is yours, now. Don't lose it."

Fawn glanced up at them both, her eyebrows climbing in surprise, then smiled and folded the peg in her firm little grip. "You bet I won't, sir."

Dag made plans to leave in the gray light of dawn, in part to get a start on a day that promised to turn cool and rainy later, but mostly to avoid any more farewells, or worse, folks who still wanted to argue with him. He and Fawn had packed their saddlebags the night before, and Dag had given away what wouldn't fit: his trunk to Sarri, his good ash spear to Razi, and his father's sword to Utau, because he sure wasn't passing it back to Dar. His winter gear in storage at Bearsford he supposed he must abandon with his camp credit. Tent Bluefield he left standing for Stores to struggle with, since they'd been so anxious for it.

Dag was surprised when Omba herself, and not one of her girls, appeared out of the mists hanging above the road leading Copperhead and Grace. She gave him a hug.

"Sneaking in a good-bye out of sight of the kin?" he inquired, hugging her back.

"Well, that, and, um . . . I have to offer an apology to Fawn."

Fawn, taking Grace's reins from her, said, "You never did me any harm that I know of, Omba. I'm glad to have met you."

Omba cleared her throat. "Not harm, exactly. More of an . . . accident." She was a bit flushed in the face, Dag was bemused to note, not at all like her usual dry briskness. "Fawn, I'm very sorry, but I'm afraid your horse is pregnant."

"What?" cried Fawn. She looked at Grace, who looked back with a mild and unrepentant eye, and snuffled her soft muzzle into Fawn's hand in search of treats. "Grace! You bad girl, what have you been up to?" She gave her reins a little shake, laughing and amazed.

"Omba," said Dag, leaning against Copperhead's shoulder and grinning despite himself, "who have you gone and let ravish my wife's mare?"

Omba sighed hugely. "Rig Crow's stallion Shadow got loose and swam over from Walnut about five nights ago. Had himself a fine old time before we caught up with him. You're not the only mares' owners I'm going to have to apologize to today, though you're the first in line. I'm not looking forward to it."

"Will they be angry?" asked Fawn. "Were they planning other mates? Was he not a good horse?"

"Oh, Shadow is a fine horse," Dag assured her. "You would not believe how many furs Rig asks for, and gets, as a stud fee for that snorty horse of his. I know. I paid through the nose last year to have him cover Swallow, for Darkling."

"And therefore," said Omba, pulling on her black-and-white braid, "everyone will *say* they are very upset, and carry on as convincingly as possible. While Rig tries to collect. It could go to the camp council."

"You'll forgive me, I trust, for wishing them all a long, tedious dispute, burning many candles," said Dag. "If Rig asks, my wife and I are just *furious* about it all." He vented an evil laugh that made even Fawn raise an eyebrow at him.

"I wasn't even going to mention Grace," Omba assured him. "I'll be having troubles enough over this."

Utau and Razi came out to help them saddle up, followed by Sarri, and Mari and Cattagus together. Dag mostly exchanged sober nods, except with his aunt Mari, whom he embraced; Fawn hugged everybody.

"Think you'll be back?" asked Utau gruffly. "For that Bearsford Council, maybe?"

"Not for that. For the rest, who can say? I've left home for good at least four times that I recall, as Mari can testify."

"I remember a spectacular one, 'bout eight years back," she allowed. "There was a lot of shouting. You managed to be gone for seventeen months."

"Maybe I'll get better at it with practice."

"Could be," she said. Then added, "But I sort of hope not."

And then it was time to mount up. Razi gave Dag a leg up and sprang away, Copperhead put in his usual tricks and was duly chastised, and Utau boosted Fawn onto Grace. On the road, Dag and Fawn both turned and gave silent waves, as silently returned. As the blurring forms left behind parted to their different tents, the mist swallowed them all.

Dag and Fawn didn't speak again till the horses had clopped over the long wooden span from the island. She watched him lean his hand on his cantle and stare over his shoulder.

She said quietly, "I didn't mean, when I fell in love with you, to burn your life to the ground."

He turned back, giving her a pensive smile. "I was dry, dry timber when you met me, Spark. It'll be well." He set his face ahead and didn't look around again.

He added after a while, "Though I'm sorry I lost all my camp credit. I really thought, when I promised your folks I would care for you, to have in hand whatever you'd need for your comfort, come this winter and on for a lot of winters more. All the plunkins in the Bearsford cold cellars won't do us much good now."

"As I understand it, your goods aren't lost, exactly. More like, held. Like my dowry."

His brows rose. "There's a way of looking at it I hadn't thought of."

"I don't know how we'd manage traveling anyhow, with a string of, what did you say—eight horses?"

He considered this picture. "I was thinking more of converting it into Tripoint gold tridens or Silver Shoals silver mussels. Their monies are good all up and down the Grace and the Gray. But if all my camp credit for the past eighteen years were converted into horses—average horses, not Copperheads or Shadows . . . hm. Let me see." He did some mental estimating, for the curiosity of it. "That would be about forty horses, roughly. Way too many for us to trail in a string, it's true."

"Forty horses!" said Fawn, sounding quite taken aback. "You could buy a farm for the price of forty horses!"

"But I wouldn't know what to do with it once I had it."

"But *I* would—oh, never mind." She added, "I'm glad I didn't know this yesterday. I'd have been a lot more upset."

"Offends your notions of economy, does it?"

"Well, yes! Or my notions of *something*."

He gave her a wink. "You're worth it at twice the price, Spark. Trust me."

"Huh." But she settled again, thumping her heels gently against Grace's wide-sprung sides to urge her to keep up, looking meditative.

They pulled their horses to a halt at the place, a mile from the bridge, where the road split in three. "So," he said. "Which way?"

"Don't you know?"

"No. Well, not north. Not this late in the season." In the meadows, the cicadas were growing noisier as the morning warmed, but the first frosts would silence them soon enough. "Whichever way we go, we'll need to travel in easy stages, see, on account of Grace's delicate condition." He suspected he could get a lot of use out of Grace's condition if he played it right.

Not fooled a bit, Fawn looked narrowly at him, and said, "Couldn't agree more." She swiveled her head. "But still . . . which road?" Her eye was caught by something, and she twisted in her saddle. "What's this?"

Dag followed her gaze, and his stomach knotted coldly at the sight of Saun and Dirla, galloping madly from the bridge and waving at them. *Please, please, not some other malice outbreak . . . I don't want to have to do all this leaving over again.* But their flushed faces, when they pulled up and sat panting on their fidgeting mounts, weren't that sort of anxious.

"I was afraid we'd missed you," gasped Dirla.

"Kindly," said Dag, touching his temple. "But I thought we'd all said good-bye yesterday?" And, while not enough . . . it had been enough.

Saun, catching his breath, waved this away. "It's not that. It's this." He stuck a hand in his vest and pulled out a leather bag, which clinked. "A lot of folks from our company, and in the patrol, weren't too pleased with how things went yesterday in the camp council. So Dirla and Griff and I took up a little collection. It's nothing compared to what Dar stripped you of, I know, but it's *something*." He thrust out the bag toward Dag, who let Copperhead shy away a step.

"I thank you kindly, Saun, but I can't take that."

"Not as many chipped in as I thought should," said Dirla, looking irate. "But at least the blighted camp council has nothing to do with this."

Dag was both touched and embarrassed. "Look, you children, I can't—"

"*Fairbolt* put in three gold tridens," Saun interrupted him. "And told us not to tell Massape."

"And *Massape* put in ten silver mussels," Dirla added, "and told us not to tell Fairbolt." She paused in reflection. "You do wonder what they'll say if they catch up with each other."

"Are you telling?" Saun asked her, interested.

"Nope."

Well . . . the Crow clan was rich. Dag sighed, looking at those earnest, eager faces. He could see he wasn't getting out of this one. "I suppose the patrol will be wearing out some of those horses I left behind."

"Likely," said Saun.

Dag smiled in defeat and held out his hand.

Saun passed the bag across, grinning. "I'll try and remember all you taught me. No more swordplay in the woods, right."

"That's a start," Dag agreed. "*Duck faster* is another good one, 'cept you learned that one all by yourself. It'll stick better that way, I do allow. Take care of each other, you two."

"The patrol looks after its own," said Dirla firmly.

Dag gave her a warm nod. "The patrol looks after everybody, Dirla."

Her return smirk was quite Spark-like. "Then you're still some kind of patroller. Aren't you. Take care—Captain."

They waved and turned away.

Dag waited till they'd stopped craning around and looking back, then hefted the bag and peeked in. "Huh. Not bad. Well, this gives us a direction."

"How so?" Fawn asked.

"South," he said definitely.

"I've been south," she objected. "All the way to Glassforge."

"Spark, south doesn't even start till you get to Silver Shoals. I'm thinkin' . . . this season, passage on a flatboat going down the river isn't too expensive. We could ride slow down as far as Silver Shoals, pick out a boat . . . load Grace and Copperhead in too. I could see a lot of farmer country *and* sit still at the same time. Very enticin', that notion. I've always wanted to do that. Follow fall all the way down to the sea, and show you the sea. Ride back easy, come spring—you can make spring last a long time, riding north at the right pace. Bet my ground will be healed by then. What do you think?"

Her mouth had fallen open at this sudden spate of what were to her, he guessed, quite fantastical visions. She shut it and swallowed. "When you say travel," she said, "you don't think small."

"Oh, that's just a jaunt, by old patroller standards," he assured her. He twisted in his saddle to tuck the leather purse away in his saddlebag, then frowned when his fingers, pushing through a fold of blanket cloth, encountered an unidentifiable lump. He traded off and pulled out the lump to hold up to the light, and gazed in some astonishment at a plunkin ear. "What's this? Did you pack this?" he asked Fawn.

She blushed. "Them. Yes. I thought you should have your food, wherever we end up."

"We don't eat the ears, love."

"*I* know that." She tossed her head. "They're for planting. Sarri told me the ears'll keep good for two or three years, dry. I snuck round last night after you fell asleep and filched some out of the feed bin on Mare Island. Not the best, maybe, but I picked out the nicest-looking that were there."

"What were you thinking, farmer girl?"

"I was thinking . . . we might have a pond, someday." And at his look, "Well, we might!"

He couldn't deny it. He threw back his head and laughed. "Smuggling plunkins! And horses! No, no, Spark, it's all clear to me now. The only future for us is going to be as road bandits!"

She grinned in exasperation and shook her head. "Just ride, Dag."

As they chirped their horses into a walk, a patrol of some two dozen wild geese flew overhead, calling hauntingly, and they both turned their faces upward to mark the beating wonder of those wings.

"A bit early," Fawn commented.

"Maybe they're out for a jaunt."

"Or lost."

"Not those fellows. It looks like a pointer to me, Spark. I say, let's follow 'em."

Stirrup to stirrup, they did.